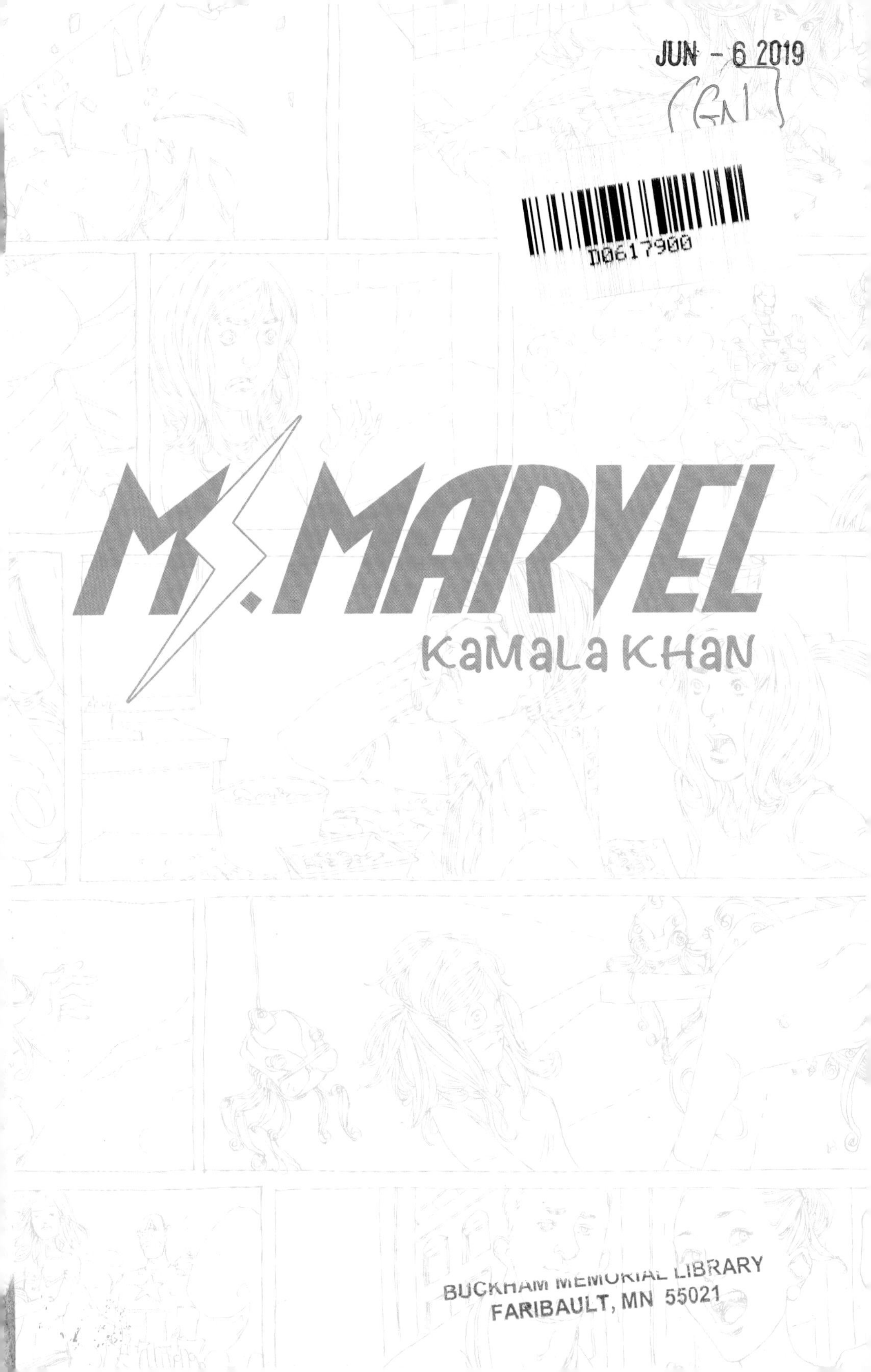

MS. MARVEL
KAMALA KHAN

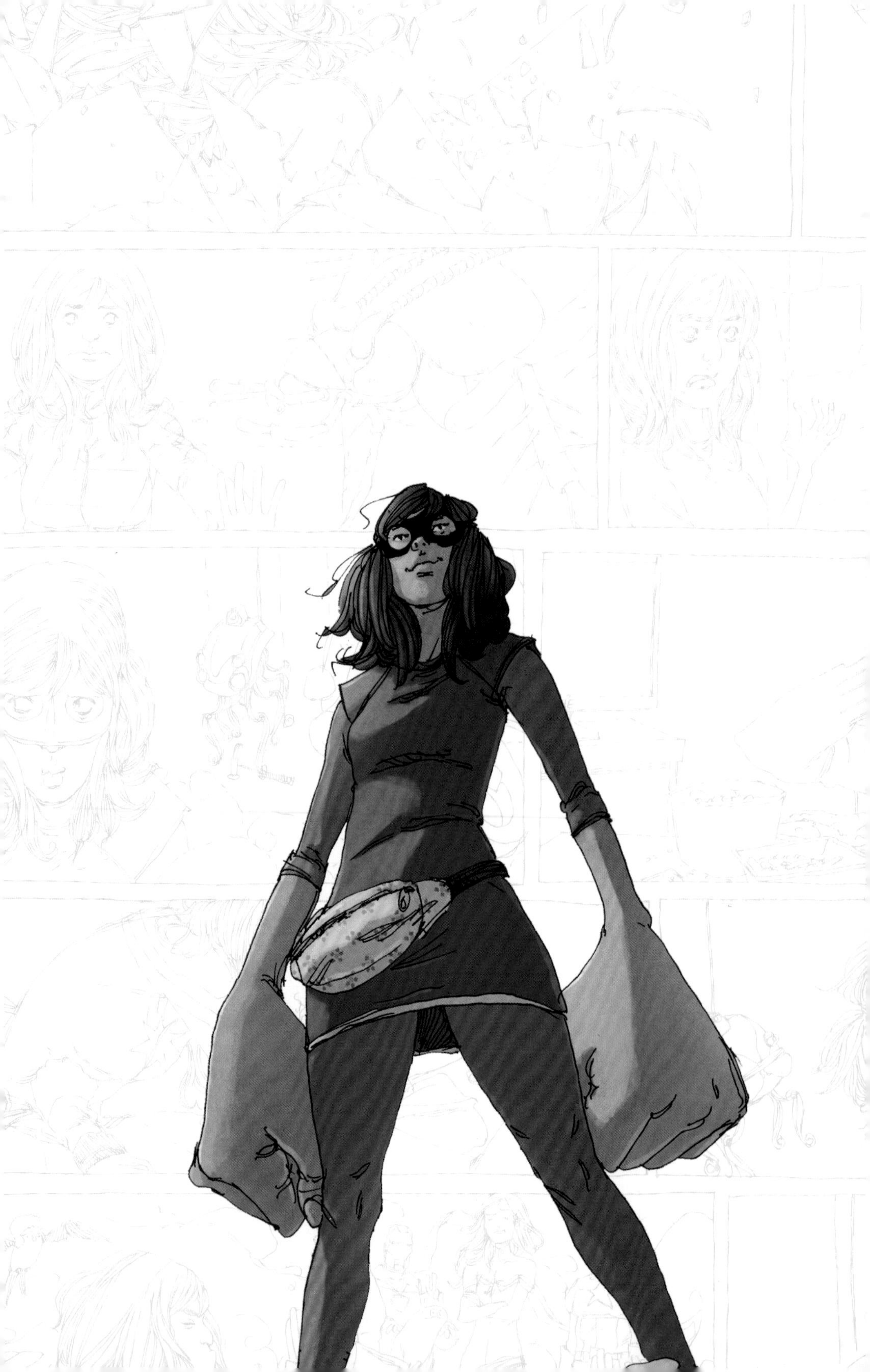

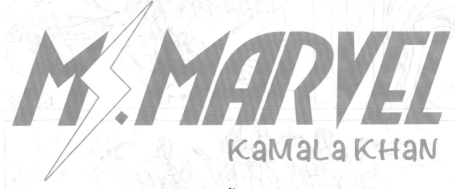

MS. MARVEL

KAMALA KHAN

writer
G. WILLOW WILSON

artists
ADRIAN ALPHONA (#1-5, #8-11)
& **JAKE WYATT** (#6-7)

color artist
IAN HERRING

letterer
VC'S JOE CARAMAGNA

cover art
SARA PICHELLI & **JUSTIN PONSOR** (#1),
JAMIE McKELVIE (#4),
JAMIE McKELVIE & **MATTHEW WILSON** (#2-3 & #5-9)
and **KRIS ANKA** (#10-11)

assistant editor
DEVIN LEWIS

editor
SANA AMANAT

senior editors
STEPHEN WACKER & **NICK LOWE**

collection editor JENNIFER GRÜNWALD
assistant editor CAILTLIN O'CONNELL • associate managing editor KATERI WOODY
editor, special projects MARK D. BEAZLEY • vp production & special projects JEFF YOUNGQUIST
svp print, sales & marketing DAVID GABRIEL

editor in chief C.B. CEBULSKI • chief creative officer JOE QUESADA
president DAN BUCKLEY • executive producer ALAN FINE

MS. MARVEL: KAMALA KHAN. Contains material originally published in magazine form as MS. MARVEL #1-11 and ALL-NEW MARVEL NOW! POINT ONE #1. First printing 2018. ISBN 978-1-302-91640-4. Published by MARVEL WORLDWIDE, INC., a subsidiary of MARVEL ENTERTAINMENT, LLC. OFFICE OF PUBLICATION: 135 West 50th Street, New York, NY 10020. **Printed in Canada.** DAN BUCKLEY, President, Marvel Entertainment; JOHN NEE, Publisher; JOE QUESADA, Chief Creative Officer; TOM BREVOORT, SVP of Publishing; DAVID BOGART, SVP of Business Affairs & Operations, Publishing & Partnership; DAVID GABRIEL, SVP of Sales & Marketing, Publishing; JEFF YOUNGQUIST, VP of Production & Special Projects; DAN CARR, Executive Director of Publishing Technology; ALEX MORALES, Director of Publishing Operations; DAN EDINGTON, Managing Editor; SUSAN CRESPI, Production Manager; STAN LEE, Chairman Emeritus. For information regarding advertising in Marvel Comics or on Marvel.com, please contact Vit DeBellis, Custom Solutions & Integrated Advertising Manager, at vdebellis@marvel.com. For Marvel subscription inquiries, please call 888-511-5480. **Manufactured between 12/14/2018 and 1/15/2019 by SOLISCO PRINTERS, SCOTT, QC, CANADA.**

10 9 8 7 6 5 4 3 2 1

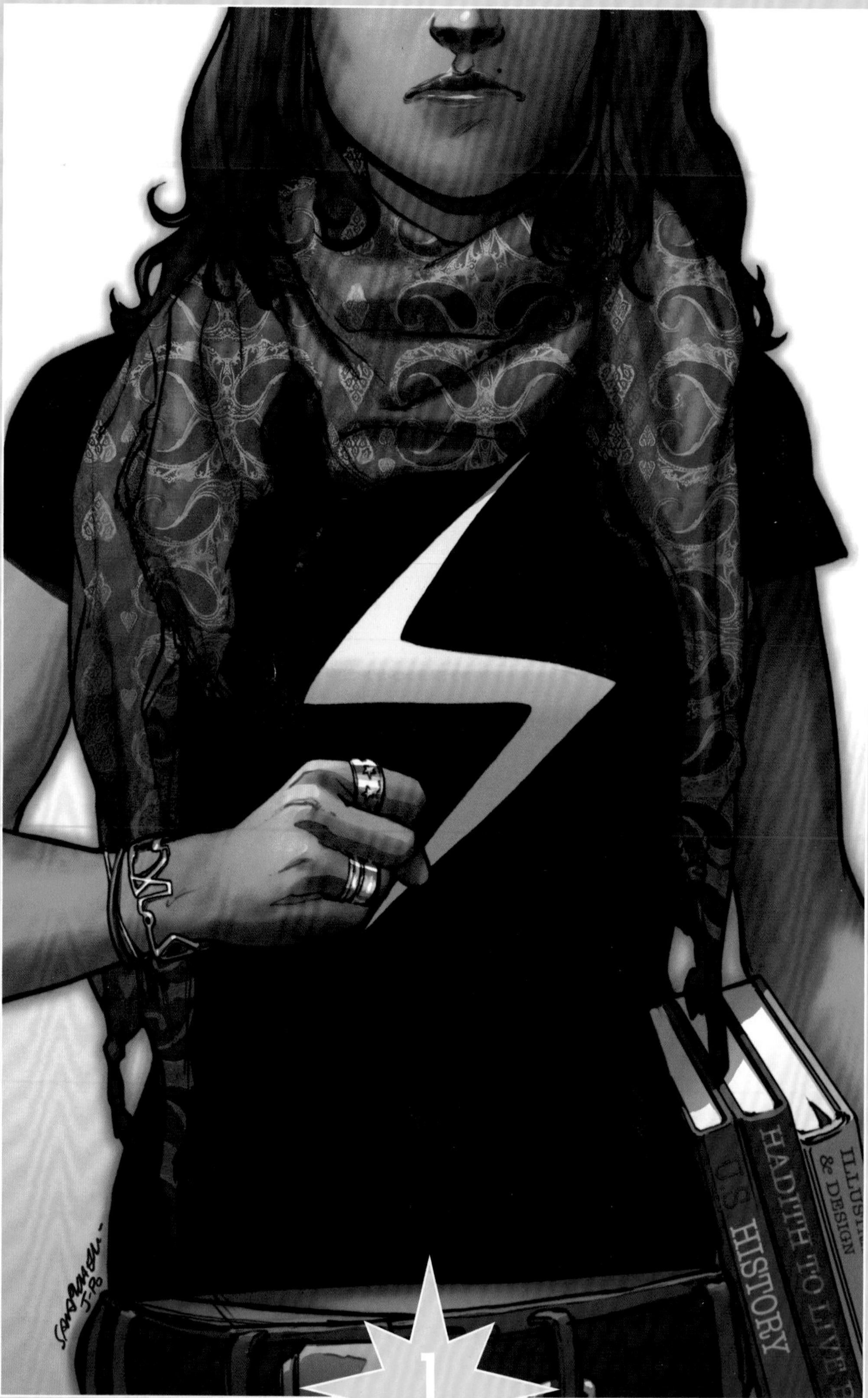
U.S. HISTORY
HADITH TO LIVE
& DESIGN
1

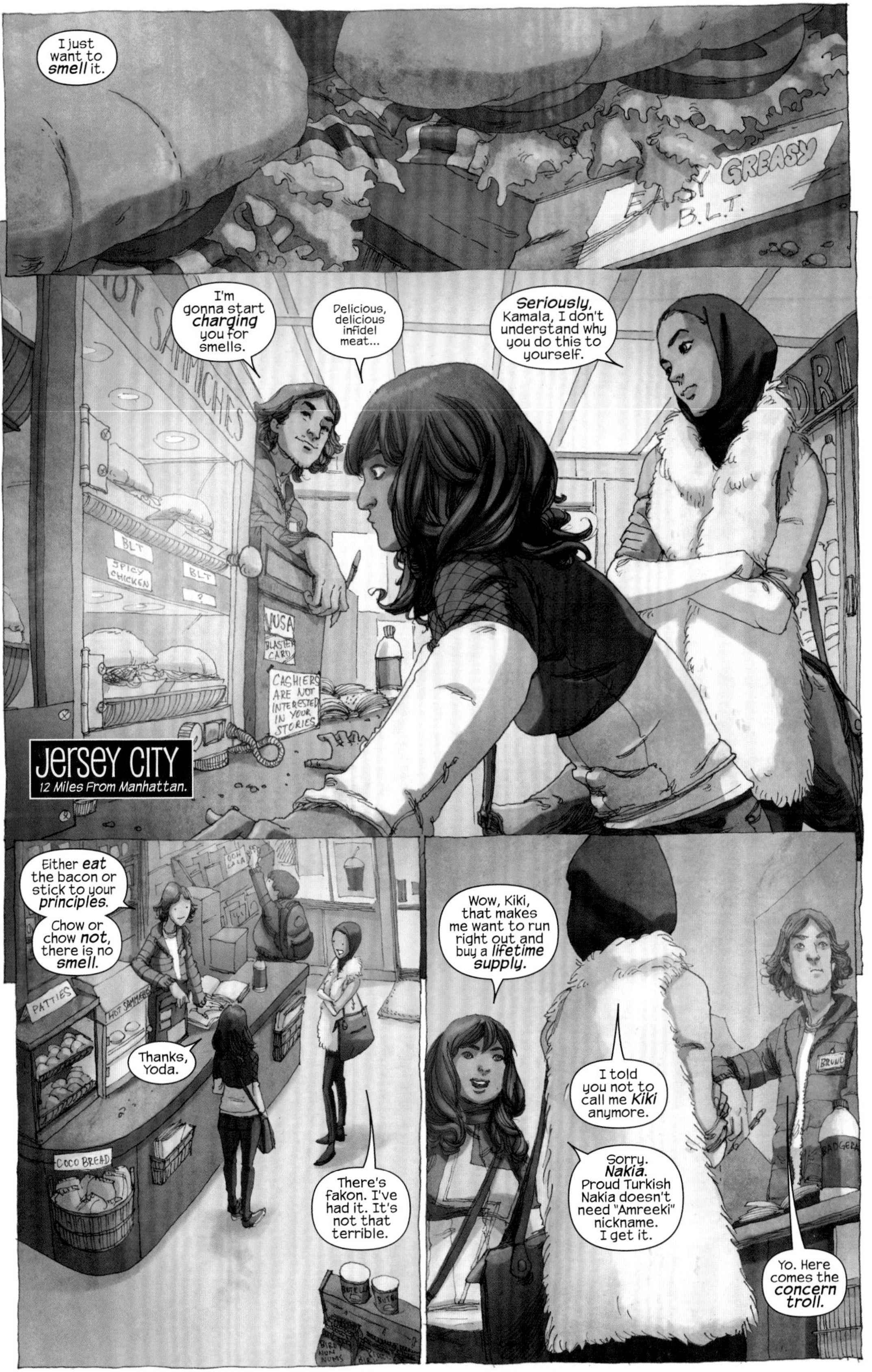
I just want to smell it.
EASY GREASY B.L.T.
I'm gonna start charging you for smells.
Delicious, delicious infidel meat...
Seriously, Kamala, I don't understand why you do this to yourself.
HOT SAMMICHES
BLT
SPICY CHICKEN
BLT
VISA
BLASTER CARD
CASHIERS ARE NOT INTERESTED IN YOUR STORIES
JERSEY CITY
12 Miles From Manhattan.
Either eat the bacon or stick to your principles.
Chow or chow not, there is no smell.
Thanks, Yoda.
PATTIES
HOT SAMMICHES
COCO BREAD
There's fakon. I've had it. It's not that terrible.
Wow, Kiki, that makes me want to run right out and buy a lifetime supply.
I told you not to call me Kiki anymore.
Sorry. Nakia. Proud Turkish Nakia doesn't need "Amreeki" nickname. I get it.
BRUNO
Yo. Here comes the concern troll.

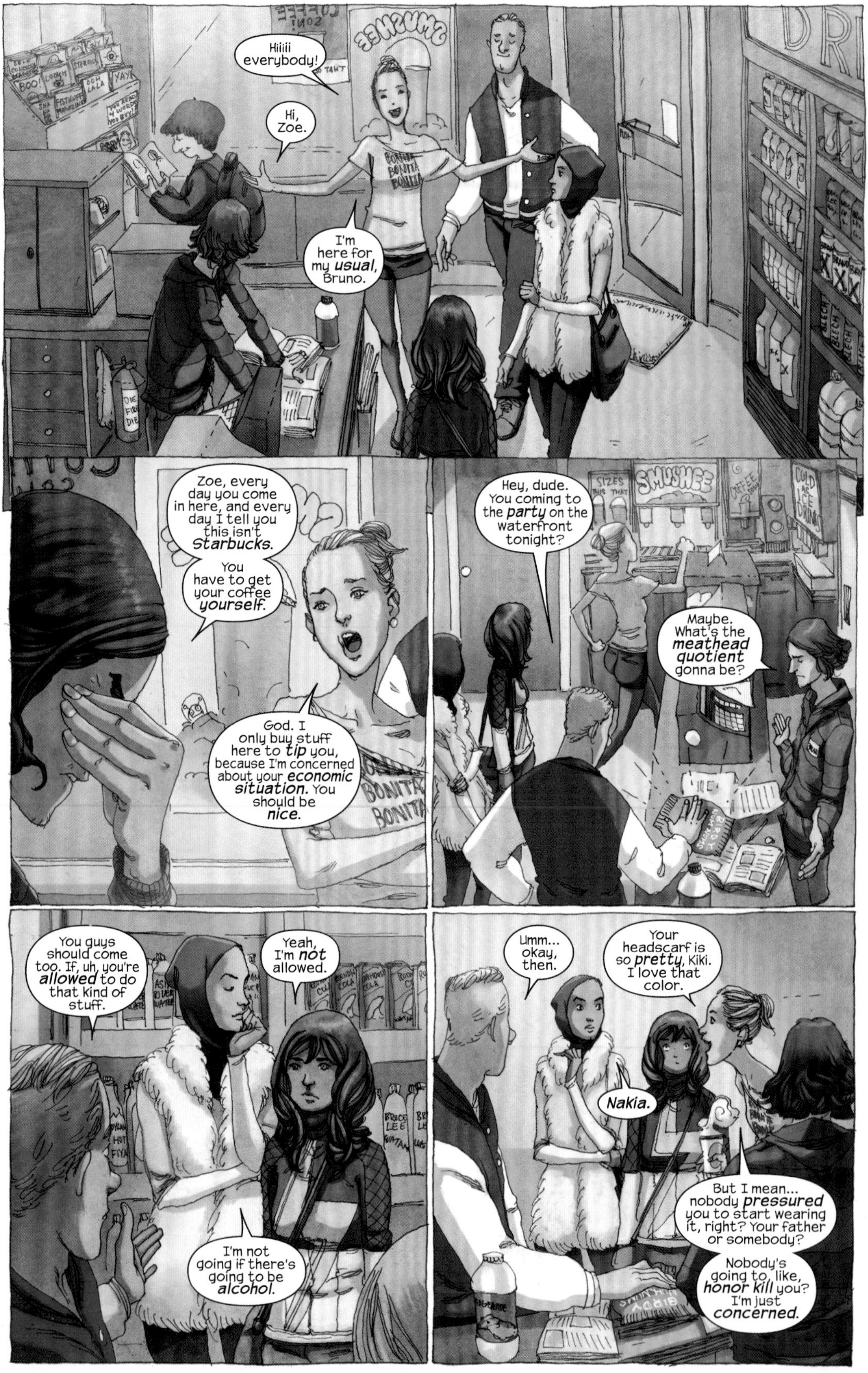
Hiiiii everybody!
Hi, Zoe.
I'm here for my *usual*, Bruno.
Zoe, every day you come in here, and every day I tell you this isn't *Starbucks*.
You have to get your coffee *yourself*.
God. I only buy stuff here to *tip* you, because I'm concerned about your *economic situation*. You should be *nice*.
Hey, dude. You coming to the *party* on the waterfront tonight?
Maybe. What's the *meathead quotient* gonna be?
You guys should come too. If, uh, you're *allowed* to do that kind of stuff.
Yeah, I'm *not* allowed.
I'm not going if there's going to be *alcohol*.
Umm... okay, then.
Your headscarf is so *pretty*, Kiki. I love that color.
Nakia.
But I mean... nobody *pressured* you to start wearing it, right? Your father or somebody?
Nobody's going to, like, *honor kill* you? I'm just *concerned*.

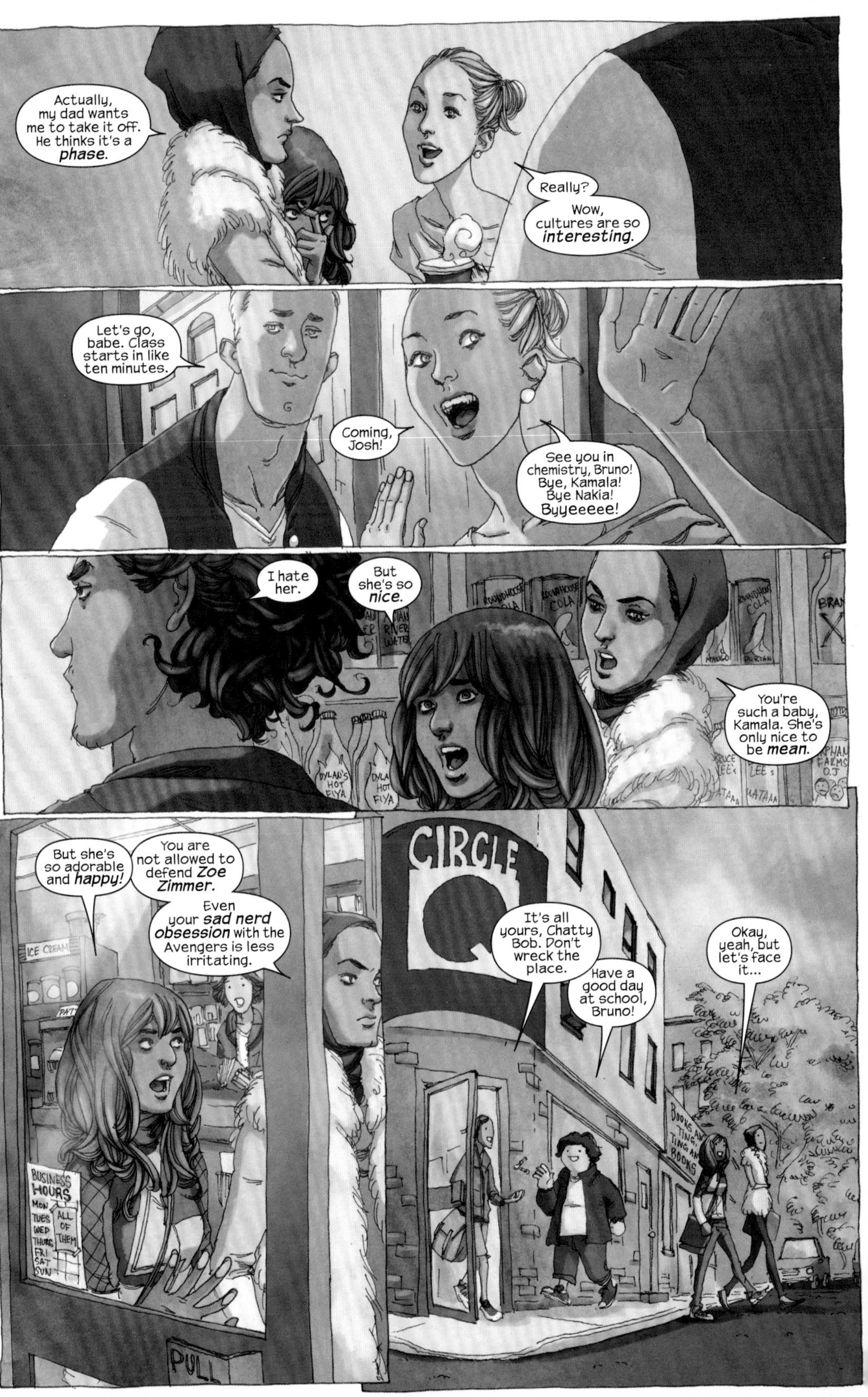
Actually, my dad wants me to take it off. He thinks it's a *phase*.
Really?
Wow, cultures are so *interesting*.
Let's go, babe. Class starts in like ten minutes.
Coming, Josh!
See you in chemistry, Bruno! Bye, Kamala! Bye Nakia! Byyeeeee!
I hate her.
But she's so *nice*.
You're such a baby, Kamala. She's only nice to be *mean*.
ROUNDHOUSE COLA
DYLAN'S HOT FLYA
But she's so adorable and *happy!*
You are not allowed to defend *Zoe Zimmer*.
Even your *sad nerd obsession* with the Avengers is less irritating.
ICE CREAM
BUSINESS HOURS
MON TUES WED THURS FRI SAT SUN
ALL OF THEM
PULL
CIRCLE Q
It's all yours, Chatty Bob. Don't wreck the place.
Have a good day at school, Bruno!
Okay, yeah, but let's face it...
BOOKS AN TING, TING AN BOOKS

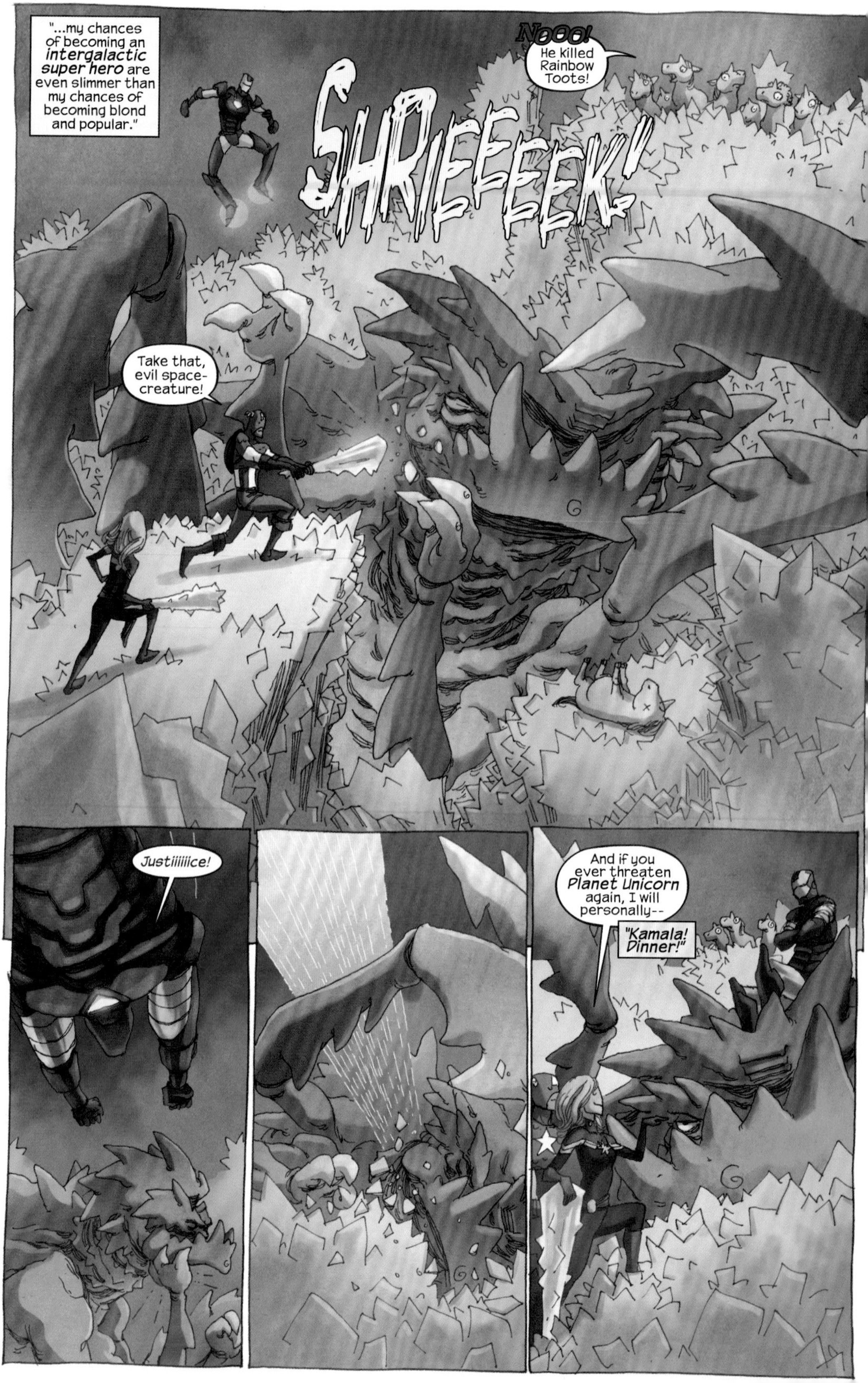
"...my chances of becoming an *intergalactic super hero* are even slimmer than my chances of becoming blond and popular."
NOOOO!
He killed Rainbow Toots!
SHRIEEEEK!
Take that, evil space-creature!
Justiiiiice!
And if you ever threaten *Planet Unicorn* again, I will personally--
"Kamala! Dinner!"

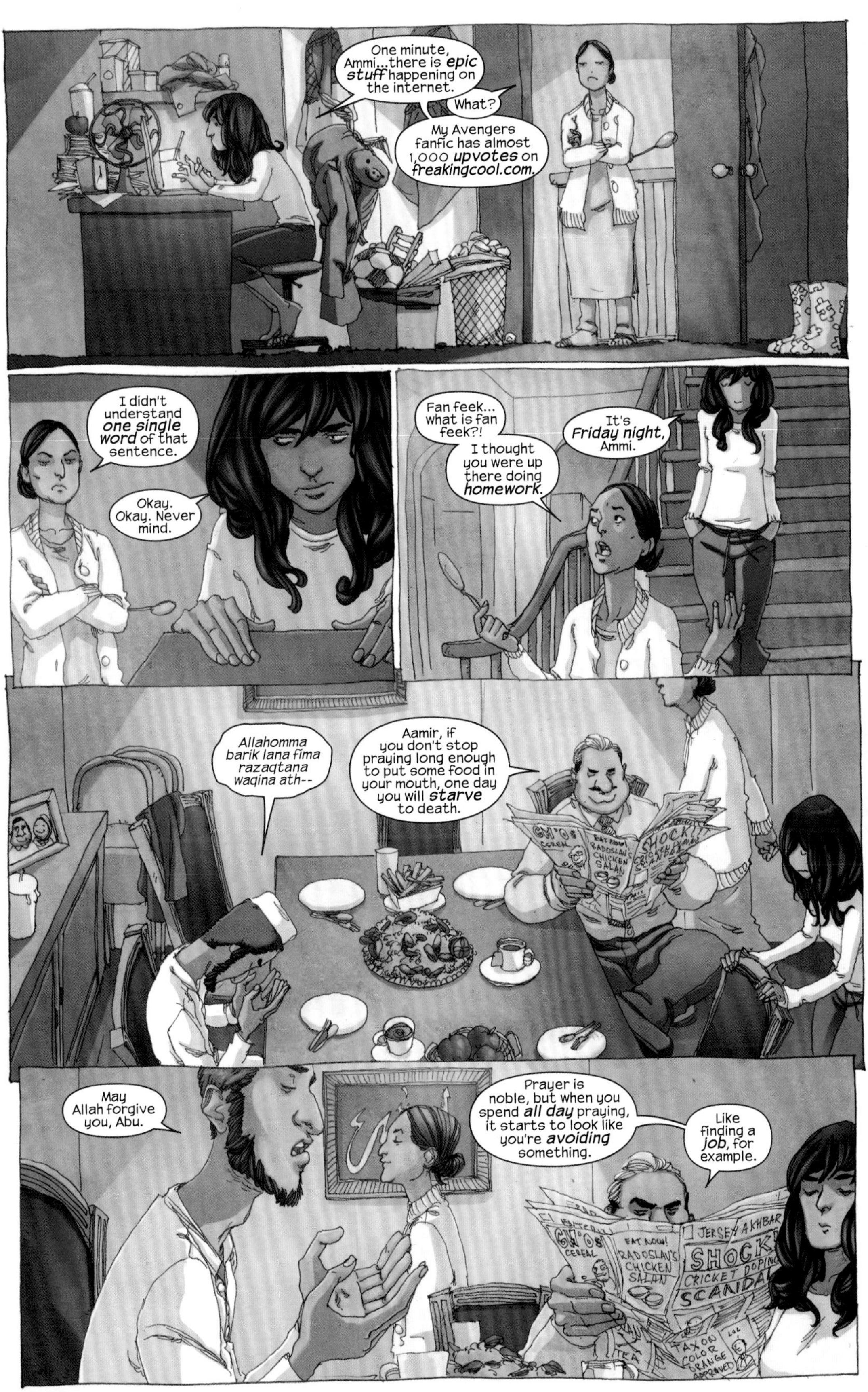

One minute, Ammi...there is *epic stuff* happening on the internet.
What?
My Avengers fanfic has almost 1,000 *upvotes* on *freakingcool.com.*
I didn't understand *one single word* of that sentence.
Okay. Okay. Never mind.
Fan feek... what is fan feek?!
I thought you were up there doing *homework*.
It's *Friday night*, Ammi.
Allahomma barik lana fima razaqtana waqina ath--
Aamir, if you don't stop praying long enough to put some food in your mouth, one day you will *starve* to death.
May Allah forgive you, Abu.
Prayer is noble, but when you spend *all day* praying, it starts to look like you're *avoiding* something.
Like finding a *job*, for example.

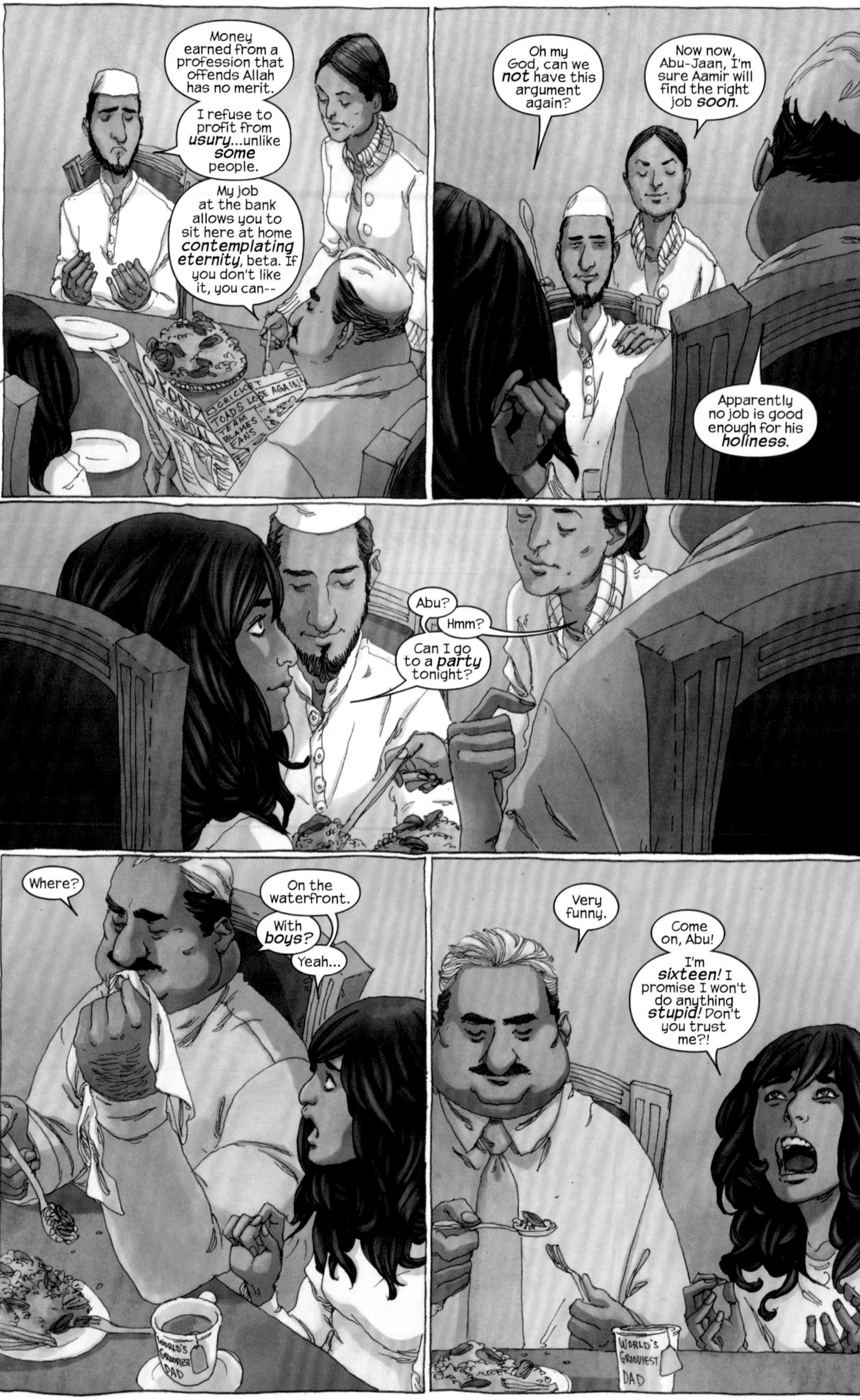
Money earned from a profession that offends Allah has no merit.
I refuse to profit from usury...unlike some people.
My job at the bank allows you to sit here at home contemplating eternity, beta. If you don't like it, you can--
SPORTS SCANDAL
CRICKET TOADS LOSE AGAIN! TEAM BLAMES FANS
Oh my God, can we not have this argument again?
Now now, Abu-Jaan, I'm sure Aamir will find the right job soon.
Apparently no job is good enough for his holiness.
Abu?
Hmm?
Can I go to a party tonight?
Where?
On the waterfront.
With boys?
Yeah...
WORLD'S GROOVIEST DAD
Very funny.
Come on, Abu!
I'm sixteen! I promise I won't do anything stupid! Don't you trust me?!
WORLD'S GROOVIEST DAD

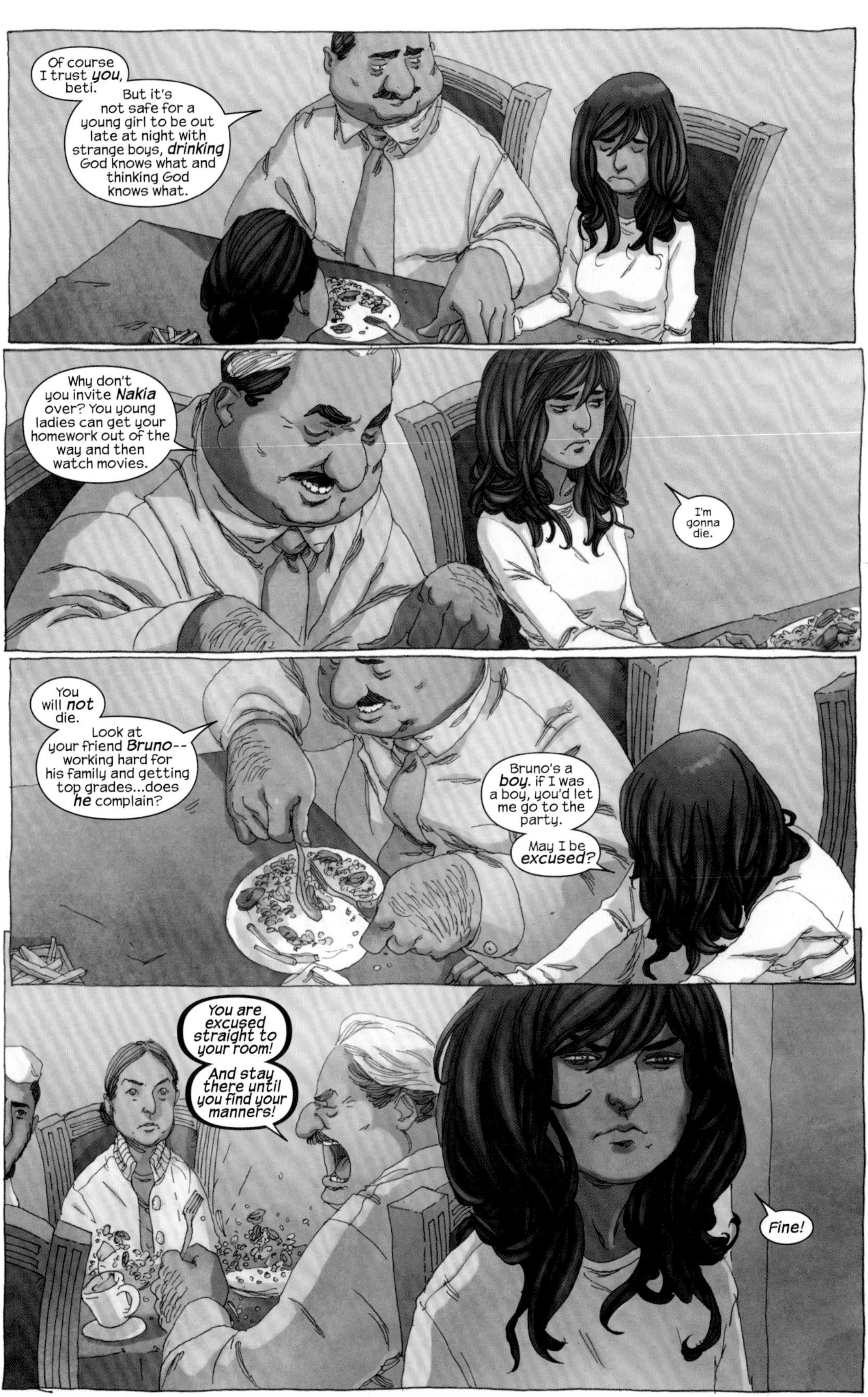
Of course I trust *you*, beti.
But it's not safe for a young girl to be out late at night with strange boys, *drinking* God knows what and thinking God knows what.
Why don't you invite *Nakia* over? You young ladies can get your homework out of the way and then watch movies.
I'm gonna die.
You will *not* die.
Look at your friend *Bruno*--working hard for his family and getting top grades...does *he* complain?
Bruno's a *boy*. If I was a boy, you'd let me go to the party.
May I be *excused*?
You are excused straight to your room!
And stay there until you find your manners!
Fine!

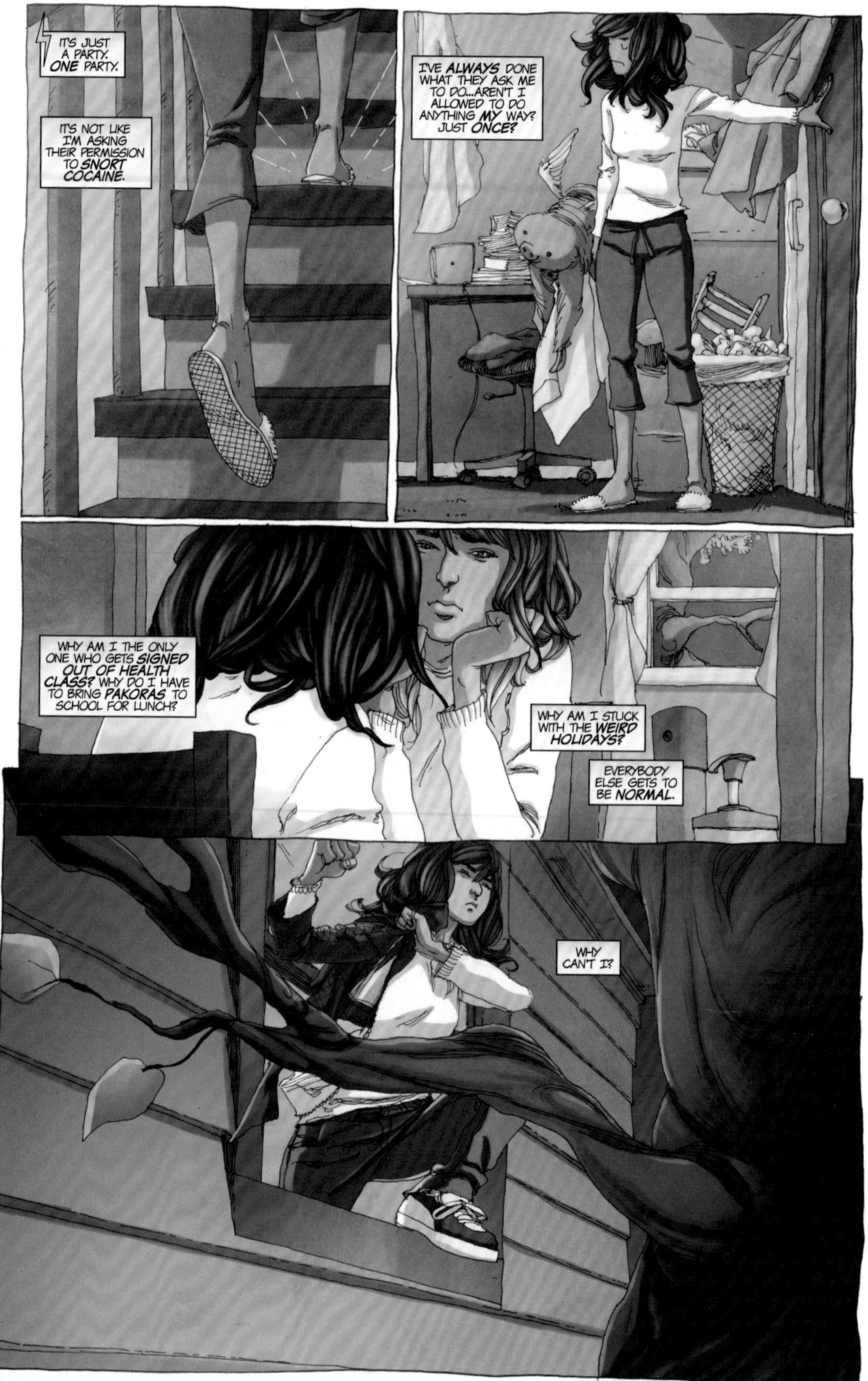
IT'S JUST A PARTY. ONE PARTY.
IT'S NOT LIKE I'M ASKING THEIR PERMISSION TO SNORT COCAINE.
I'VE ALWAYS DONE WHAT THEY ASK ME TO DO...AREN'T I ALLOWED TO DO ANYTHING MY WAY? JUST ONCE?
WHY AM I THE ONLY ONE WHO GETS SIGNED OUT OF HEALTH CLASS? WHY DO I HAVE TO BRING PAKORAS TO SCHOOL FOR LUNCH?
WHY AM I STUCK WITH THE WEIRD HOLIDAYS?
EVERYBODY ELSE GETS TO BE NORMAL.
WHY CAN'T I?

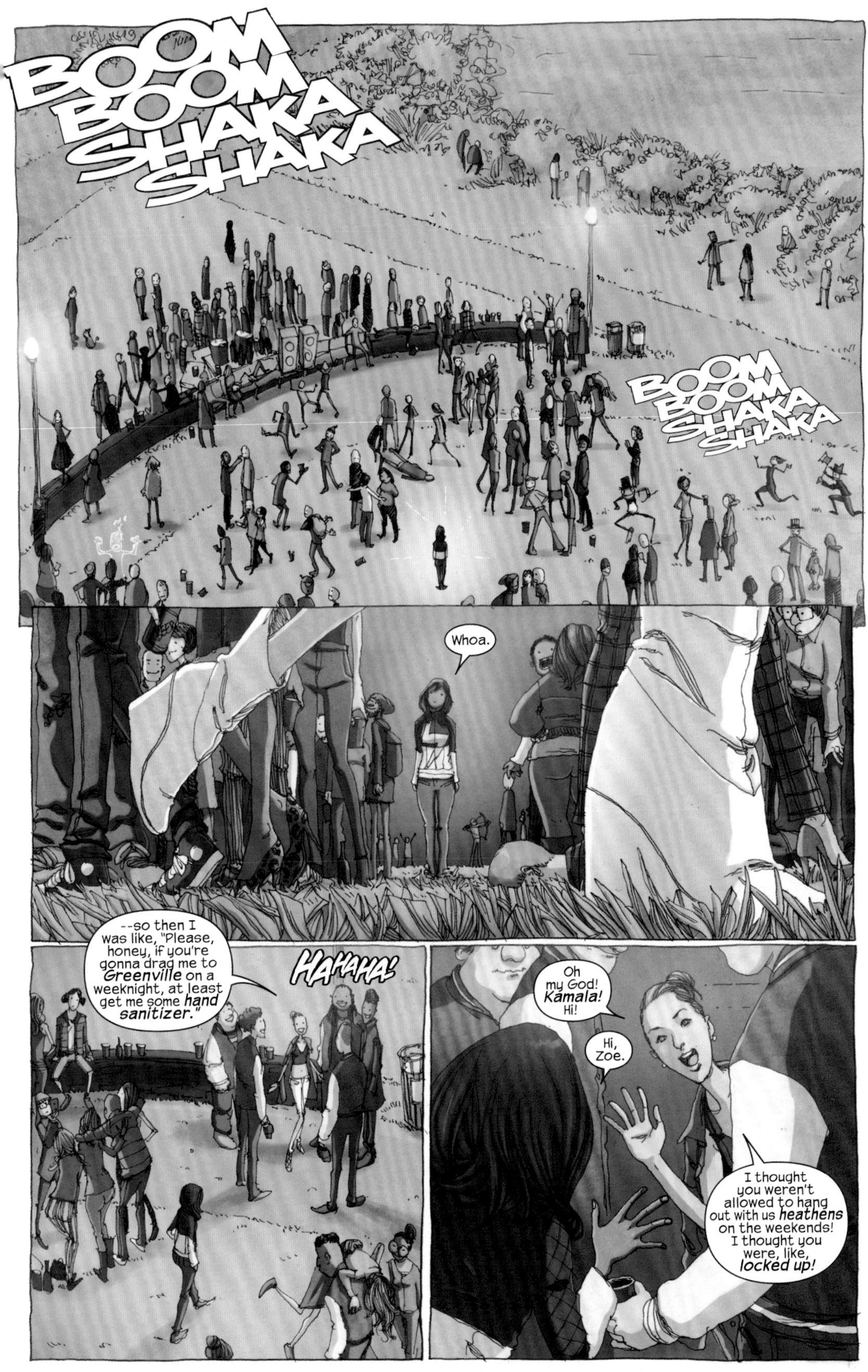
BOOM BOOM SHAKA SHAKA
BOOM BOOM SHAKA SHAKA
Whoa.
--so then I was like, "Please, honey, if you're gonna drag me to Greenville on a weeknight, at least get me some hand sanitizer."
HAHAHA!
Oh my God! Kamala! Hi!
Hi, Zoe.
I thought you weren't allowed to hang out with us heathens on the weekends! I thought you were, like, locked up!

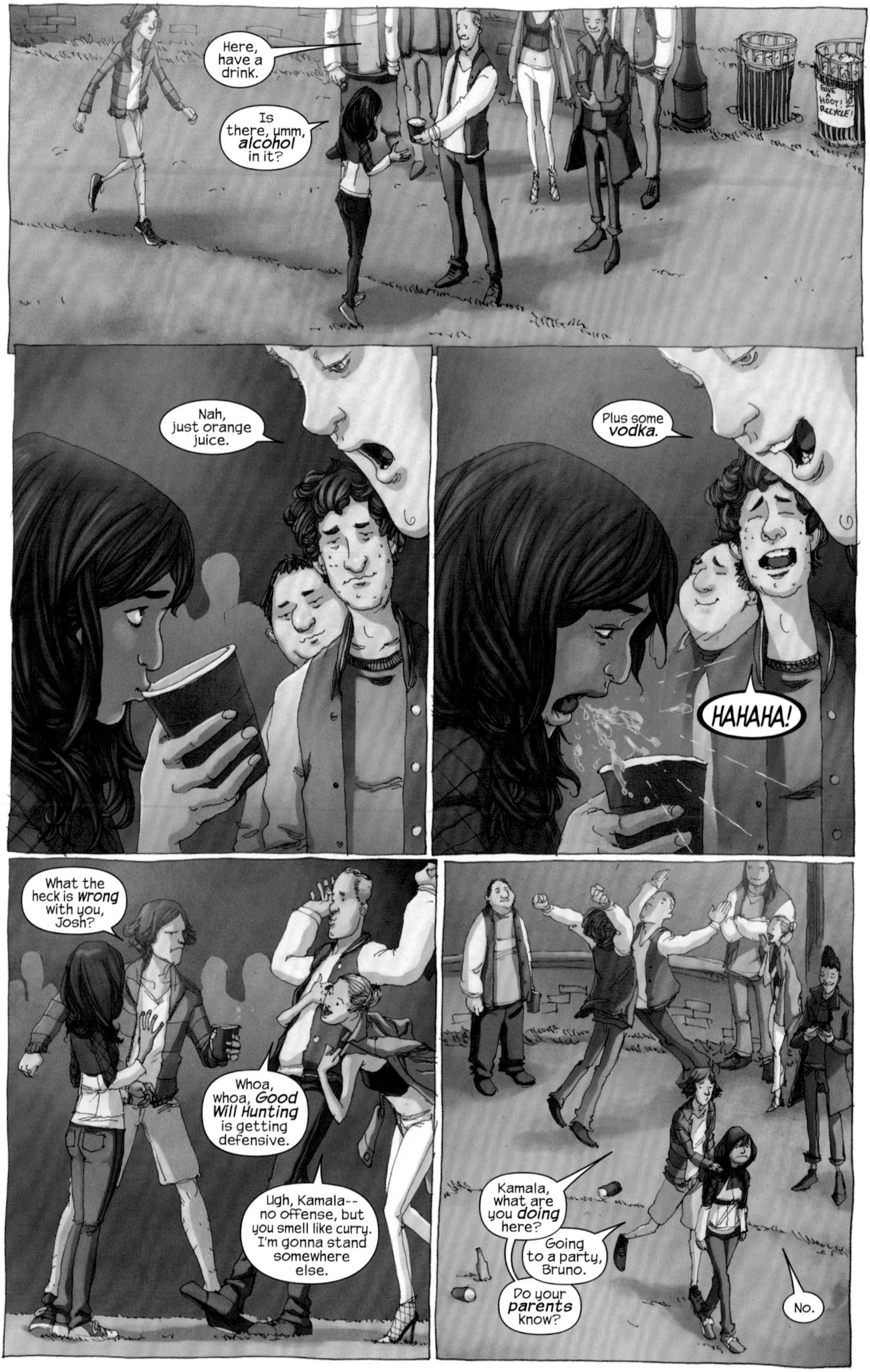
Here, have a drink.
Is there, umm, alcohol in it?
GIVE A HOOT! RECYCLE!
Nah, just orange juice.
Plus some vodka.
HAHAHA!
What the heck is wrong with you, Josh?
Whoa, whoa, Good Will Hunting is getting defensive.
Ugh, Kamala-- no offense, but you smell like curry. I'm gonna stand somewhere else.
Kamala, what are you doing here?
Going to a party, Bruno.
Do your parents know?
No.

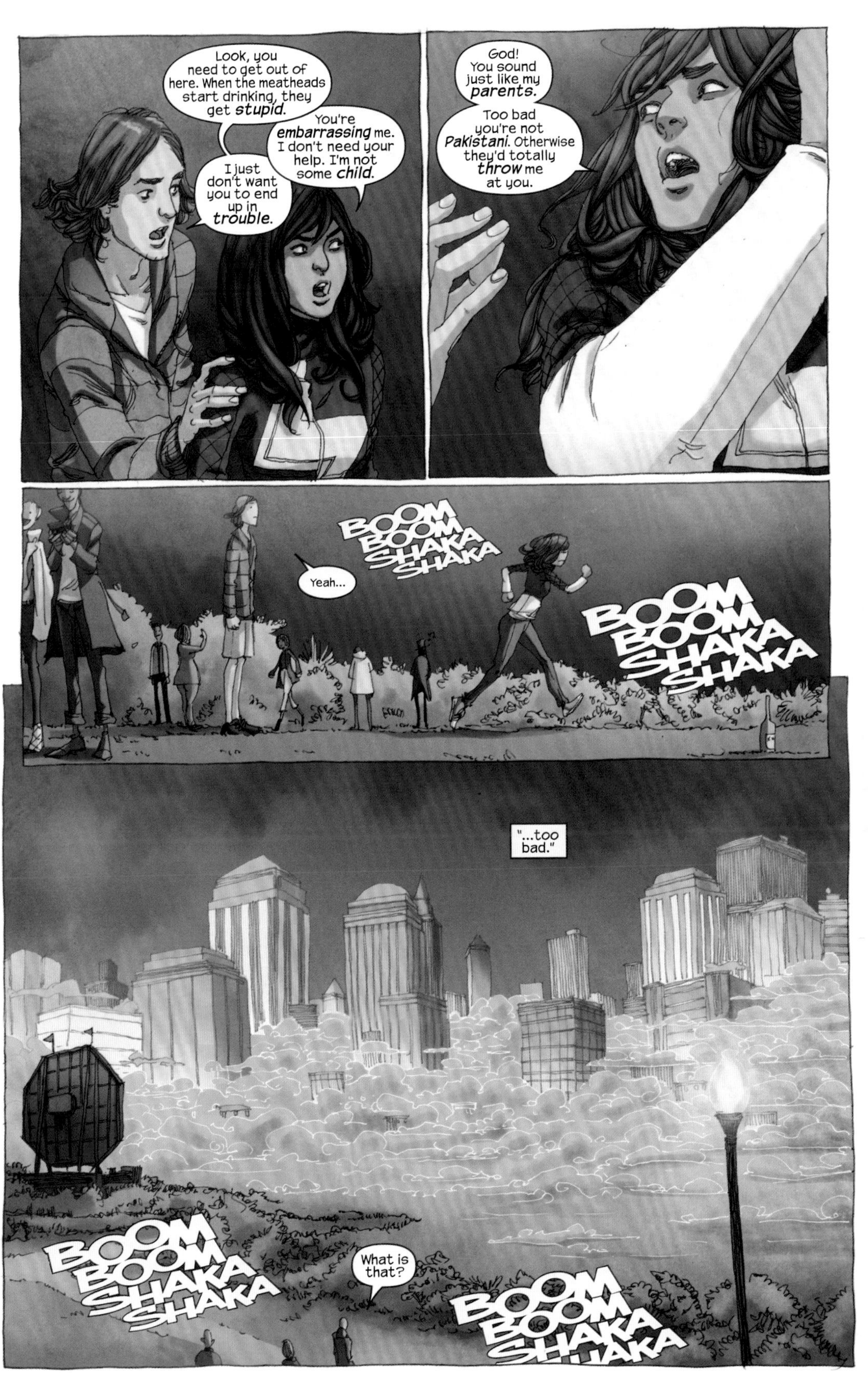
Look, you need to get out of here. When the meatheads start drinking, they get *stupid*.
You're *embarrassing* me. I don't need your help. I'm not some *child*.
I just don't want you to end up in *trouble*.
God! You sound just like my *parents*.
Too bad you're not *Pakistani*. Otherwise they'd totally *throw* me at you.
BOOM BOOM SHAKA SHAKA
Yeah...
BOOM BOOM SHAKA SHAKA
"...too bad."
BOOM BOOM SHAKA SHAKA
What is that?
BOOM BOOM SHAKA SHAKA

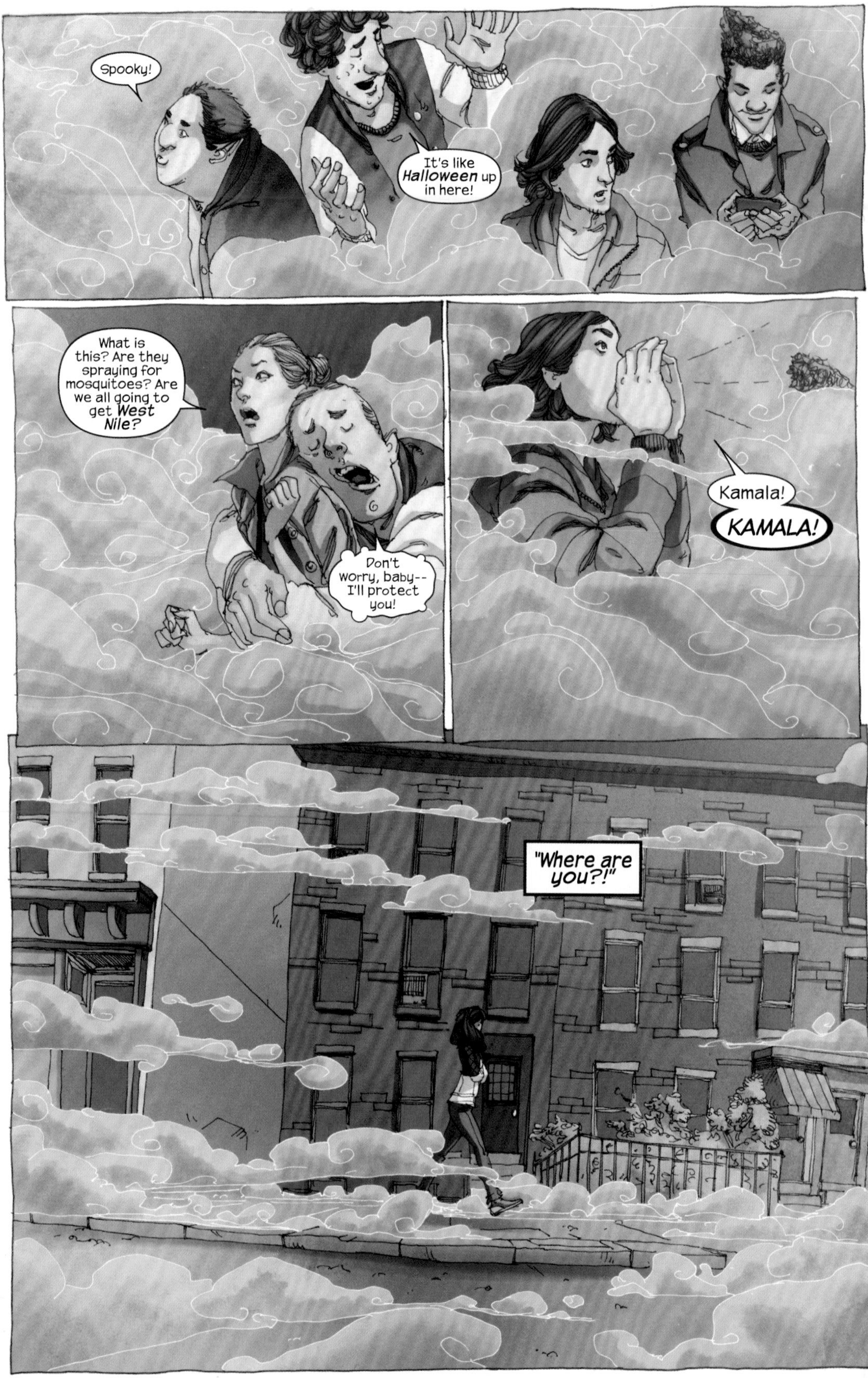
Spooky!
It's like Halloween up in here!
What is this? Are they spraying for mosquitoes? Are we all going to get West Nile?
Don't worry, baby-- I'll protect you!
Kamala!
KAMALA!
"Where are you?!"

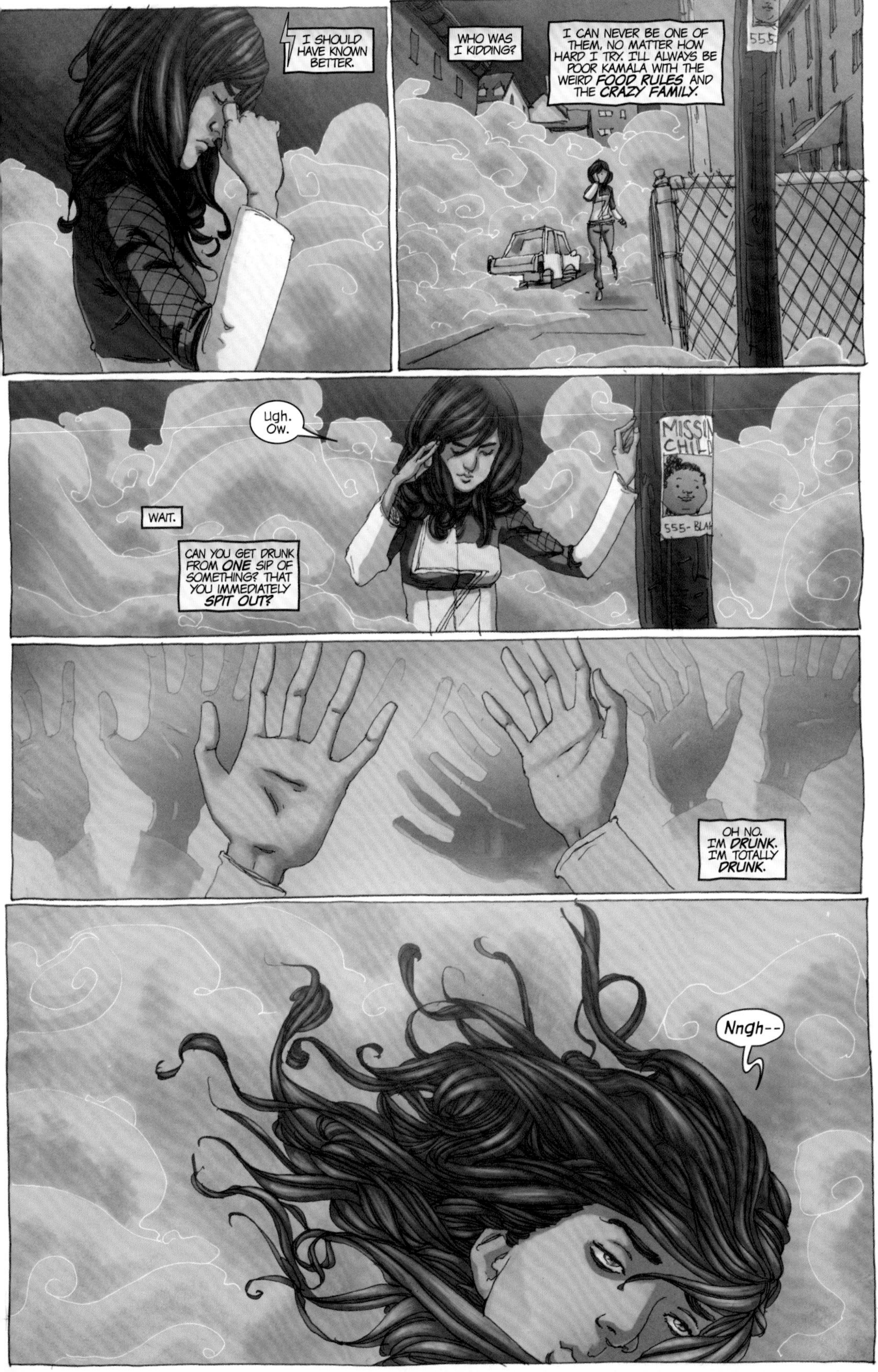
I SHOULD HAVE KNOWN BETTER.
WHO WAS I KIDDING?
I CAN NEVER BE ONE OF THEM, NO MATTER HOW HARD I TRY. I'LL ALWAYS BE POOR KAMALA WITH THE WEIRD FOOD RULES AND THE CRAZY FAMILY.
555
Ugh. Ow.
MISSIN CHILD
555-BLAH
WAIT.
CAN YOU GET DRUNK FROM ONE SIP OF SOMETHING? THAT YOU IMMEDIATELY SPIT OUT?
OH NO. I'M DRUNK. I'M TOTALLY DRUNK.
Nngh--

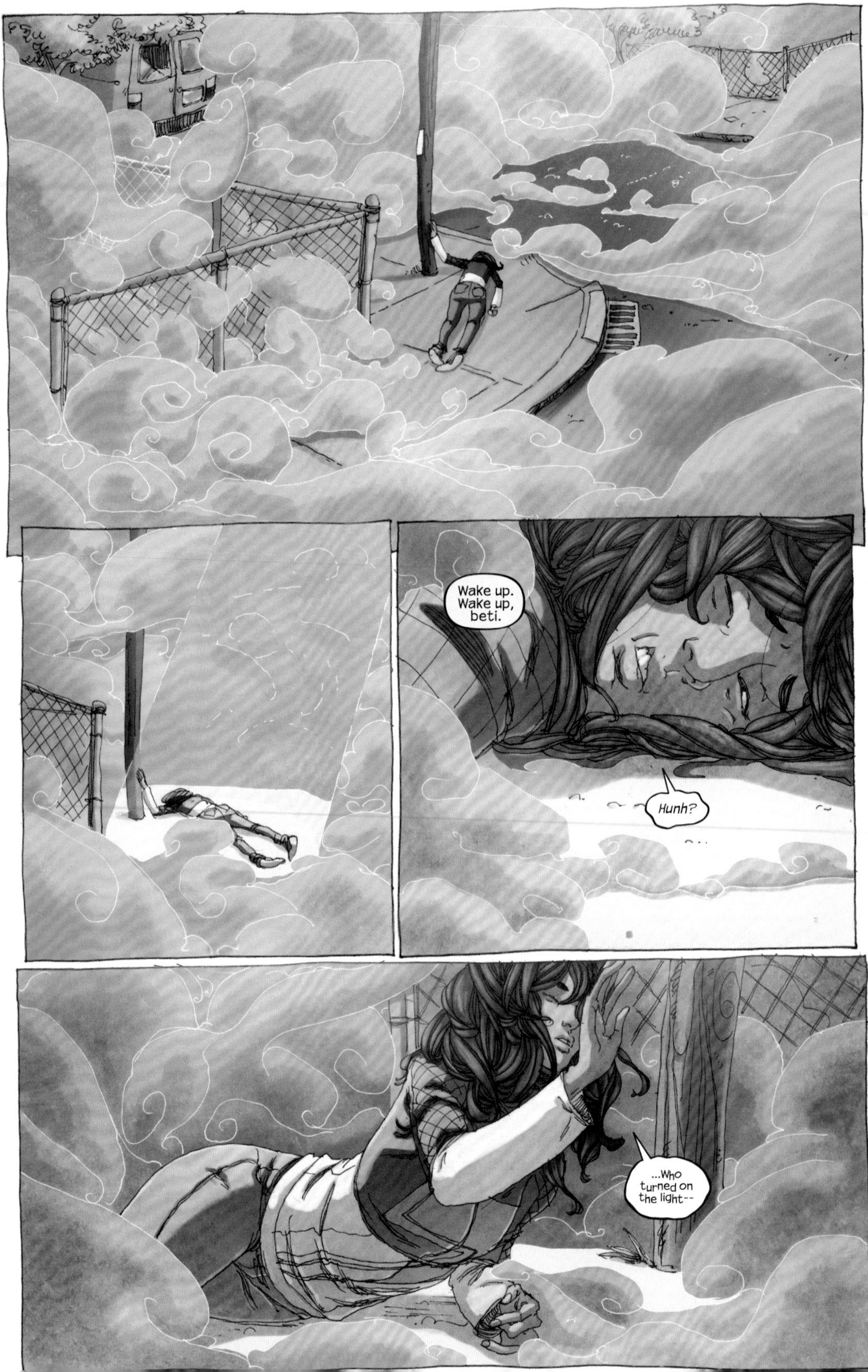
Wake up. Wake up, beti.
Hunh?
...Who turned on the light--

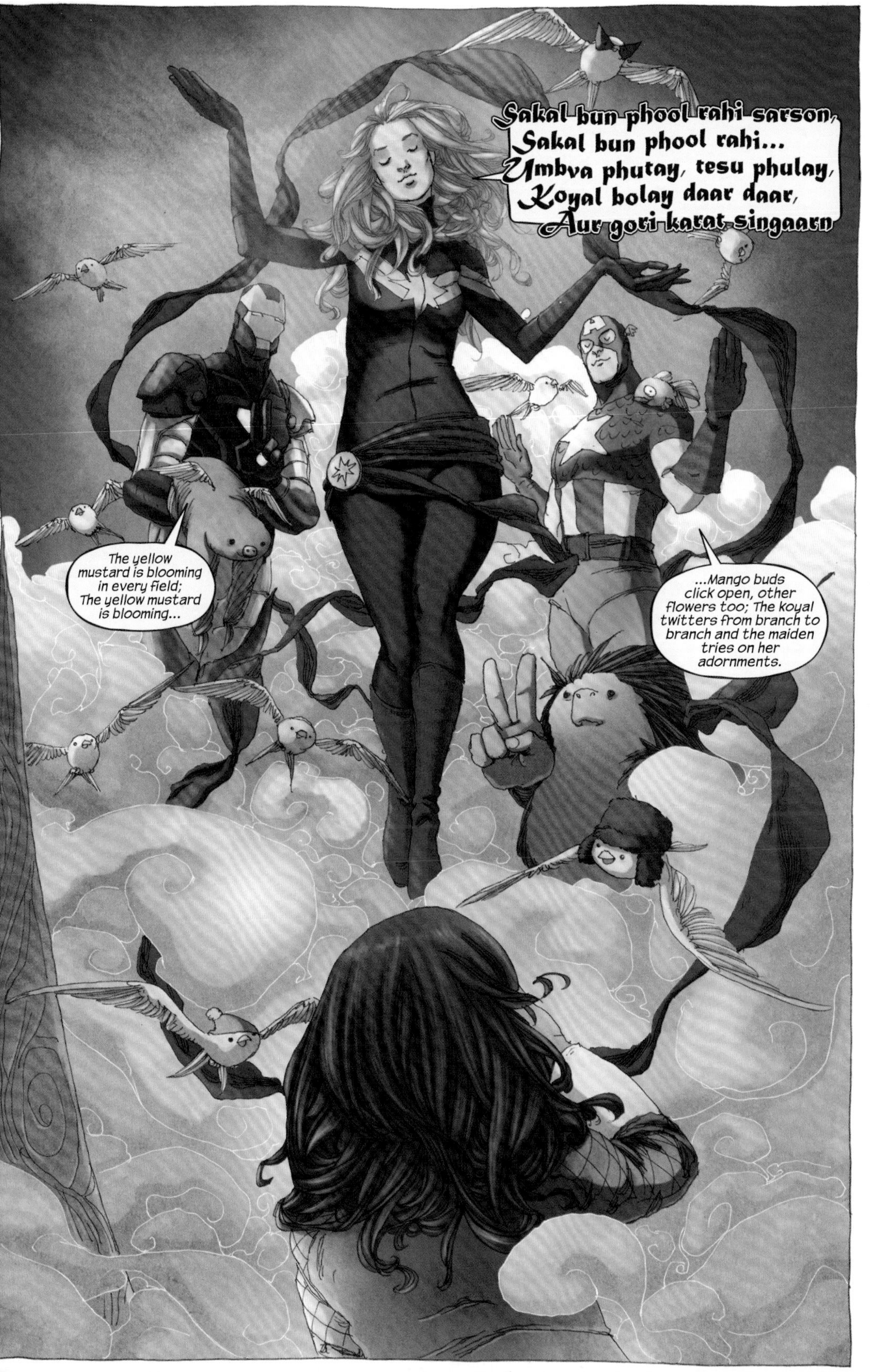
Sakal bun phool rahi sarson, Sakal bun phool rahi... Umbva phutay, tesu phulay, Koyal bolay daar daar, Aur gori karat singaarn
The yellow mustard is blooming in every field; The yellow mustard is blooming...
...Mango buds click open, other flowers too; The koyal twitters from branch to branch and the maiden tries on her adornments.

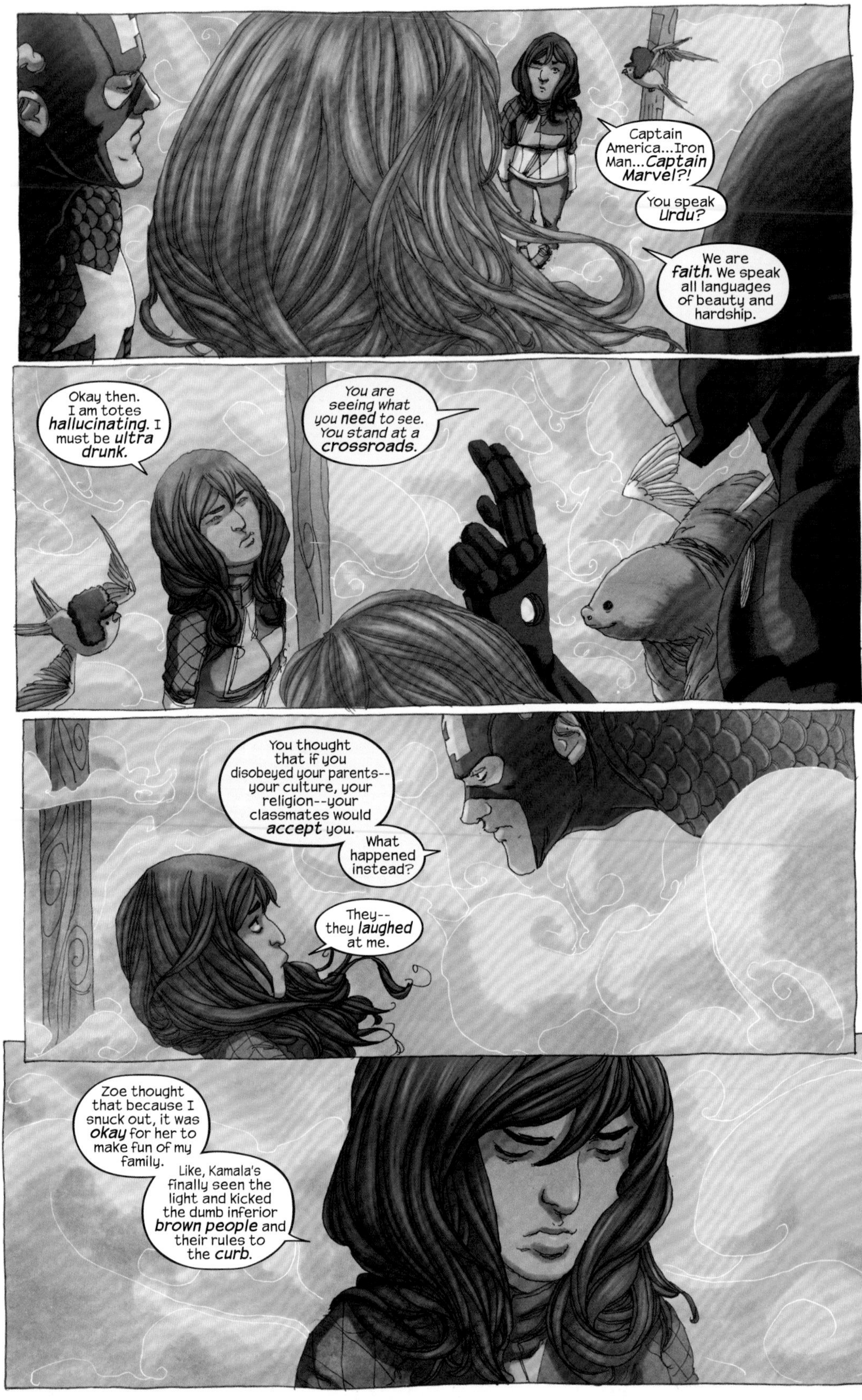

Captain America...Iron Man...Captain Marvel?!
You speak Urdu?
We are faith. We speak all languages of beauty and hardship.
Okay then. I am totes hallucinating. I must be ultra drunk.
You are seeing what you need to see. You stand at a crossroads.
You thought that if you disobeyed your parents--your culture, your religion--your classmates would accept you.
What happened instead?
They--they laughed at me.
Zoe thought that because I snuck out, it was okay for her to make fun of my family.
Like, Kamala's finally seen the light and kicked the dumb inferior brown people and their rules to the curb.

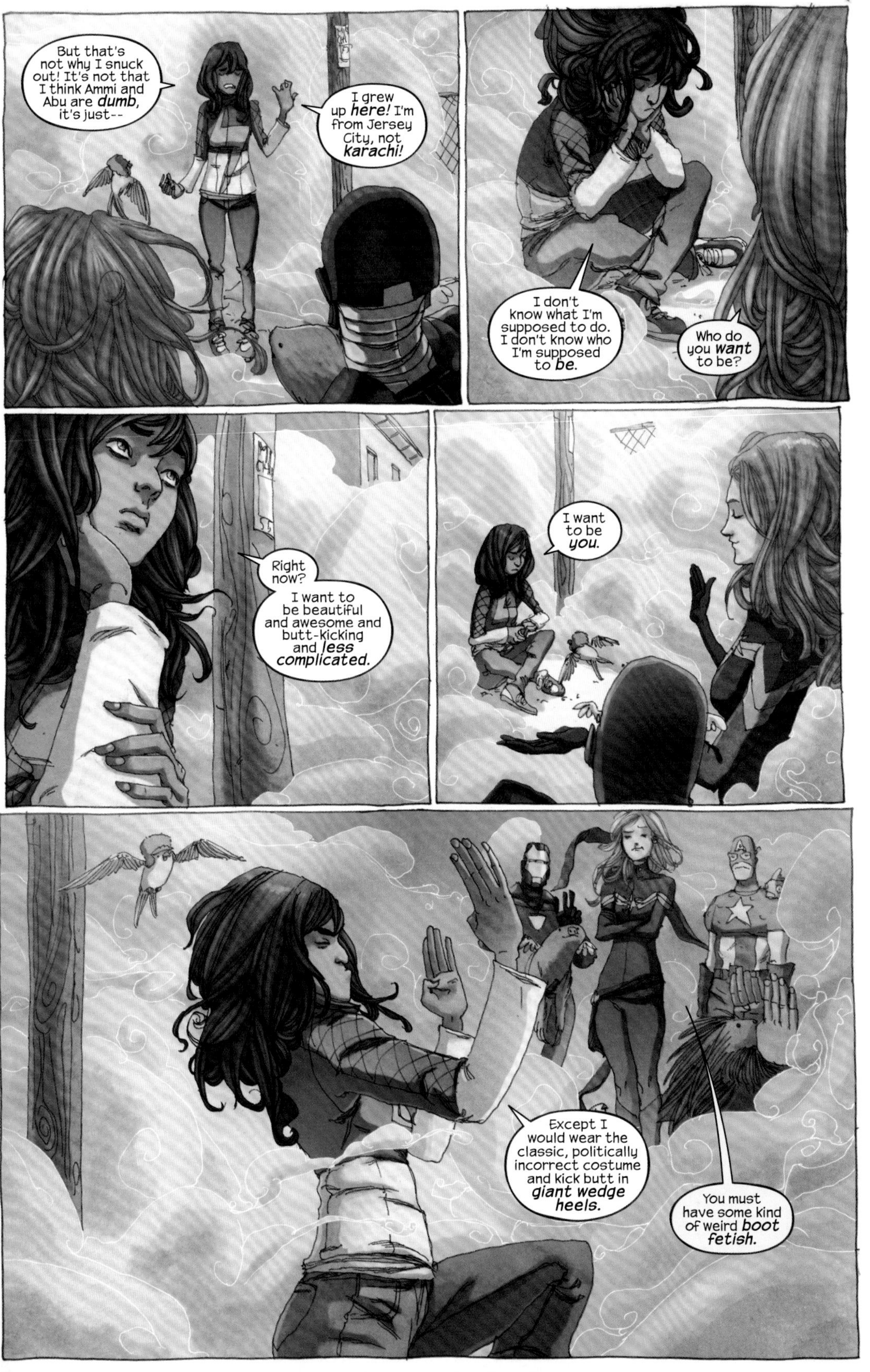

But that's not why I snuck out! It's not that I think Ammi and Abu are *dumb*, it's just--
I grew up *here!* I'm from Jersey City, not *karachi!*
I don't know what I'm supposed to do. I don't know who I'm supposed to *be*.
Who do you *want* to be?
Right now?
I want to be beautiful and awesome and butt-kicking and *less complicated*.
I want to be *you*.
Except I would wear the classic, politically incorrect costume and kick butt in *giant wedge heels*.
You must have some kind of weird *boot fetish*.

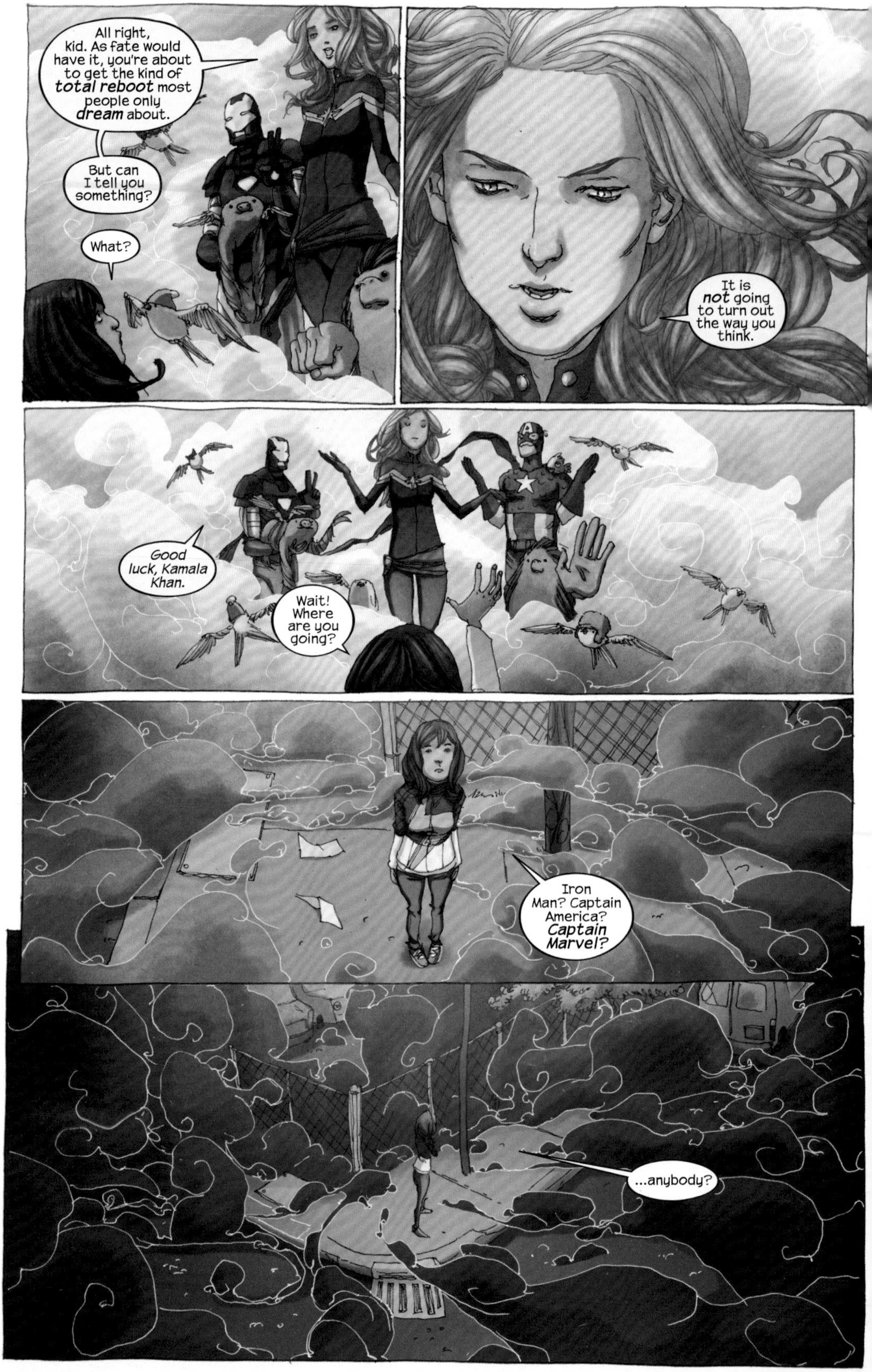
All right, kid. As fate would have it, you're about to get the kind of **total reboot** most people only **dream** about.
But can I tell you something?
What?
It is **not** going to turn out the way you think.
Good luck, Kamala Khan.
Wait! Where are you going?
Iron Man? Captain America? **Captain Marvel?**
...anybody?

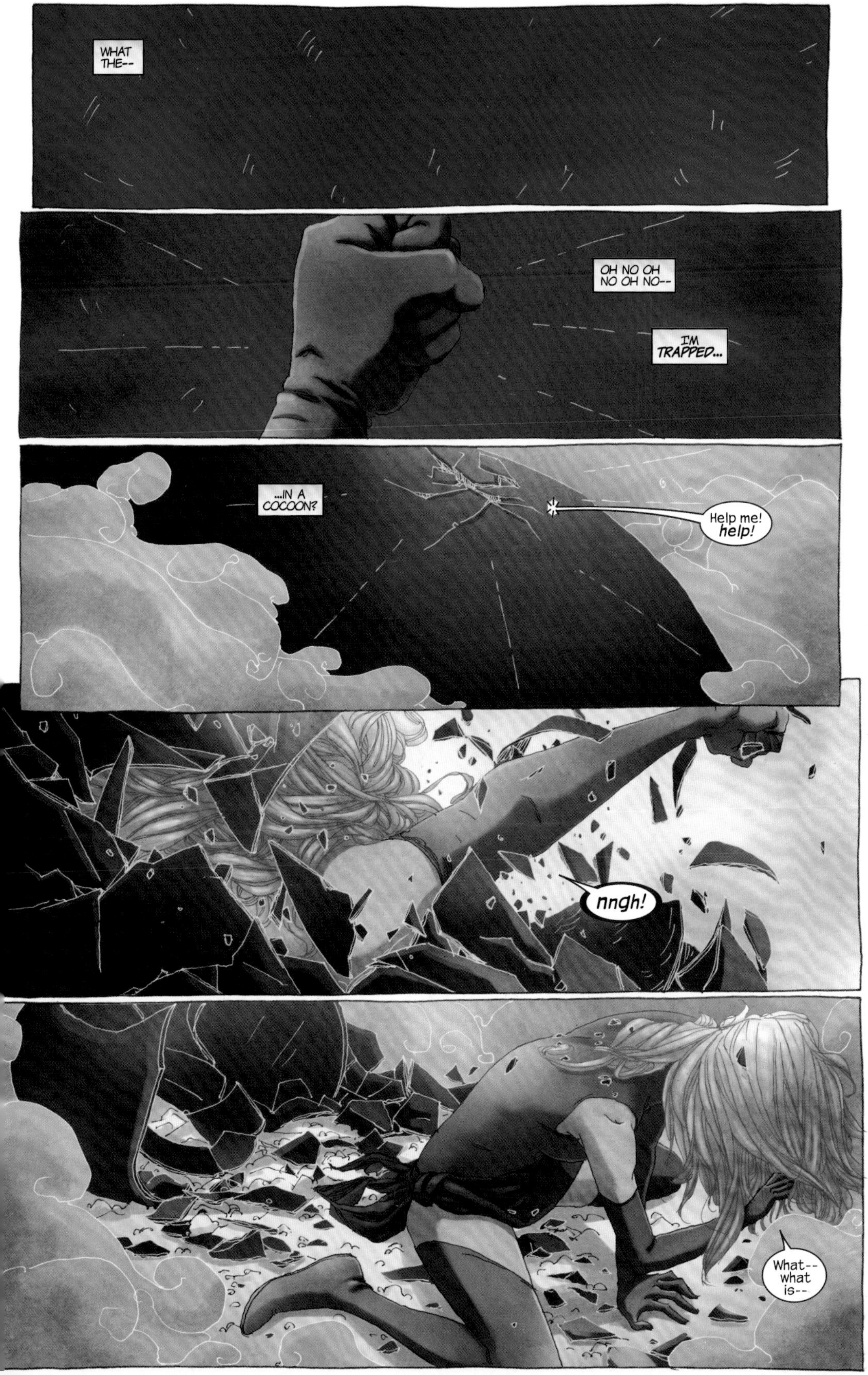

WHAT THE--
OH NO OH NO OH NO--
I'M TRAPPED...
...IN A COCOON?
Help me! help!
nngh!
What-- what is--

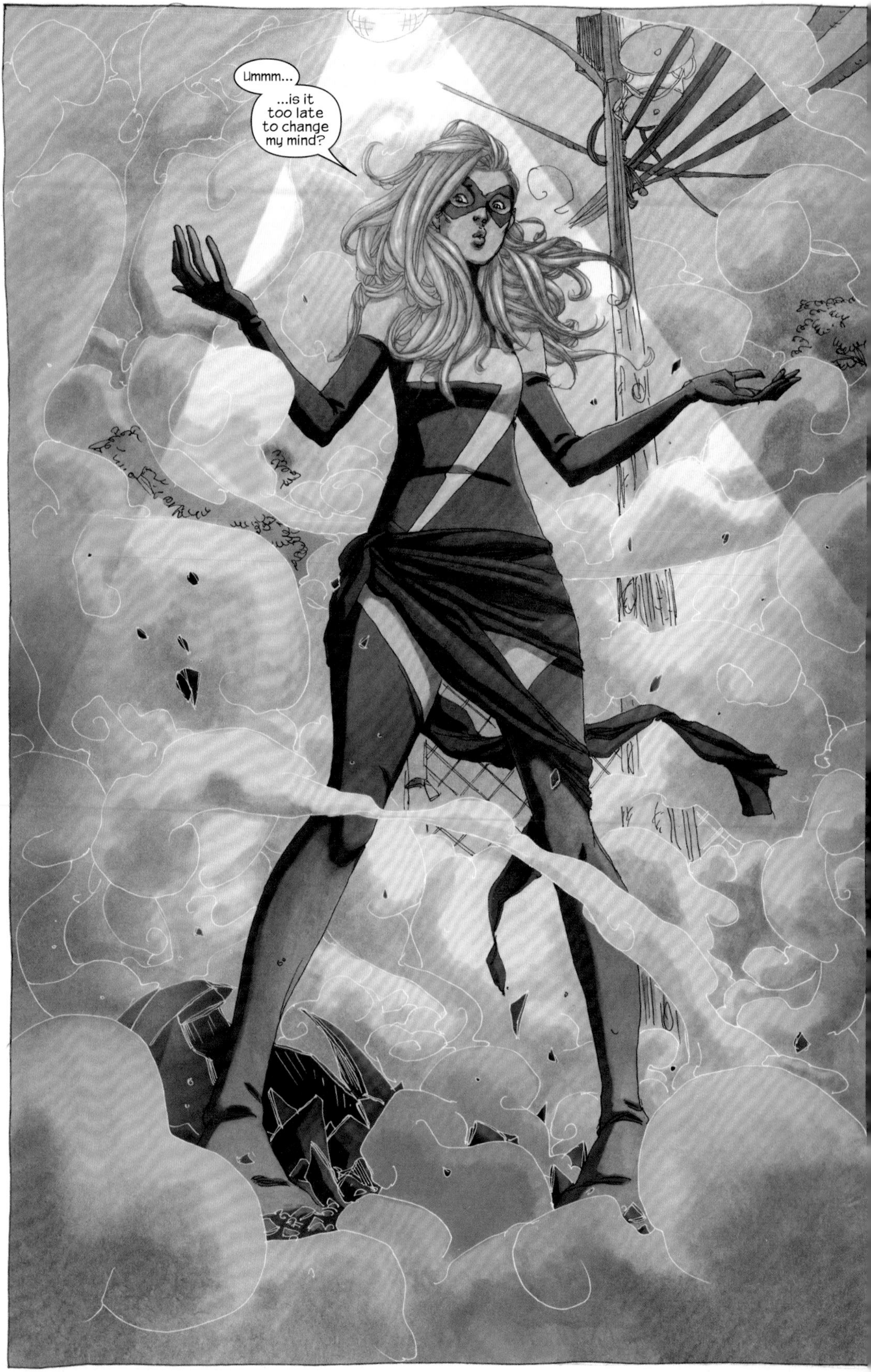
Ummm...
...is it too late to change my mind?

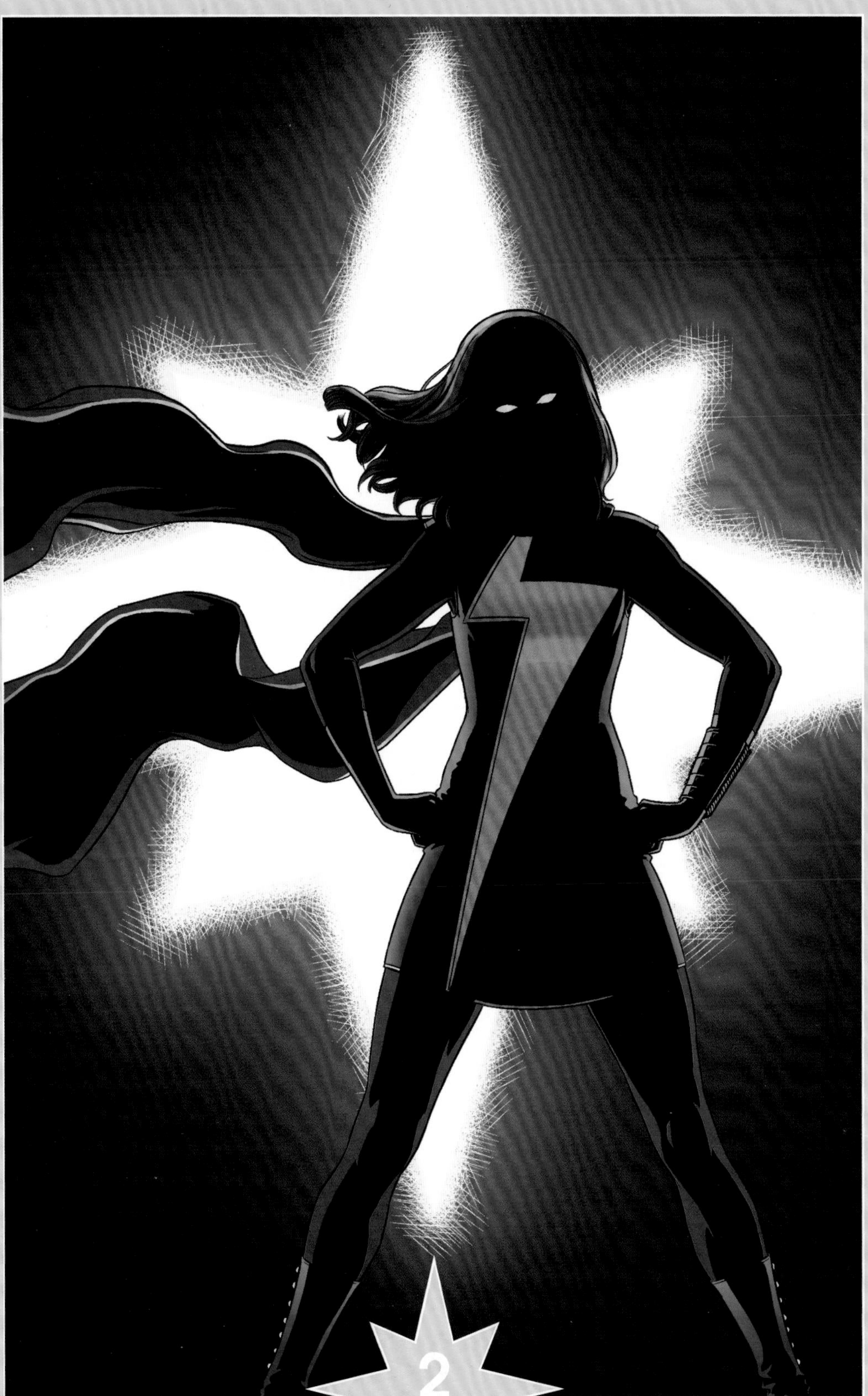
2

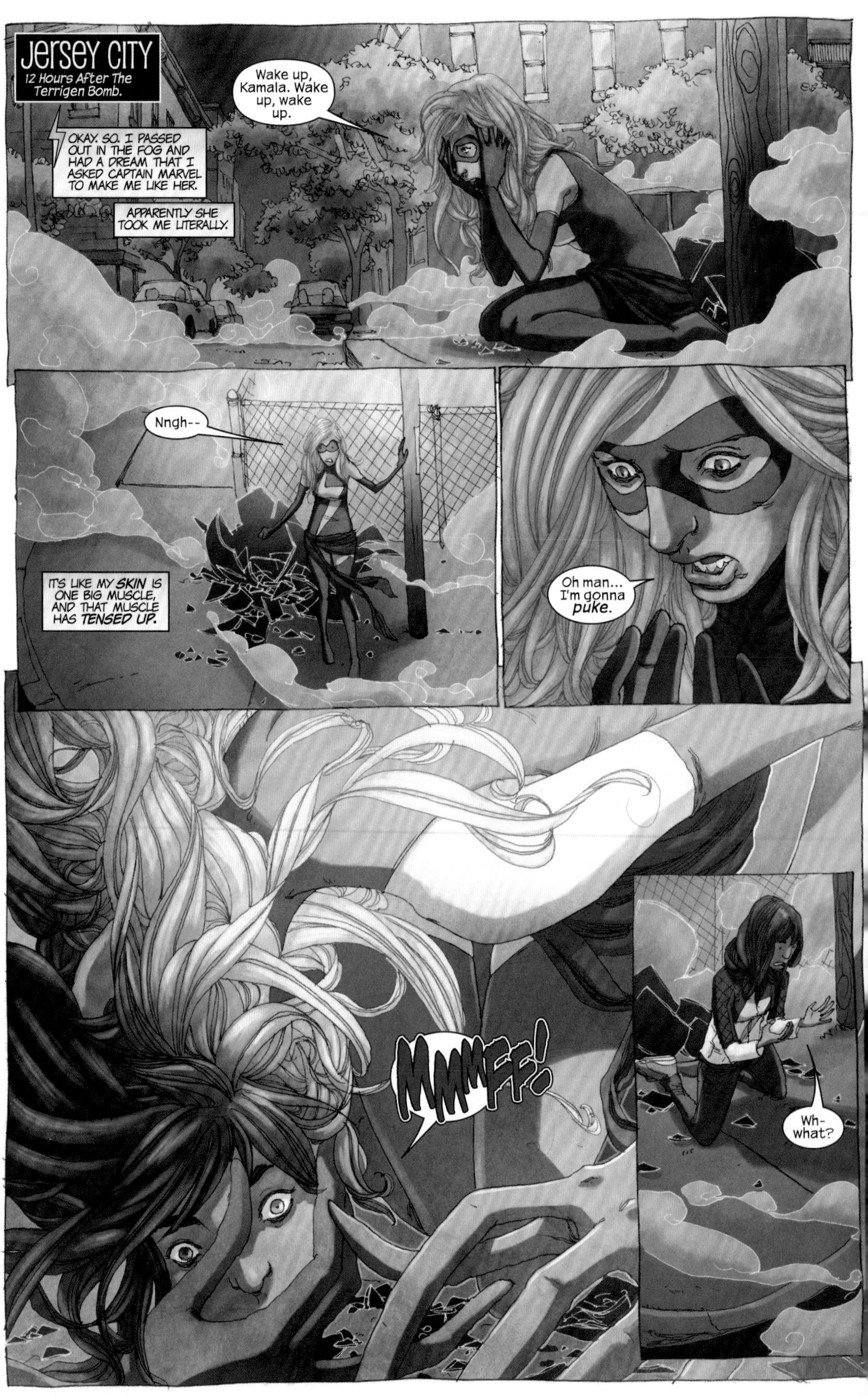
JERSEY CITY
12 Hours After The Terrigen Bomb.
Wake up, Kamala. Wake up, wake up.
OKAY. SO. I PASSED OUT IN THE FOG AND HAD A DREAM THAT I ASKED CAPTAIN MARVEL TO MAKE ME LIKE HER.
APPARENTLY SHE TOOK ME LITERALLY.
Nngh--
IT'S LIKE MY SKIN IS ONE BIG MUSCLE, AND THAT MUSCLE HAS TENSED UP.
Oh man... I'm gonna puke.
MMMFF!
Wh-what?

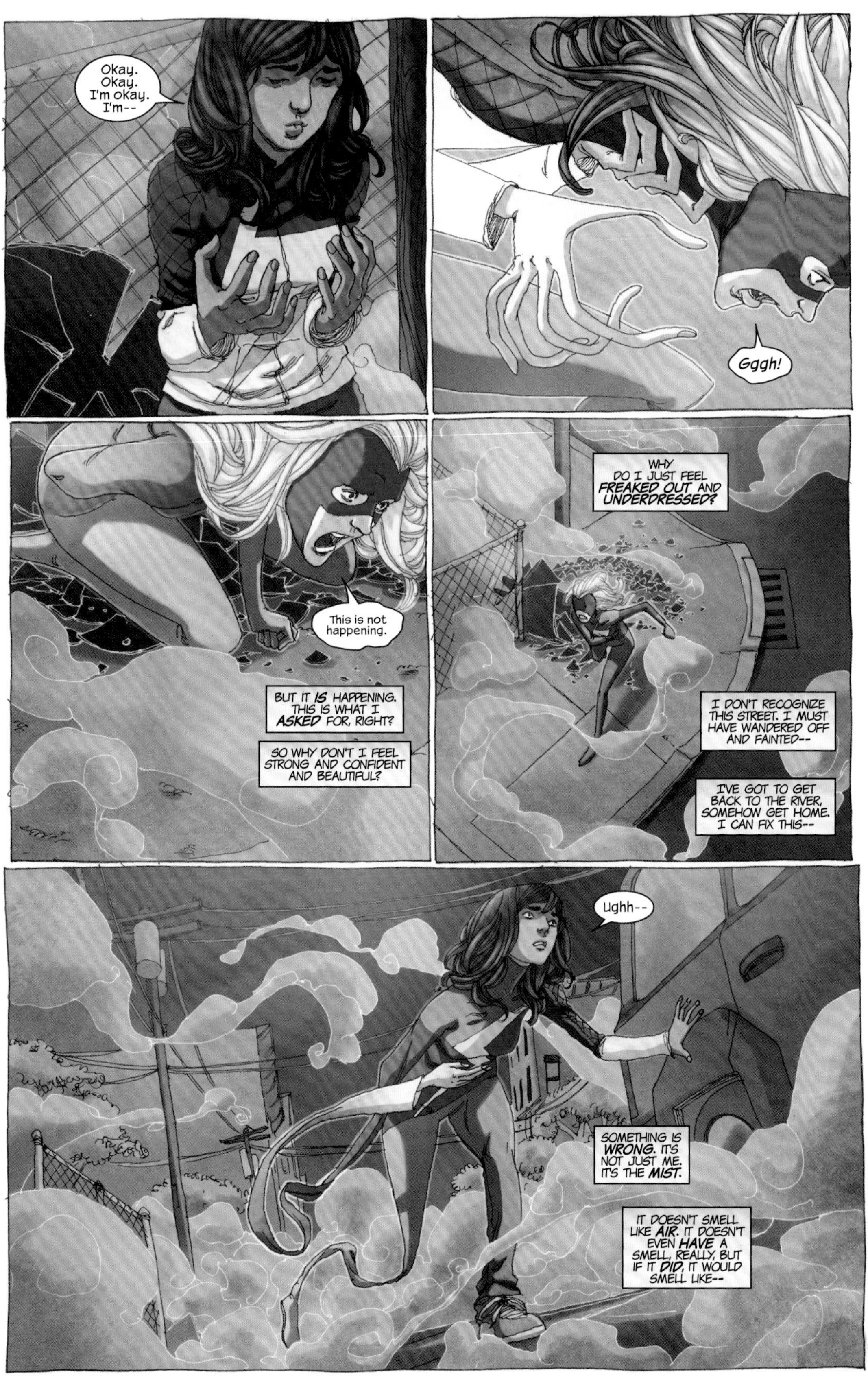

Okay. Okay. I'm okay. I'm--
Gggh!
This is not happening.
BUT IT IS HAPPENING. THIS IS WHAT I ASKED FOR, RIGHT?
SO WHY DON'T I FEEL STRONG AND CONFIDENT AND BEAUTIFUL?
WHY DO I JUST FEEL FREAKED OUT AND UNDERDRESSED?
I DON'T RECOGNIZE THIS STREET. I MUST HAVE WANDERED OFF AND FAINTED--
I'VE GOT TO GET BACK TO THE RIVER, SOMEHOW GET HOME. I CAN FIX THIS--
Ughh--
SOMETHING IS WRONG. IT'S NOT JUST ME. IT'S THE MIST.
IT DOESN'T SMELL LIKE AIR. IT DOESN'T EVEN HAVE A SMELL, REALLY, BUT IF IT DID, IT WOULD SMELL LIKE--

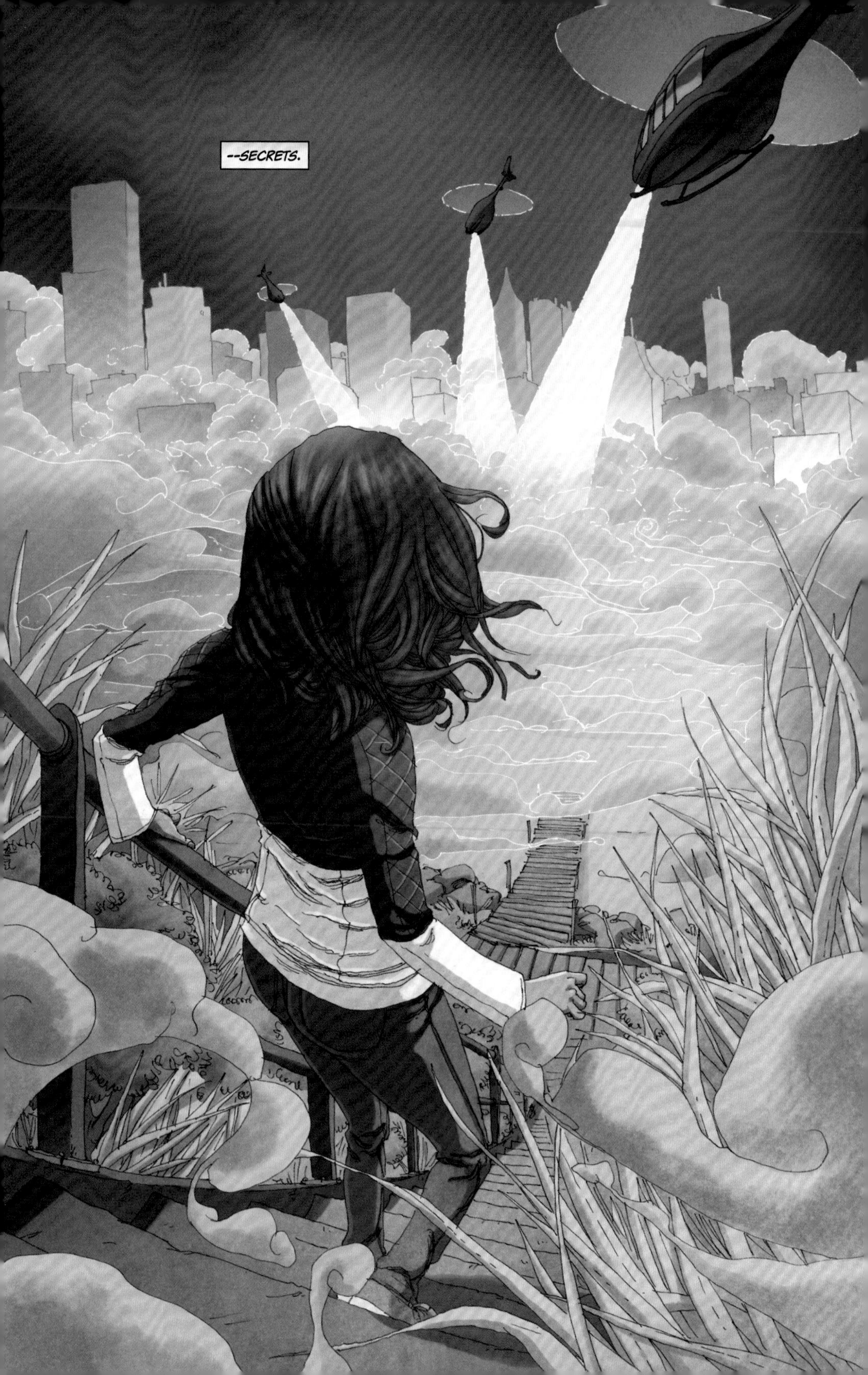
--SECRETS.

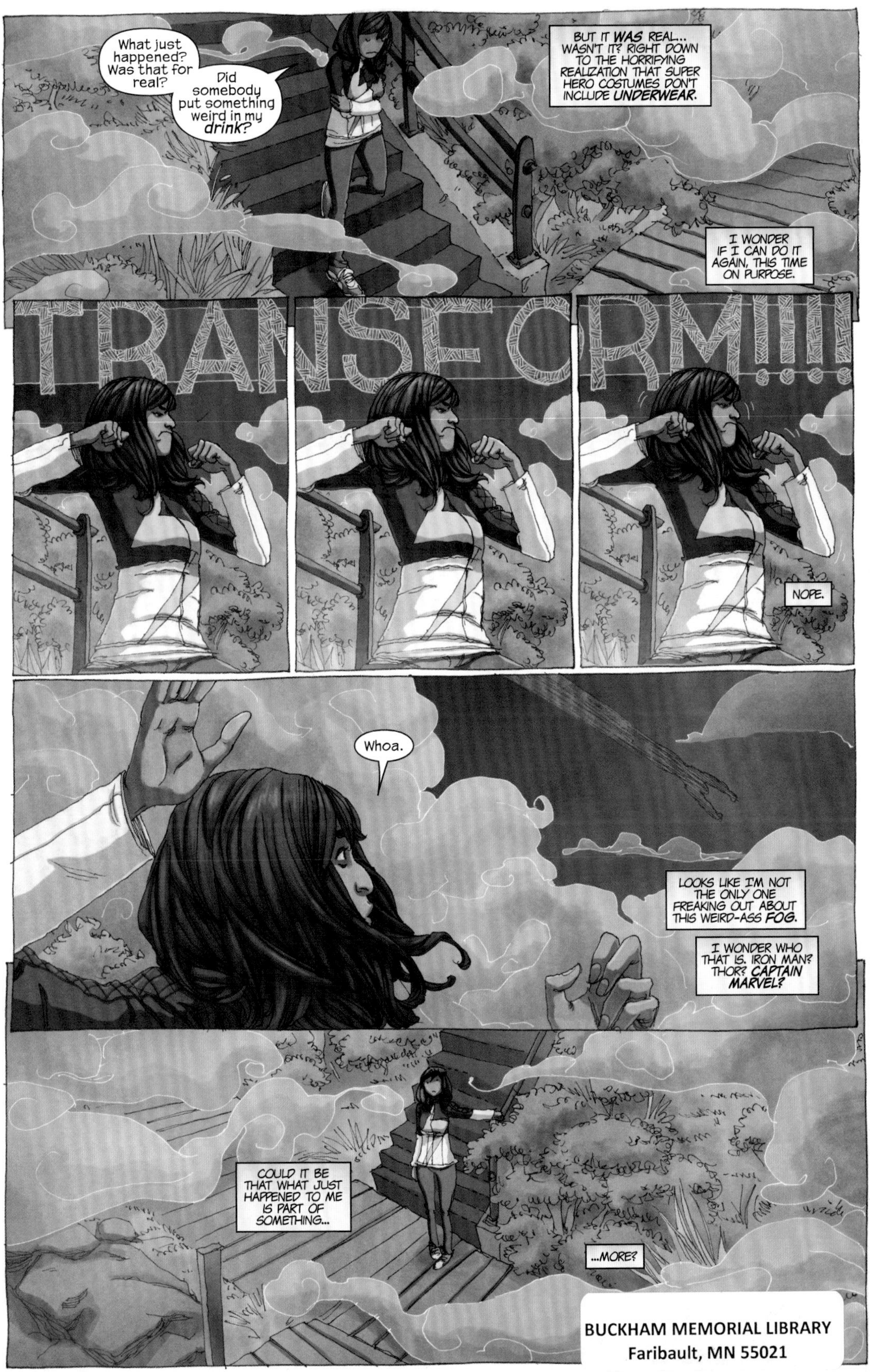

What just happened? Was that for real?
Did somebody put something weird in my drink?
BUT IT WAS REAL... WASN'T IT? RIGHT DOWN TO THE HORRIFYING REALIZATION THAT SUPER HERO COSTUMES DON'T INCLUDE UNDERWEAR.
I WONDER IF I CAN DO IT AGAIN, THIS TIME ON PURPOSE.
TRANSFORM!!!!
NOPE.
Whoa.
LOOKS LIKE I'M NOT THE ONLY ONE FREAKING OUT ABOUT THIS WEIRD-ASS FOG.
I WONDER WHO THAT IS. IRON MAN? THOR? CAPTAIN MARVEL?
COULD IT BE THAT WHAT JUST HAPPENED TO ME IS PART OF SOMETHING...
...MORE?

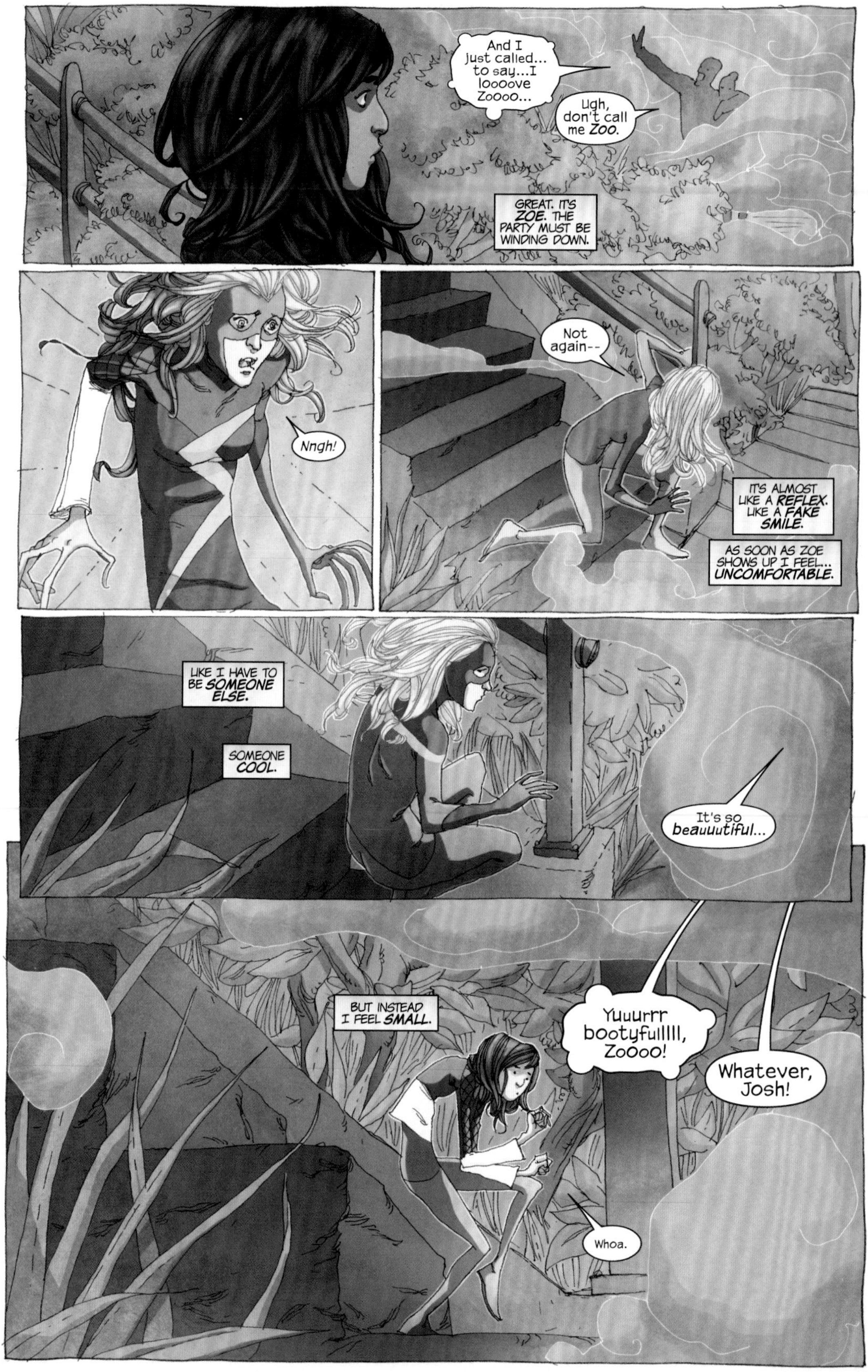

And I just called... to say...I loooove Zoooo...
Ugh, don't call me *ZOO*.
GREAT. IT'S *ZOE*. THE PARTY MUST BE WINDING DOWN.
Nngh!
Not again--
IT'S ALMOST LIKE A *REFLEX*. LIKE A *FAKE SMILE*.
AS SOON AS ZOE SHOWS UP I FEEL... *UNCOMFORTABLE*.
LIKE I HAVE TO BE *SOMEONE ELSE*.
SOMEONE *COOL*.
It's so *beauuutiful*...
BUT INSTEAD I FEEL *SMALL*.
Yuuurrr bootyfullllll, Zoooo!
Whatever, Josh!
Whoa.

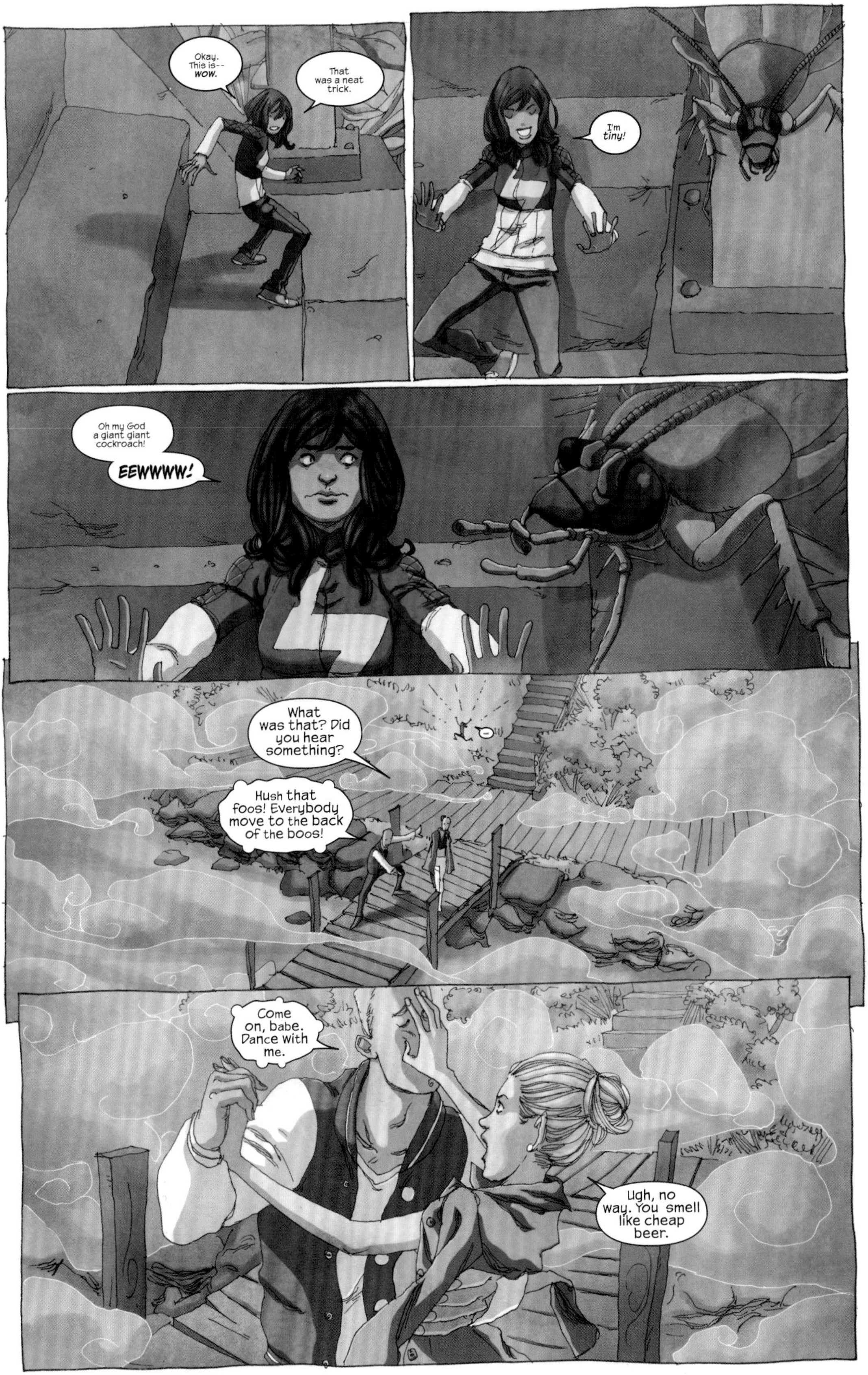
Okay. This is-- WOW.
That was a neat trick.
I'm tiny!
Oh my God a giant giant cockroach!
EEWWWW!
What was that? Did you hear something?
Hush that foos! Everybody move to the back of the boos!
Come on, babe. Dance with me.
Ugh, no way. You smell like cheap beer.

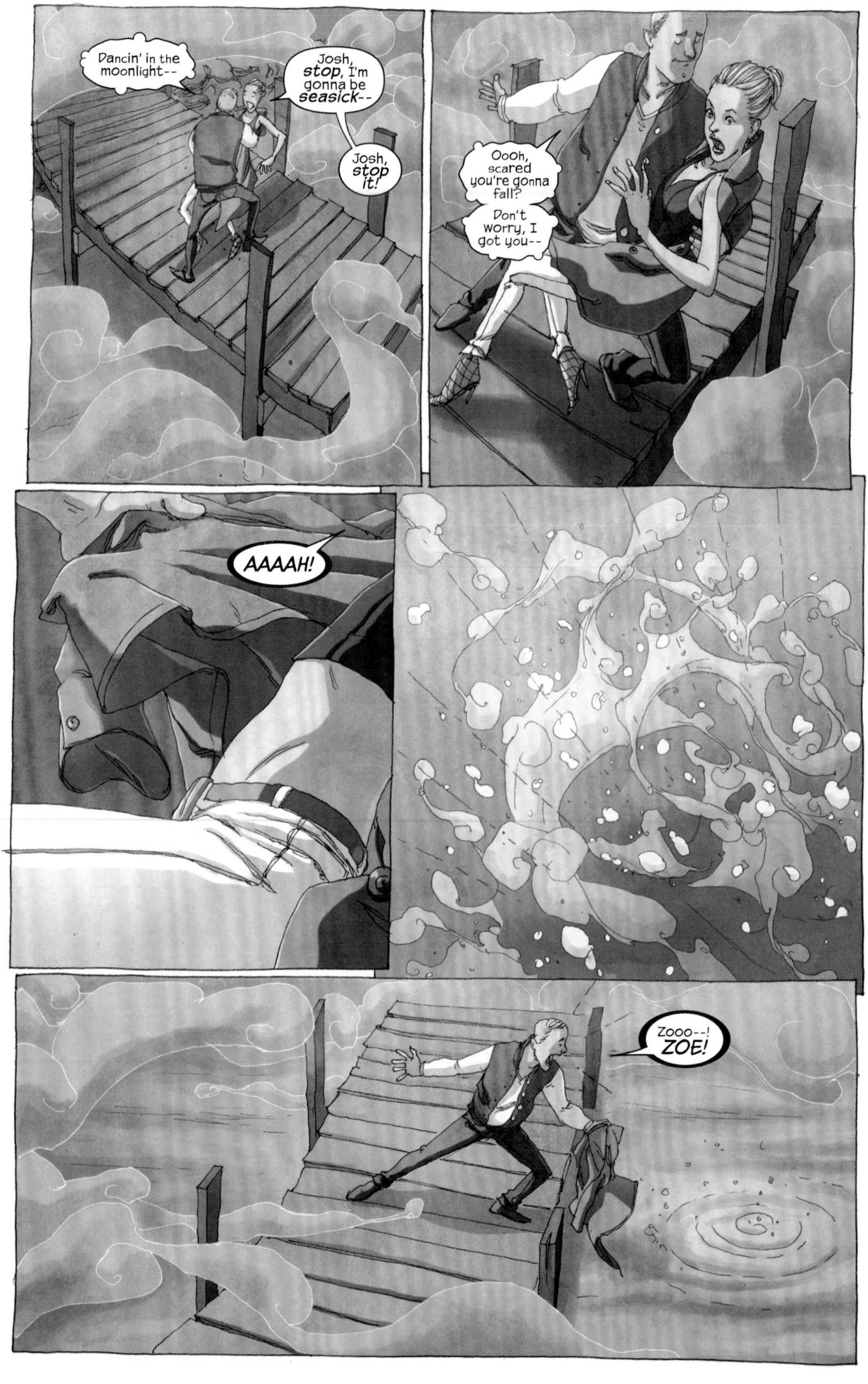
Dancin' in the moonlight--
Josh, stop, I'm gonna be seasick--
Josh, stop it!
Oooh, scared you're gonna fall?
Don't worry, I got you--
AAAAH!
Zooo--! ZOE!

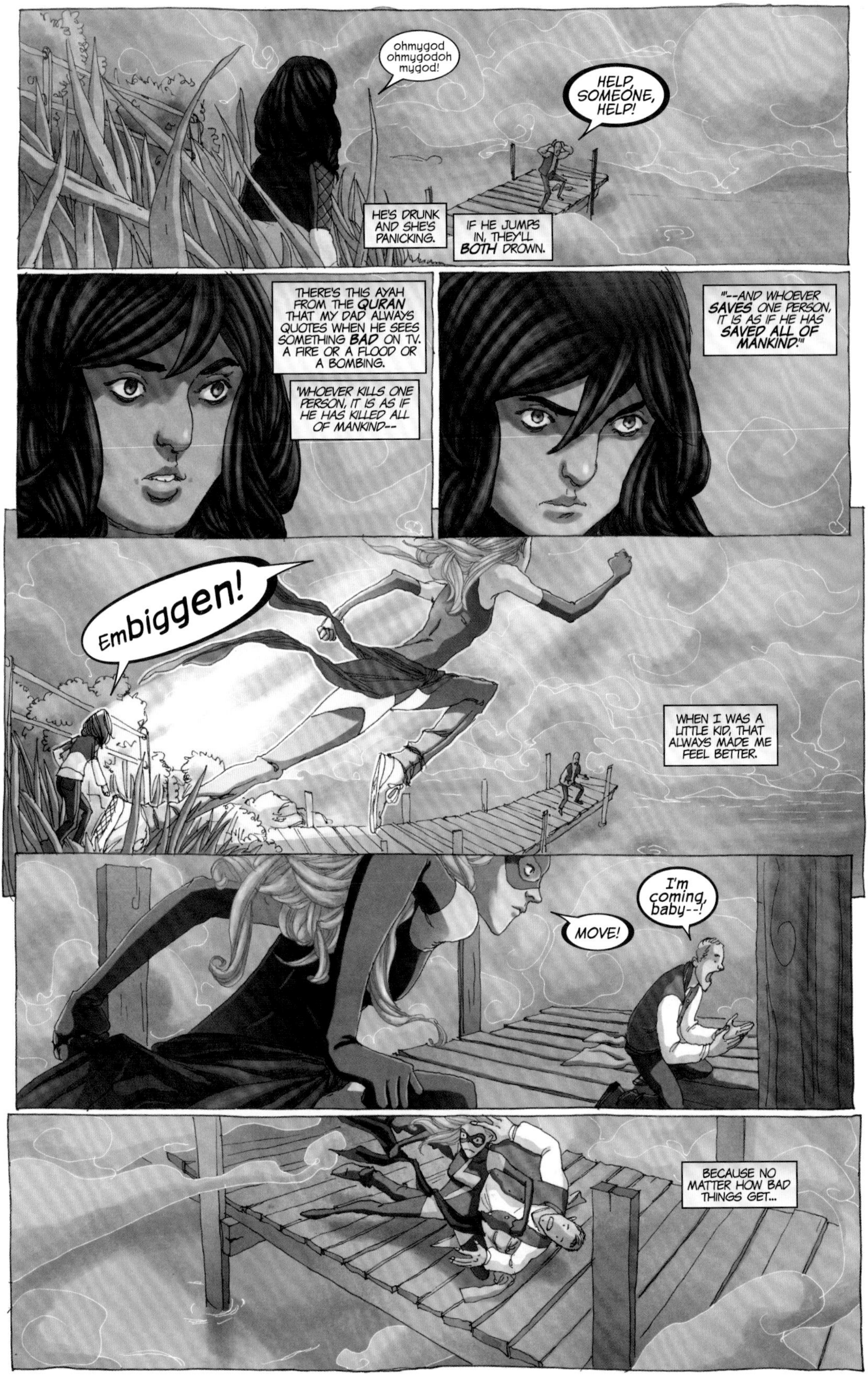
ohmygod ohmygodoh mygod!
HELP, SOMEONE, HELP!
HE'S DRUNK AND SHE'S PANICKING.
IF HE JUMPS IN, THEY'LL BOTH DROWN.
THERE'S THIS AYAH FROM THE QURAN THAT MY DAD ALWAYS QUOTES WHEN HE SEES SOMETHING BAD ON TV. A FIRE OR A FLOOD OR A BOMBING.
'WHOEVER KILLS ONE PERSON, IT IS AS IF HE HAS KILLED ALL OF MANKIND--
"--AND WHOEVER SAVES ONE PERSON, IT IS AS IF HE HAS SAVED ALL OF MANKIND."
Embiggen!
WHEN I WAS A LITTLE KID, THAT ALWAYS MADE ME FEEL BETTER.
I'm coming, baby--!
MOVE!
BECAUSE NO MATTER HOW BAD THINGS GET...

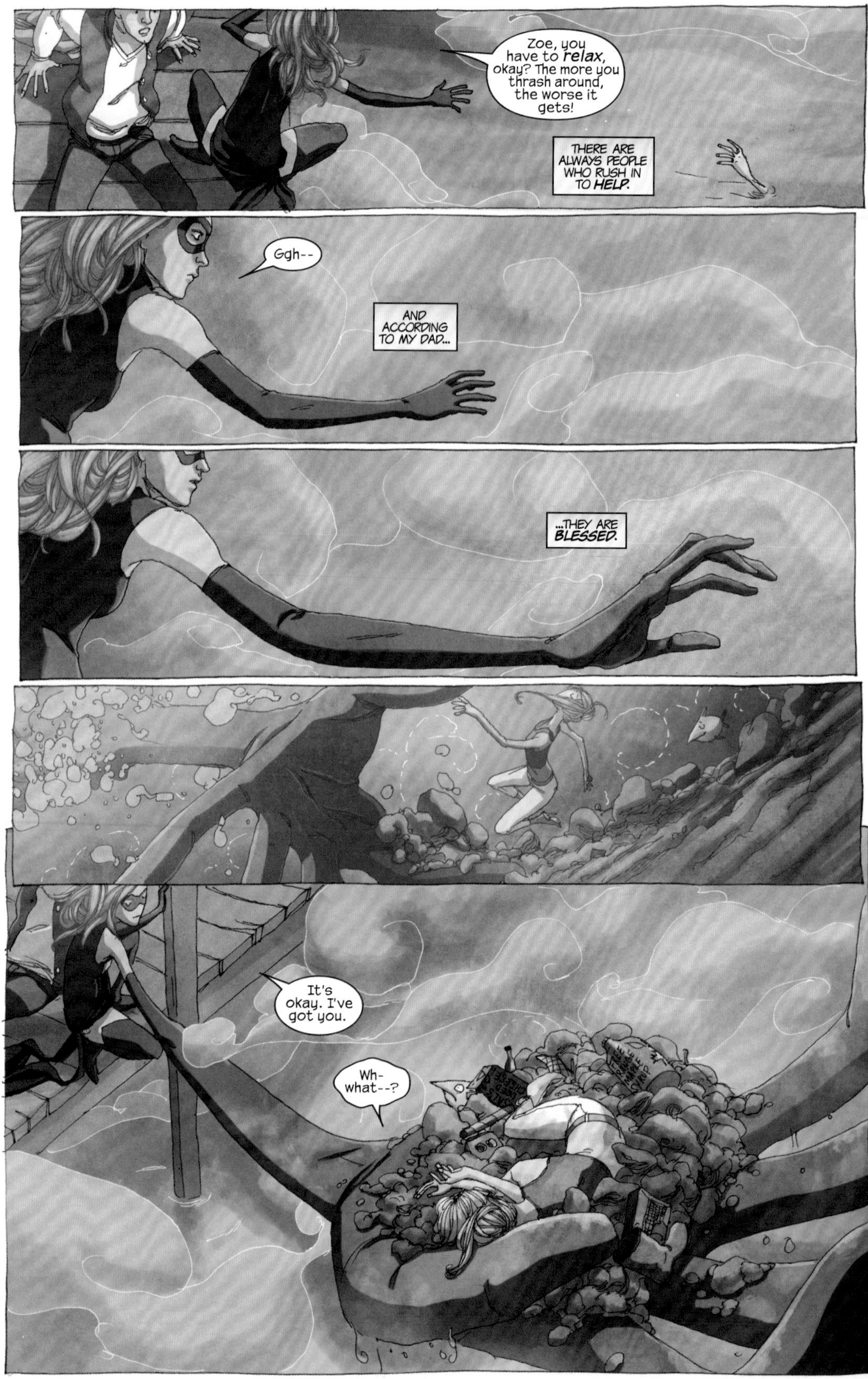
Zoe, you have to relax, okay? The more you thrash around, the worse it gets!
THERE ARE ALWAYS PEOPLE WHO RUSH IN TO HELP.
Ggh--
AND ACCORDING TO MY DAD...
...THEY ARE BLESSED.
It's okay. I've got you.
Wh-what--?

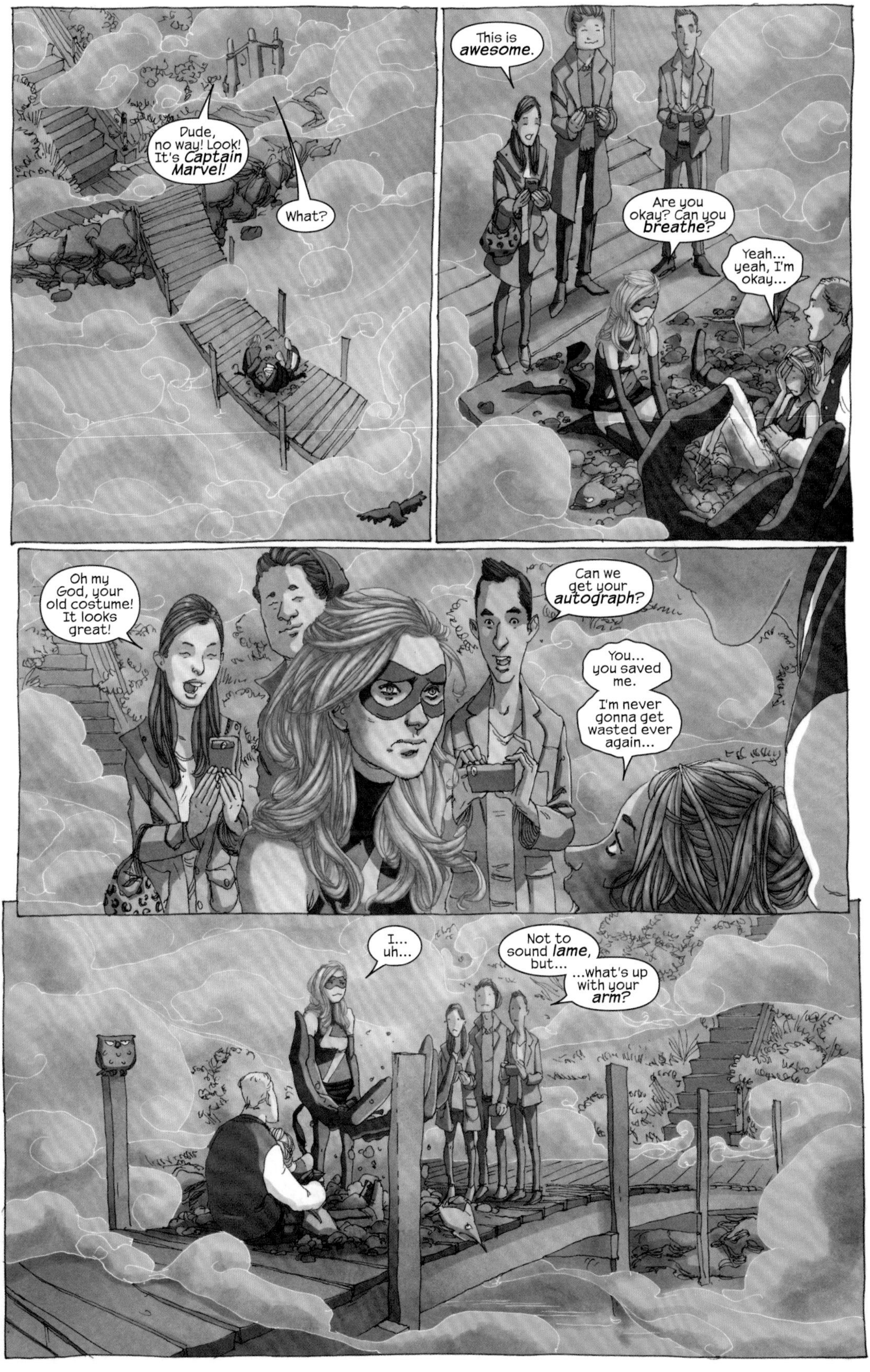
Dude, no way! Look! It's Captain Marvel!
What?
This is awesome.
Are you okay? Can you breathe?
Yeah... yeah, I'm okay...
Oh my God, your old costume! It looks great!
Can we get your autograph?
You... you saved me.
I'm never gonna get wasted ever again...
I... uh...
Not to sound lame, but... ...what's up with your arm?

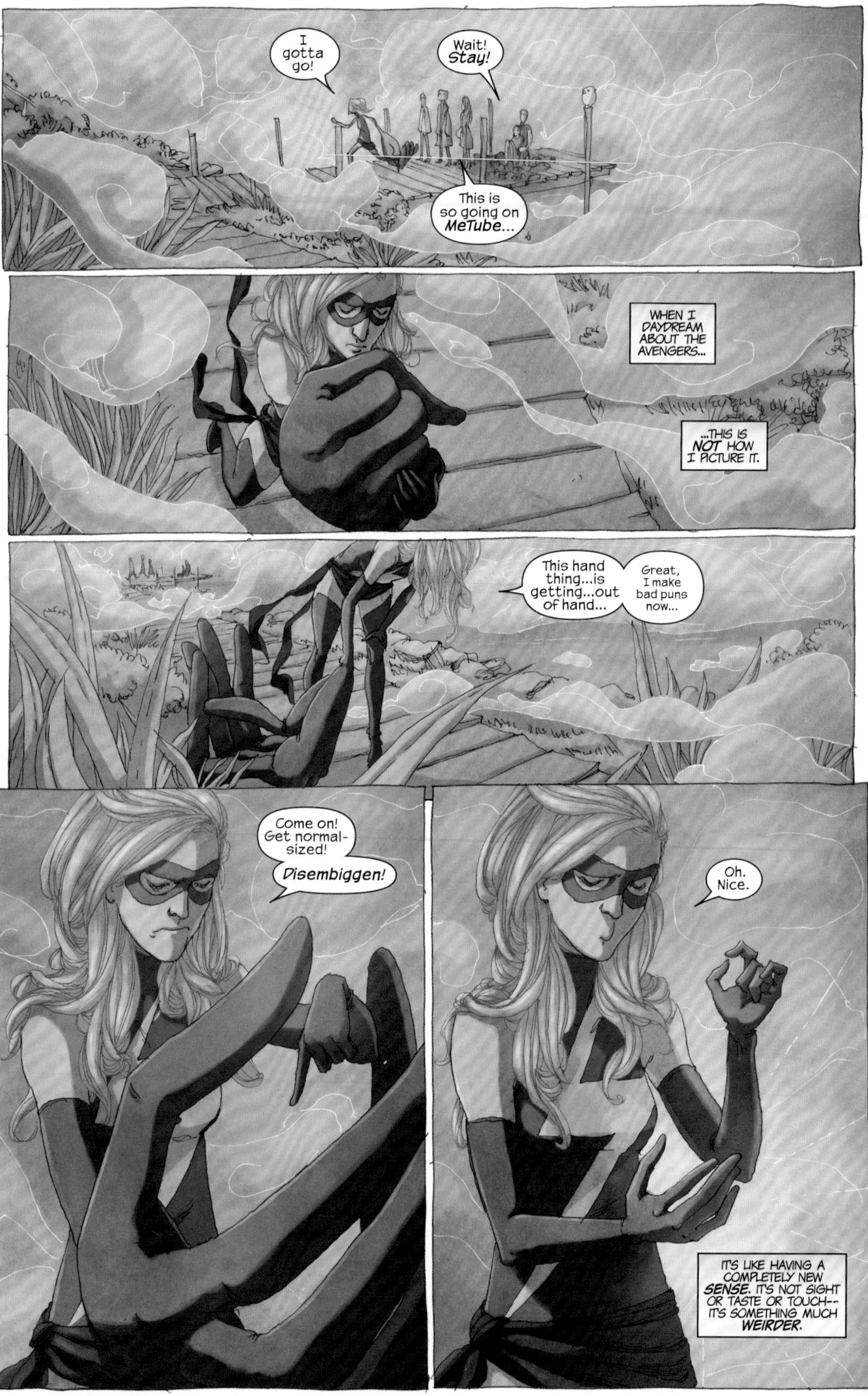
I gotta go!
Wait! Stay!
This is so going on MeTube...
WHEN I DAYDREAM ABOUT THE AVENGERS...
...THIS IS NOT HOW I PICTURE IT.
This hand thing...is getting...out of hand...
Great, I make bad puns now...
Come on! Get normal-sized!
Disembiggen!
Oh. Nice.
IT'S LIKE HAVING A COMPLETELY NEW SENSE. IT'S NOT SIGHT OR TASTE OR TOUCH--IT'S SOMETHING MUCH WEIRDER.

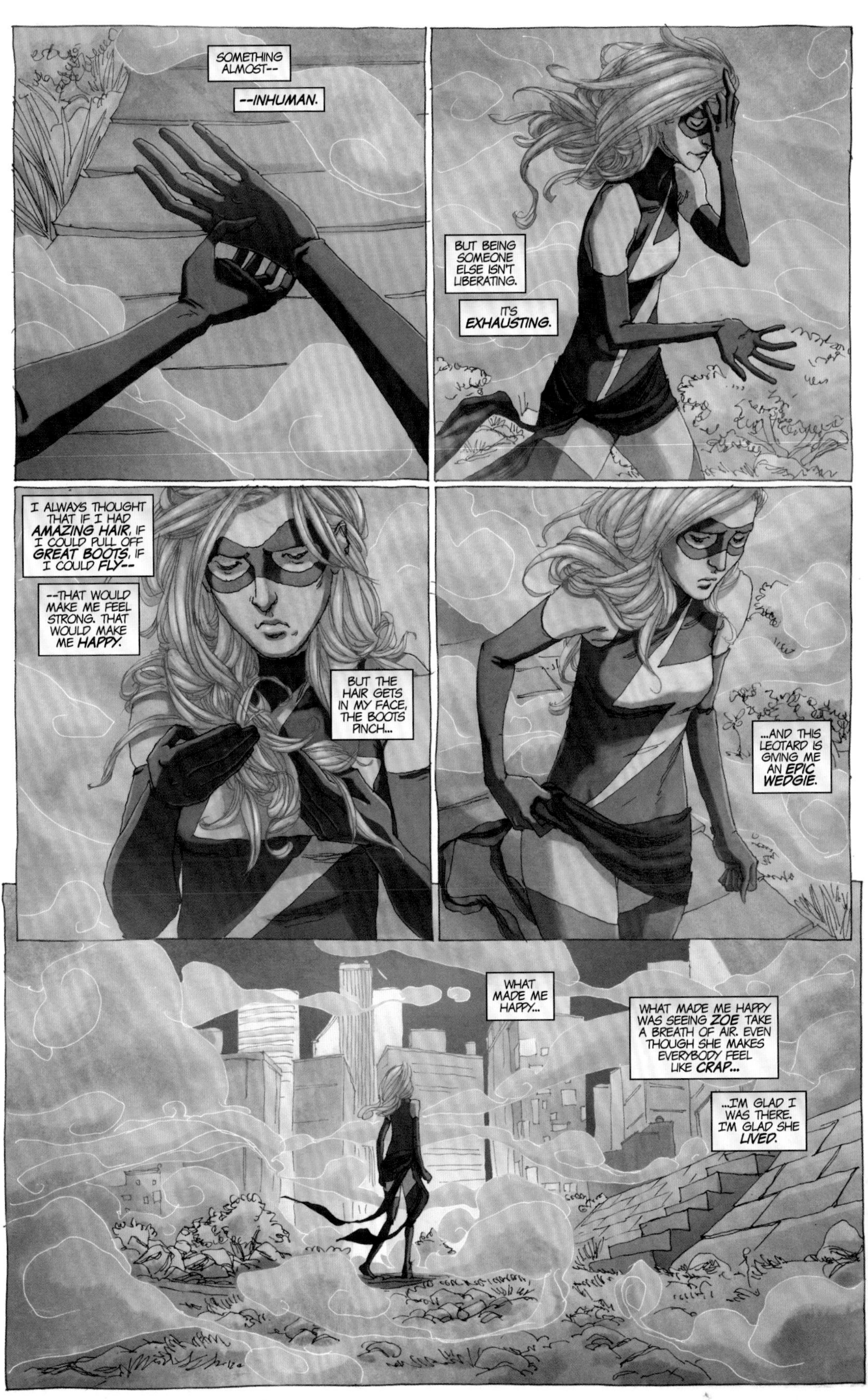
SOMETHING ALMOST--
--INHUMAN.
BUT BEING SOMEONE ELSE ISN'T LIBERATING.
IT'S EXHAUSTING.
I ALWAYS THOUGHT THAT IF I HAD AMAZING HAIR, IF I COULD PULL OFF GREAT BOOTS, IF I COULD FLY--
--THAT WOULD MAKE ME FEEL STRONG. THAT WOULD MAKE ME HAPPY.
BUT THE HAIR GETS IN MY FACE, THE BOOTS PINCH...
...AND THIS LEOTARD IS GIVING ME AN EPIC WEDGIE.
WHAT MADE ME HAPPY...
WHAT MADE ME HAPPY WAS SEEING ZOE TAKE A BREATH OF AIR. EVEN THOUGH SHE MAKES EVERYBODY FEEL LIKE CRAP...
...I'M GLAD I WAS THERE. I'M GLAD SHE LIVED.

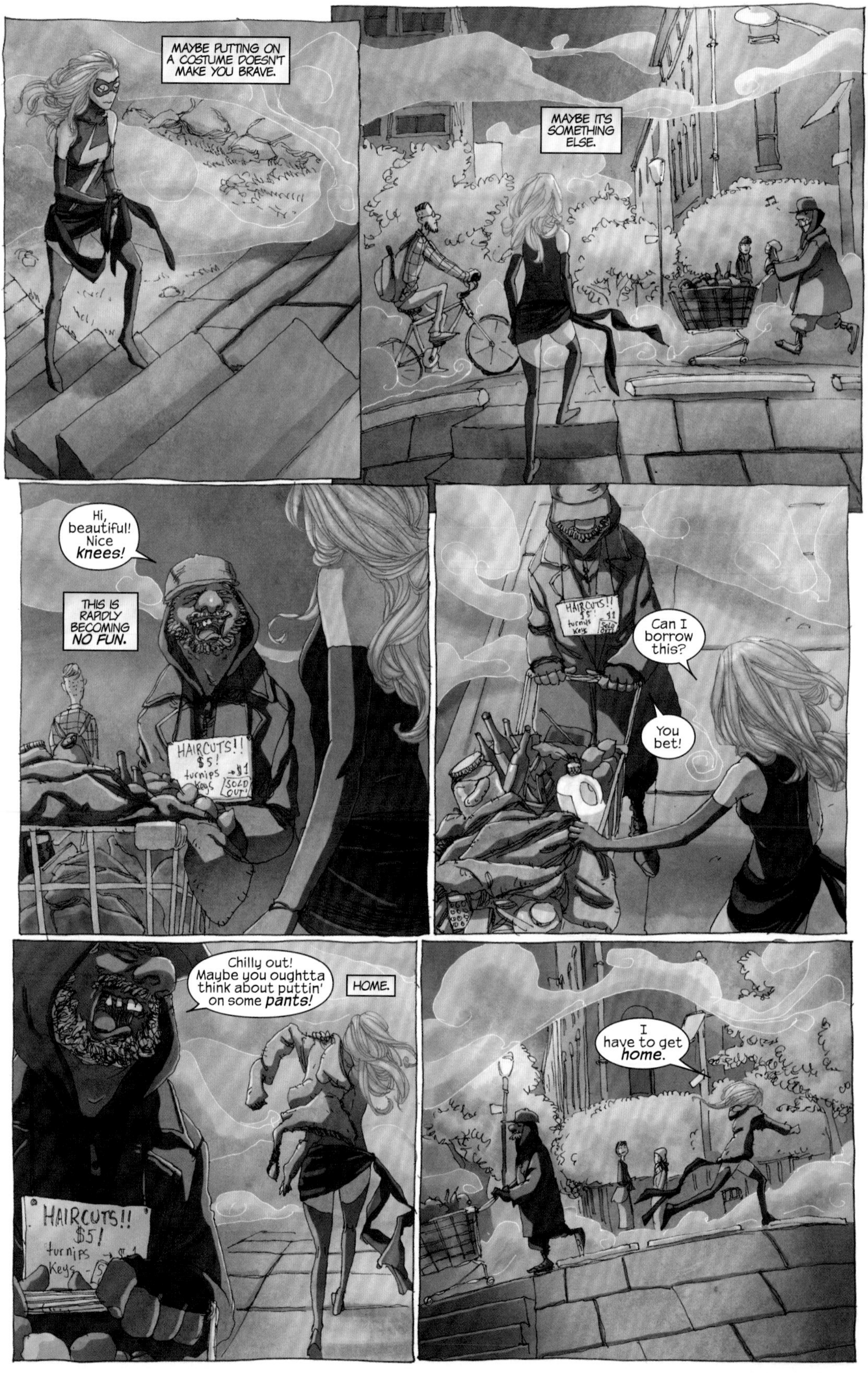
MAYBE PUTTING ON A COSTUME DOESN'T MAKE YOU BRAVE.
MAYBE IT'S SOMETHING ELSE.
Hi, beautiful! Nice knees!
THIS IS RAPIDLY BECOMING NO FUN.
HAIRCUTS!! $5! turnips → $1 Keys SOLD OUT
Can I borrow this?
You bet!
Chilly out! Maybe you oughtta think about puttin' on some pants!
HOME.
HAIRCUTS!! $5!
I have to get home.

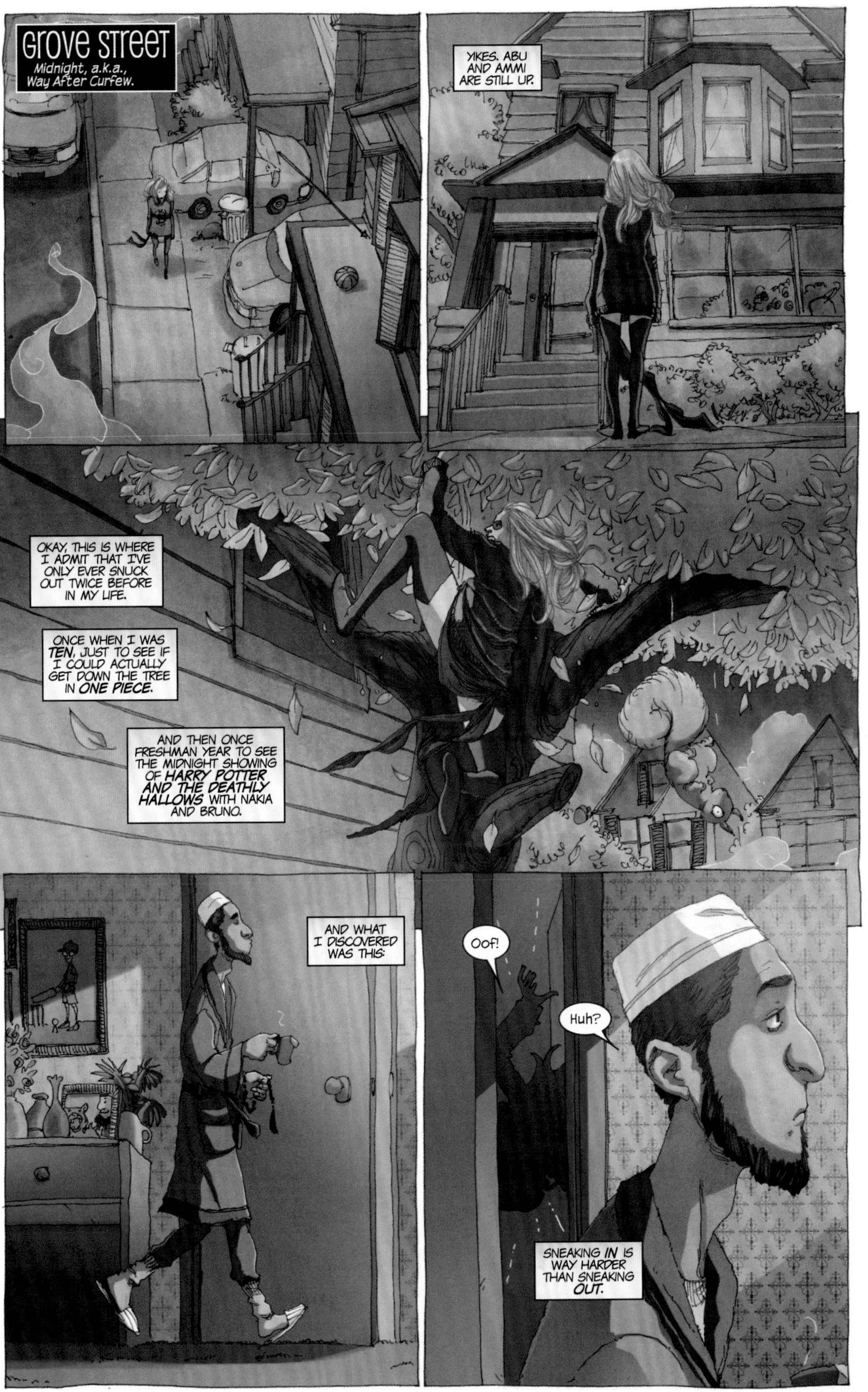
GROVE STREET
Midnight, a.k.a., Way After Curfew.
YIKES. ABU AND AMMI ARE STILL UP.
OKAY, THIS IS WHERE I ADMIT THAT I'VE ONLY EVER SNUCK OUT TWICE BEFORE IN MY LIFE.
ONCE WHEN I WAS TEN, JUST TO SEE IF I COULD ACTUALLY GET DOWN THE TREE IN ONE PIECE.
AND THEN ONCE FRESHMAN YEAR TO SEE THE MIDNIGHT SHOWING OF HARRY POTTER AND THE DEATHLY HALLOWS WITH NAKIA AND BRUNO.
AND WHAT I DISCOVERED WAS THIS:
Oof!
Huh?
SNEAKING IN IS WAY HARDER THAN SNEAKING OUT.

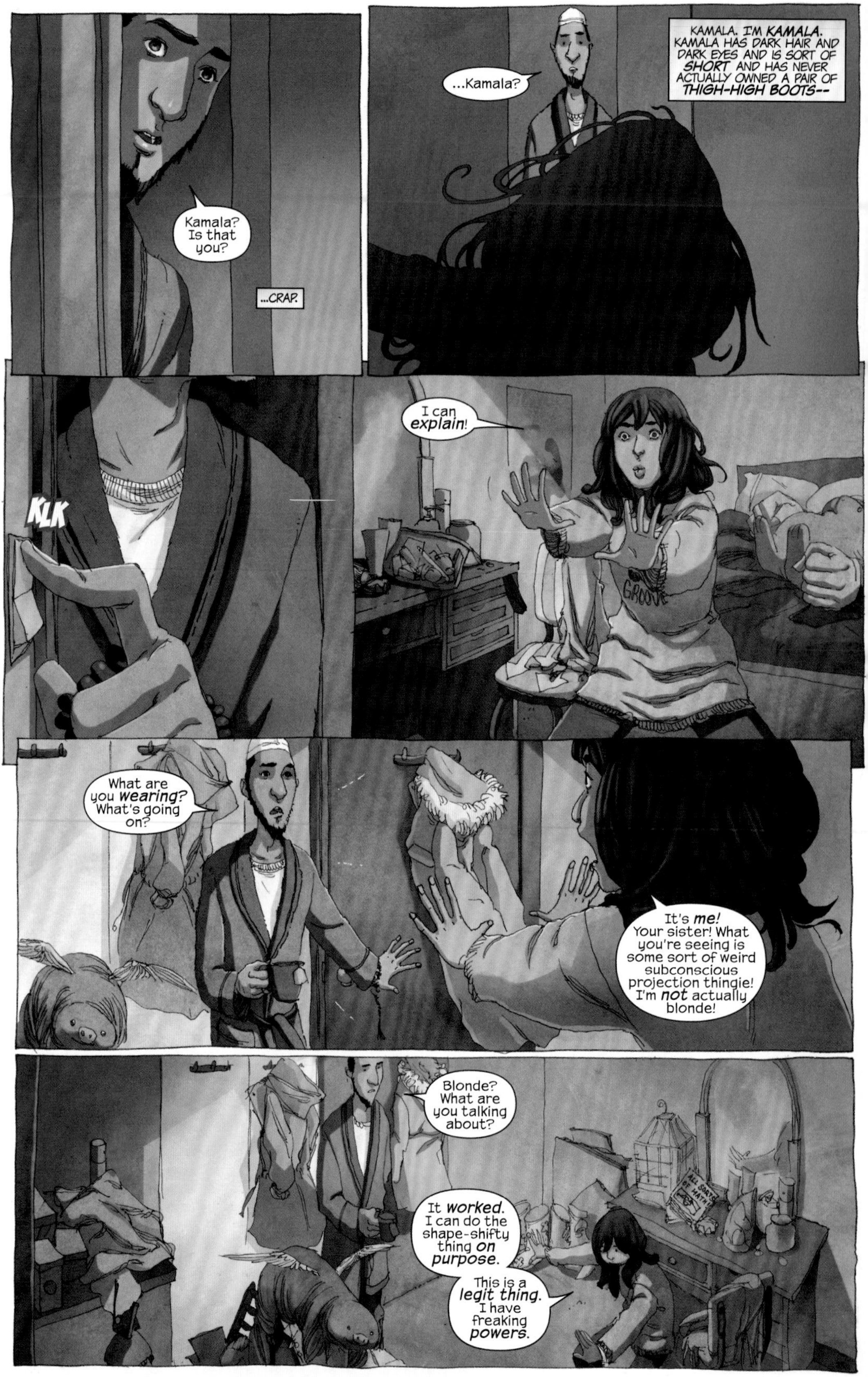
Kamala? Is that you?
...CRAP.
...Kamala?
KAMALA. I'M KAMALA. KAMALA HAS DARK HAIR AND DARK EYES AND IS SORT OF SHORT AND HAS NEVER ACTUALLY OWNED A PAIR OF THIGH-HIGH BOOTS--
KLK
I can explain!
GROOVE
What are you wearing? What's going on?
It's me! Your sister! What you're seeing is some sort of weird subconscious projection thingie! I'm not actually blonde!
Blonde? What are you talking about?
It worked. I can do the shape-shifty thing on purpose.
This is a legit thing. I have freaking powers.

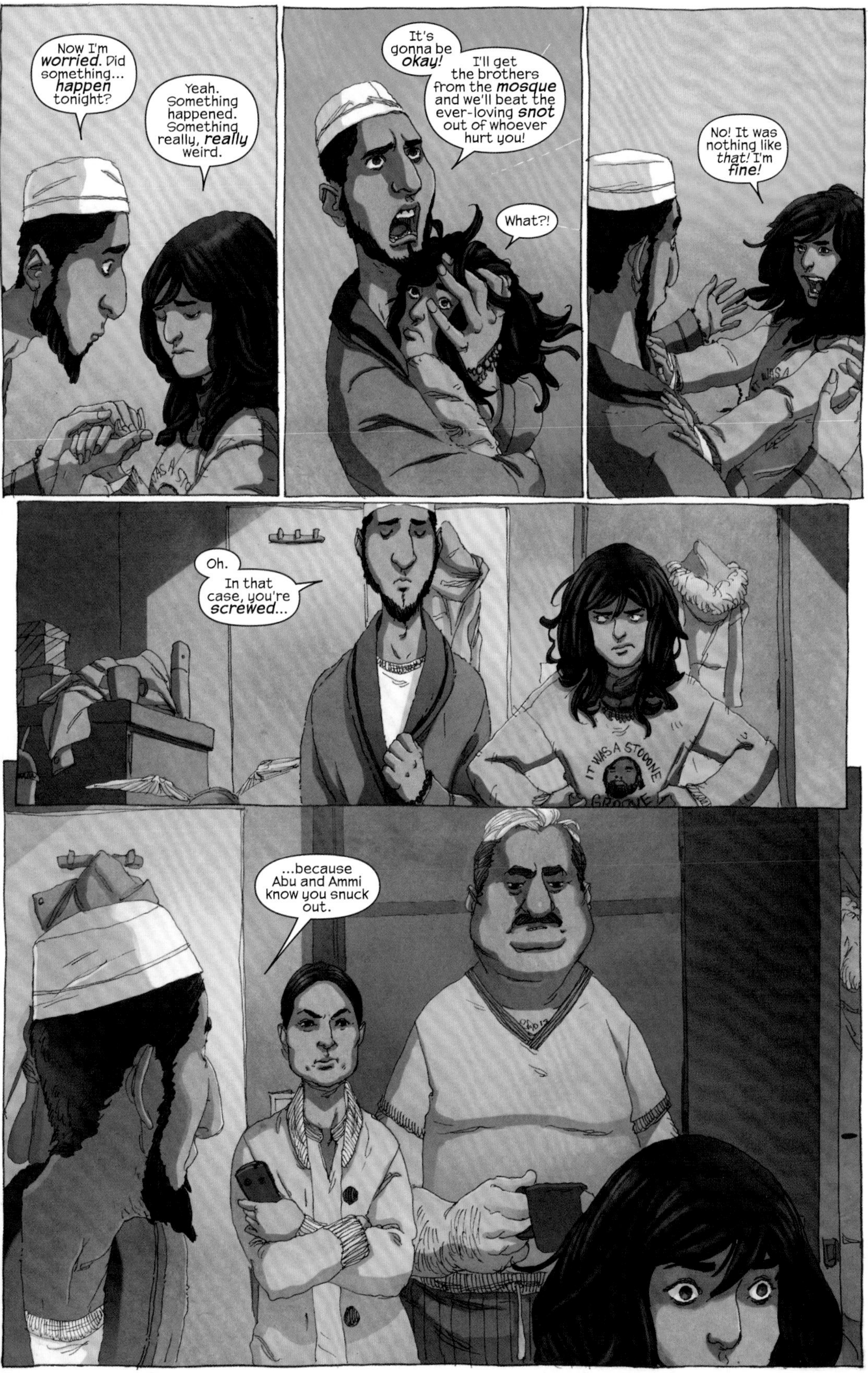
Now I'm worried. Did something... happen tonight?
Yeah. Something happened. Something really, really weird.
It's gonna be okay!
I'll get the brothers from the mosque and we'll beat the ever-loving snot out of whoever hurt you!
What?!
No! It was nothing like that! I'm fine!
Oh.
In that case, you're screwed...
...because Abu and Ammi know you snuck out.

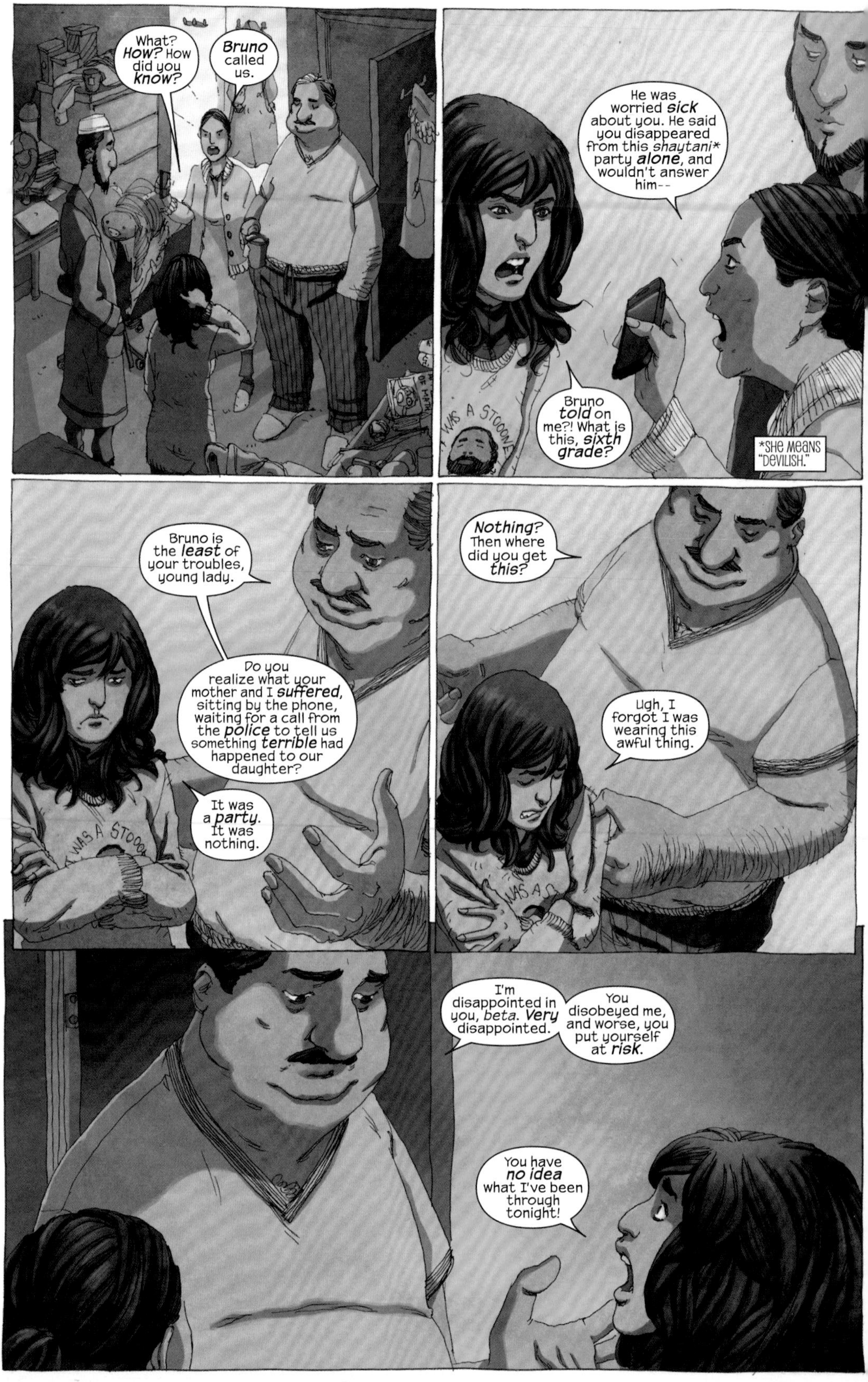
What? How? How did you know?
Bruno called us.
He was worried sick about you. He said you disappeared from this shaytani* party alone, and wouldn't answer him--
Bruno told on me?! What is this, sixth grade?
*SHE MEANS "DEVILISH."
I WAS A STOOOONE
Bruno is the least of your troubles, young lady.
Do you realize what your mother and I suffered, sitting by the phone, waiting for a call from the police to tell us something terrible had happened to our daughter?
It was a party. It was nothing.
Nothing? Then where did you get this?
Ugh, I forgot I was wearing this awful thing.
I'm disappointed in you, beta. Very disappointed.
You disobeyed me, and worse, you put yourself at risk.
You have no idea what I've been through tonight!

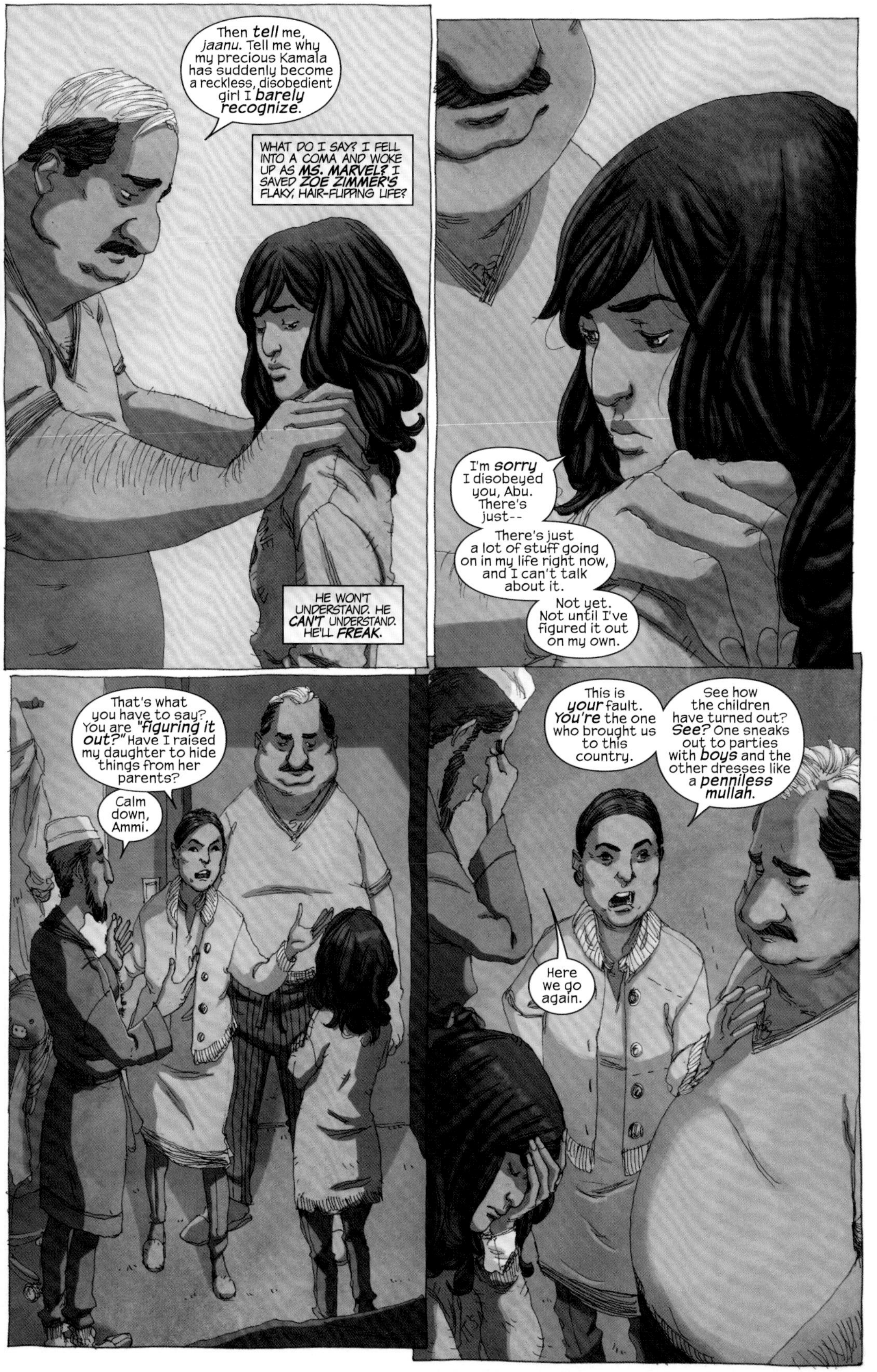
Then *tell* me, *jaanu*. Tell me why my precious Kamala has suddenly become a reckless, disobedient girl I *barely recognize*.
WHAT DO I SAY? I FELL INTO A COMA AND WOKE UP AS *MS. MARVEL?* I SAVED *ZOE ZIMMER'S* FLAKY, HAIR-FLIPPING LIFE?
HE WON'T UNDERSTAND. HE *CAN'T* UNDERSTAND. HE'LL *FREAK*.
I'm *sorry* I disobeyed you, Abu. There's just--
There's just a lot of stuff going on in my life right now, and I can't talk about it.
Not yet. Not until I've figured it out on my own.
That's what you have to say? You are "*figuring it out?*" Have I raised my daughter to hide things from her parents?
Calm down, Ammi.
This is *your* fault. *You're* the one who brought us to this country.
See how the children have turned out? *See?* One sneaks out to parties with *boys* and the other dresses like a *penniless mullah*.
Here we go again.

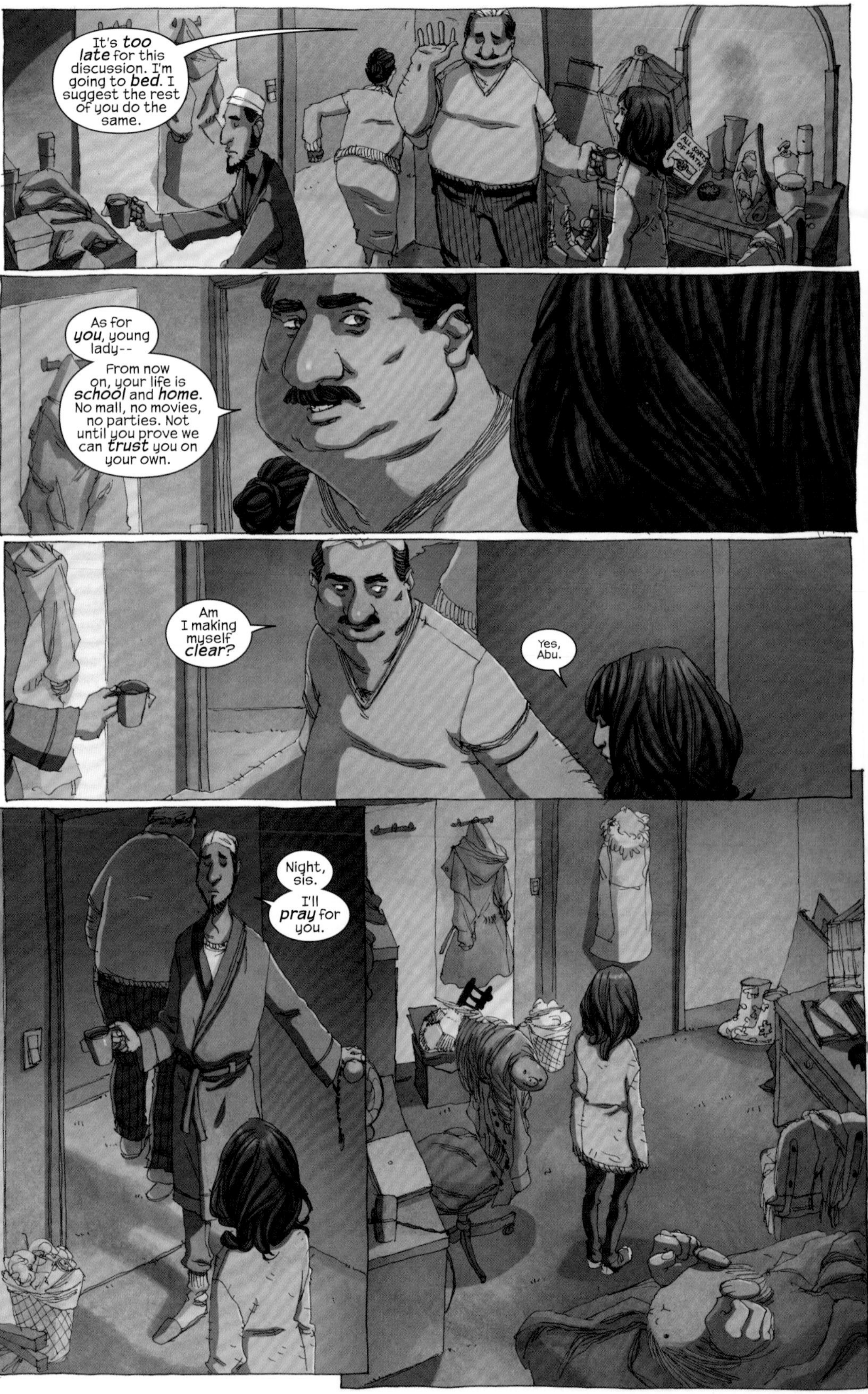
It's too late for this discussion. I'm going to bed. I suggest the rest of you do the same.
ALL SORTS OF FAITH!
As for you, young lady--
From now on, your life is school and home. No mall, no movies, no parties. Not until you prove we can trust you on your own.
Am I making myself clear?
Yes, Abu.
Night, sis.
I'll pray for you.

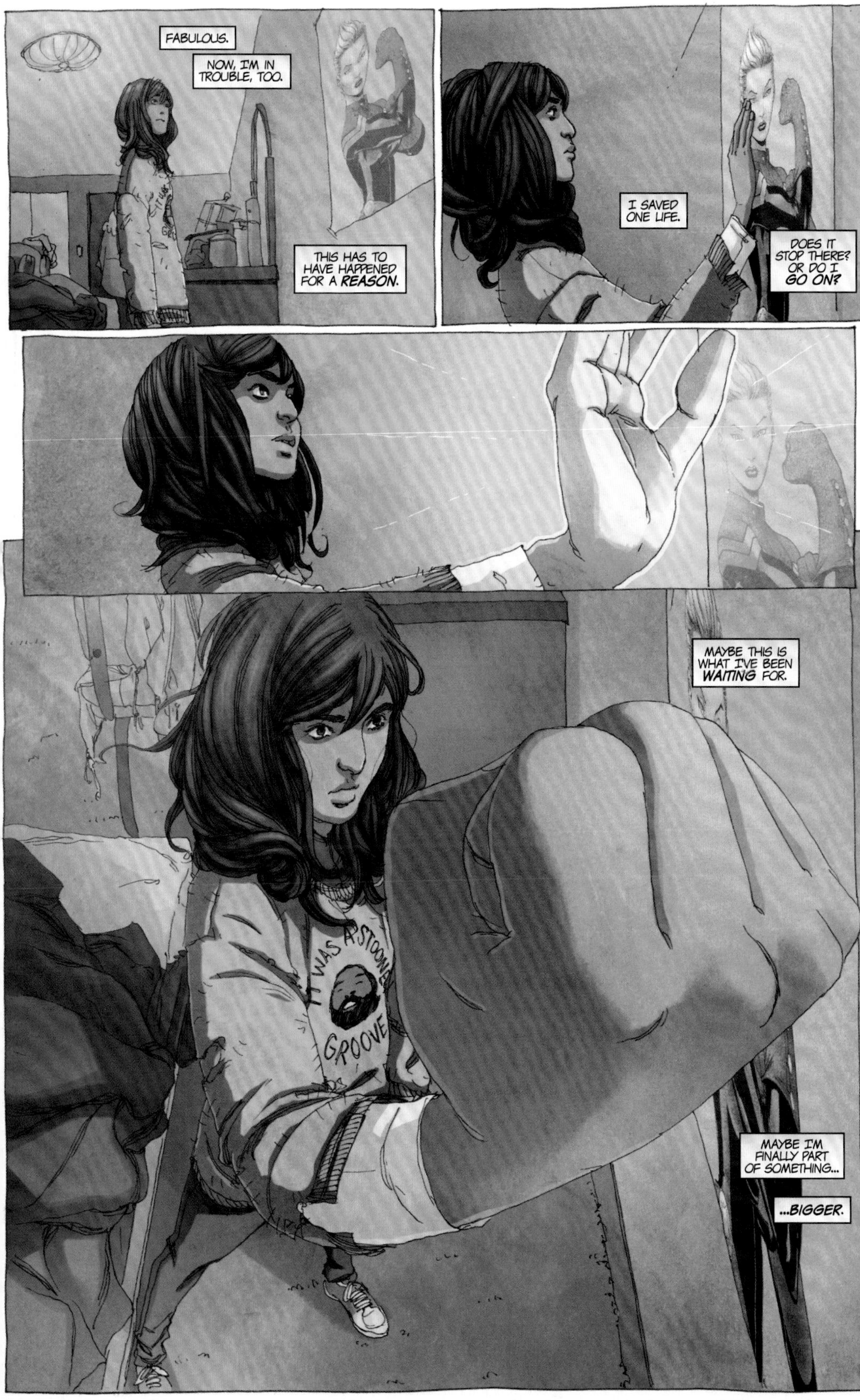
FABULOUS.
NOW, I'M IN TROUBLE, TOO.
THIS HAS TO HAVE HAPPENED FOR A **REASON**.
I SAVED ONE LIFE.
DOES IT STOP THERE? OR DO I **GO ON?**
MAYBE THIS IS WHAT I'VE BEEN **WAITING** FOR.
IT WAS A STOOPENDOUS GROOVE
MAYBE I'M FINALLY PART OF SOMETHING...
...**BIGGER**.

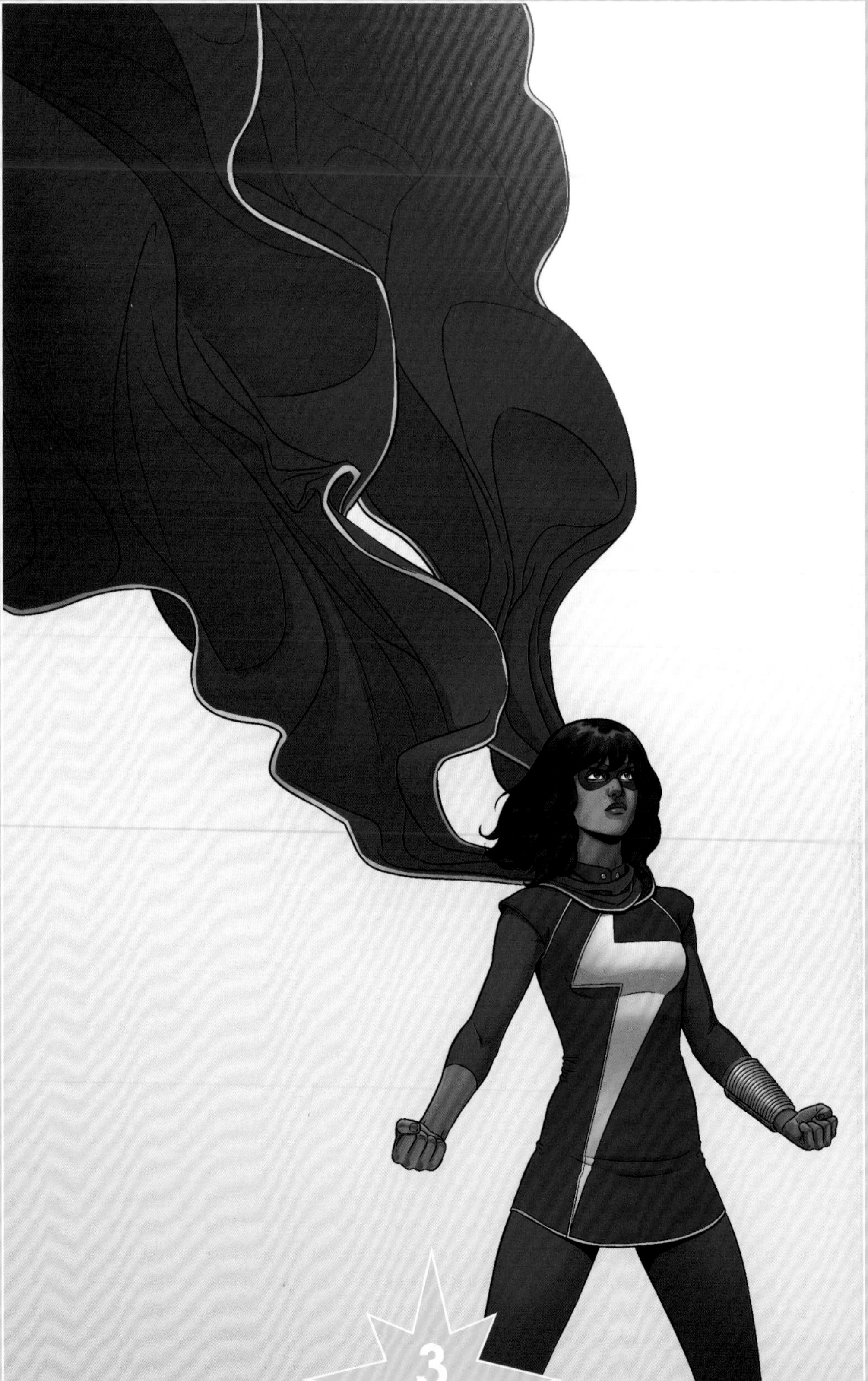
3

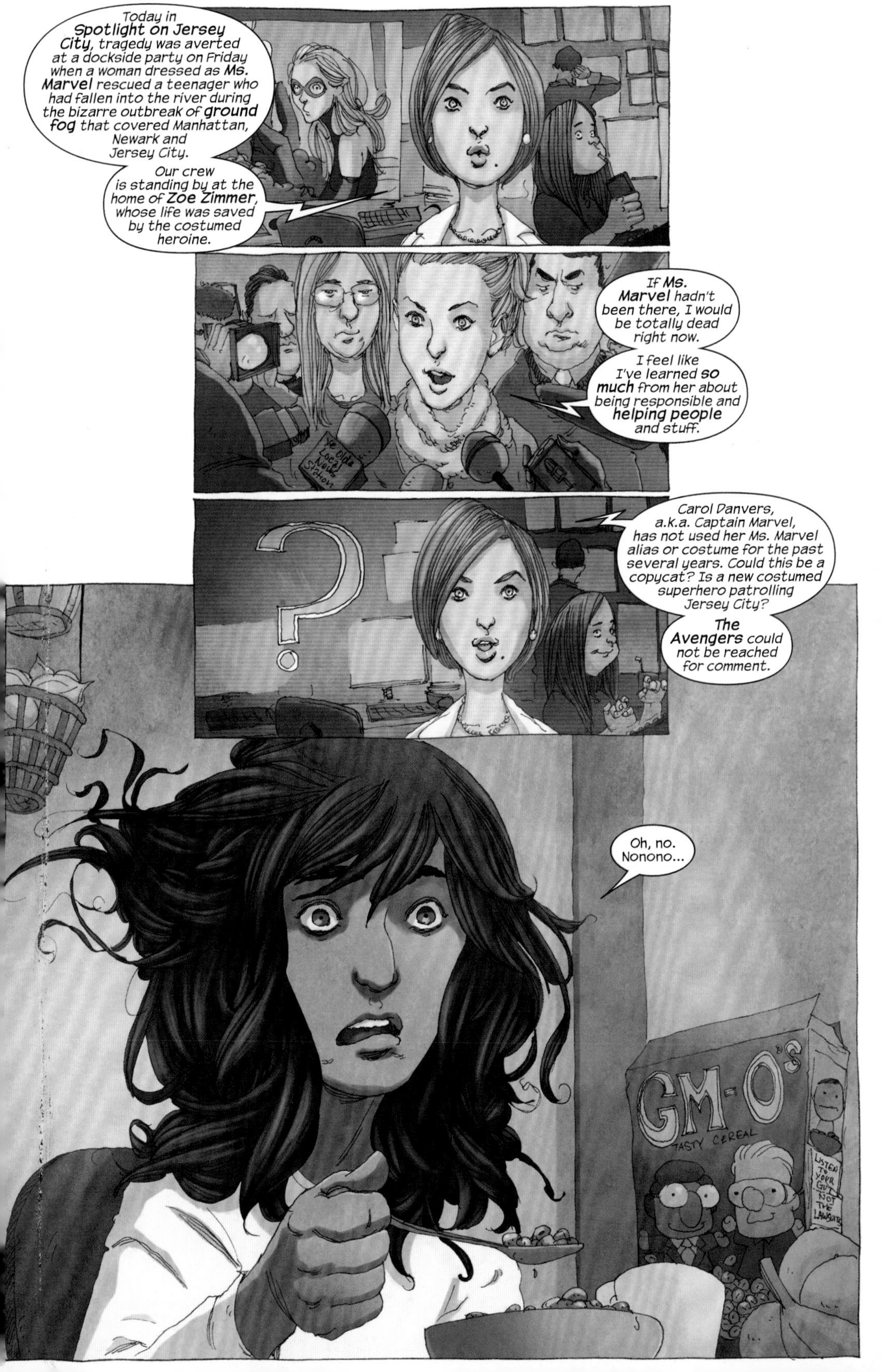
Today in Spotlight on Jersey City, tragedy was averted at a dockside party on Friday when a woman dressed as Ms. Marvel rescued a teenager who had fallen into the river during the bizarre outbreak of ground fog that covered Manhattan, Newark and Jersey City.
Our crew is standing by at the home of Zoe Zimmer, whose life was saved by the costumed heroine.
If Ms. Marvel hadn't been there, I would be totally dead right now.
I feel like I've learned so much from her about being responsible and helping people and stuff.
Ye Olde Local News Station
Carol Danvers, a.k.a. Captain Marvel, has not used her Ms. Marvel alias or costume for the past several years. Could this be a copycat? Is a new costumed superhero patrolling Jersey City?
The Avengers could not be reached for comment.
Oh, no. Nonono...
GM-O's
TASTY CEREAL
LISTEN TO YOUR GUT NOT THE LAWSUITS

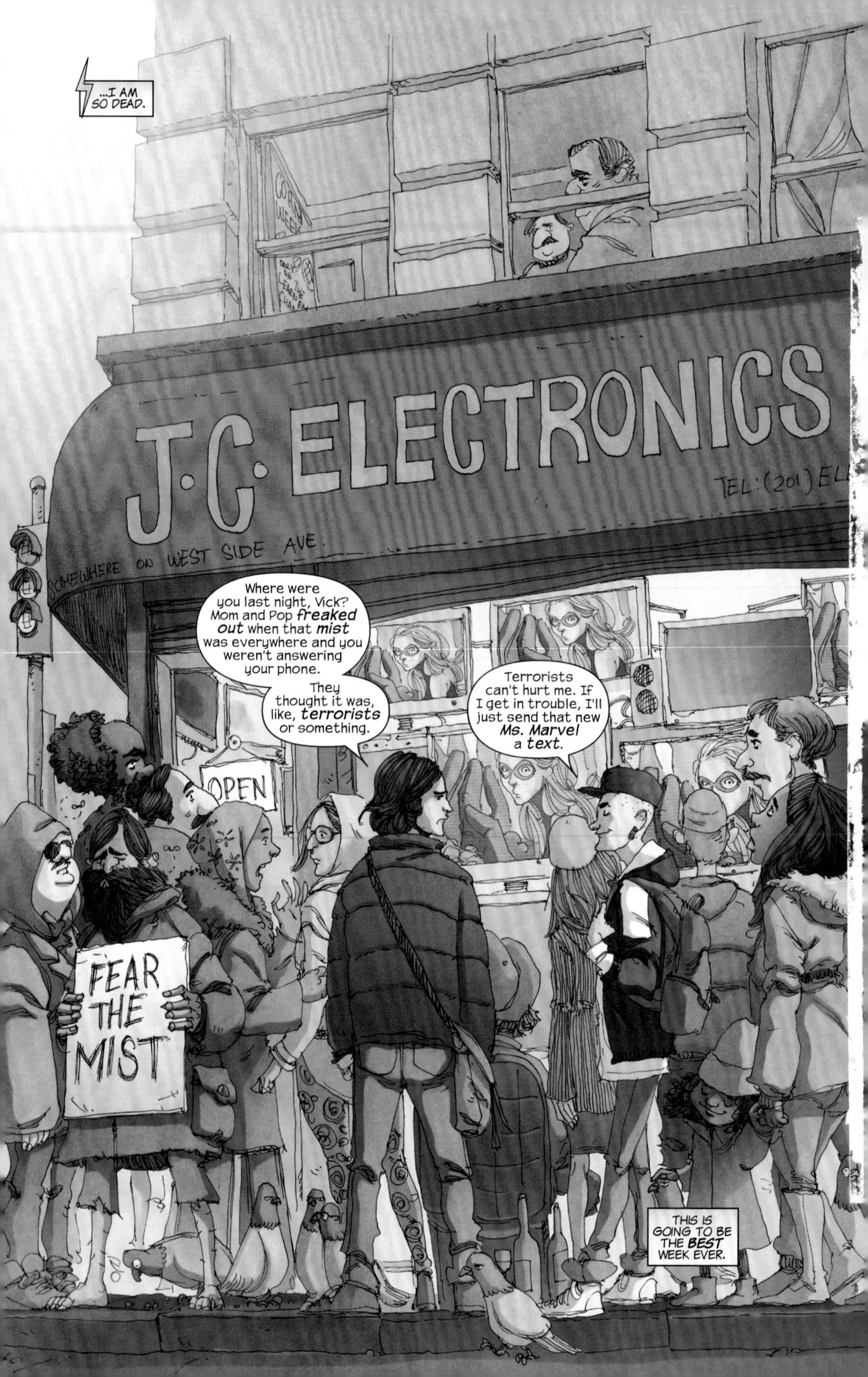

...I AM SO DEAD.
J·C· ELECTRONICS
SOMEWHERE ON WEST SIDE AVE.
Where were you last night, Vick? Mom and Pop freaked out when that mist was everywhere and you weren't answering your phone.
They thought it was, like, terrorists or something.
Terrorists can't hurt me. If I get in trouble, I'll just send that new Ms. Marvel a text.
OPEN
FEAR THE MIST
THIS IS GOING TO BE THE BEST WEEK EVER.

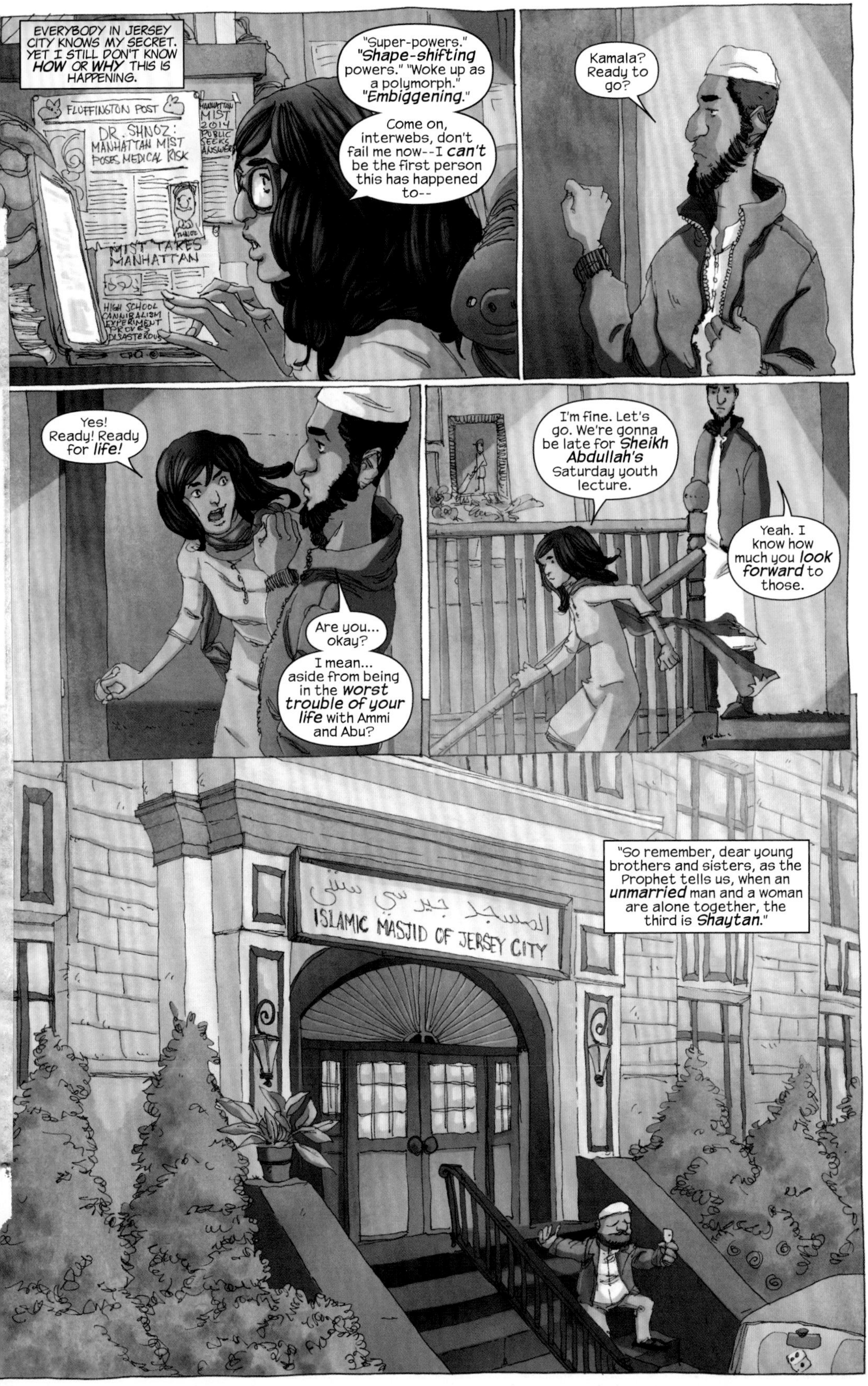

EVERYBODY IN JERSEY CITY KNOWS MY SECRET. YET I STILL DON'T KNOW *HOW* OR *WHY* THIS IS HAPPENING.
FLUFFINGTON POST
DR. SHNOZ: MANHATTAN MIST POSES MEDICAL RISK
MANHATTAN MIST 2014 PUBLIC SEEKS
MIST TAKES MANHATTAN
HIGH SCHOOL CANNIBALISM EXPERIMENT PROVES DISASTEROUS
"Super-powers." "*Shape-shifting* powers." "Woke up as a polymorph." "*Embiggening*."
Come on, interwebs, don't fail me now--I *can't* be the first person this has happened to--
Kamala? Ready to go?
Yes! Ready! Ready for *life!*
Are you... okay?
I mean... aside from being in the *worst trouble of your life* with Ammi and Abu?
I'm fine. Let's go. We're gonna be late for *Sheikh Abdullah's* Saturday youth lecture.
Yeah. I know how much you *look forward* to those.
المسجد جيرسي ستي
ISLAMIC MASJID OF JERSEY CITY
"So remember, dear young brothers and sisters, as the Prophet tells us, when an *unmarried* man and a woman are alone together, the third is *Shaytan*."

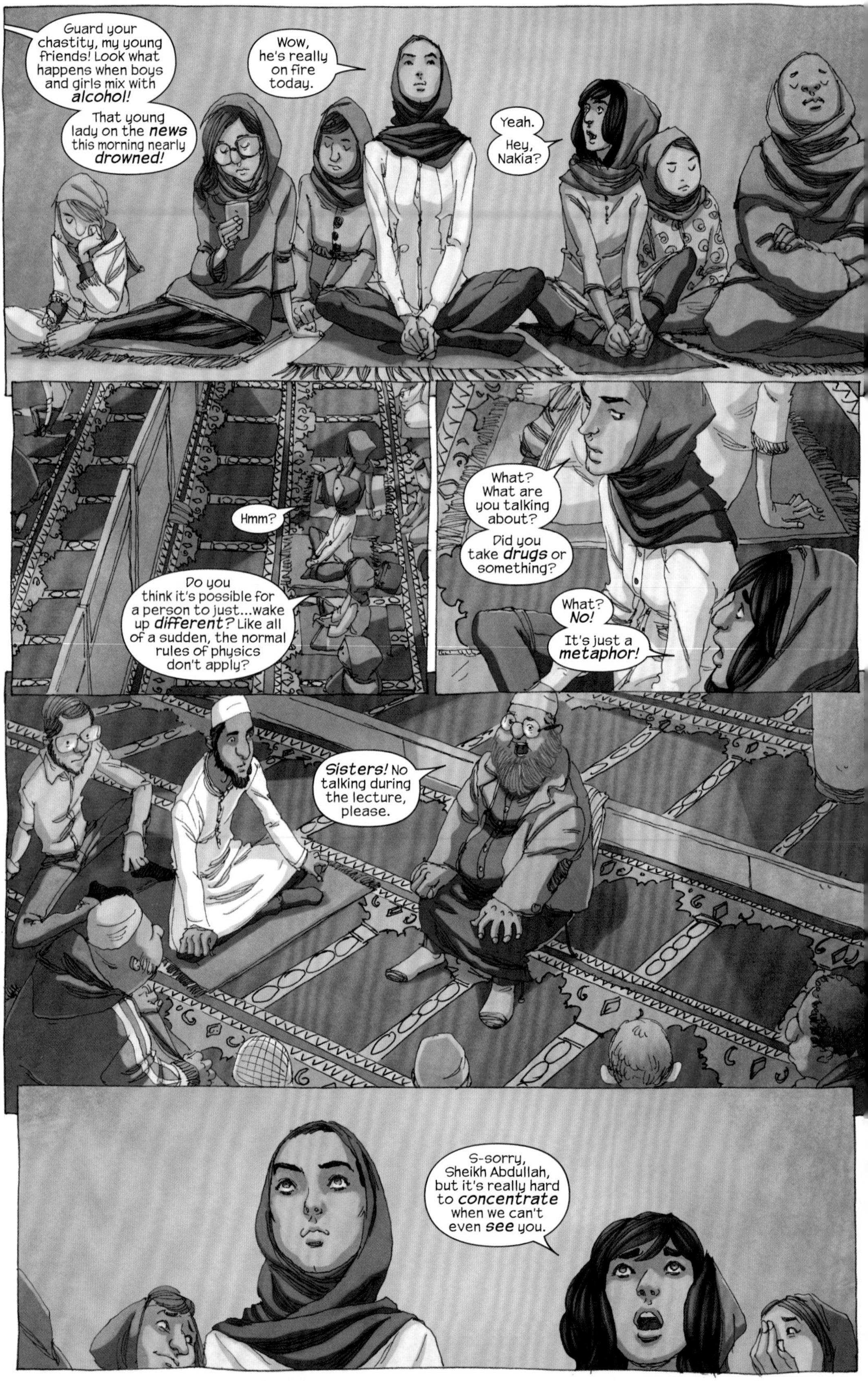

Guard your chastity, my young friends! Look what happens when boys and girls mix with *alcohol!*
That young lady on the *news* this morning nearly *drowned!*
Wow, he's really on fire today.
Yeah.
Hey, Nakia?
Hmm?
Do you think it's possible for a person to just...wake up *different?* Like all of a sudden, the normal rules of physics don't apply?
What? What are you talking about?
Did you take *drugs* or something?
What? *No!*
It's just a *metaphor!*
Sisters! No talking during the lecture, please.
S-sorry, Sheikh Abdullah, but it's really hard to *concentrate* when we can't even *see* you.

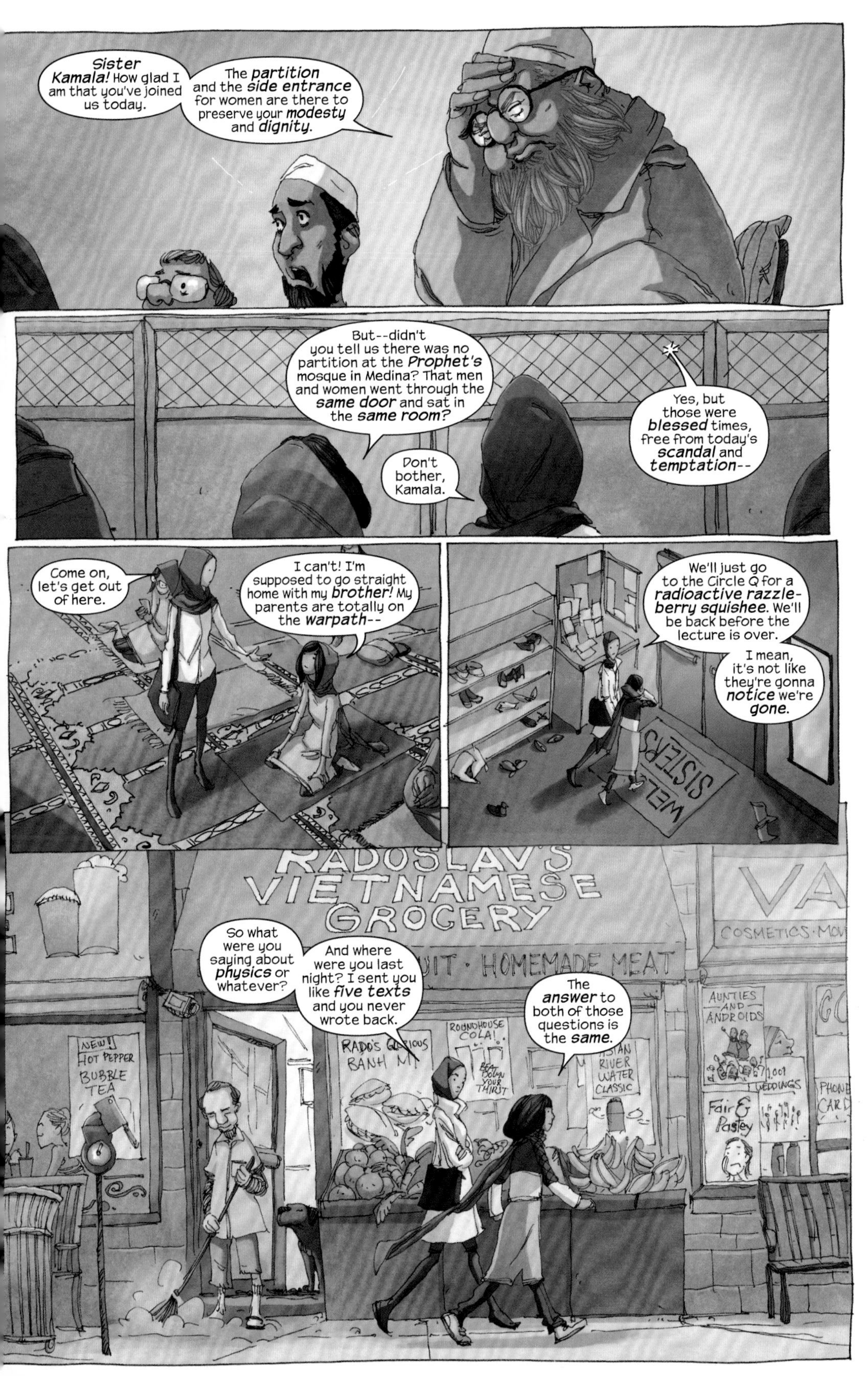
Sister Kamala! How glad I am that you've joined us today.
The partition and the side entrance for women are there to preserve your modesty and dignity.
But--didn't you tell us there was no partition at the Prophet's mosque in Medina? That men and women went through the same door and sat in the same room?
Yes, but those were blessed times, free from today's scandal and temptation--
Don't bother, Kamala.
Come on, let's get out of here.
I can't! I'm supposed to go straight home with my brother! My parents are totally on the warpath--
We'll just go to the Circle Q for a radioactive razzleberry squishee. We'll be back before the lecture is over.
I mean, it's not like they're gonna notice we're gone.
WEL
SISTERS
RADOSLAV'S VIETNAMESE GROCERY
HOMEMADE MEAT
COSMETICS·MOV
NEW! HOT PEPPER BUBBLE TEA
RADO'S BANH MI
ROUNDHOUSE COLA! BEAT DOWN YOUR THIRST
RIVER WATER CLASSIC
AUNTIES AND ANDROIDS
1,001 WEDDINGS
Fair & Pasty
PHONE CARD
So what were you saying about physics or whatever?
And where were you last night? I sent you like five texts and you never wrote back.
The answer to both of those questions is the same.

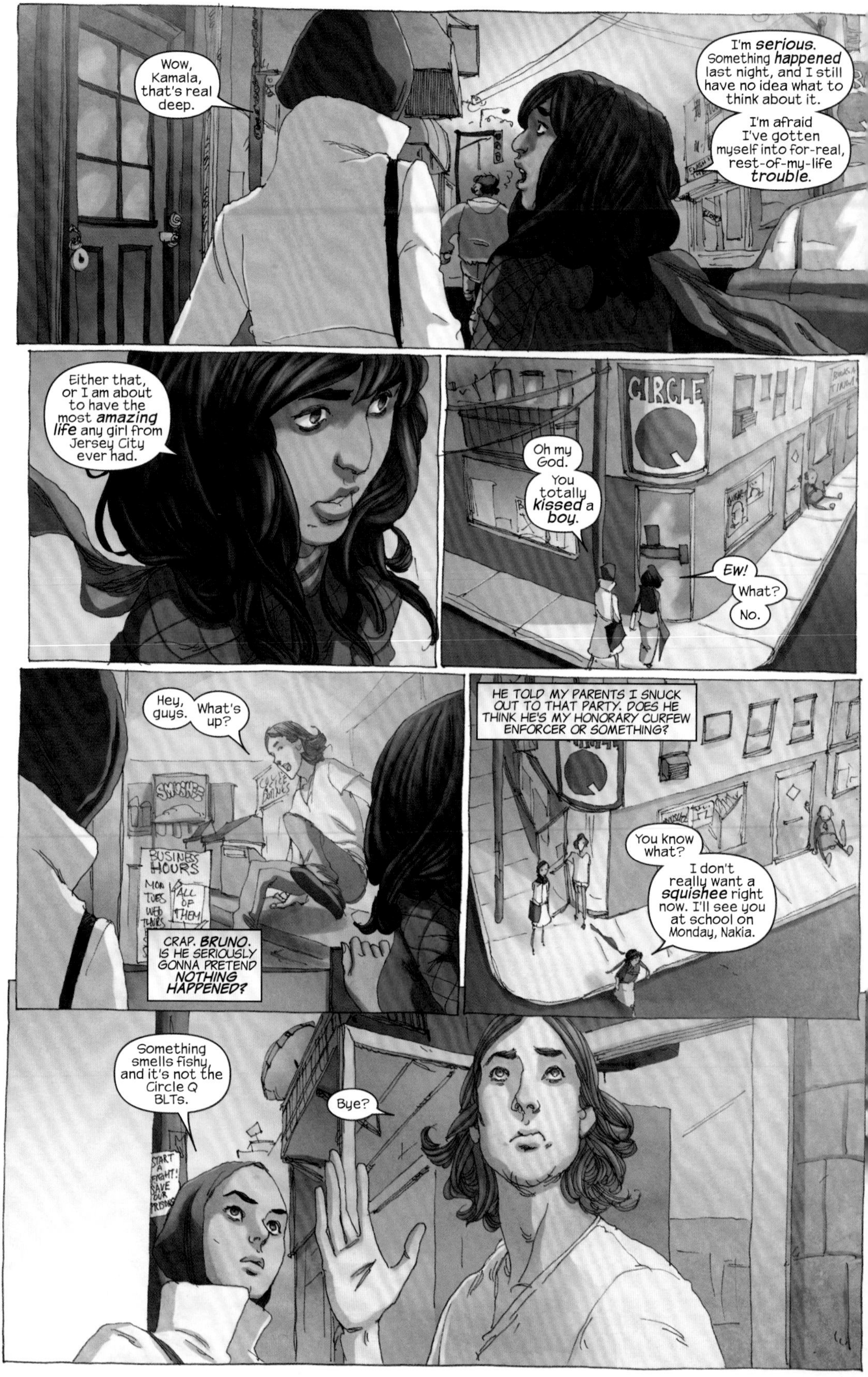

Wow, Kamala, that's real deep.
I'm serious. Something happened last night, and I still have no idea what to think about it.
I'm afraid I've gotten myself into for-real, rest-of-my-life trouble.
Either that, or I am about to have the most amazing life any girl from Jersey City ever had.
CIRCLE Q
Oh my God.
You totally kissed a boy.
Ew!
What?
No.
Hey, guys.
What's up?
BUSINESS HOURS MON TUES WED THURS ALL OF THEM
CRAP. BRUNO. IS HE SERIOUSLY GONNA PRETEND NOTHING HAPPENED?
HE TOLD MY PARENTS I SNUCK OUT TO THAT PARTY. DOES HE THINK HE'S MY HONORARY CURFEW ENFORCER OR SOMETHING?
You know what?
I don't really want a squishee right now. I'll see you at school on Monday, Nakia.
Something smells fishy and it's not the Circle Q BLTs.
Bye?

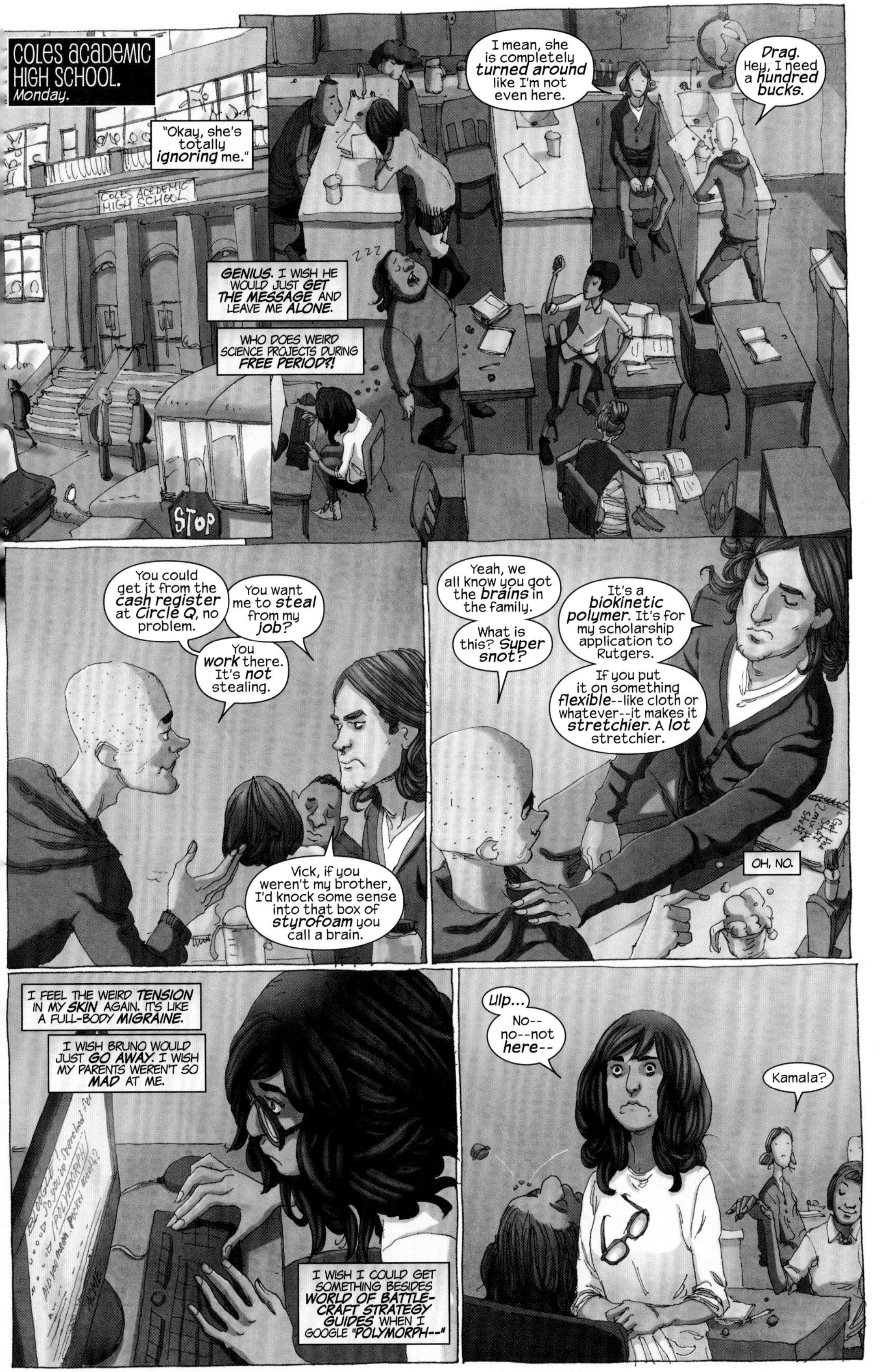
COLES ACADEMIC HIGH SCHOOL. Monday.
COLES ACADEMIC HIGH SCHOOL
"Okay, she's totally ignoring me."
I mean, she is completely turned around like I'm not even here.
Drag. Hey, I need a hundred bucks.
GENIUS. I WISH HE WOULD JUST GET THE MESSAGE AND LEAVE ME ALONE.
WHO DOES WEIRD SCIENCE PROJECTS DURING FREE PERIOD?!
STOP
You could get it from the cash register at Circle Q, no problem.
You want me to steal from my job?
You work there. It's not stealing.
Vick, if you weren't my brother, I'd knock some sense into that box of styrofoam you call a brain.
Yeah, we all know you got the brains in the family.
What is this? Super snot?
It's a biokinetic polymer. It's for my scholarship application to Rutgers.
If you put it on something flexible--like cloth or whatever--it makes it stretchier. A lot stretchier.
OH, NO.
I FEEL THE WEIRD TENSION IN MY SKIN AGAIN. IT'S LIKE A FULL-BODY MIGRAINE.
I WISH BRUNO WOULD JUST GO AWAY. I WISH MY PARENTS WEREN'T SO MAD AT ME.
I WISH I COULD GET SOMETHING BESIDES WORLD OF BATTLE-CRAFT STRATEGY GUIDES WHEN I GOOGLE "POLYMORPH--"
Ulp...
No-- no--not here--
Kamala?

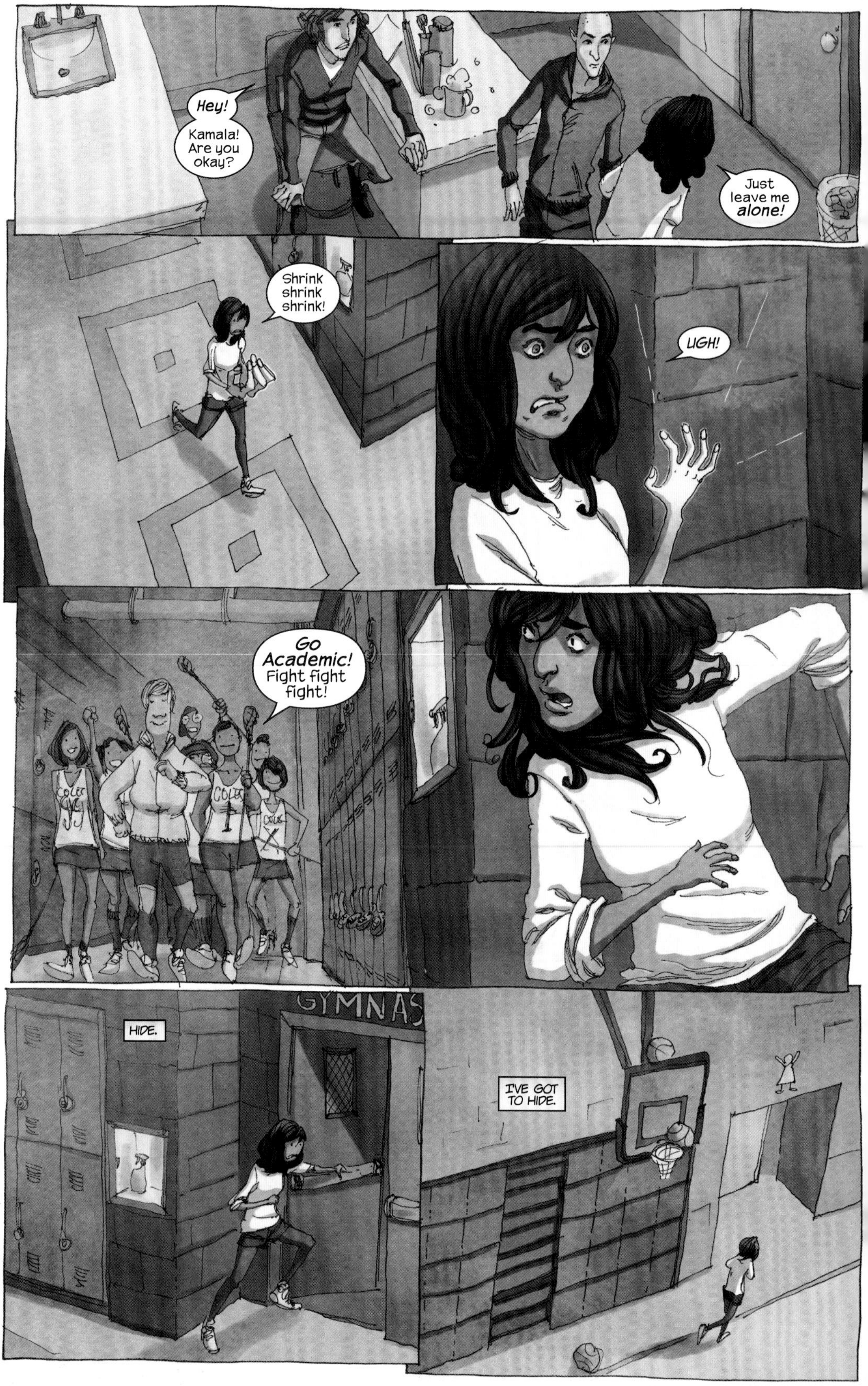
Hey!
Kamala! Are you okay?
Just leave me alone!
Shrink shrink shrink!
UGH!
Go Academic! Fight fight fight!
HIDE.
GYMNAS
I'VE GOT TO HIDE.

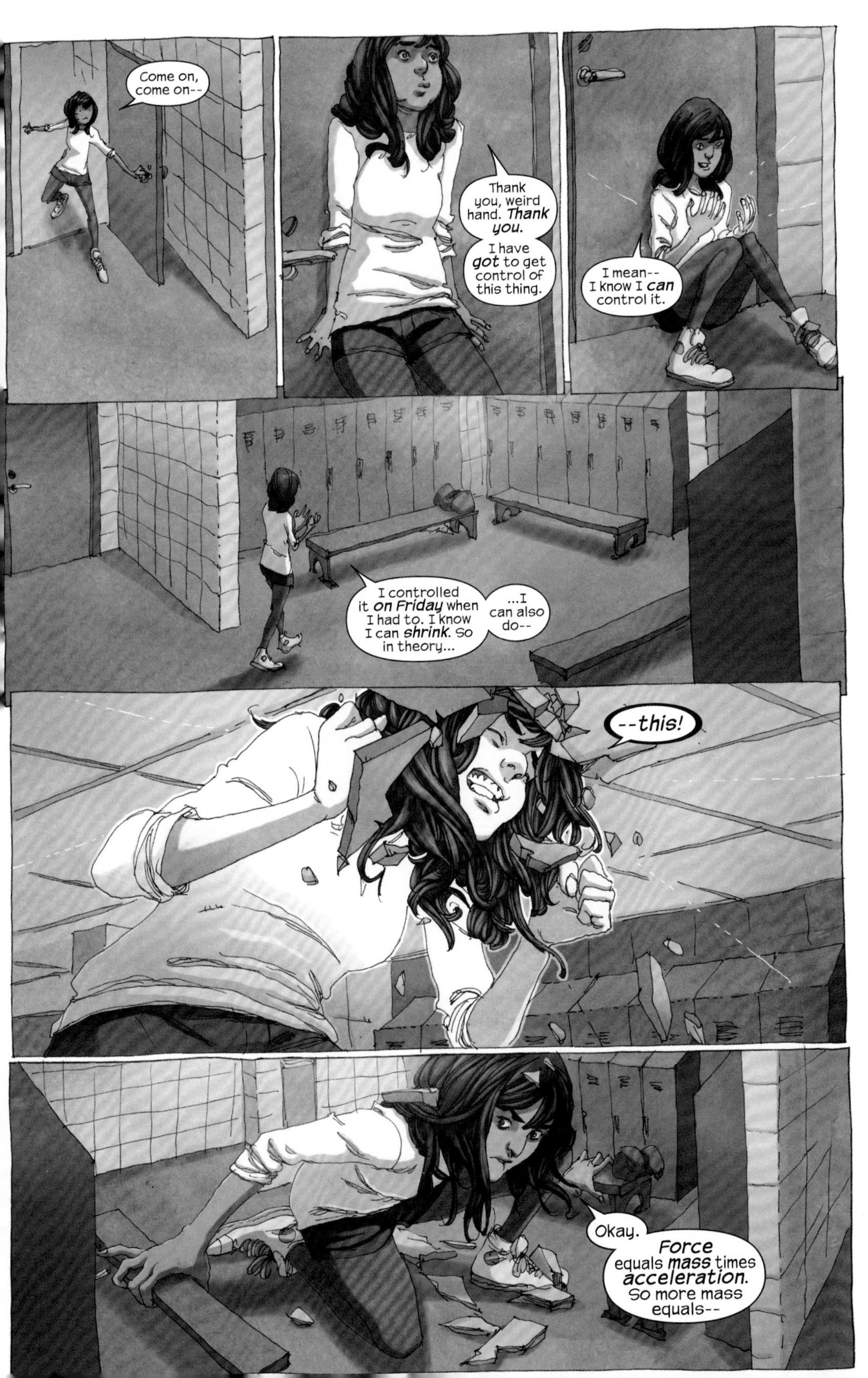
Come on, come on--
Thank you, weird hand. Thank you.
I have got to get control of this thing.
I mean-- I know I can control it.
I controlled it on Friday when I had to. I know I can shrink. So in theory...
...I can also do--
--this!
Okay.
Force equals mass times acceleration. So more mass equals--

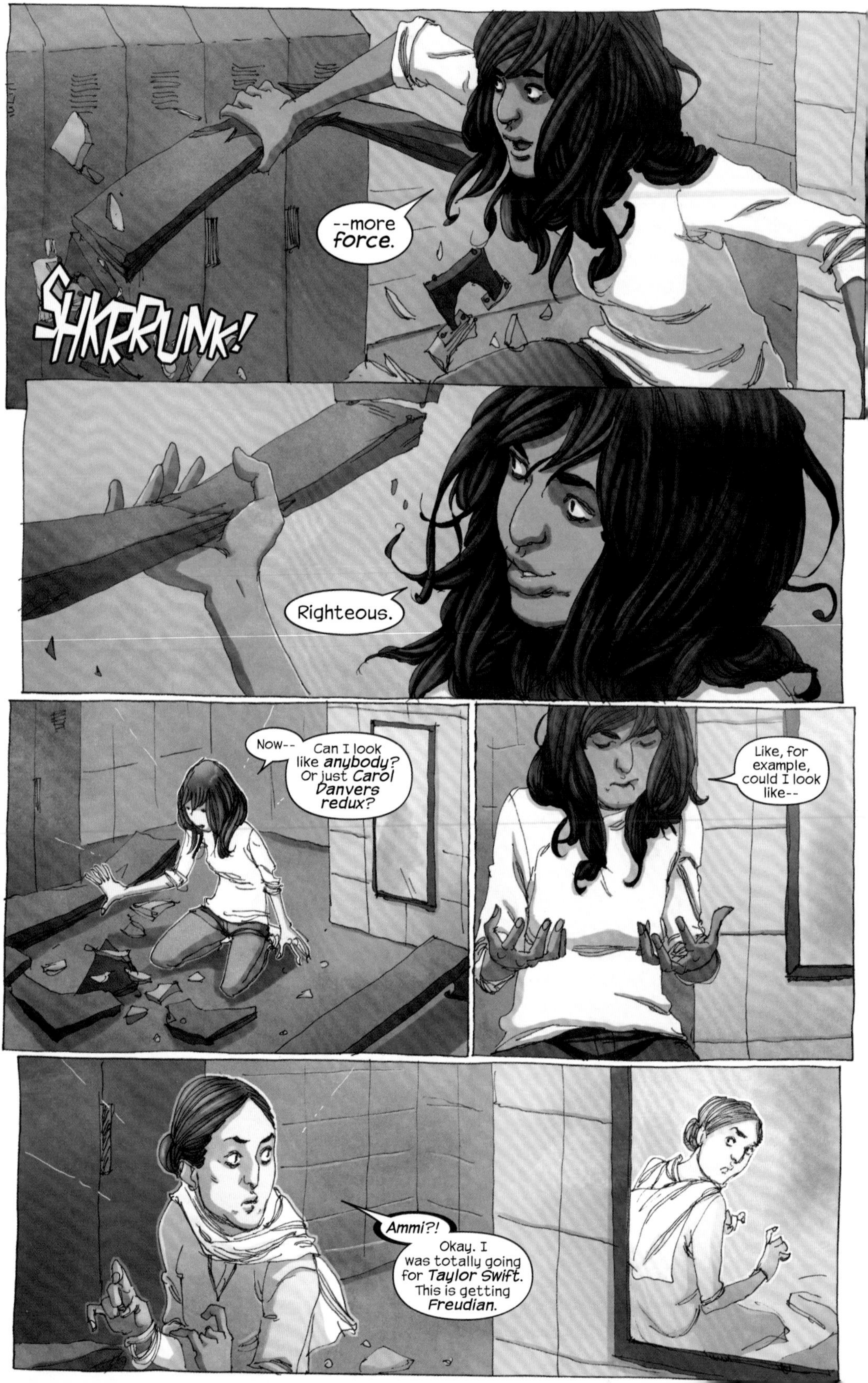
--more force.
SHKRRUNK!
Righteous.
Now--
Can I look like anybody? Or just Carol Danvers redux?
Like, for example, could I look like--
Ammi?!
Okay. I was totally going for Taylor Swift. This is getting Freudian.

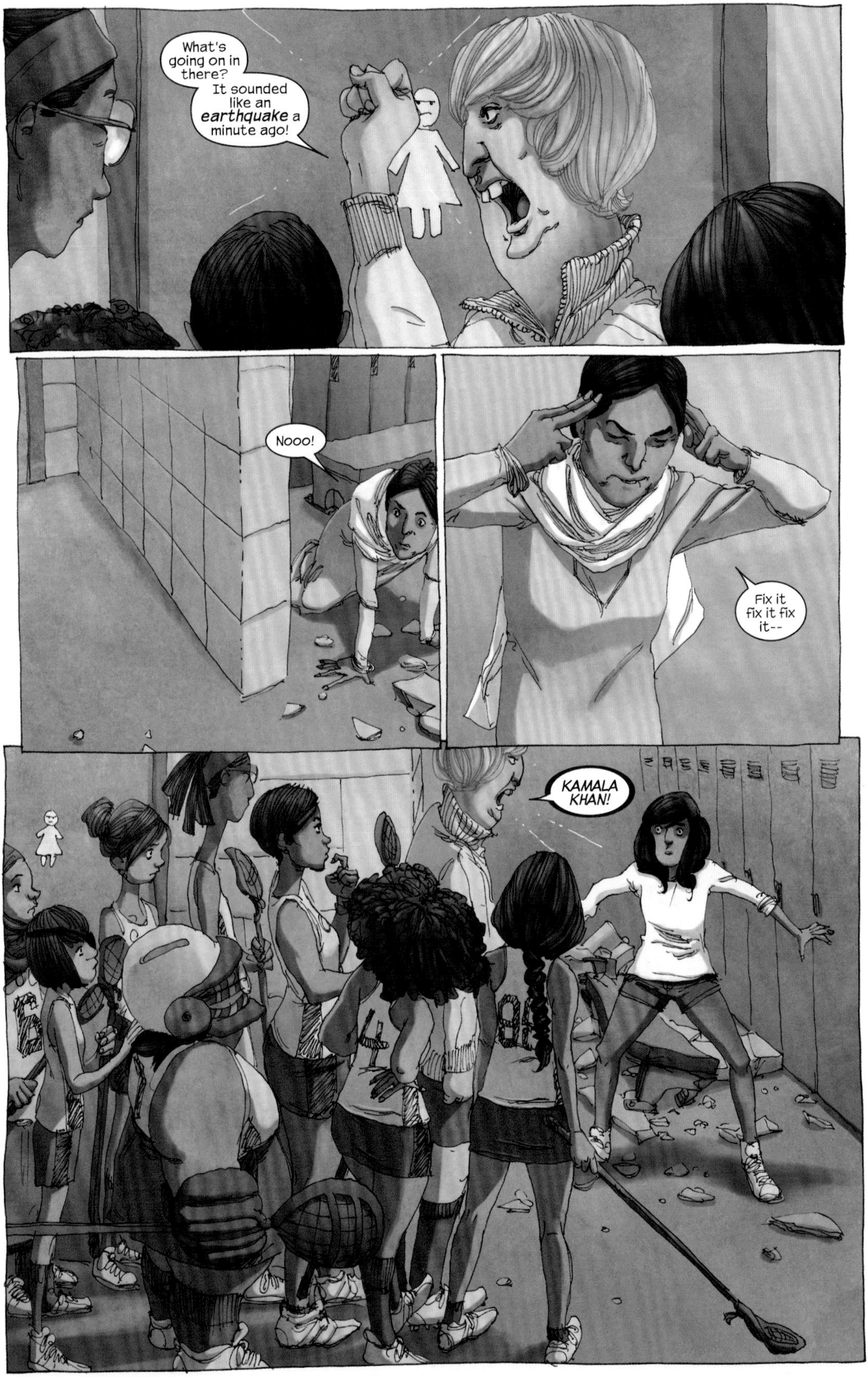
What's going on in there?
It sounded like an *earthquake* a minute ago!
Nooo!
Fix it fix it fix it--
KAMALA KHAN!

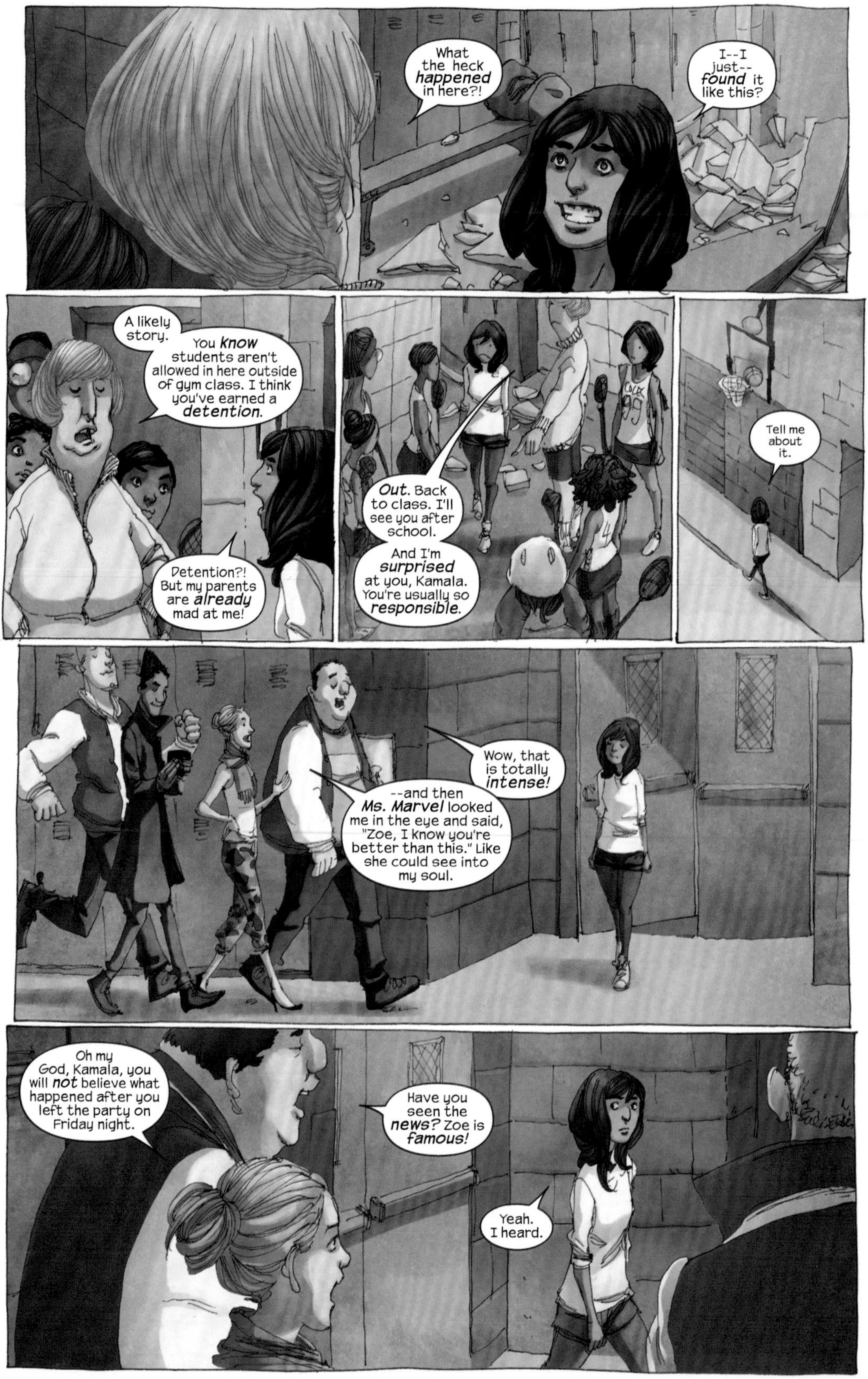
What the heck happened in here?!
I--I just-- found it like this?
A likely story.
You know students aren't allowed in here outside of gym class. I think you've earned a detention.
Detention?! But my parents are already mad at me!
Out. Back to class. I'll see you after school.
And I'm surprised at you, Kamala. You're usually so responsible.
Tell me about it.
Wow, that is totally intense!
--and then Ms. Marvel looked me in the eye and said, "Zoe, I know you're better than this." Like she could see into my soul.
Oh my God, Kamala, you will not believe what happened after you left the party on Friday night.
Have you seen the news? Zoe is famous!
Yeah. I heard.

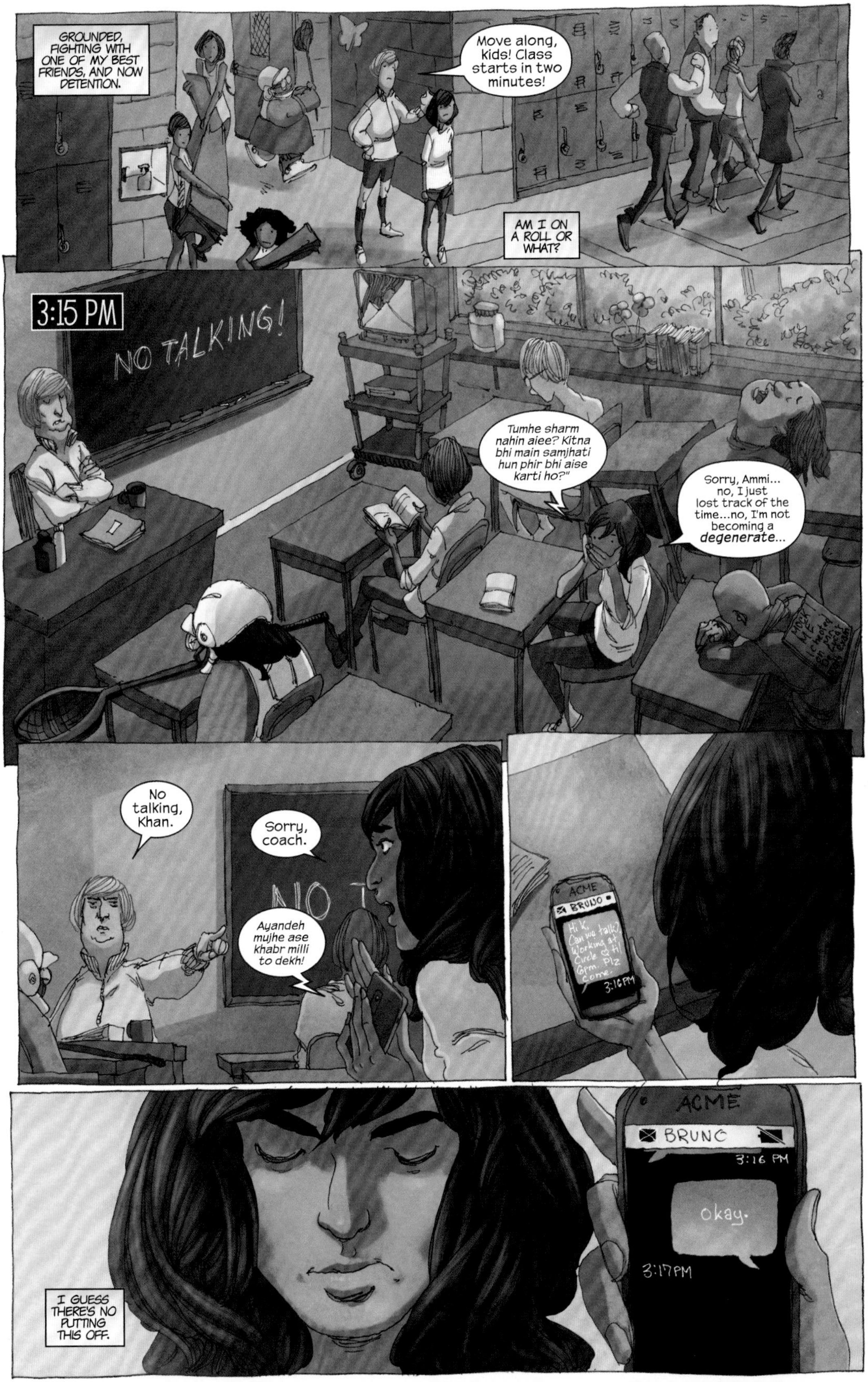

GROUNDED, FIGHTING WITH ONE OF MY BEST FRIENDS, AND NOW DETENTION.
Move along, kids! Class starts in two minutes!
AM I ON A ROLL OR WHAT?
3:15 PM
NO TALKING!
Tumhe sharm nahin aiee? Kitna bhi main samjhati hun phir bhi aise karti ho?"
Sorry, Ammi... no, I just lost track of the time...no, I'm not becoming a *degenerate*...
No talking, Khan.
Sorry, coach.
Ayandeh mujhe ase khabr milli to dekh!
ACME
BRUNO
Hi K, Can we talk? Working at Circle Q til 6pm. Plz come.
3:16 PM
ACME
BRUNO
3:16 PM
okay.
3:17PM
I GUESS THERE'S NO PUTTING THIS OFF.

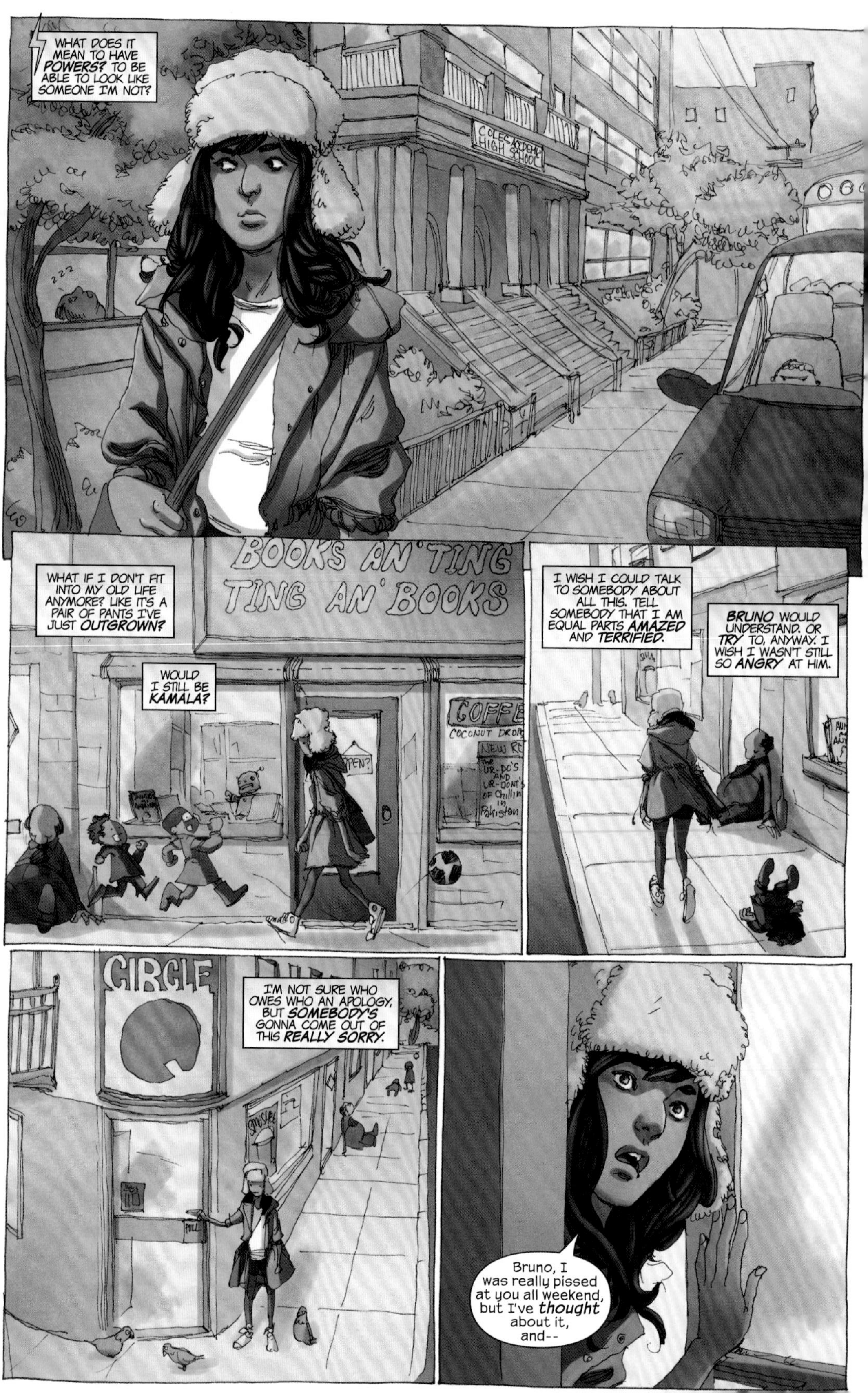
WHAT DOES IT MEAN TO HAVE POWERS? TO BE ABLE TO LOOK LIKE SOMEONE I'M NOT?
COLES ACADEMIC HIGH SCHOOL
BOOKS AN' TING TING AN' BOOKS
WHAT IF I DON'T FIT INTO MY OLD LIFE ANYMORE? LIKE IT'S A PAIR OF PANTS I'VE JUST OUTGROWN?
WOULD I STILL BE KAMALA?
COFFE
COCONUT DROPS
OPEN?
THE UR-DO'S AND UR-DONT'S OF CHILLIN IN PAKISTAN
I WISH I COULD TALK TO SOMEBODY ABOUT ALL THIS. TELL SOMEBODY THAT I AM EQUAL PARTS AMAZED AND TERRIFIED.
BRUNO WOULD UNDERSTAND. OR TRY TO, ANYWAY. I WISH I WASN'T STILL SO ANGRY AT HIM.
CIRCLE
I'M NOT SURE WHO OWES WHO AN APOLOGY, BUT SOMEBODY'S GONNA COME OUT OF THIS REALLY SORRY.
PULL
Bruno, I was really pissed at you all weekend, but I've thought about it, and--

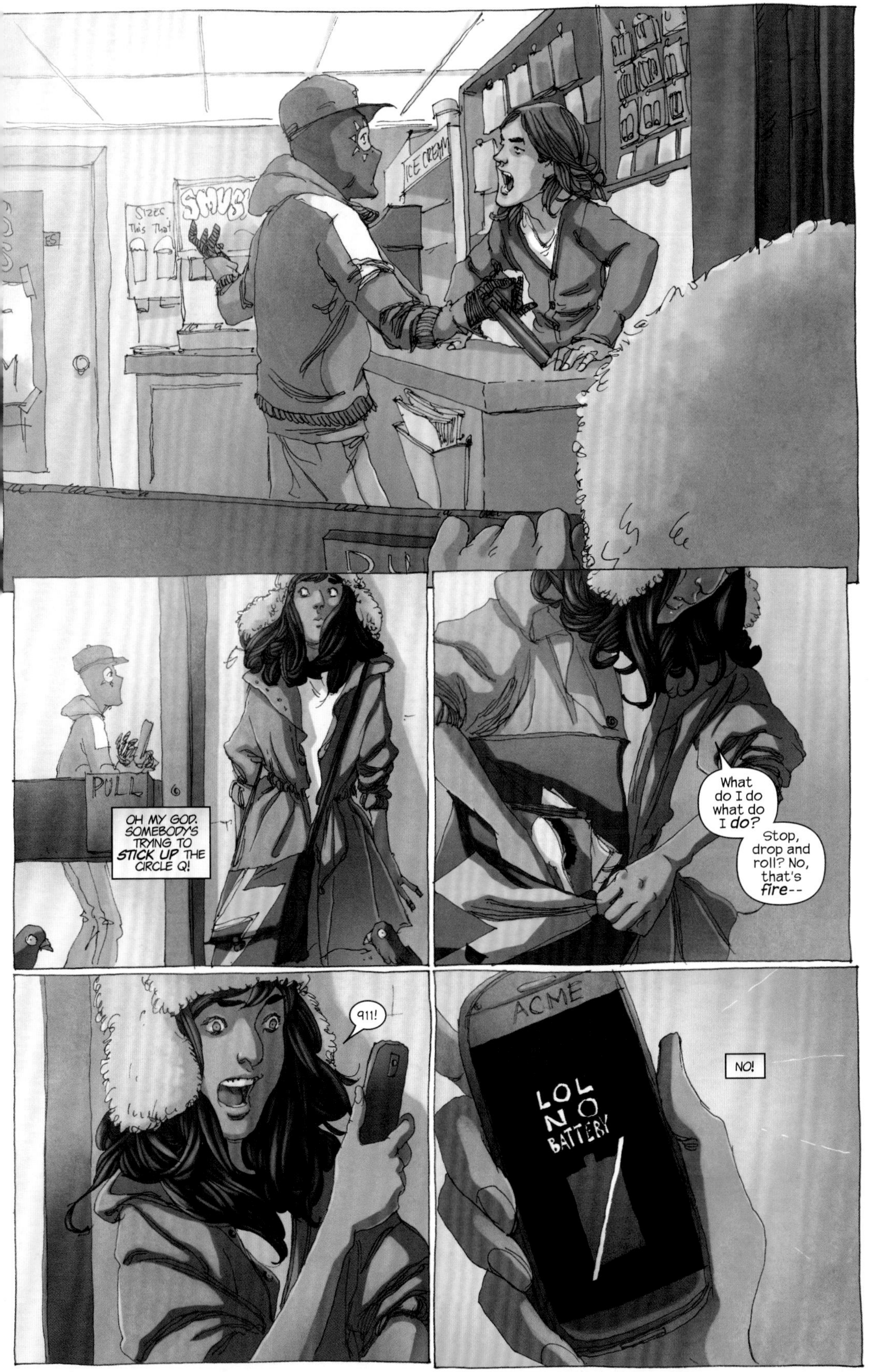

ICE CREAM
Sizes
This That
PULL
OH MY GOD. SOMEBODY'S TRYING TO STICK UP THE CIRCLE Q!
What do I do what do I do?
Stop, drop and roll? No, that's fire--
911!
ACME
LOL NO BATTERY
NO!

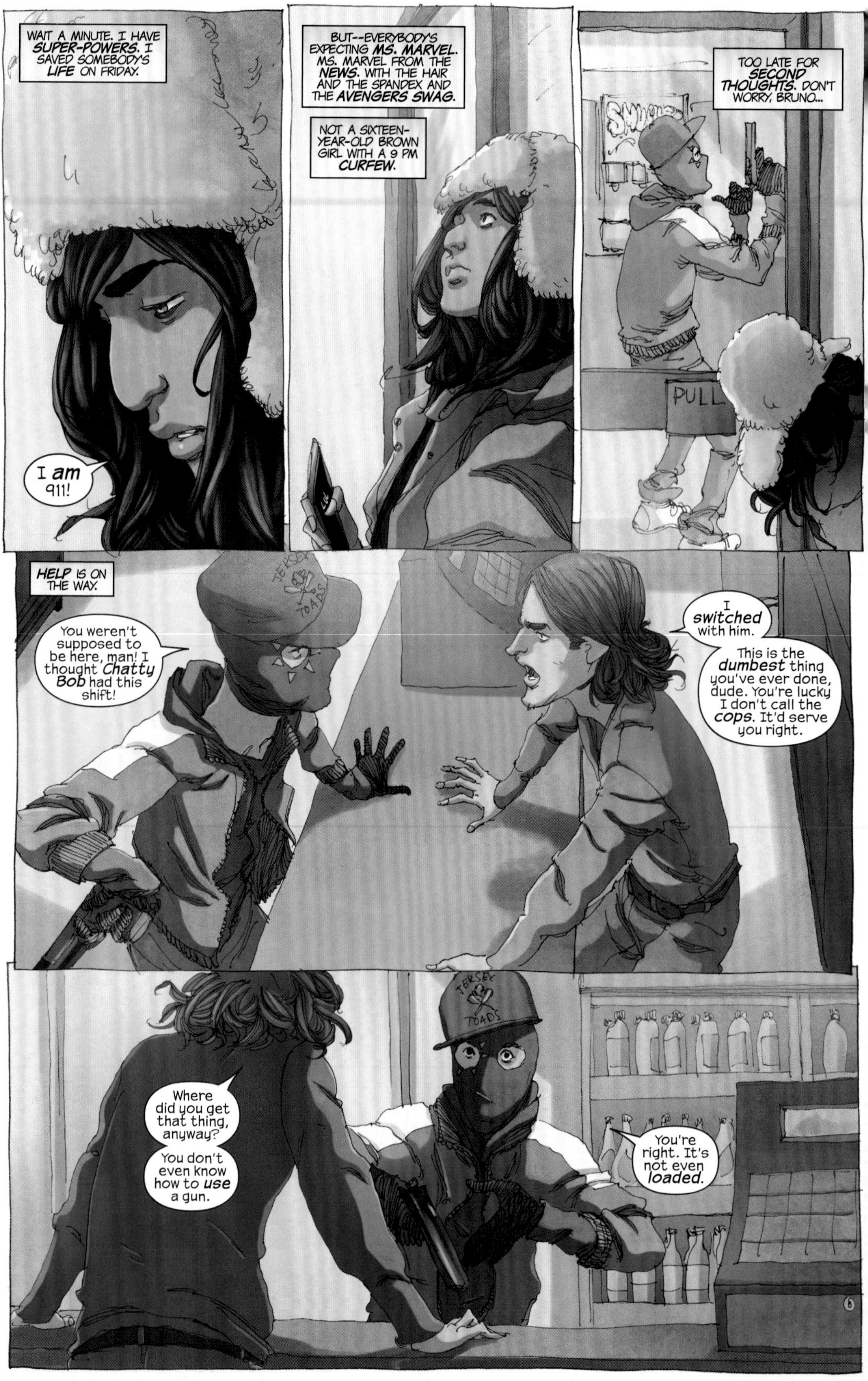
WAIT A MINUTE. I HAVE SUPER-POWERS. I SAVED SOMEBODY'S LIFE ON FRIDAY.
I am 911!
BUT--EVERYBODY'S EXPECTING MS. MARVEL. MS. MARVEL FROM THE NEWS. WITH THE HAIR AND THE SPANDEX AND THE AVENGERS SWAG.
NOT A SIXTEEN-YEAR-OLD BROWN GIRL WITH A 9 PM CURFEW.
TOO LATE FOR SECOND THOUGHTS. DON'T WORRY, BRUNO...
PULL
HELP IS ON THE WAY.
JERSEY TOADS
You weren't supposed to be here, man! I thought Chatty Bob had this shift!
I switched with him.
This is the dumbest thing you've ever done, dude. You're lucky I don't call the cops. It'd serve you right.
JERSEY TOADS
Where did you get that thing, anyway?
You don't even know how to use a gun.
You're right. It's not even loaded.
6

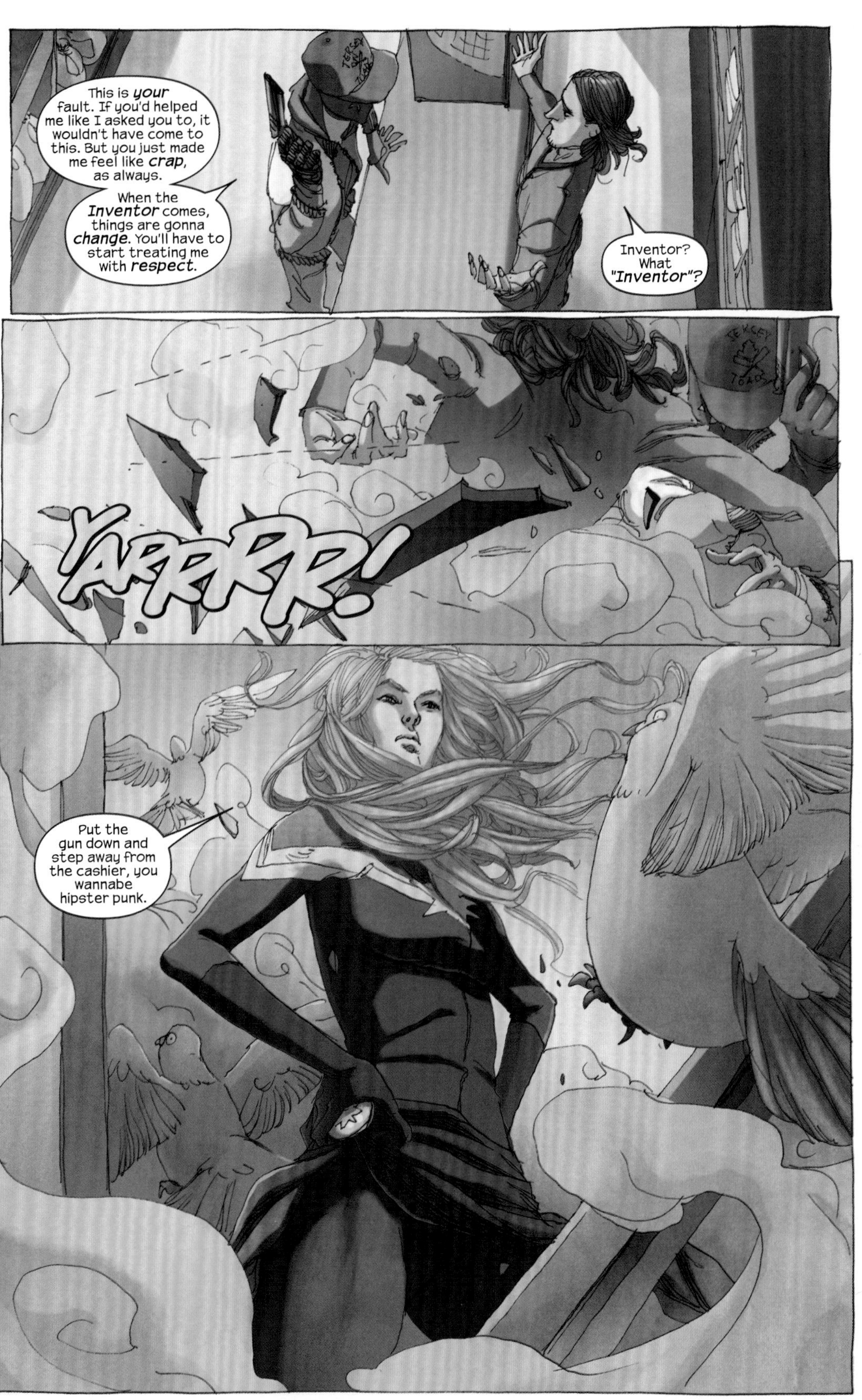

This is your fault. If you'd helped me like I asked you to, it wouldn't have come to this. But you just made me feel like crap, as always.
When the Inventor comes, things are gonna change. You'll have to start treating me with respect.
Inventor? What "Inventor"?
YARRRR!
Put the gun down and step away from the cashier, you wannabe hipster punk.

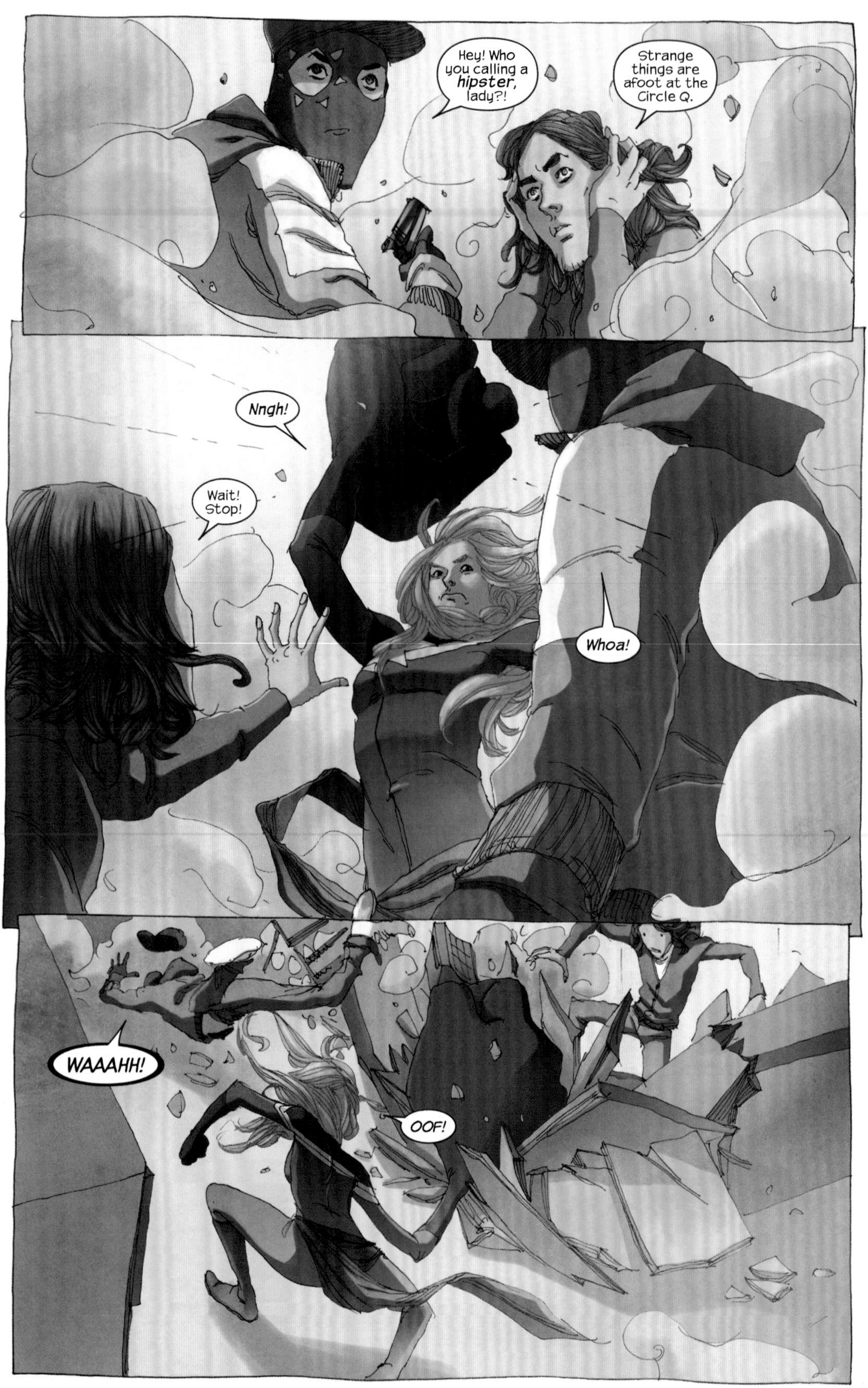

Hey! Who you calling a *hipster*, lady?!
Strange things are afoot at the Circle Q.
Nngh!
Wait! Stop!
Whoa!
WAAAHH!
OOF!

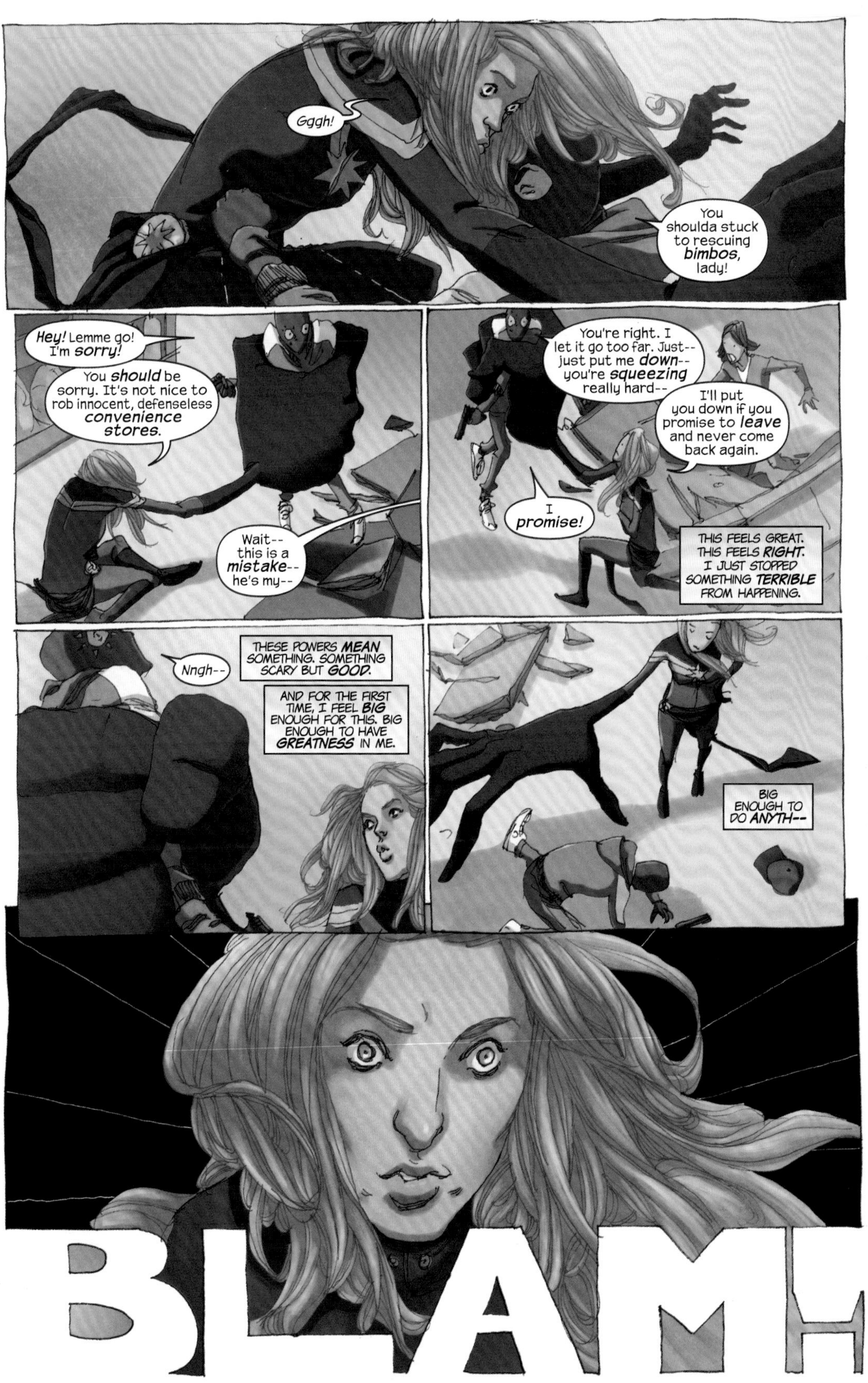
Gggh!
You shoulda stuck to rescuing bimbos, lady!
Hey! Lemme go! I'm sorry!
You should be sorry. It's not nice to rob innocent, defenseless convenience stores.
Wait--this is a mistake--he's my--
You're right. I let it go too far. Just--just put me down--you're squeezing really hard--
I'll put you down if you promise to leave and never come back again.
I promise!
THIS FEELS GREAT. THIS FEELS RIGHT. I JUST STOPPED SOMETHING TERRIBLE FROM HAPPENING.
Nngh--
THESE POWERS MEAN SOMETHING. SOMETHING SCARY BUT GOOD.
AND FOR THE FIRST TIME, I FEEL BIG ENOUGH FOR THIS. BIG ENOUGH TO HAVE GREATNESS IN ME.
BIG ENOUGH TO DO ANYTH--
BLAMH

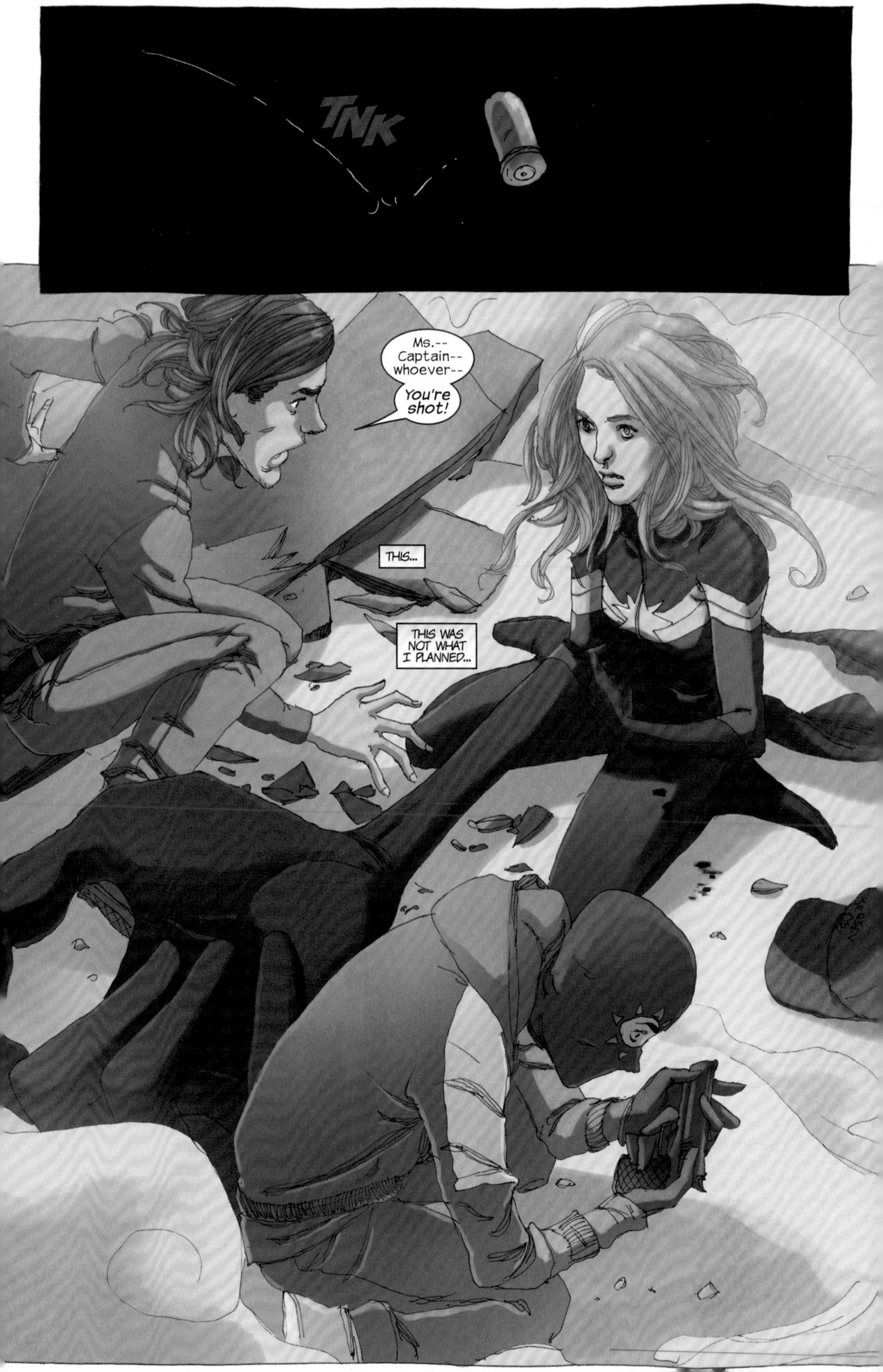
TNK
Ms.-- Captain-- whoever-- You're shot!
THIS...
THIS WAS NOT WHAT I PLANNED...

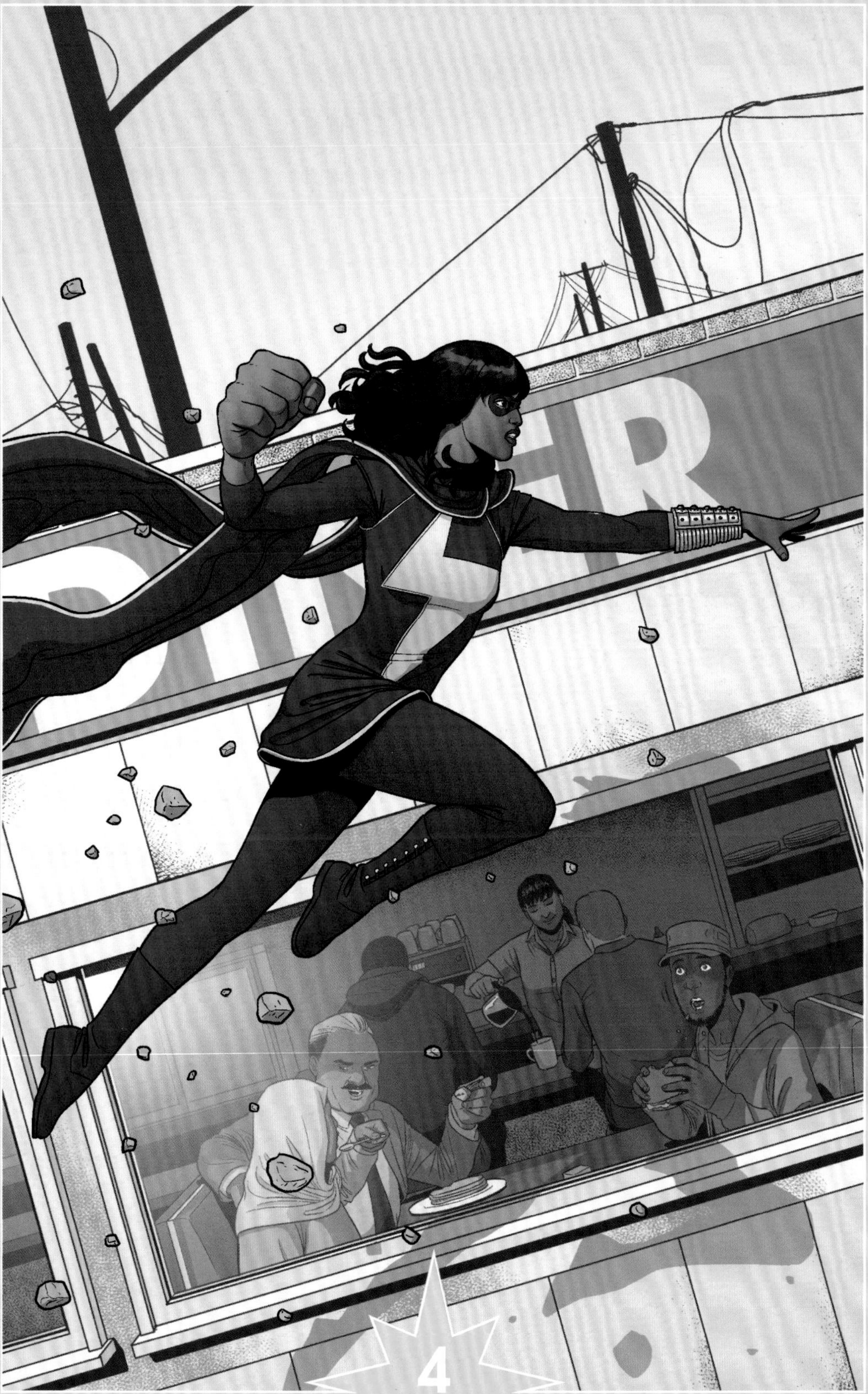
4

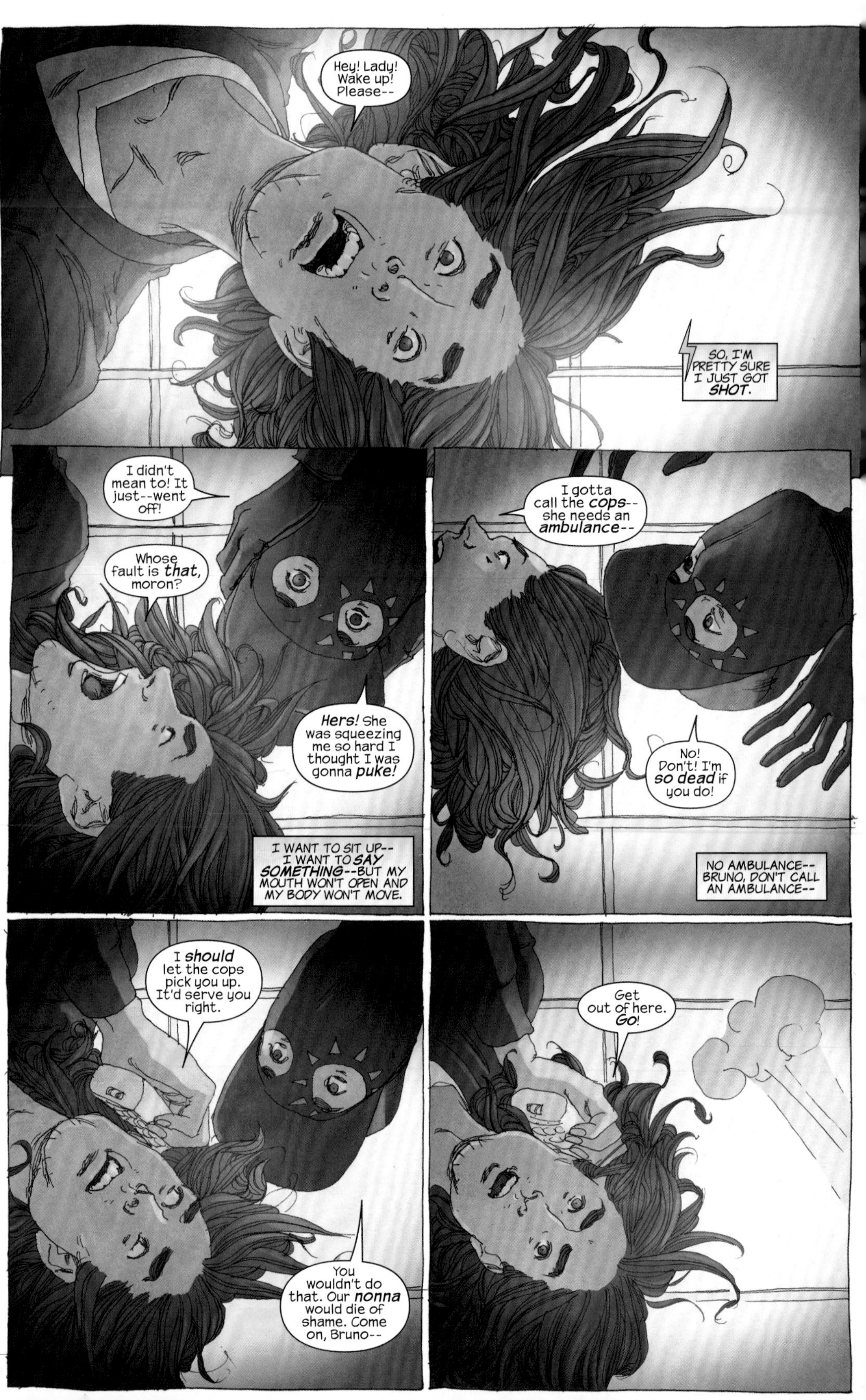
Hey! Lady! Wake up! Please--
SO, I'M PRETTY SURE I JUST GOT SHOT.
I didn't mean to! It just--went off!
Whose fault is that, moron?
Hers! She was squeezing me so hard I thought I was gonna puke!
I WANT TO SIT UP-- I WANT TO SAY SOMETHING--BUT MY MOUTH WON'T OPEN AND MY BODY WON'T MOVE.
I gotta call the cops-- she needs an ambulance--
No! Don't! I'm so dead if you do!
NO AMBULANCE-- BRUNO, DON'T CALL AN AMBULANCE--
I should let the cops pick you up. It'd serve you right.
You wouldn't do that. Our nonna would die of shame. Come on, Bruno--
Get out of here. Go!

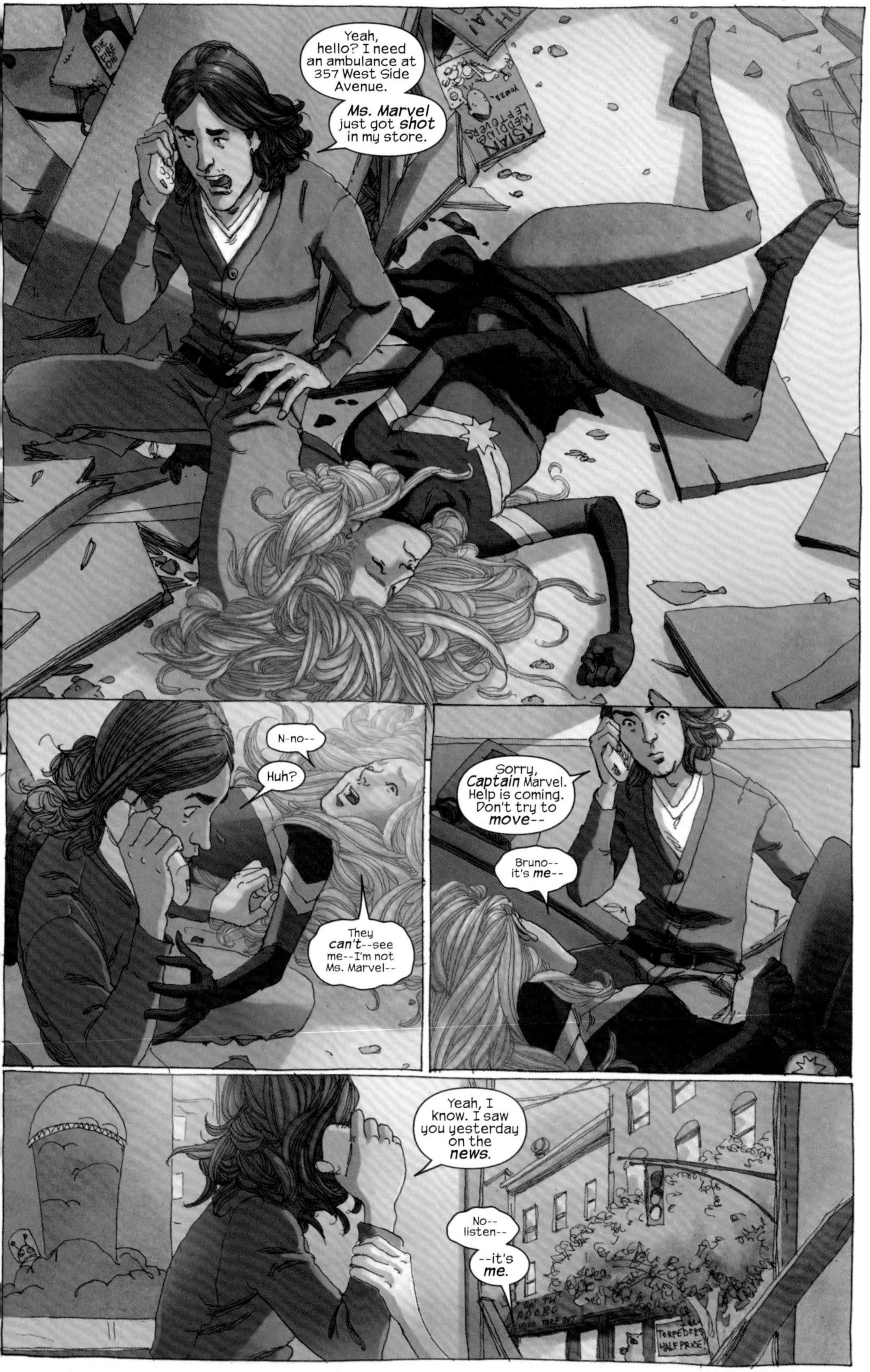

Yeah, hello? I need an ambulance at 357 West Side Avenue.
Ms. Marvel just got shot in my store.
ASIAN WEDDING LEFTOVERS
DIE FIRE DIE
N-no--
Huh?
They can't--see me--I'm not Ms. Marvel--
Sorry, Captain Marvel. Help is coming. Don't try to move--
Bruno-- it's me--
Yeah, I know. I saw you yesterday on the news.
No-- listen--
--it's me.
ADOBO
TORPEDOES HALF PRICE

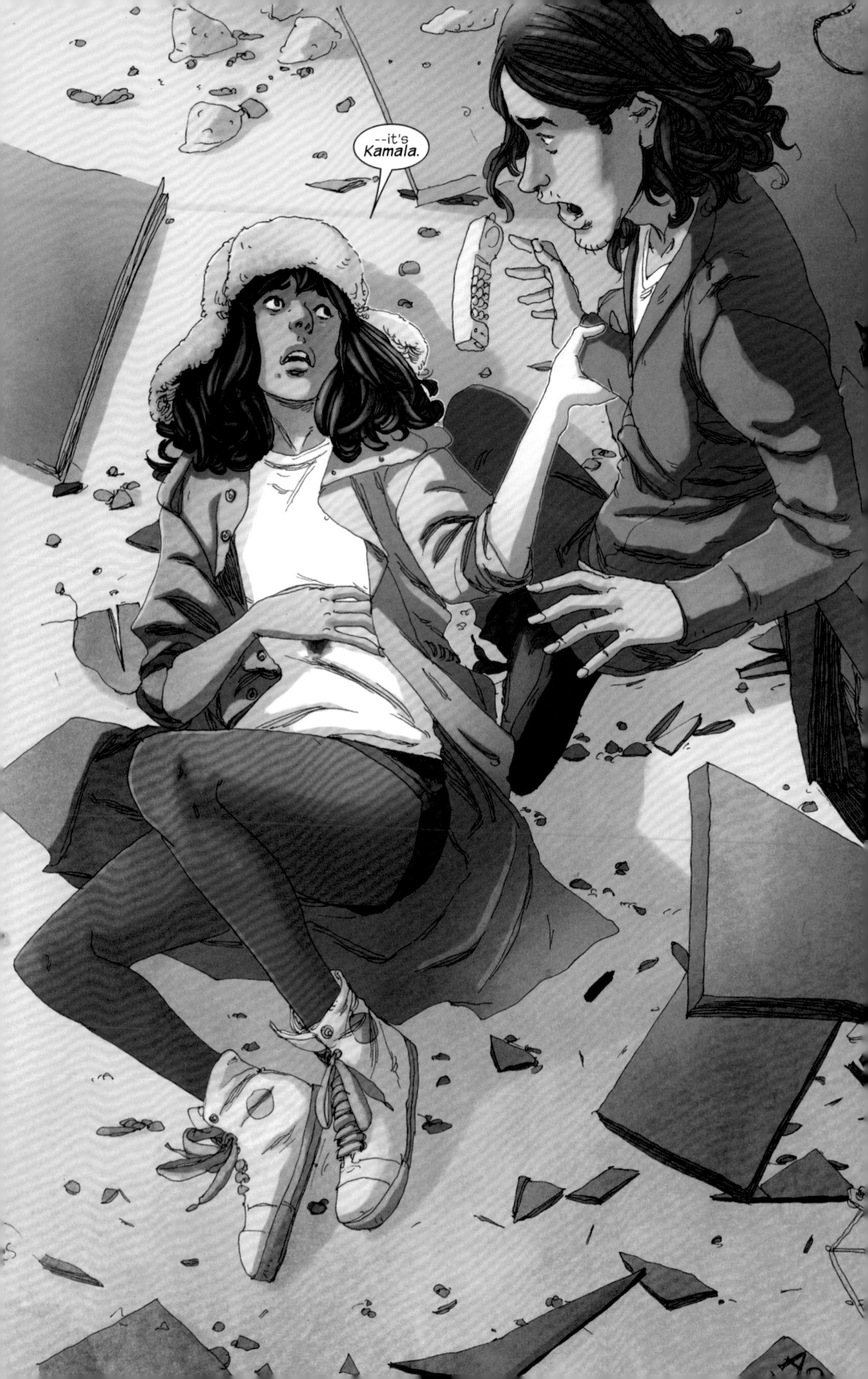
--it's Kamala.

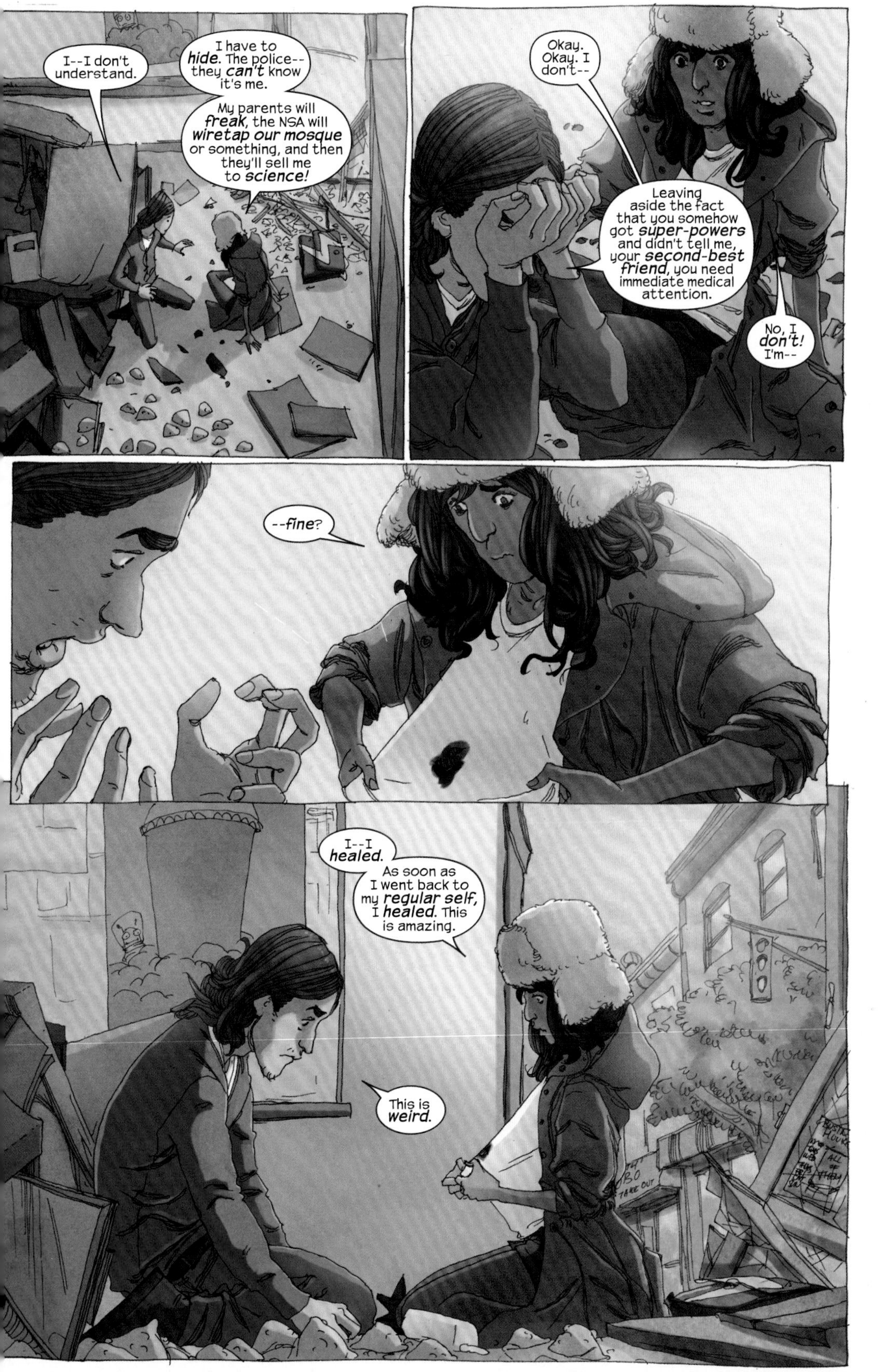
I--I don't understand.
I have to hide. The police--they can't know it's me.
My parents will freak, the NSA will wiretap our mosque or something, and then they'll sell me to science!
Okay. Okay. I don't--
Leaving aside the fact that you somehow got super-powers and didn't tell me, your second-best friend, you need immediate medical attention.
No, I don't! I'm--
--fine?
I--I healed.
As soon as I went back to my regular self, I healed. This is amazing.
This is weird.
TAKE OUT

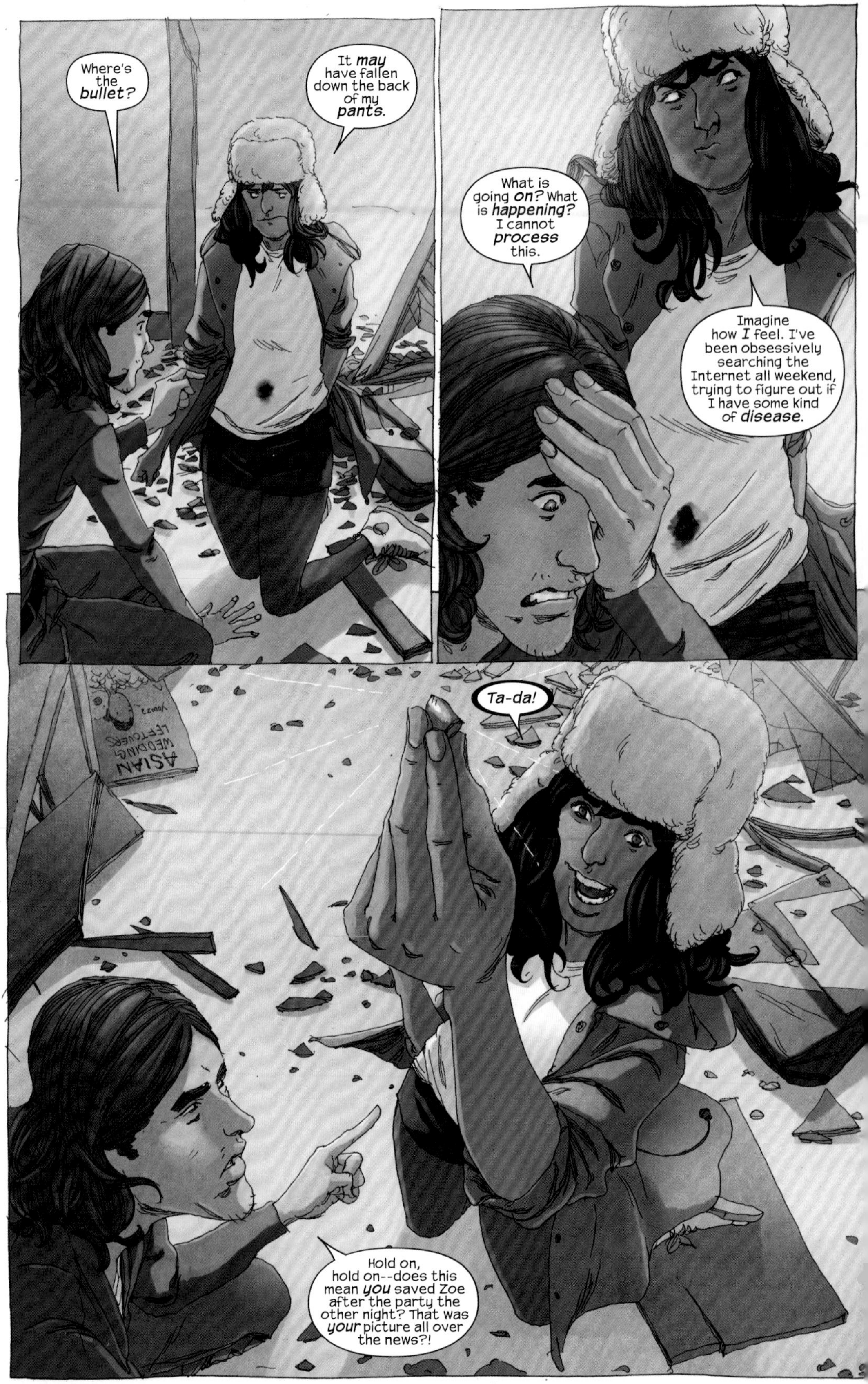
Where's the bullet?
It may have fallen down the back of my pants.
What is going on? What is happening? I cannot process this.
Imagine how I feel. I've been obsessively searching the Internet all weekend, trying to figure out if I have some kind of disease.
ASIAN WEDDING LEFTOVERS
Ta-da!
Hold on, hold on--does this mean you saved Zoe after the party the other night? That was your picture all over the news?!

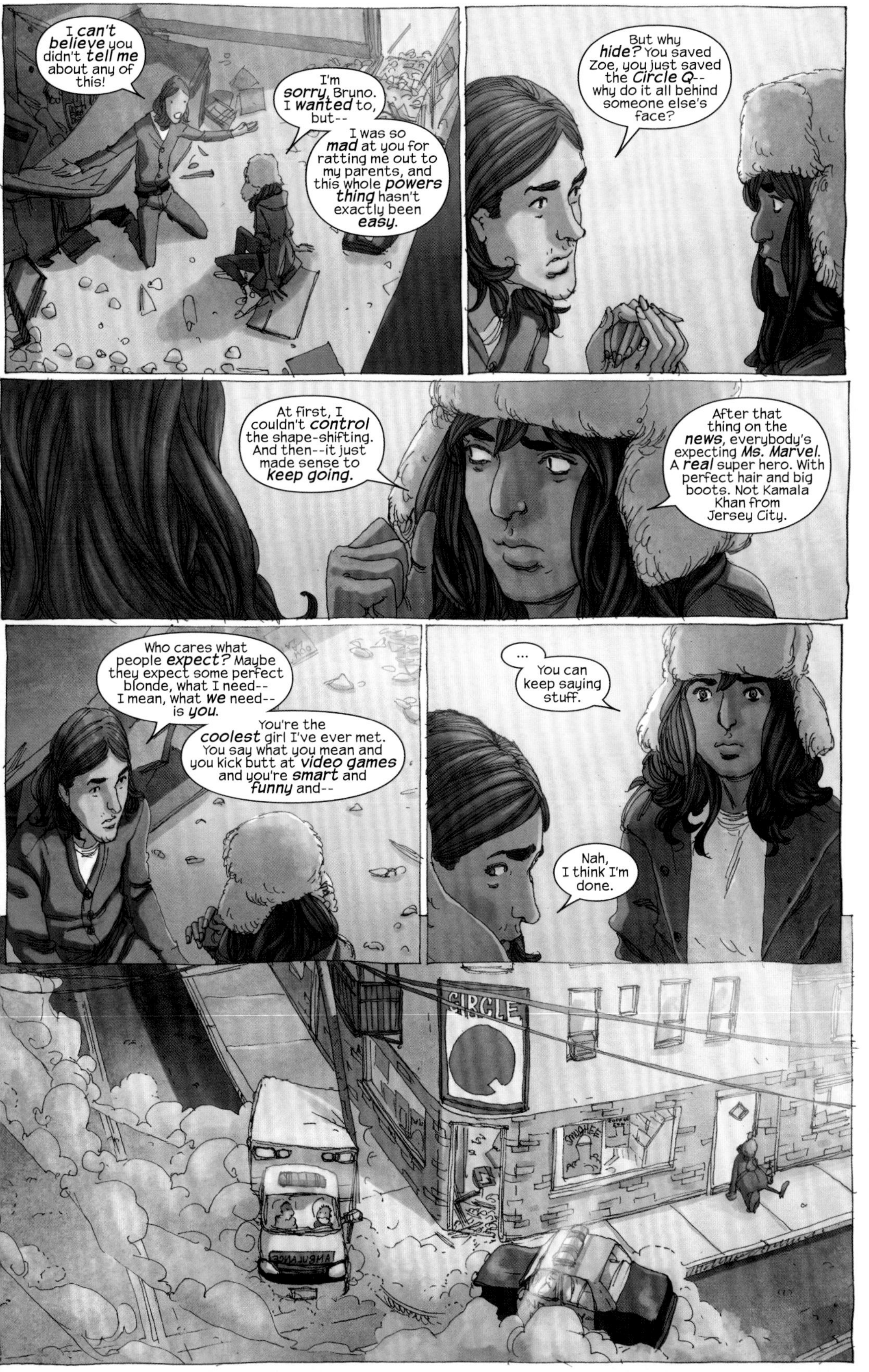
I can't believe you didn't tell me about any of this!
I'm sorry, Bruno. I wanted to, but--
I was so mad at you for ratting me out to my parents, and this whole powers thing hasn't exactly been easy.
But why hide? You saved Zoe, you just saved the Circle Q-- why do it all behind someone else's face?
At first, I couldn't control the shape-shifting. And then--it just made sense to keep going.
After that thing on the news, everybody's expecting Ms. Marvel. A real super hero. With perfect hair and big boots. Not Kamala Khan from Jersey City.
Who cares what people expect? Maybe they expect some perfect blonde, what I need-- I mean, what we need-- is you.
You're the coolest girl I've ever met. You say what you mean and you kick butt at video games and you're smart and funny and--
... You can keep saying stuff.
Nah, I think I'm done.
CIRCLE

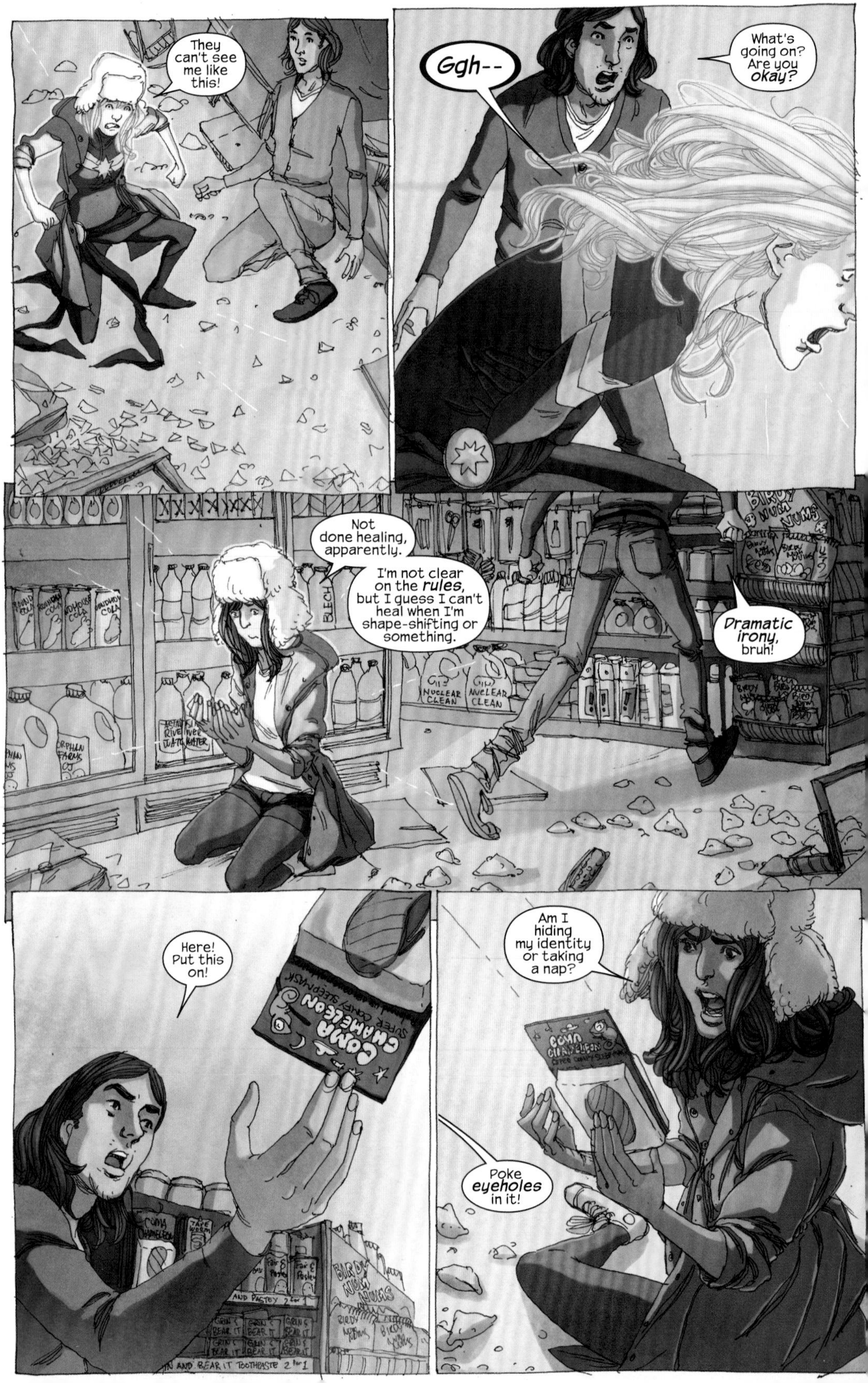
They can't see me like this!
Ggh--
What's going on? Are you *okay?*
Not done healing, apparently.
I'm not clear on the *rules*, but I guess I can't heal when I'm shape-shifting or something.
Dramatic irony, bruh!
Here! Put this on!
COMA CHAMELEON
SUPER COMFY SLEEPMASK
Am I hiding my identity or taking a nap?
Poke *eyeholes* in it!
NUCLEAR CLEAN
BIRDY NUM NUMS
GRIN & BEAR IT
AND BEAR IT TOOTHPASTE 2 for 1

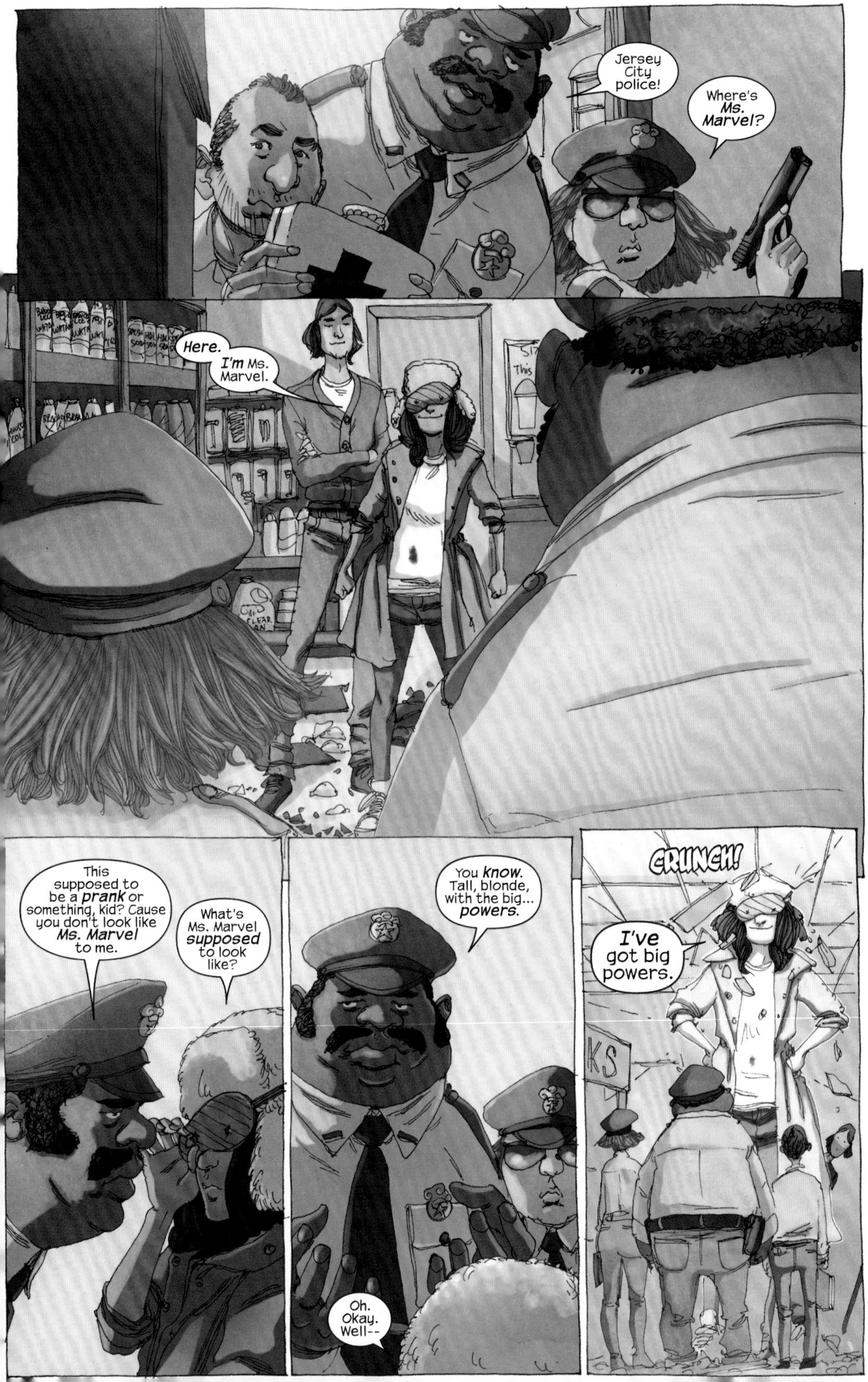

Jersey City police!
Where's *Ms. Marvel?*
Here. *I'm* Ms. Marvel.
This supposed to be a *prank* or something, kid? Cause you don't look like *Ms. Marvel* to me.
What's Ms. Marvel *supposed* to look like?
You *know.* Tall, blonde, with the big... *powers.*
Oh. Okay. Well--
CRUNCH!
I've got big powers.

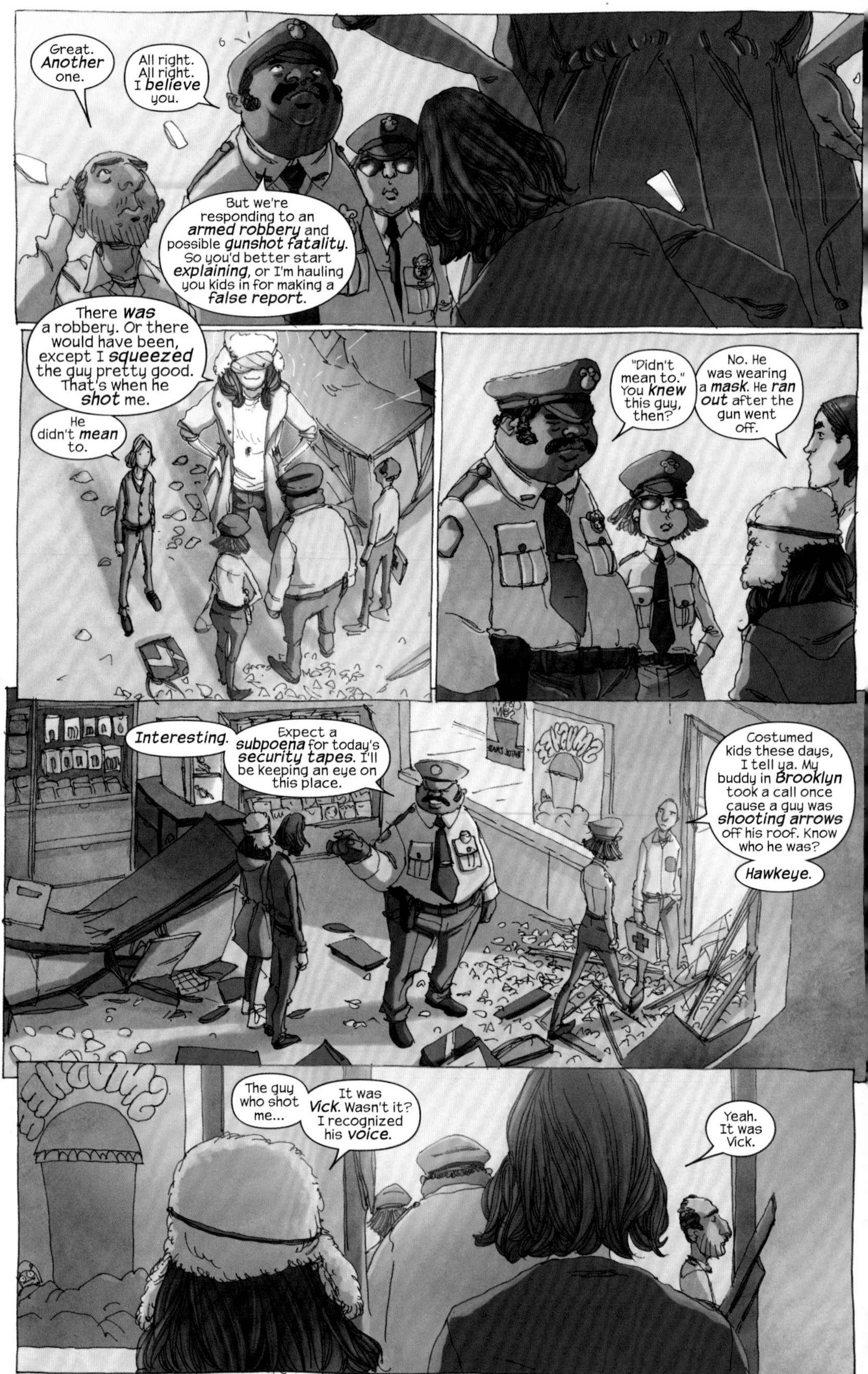

Great. Another one.
All right. All right. I believe you.
But we're responding to an armed robbery and possible gunshot fatality. So you'd better start explaining, or I'm hauling you kids in for making a false report.
There was a robbery. Or there would have been, except I squeezed the guy pretty good. That's when he shot me.
He didn't mean to.
"Didn't mean to." You knew this guy, then?
No. He was wearing a mask. He ran out after the gun went off.
Interesting.
Expect a subpoena for today's security tapes. I'll be keeping an eye on this place.
Costumed kids these days, I tell ya. My buddy in Brooklyn took a call once cause a guy was shooting arrows off his roof. Know who he was?
Hawkeye.
The guy who shot me...
It was Vick. Wasn't it? I recognized his voice.
Yeah. It was Vick.

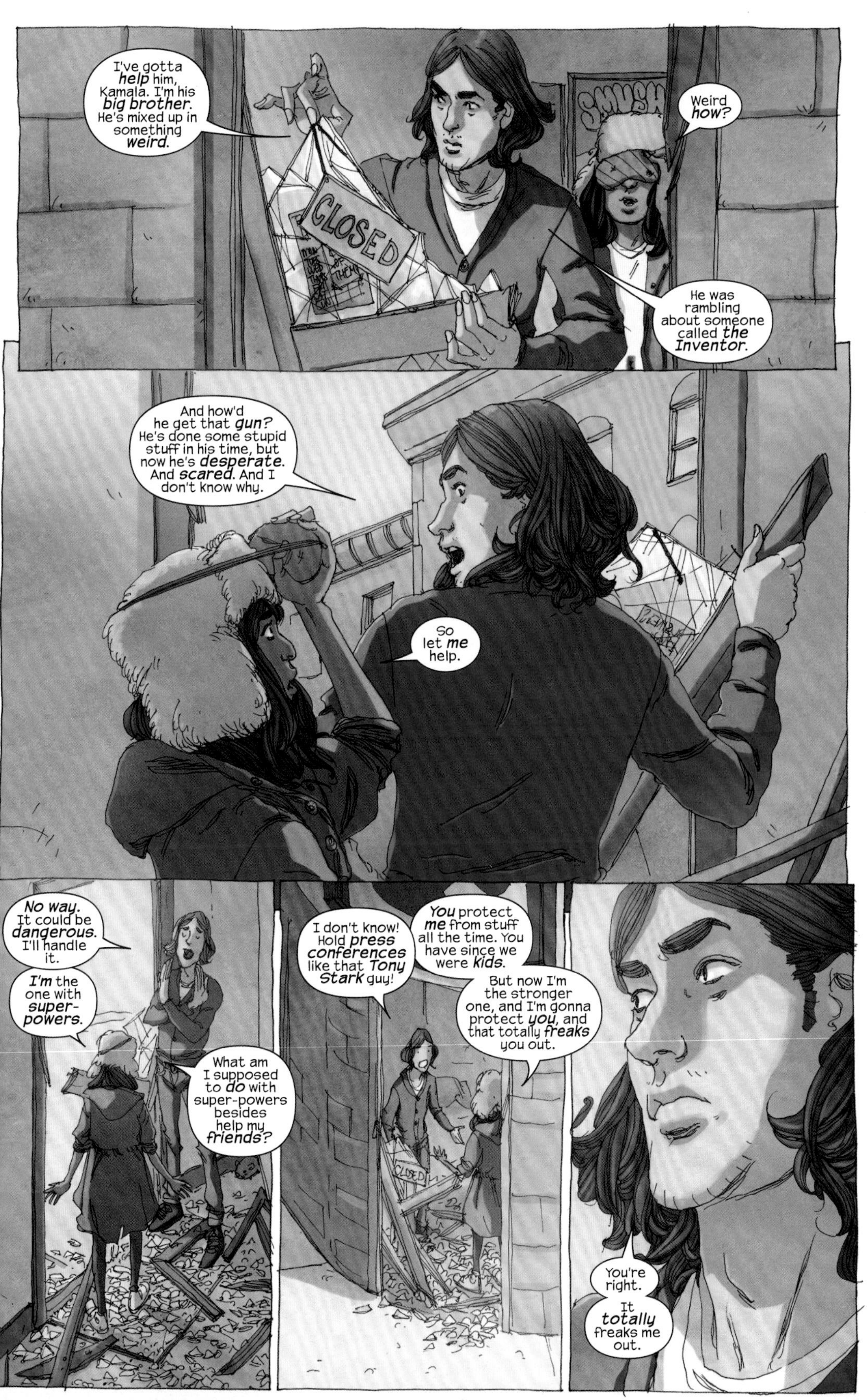

I've gotta help him, Kamala. I'm his big brother. He's mixed up in something weird.
Weird how?
He was rambling about someone called the Inventor.
SMUSH
CLOSED
And how'd he get that gun? He's done some stupid stuff in his time, but now he's desperate. And scared. And I don't know why.
So let me help.
No way. It could be dangerous. I'll handle it.
I'm the one with super-powers.
What am I supposed to do with super-powers besides help my friends?
I don't know! Hold press conferences like that Tony Stark guy!
You protect me from stuff all the time. You have since we were kids.
But now I'm the stronger one, and I'm gonna protect you, and that totally freaks you out.
CLOSED
You're right.
It totally freaks me out.

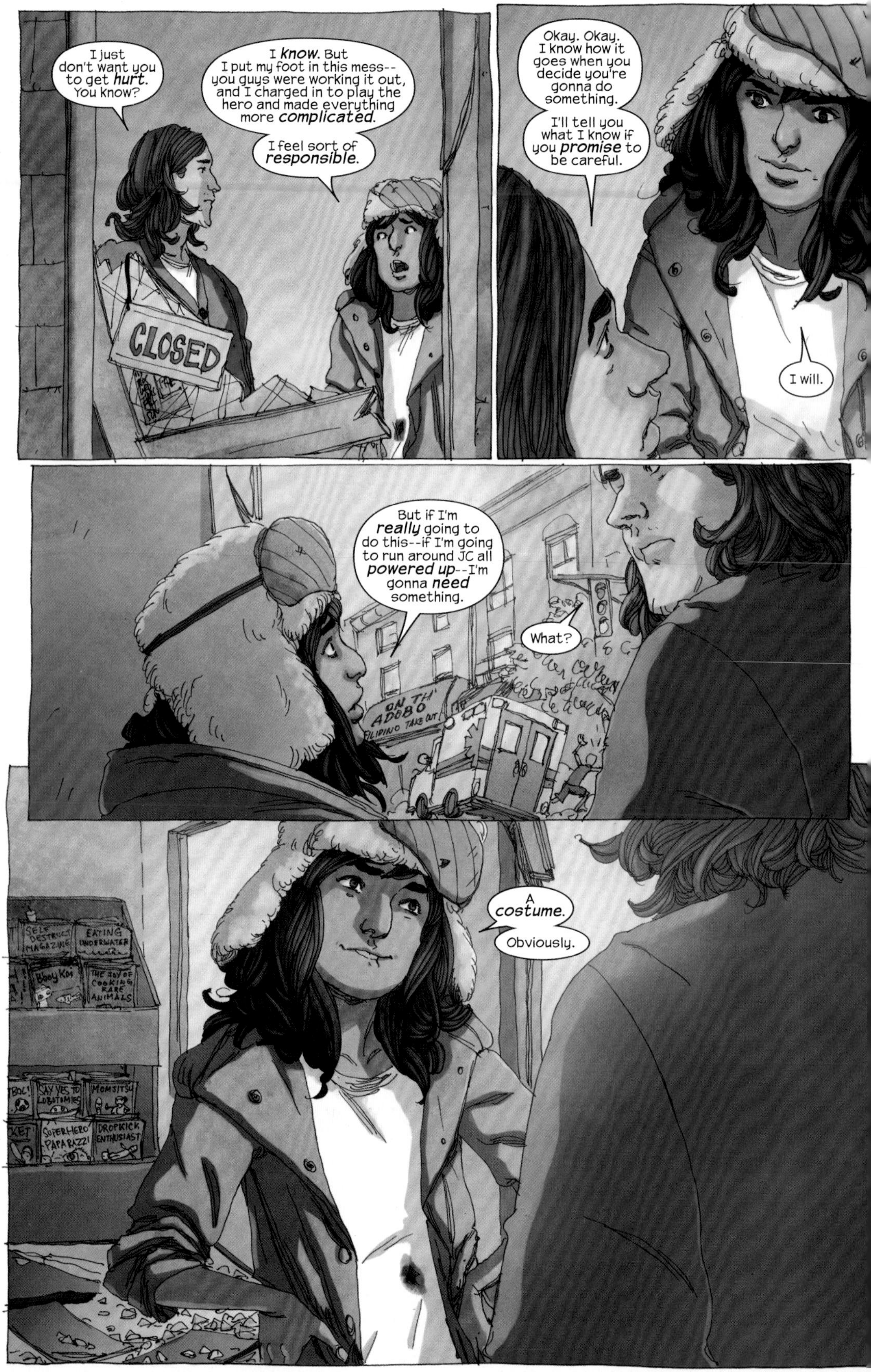
I just don't want you to get *hurt*. You know?
I *know*. But I put my foot in this mess--you guys were working it out, and I charged in to play the hero and made everything more *complicated*.
I feel sort of *responsible*.
CLOSED
Okay. Okay. I know how it goes when you decide you're gonna do something.
I'll tell you what I know if you *promise* to be careful.
I will.
But if I'm *really* going to do this--if I'm going to run around JC all *powered up*--I'm gonna *need* something.
What?
ON TH' ADOBO
FILIPINO TAKE OUT
A *costume*.
Obviously.
SELF DESTRUCT MAGAZINE
EATING UNDERWATER
THE JOY OF COOKING RARE ANIMALS
SAY YES TO LOBOTOMIES
MOMJITSU
SUPERHERO PAPARAZZI
DROPKICK ENTHUSIAST

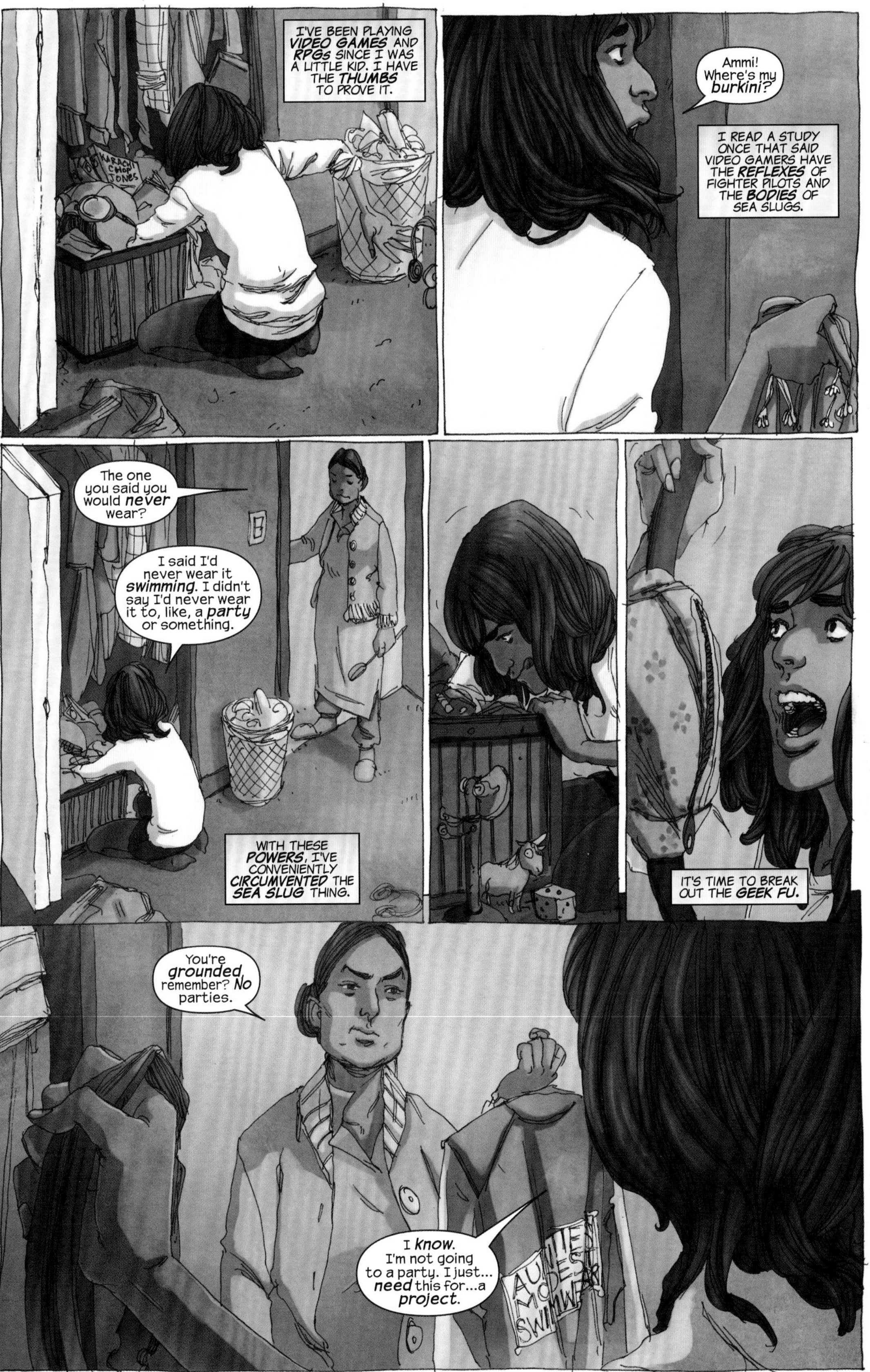
I'VE BEEN PLAYING VIDEO GAMES AND RPGs SINCE I WAS A LITTLE KID. I HAVE THE THUMBS TO PROVE IT.
KARACHI CHOP JONES
Ammi! Where's my burkini?
I READ A STUDY ONCE THAT SAID VIDEO GAMERS HAVE THE REFLEXES OF FIGHTER PILOTS AND THE BODIES OF SEA SLUGS.
The one you said you would never wear?
I said I'd never wear it swimming. I didn't say I'd never wear it to, like, a party or something.
WITH THESE POWERS, I'VE CONVENIENTLY CIRCUMVENTED THE SEA SLUG THING.
IT'S TIME TO BREAK OUT THE GEEK FU.
You're grounded, remember? No parties.
I know. I'm not going to a party. I just... need this for...a project.
AUNTIE'S MODEST SWIMWEAR

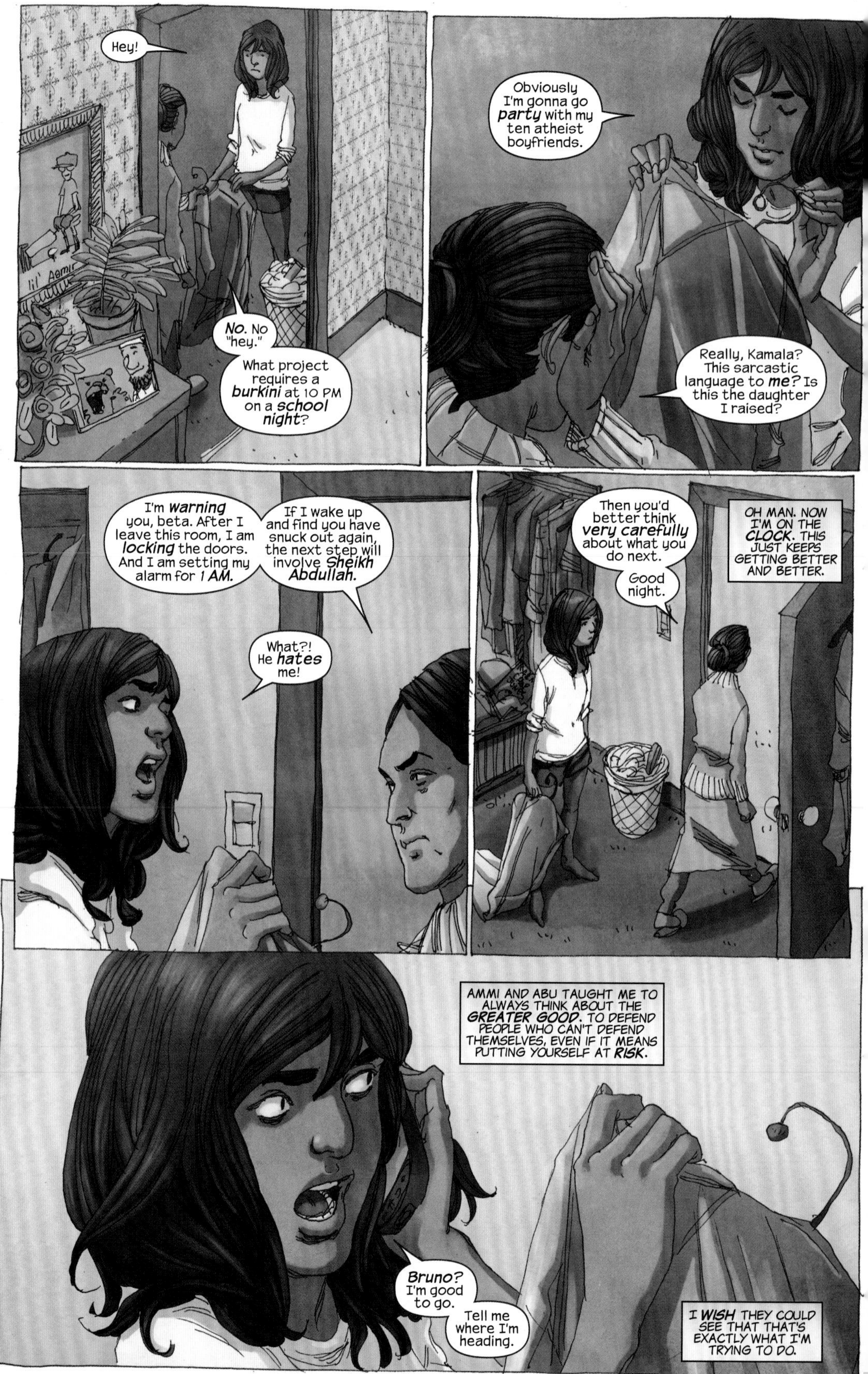

Hey!
No. No "hey."
What project requires a burkini at 10 PM on a school night?
Obviously I'm gonna go party with my ten atheist boyfriends.
Really, Kamala? This sarcastic language to me? Is this the daughter I raised?
I'm warning you, beta. After I leave this room, I am locking the doors. And I am setting my alarm for 1 AM.
If I wake up and find you have snuck out again, the next step will involve Sheikh Abdullah.
What?! He hates me!
Then you'd better think very carefully about what you do next.
Good night.
OH MAN. NOW I'M ON THE CLOCK. THIS JUST KEEPS GETTING BETTER AND BETTER.
AMMI AND ABU TAUGHT ME TO ALWAYS THINK ABOUT THE GREATER GOOD. TO DEFEND PEOPLE WHO CAN'T DEFEND THEMSELVES, EVEN IF IT MEANS PUTTING YOURSELF AT RISK.
Bruno? I'm good to go.
Tell me where I'm heading.
I WISH THEY COULD SEE THAT THAT'S EXACTLY WHAT I'M TRYING TO DO.

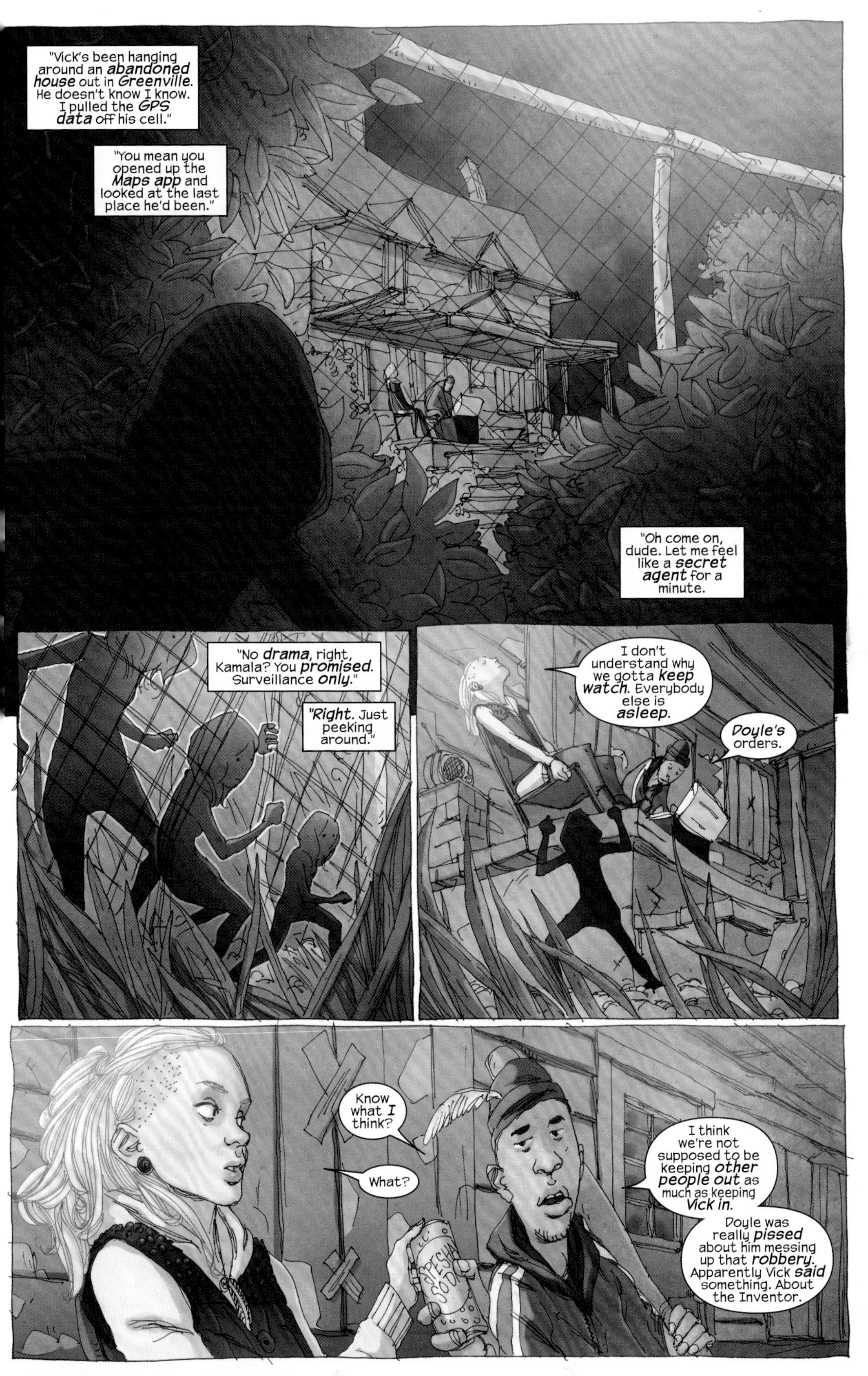
"Vick's been hanging around an *abandoned house* out in *Greenville*. He doesn't know I know. I pulled the *GPS data* off his cell."
"You mean you opened up the *Maps app* and looked at the last place he'd been."
"Oh come on, dude. Let me feel like a *secret agent* for a minute.
"No *drama*, right, Kamala? You *promised*. Surveillance *only*."
"*Right*. Just peeking around."
I don't understand why we gotta *keep watch*. Everybody else is *asleep*.
Doyle's orders.
Know what *I* think?
What?
I think we're not supposed to be keeping *other people out* as much as keeping *Vick in*.
Doyle was really *pissed* about him messing up that *robbery*. Apparently Vick *said* something. About the Inventor.

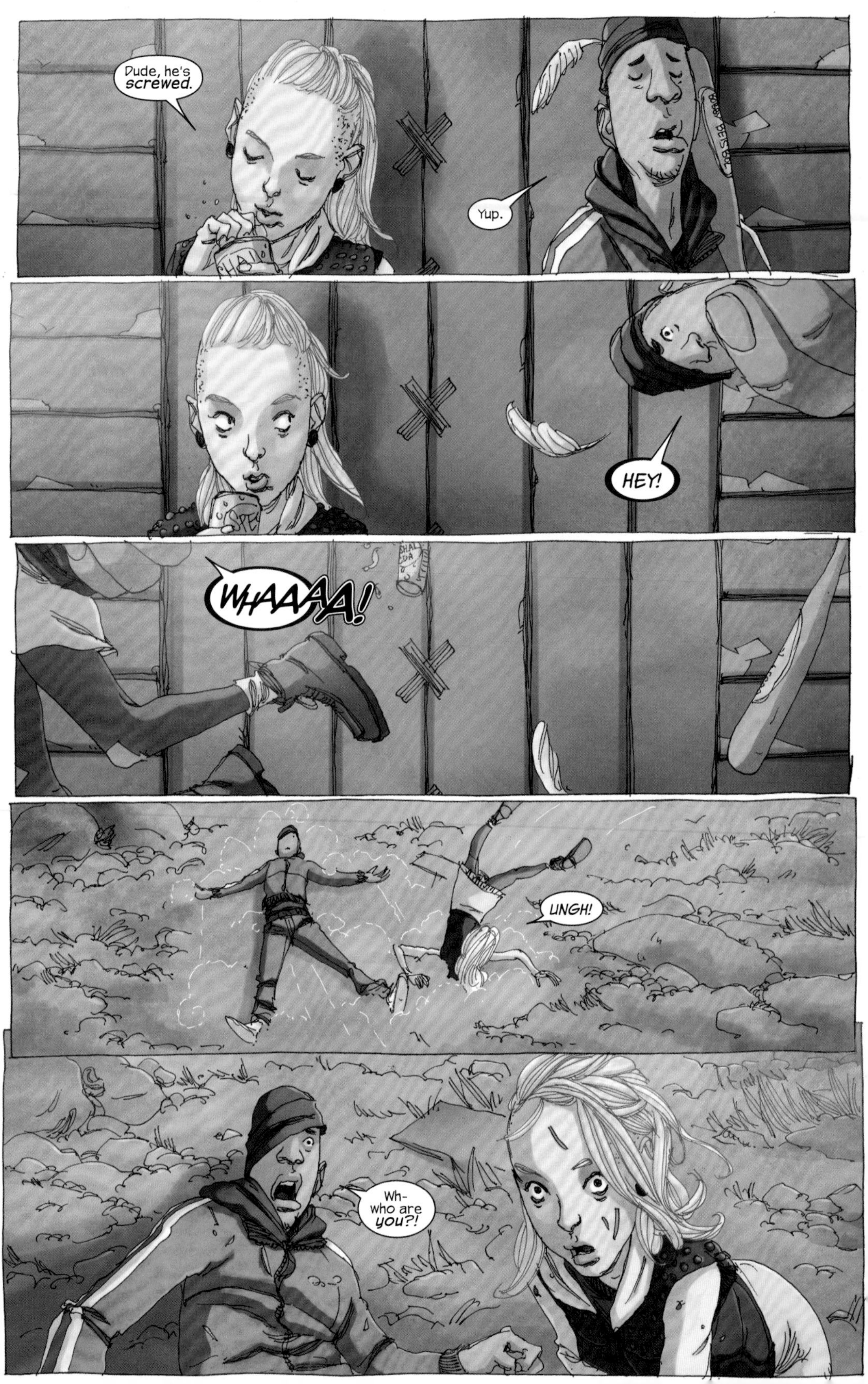
Dude, he's *screwed*.
Yup.
HEY!
WHAAAAA!
UNGH!
Wh- who are *you*?!

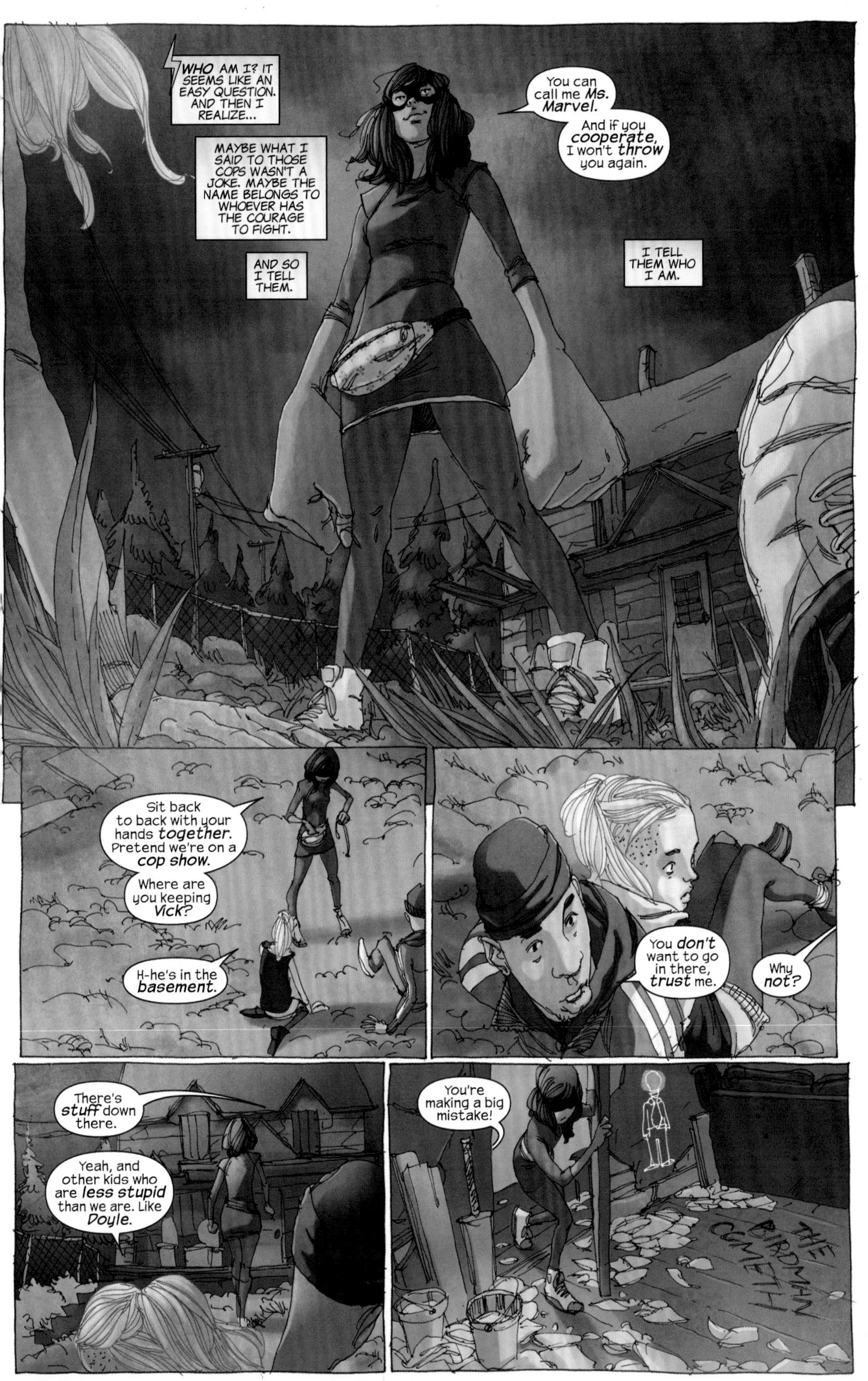
WHO AM I? IT SEEMS LIKE AN EASY QUESTION. AND THEN I REALIZE...
MAYBE WHAT I SAID TO THOSE COPS WASN'T A JOKE. MAYBE THE NAME BELONGS TO WHOEVER HAS THE COURAGE TO FIGHT.
AND SO I TELL THEM.
You can call me Ms. Marvel.
And if you cooperate, I won't throw you again.
I TELL THEM WHO I AM.
Sit back to back with your hands together. Pretend we're on a cop show.
Where are you keeping Vick?
H-he's in the basement.
You don't want to go in there, trust me.
Why not?
There's stuff down there.
Yeah, and other kids who are less stupid than we are. Like Doyle.
You're making a big mistake!
THE BIRDMAN COMETH

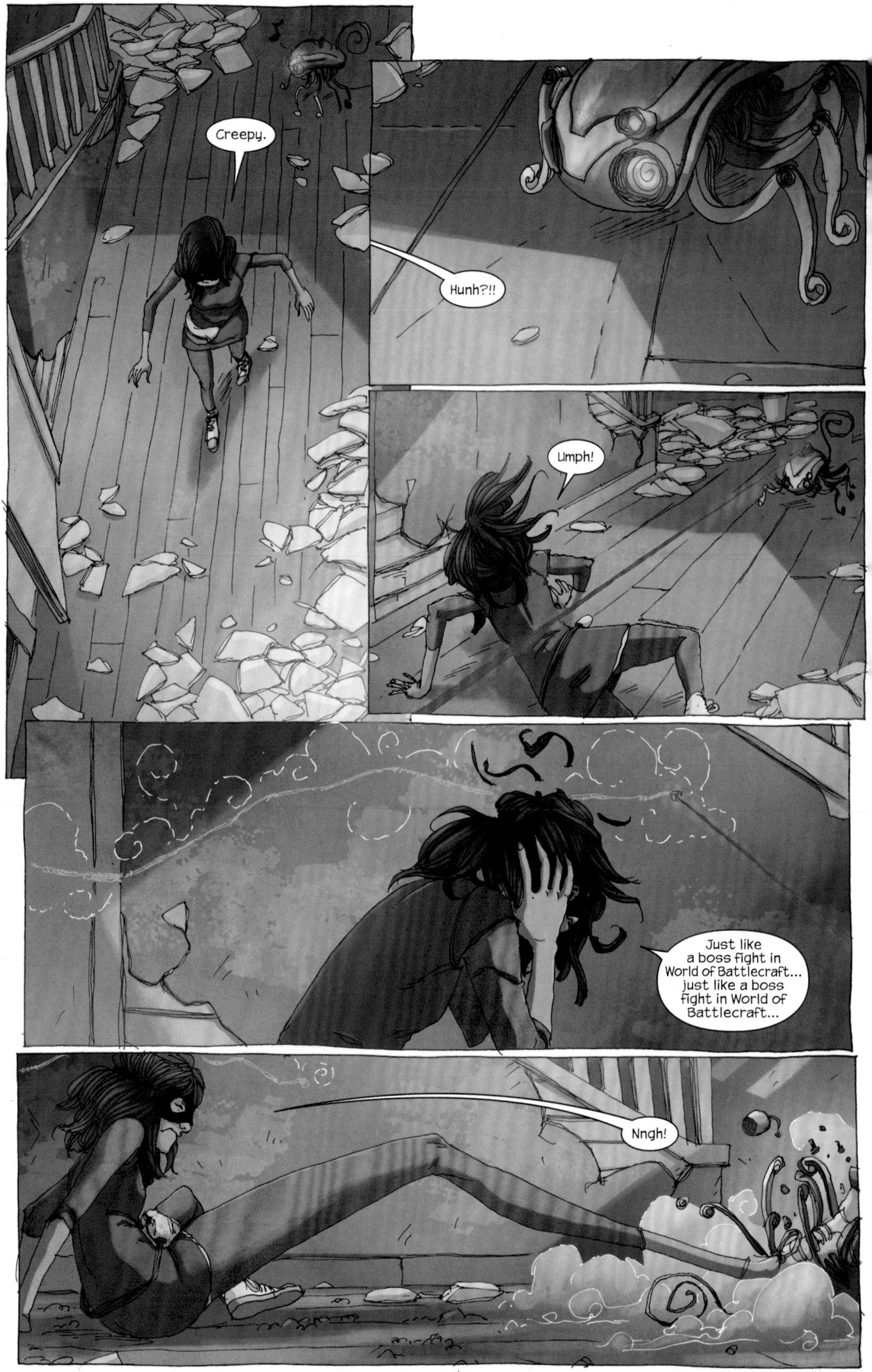
Creepy.
Hunh?!!
Umph!
Just like a boss fight in World of Battlecraft... just like a boss fight in World of Battlecraft...
Nngh!

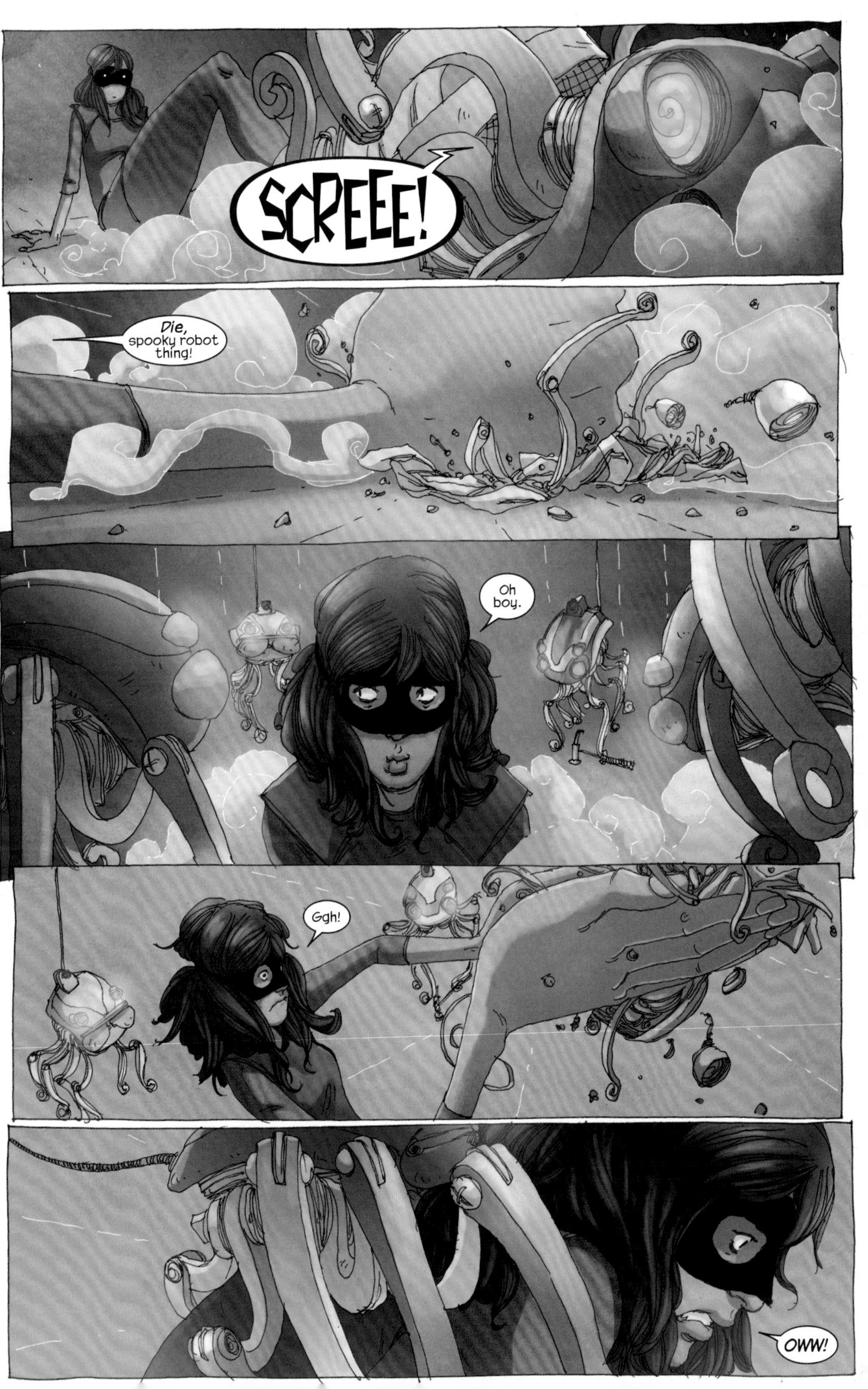
SCREEE!
Die, spooky robot thing!
Oh boy.
Ggh!
OWW!

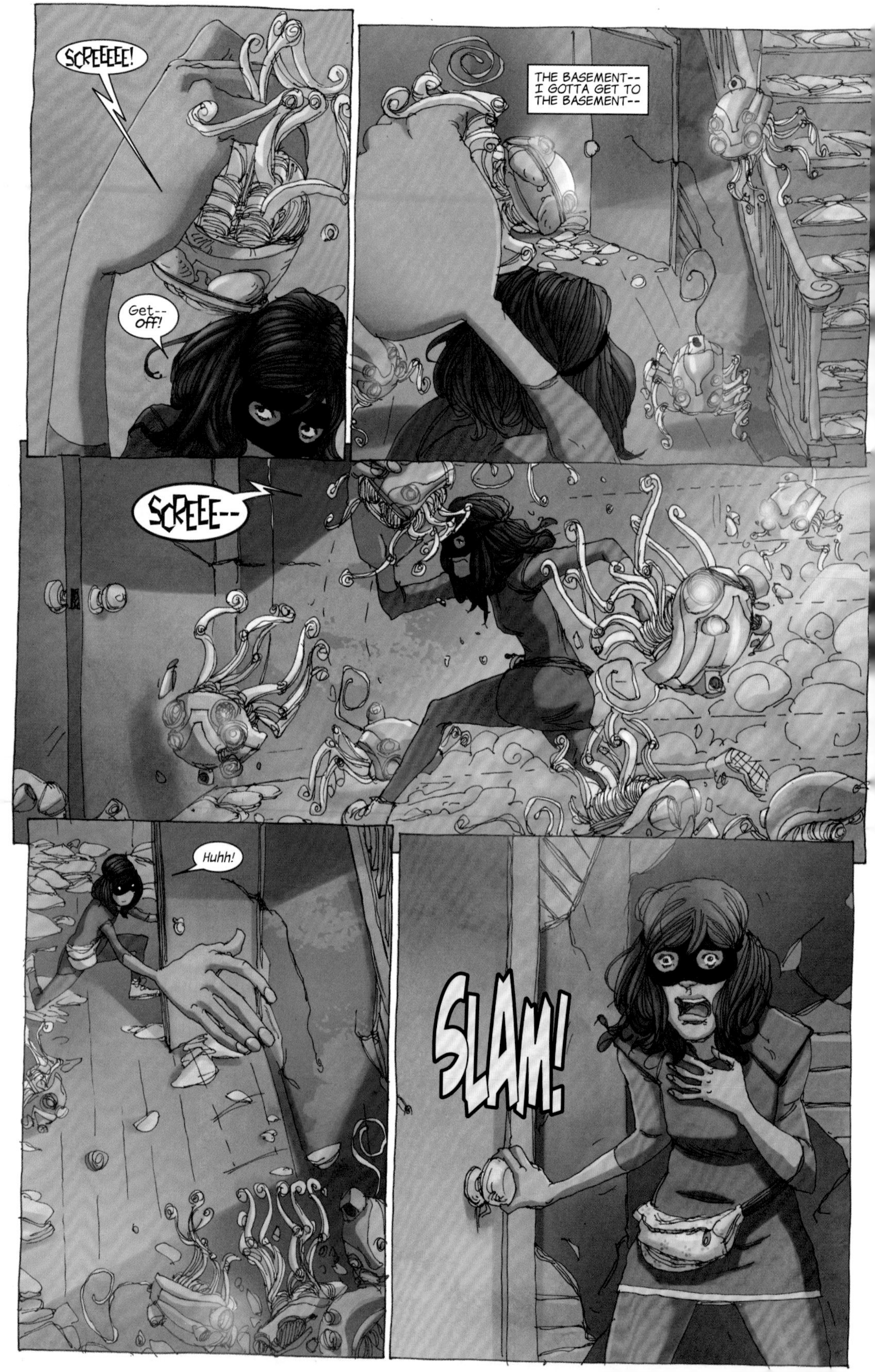
SCREEEEE!
Get-- off!
THE BASEMENT-- I GOTTA GET TO THE BASEMENT--
SCREEE--
Huhh!
SLAM!

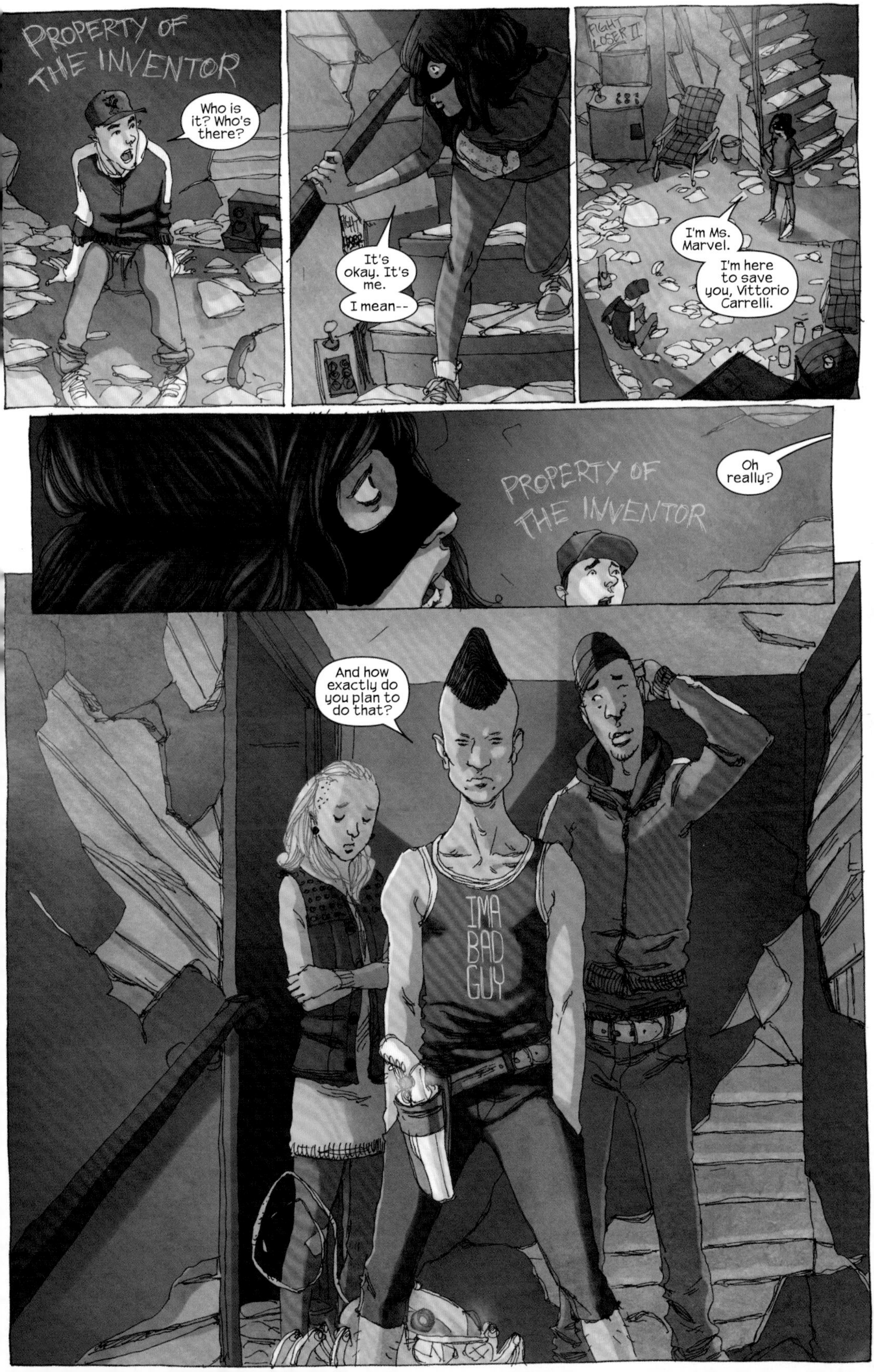
PROPERTY OF THE INVENTOR
Who is it? Who's there?
It's okay. It's me.
I mean--
FIGHT LOSER II
I'm Ms. Marvel.
I'm here to save you, Vittorio Carrelli.
PROPERTY OF THE INVENTOR
Oh really?
And how exactly do you plan to do that?
IMA BAD GUY

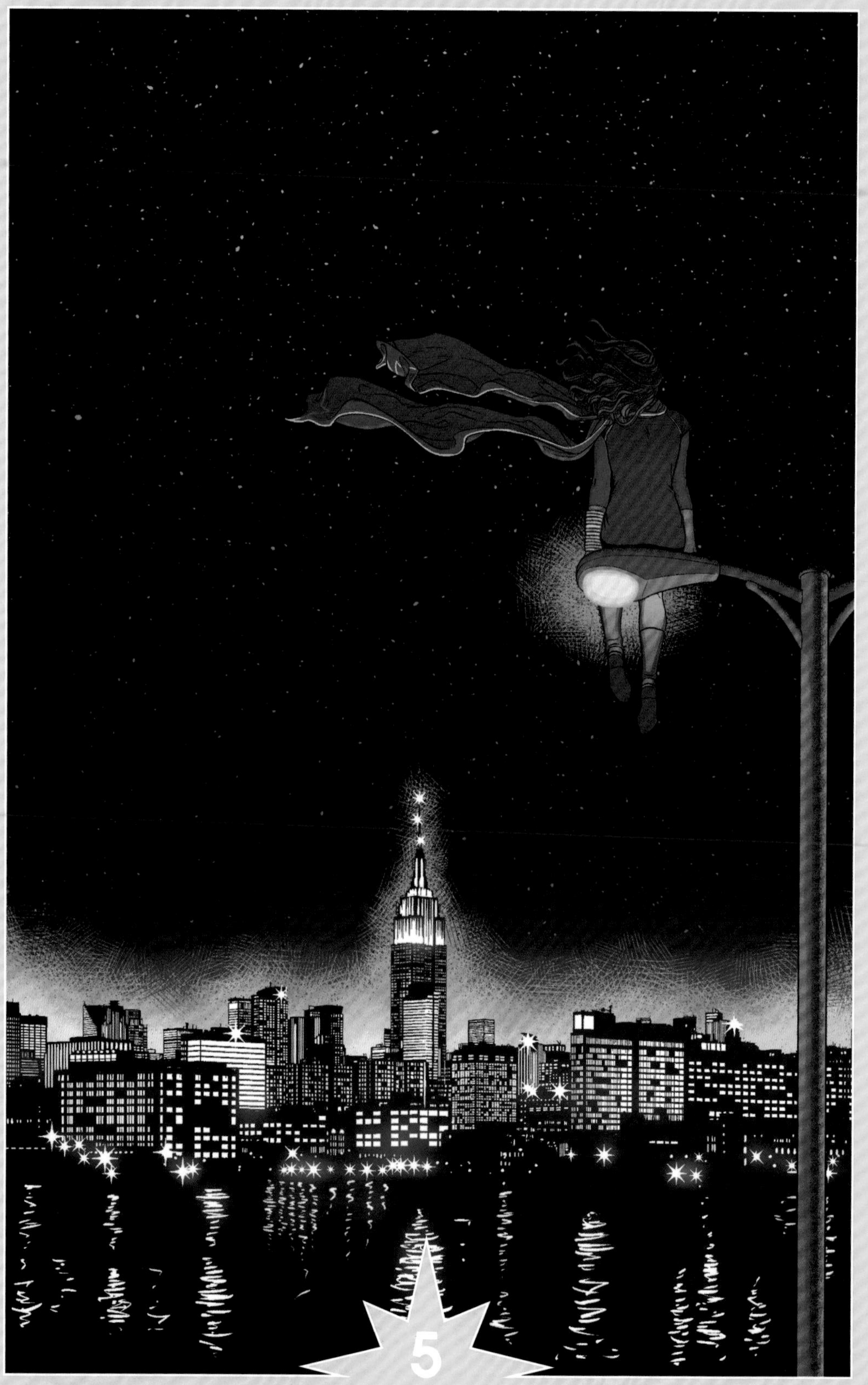
5

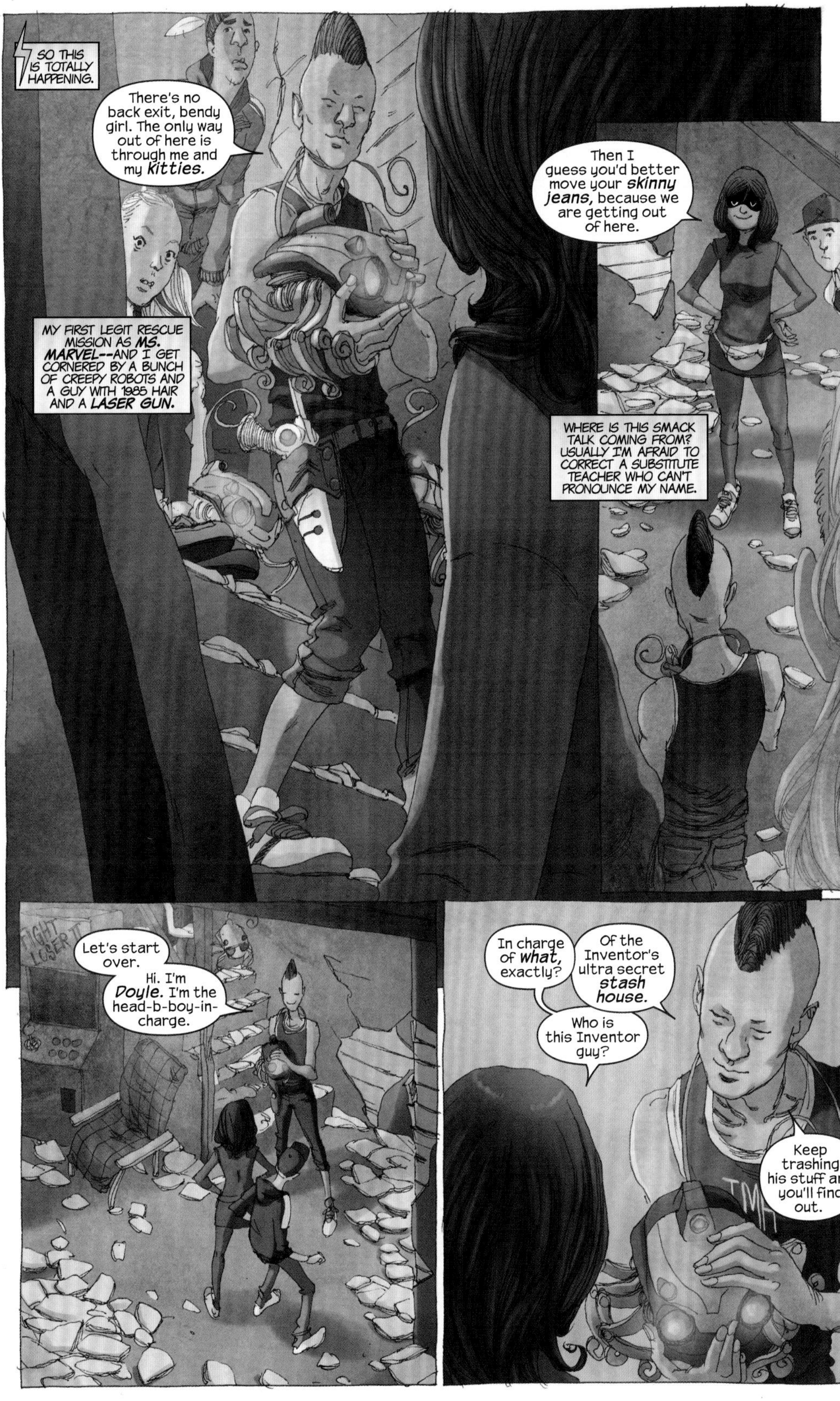
SO THIS IS TOTALLY HAPPENING.
There's no back exit, bendy girl. The only way out of here is through me and my kitties.
MY FIRST LEGIT RESCUE MISSION AS MS. MARVEL--AND I GET CORNERED BY A BUNCH OF CREEPY ROBOTS AND A GUY WITH 1985 HAIR AND A LASER GUN.
Then I guess you'd better move your skinny jeans, because we are getting out of here.
WHERE IS THIS SMACK TALK COMING FROM? USUALLY I'M AFRAID TO CORRECT A SUBSTITUTE TEACHER WHO CAN'T PRONOUNCE MY NAME.
FIGHT LOSER II
Let's start over.
Hi. I'm Doyle. I'm the head-b-boy-in-charge.
In charge of what, exactly?
Of the Inventor's ultra secret stash house.
Who is this Inventor guy?
Keep trashing his stuff and you'll find out.

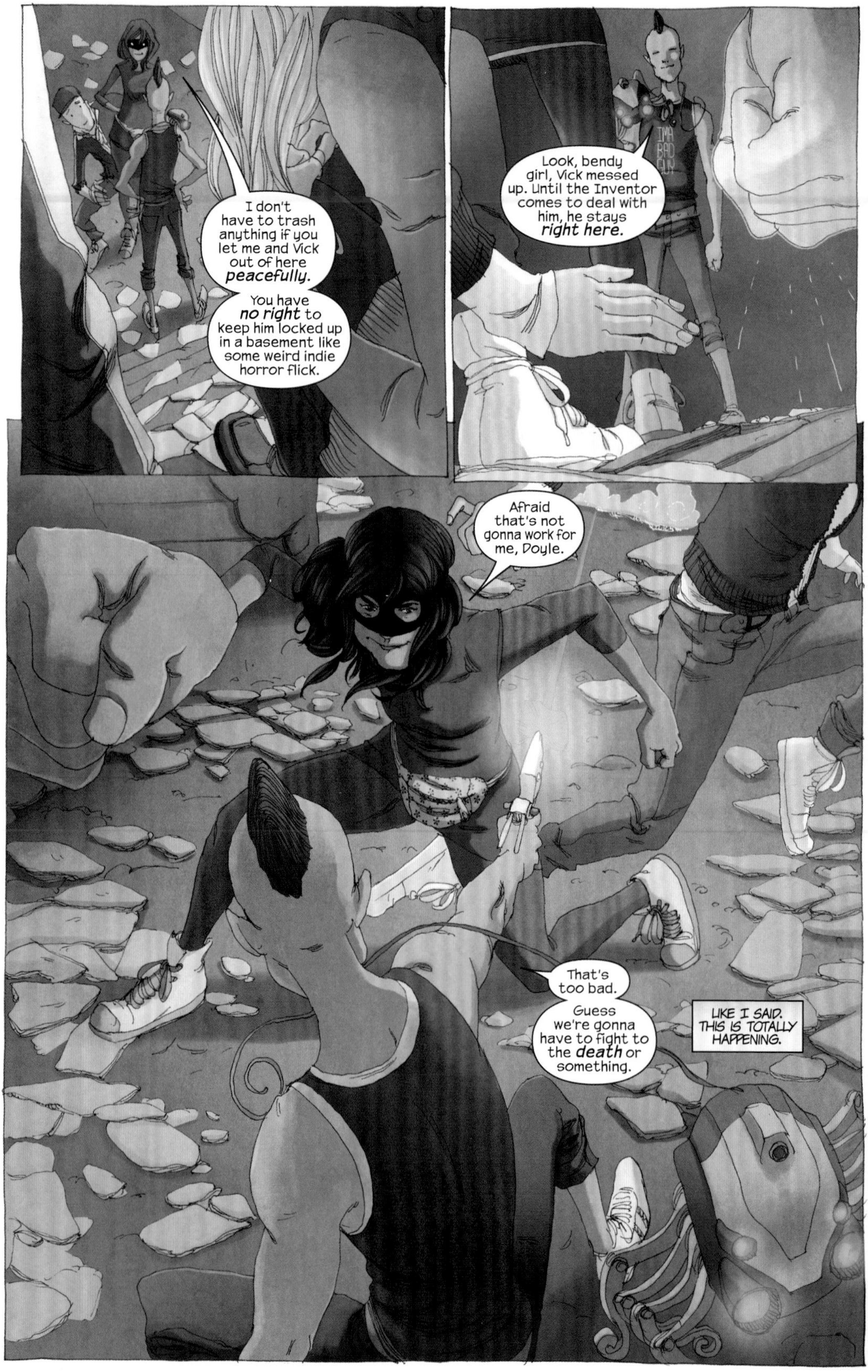
I don't have to trash anything if you let me and Vick out of here *peacefully*.
You have *no right* to keep him locked up in a basement like some weird indie horror flick.
Look, bendy girl, Vick messed up. Until the Inventor comes to deal with him, he stays *right here*.
IMA BAD GUY
Afraid that's not gonna work for me, Doyle.
That's too bad.
Guess we're gonna have to fight to the *death* or something.
LIKE I SAID. THIS IS TOTALLY HAPPENING.

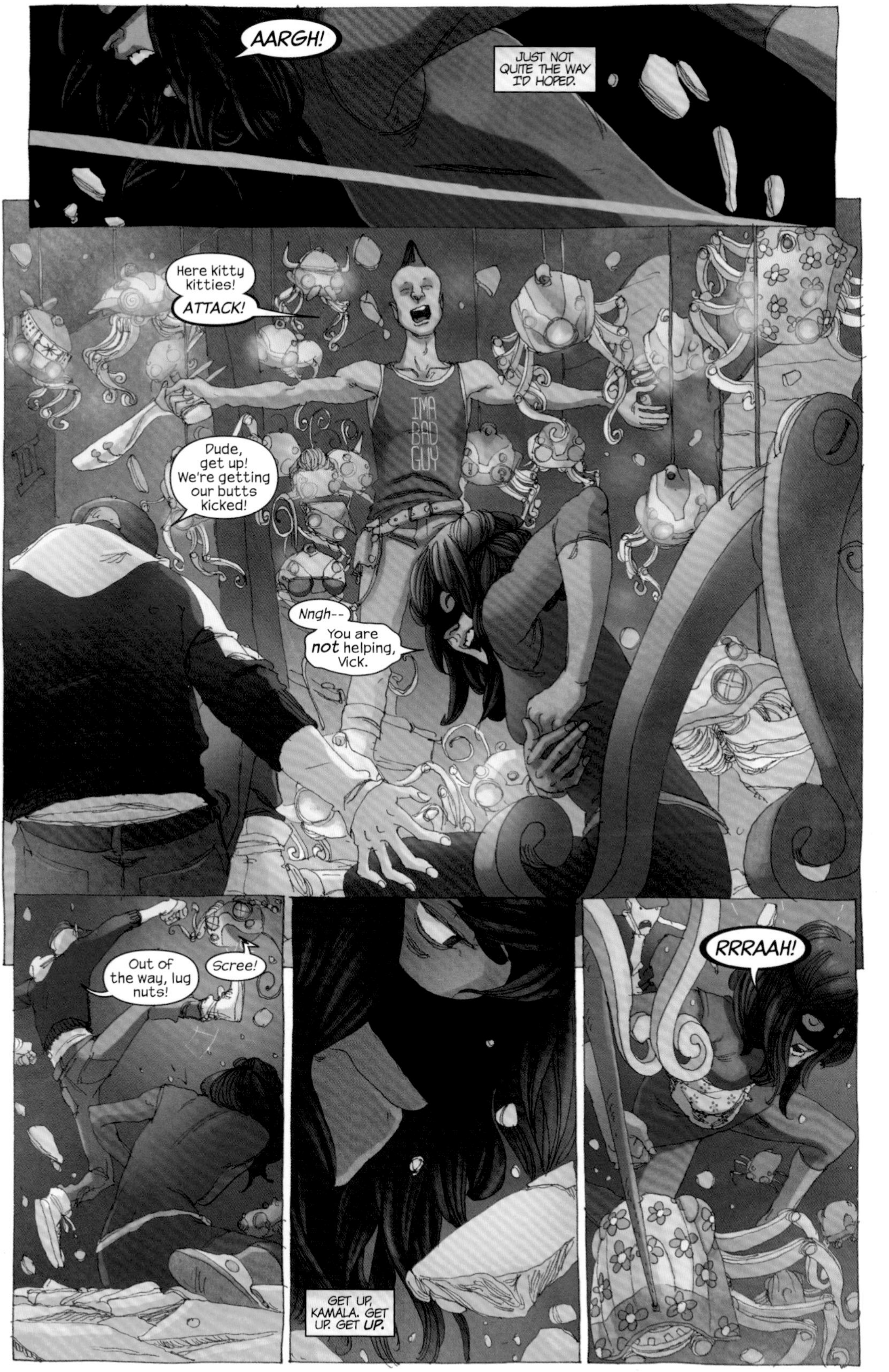
AARGH!
JUST NOT QUITE THE WAY I'D HOPED.
Here kitty kitties! ATTACK!
IMA BAD GUY
Dude, get up! We're getting our butts kicked!
Nngh-- You are not helping, Vick.
Out of the way, lug nuts!
Scree!
GET UP, KAMALA. GET UP. GET UP.
RRRAAH!

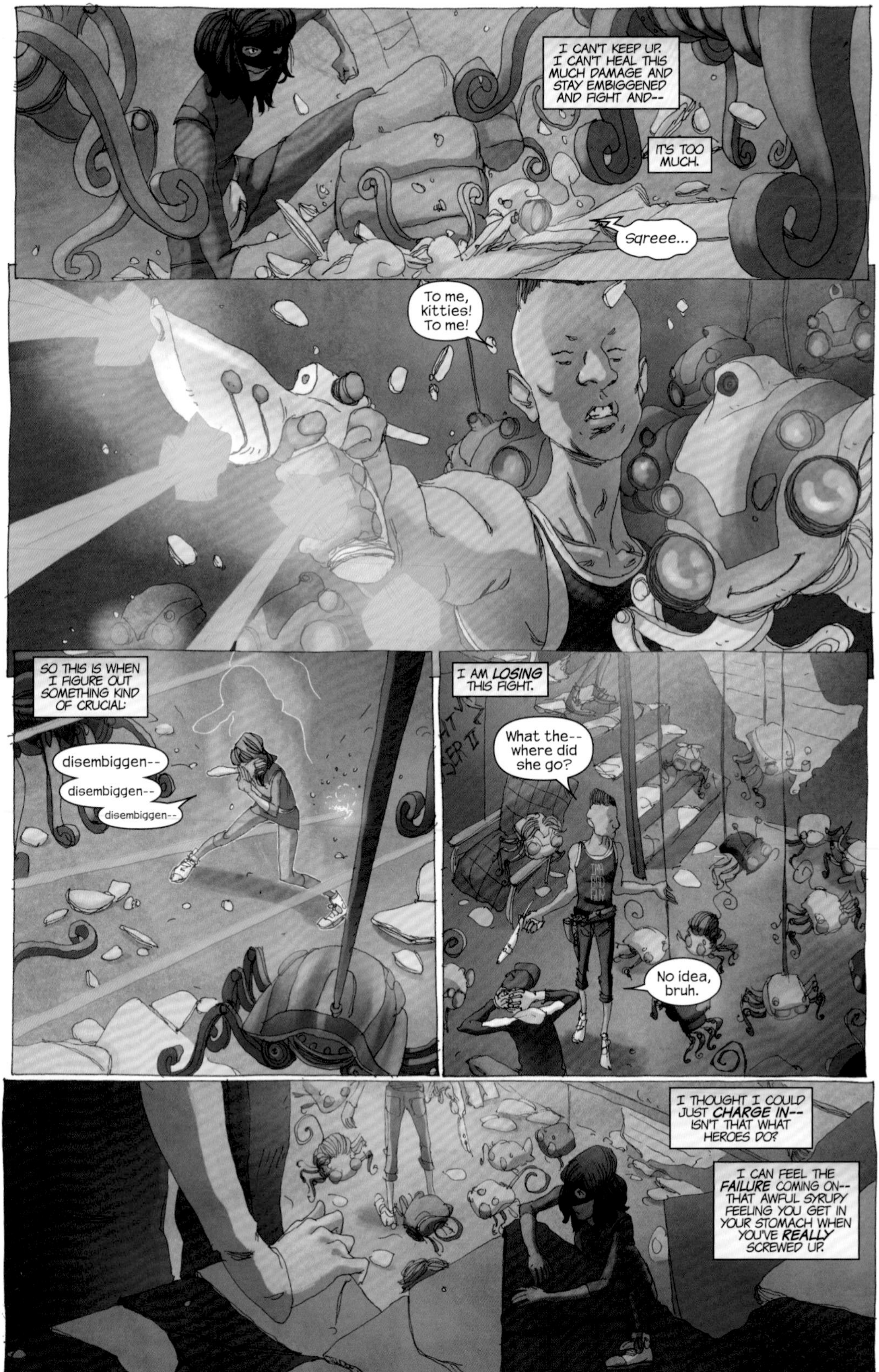
I CAN'T KEEP UP. I CAN'T HEAL THIS MUCH DAMAGE AND STAY EMBIGGENED AND FIGHT AND--
IT'S TOO MUCH.
Sqreee...
To me, kitties! To me!
SO THIS IS WHEN I FIGURE OUT SOMETHING KIND OF CRUCIAL:
disembiggen--
disembiggen--
disembiggen--
I AM LOSING THIS FIGHT.
What the-- where did she go?
No idea, bruh.
I THOUGHT I COULD JUST CHARGE IN-- ISN'T THAT WHAT HEROES DO?
I CAN FEEL THE FAILURE COMING ON-- THAT AWFUL SYRUPY FEELING YOU GET IN YOUR STOMACH WHEN YOU'VE REALLY SCREWED UP.

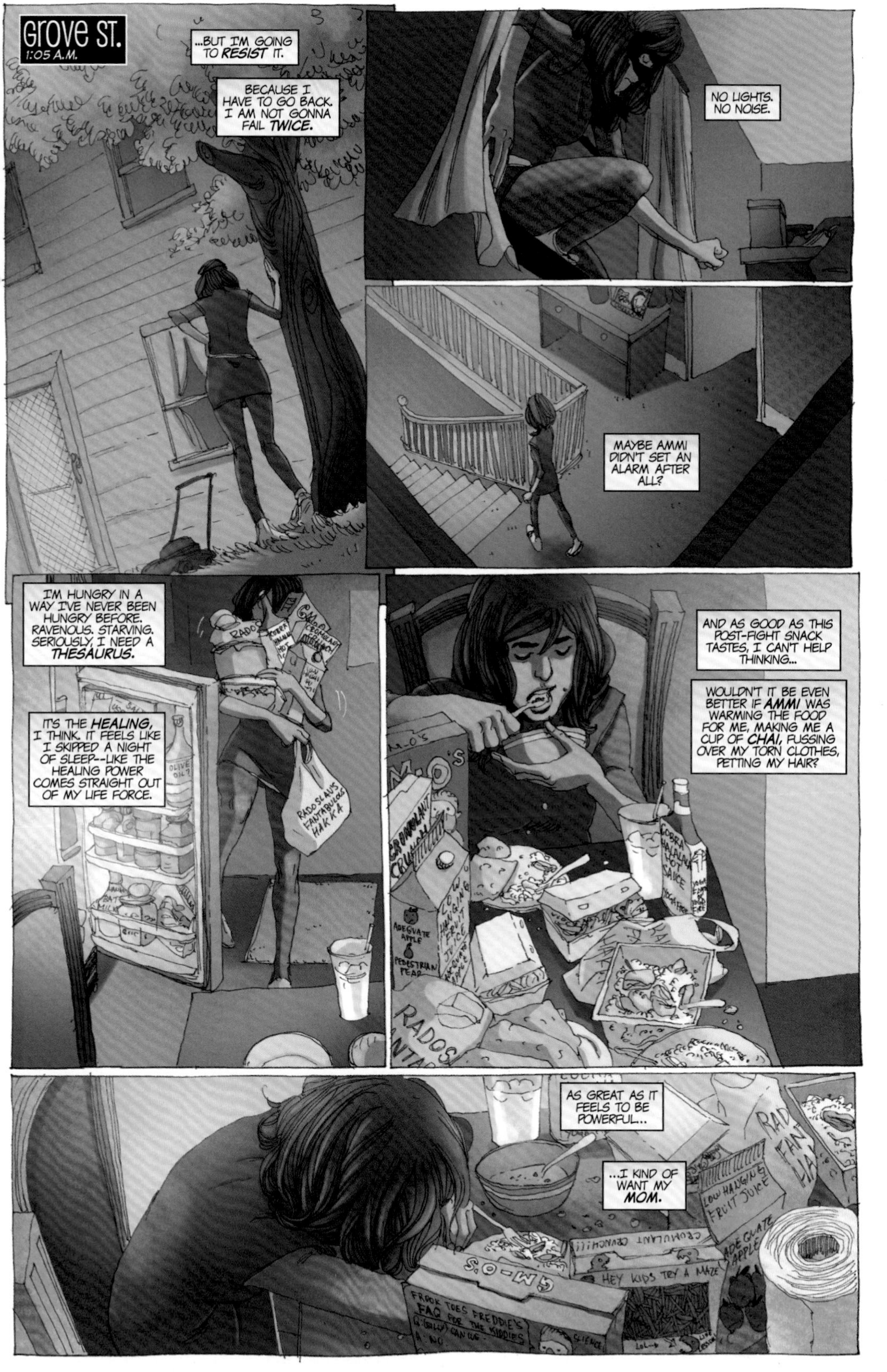
GROVE ST.
1:05 A.M.
...BUT I'M GOING TO RESIST IT.
BECAUSE I HAVE TO GO BACK. I AM NOT GONNA FAIL TWICE.
NO LIGHTS. NO NOISE.
MAYBE AMMI DIDN'T SET AN ALARM AFTER ALL?
I'M HUNGRY IN A WAY I'VE NEVER BEEN HUNGRY BEFORE. RAVENOUS. STARVING. SERIOUSLY, I NEED A THESAURUS.
IT'S THE HEALING, I THINK. IT FEELS LIKE I SKIPPED A NIGHT OF SLEEP--LIKE THE HEALING POWER COMES STRAIGHT OUT OF MY LIFE FORCE.
RADOSLAV'S FANTABULOUS HAKKA
AND AS GOOD AS THIS POST-FIGHT SNACK TASTES, I CAN'T HELP THINKING...
WOULDN'T IT BE EVEN BETTER IF AMMI WAS WARMING THE FOOD FOR ME, MAKING ME A CUP OF CHAI, FUSSING OVER MY TORN CLOTHES, PETTING MY HAIR?
ADEQUATE APPLE
PEDESTRIAN PEAR
AS GREAT AS IT FEELS TO BE POWERFUL...
...I KIND OF WANT MY MOM.
LOW HANGING FRUIT JUICE
HEY KIDS TRY A MAZE

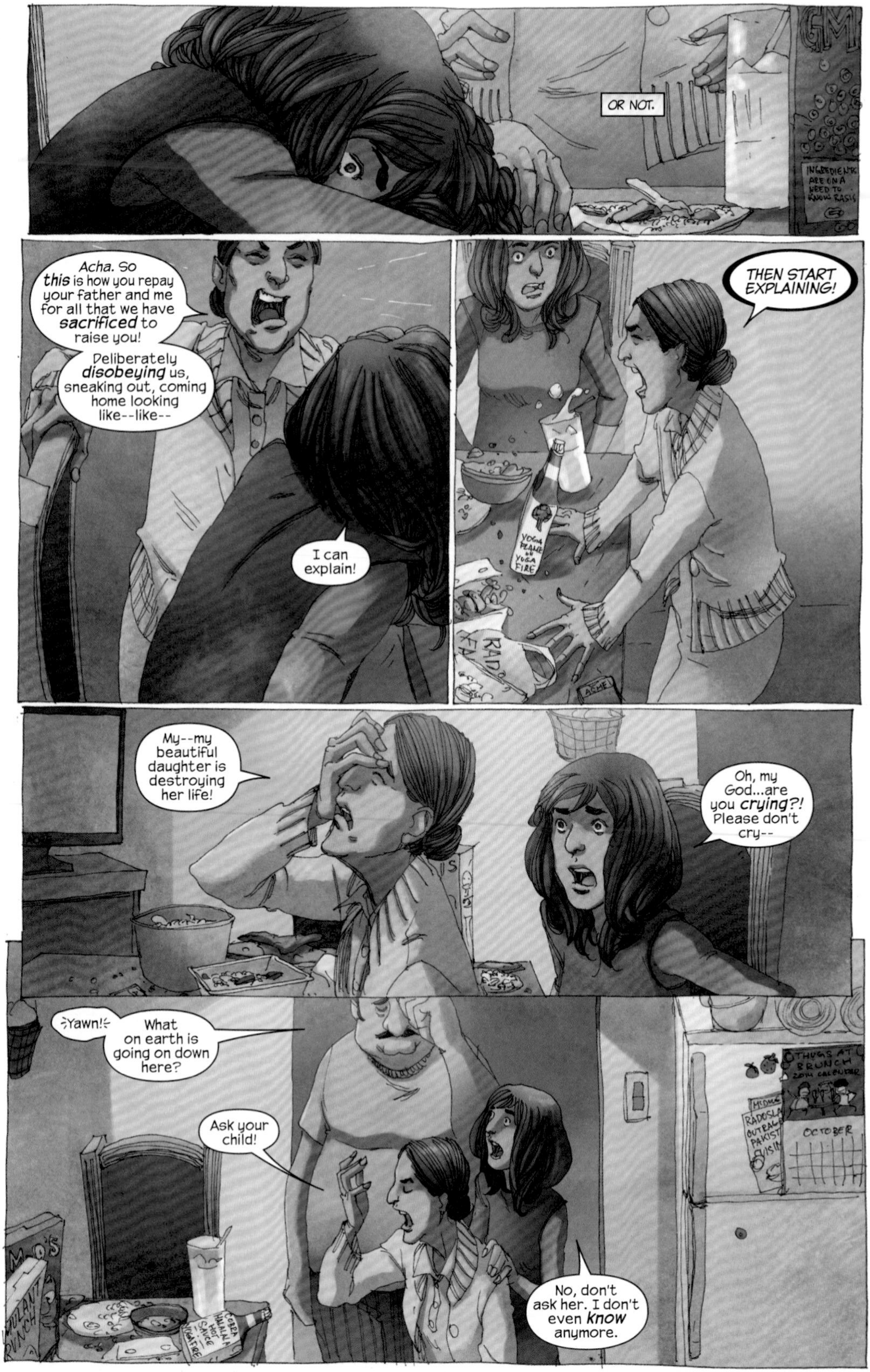
OR NOT.
INGREDIENTS ARE ON A NEED TO KNOW BASIS
Acha. So this is how you repay your father and me for all that we have sacrificed to raise you!
Deliberately disobeying us, sneaking out, coming home looking like--like--
I can explain!
THEN START EXPLAINING!
YOGA FLAME ON YOGA FIRE
My--my beautiful daughter is destroying her life!
Oh, my God...are you crying?! Please don't cry--
-Yawn!-
What on earth is going on down here?
Ask your child!
No, don't ask her. I don't even know anymore.
OCTOBER

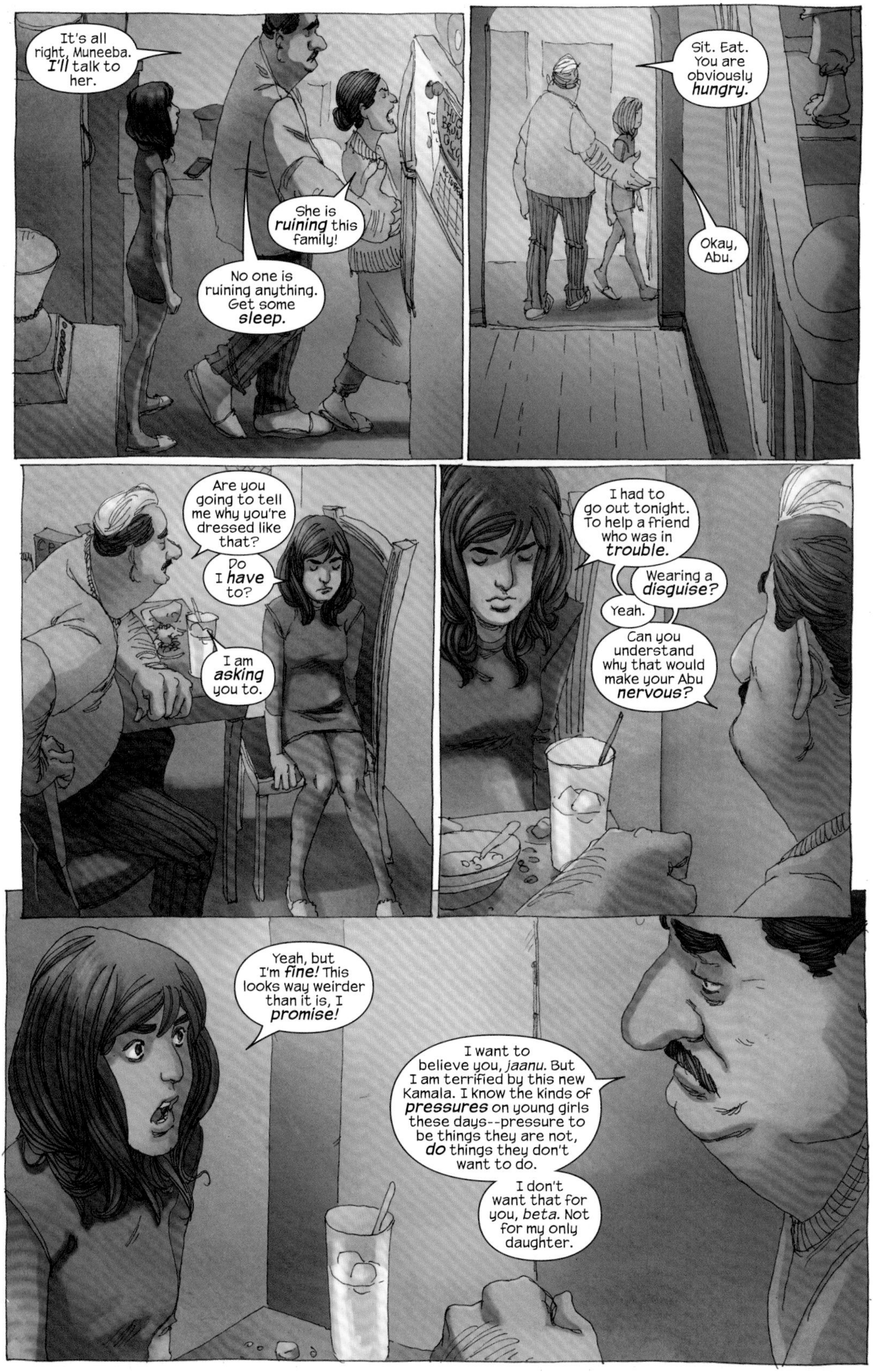

It's all right, Muneeba. *I'll* talk to her.
She is *ruining* this family!
No one is ruining anything. Get some *sleep.*
Sit. Eat. You are obviously *hungry.*
Okay, Abu.
Are you going to tell me why you're dressed like that?
Do I *have* to?
I am *asking* you to.
I had to go out tonight. To help a friend who was in *trouble.*
Wearing a *disguise?*
Yeah.
Can you understand why that would make your Abu *nervous?*
Yeah, but I'm *fine!* This looks way weirder than it is, I *promise!*
I want to believe you, *jaanu.* But I am terrified by this new Kamala. I know the kinds of *pressures* on young girls these days--pressure to be things they are not, *do* things they don't want to do.
I don't want that for you, *beta.* Not for my only daughter.

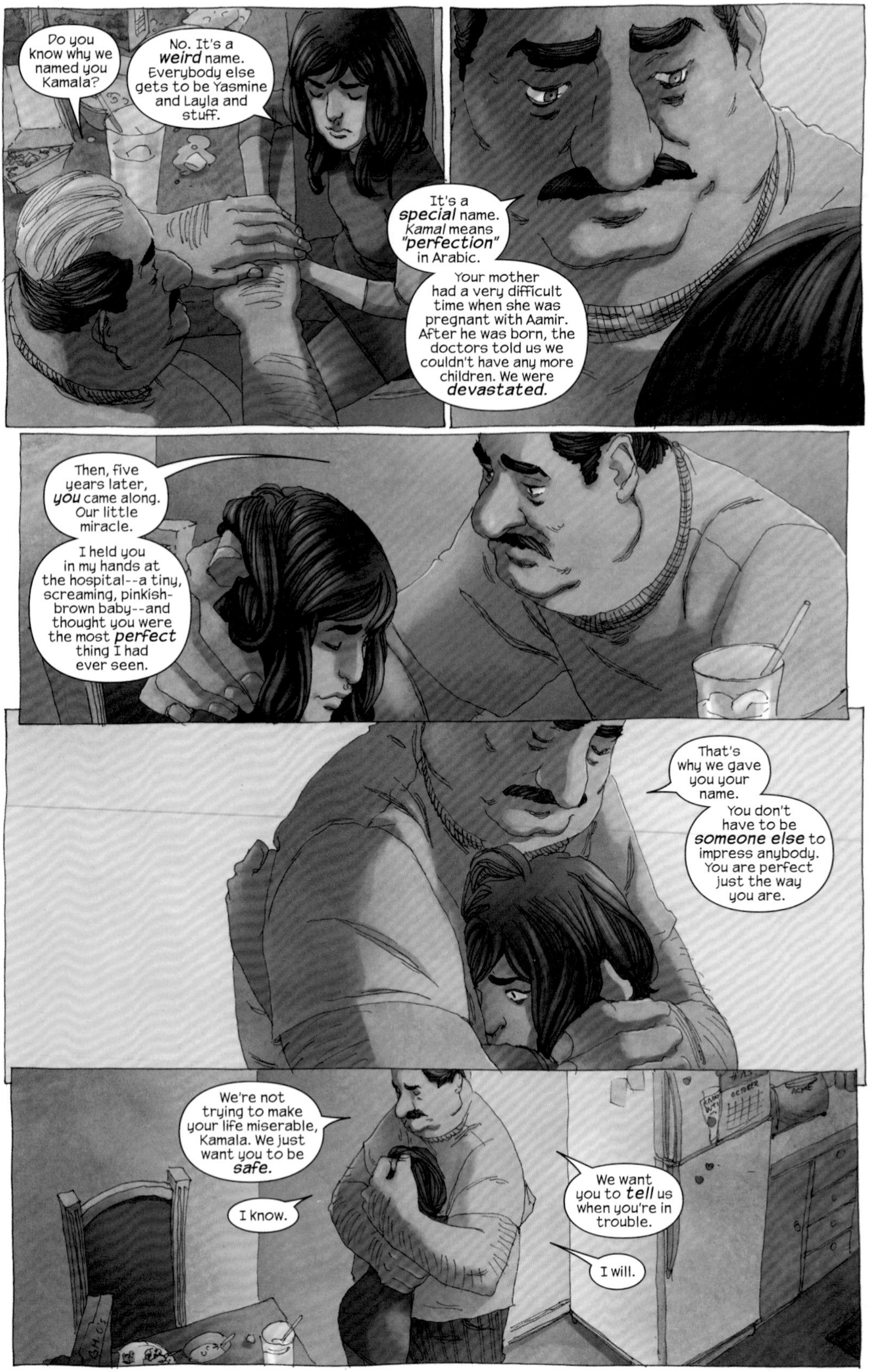
Do you know why we named you Kamala?
No. It's a weird name. Everybody else gets to be Yasmine and Layla and stuff.
It's a special name. Kamal means "perfection" in Arabic.
Your mother had a very difficult time when she was pregnant with Aamir. After he was born, the doctors told us we couldn't have any more children. We were devastated.
Then, five years later, you came along. Our little miracle.
I held you in my hands at the hospital--a tiny, screaming, pinkish-brown baby--and thought you were the most perfect thing I had ever seen.
That's why we gave you your name.
You don't have to be someone else to impress anybody. You are perfect just the way you are.
We're not trying to make your life miserable, Kamala. We just want you to be safe.
I know.
We want you to tell us when you're in trouble.
I will.

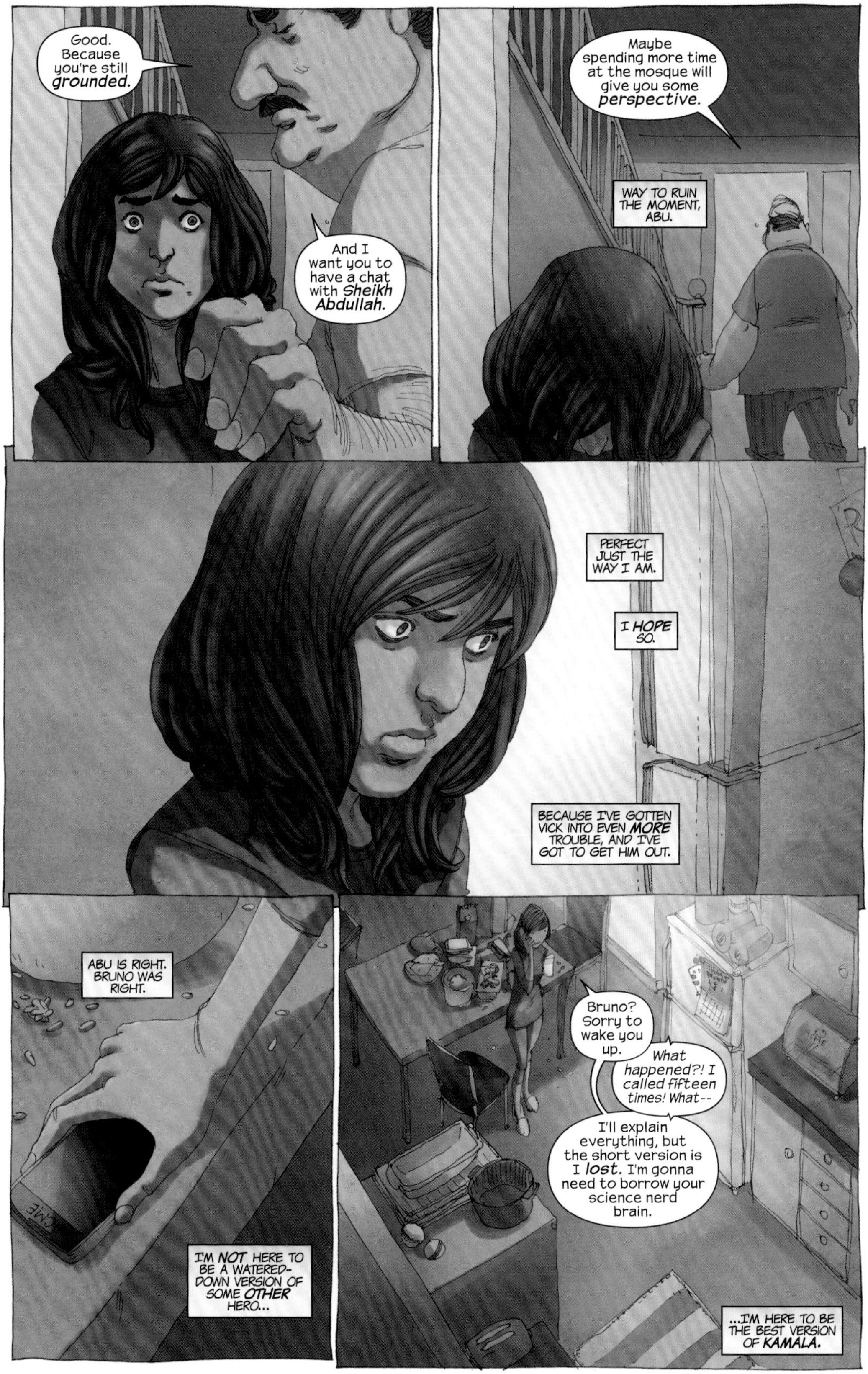
Good. Because you're still *grounded.*
And I want you to have a chat with *Sheikh Abdullah.*
Maybe spending more time at the mosque will give you some *perspective.*
WAY TO RUIN THE MOMENT, ABU.
PERFECT JUST THE WAY I AM.
I *HOPE* SO.
BECAUSE I'VE GOTTEN VICK INTO EVEN *MORE* TROUBLE, AND I'VE GOT TO GET HIM OUT.
ABU IS RIGHT. BRUNO WAS RIGHT.
I'M *NOT* HERE TO BE A WATERED-DOWN VERSION OF SOME *OTHER* HERO...
Bruno? Sorry to wake you up.
What happened?! I called fifteen times! What--
I'll explain everything, but the short version is I *lost.* I'm gonna need to borrow your science nerd brain.
...I'M HERE TO BE THE BEST VERSION OF *KAMALA.*

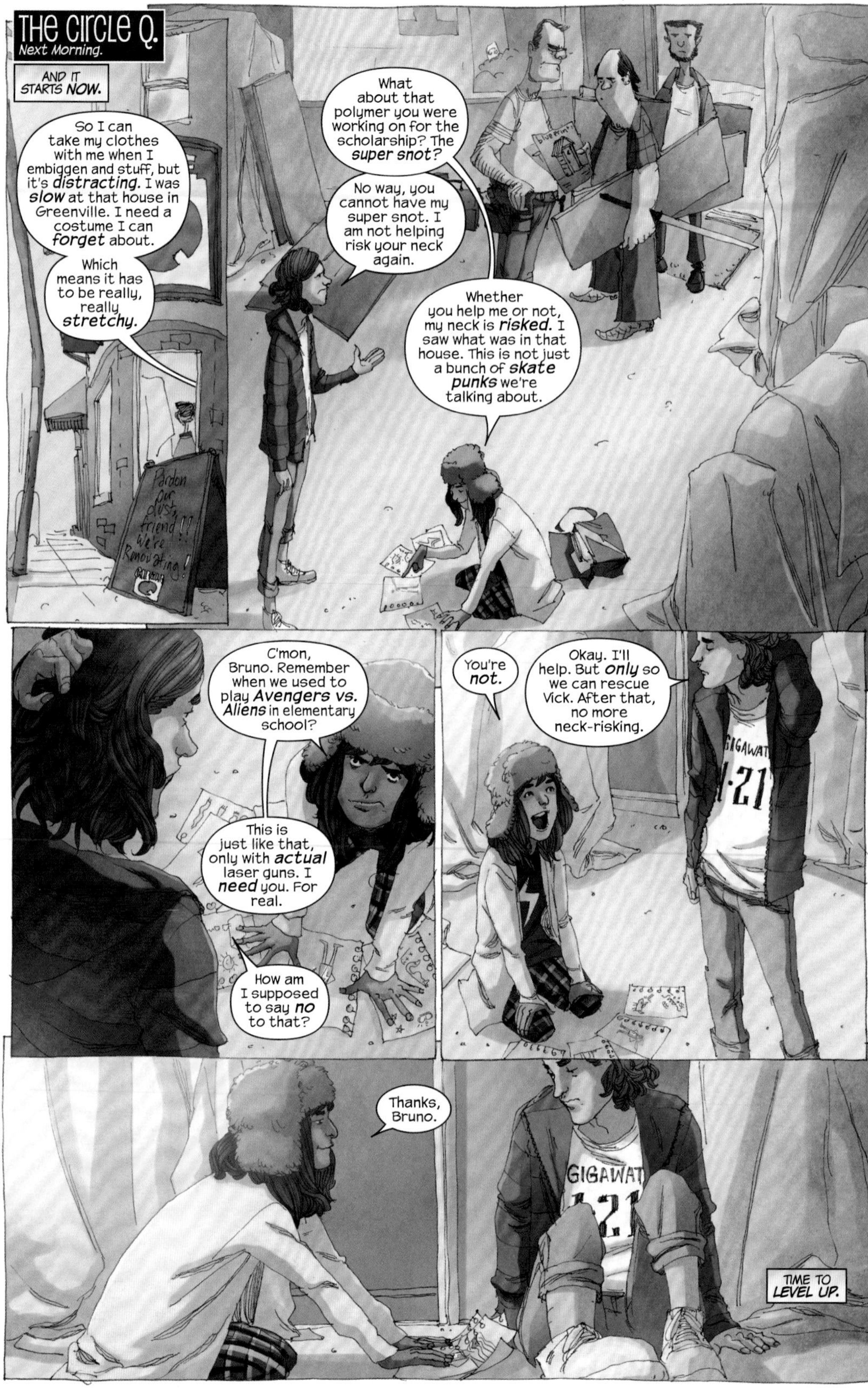
THE CIRCLE Q. Next Morning.
AND IT STARTS NOW.
So I can take my clothes with me when I embiggen and stuff, but it's distracting. I was slow at that house in Greenville. I need a costume I can forget about.
Which means it has to be really, really stretchy.
What about that polymer you were working on for the scholarship? The super snot?
No way, you cannot have my super snot. I am not helping risk your neck again.
Whether you help me or not, my neck is risked. I saw what was in that house. This is not just a bunch of skate punks we're talking about.
Pardon our dust, friend!! We're Renovating!
C'mon, Bruno. Remember when we used to play Avengers vs. Aliens in elementary school?
This is just like that, only with actual laser guns. I need you. For real.
How am I supposed to say no to that?
You're not.
Okay. I'll help. But only so we can rescue Vick. After that, no more neck-risking.
Thanks, Bruno.
TIME TO LEVEL UP.

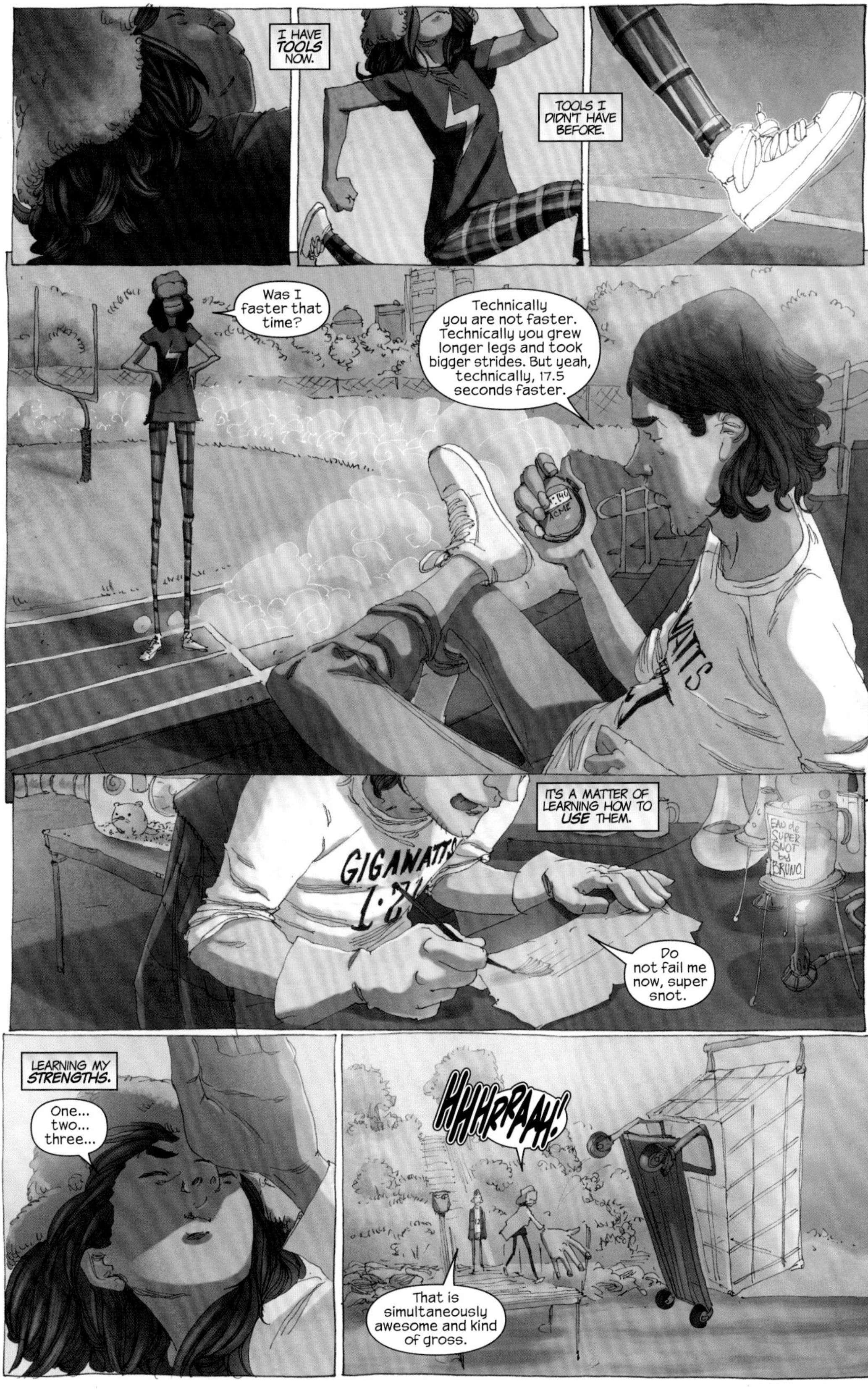
I HAVE TOOLS NOW.
TOOLS I DIDN'T HAVE BEFORE.
Was I faster that time?
Technically you are not faster. Technically you grew longer legs and took bigger strides. But yeah, technically, 17.5 seconds faster.
ACME
IT'S A MATTER OF LEARNING HOW TO USE THEM.
GIGANATTS
EAU de SUPER SNOT by BRUNO
Do not fail me now, super snot.
LEARNING MY STRENGTHS.
One... two... three...
HHHRRAAH!
That is simultaneously awesome and kind of gross.

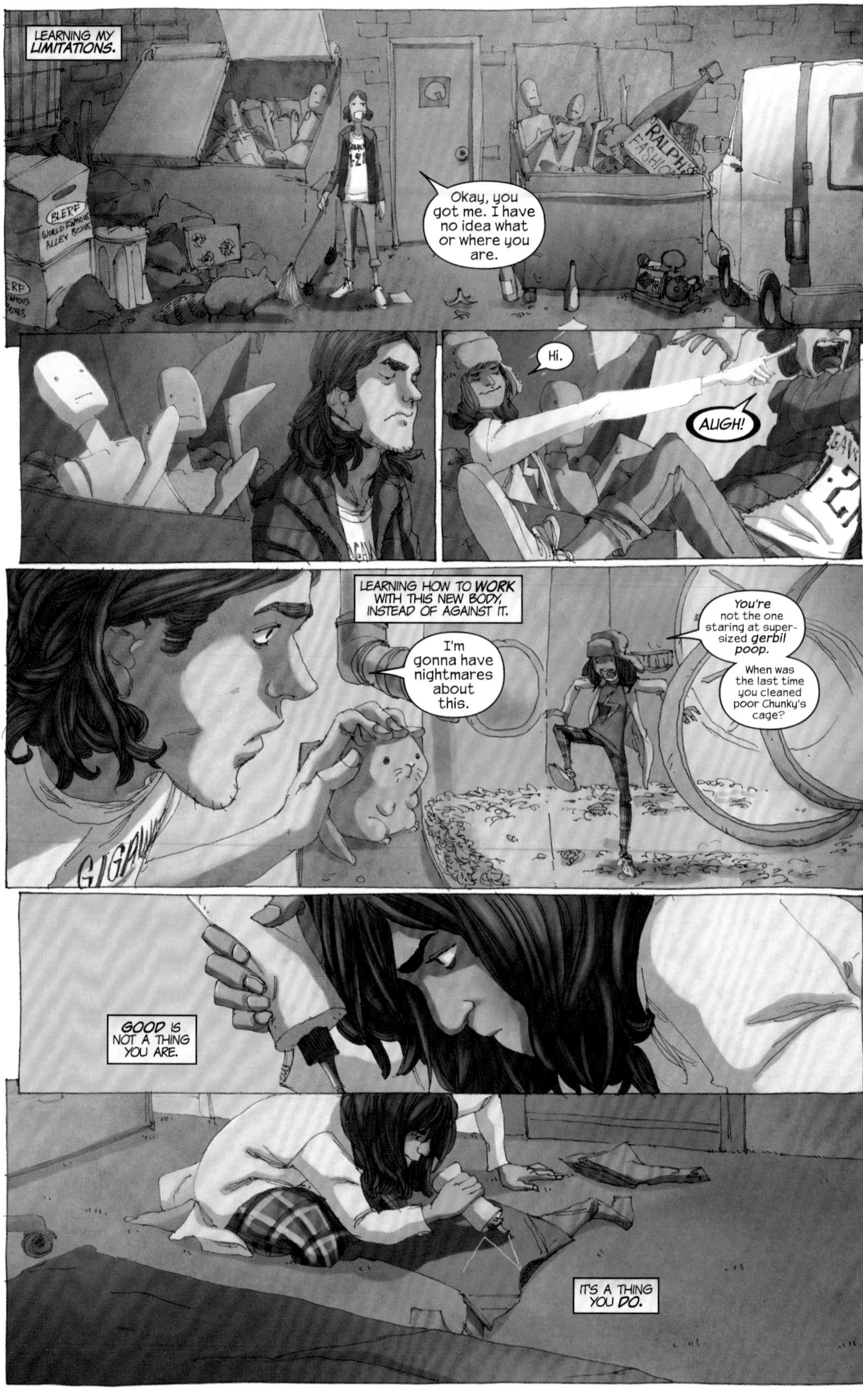
LEARNING MY LIMITATIONS.
BLERF WORLD FAMOUS ALLEY BOXES
RALPH'S FASHION
Okay, you got me. I have no idea what or where you are.
Hi.
AUGH!
LEARNING HOW TO WORK WITH THIS NEW BODY, INSTEAD OF AGAINST IT.
I'm gonna have nightmares about this.
You're not the one staring at super-sized gerbil poop.
When was the last time you cleaned poor Chunky's cage?
GOOD IS NOT A THING YOU ARE.
IT'S A THING YOU DO.

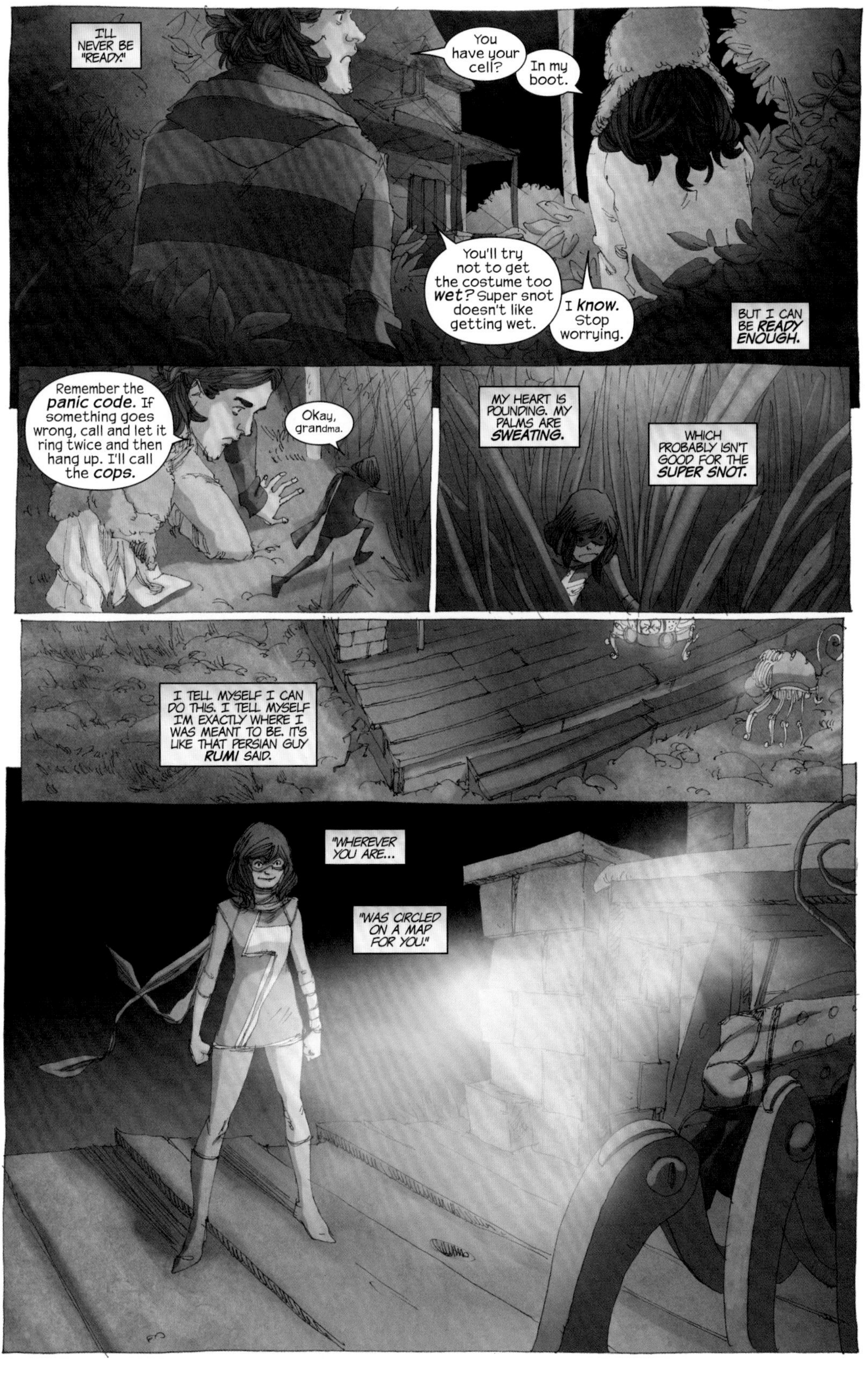
I'LL NEVER BE "READY."
You have your cell?
In my boot.
You'll try not to get the costume too wet? Super snot doesn't like getting wet.
I know. Stop worrying.
BUT I CAN BE READY ENOUGH.
Remember the panic code. If something goes wrong, call and let it ring twice and then hang up. I'll call the cops.
Okay, grandma.
MY HEART IS POUNDING. MY PALMS ARE SWEATING.
WHICH PROBABLY ISN'T GOOD FOR THE SUPER SNOT.
I TELL MYSELF I CAN DO THIS. I TELL MYSELF I'M EXACTLY WHERE I WAS MEANT TO BE. IT'S LIKE THAT PERSIAN GUY RUMI SAID.
"WHEREVER YOU ARE...
"WAS CIRCLED ON A MAP FOR YOU."

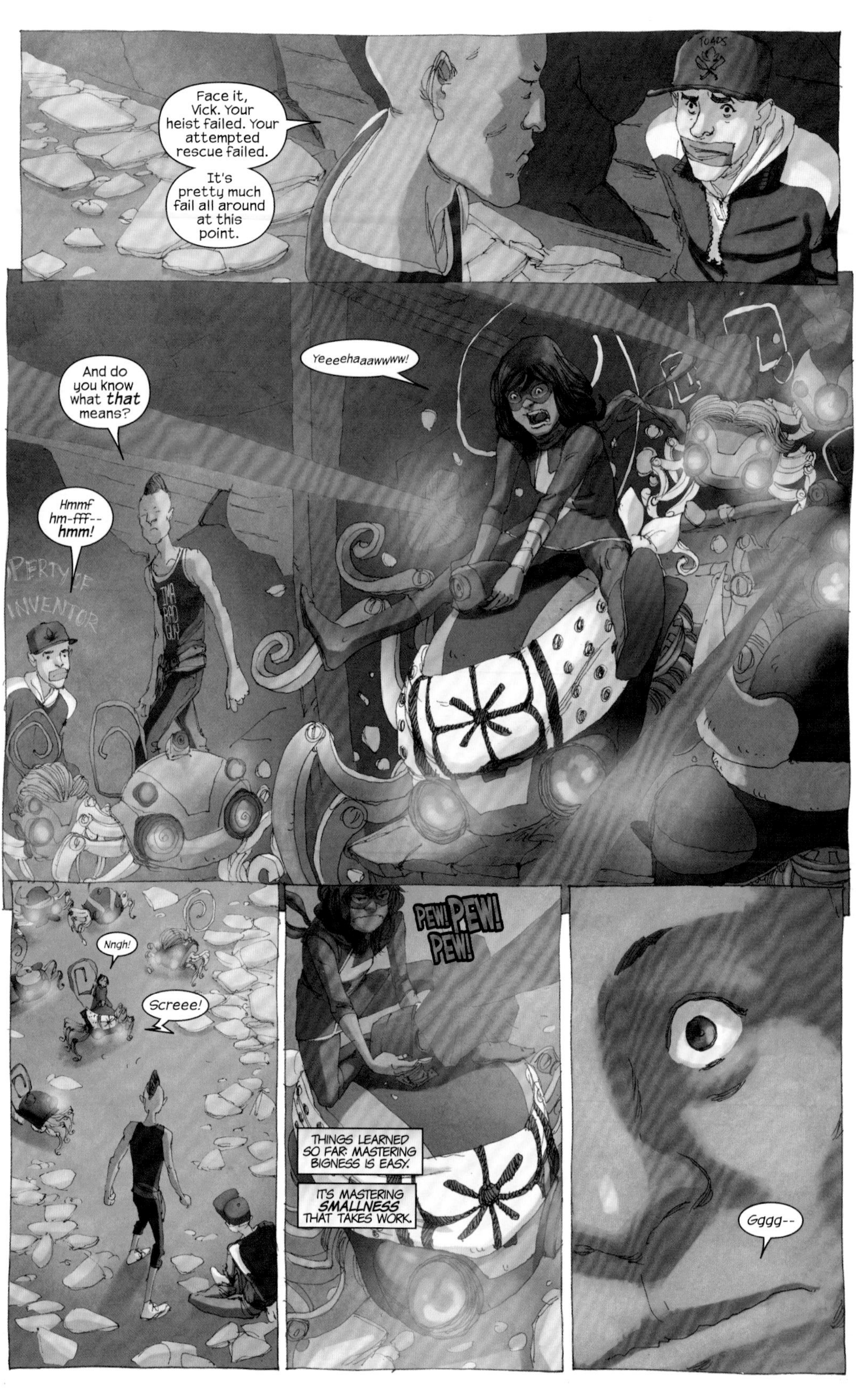

Face it, Vick. Your heist failed. Your attempted rescue failed.
It's pretty much fail all around at this point.
And do you know what *that* means?
Yeeeehaaawwww!
Hmmf hm-fff-- hmm!
PERTY OF INVENTOR
Nngh!
Screee!
PEW! PEW! PEW!
THINGS LEARNED SO FAR: MASTERING BIGNESS IS EASY.
IT'S MASTERING SMALLNESS THAT TAKES WORK.
Gggg--

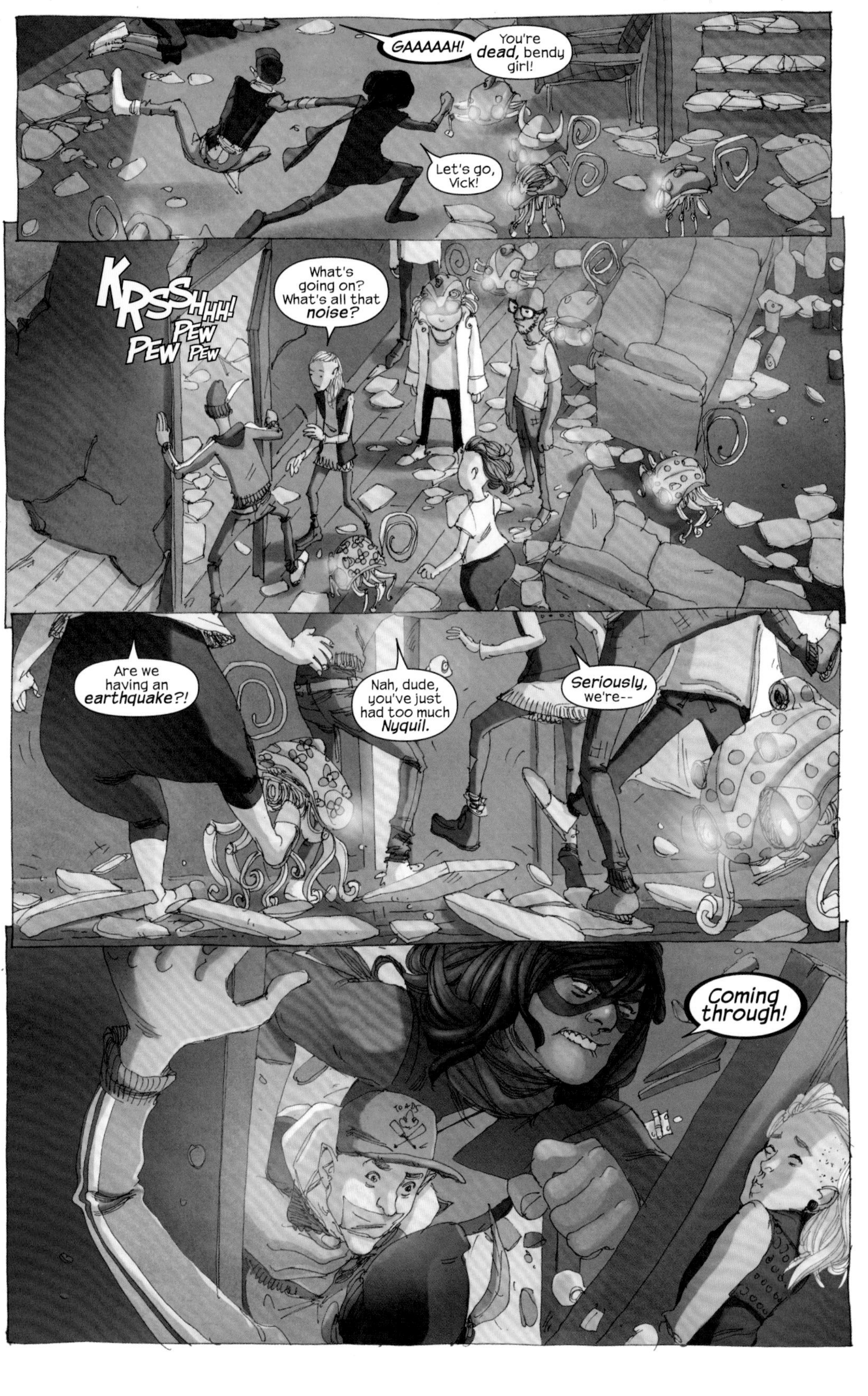

GAAAAAH!
You're dead, bendy girl!
Let's go, Vick!
KRSSHHH! PEW PEW PEW
What's going on? What's all that noise?
Are we having an earthquake?!
Nah, dude, you've just had too much Nyquil.
Seriously, we're--
Coming through!

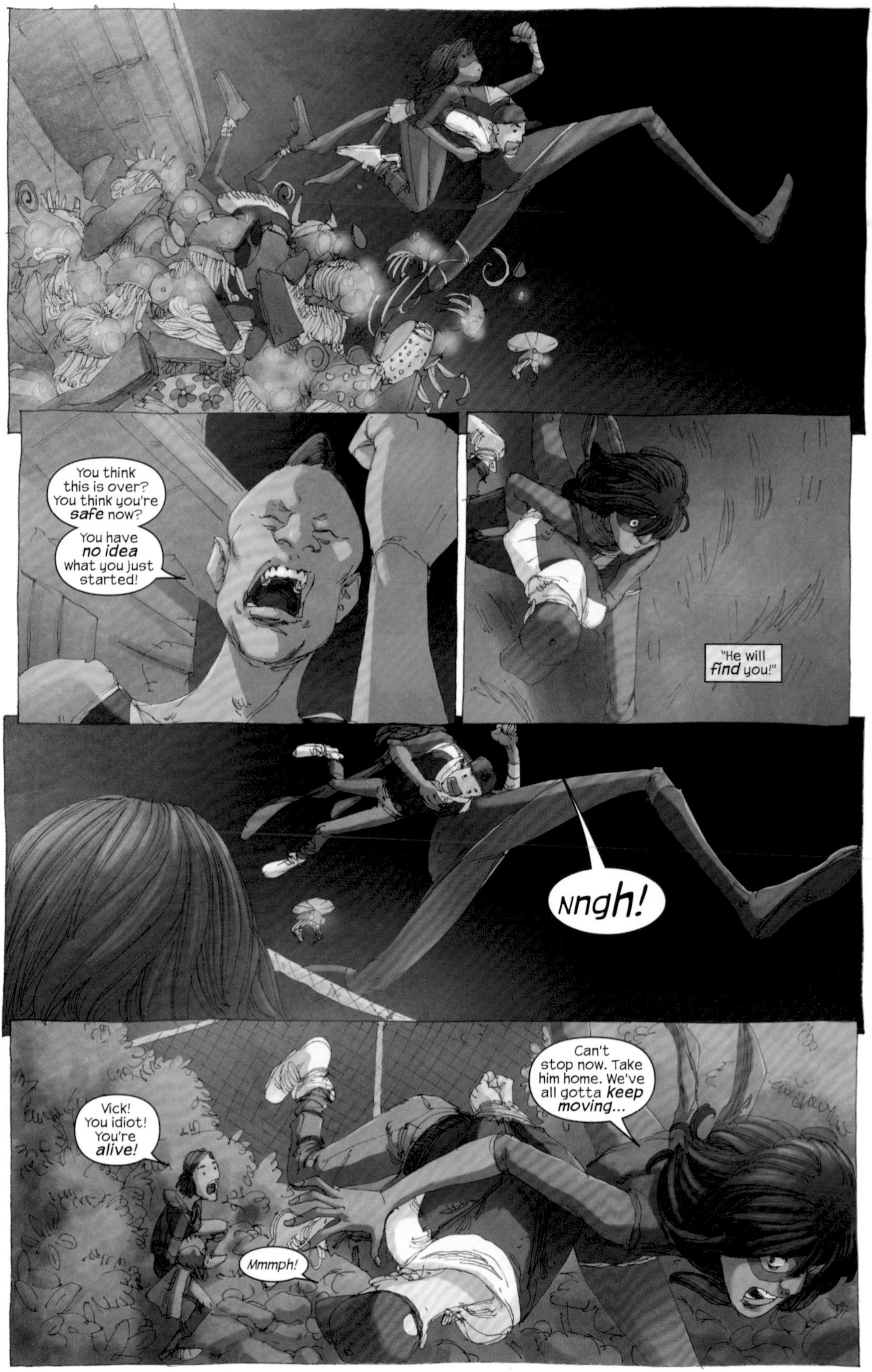

You think this is over? You think you're *safe* now?
You have ***no idea*** what you just started!
"He will ***find*** you!"
Nngh!
Vick! You idiot! You're *alive!*
Can't stop now. Take him home. We've all gotta ***keep moving...***
Mmmph!

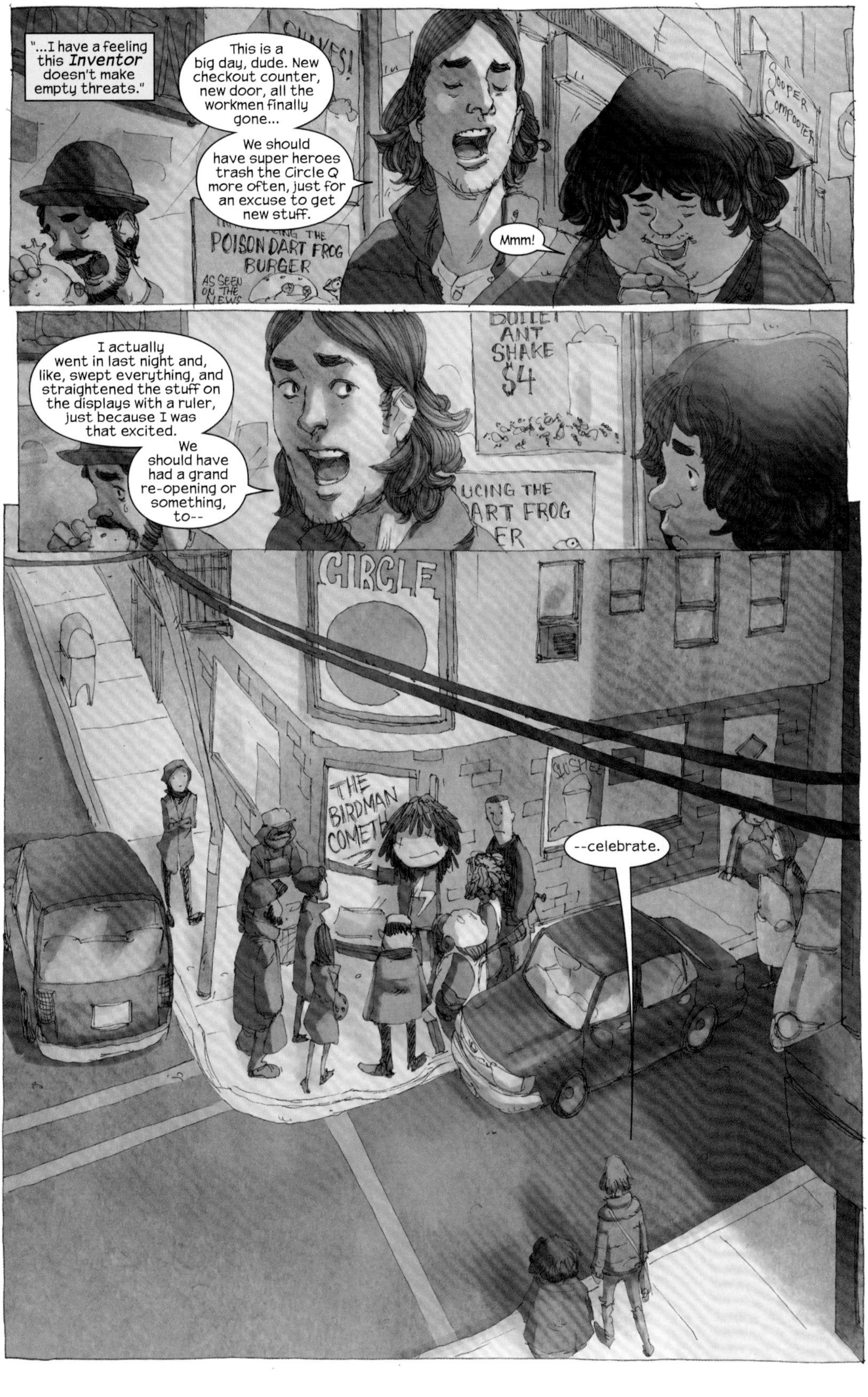
"...I have a feeling this *Inventor* doesn't make empty threats."
This is a big day, dude. New checkout counter, new door, all the workmen finally gone...
We should have super heroes trash the Circle Q more often, just for an excuse to get new stuff.
POISON DART FROG BURGER
AS SEEN ON THE NEWS
SOOPER COMPOOTER
Mmm!
I actually went in last night and, like, swept everything, and straightened the stuff on the displays with a ruler, just because I was that excited.
We should have had a grand re-opening or something, to--
ANT SHAKE $4
CIRCLE
THE BIRDMAN COMETH
--celebrate.

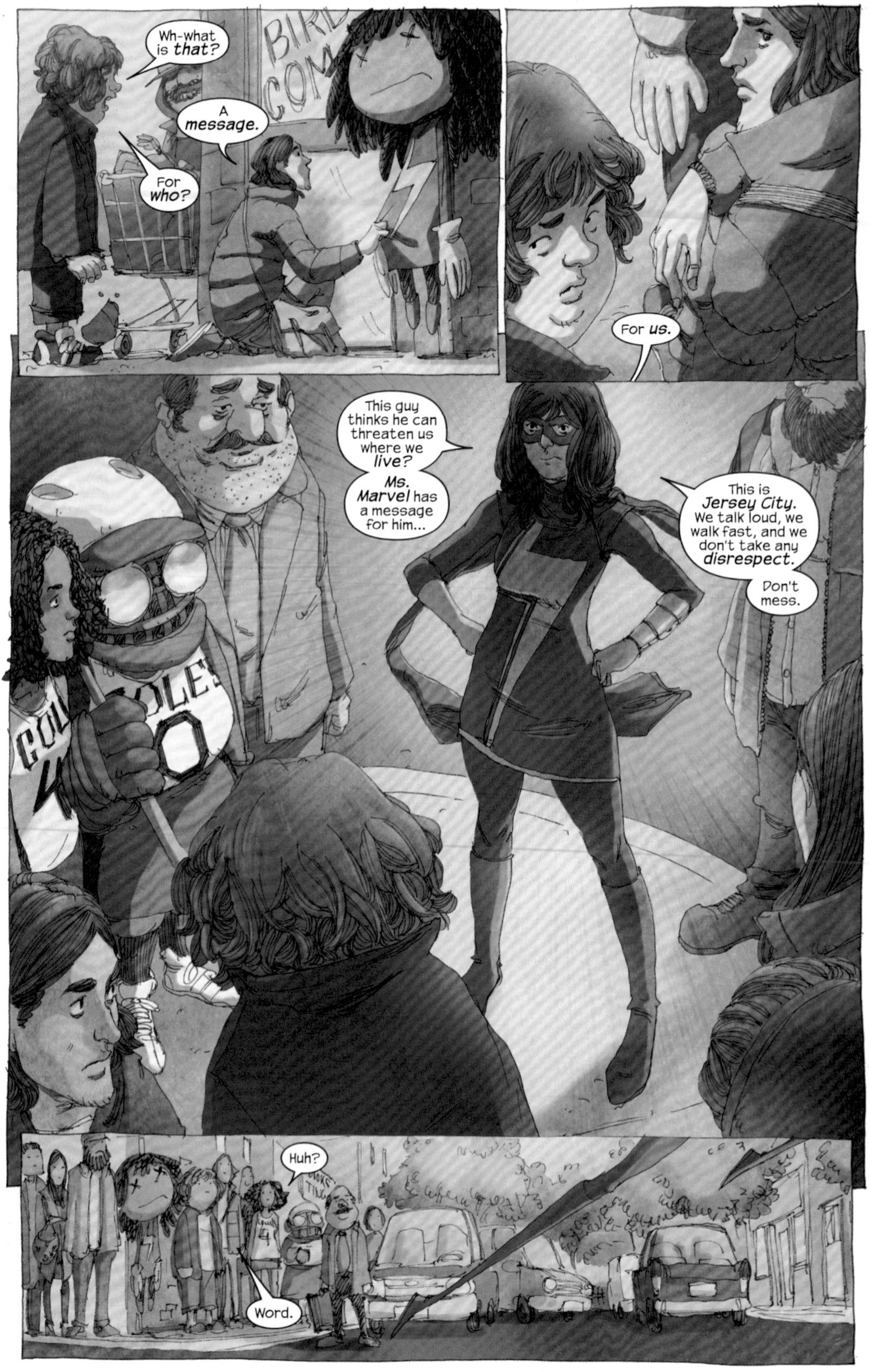
Wh-what is that?
A message.
For who?
For us.
This guy thinks he can threaten us where we live? Ms. Marvel has a message for him...
This is Jersey City. We talk loud, we walk fast, and we don't take any disrespect.
Don't mess.
Huh?
Word.

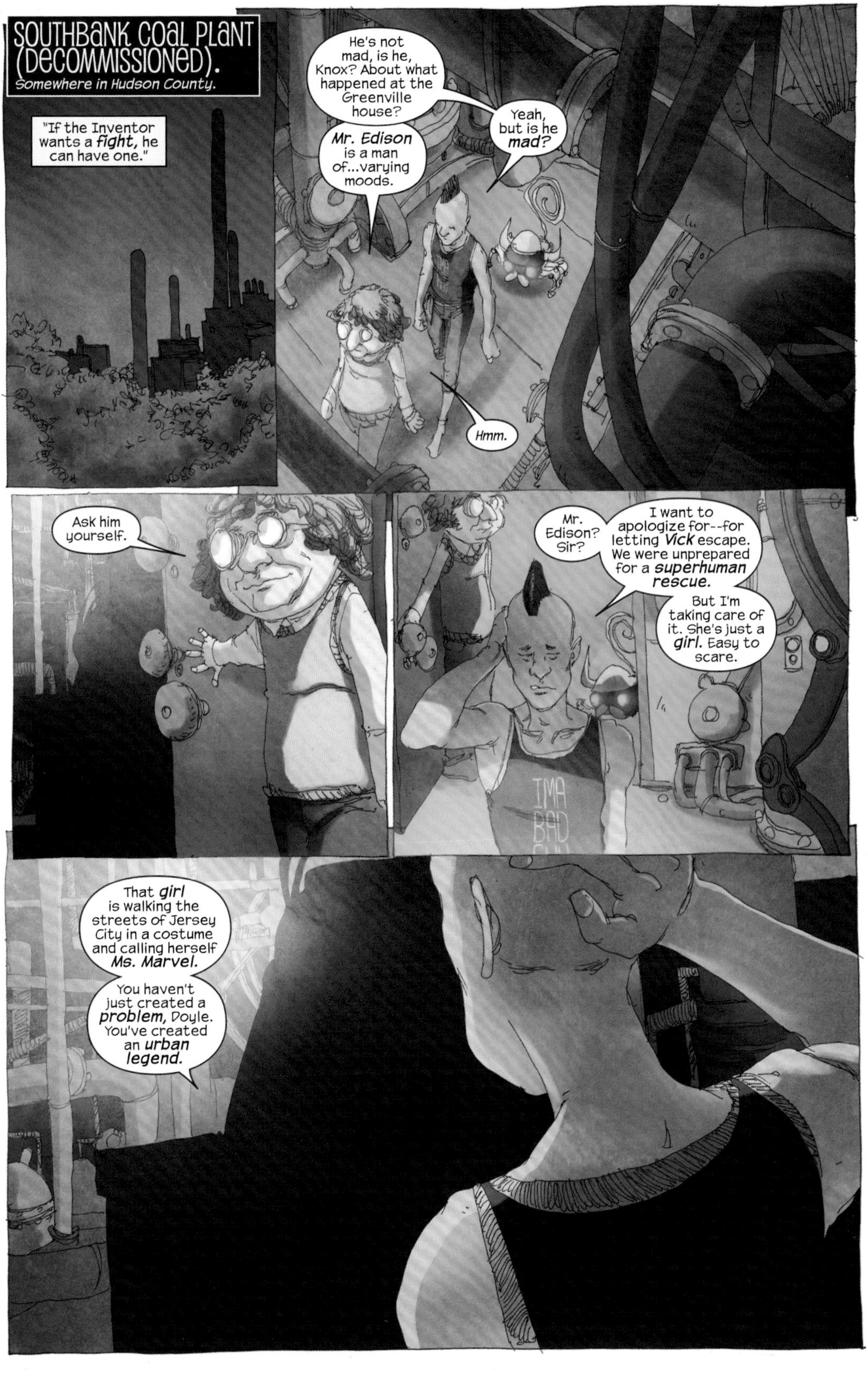
SOUTHBANK COAL PLANT (DECOMMISSIONED).
Somewhere in Hudson County.
"If the Inventor wants a *fight,* he can have one."
He's not mad, is he, Knox? About what happened at the Greenville house?
Mr. Edison is a man of...varying moods.
Yeah, but is he *mad?*
Hmm.
Ask him yourself.
Mr. Edison? Sir?
I want to apologize for--for letting *Vick* escape. We were unprepared for a *superhuman rescue.*
But I'm taking care of it. She's just a *girl.* Easy to scare.
IMA BAD
That *girl* is walking the streets of Jersey City in a costume and calling herself *Ms. Marvel.*
You haven't just created a *problem,* Doyle. You've created an *urban legend.*

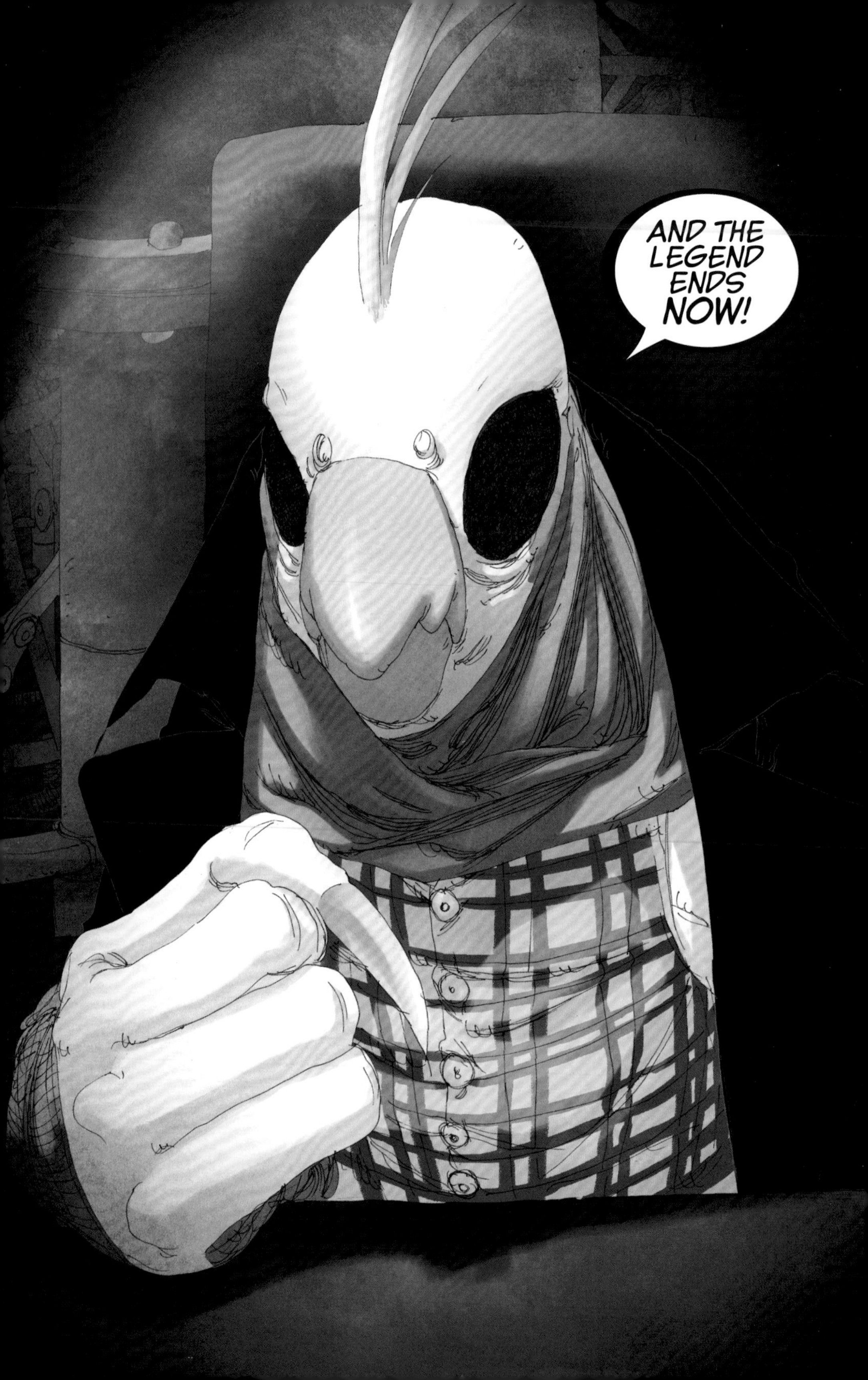
AND THE LEGEND ENDS NOW!

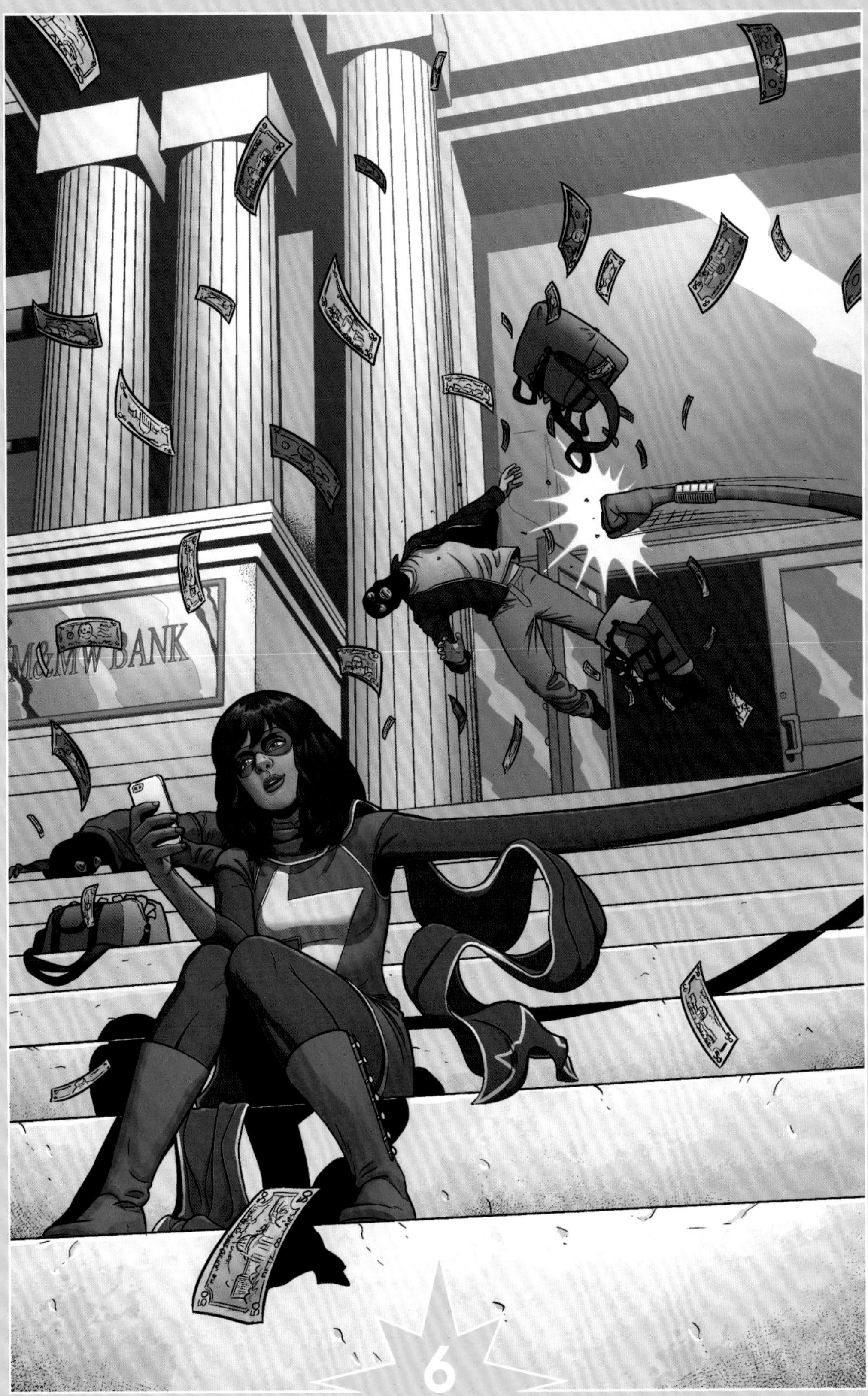
M&MW BANK

6

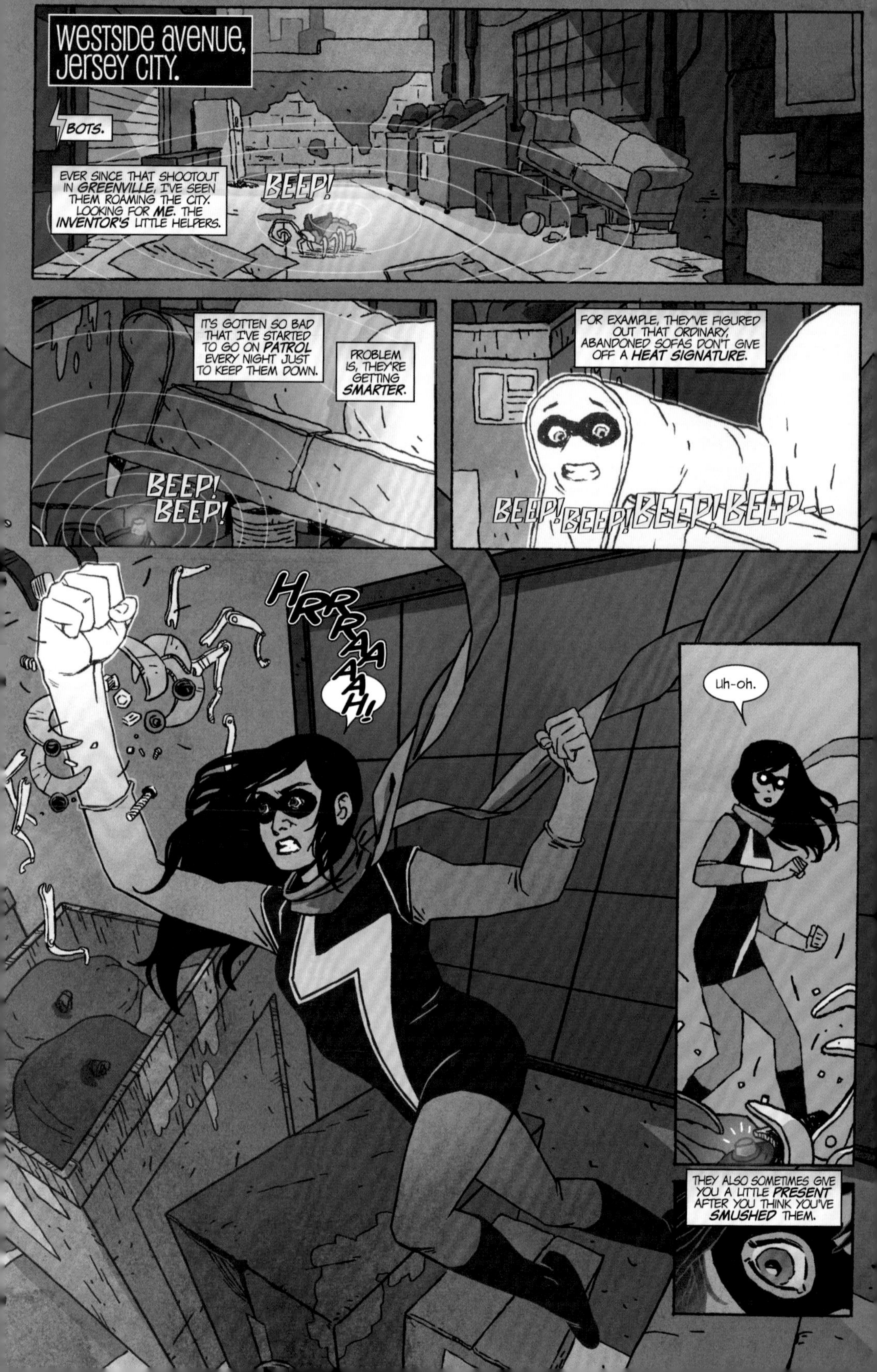
WESTSIDE AVENUE, JERSEY CITY.
BOTS.
EVER SINCE THAT SHOOTOUT IN GREENVILLE, I'VE SEEN THEM ROAMING THE CITY. LOOKING FOR ME. THE INVENTOR'S LITTLE HELPERS.
BEEP!
IT'S GOTTEN SO BAD THAT I'VE STARTED TO GO ON PATROL EVERY NIGHT JUST TO KEEP THEM DOWN.
PROBLEM IS, THEY'RE GETTING SMARTER.
BEEP! BEEP!
FOR EXAMPLE, THEY'VE FIGURED OUT THAT ORDINARY, ABANDONED SOFAS DON'T GIVE OFF A HEAT SIGNATURE.
BEEP! BEEP! BEEP! BEEP--
HRRRAAAAH!
Uh-oh.
THEY ALSO SOMETIMES GIVE YOU A LITTLE PRESENT AFTER YOU THINK YOU'VE SMUSHED THEM.

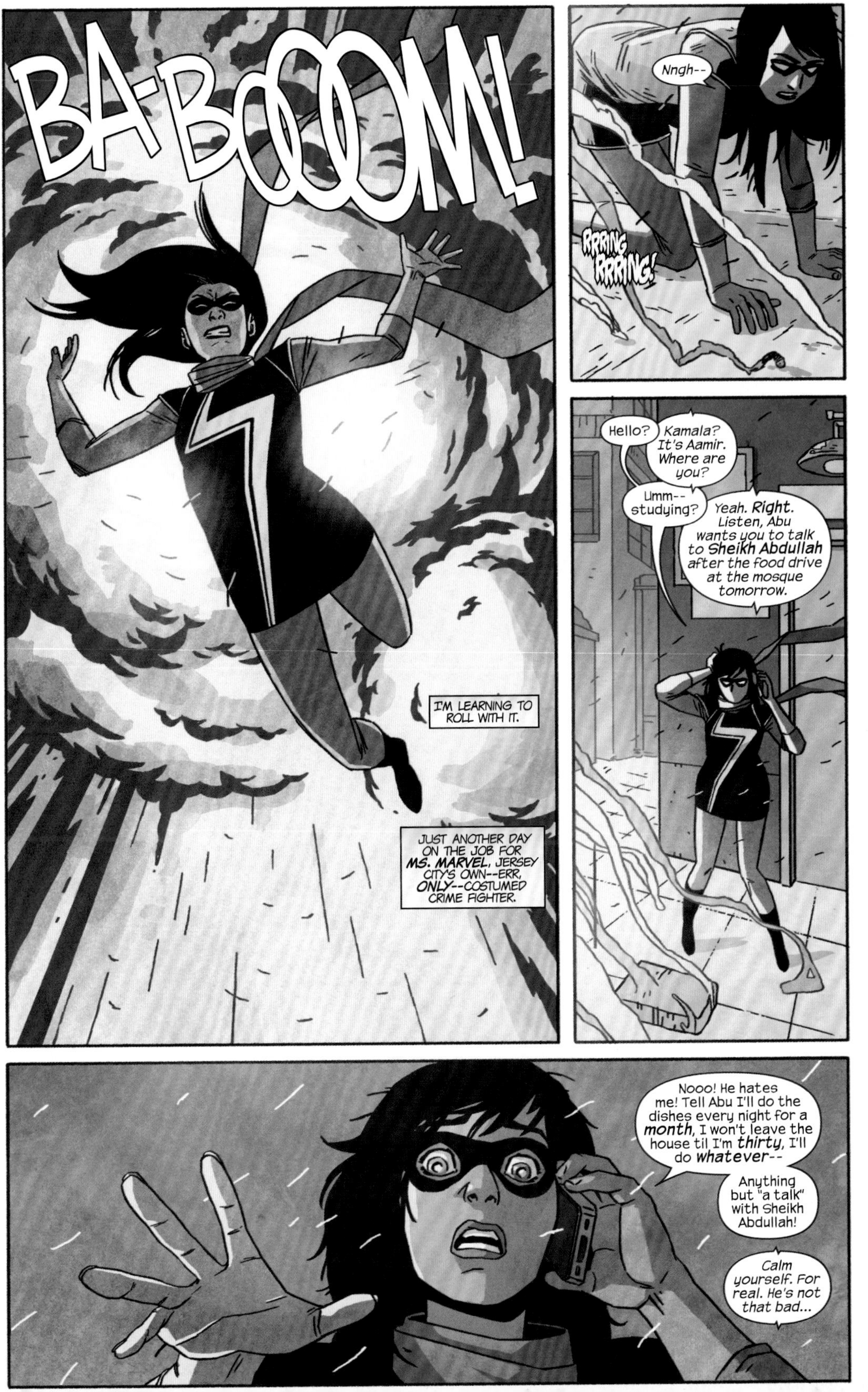

BA-BOOOOM!
I'M LEARNING TO ROLL WITH IT.
JUST ANOTHER DAY ON THE JOB FOR MS. MARVEL, JERSEY CITY'S OWN--ERR, ONLY--COSTUMED CRIME FIGHTER.
Nngh--
RRRING RRRING!
Hello?
Kamala? It's Aamir. Where are you?
Umm-- studying?
Yeah. Right. Listen, Abu wants you to talk to Sheikh Abdullah after the food drive at the mosque tomorrow.
Nooo! He hates me! Tell Abu I'll do the dishes every night for a month, I won't leave the house til I'm thirty, I'll do whatever--
Anything but "a talk" with Sheikh Abdullah!
Calm yourself. For real. He's not that bad...

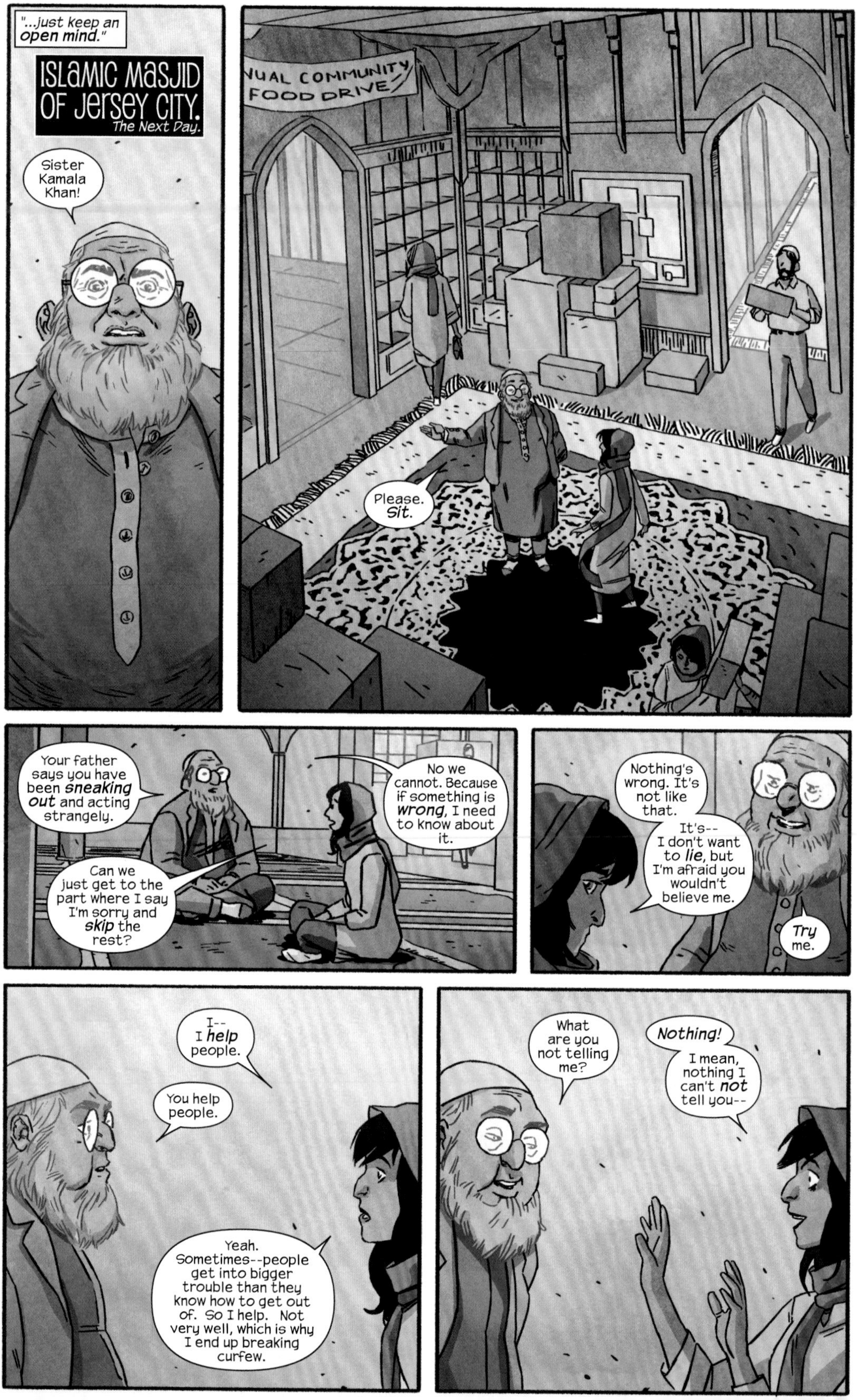
"...just keep an open mind."
ISLAMIC MASJID OF JERSEY CITY. The Next Day.
Sister Kamala Khan!
NUAL COMMUNITY FOOD DRIVE
Please. *Sit*.
Your father says you have been *sneaking out* and acting strangely.
Can we just get to the part where I say I'm sorry and *skip* the rest?
No we cannot. Because if something is *wrong*, I need to know about it.
Nothing's wrong. It's not like that.
It's-- I don't want to *lie*, but I'm afraid you wouldn't believe me.
Try me.
I-- I *help* people.
You help people.
Yeah. Sometimes--people get into bigger trouble than they know how to get out of. So I help. Not very well, which is why I end up breaking curfew.
What are you not telling me?
Nothing!
I mean, nothing I can't *not* tell you--

I don't **mean** to disobey Abu and Ammi. It's just that sometimes I **have to** in order to do the right thing.

I see.

Well, if you're not very **good** at it--**helping** people, that is--perhaps you need a **teacher**.

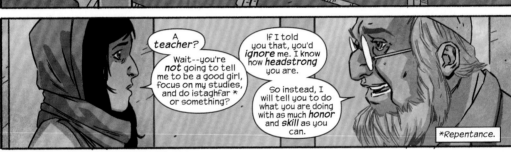

A **teacher**?

Wait--you're **not** going to tell me to be a good girl, focus on my studies, and do istaghfar * or something?

If I told you that, you'd **ignore** me. I know how **headstrong** you are.

So instead, I will tell you to do what you are doing with as much **honor** and **skill** as you can.

*Repentance.

I can't believe it. I thought you were going to warn me about **Satan** and **boys**.

I've been giving **youth lectures** at this mosque for ten years. If I still have to warn you about Satan and boys, I should lose my job.

I am asking you for something more **difficult**. If you insist on pursuing this thing you will not tell me about, do it with the qualities befitting an upright young woman:

Courage, strength, honesty, compassion and **self-respect**.

Do we have a **deal**?

Yeah. I mean **yes**, hazrat sahib. Thank you, hazrat sahib.

But--about finding a **teacher**. How am I supposed to find someone to teach me how to--you know--be better? At **helping**?

As the ancient saying goes:

"When the student is ready...

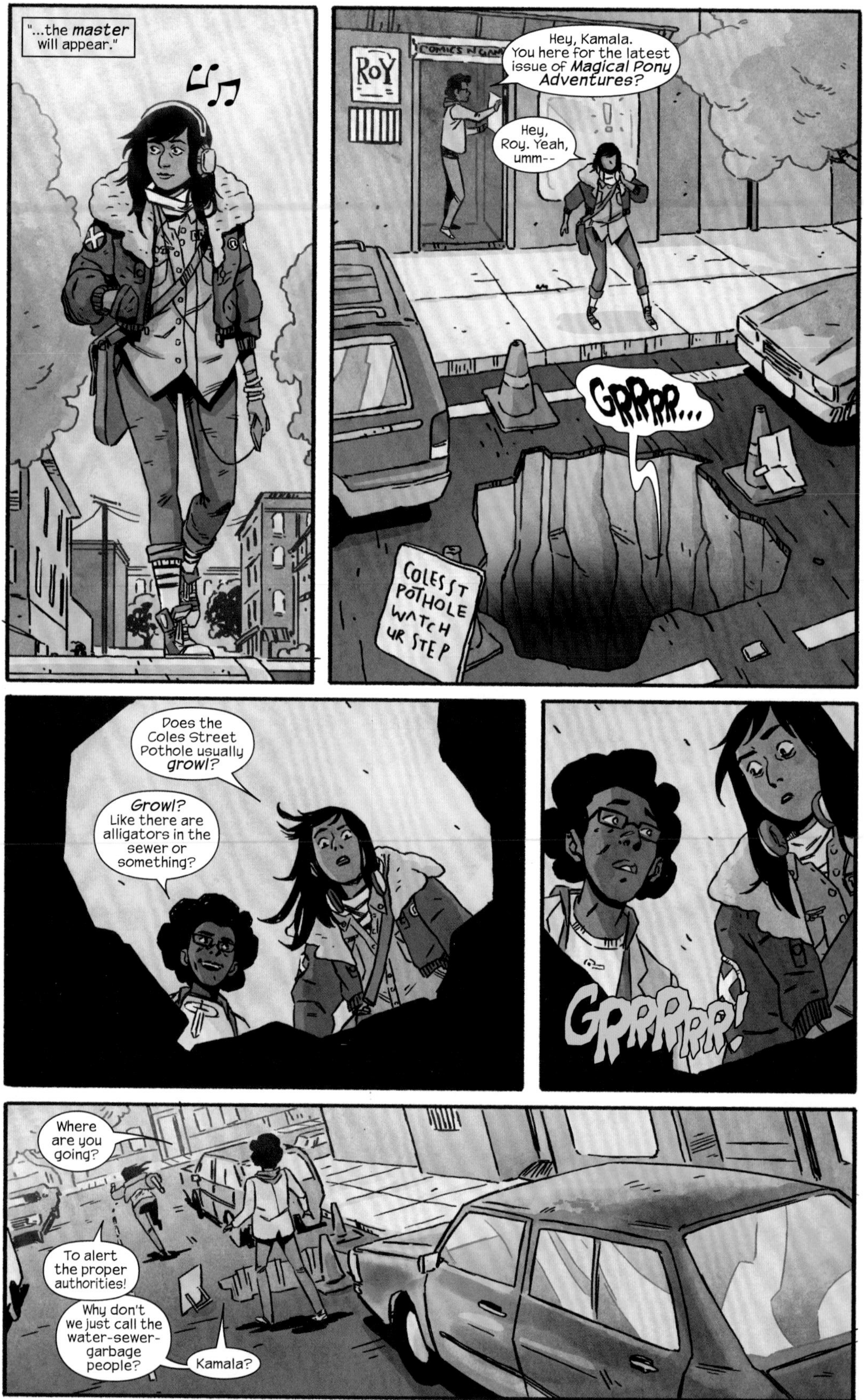
"...the *master* will appear."
Hey, Kamala. You here for the latest issue of *Magical Pony Adventures*?
Hey, Roy. Yeah, umm--
ROY
GRRRR...
COLES ST POTHOLE WATCH UR STEP
Does the Coles Street Pothole usually *growl*?
Growl? Like there are alligators in the sewer or something?
GRRRRRR!
Where are you going?
To alert the proper authorities!
Why don't we just call the water-sewer-garbage people?
Kamala?

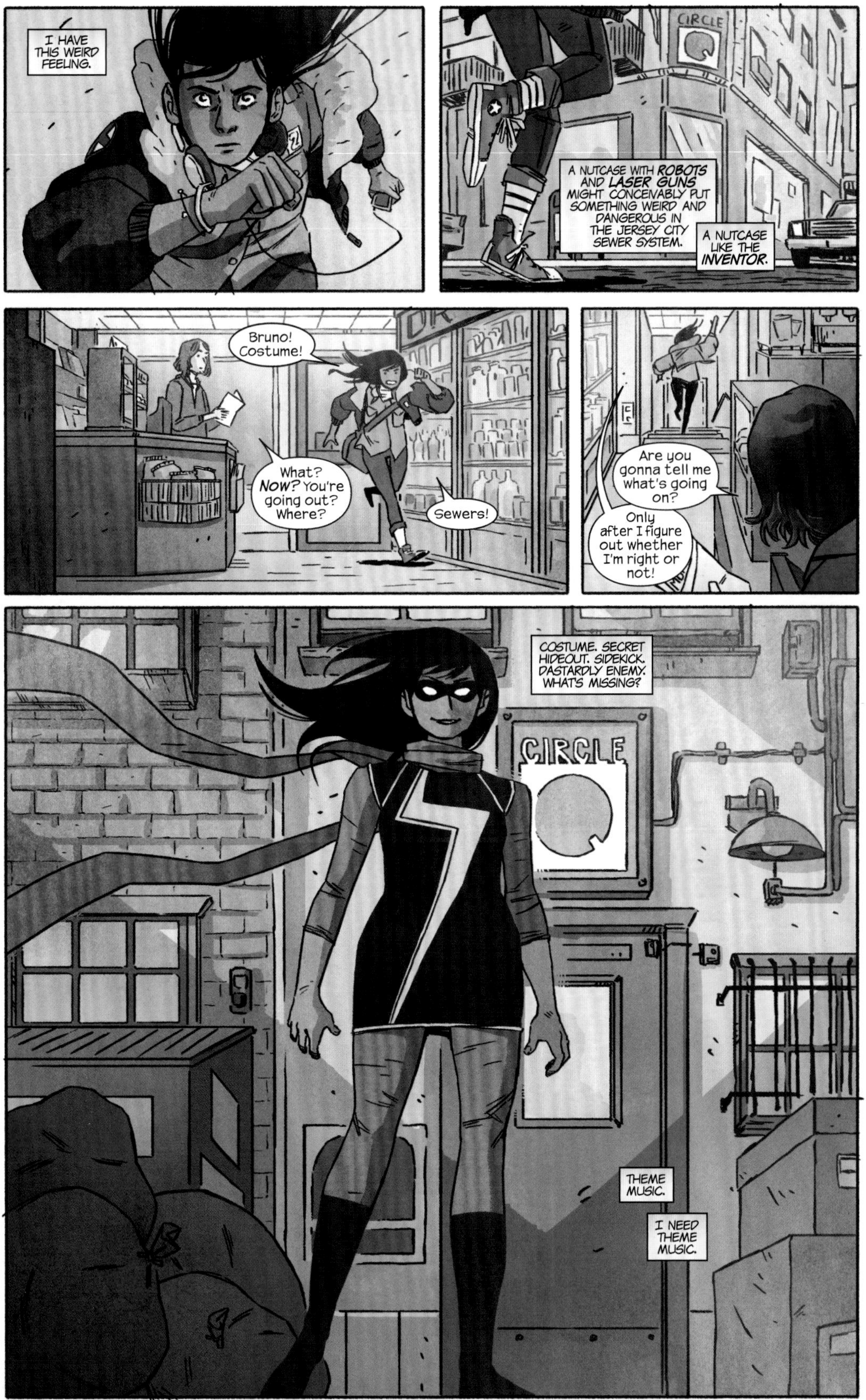
I HAVE THIS WEIRD FEELING.
CIRCLE
A NUTCASE WITH ROBOTS AND LASER GUNS MIGHT CONCEIVABLY PUT SOMETHING WEIRD AND DANGEROUS IN THE JERSEY CITY SEWER SYSTEM.
A NUTCASE LIKE THE INVENTOR.
Bruno! Costume!
What? NOW? You're going out? Where?
Sewers!
Are you gonna tell me what's going on?
Only after I figure out whether I'm right or not!
COSTUME. SECRET HIDEOUT. SIDEKICK. DASTARDLY ENEMY. WHAT'S MISSING?
CIRCLE
THEME MUSIC.
I NEED THEME MUSIC.

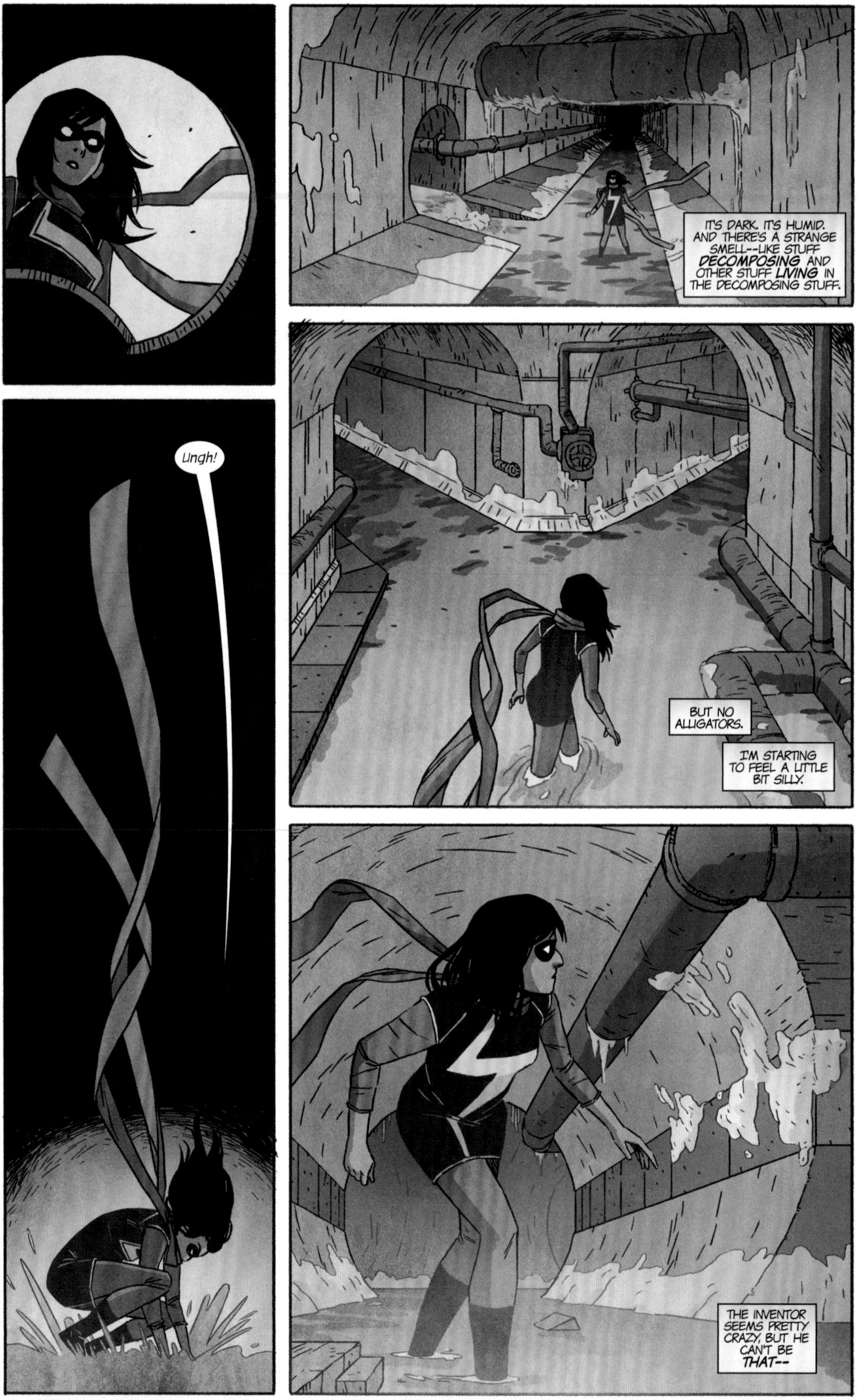
Ungh!
IT'S DARK. IT'S HUMID. AND THERE'S A STRANGE SMELL--LIKE STUFF DECOMPOSING AND OTHER STUFF LIVING IN THE DECOMPOSING STUFF.
BUT NO ALLIGATORS.
I'M STARTING TO FEEL A LITTLE BIT SILLY.
THE INVENTOR SEEMS PRETTY CRAZY, BUT HE CAN'T BE THAT--

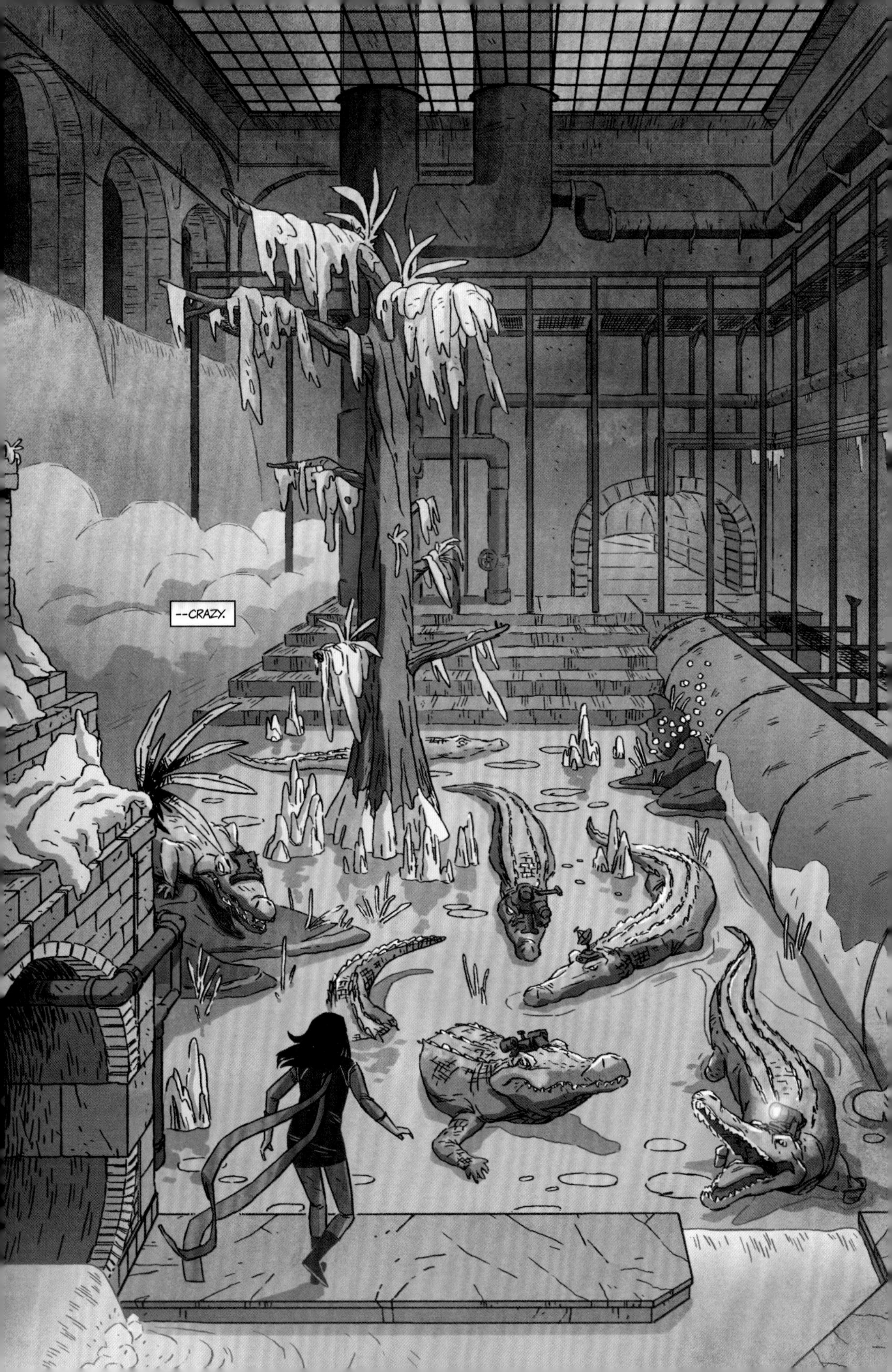
--CRAZY.

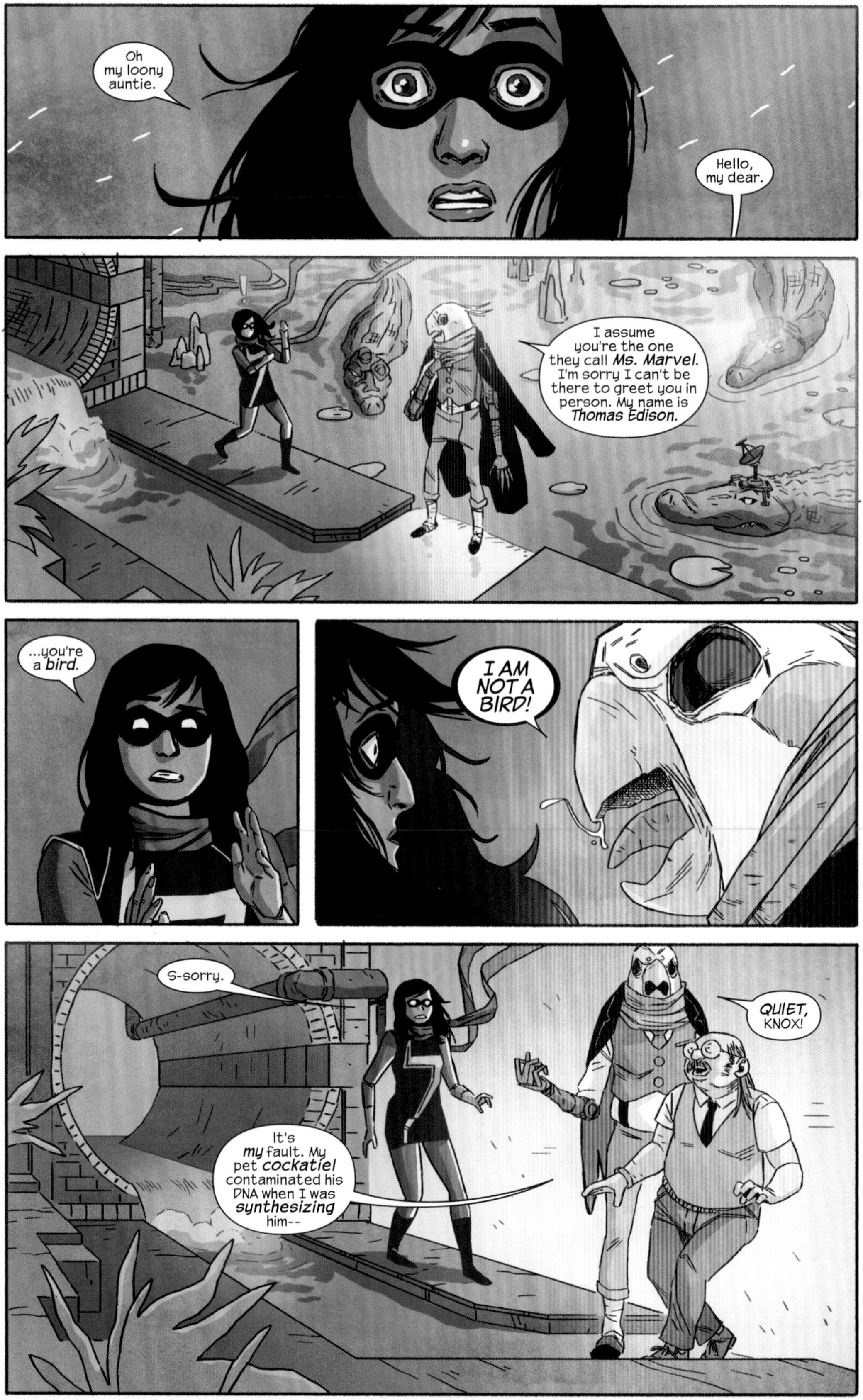
Oh my loony auntie.
Hello, my dear.
I assume you're the one they call *Ms. Marvel*. I'm sorry I can't be there to greet you in person. My name is *Thomas Edison*.
...you're a *bird*.
I AM NOT A BIRD!
S-sorry.
QUIET, KNOX!
It's *my* fault. My pet *cockatiel* contaminated his DNA when I was *synthesizing* him--

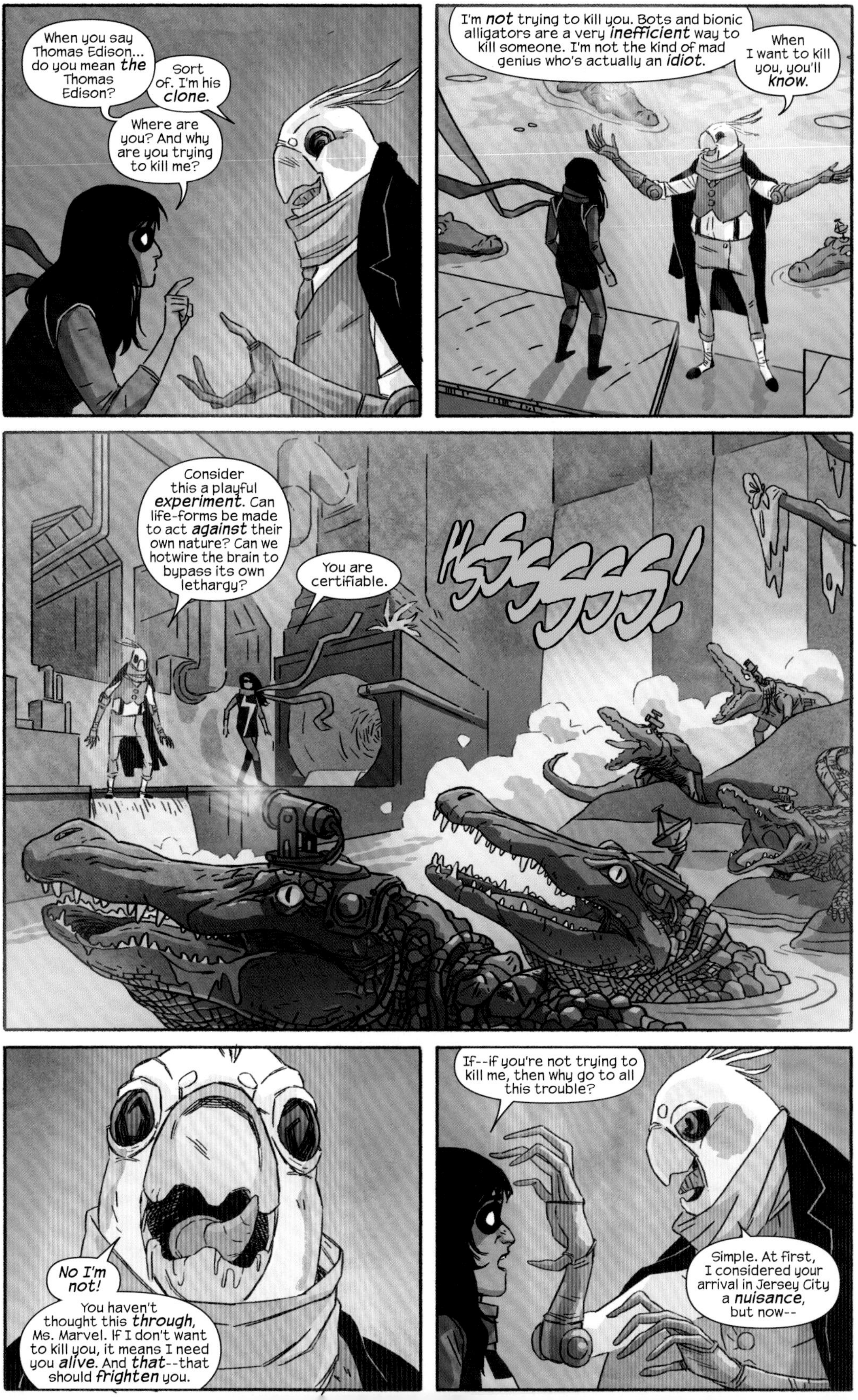
When you say Thomas Edison... do you mean the Thomas Edison?
Sort of. I'm his clone.
Where are you? And why are you trying to kill me?
I'm not trying to kill you. Bots and bionic alligators are a very inefficient way to kill someone. I'm not the kind of mad genius who's actually an idiot.
When I want to kill you, you'll know.
Consider this a playful experiment. Can life-forms be made to act against their own nature? Can we hotwire the brain to bypass its own lethargy?
You are certifiable.
HSSSSSS!
No I'm not!
You haven't thought this through, Ms. Marvel. If I don't want to kill you, it means I need you alive. And that--that should frighten you.
If--if you're not trying to kill me, then why go to all this trouble?
Simple. At first, I considered your arrival in Jersey City a nuisance, but now--

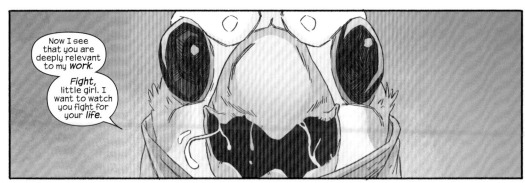

Now I see that you are deeply relevant to my *work.*

Fight, little girl. I want to watch you fight for your *life.*

Sir! Infrared has detected someone else approaching the holding tank!

Someone? What do you mean, *"someone?"* This place was supposed to be locked down!

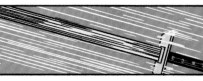

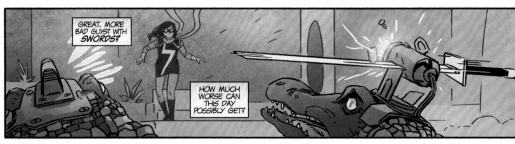

GREAT. MORE BAD GUYS? WITH *SWORDS?*

HOW MUCH WORSE CAN THIS DAY POSSIBLY GET?

GET READY TO *LOSE,* WEIRD SHORT DUDE. I'VE GOT +10 HEALS.

POWER ATTACK!

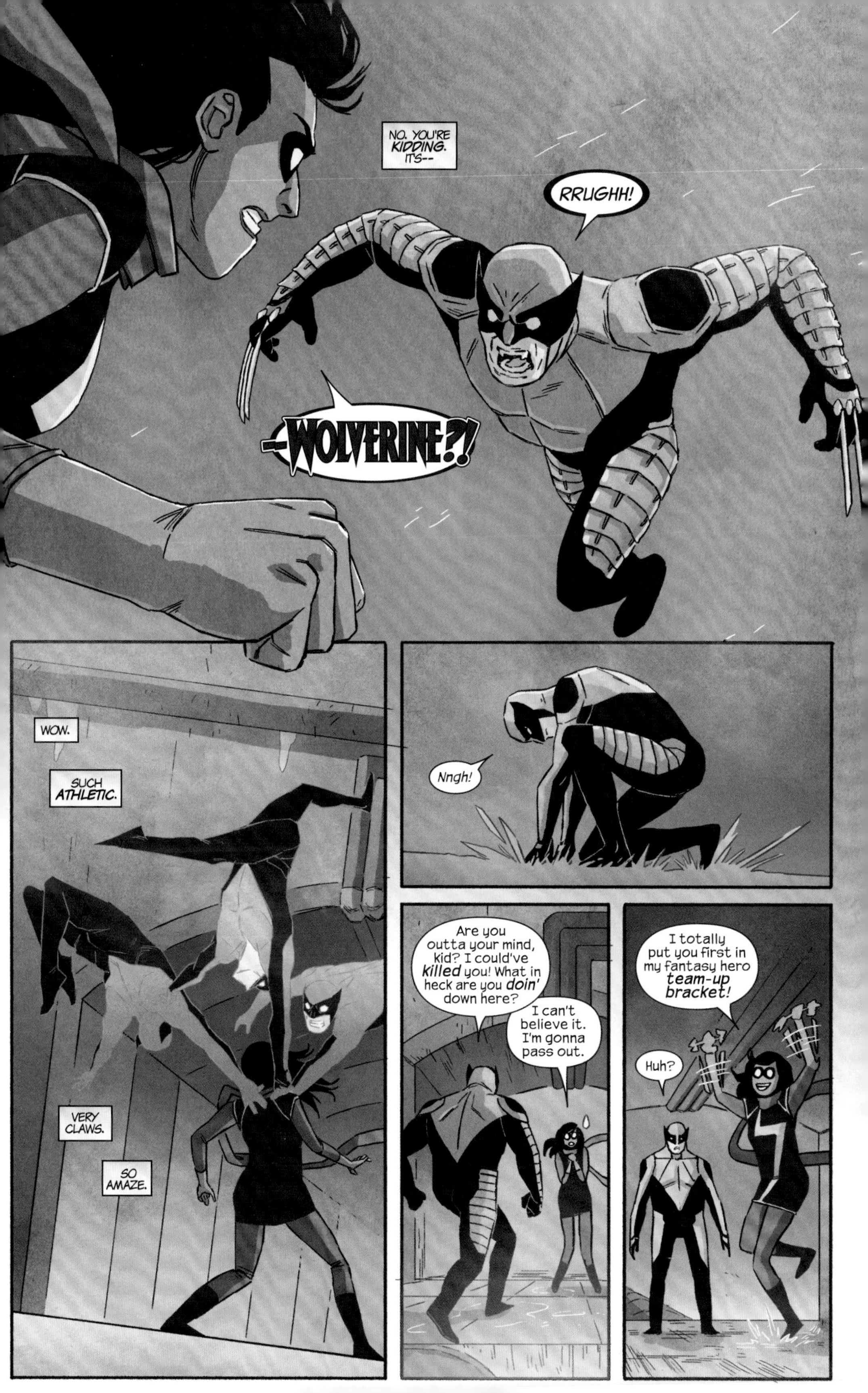
NO. YOU'RE KIDDING. IT'S--
RRUGHH!
--WOLVERINE?!
WOW.
SUCH ATHLETIC.
VERY CLAWS.
SO AMAZE.
Nngh!
Are you outta your mind, kid? I could've killed you! What in heck are you doin' down here?
I can't believe it. I'm gonna pass out.
I totally put you first in my fantasy hero team-up bracket!
Huh?

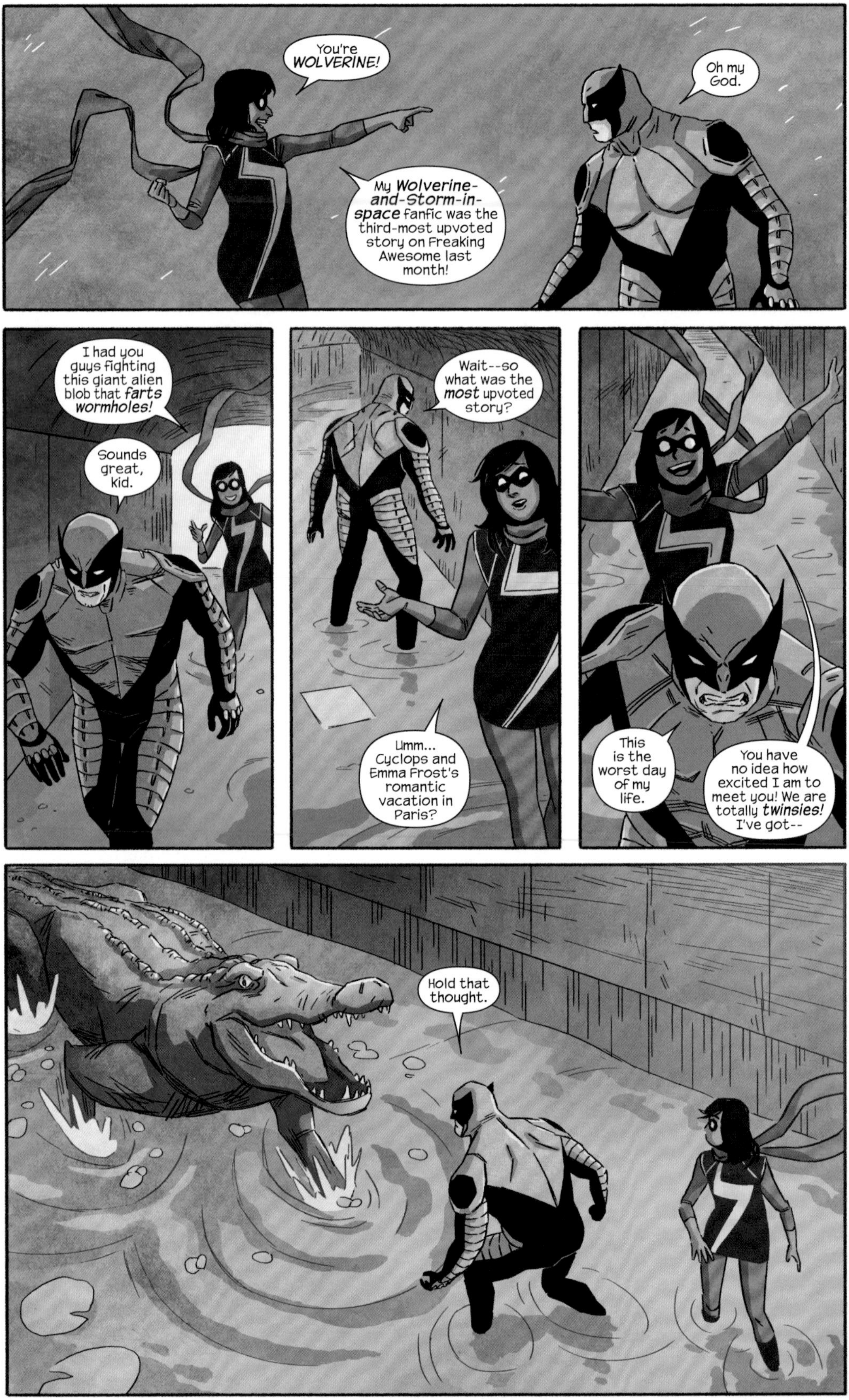
You're WOLVERINE!
Oh my God.
My Wolverine-and-Storm-in-space fanfic was the third-most upvoted story on Freaking Awesome last month!
I had you guys fighting this giant alien blob that farts wormholes!
Sounds great, kid.
Wait--so what was the most upvoted story?
Umm... Cyclops and Emma Frost's romantic vacation in Paris?
You have no idea how excited I am to meet you! We are totally twinsies! I've got--
This is the worst day of my life.
Hold that thought.

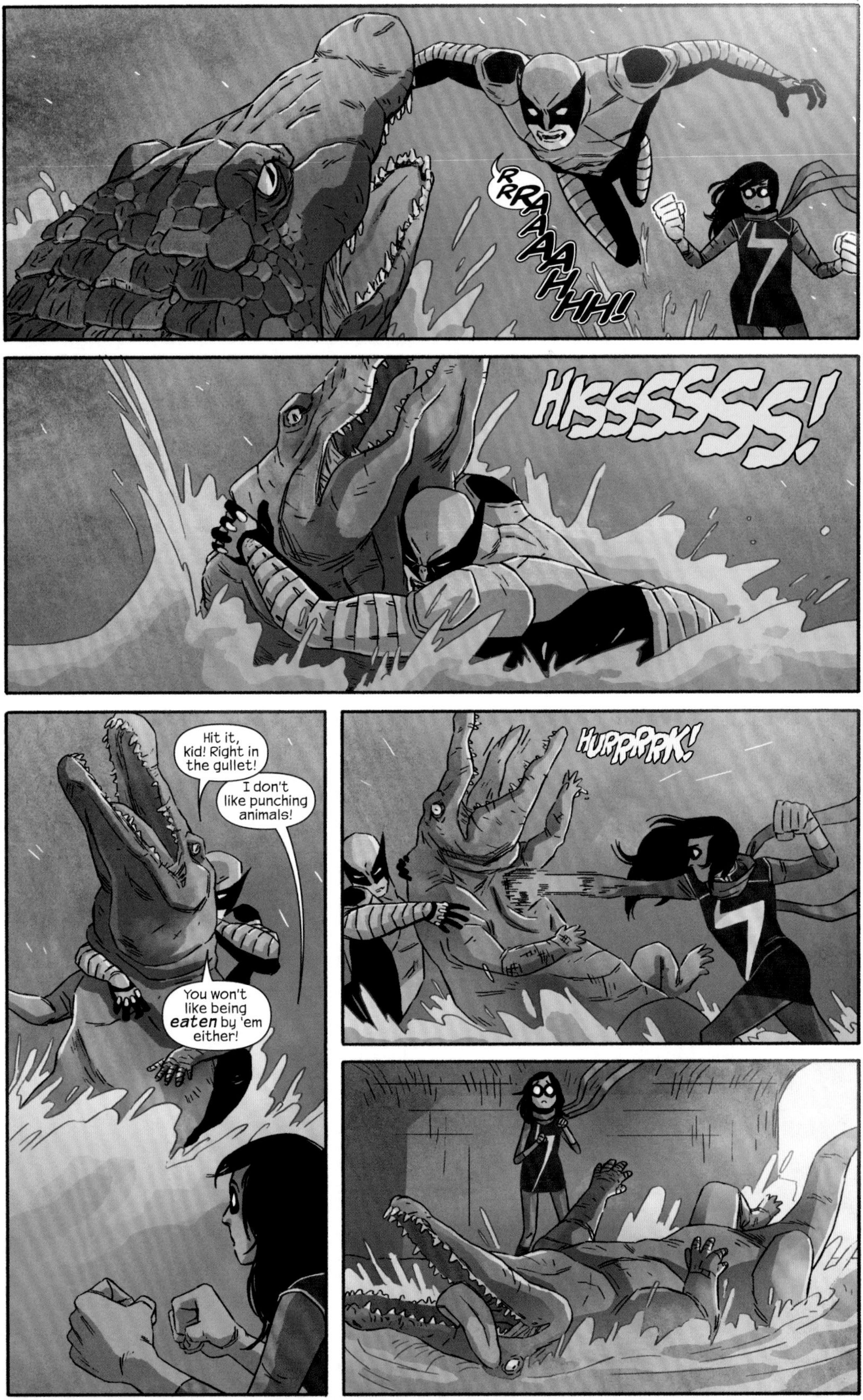
RRRAAAAHHH!
HISSSSSS!
Hit it, kid! Right in the gullet!
I don't like punching animals!
You won't like being *eaten* by 'em either!
HURRRRK!

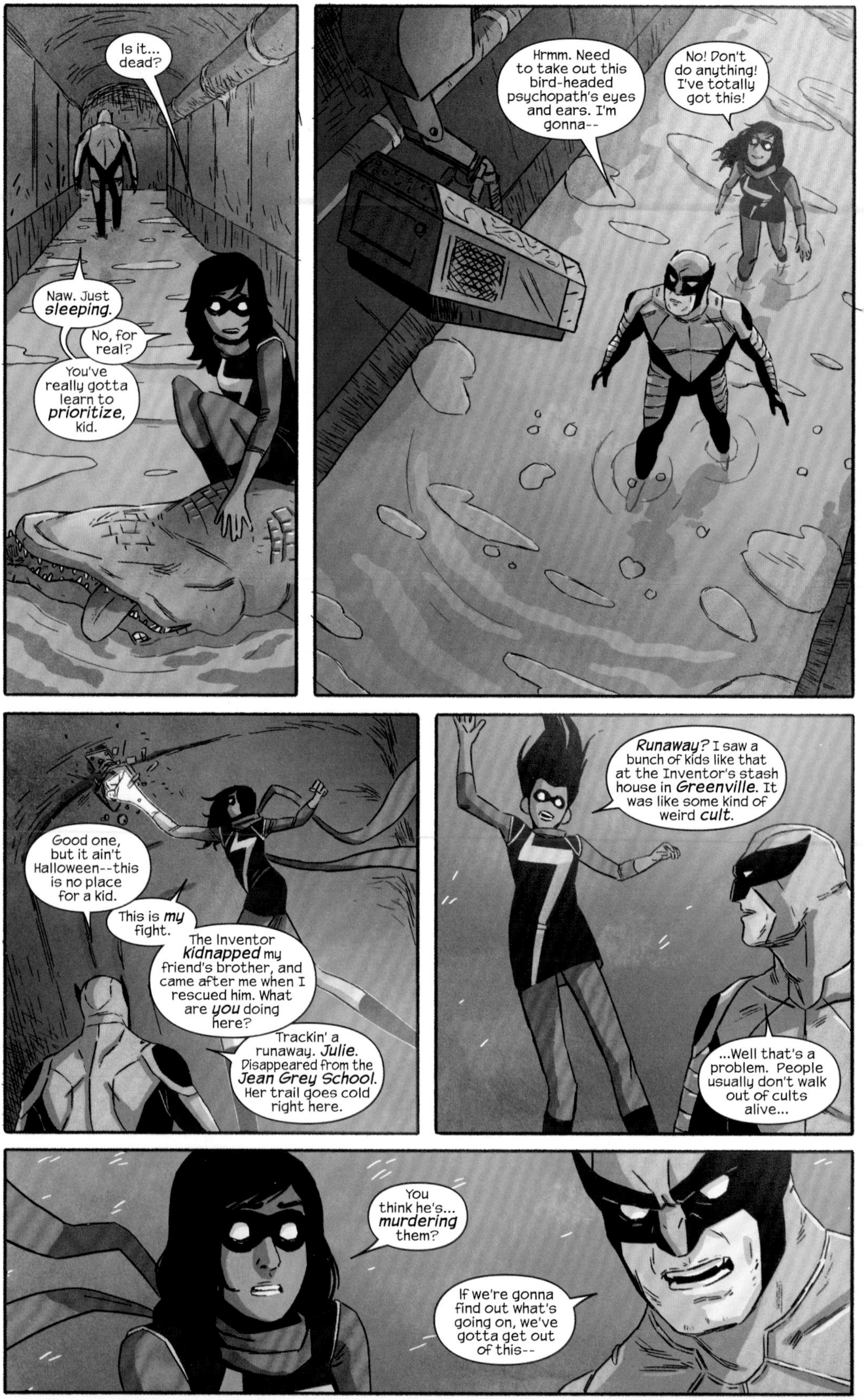

Is it... dead?
Naw. Just *sleeping*.
No, for real?
You've really gotta learn to *prioritize*, kid.
Hrmm. Need to take out this bird-headed psychopath's eyes and ears. I'm gonna--
No! Don't do anything! I've totally got this!
Good one, but it ain't Halloween--this is no place for a kid.
This is *my* fight.
The Inventor *kidnapped* my friend's brother, and came after me when I rescued him. What are *you* doing here?
Trackin' a runaway. *Julie*. Disappeared from the *Jean Grey School*. Her trail goes cold right here.
Runaway? I saw a bunch of kids like that at the Inventor's stash house in *Greenville*. It was like some kind of weird *cult*.
...Well that's a problem. People usually don't walk out of cults alive...
You think he's... *murdering* them?
If we're gonna find out what's going on, we've gotta get out of this--

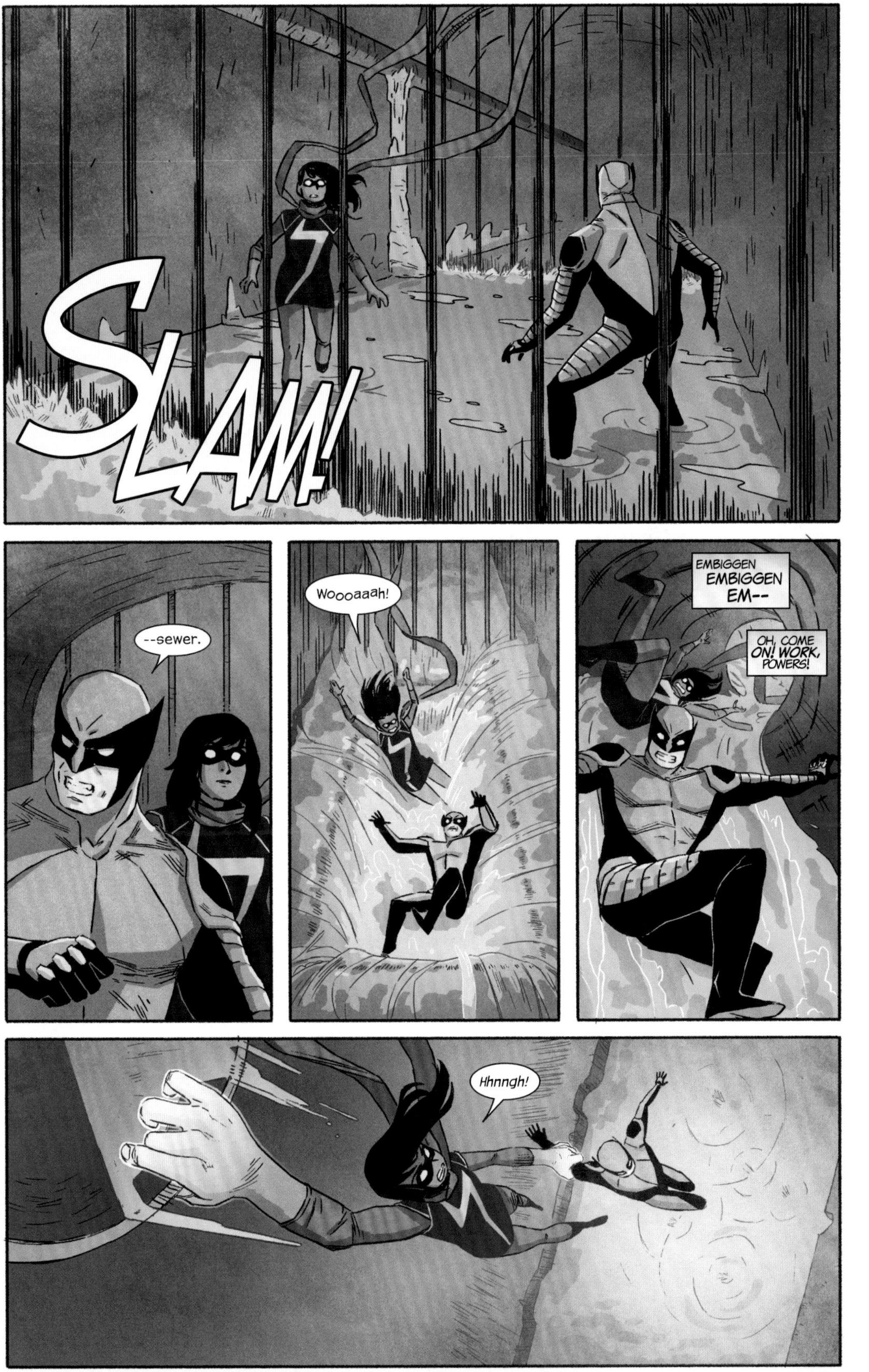
SLAM!
--sewer.
Woooaaah!
EMBIGGEN
EMBIGGEN
EM--
OH, COME ON! WORK, POWERS!
Hhnngh!

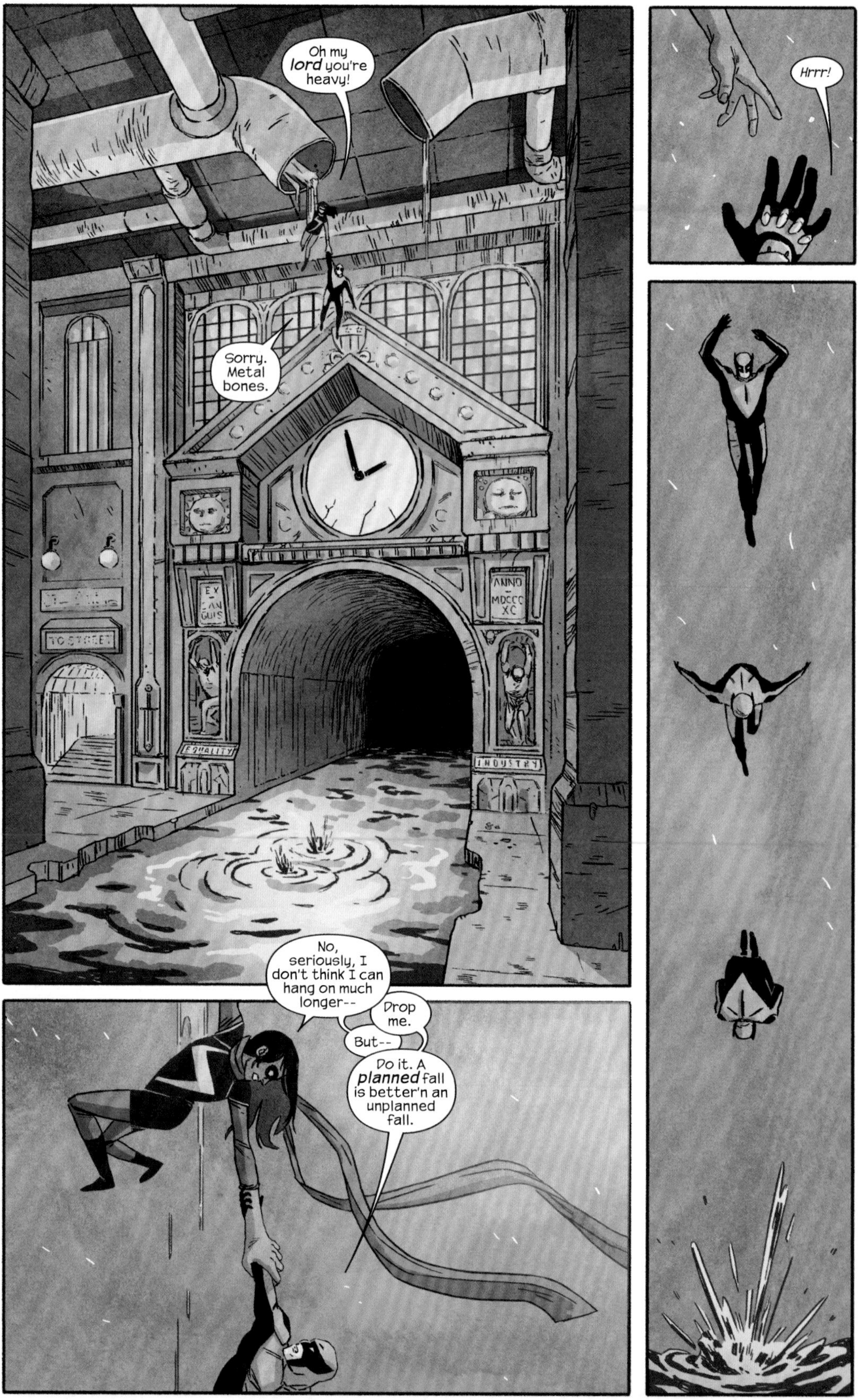

Oh my *lord* you're heavy!
Sorry. Metal bones.
EX SAN GUIS
ANNO MDCCC XC
TO STREET
EQUALITY
INDUSTRY
No, seriously, I don't think I can hang on much longer--
Drop me.
But--
Do it. A *planned* fall is better'n an unplanned fall.
Hrrr!

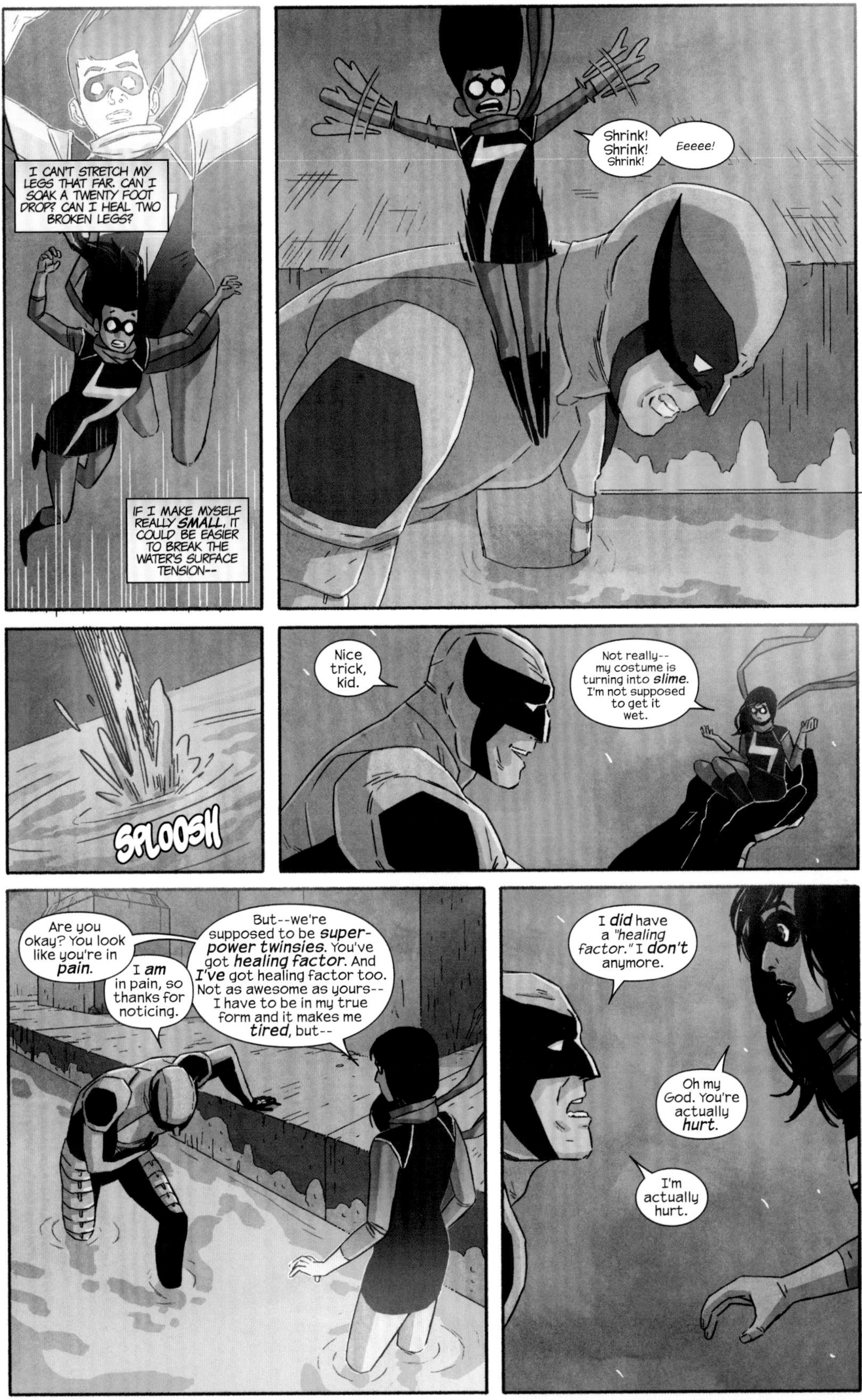
I CAN'T STRETCH MY LEGS THAT FAR. CAN I SOAK A TWENTY FOOT DROP? CAN I HEAL TWO BROKEN LEGS?
IF I MAKE MYSELF REALLY SMALL, IT COULD BE EASIER TO BREAK THE WATER'S SURFACE TENSION--
Shrink! Shrink! Shrink!
Eeeee!
SPLOOSH
Nice trick, kid.
Not really-- my costume is turning into slime. I'm not supposed to get it wet.
Are you okay? You look like you're in pain.
I am in pain, so thanks for noticing.
But--we're supposed to be super-power twinsies. You've got healing factor. And I've got healing factor too. Not as awesome as yours-- I have to be in my true form and it makes me tired, but--
I did have a "healing factor." I don't anymore.
Oh my God. You're actually hurt.
I'm actually hurt.

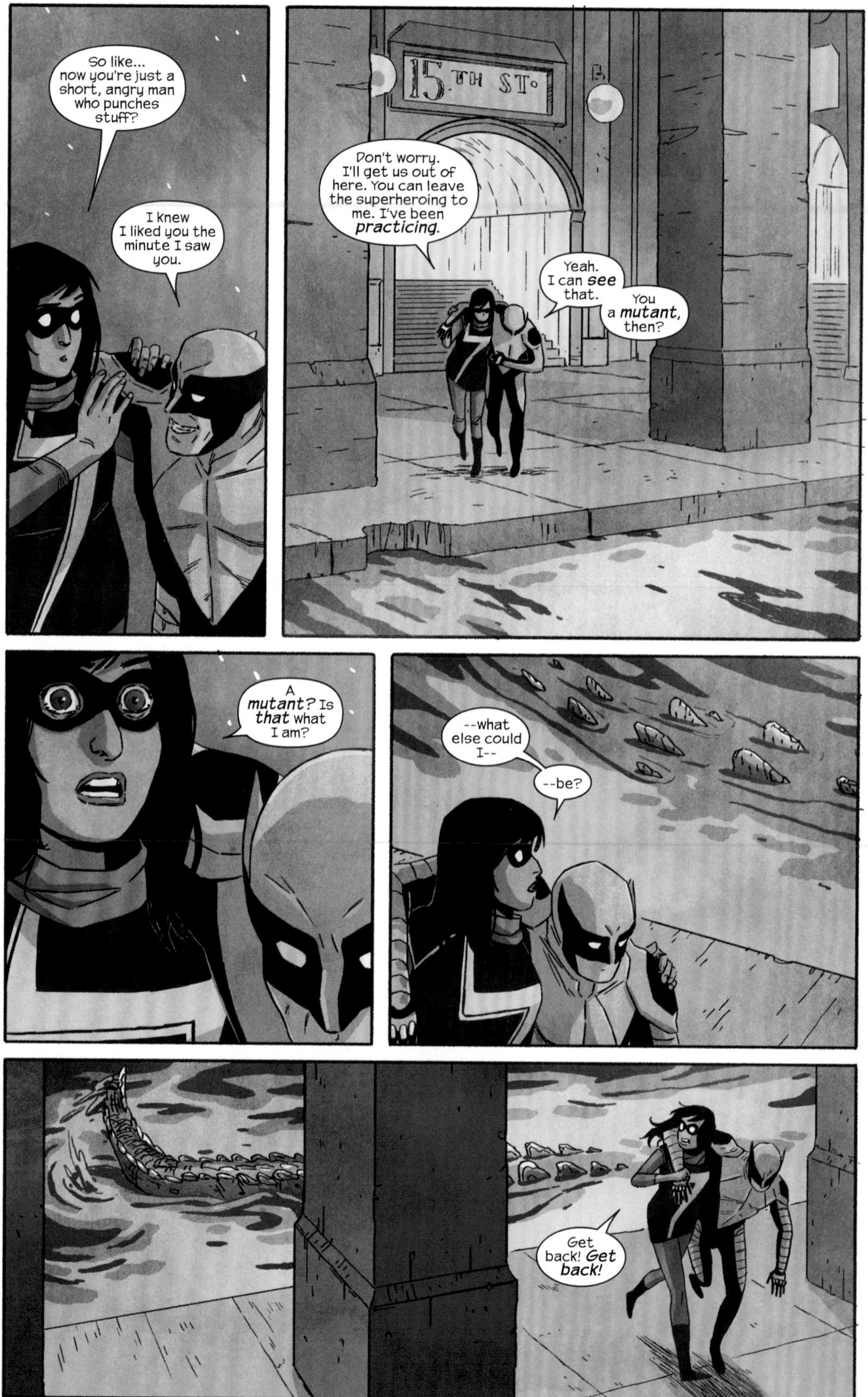
So like... now you're just a short, angry man who punches stuff?
I knew I liked you the minute I saw you.
15TH ST.
Don't worry. I'll get us out of here. You can leave the superheroing to me. I've been practicing.
Yeah. I can see that.
You a mutant, then?
A mutant? Is that what I am?
--what else could I--
--be?
Get back! Get back!

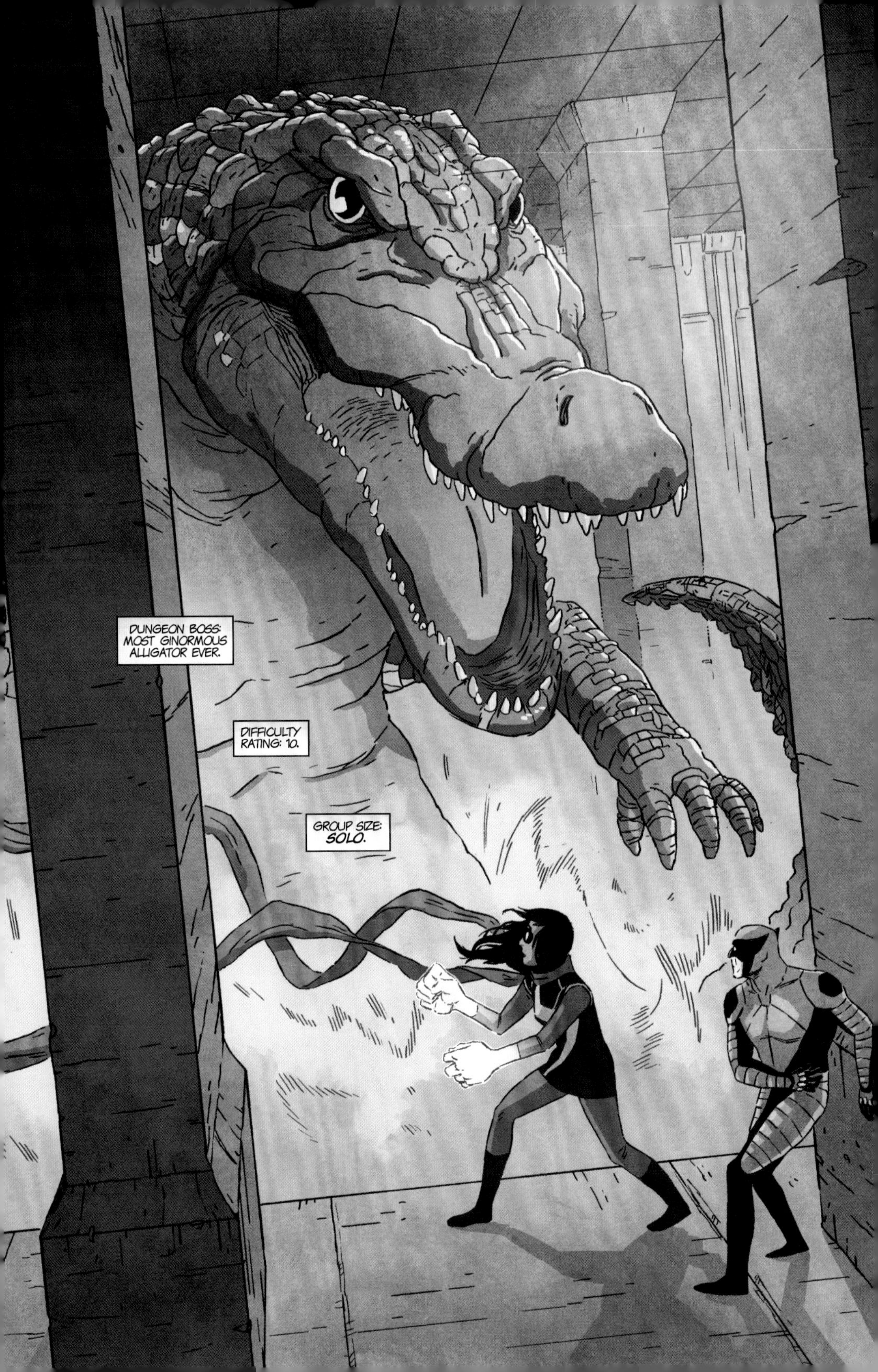
DUNGEON BOSS: MOST GINORMOUS ALLIGATOR EVER.
DIFFICULTY RATING: 10.
GROUP SIZE: SOLO.

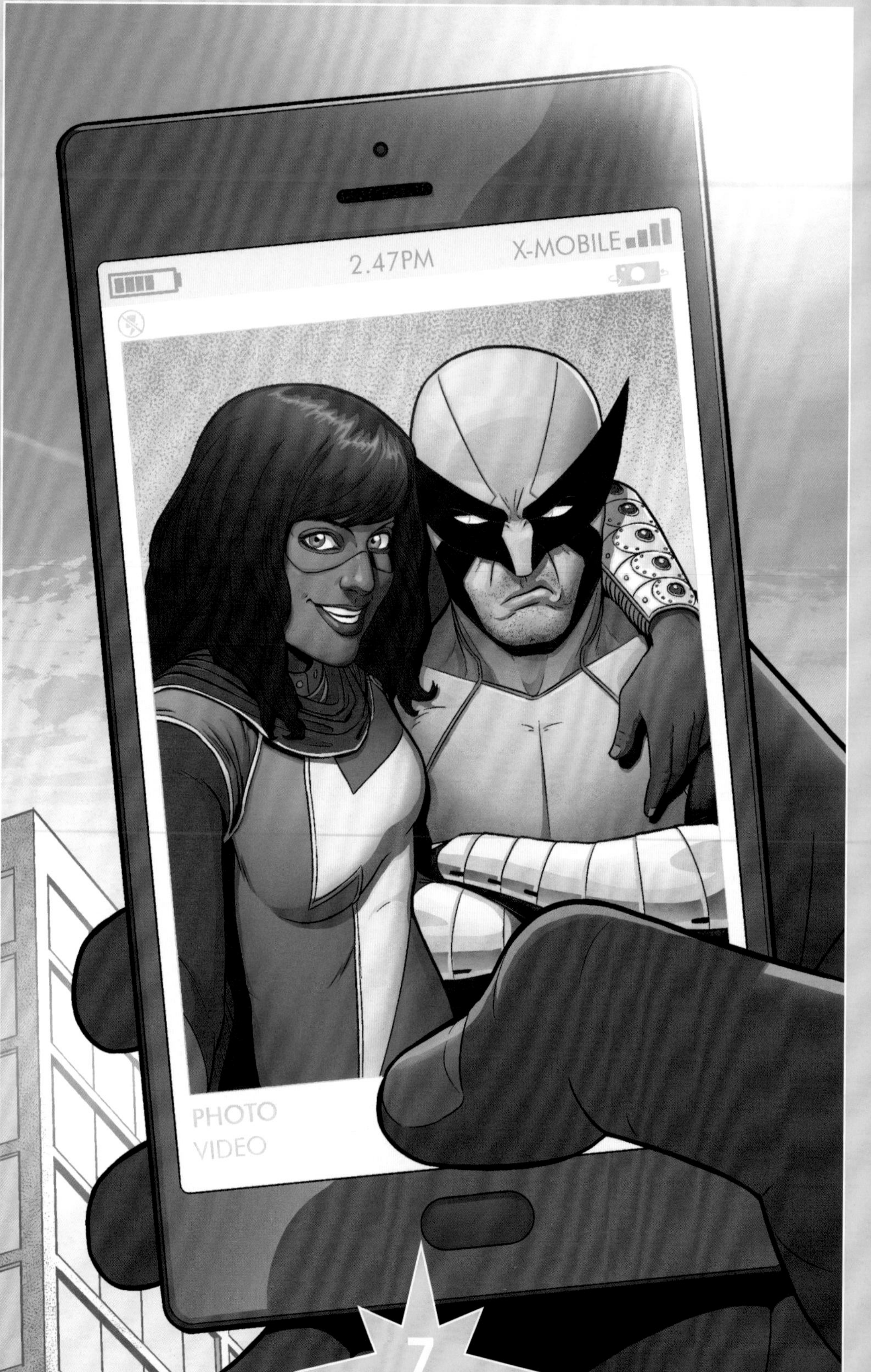
2.47PM
X-MOBILE
PHOTO
VIDEO
7

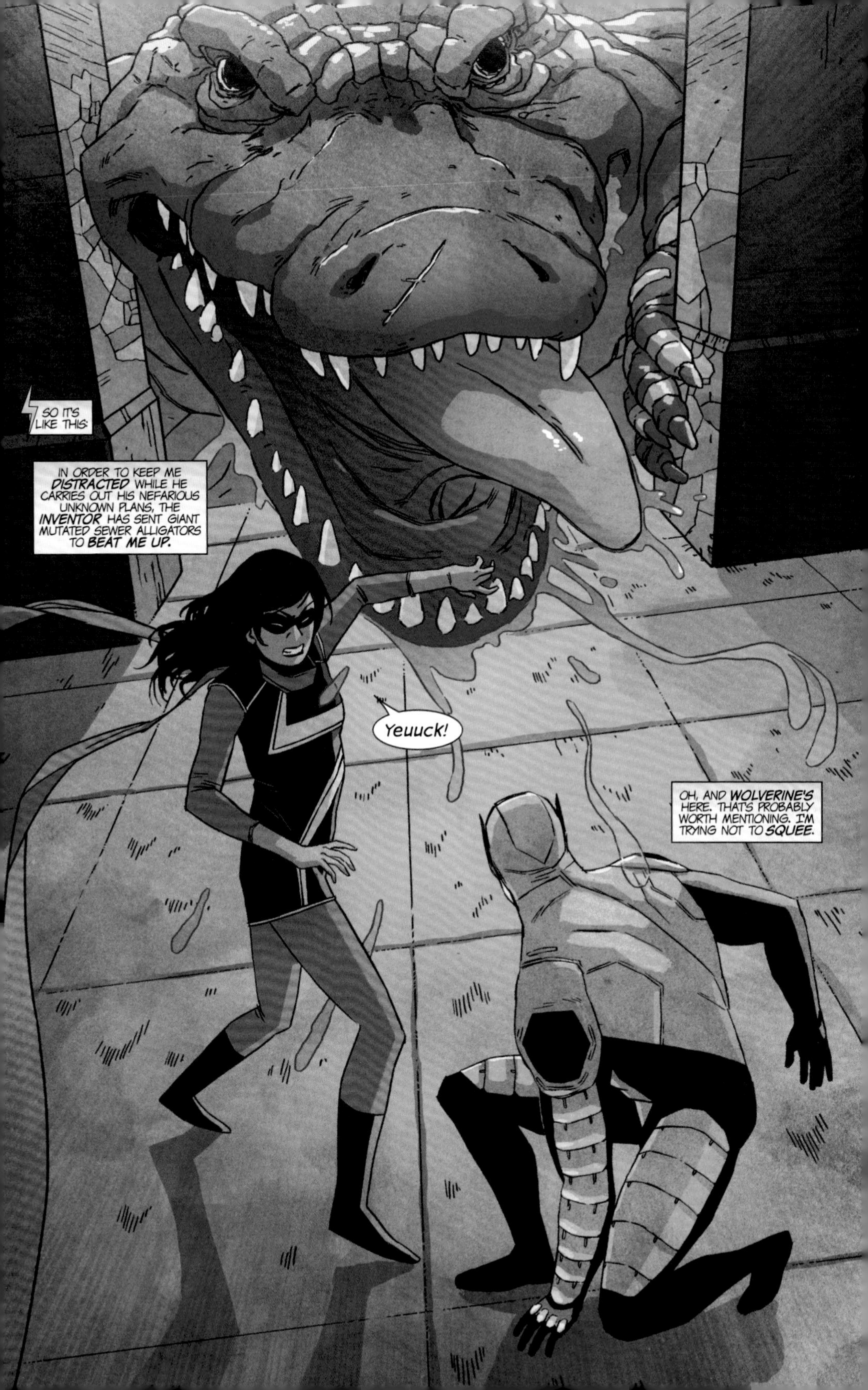
SO IT'S LIKE THIS:
IN ORDER TO KEEP ME DISTRACTED WHILE HE CARRIES OUT HIS NEFARIOUS UNKNOWN PLANS, THE INVENTOR HAS SENT GIANT MUTATED SEWER ALLIGATORS TO BEAT ME UP.
Yeuuck!
OH, AND WOLVERINE'S HERE. THAT'S PROBABLY WORTH MENTIONING. I'M TRYING NOT TO SQUEE.

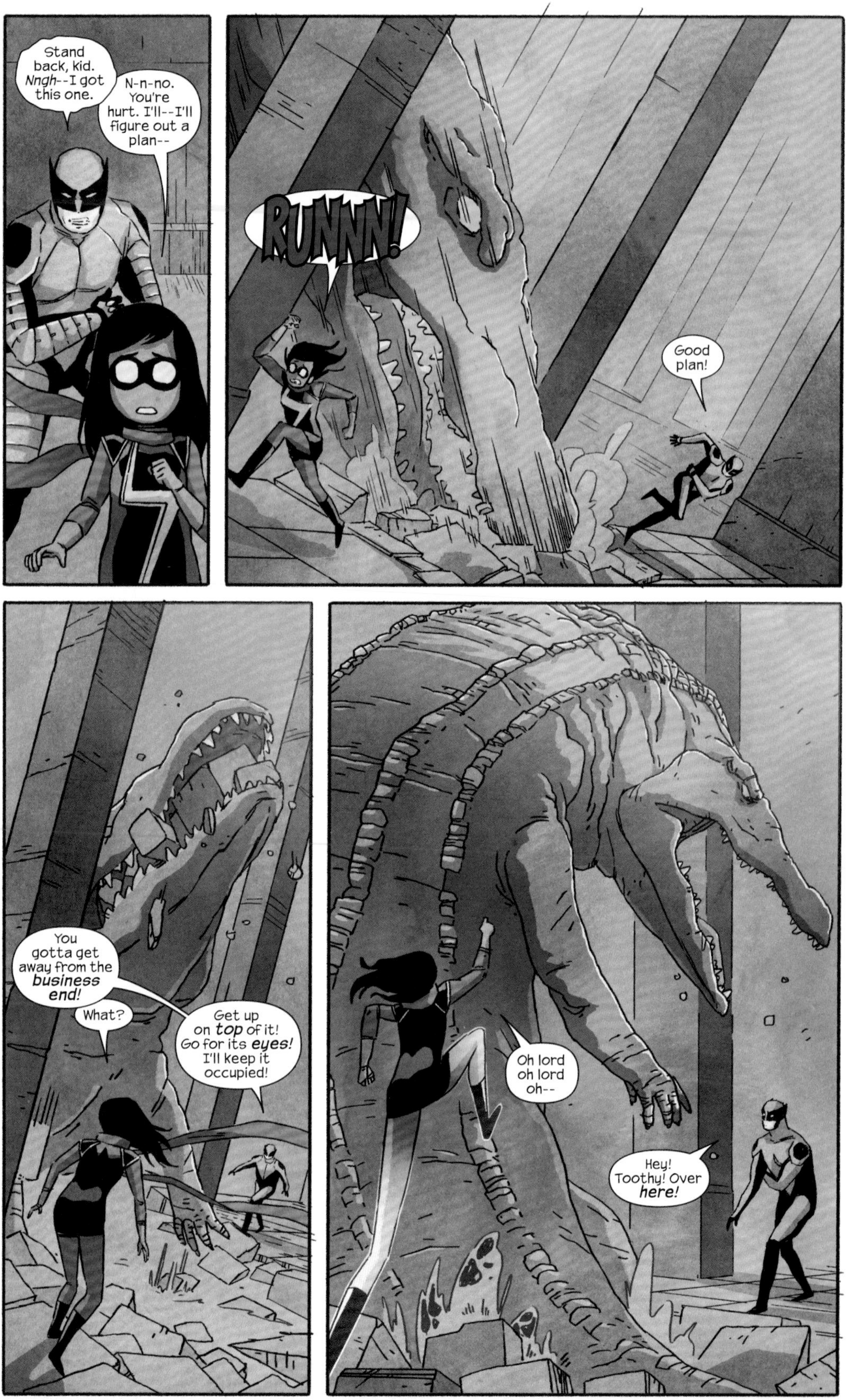

Stand back, kid. *Nngh*--I got this one.
N-n-no. You're hurt. I'll--I'll figure out a plan--
RUNNN!
Good plan!
You gotta get away from the *business end!*
What?
Get up on *top* of it! Go for its *eyes!* I'll keep it occupied!
Oh lord oh lord oh--
Hey! Toothy! Over *here!*

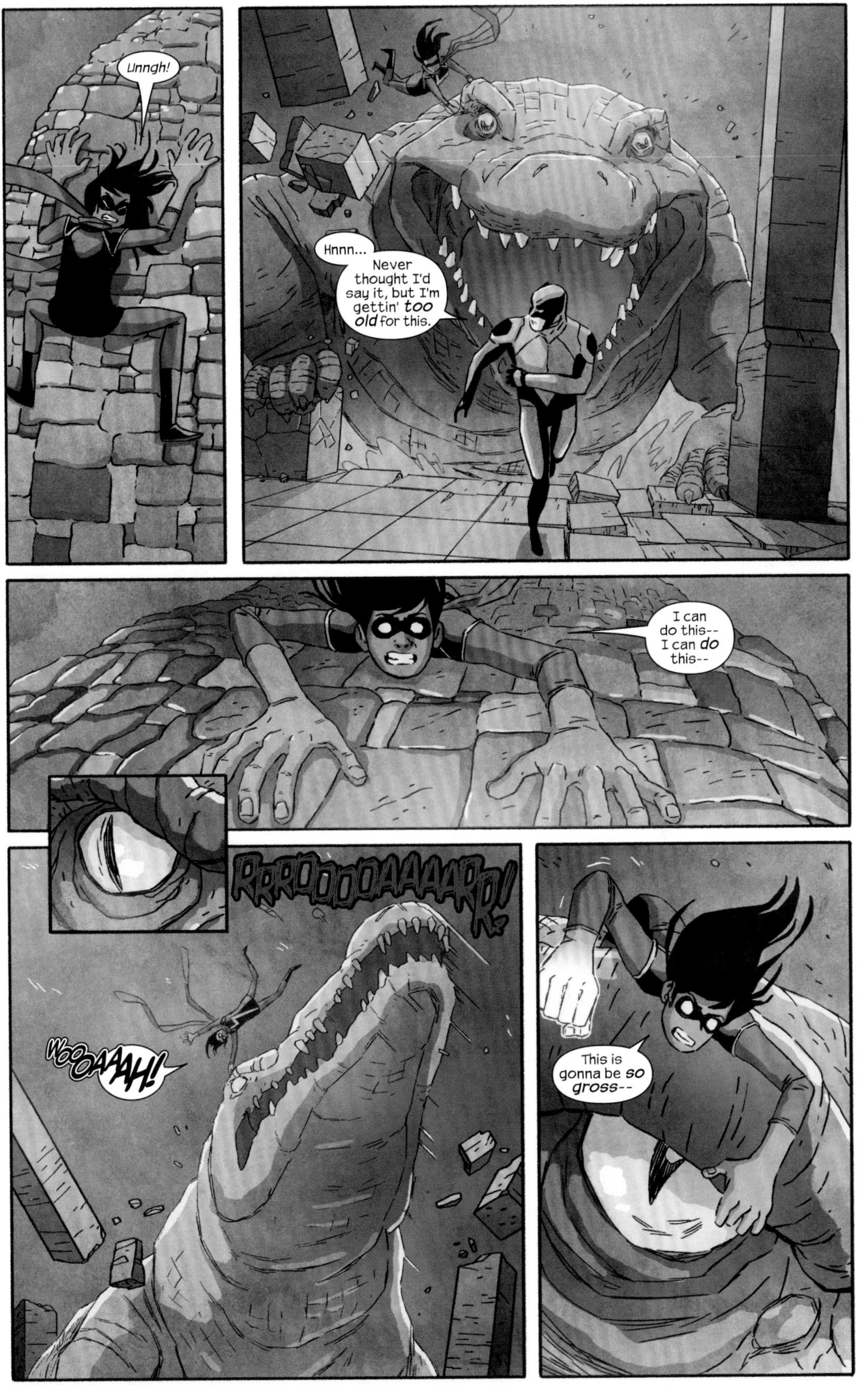
Unngh!
Hnnn...
Never thought I'd say it, but I'm gettin' too old for this.
I can do this-- I can do this--
RRROOOOAAAARR!
WOOOAAAH!
This is gonna be so gross--

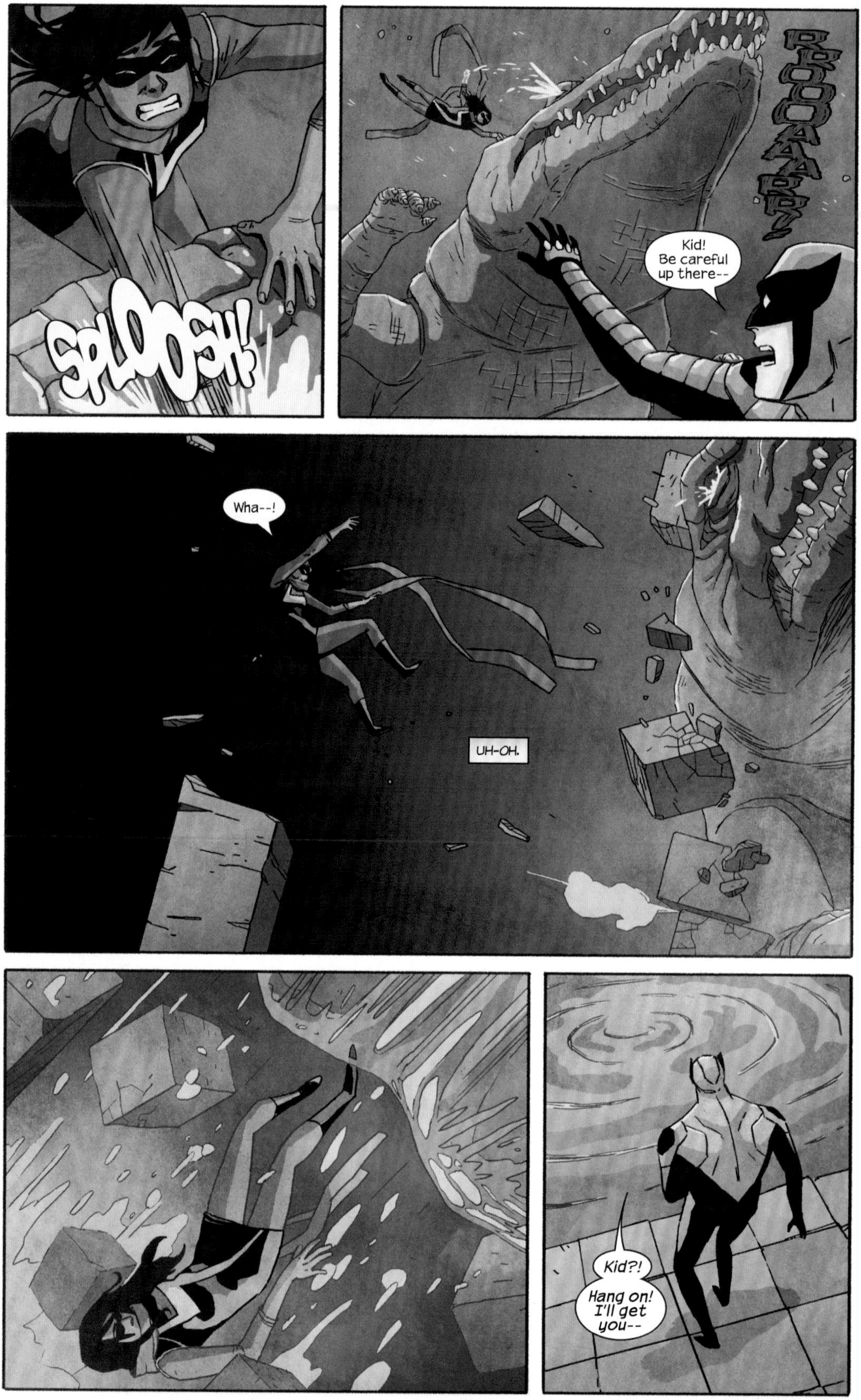
SPLOOSH!
RROOOAAARR!
Kid! Be careful up there--
Wha--!
UH-OH.
Kid?!
Hang on! I'll get you--

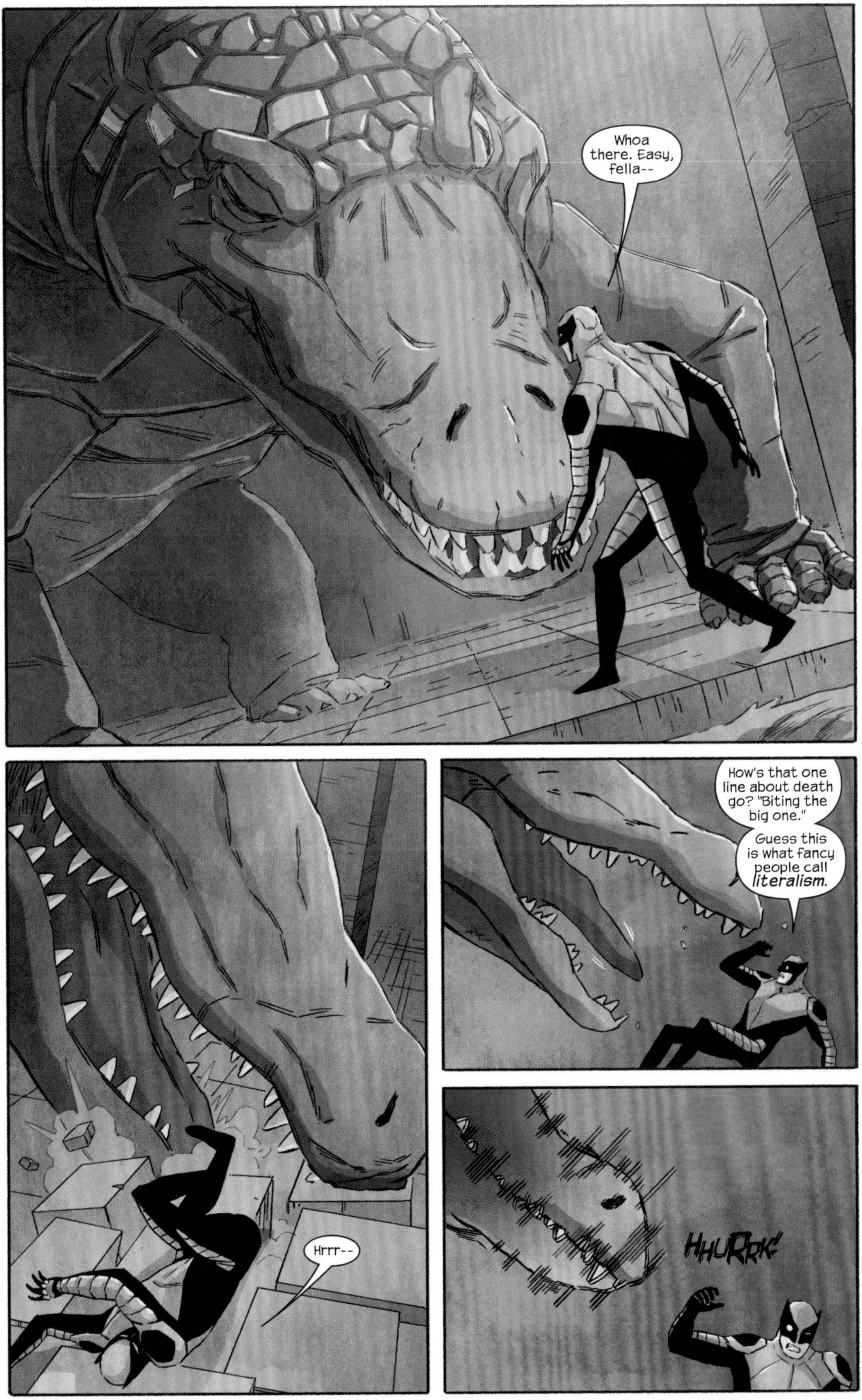
Whoa there. Easy, fella--
Hrrr--
How's that one line about death go? "Biting the big one."
Guess this is what fancy people call *literalism*.
HHURRK!

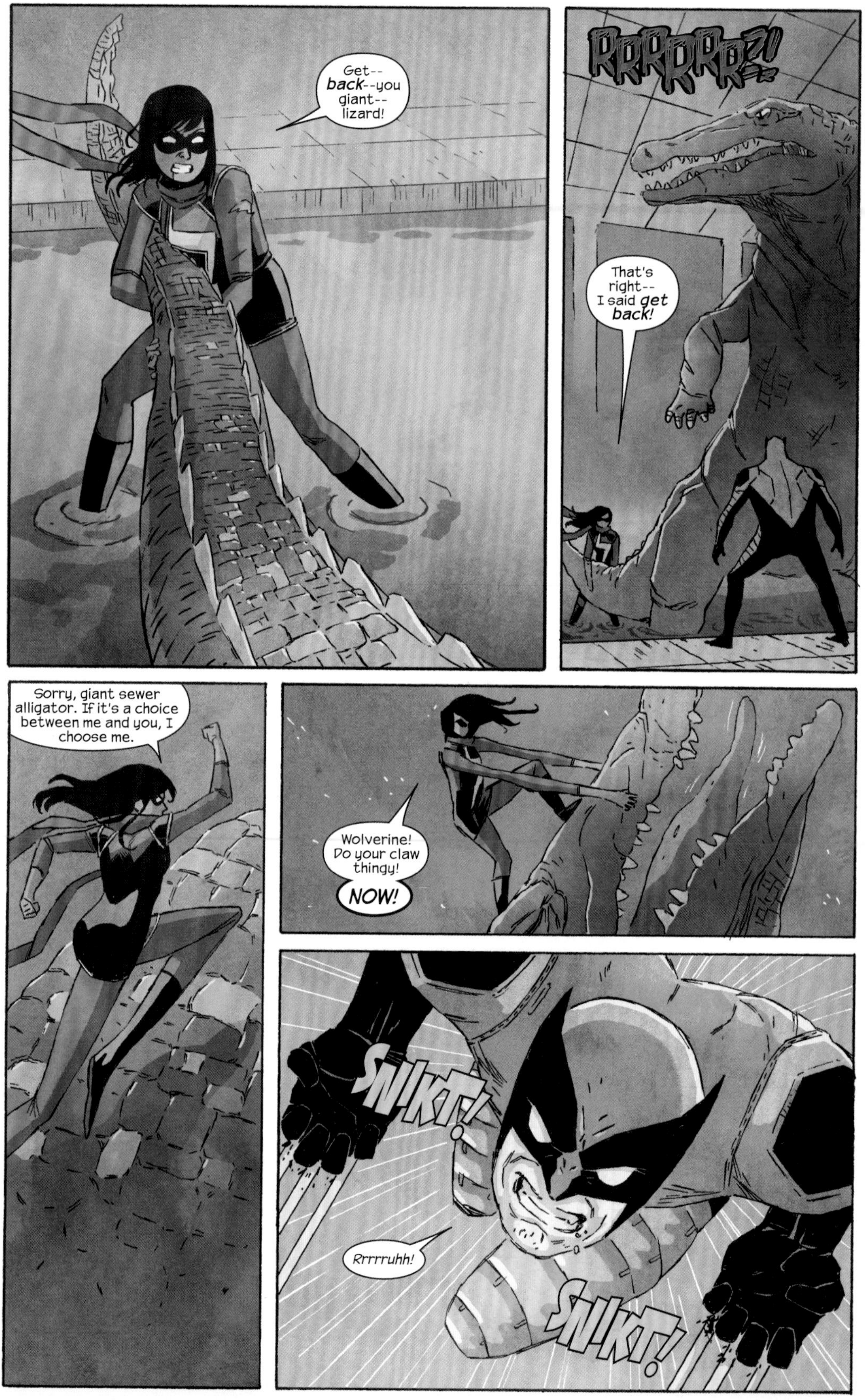
Get--
back--you
giant--
lizard!
RRRRRRRZ!!
That's
right--
I said get
back!
Sorry, giant sewer alligator. If it's a choice between me and you, I choose me.
Wolverine!
Do your claw
thingy!
NOW!
SNIKT!
Rrrrruhh!
SNIKT!

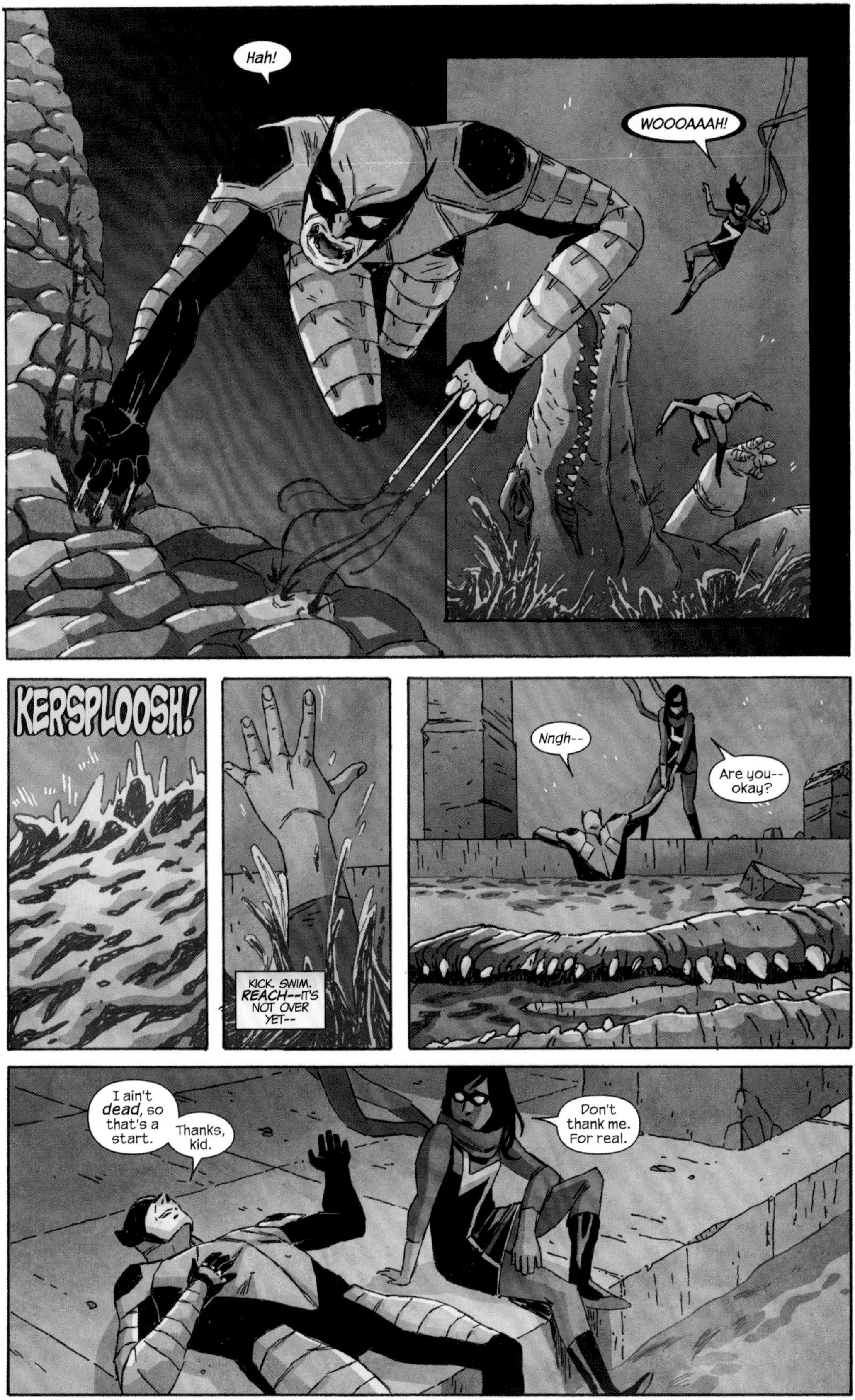
Hah!
WOOOAAAH!
KERSPLOOSH!
KICK. SWIM. REACH--IT'S NOT OVER YET--
Nngh--
Are you-- okay?
I ain't dead, so that's a start.
Thanks, kid.
Don't thank me. For real.

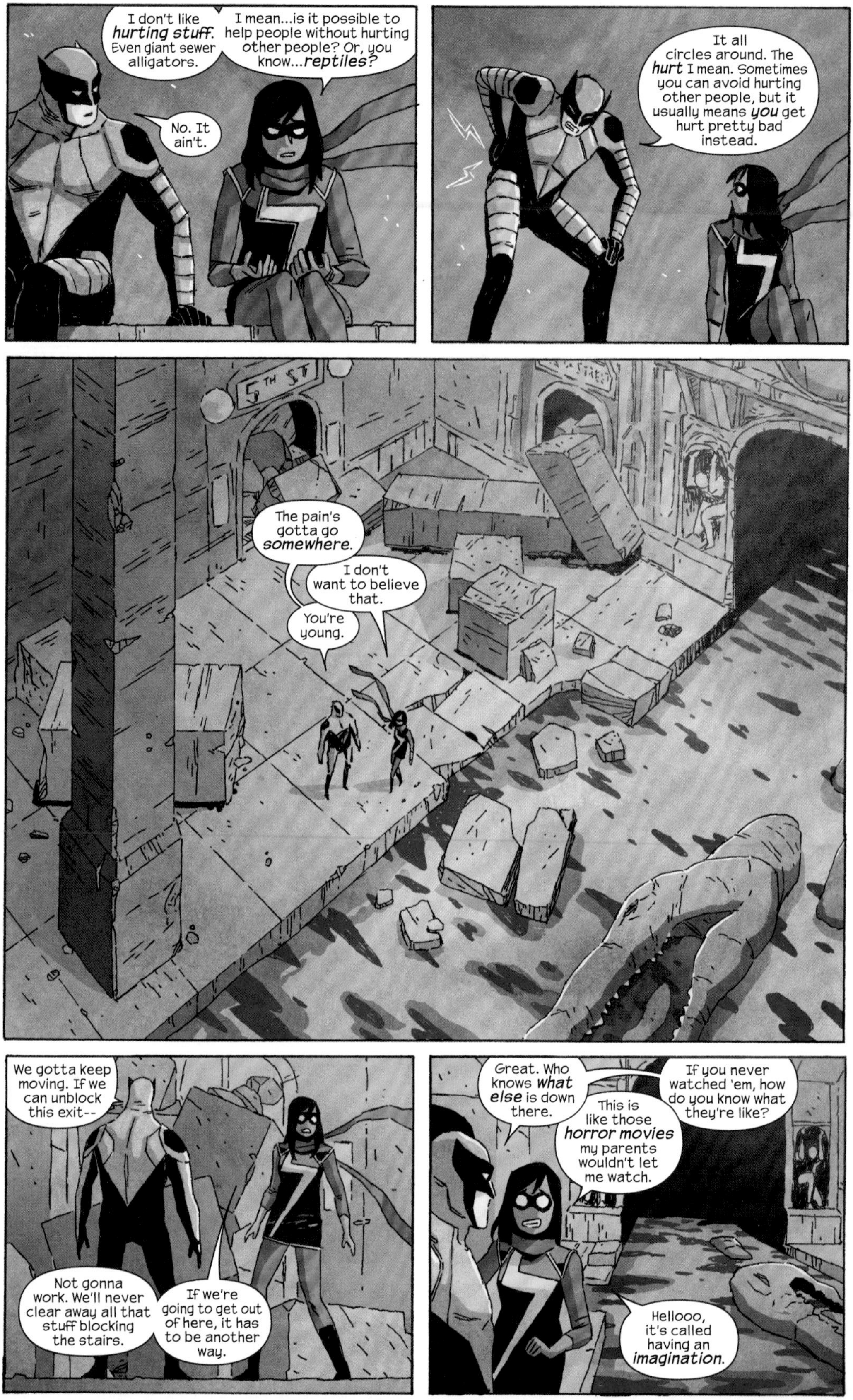
I don't like *hurting stuff*. Even giant sewer alligators.
I mean...is it possible to help people without hurting other people? Or, you know...*reptiles?*
No. It ain't.
It all circles around. The *hurt* I mean. Sometimes you can avoid hurting other people, but it usually means *you* get hurt pretty bad instead.
5TH ST
The pain's gotta go *somewhere*.
I don't want to believe that.
You're young.
We gotta keep moving. If we can unblock this exit--
Not gonna work. We'll never clear away all that stuff blocking the stairs.
If we're going to get out of here, it has to be another way.
Great. Who knows *what else* is down there.
This is like those *horror movies* my parents wouldn't let me watch.
If you never watched 'em, how do you know what they're like?
Hellooo, it's called having an *imagination*.

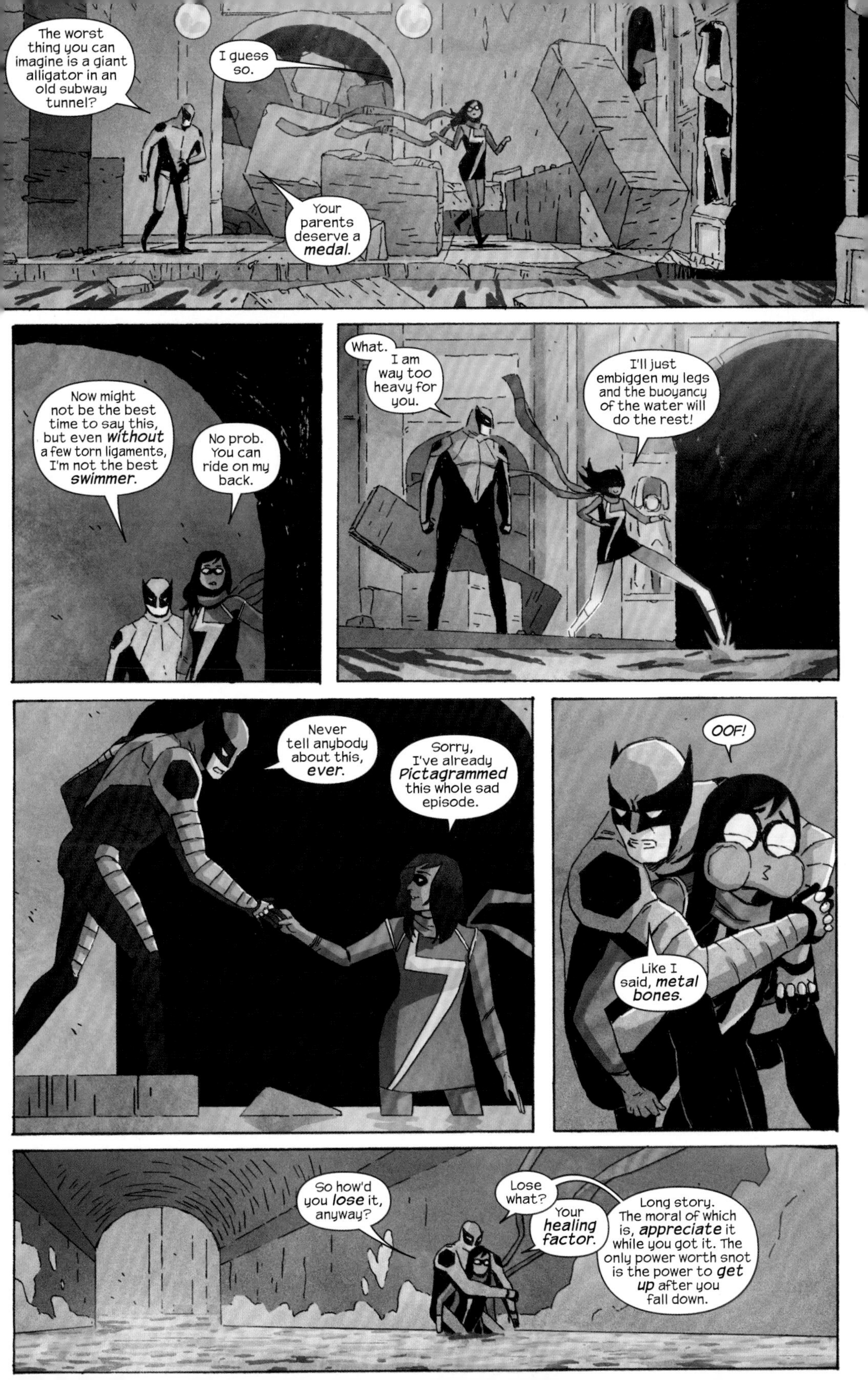
The worst thing you can imagine is a giant alligator in an old subway tunnel?
I guess so.
Your parents deserve a *medal*.
Now might not be the best time to say this, but even *without* a few torn ligaments, I'm not the best *swimmer*.
No prob. You can ride on my back.
What. I am way too heavy for you.
I'll just embiggen my legs and the buoyancy of the water will do the rest!
Never tell anybody about this, *ever*.
Sorry, I've already *Pictagrammed* this whole sad episode.
OOF!
Like I said, *metal bones*.
So how'd you *lose* it, anyway?
Lose what?
Your *healing factor*.
Long story. The moral of which is, *appreciate* it while you got it. The only power worth snot is the power to *get up* after you fall down.

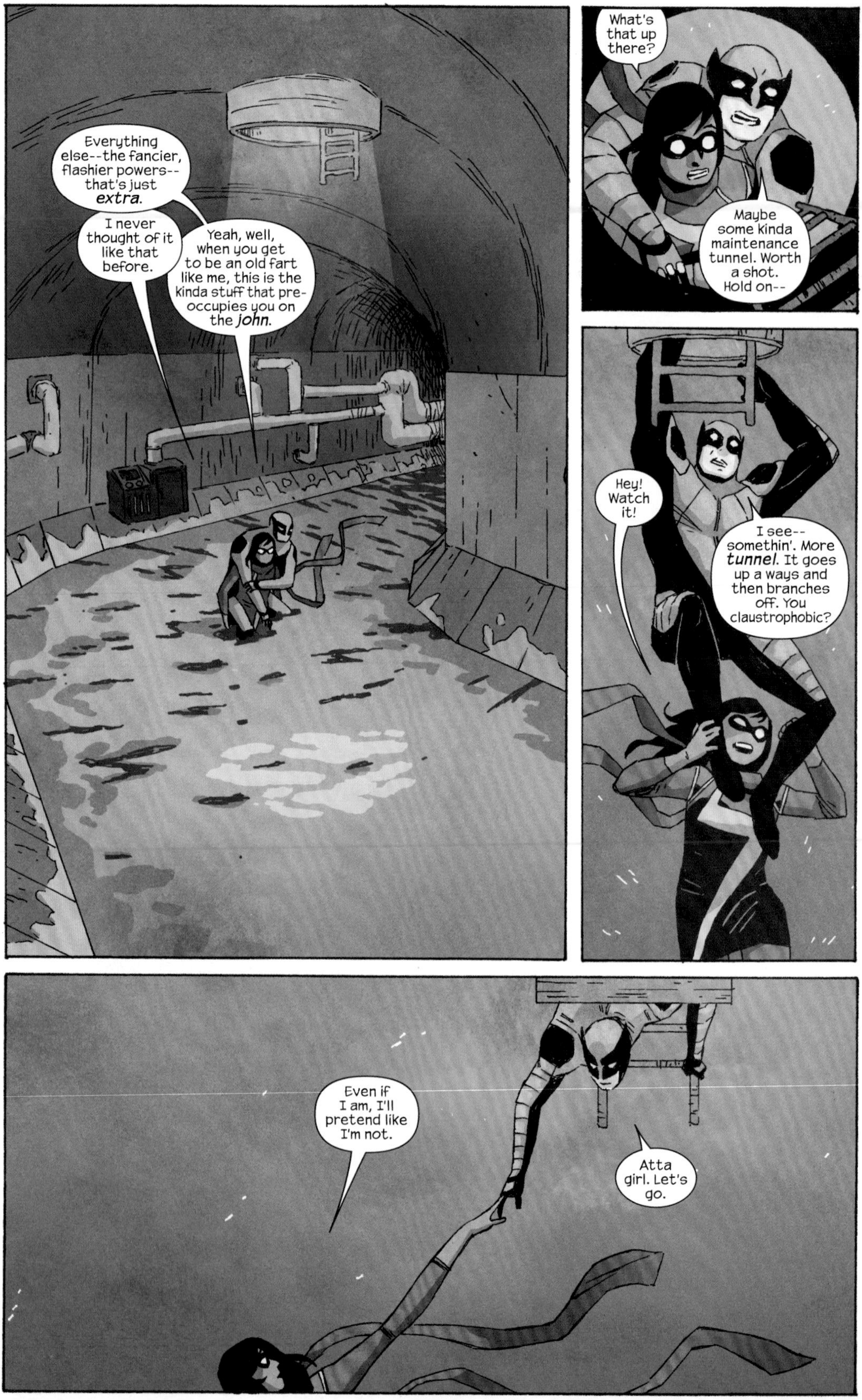
Everything else--the fancier, flashier powers--that's just *extra*.
I never thought of it like that before.
Yeah, well, when you get to be an old fart like me, this is the kinda stuff that pre-occupies you on the *john*.
What's that up there?
Maybe some kinda maintenance tunnel. Worth a shot. Hold on--
Hey! Watch it!
I see--somethin'. More *tunnel*. It goes up a ways and then branches off. You claustrophobic?
Even if I am, I'll pretend like I'm not.
Atta girl. Let's go.

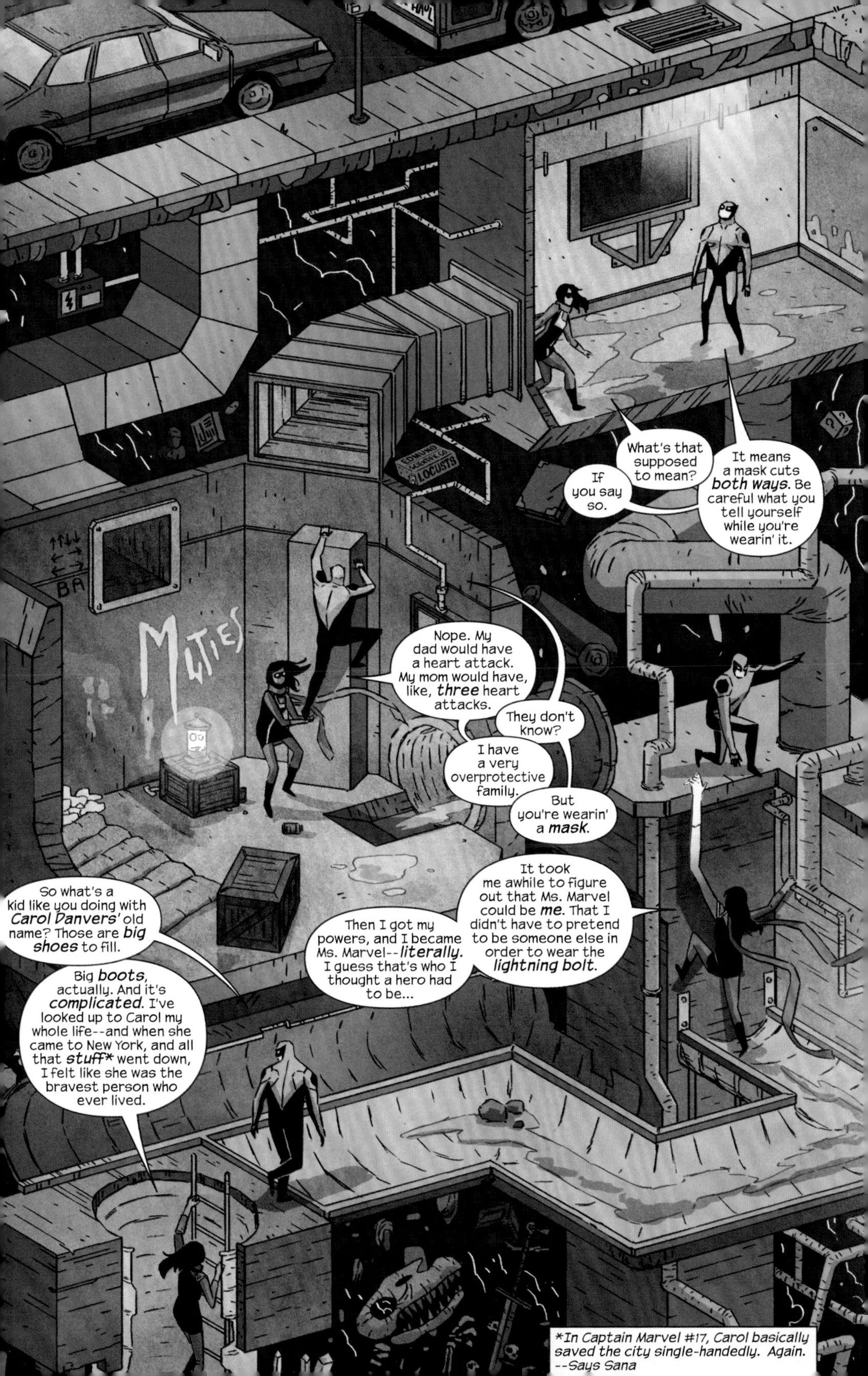

So what's a kid like you doing with *Carol Danvers'* old name? Those are *big shoes* to fill.
Big *boots*, actually. And it's *complicated*. I've looked up to Carol my whole life--and when she came to New York, and all that *stuff** went down, I felt like she was the bravest person who ever lived.
Then I got my powers, and I became Ms. Marvel--*literally*. I guess that's who I thought a hero had to be...
It took me awhile to figure out that Ms. Marvel could be *me*. That I didn't have to pretend to be someone else in order to wear the *lightning bolt*.
Nope. My dad would have a heart attack. My mom would have, like, *three* heart attacks.
They don't know?
I have a very overprotective family.
But you're wearin' a *mask*.
What's that supposed to mean?
It means a mask cuts *both ways*. Be careful what you tell yourself while you're wearin' it.
If you say so.
MUTIES
LOCUSTS
*In Captain Marvel #17, Carol basically saved the city single-handedly. Again. --Says Sana

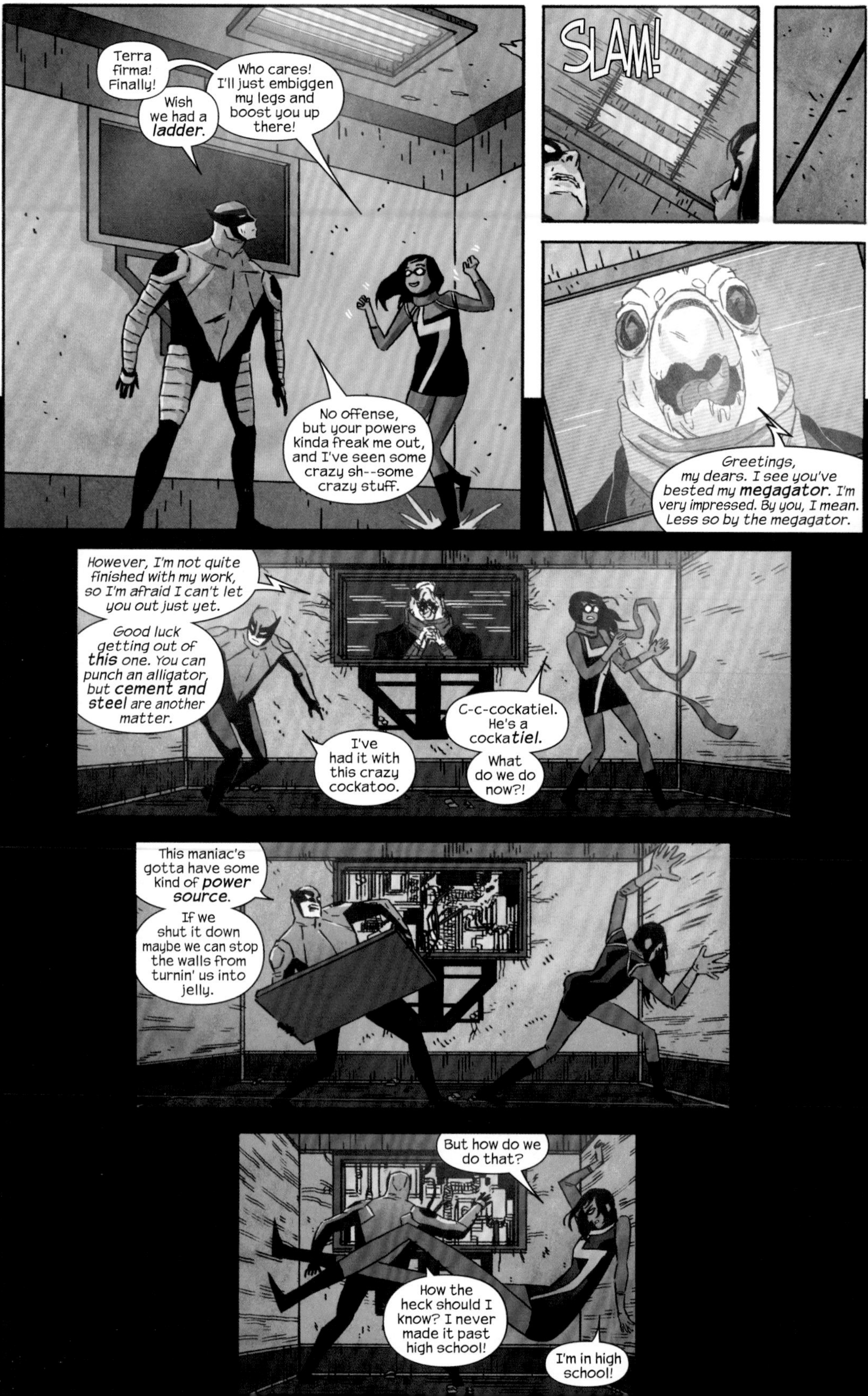
Terra firma! Finally!
Wish we had a *ladder*.
Who cares! I'll just embiggen my legs and boost you up there!
No offense, but your powers kinda freak me out, and I've seen some crazy sh--some crazy stuff.
SLAM!
Greetings, my dears. I see you've bested my **megagator**. *I'm very impressed. By you, I mean. Less so by the megagator.*
However, I'm not quite finished with my work, so I'm afraid I can't let you out just yet.
Good luck getting out of **this** *one. You can punch an alligator, but* **cement and steel** *are another matter.*
I've had it with this crazy cockatoo.
C-c-cockatiel. He's a cocka***tiel***.
What do we do now?!
This maniac's gotta have some kind of ***power source***.
If we shut it down maybe we can stop the walls from turnin' us into jelly.
But how do we do that?
How the heck should I know? I never made it past high school!
I'm in high school!

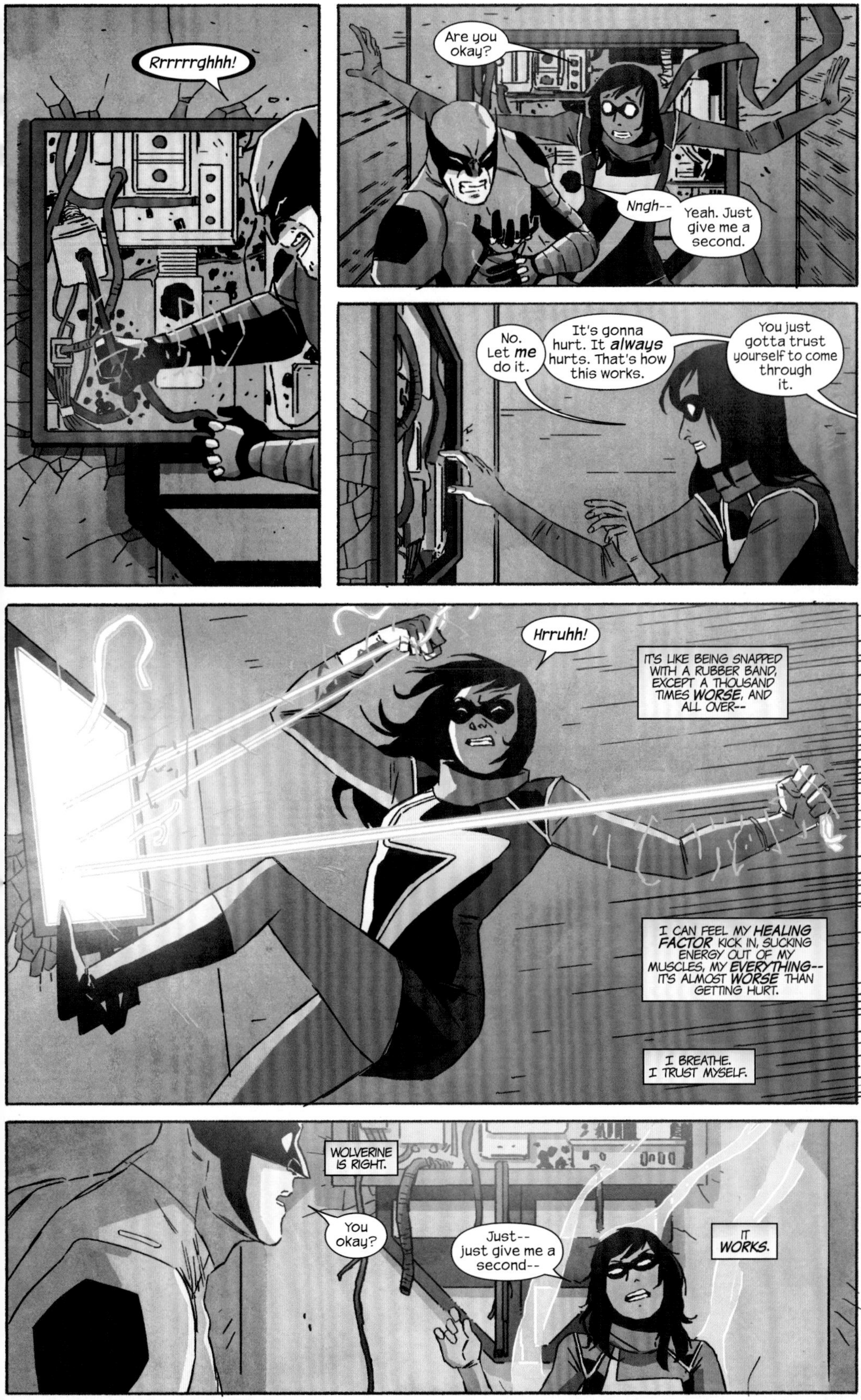
Rrrrrrghhh!
Are you okay?
Nngh--
Yeah. Just give me a second.
No. Let *me* do it.
It's gonna hurt. It *always* hurts. That's how this works.
You just gotta trust yourself to come through it.
Hrruhh!
IT'S LIKE BEING SNAPPED WITH A RUBBER BAND, EXCEPT A THOUSAND TIMES *WORSE*, AND ALL OVER--
I CAN FEEL MY *HEALING FACTOR* KICK IN, SUCKING ENERGY OUT OF MY MUSCLES, MY *EVERYTHING*-- IT'S ALMOST *WORSE* THAN GETTING HURT.
I BREATHE. I TRUST MYSELF.
WOLVERINE IS RIGHT.
You okay?
Just-- just give me a second--
IT *WORKS*.

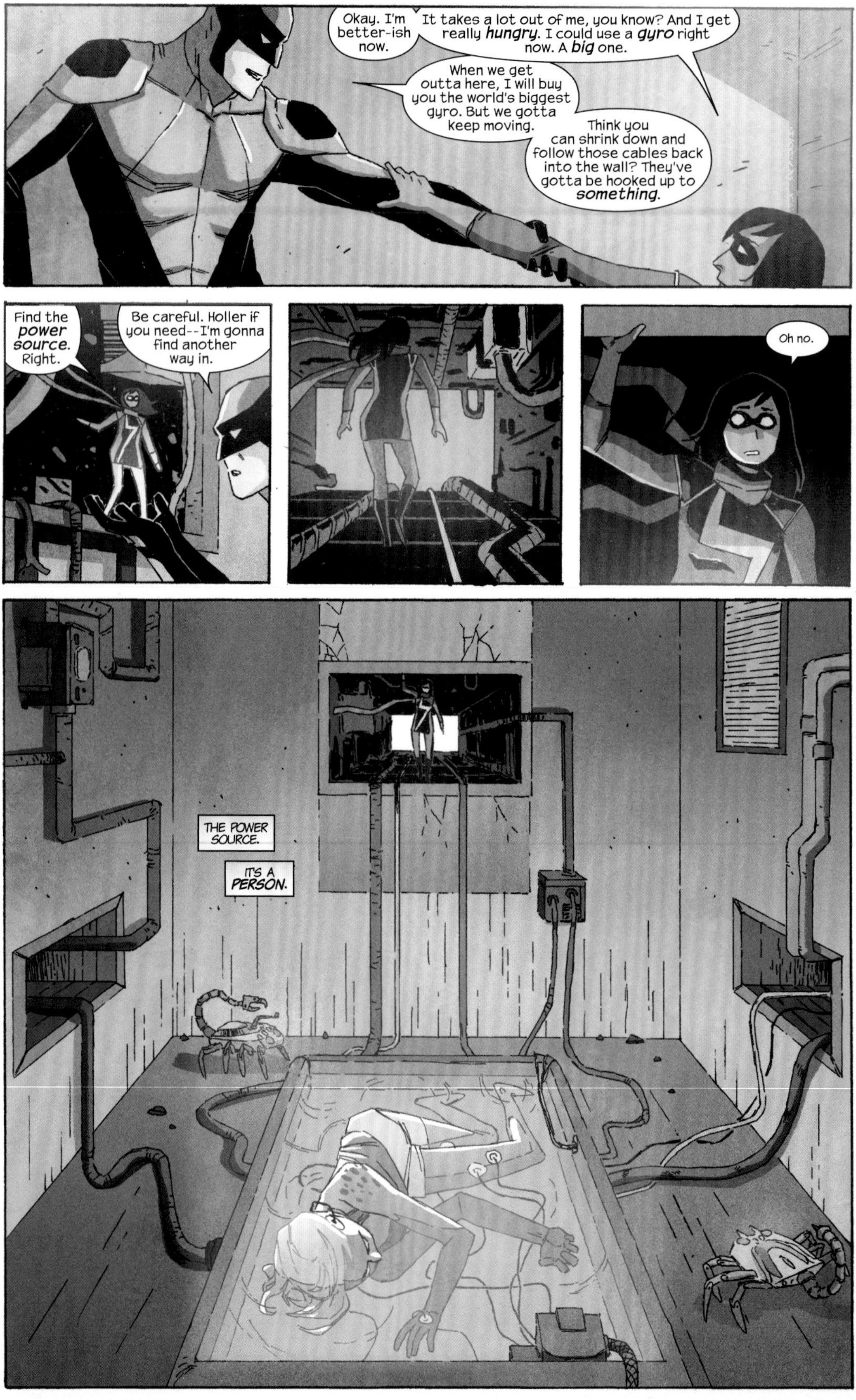
Okay. I'm better-ish now.
It takes a lot out of me, you know? And I get really *hungry*. I could use a *gyro* right now. A *big* one.
When we get outta here, I will buy you the world's biggest gyro. But we gotta keep moving.
Think you can shrink down and follow those cables back into the wall? They've gotta be hooked up to *something*.
Find the *power source*. Right.
Be careful. Holler if you need--I'm gonna find another way in.
Oh no.
THE POWER SOURCE.
IT'S A *PERSON*.

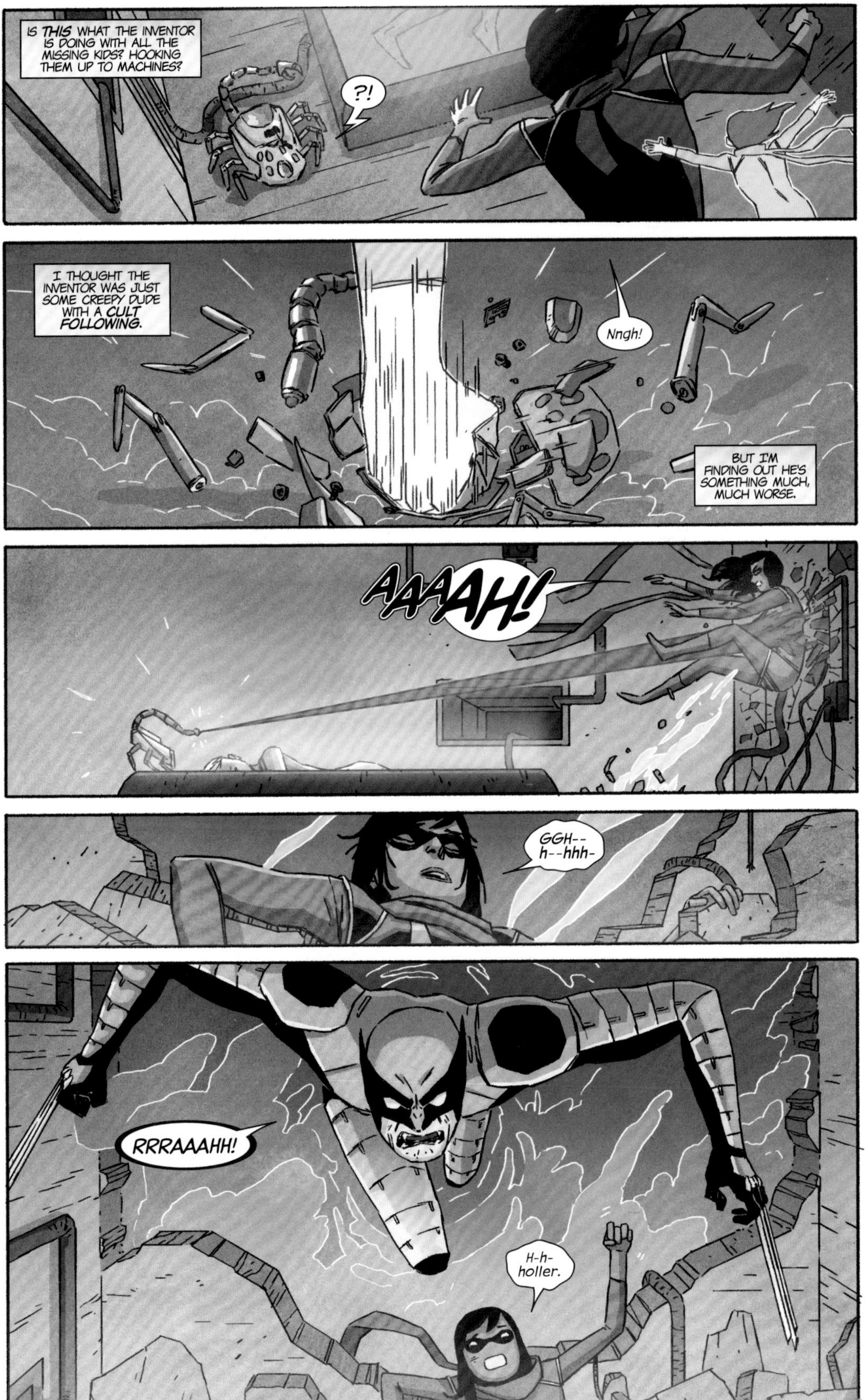
IS THIS WHAT THE INVENTOR IS DOING WITH ALL THE MISSING KIDS? HOOKING THEM UP TO MACHINES?
?!
I THOUGHT THE INVENTOR WAS JUST SOME CREEPY DUDE WITH A CULT FOLLOWING.
Nngh!
BUT I'M FINDING OUT HE'S SOMETHING MUCH, MUCH WORSE.
AAAAH!
GGH-- h--hhh-
RRRAAAHH!
H-h- holler.

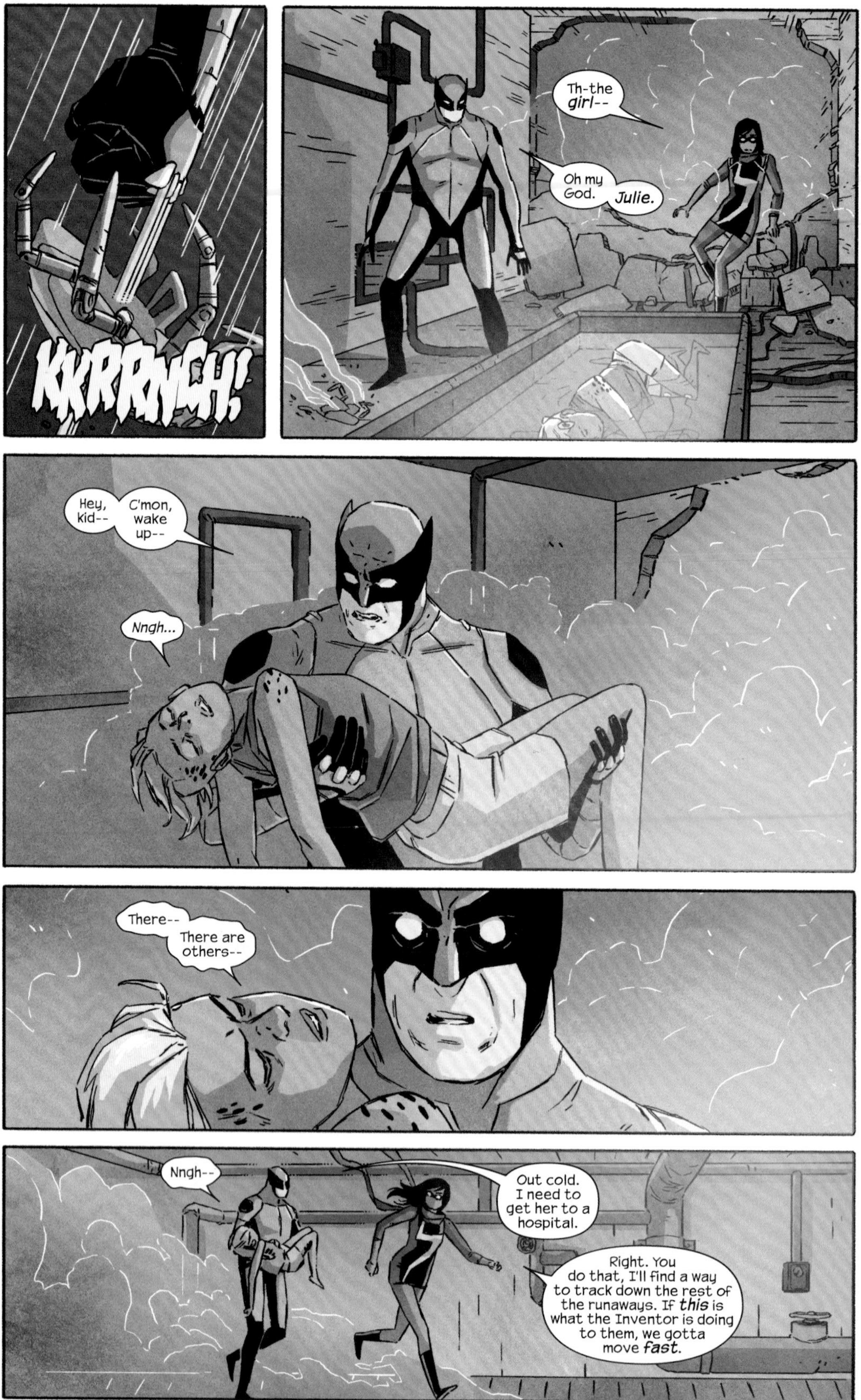
KKRRNCH!
Th-the girl--
Oh my God.
Julie.
Hey, kid--
C'mon, wake up--
Nngh...
There--
There are others--
Nngh--
Out cold. I need to get her to a hospital.
Right. You do that, I'll find a way to track down the rest of the runaways. If this is what the Inventor is doing to them, we gotta move fast.

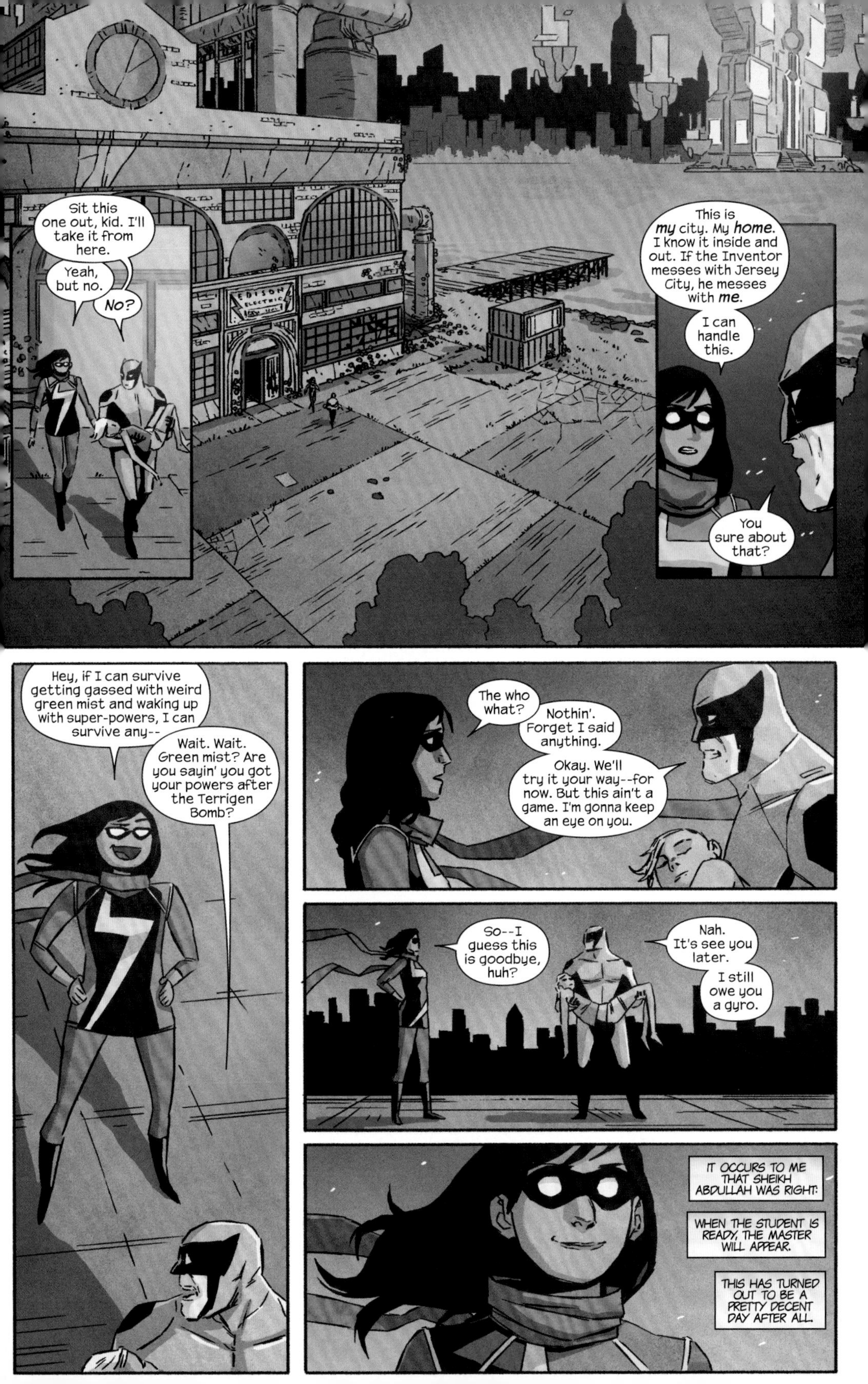

Sit this one out, kid. I'll take it from here.
Yeah, but no.
No?
This is my city. My home. I know it inside and out. If the Inventor messes with Jersey City, he messes with me.
I can handle this.
You sure about that?
EDISON ELECTRIC
Hey, if I can survive getting gassed with weird green mist and waking up with super-powers, I can survive any--
Wait. Wait. Green mist? Are you sayin' you got your powers after the Terrigen Bomb?
The who what?
Nothin'. Forget I said anything.
Okay. We'll try it your way--for now. But this ain't a game. I'm gonna keep an eye on you.
So--I guess this is goodbye, huh?
Nah. It's see you later.
I still owe you a gyro.
IT OCCURS TO ME THAT SHEIKH ABDULLAH WAS RIGHT:
WHEN THE STUDENT IS READY, THE MASTER WILL APPEAR.
THIS HAS TURNED OUT TO BE A PRETTY DECENT DAY AFTER ALL.

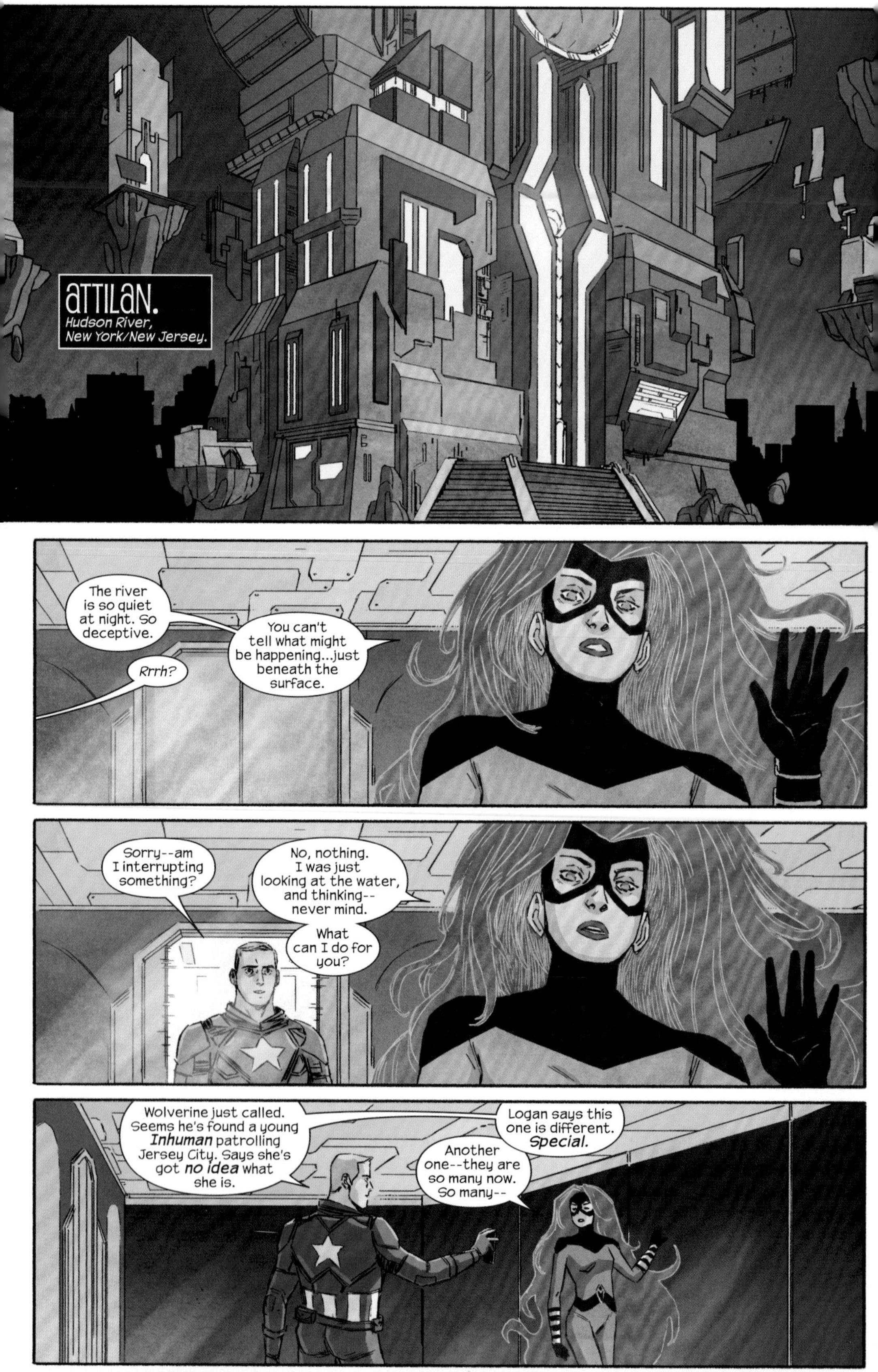
Attilan.
Hudson River, New York/New Jersey.
The river is so quiet at night. So deceptive.
You can't tell what might be happening...just beneath the surface.
Rrrh?
Sorry--am I interrupting something?
No, nothing. I was just looking at the water, and thinking-- never mind.
What can I do for you?
Wolverine just called. Seems he's found a young Inhuman patrolling Jersey City. Says she's got no idea what she is.
Logan says this one is different. Special.
Another one--they are so many now. So many--

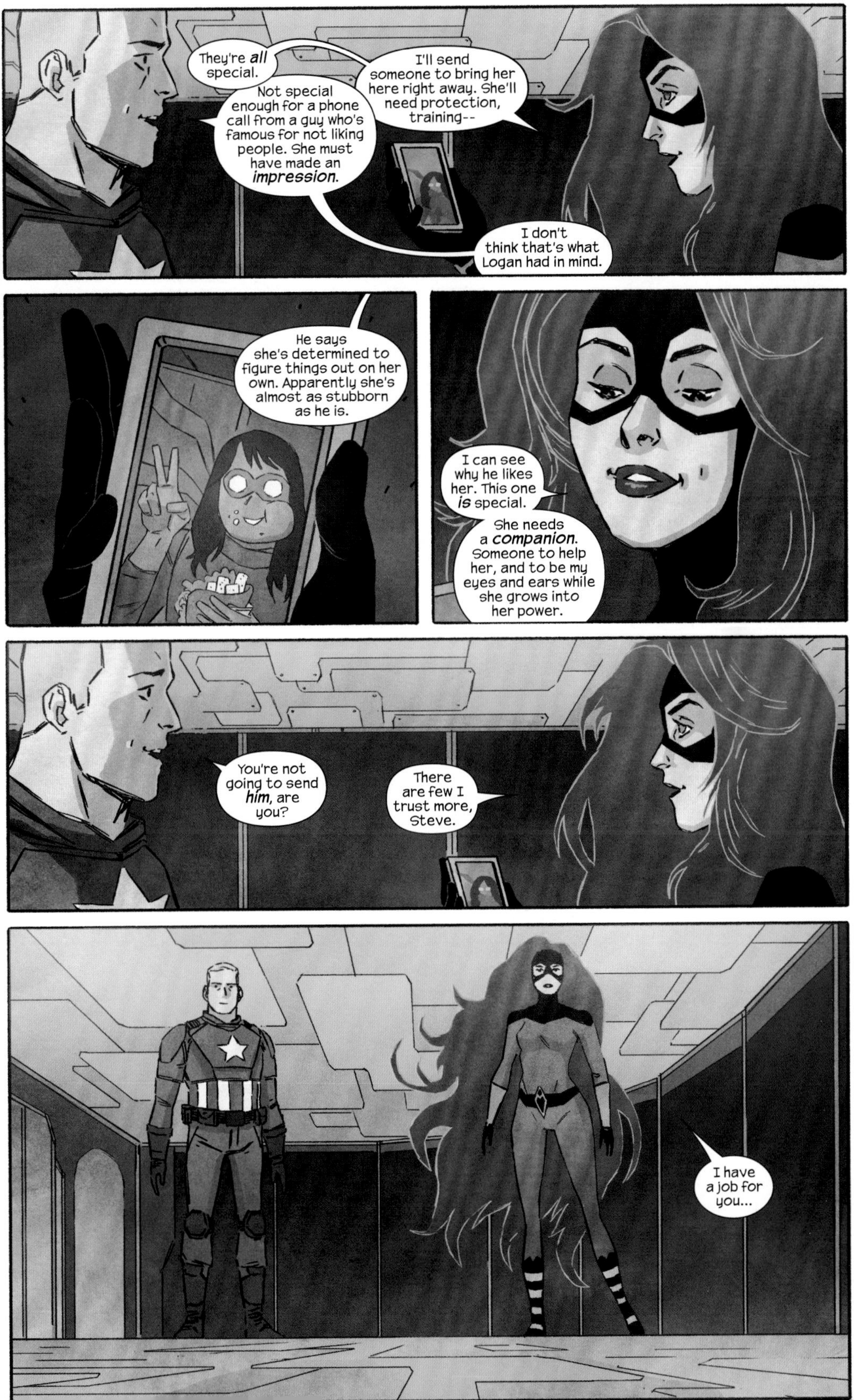
They're *all* special.
Not special enough for a phone call from a guy who's famous for not liking people. She must have made an *impression*.
I'll send someone to bring her here right away. She'll need protection, training--
I don't think that's what Logan had in mind.
He says she's determined to figure things out on her own. Apparently she's almost as stubborn as he is.
I can see why he likes her. This one *is* special.
She needs a **companion**. Someone to help her, and to be my eyes and ears while she grows into her power.
You're not going to send *him*, are you?
There are few I trust more, Steve.
I have a job for you...

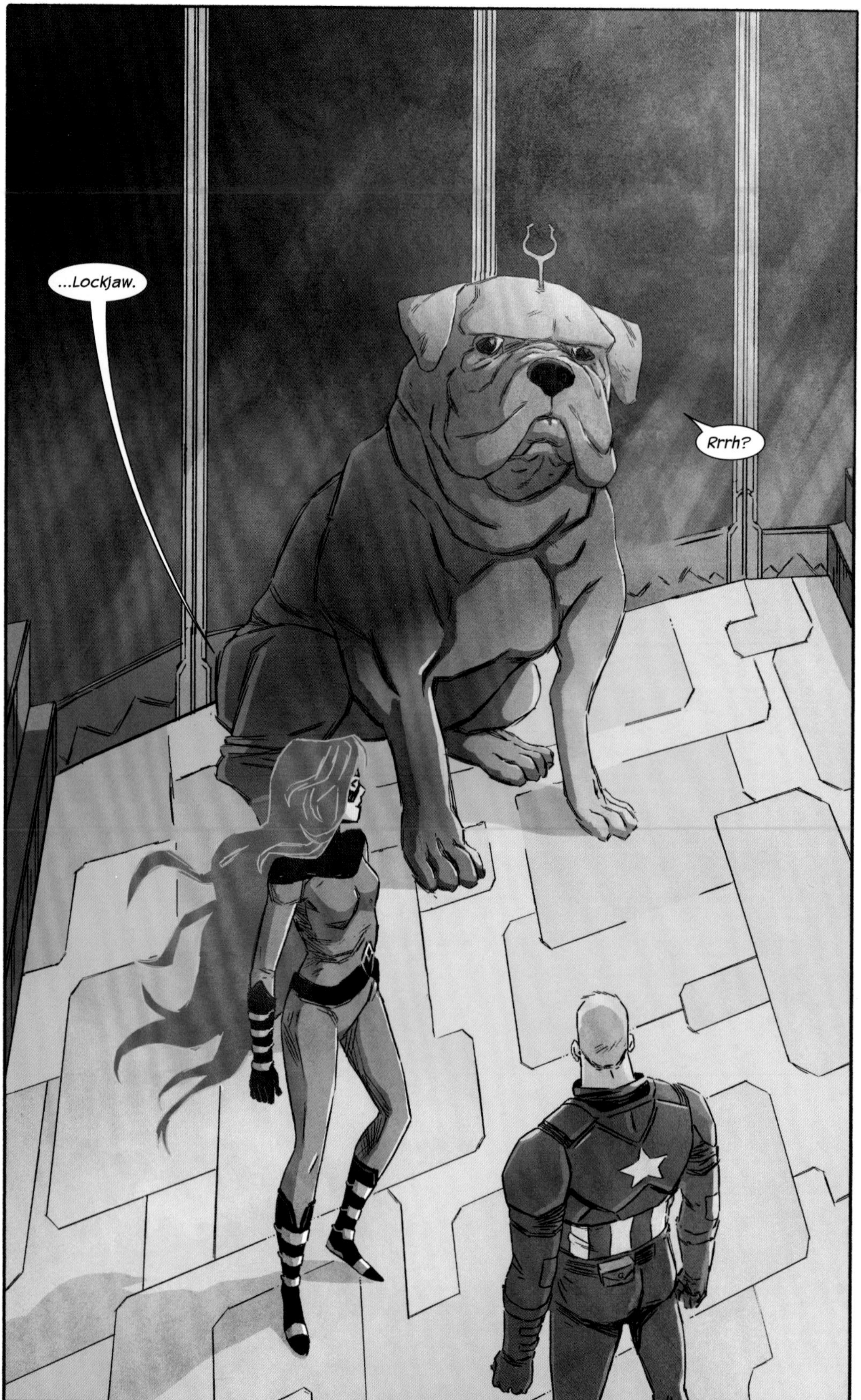
...Lockjaw.
Rrrh?

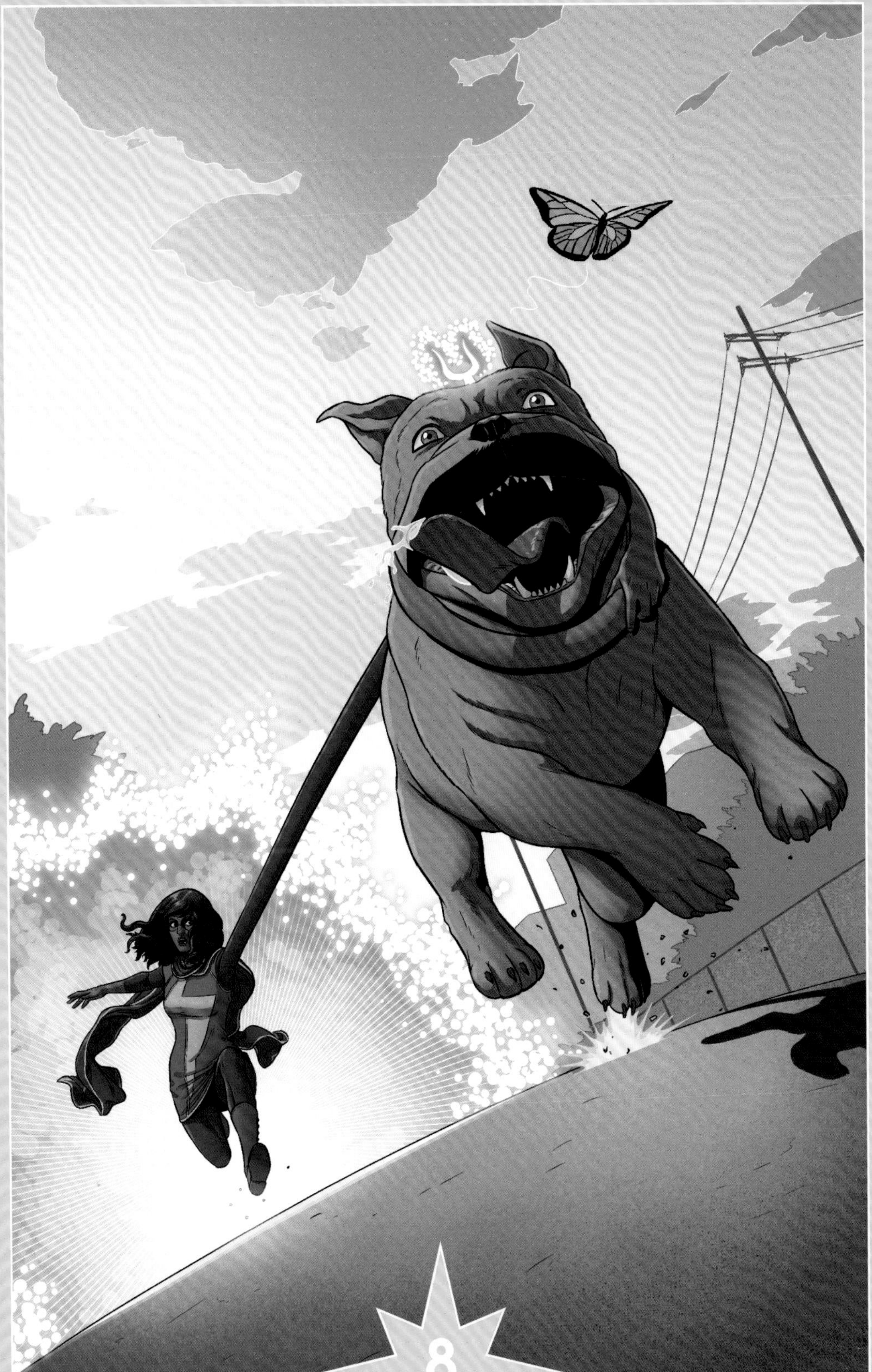
8

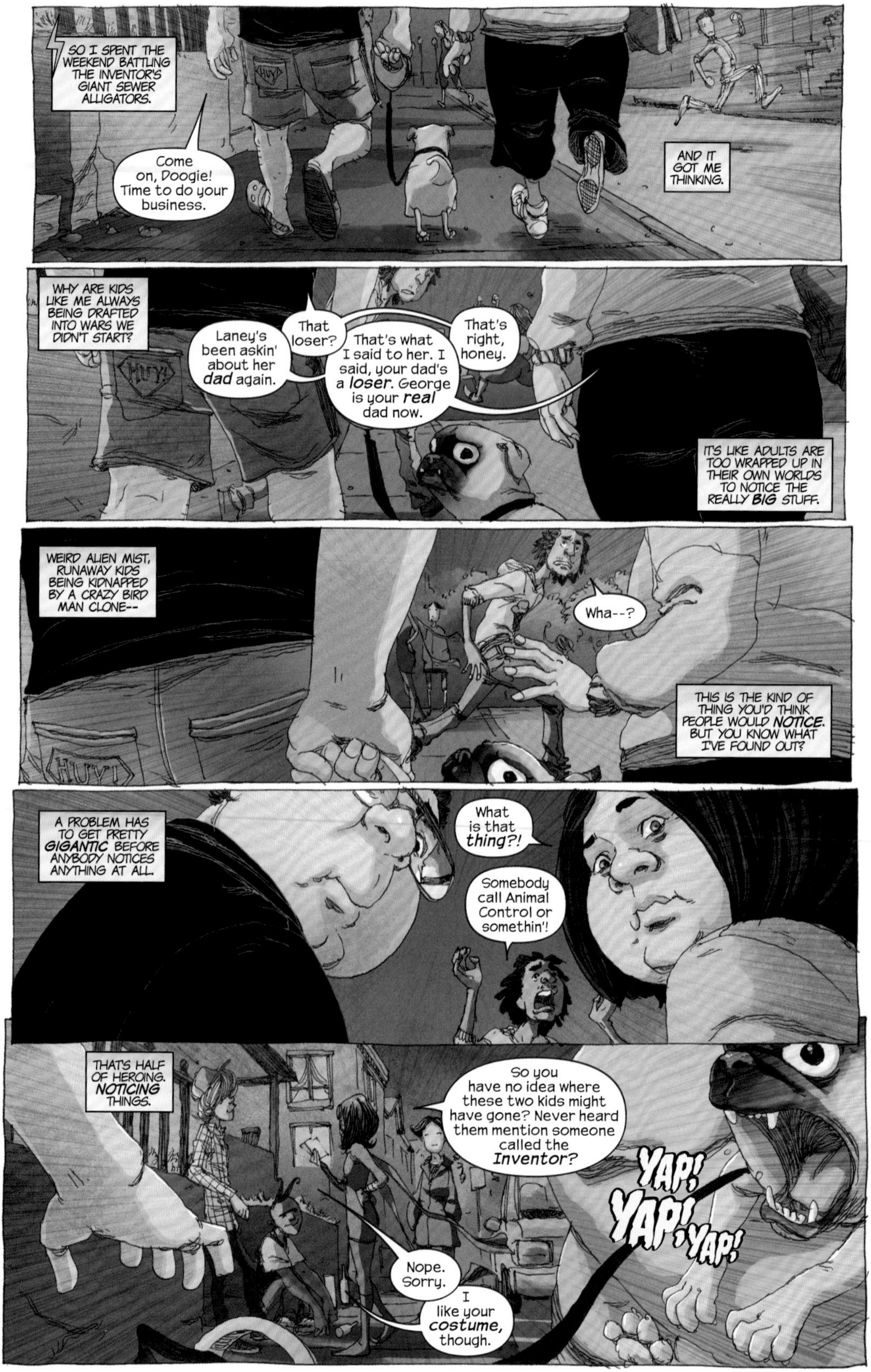

SO I SPENT THE WEEKEND BATTLING THE INVENTOR'S GIANT SEWER ALLIGATORS.
Come on, Doogie! Time to do your business.
AND IT GOT ME THINKING.
WHY ARE KIDS LIKE ME ALWAYS BEING DRAFTED INTO WARS WE DIDN'T START?
Laney's been askin' about her dad again.
That loser?
That's what I said to her. I said, your dad's a loser. George is your real dad now.
That's right, honey.
IT'S LIKE ADULTS ARE TOO WRAPPED UP IN THEIR OWN WORLDS TO NOTICE THE REALLY BIG STUFF.
WEIRD ALIEN MIST, RUNAWAY KIDS BEING KIDNAPPED BY A CRAZY BIRD MAN CLONE--
Wha--?
THIS IS THE KIND OF THING YOU'D THINK PEOPLE WOULD NOTICE. BUT YOU KNOW WHAT I'VE FOUND OUT?
A PROBLEM HAS TO GET PRETTY GIGANTIC BEFORE ANYBODY NOTICES ANYTHING AT ALL.
What is that thing?!
Somebody call Animal Control or somethin'!
THAT'S HALF OF HEROING. NOTICING THINGS.
So you have no idea where these two kids might have gone? Never heard them mention someone called the Inventor?
YAP! YAP! YAP!
Nope. Sorry.
I like your costume, though.

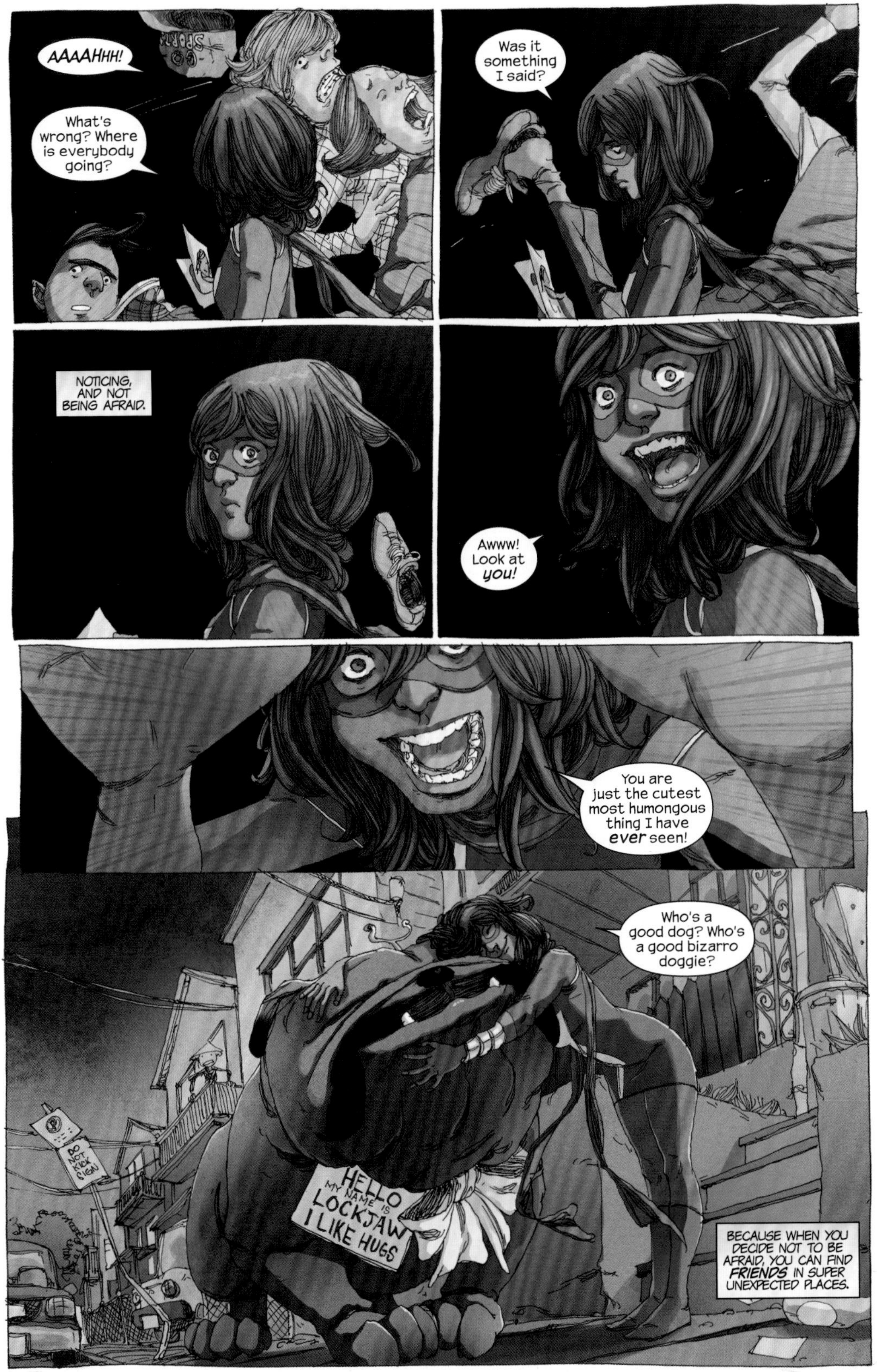
AAAAHHH!
What's wrong? Where is everybody going?
SPORTS
Was it something I said?
NOTICING, AND NOT BEING AFRAID.
Awww! Look at *you!*
You are just the cutest most humongous thing I have *ever* seen!
Who's a good dog? Who's a good bizarro doggie?
DO NOT KICK SIGN
HELLO MY NAME IS LOCKJAW I LIKE HUGS
BECAUSE WHEN YOU DECIDE NOT TO BE AFRAID, YOU CAN FIND *FRIENDS* IN SUPER UNEXPECTED PLACES.

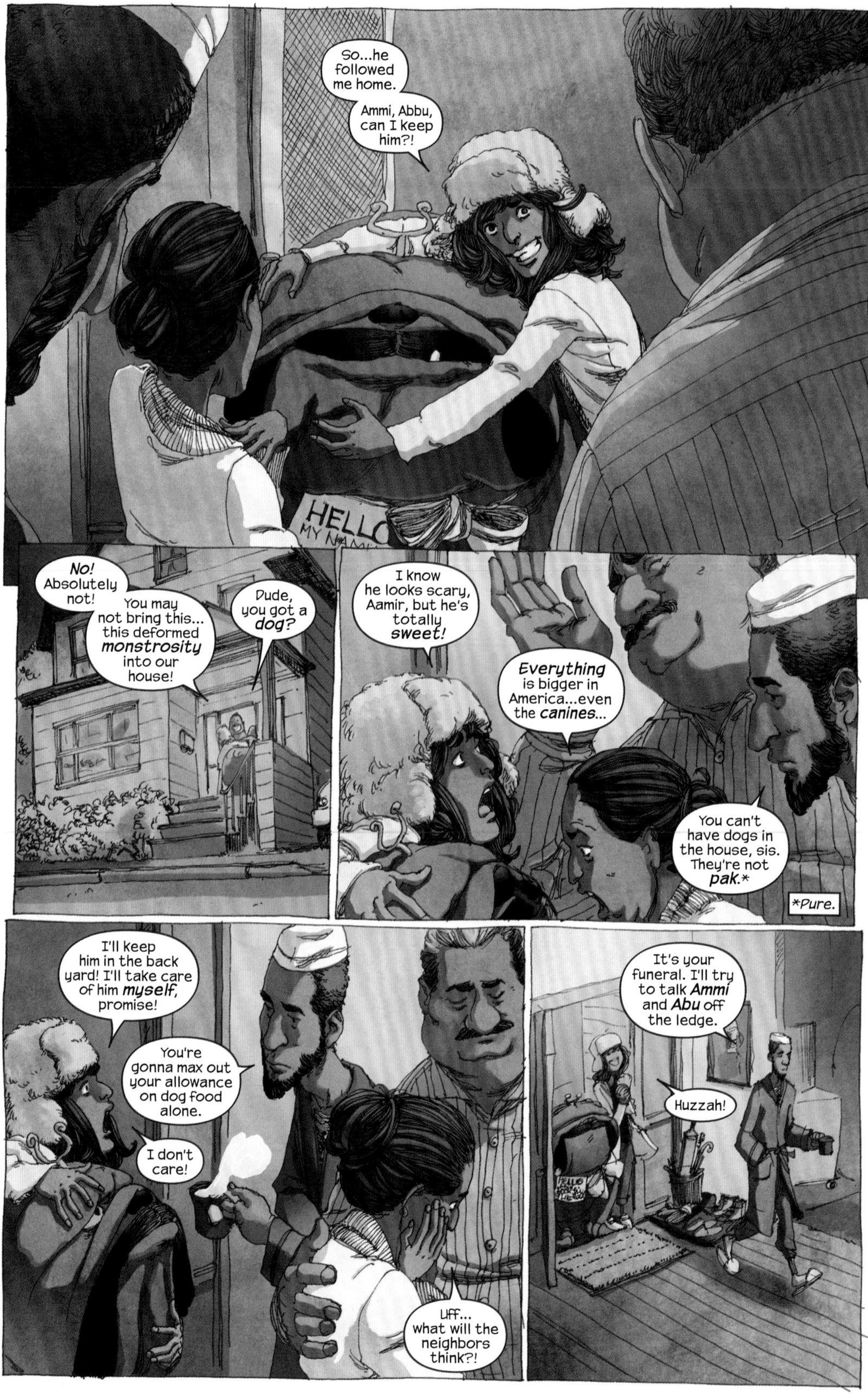

So...he followed me home.
Ammi, Abbu, can I keep him?!
HELLO MY NAME
No! Absolutely not!
You may not bring this... this deformed monstrosity into our house!
Dude, you got a dog?
I know he looks scary, Aamir, but he's totally sweet!
Everything is bigger in America...even the canines...
You can't have dogs in the house, sis. They're not pak.*
*Pure.
I'll keep him in the back yard! I'll take care of him myself, promise!
You're gonna max out your allowance on dog food alone.
I don't care!
Uff... what will the neighbors think?!
It's your funeral. I'll try to talk Ammi and Abu off the ledge.
Huzzah!

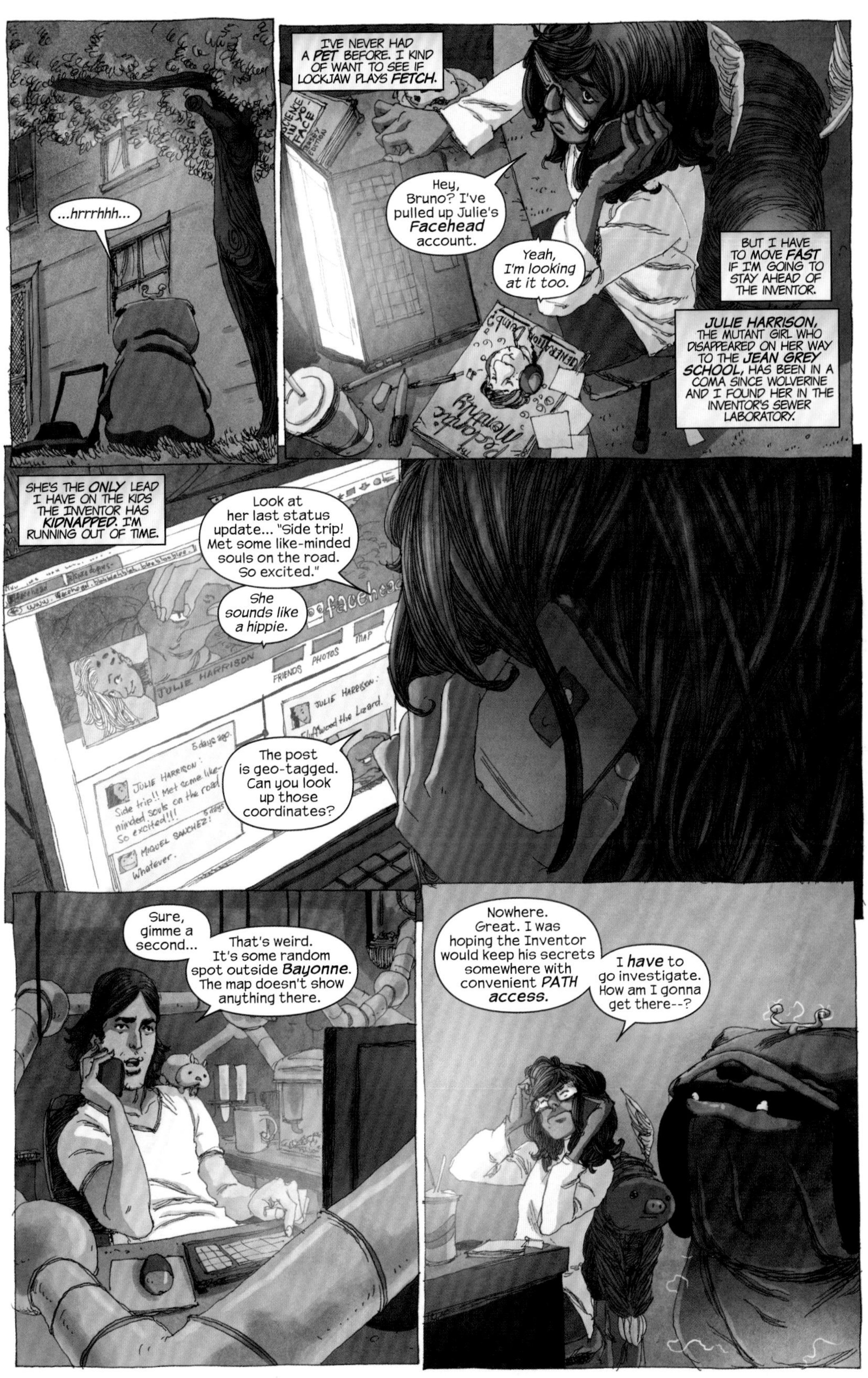
...hrrrhhh...
I'VE NEVER HAD A PET BEFORE. I KIND OF WANT TO SEE IF LOCKJAW PLAYS FETCH.
Hey, Bruno? I've pulled up Julie's Facehead account.
Yeah, I'm looking at it too.
BUT I HAVE TO MOVE FAST IF I'M GOING TO STAY AHEAD OF THE INVENTOR.
JULIE HARRISON, THE MUTANT GIRL WHO DISAPPEARED ON HER WAY TO THE JEAN GREY SCHOOL, HAS BEEN IN A COMA SINCE WOLVERINE AND I FOUND HER IN THE INVENTOR'S SEWER LABORATORY.
SHE'S THE ONLY LEAD I HAVE ON THE KIDS THE INVENTOR HAS KIDNAPPED. I'M RUNNING OUT OF TIME.
Look at her last status update... "Side trip! Met some like-minded souls on the road. So excited."
She sounds like a hippie.
facehead
JULIE HARRISON
FRIENDS
PHOTOS
MAP
JULIE HARRISON: Fluffwood the Lizard.
5 days ago.
JULIE HARRISON: Side trip!! Met some like-minded souls on the road. So excited!!!
MIGUEL SANCHEZ: Whatever.
The post is geo-tagged. Can you look up those coordinates?
Sure, gimme a second...
That's weird. It's some random spot outside Bayonne. The map doesn't show anything there.
Nowhere. Great. I was hoping the Inventor would keep his secrets somewhere with convenient PATH access.
I have to go investigate. How am I gonna get there--?

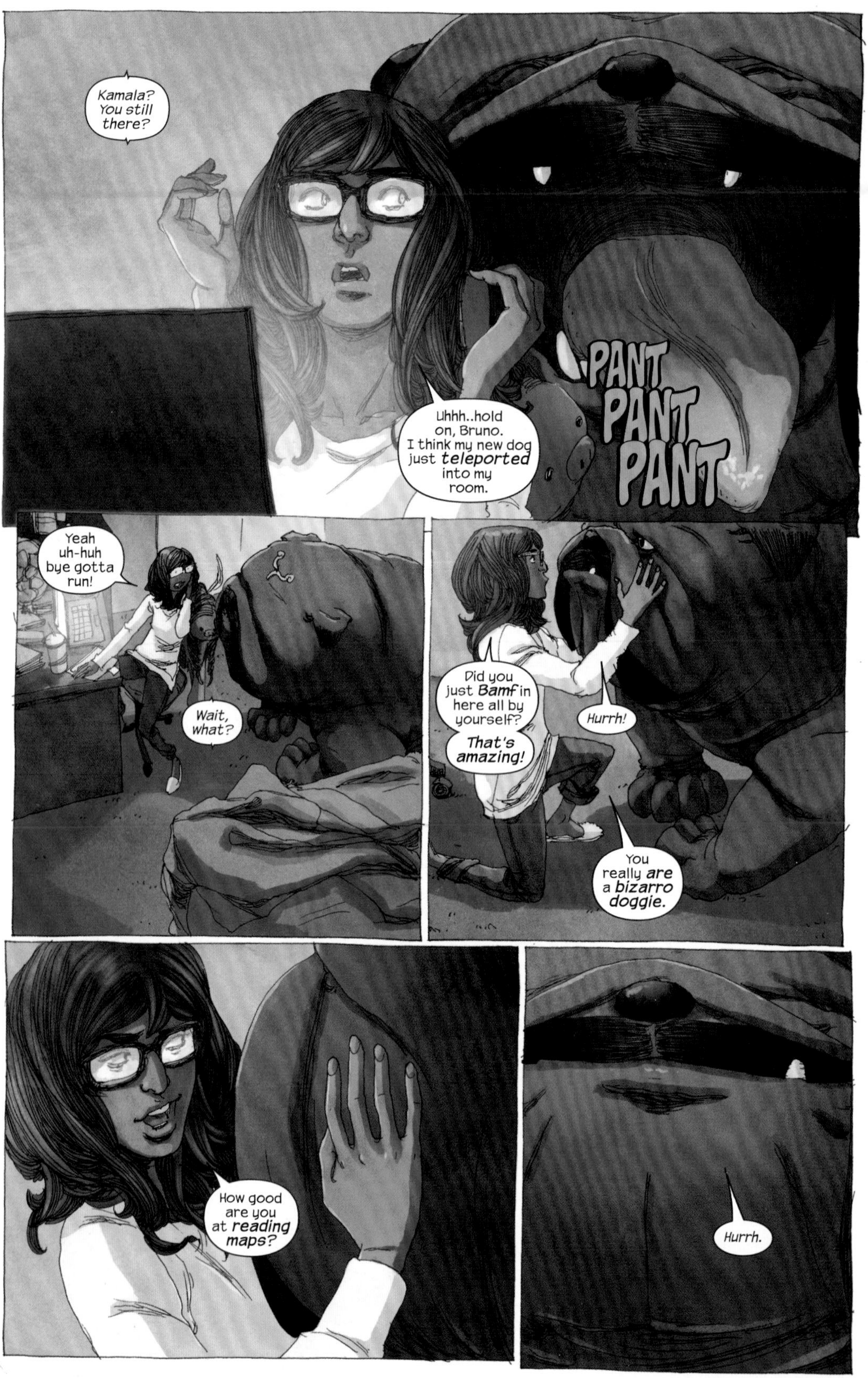
Kamala? You still there?
Uhhh..hold on, Bruno. I think my new dog just teleported into my room.
PANT PANT PANT
Yeah uh-huh bye gotta run!
Wait, what?
Did you just Bamf in here all by yourself?
That's amazing!
Hurrh!
You really are a bizarro doggie.
How good are you at reading maps?
Hurrh.

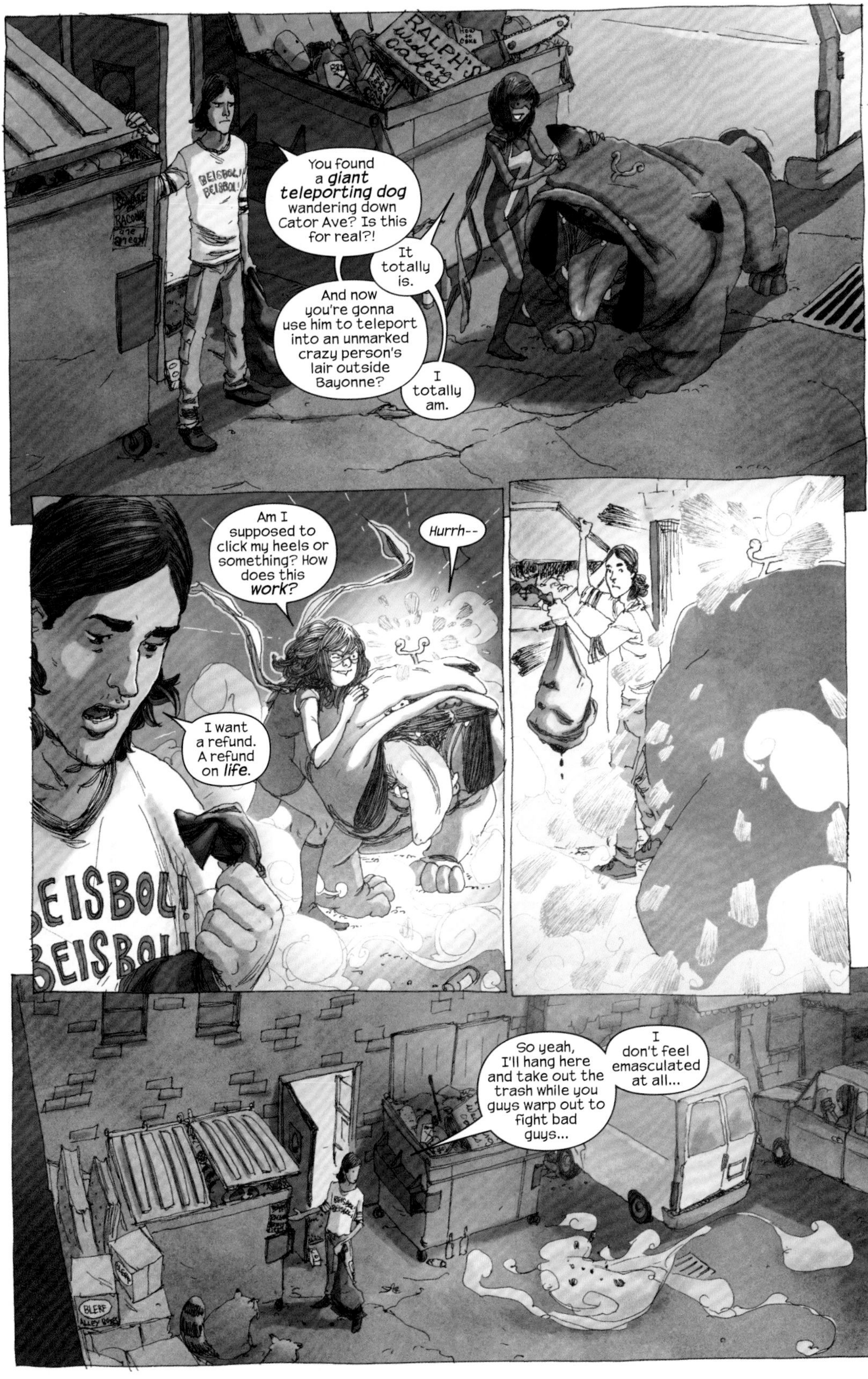

RALPH'S Wedding Cakes
You found a *giant teleporting dog* wandering down Cator Ave? Is this for real?!
It totally is.
And now you're gonna use him to teleport into an unmarked crazy person's lair outside Bayonne?
I totally am.
Am I supposed to click my heels or something? How does this *work*?
Hurrh--
I want a refund. A refund on *life*.
BEISBOL! BEISBOL!
So yeah, I'll hang here and take out the trash while you guys warp out to fight bad guys...
I don't feel emasculated at all...

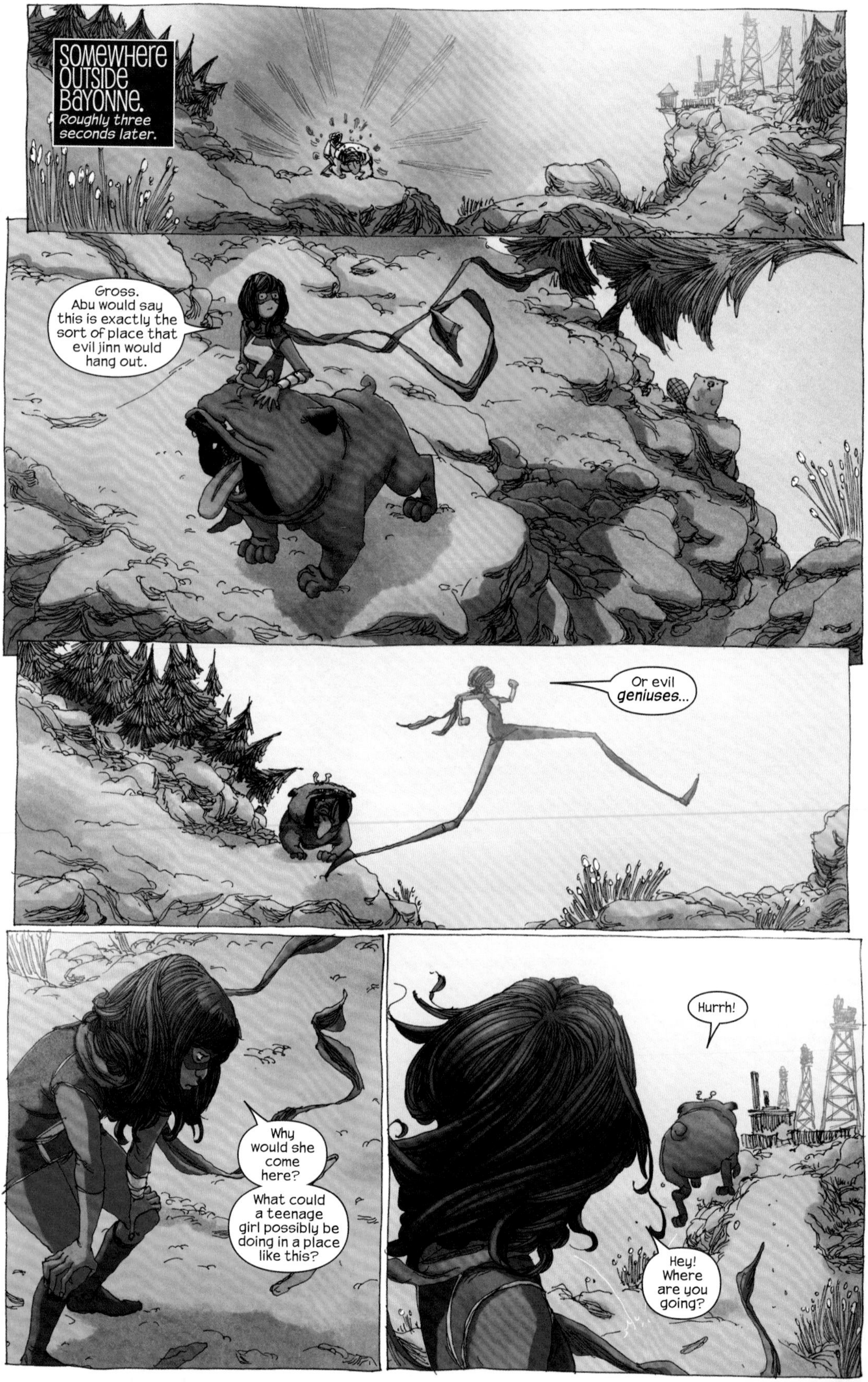
SOMEWHERE OUTSIDE BAYONNE.
Roughly three seconds later.
Gross. Abu would say this is exactly the sort of place that evil jinn would hang out.
Or evil geniuses...
Why would she come here?
What could a teenage girl possibly be doing in a place like this?
Hurrh!
Hey! Where are you going?

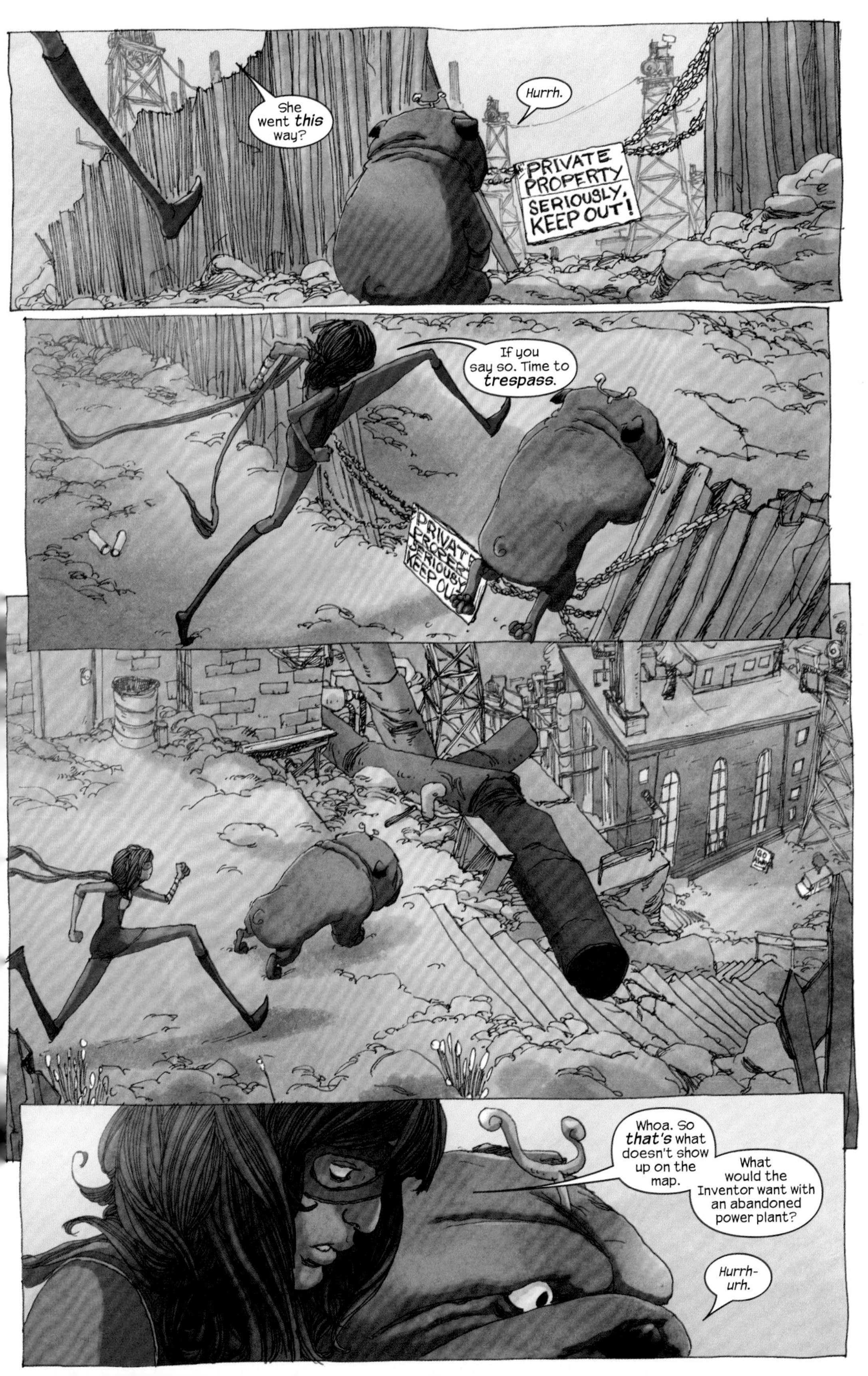
She went this way?
Hurrh.
PRIVATE PROPERTY SERIOUSLY, KEEP OUT!
If you say so. Time to trespass.
Whoa. So that's what doesn't show up on the map.
What would the Inventor want with an abandoned power plant?
Hurrh-urh.

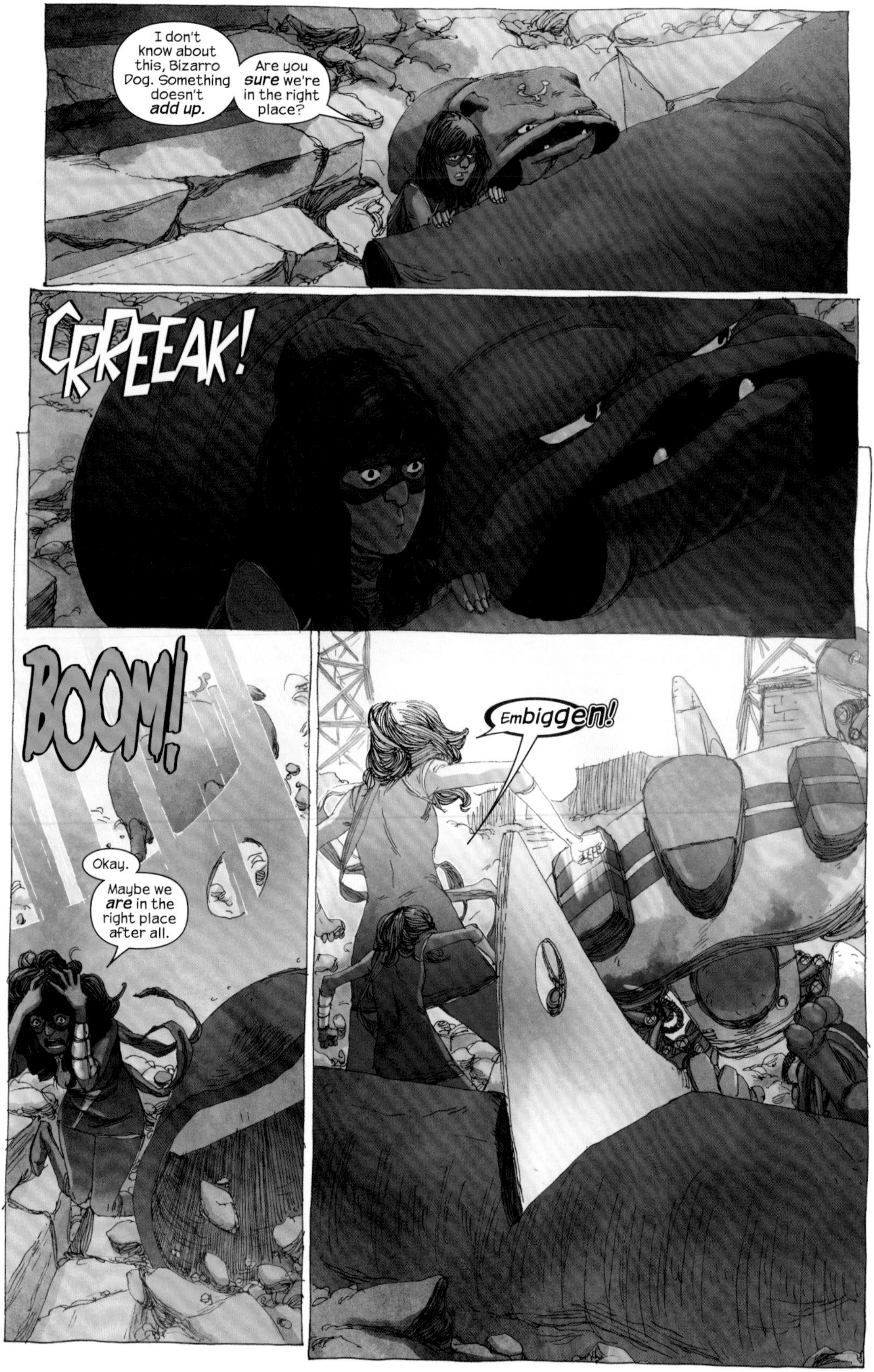
I don't know about this, Bizarro Dog. Something doesn't add up.
Are you sure we're in the right place?
CRREEAK!
BOOM!
Okay.
Maybe we are in the right place after all.
Embiggen!

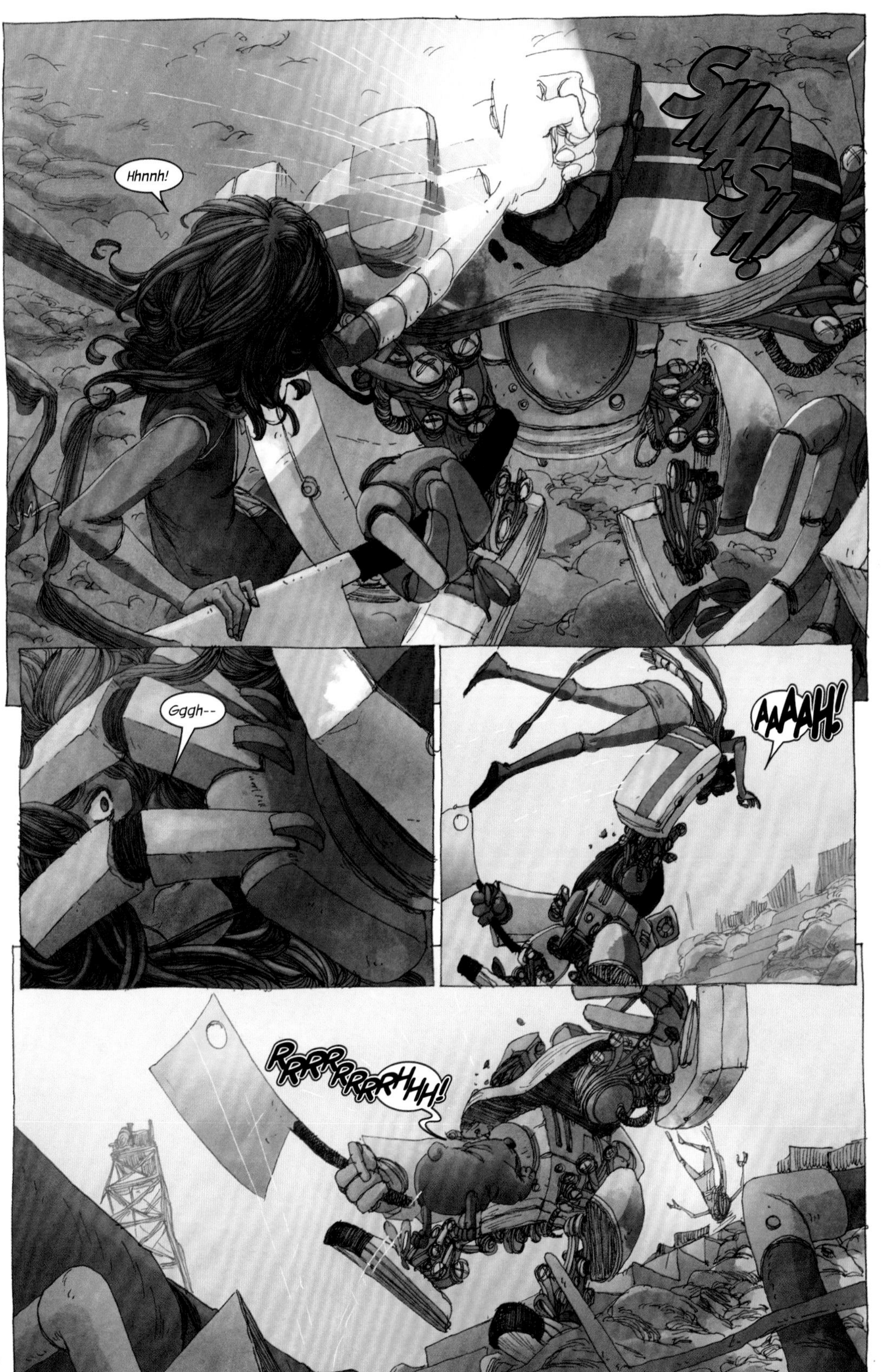
Hhnnh!
SMASH!
Gggh--
AAAAH!
RRRRRRRRRHHH!

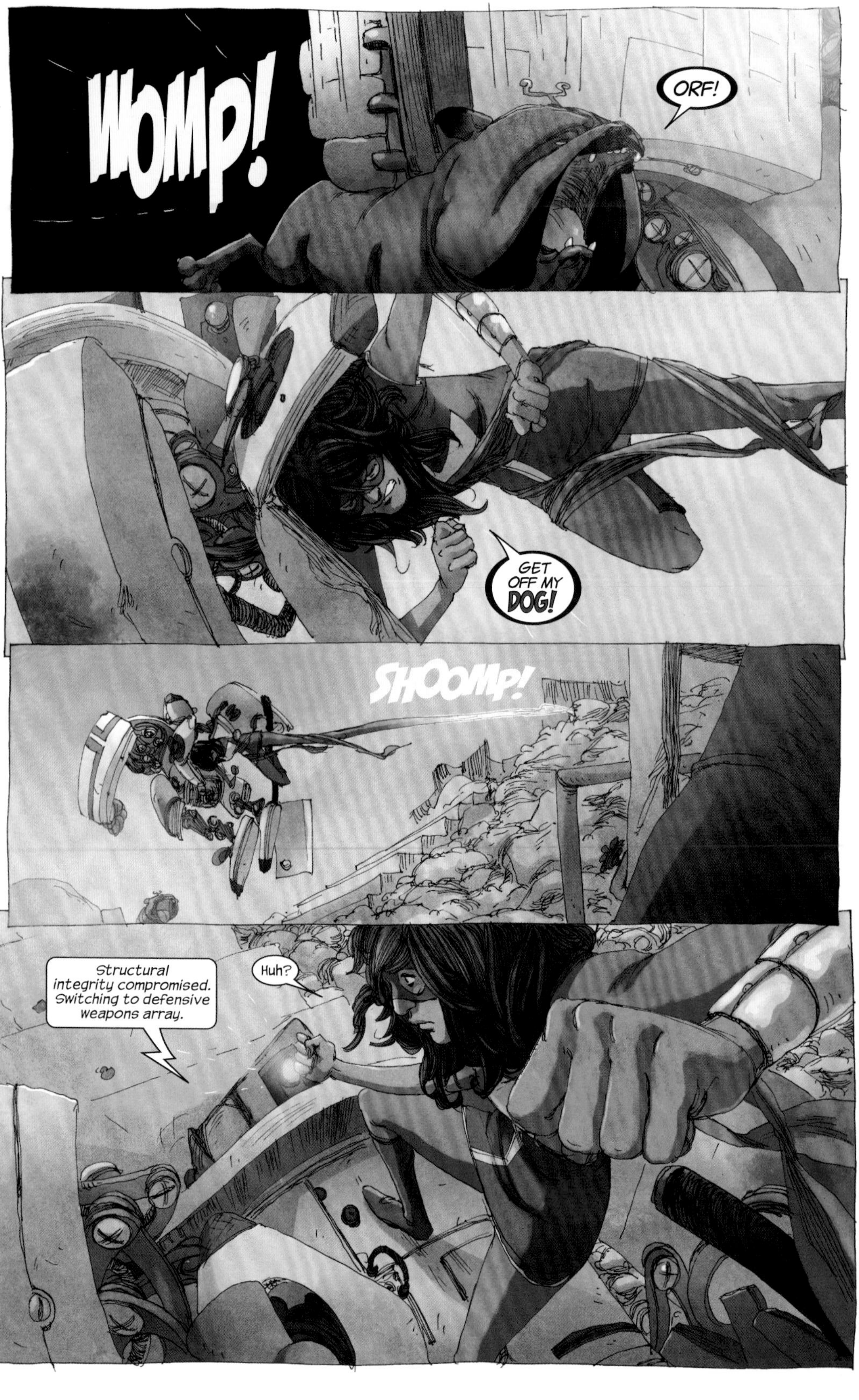
WOMP!
ORF!
GET OFF MY DOG!
SHOOMP!
Structural integrity compromised. Switching to defensive weapons array.
Huh?

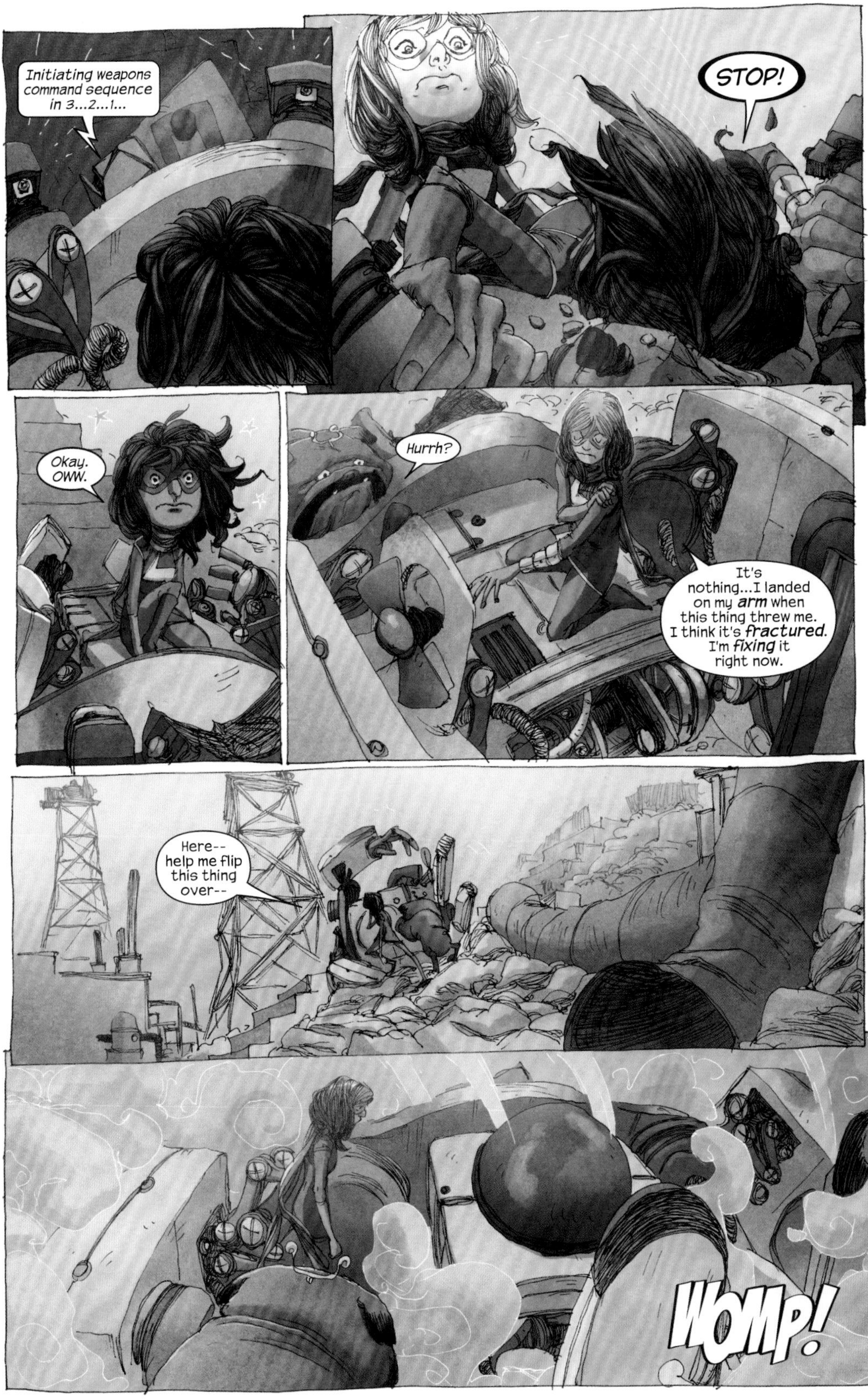
Initiating weapons command sequence in 3...2...1...
STOP!
Okay. OWW.
Hurrh?
It's nothing...I landed on my arm when this thing threw me. I think it's fractured. I'm fixing it right now.
Here-- help me flip this thing over--
WOMP!

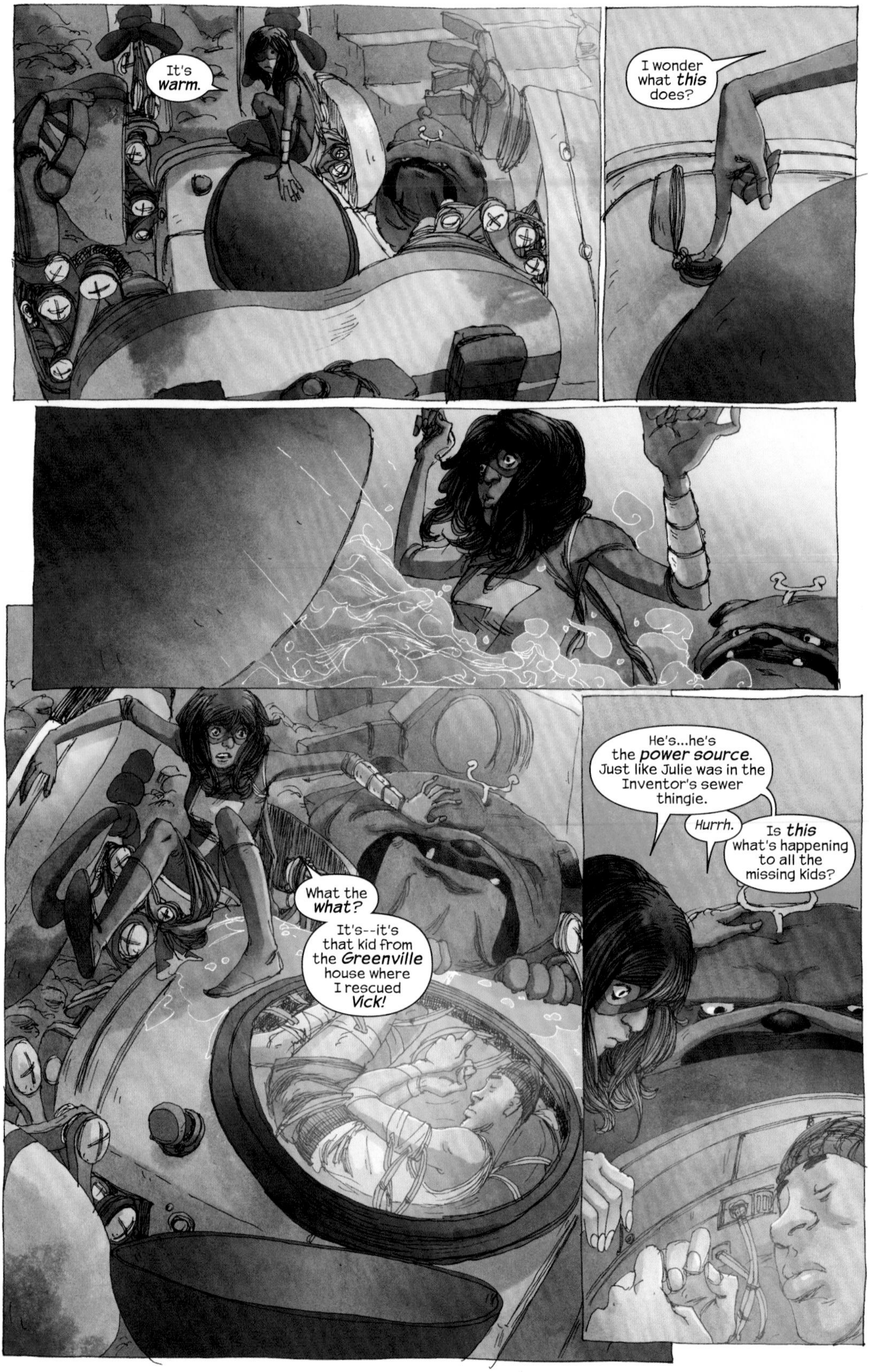
It's *warm.*
I wonder what *this* does?
What the *what?*
It's--it's that kid from the *Greenville* house where I rescued *Vick!*
He's...he's the *power source.* Just like Julie was in the Inventor's sewer thingie.
Hurrh.
Is *this* what's happening to all the missing kids?

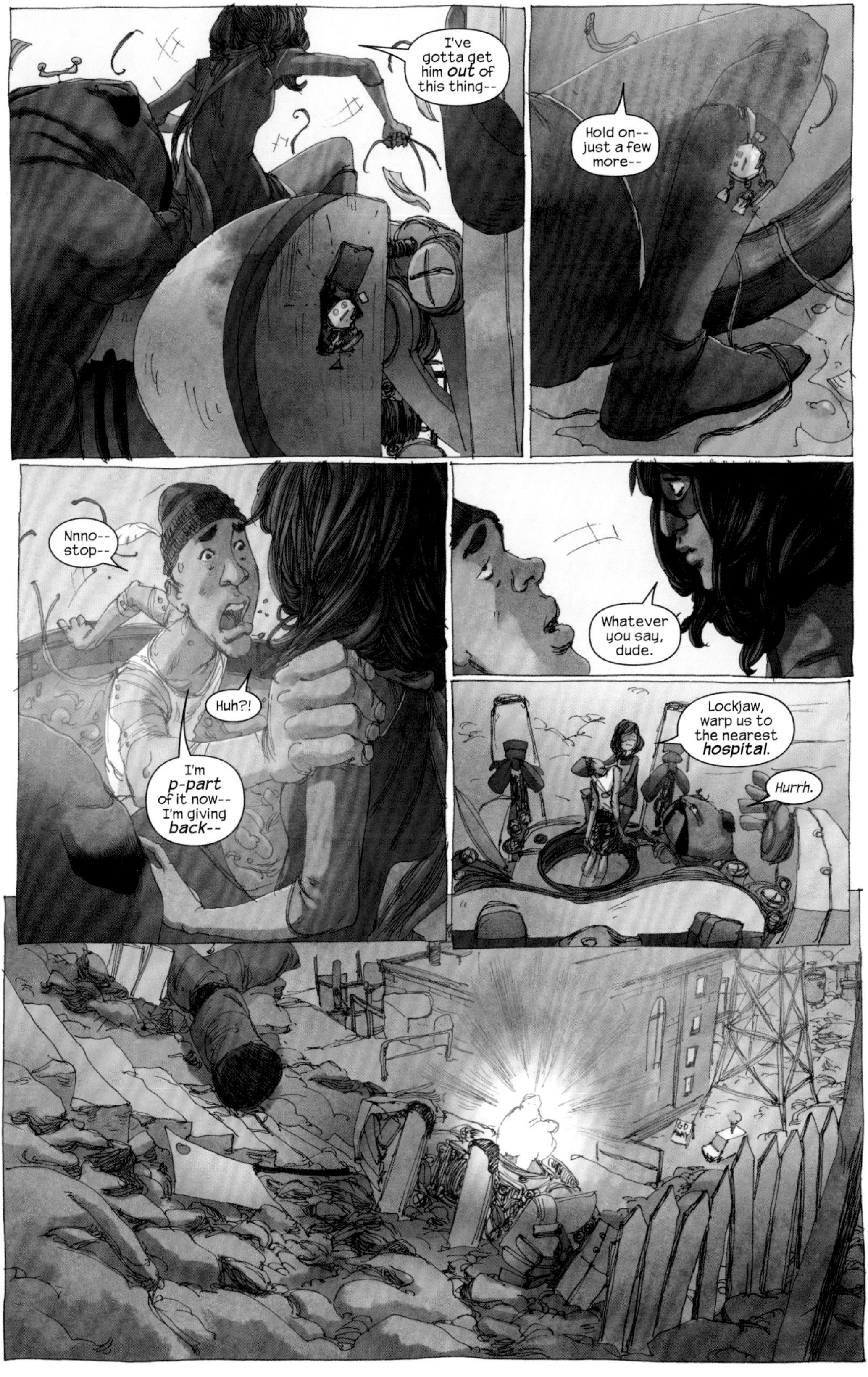
I've gotta get him out of this thing--
Hold on-- just a few more--
Nnno-- stop--
Huh?!
I'm p-part of it now-- I'm giving back--
Whatever you say, dude.
Lockjaw, warp us to the nearest hospital.
Hurrh.
GO AWAY

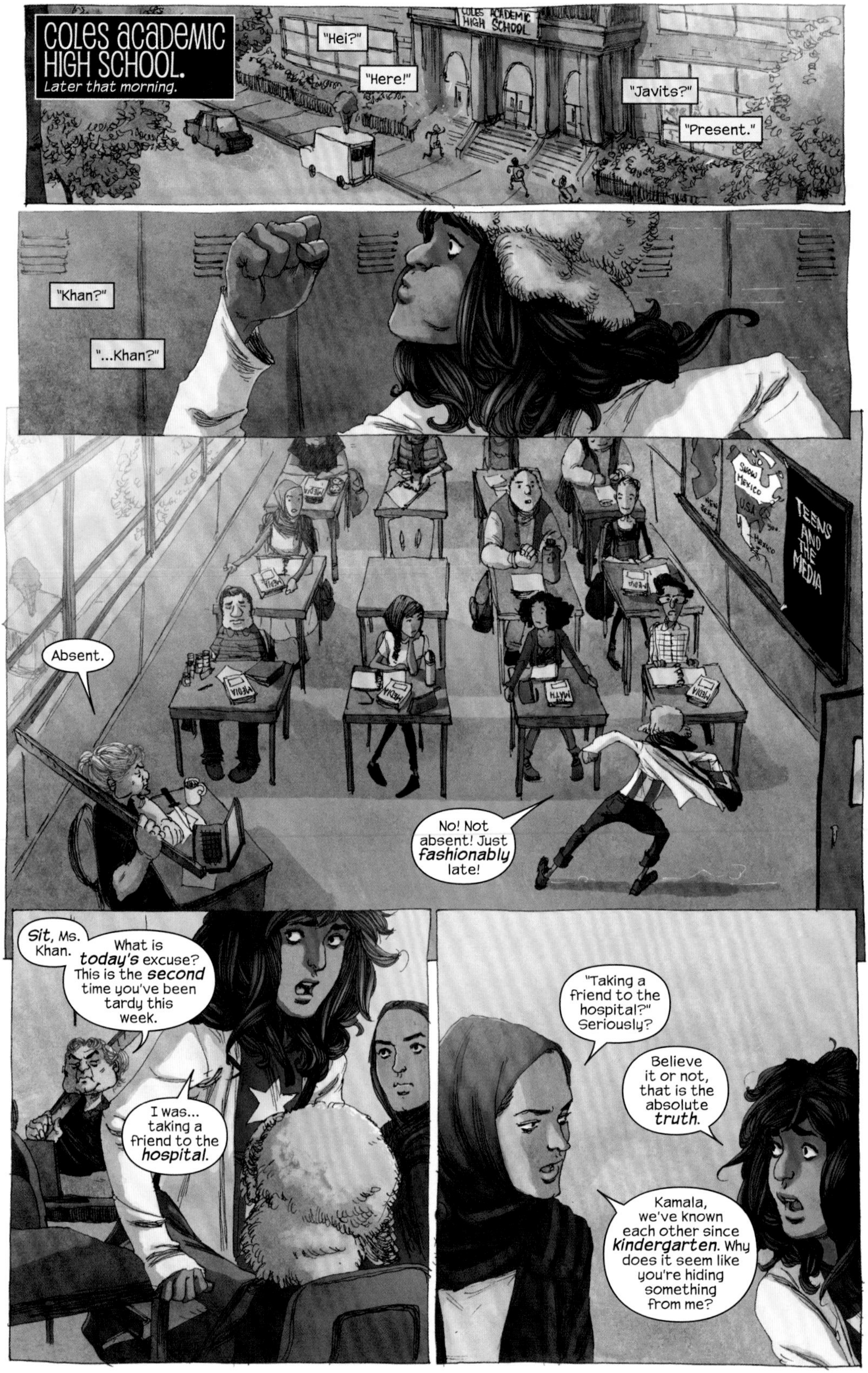

COLES ACADEMIC HIGH SCHOOL.
Later that morning.
COLES ACADEMIC HIGH SCHOOL
"Hei?"
"Here!"
"Javits?"
"Present."
"Khan?"
"...Khan?"
TEENS AND THE MEDIA
Absent.
No! Not absent! Just *fashionably* late!
Sit, Ms. Khan.
What is *today's* excuse? This is the *second* time you've been tardy this week.
I was... taking a friend to the *hospital*.
"Taking a friend to the hospital?" Seriously?
Believe it or not, that is the absolute *truth*.
Kamala, we've known each other since *kindergarten*. Why does it seem like you're hiding something from me?

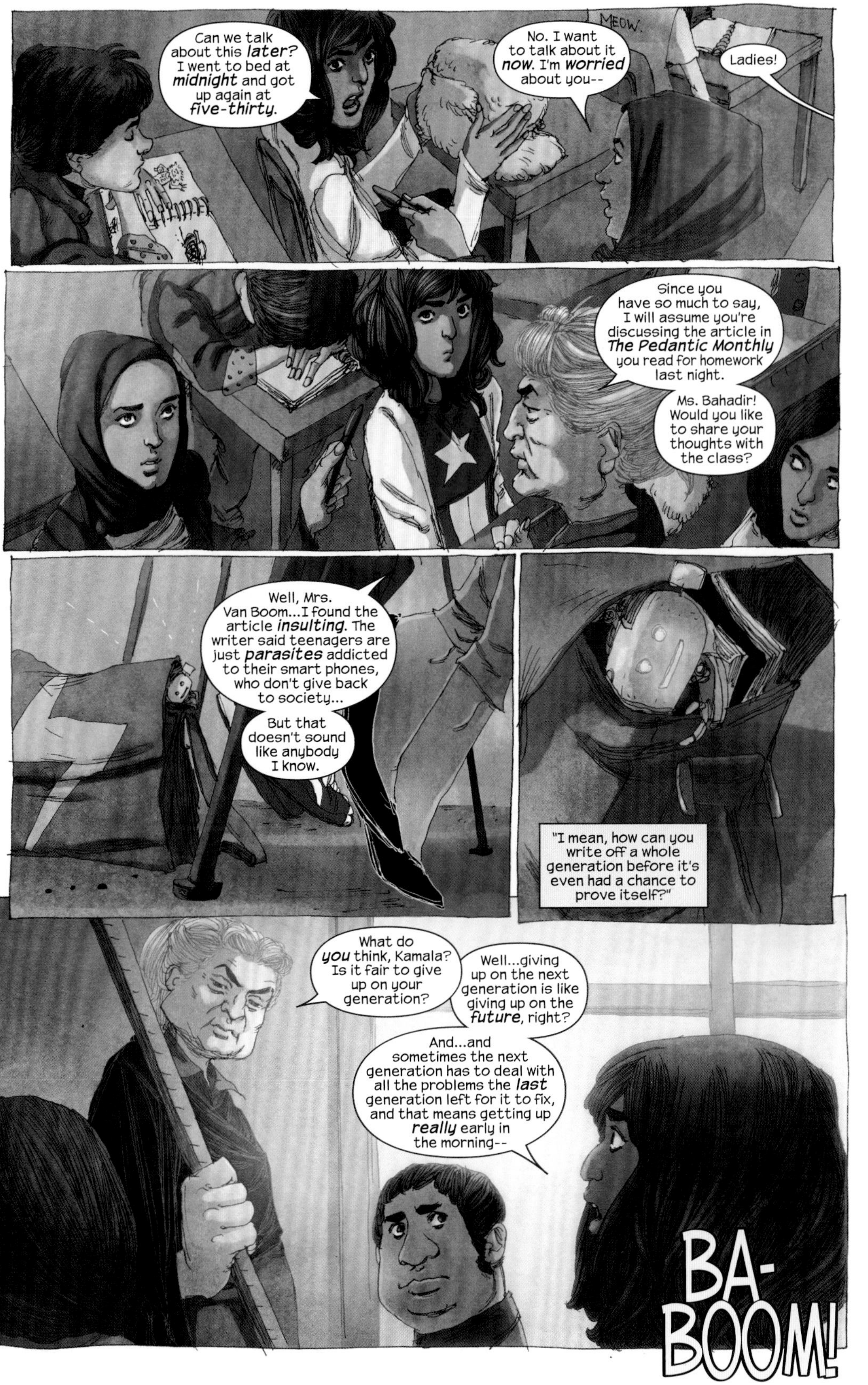

MEOW.
Can we talk about this *later*? I went to bed at *midnight* and got up again at *five-thirty*.
No. I want to talk about it *now*. I'm *worried* about you--
Ladies!
Since you have so much to say, I will assume you're discussing the article in *The Pedantic Monthly* you read for homework last night.
Ms. Bahadir! Would you like to share your thoughts with the class?
Well, Mrs. Van Boom...I found the article *insulting*. The writer said teenagers are just *parasites* addicted to their smart phones, who don't give back to society...
But that doesn't sound like anybody I know.
"I mean, how can you write off a whole generation before it's even had a chance to prove itself?"
What do *you* think, Kamala? Is it fair to give up on your generation?
Well...giving up on the next generation is like giving up on the *future*, right?
And...and sometimes the next generation has to deal with all the problems the *last* generation left for it to fix, and that means getting up *really* early in the morning--
BA-BOOM!

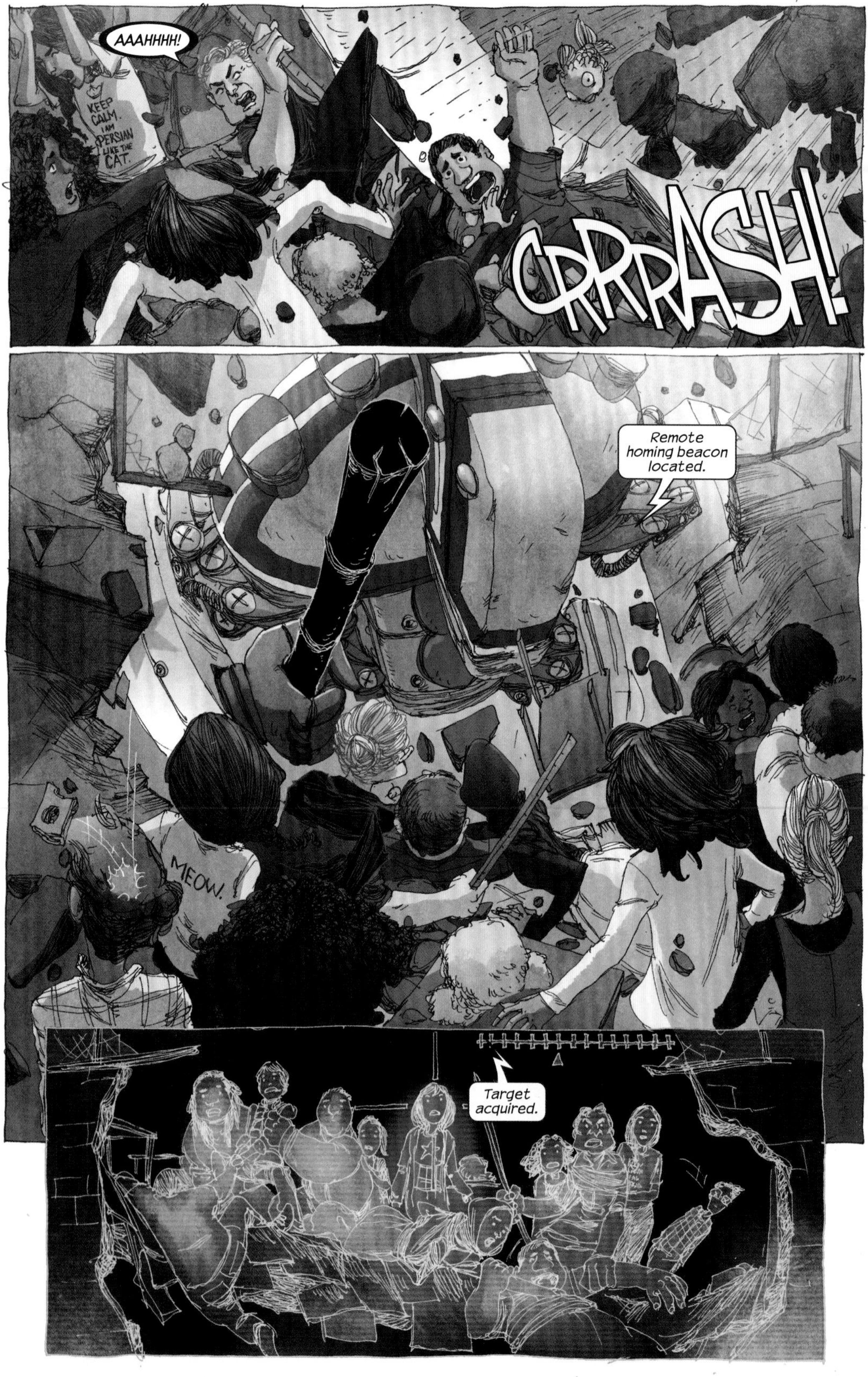
AAAHHHH!
KEEP CALM. I AM PERSIAN LIKE THE CAT.
CRRRASH!
Remote homing beacon located.
MEOW.
Target acquired.

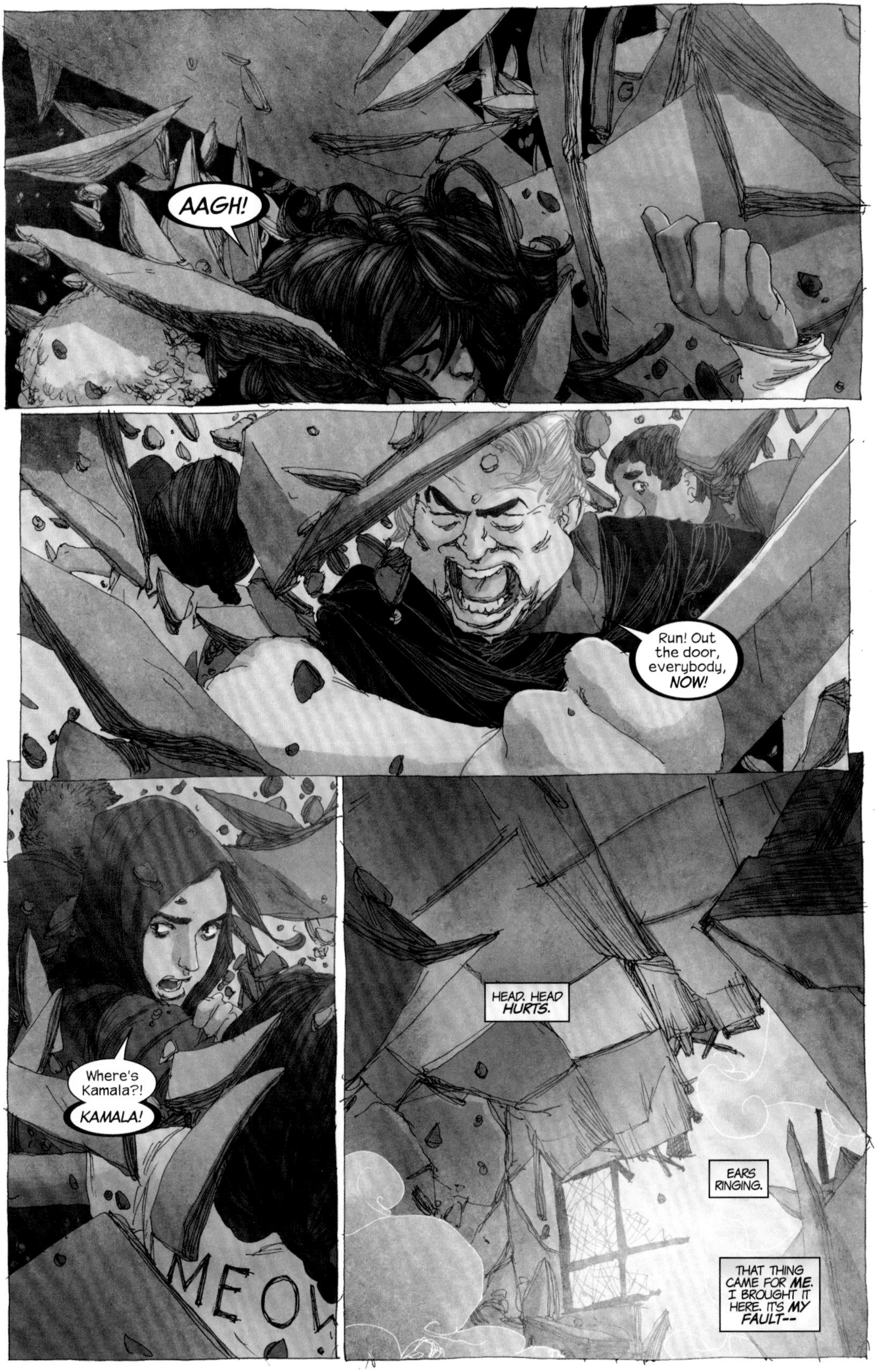
AAGH!
Run! Out the door, everybody, NOW!
Where's Kamala?!
KAMALA!
MEO
HEAD. HEAD HURTS.
EARS RINGING.
THAT THING CAME FOR ME. I BROUGHT IT HERE. IT'S MY FAULT--

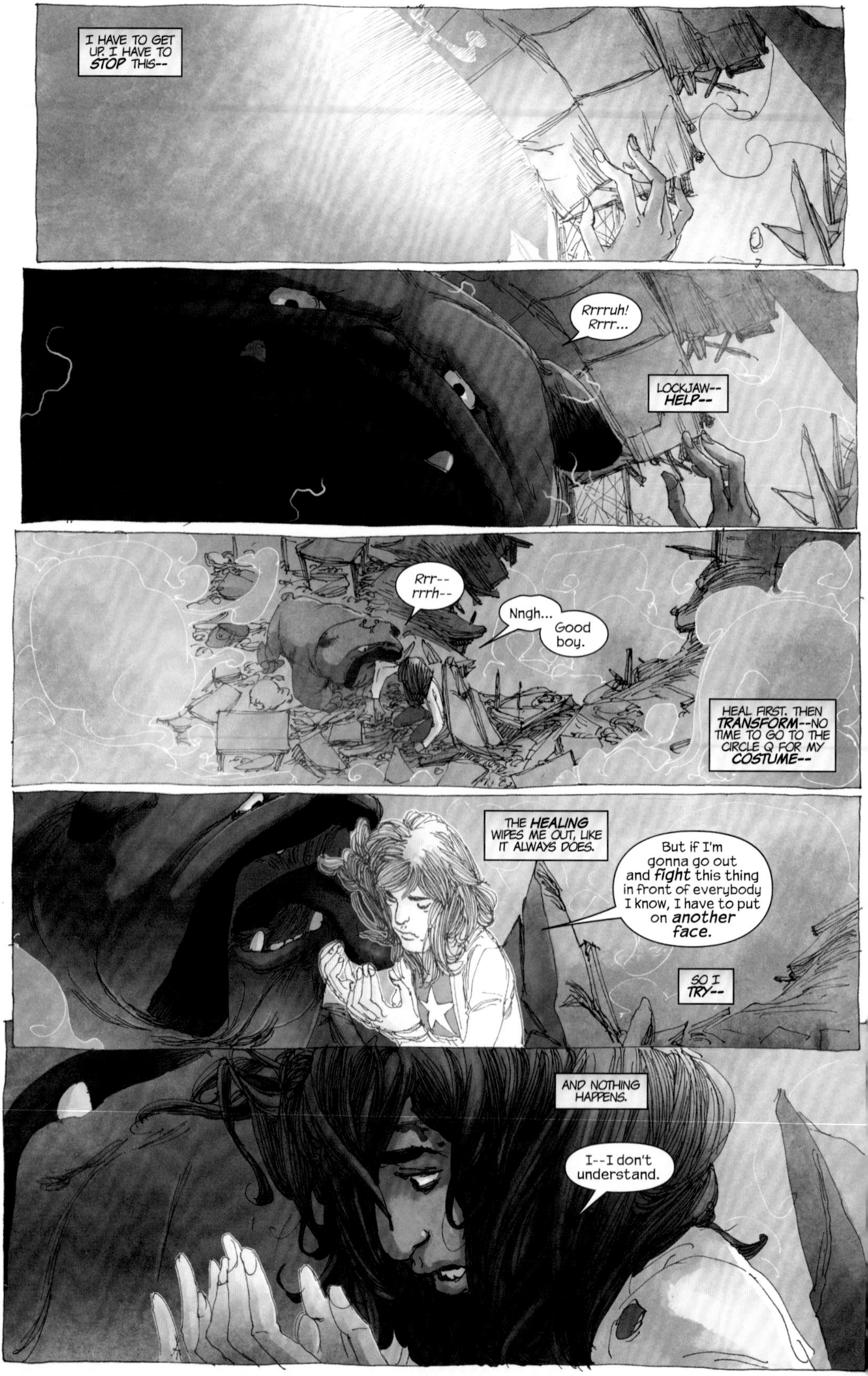
I HAVE TO GET UP. I HAVE TO STOP THIS--
Rrrruh! Rrrr...
LOCKJAW-- HELP--
Rrr-- rrrh--
Nngh... Good boy.
HEAL FIRST. THEN TRANSFORM--NO TIME TO GO TO THE CIRCLE Q FOR MY COSTUME--
THE HEALING WIPES ME OUT, LIKE IT ALWAYS DOES.
But if I'm gonna go out and fight this thing in front of everybody I know, I have to put on another face.
SO I TRY--
AND NOTHING HAPPENS.
I--I don't understand.

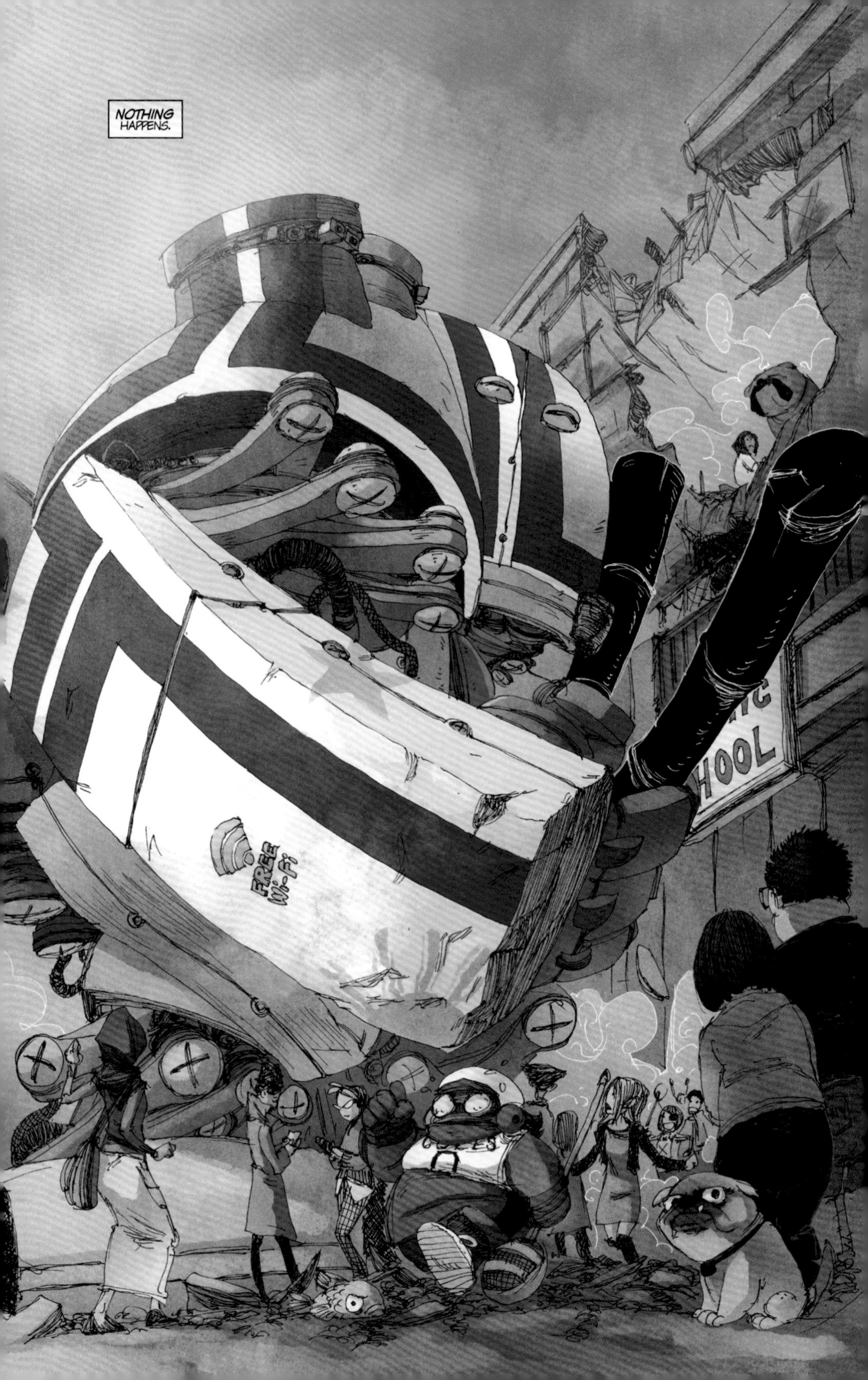
NOTHING HAPPENS.
FREE Wi-Fi
HOOL

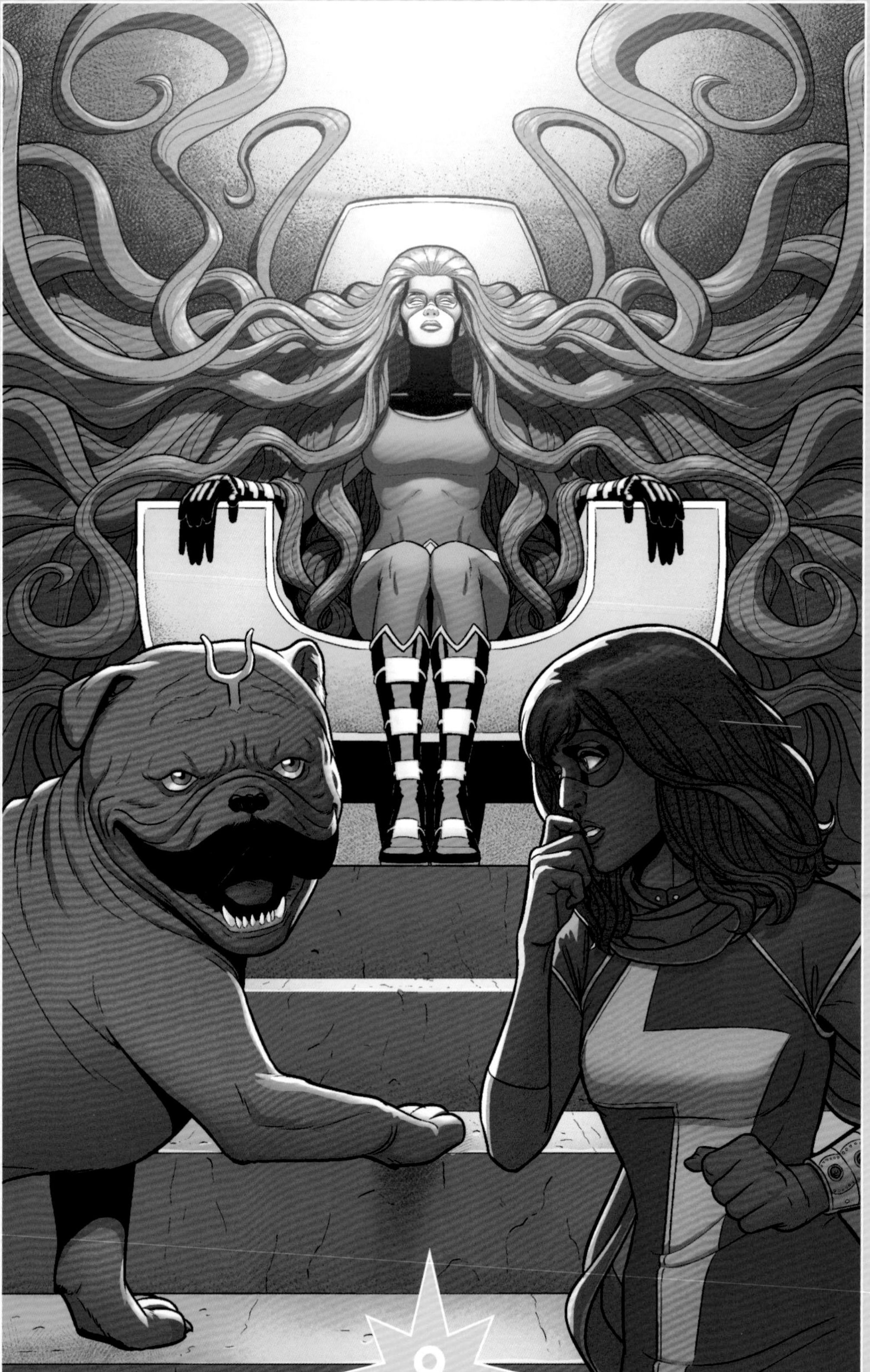
9

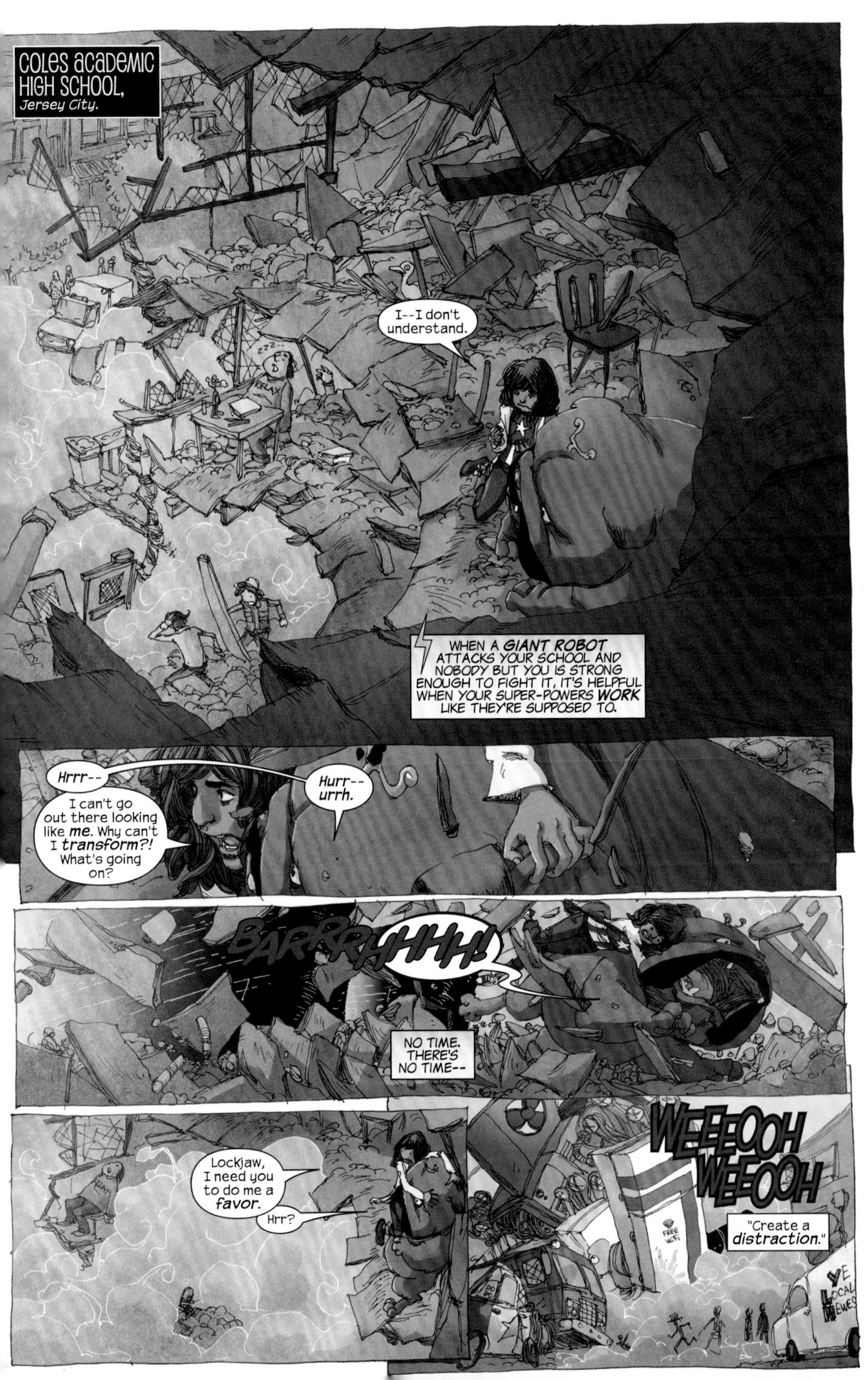
COLES ACADEMIC HIGH SCHOOL, Jersey City.
I--I don't understand.
WHEN A GIANT ROBOT ATTACKS YOUR SCHOOL AND NOBODY BUT YOU IS STRONG ENOUGH TO FIGHT IT, IT'S HELPFUL WHEN YOUR SUPER-POWERS WORK LIKE THEY'RE SUPPOSED TO.
Hrrr--
Hurr--urrh.
I can't go out there looking like me. Why can't I transform?! What's going on?
BARRRHHHH!
NO TIME. THERE'S NO TIME--
Lockjaw, I need you to do me a favor.
Hrr?
WEEEOOH WEEEOOH
"Create a distraction."
FREE WIFI
YE LOCAL NEWES

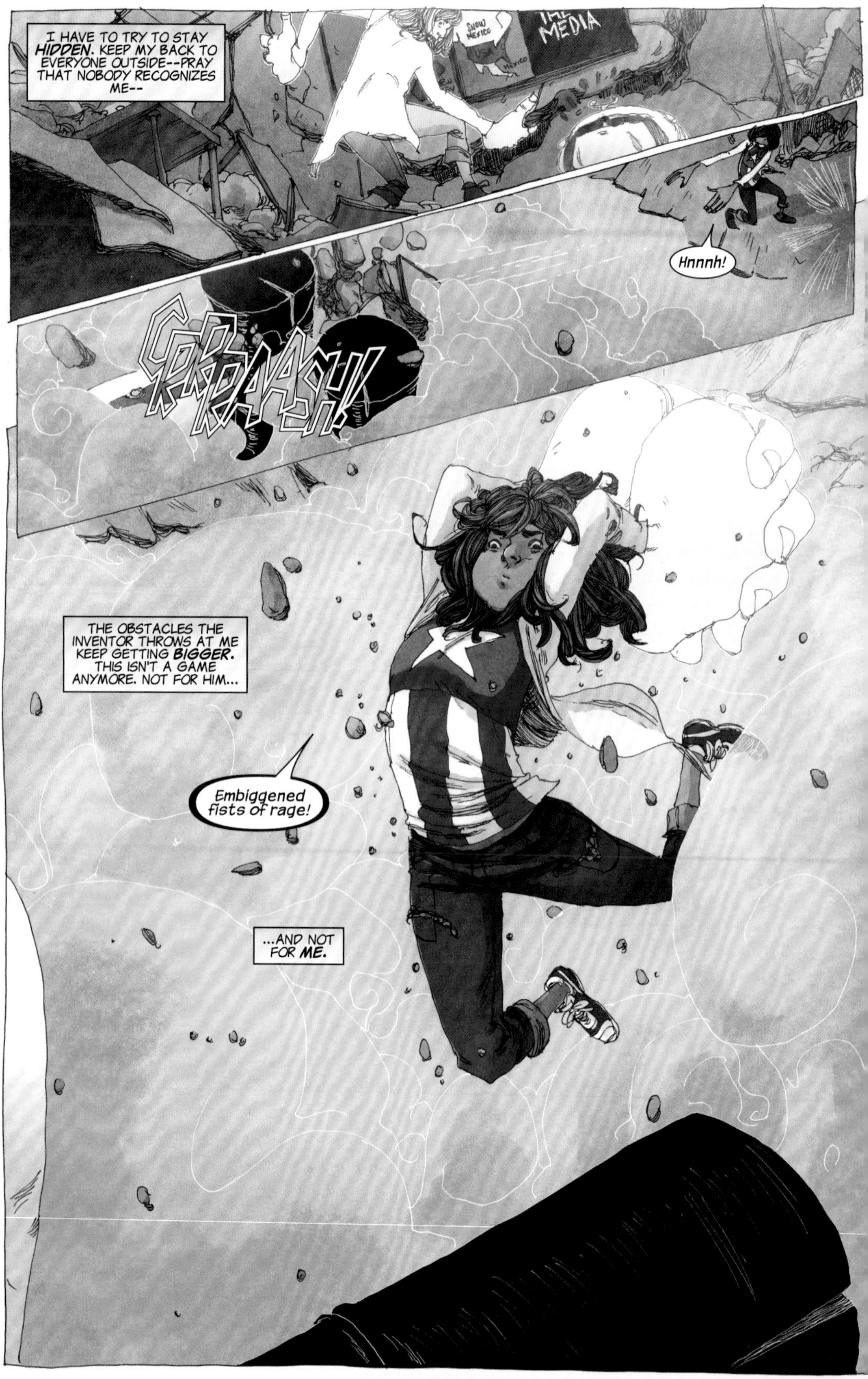
I HAVE TO TRY TO STAY HIDDEN. KEEP MY BACK TO EVERYONE OUTSIDE--PRAY THAT NOBODY RECOGNIZES ME--
THE MEDIA
Hnnnh!
KRRAASH!
THE OBSTACLES THE INVENTOR THROWS AT ME KEEP GETTING BIGGER. THIS ISN'T A GAME ANYMORE. NOT FOR HIM...
Embiggened fists of rage!
...AND NOT FOR ME.

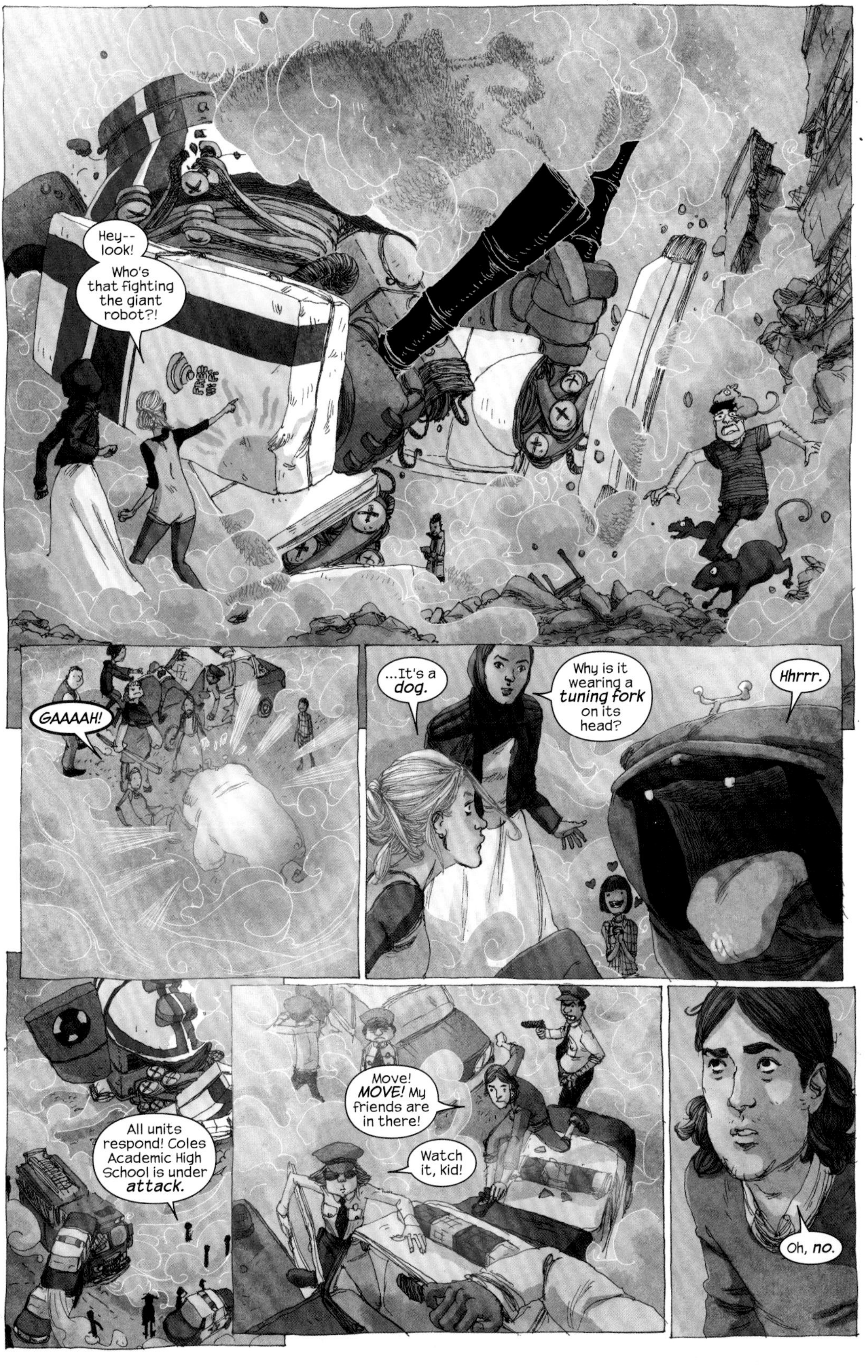
Hey-- look!
Who's that fighting the giant robot?!
GAAAAH!
...It's a dog.
Why is it wearing a tuning fork on its head?
Hhrrr.
All units respond! Coles Academic High School is under attack.
Move! MOVE! My friends are in there!
Watch it, kid!
Oh, no.

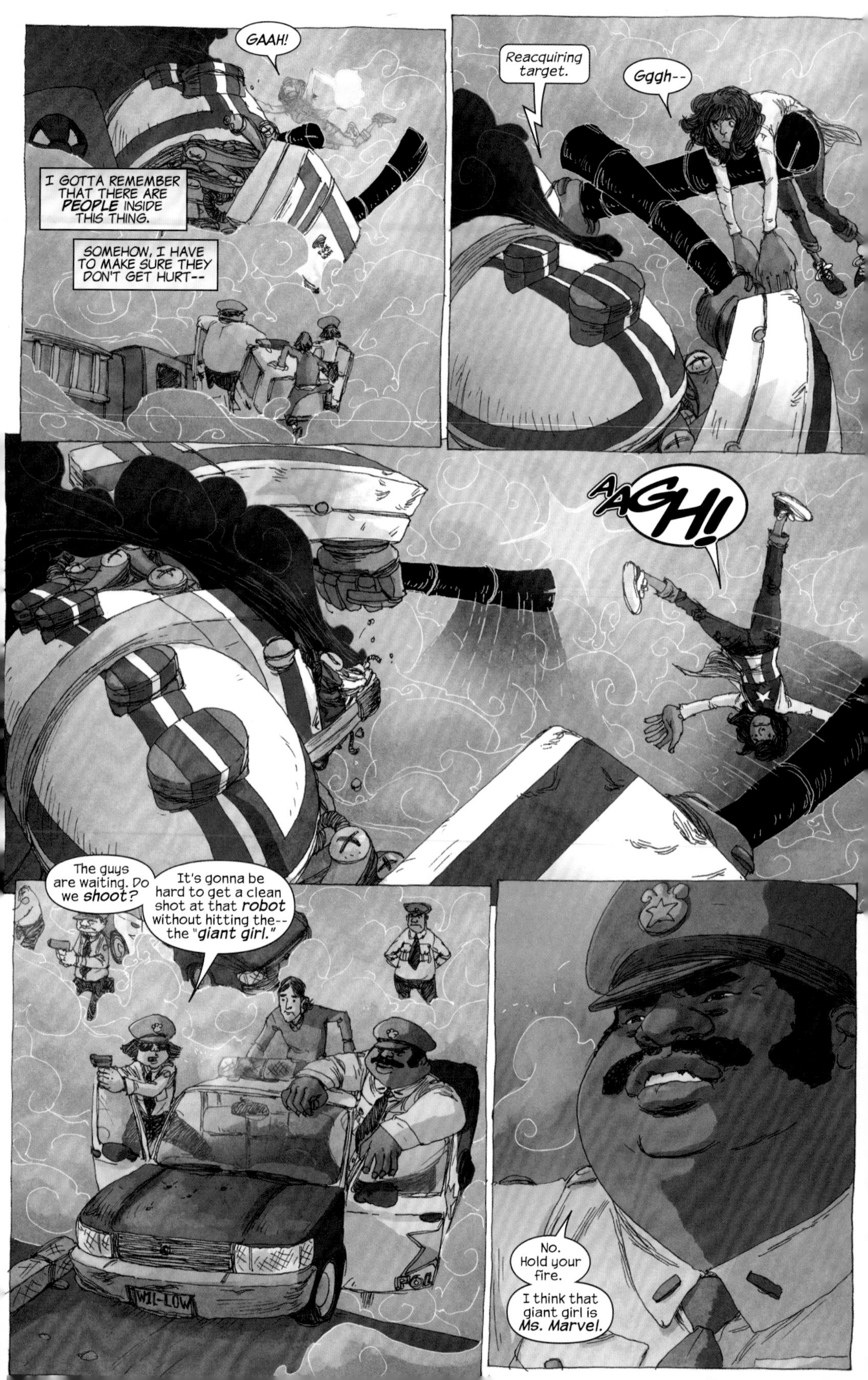
GAAH!
I GOTTA REMEMBER THAT THERE ARE PEOPLE INSIDE THIS THING.
SOMEHOW, I HAVE TO MAKE SURE THEY DON'T GET HURT--
Reacquiring target.
Gggh--
AAGH!
The guys are waiting. Do we shoot?
It's gonna be hard to get a clean shot at that robot without hitting the-- the "giant girl."
W1I-LOW
No. Hold your fire.
I think that giant girl is Ms. Marvel.

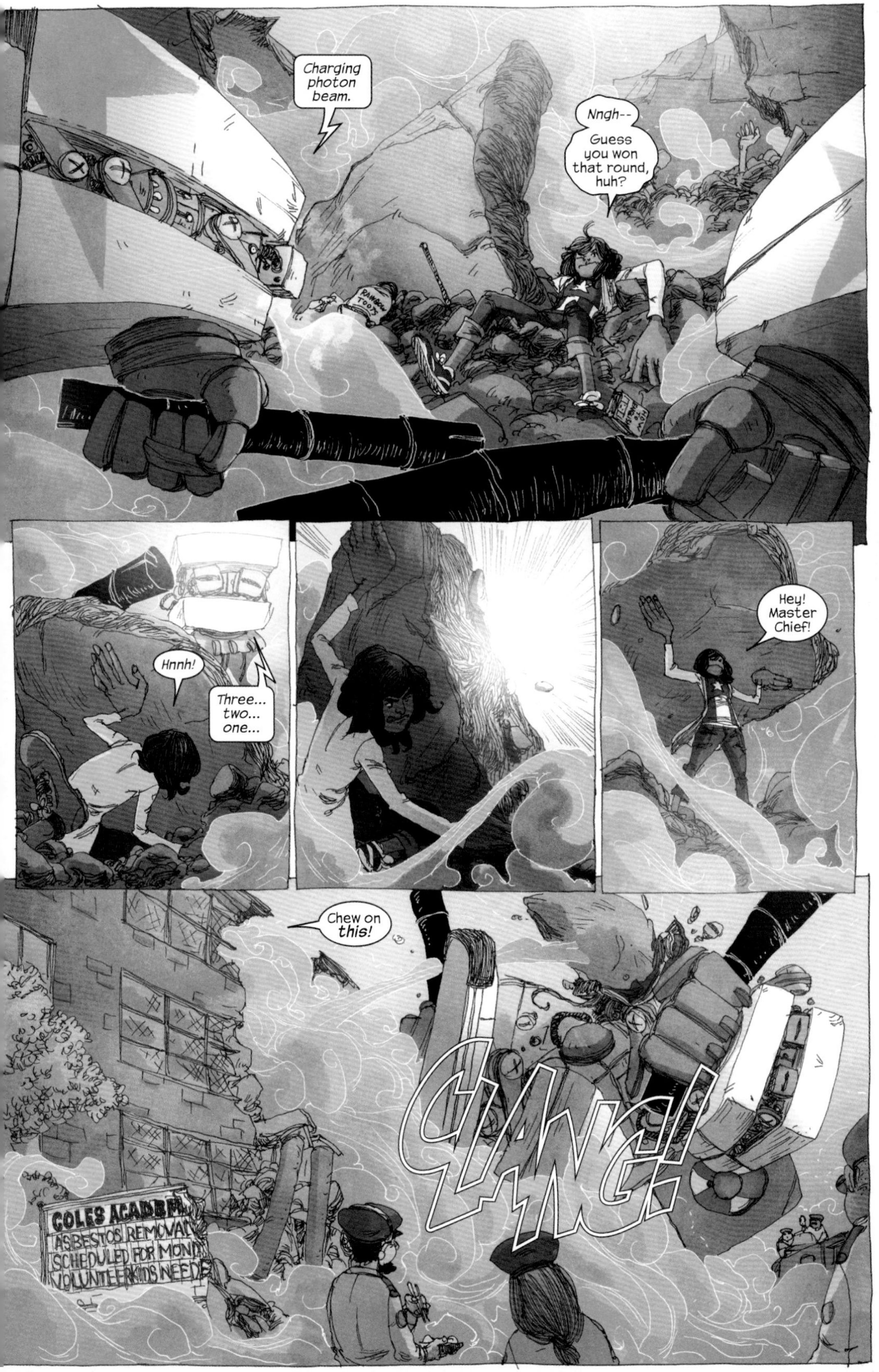
Charging photon beam.
Nngh--
Guess you won that round, huh?
Hnnh!
Three... two... one...
Hey! Master Chief!
Chew on this!
CLANG!
COLES ACADE
ASBESTOS REMOVAL
SCHEDULED FOR MOND
VOLUNTEER KIDS NEEDE

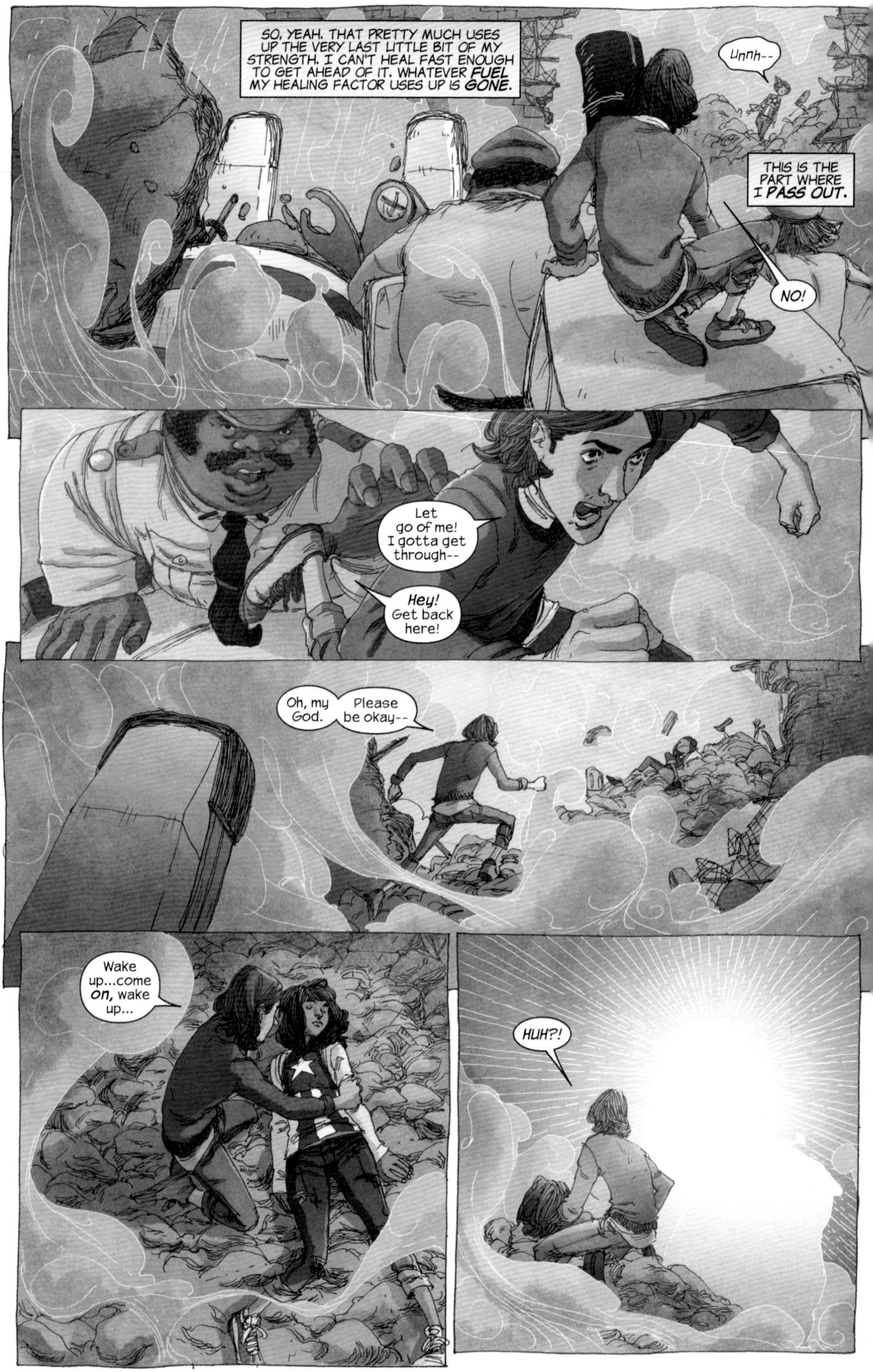
SO, YEAH. THAT PRETTY MUCH USES UP THE VERY LAST LITTLE BIT OF MY STRENGTH. I CAN'T HEAL FAST ENOUGH TO GET AHEAD OF IT. WHATEVER *FUEL* MY HEALING FACTOR USES UP IS *GONE*.
Unnh--
THIS IS THE PART WHERE I *PASS OUT*.
NO!
Let go of me! I gotta get through--
Hey! Get back here!
Oh, my God.
Please be okay--
Wake up...come *on,* wake up...
HUH?!

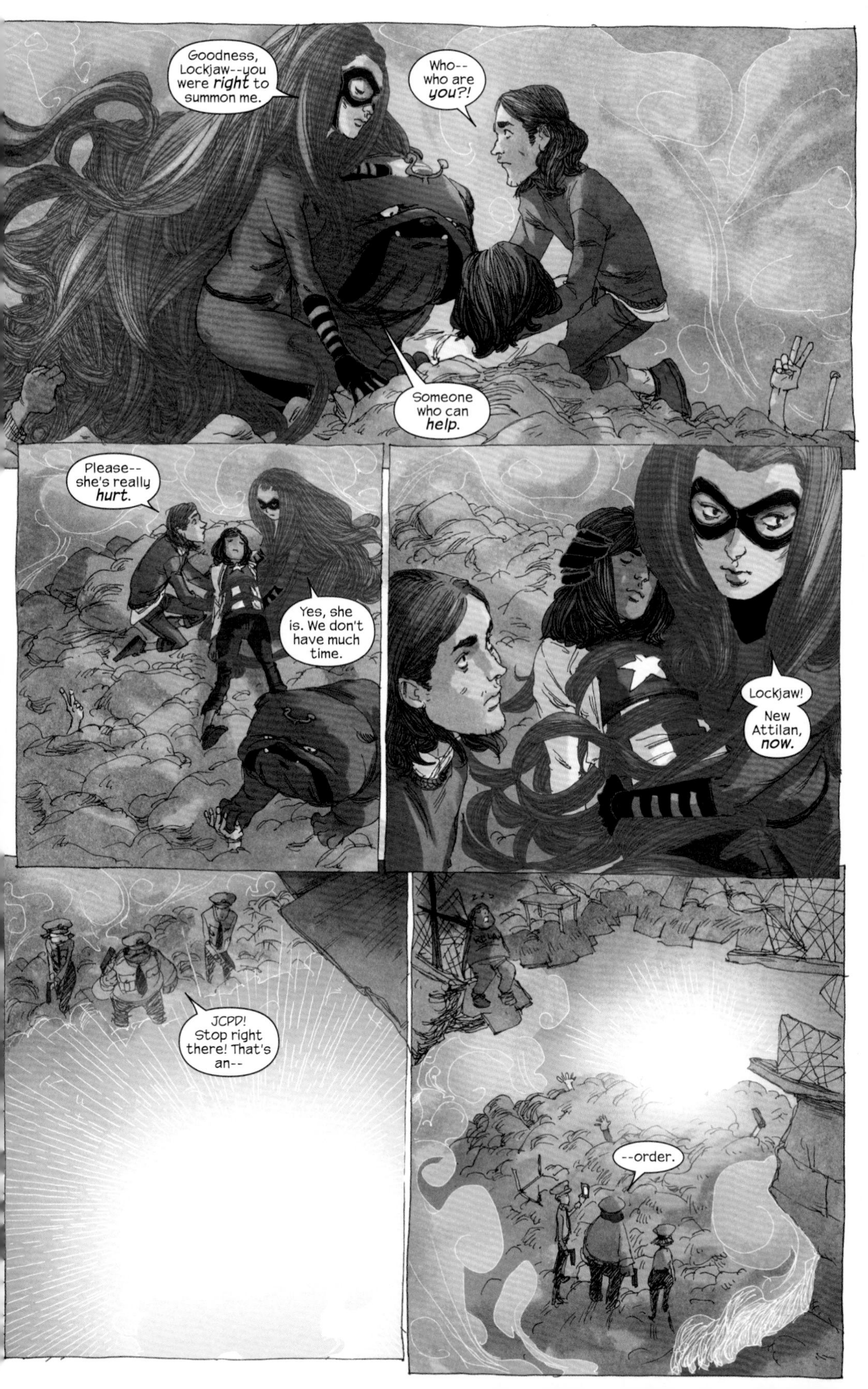

Goodness, Lockjaw--you were *right* to summon me.
Who--who are *you?!*
Someone who can *help*.
Please--she's really *hurt*.
Yes, she is. We don't have much time.
Lockjaw! New Attilan, *now.*
JCPD! Stop right there! That's an--
--order.

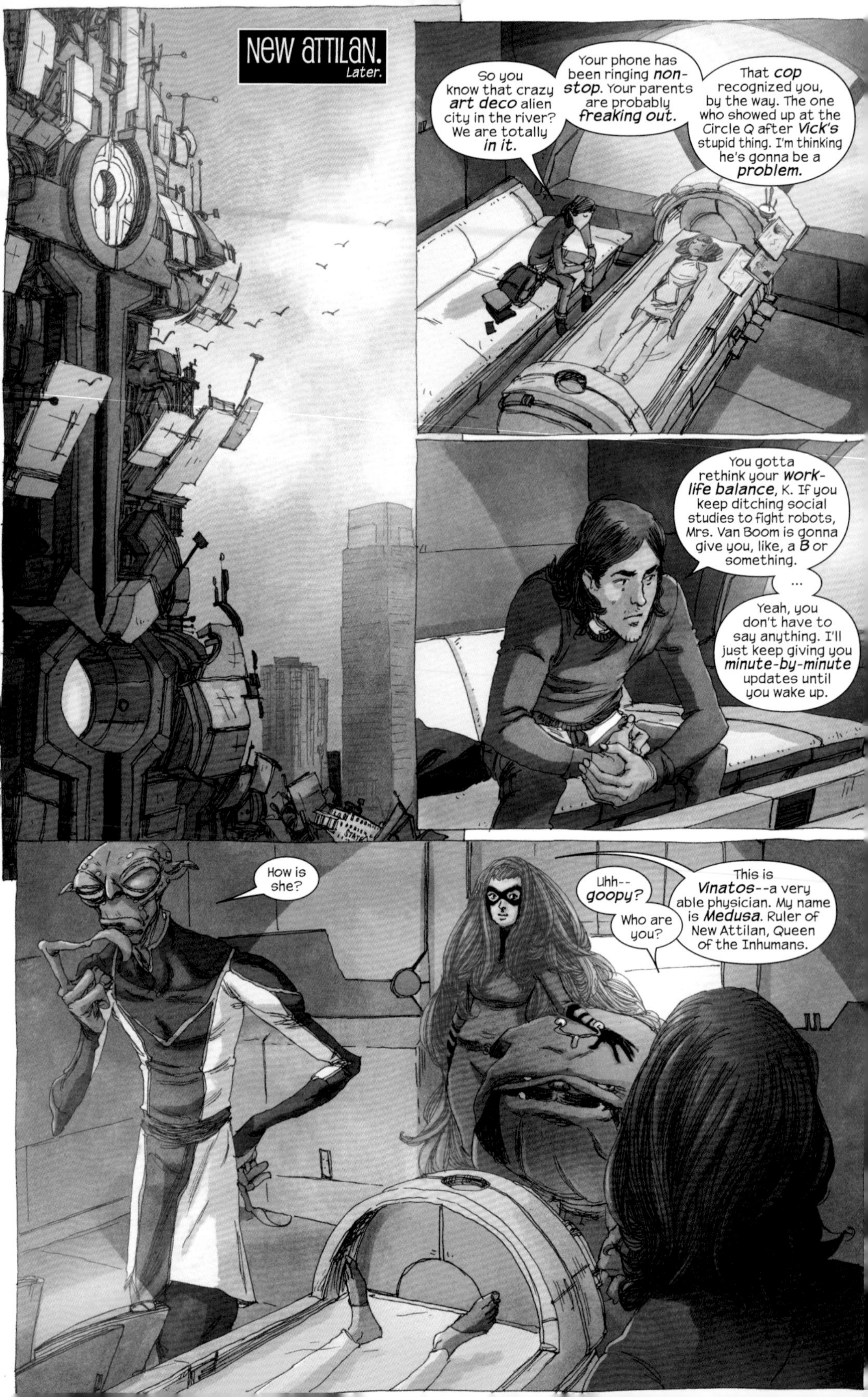
NEW ATTILAN. Later.
So you know that crazy art deco alien city in the river? We are totally in it.
Your phone has been ringing non-stop. Your parents are probably freaking out.
That cop recognized you, by the way. The one who showed up at the Circle Q after Vick's stupid thing. I'm thinking he's gonna be a problem.
You gotta rethink your work-life balance, K. If you keep ditching social studies to fight robots, Mrs. Van Boom is gonna give you, like, a B or something.
...
Yeah, you don't have to say anything. I'll just keep giving you minute-by-minute updates until you wake up.
How is she?
Uhh-- goopy?
Who are you?
This is Vinatos--a very able physician. My name is Medusa. Ruler of New Attilan, Queen of the Inhumans.

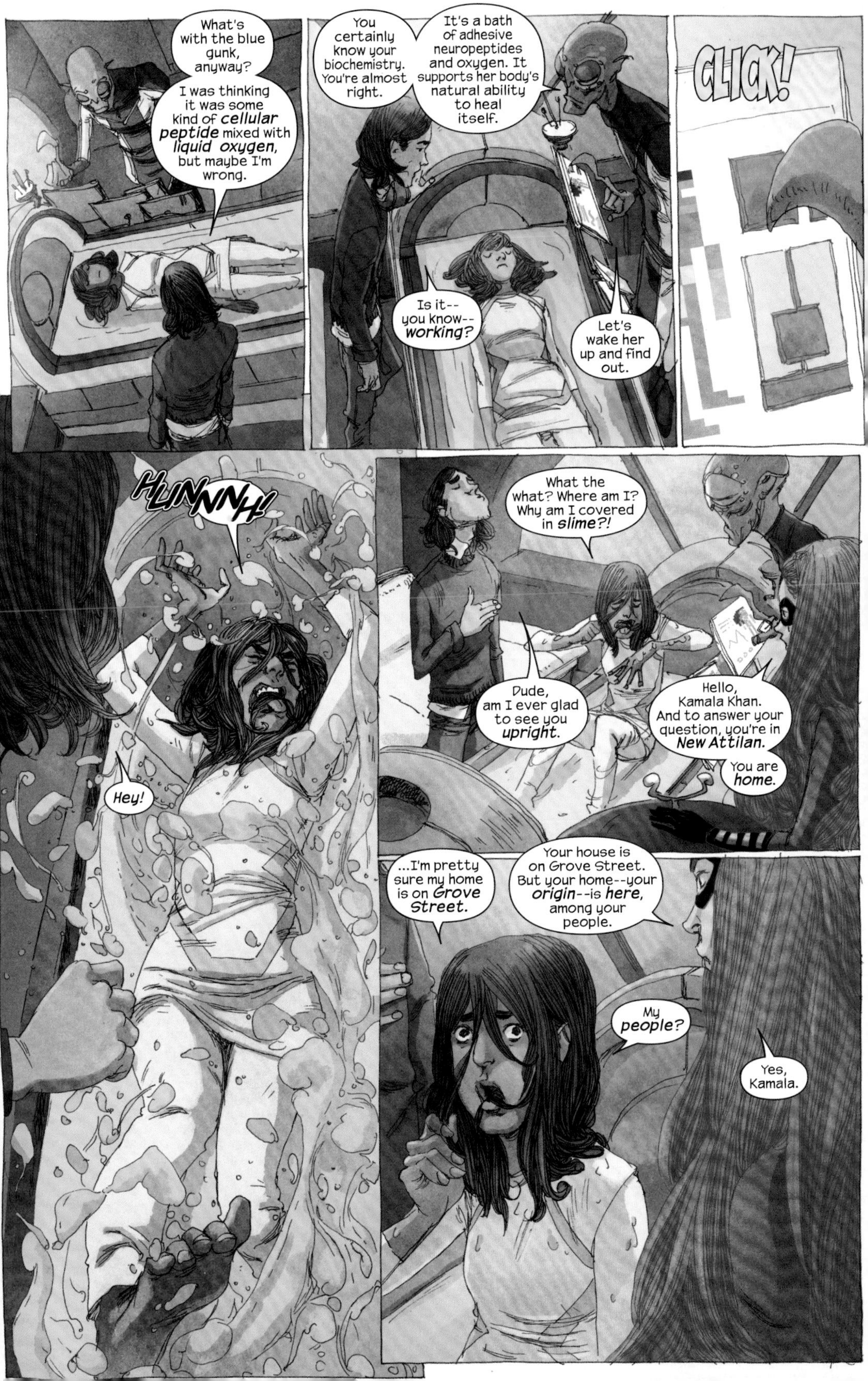

What's with the blue gunk, anyway?
I was thinking it was some kind of cellular peptide mixed with liquid oxygen, but maybe I'm wrong.
You certainly know your biochemistry. You're almost right.
It's a bath of adhesive neuropeptides and oxygen. It supports her body's natural ability to heal itself.
Is it--you know--working?
Let's wake her up and find out.
CLICK!
HUNNNH!
Hey!
What the what? Where am I? Why am I covered in slime?!
Dude, am I ever glad to see you upright.
Hello, Kamala Khan. And to answer your question, you're in New Attilan.
You are home.
...I'm pretty sure my home is on Grove Street.
Your house is on Grove Street. But your home--your origin--is here, among your people.
My people?
Yes, Kamala.

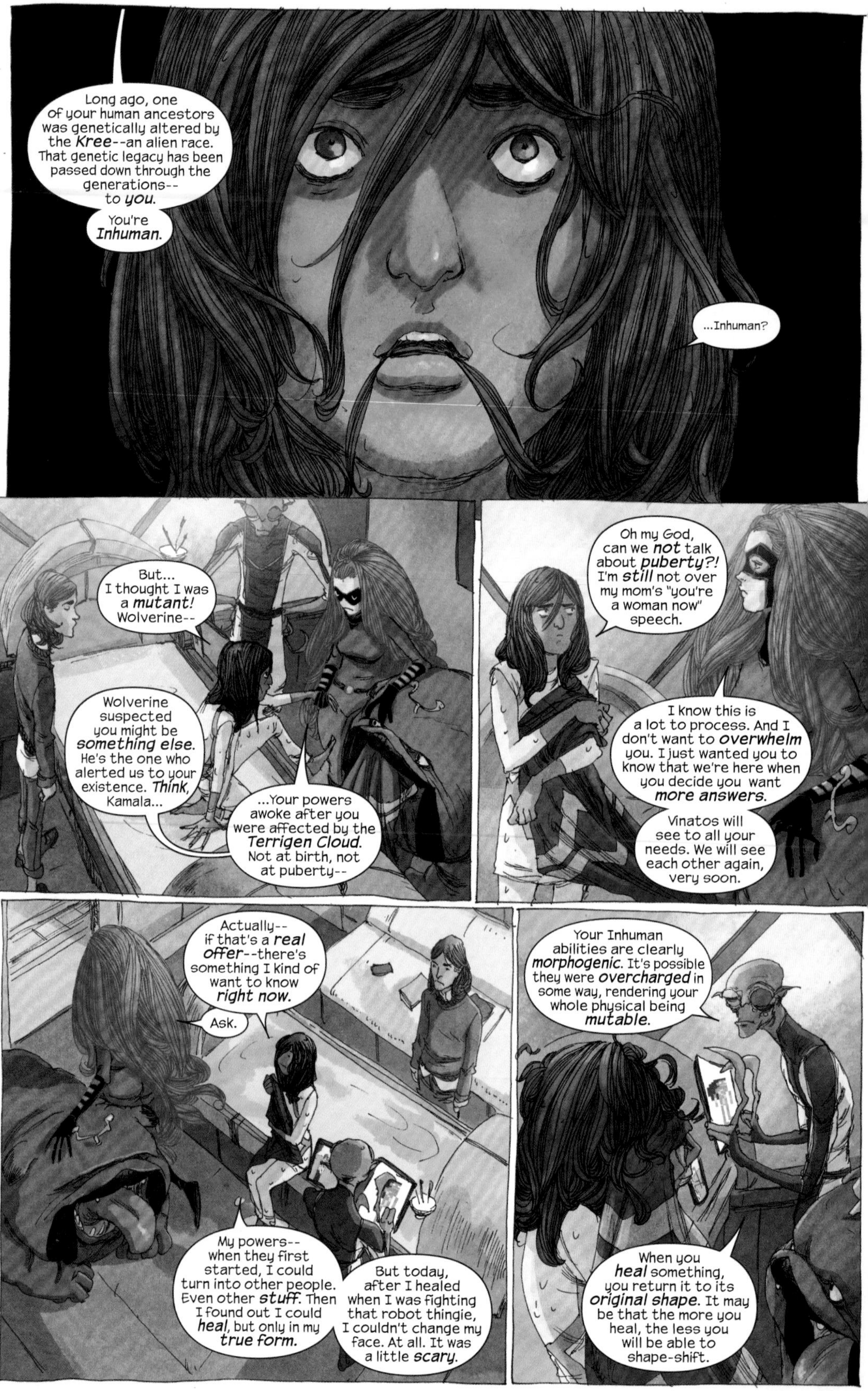
Long ago, one of your human ancestors was genetically altered by the Kree--an alien race. That genetic legacy has been passed down through the generations-- to you.
You're Inhuman.
...Inhuman?
But... I thought I was a mutant! Wolverine--
Wolverine suspected you might be something else. He's the one who alerted us to your existence. Think, Kamala...
...Your powers awoke after you were affected by the Terrigen Cloud. Not at birth, not at puberty--
Oh my God, can we not talk about puberty?! I'm still not over my mom's "you're a woman now" speech.
I know this is a lot to process. And I don't want to overwhelm you. I just wanted you to know that we're here when you decide you want more answers.
Vinatos will see to all your needs. We will see each other again, very soon.
Actually-- if that's a real offer--there's something I kind of want to know right now.
Ask.
My powers-- when they first started, I could turn into other people. Even other stuff. Then I found out I could heal, but only in my true form.
But today, after I healed when I was fighting that robot thingie, I couldn't change my face. At all. It was a little scary.
Your Inhuman abilities are clearly morphogenic. It's possible they were overcharged in some way, rendering your whole physical being mutable.
When you heal something, you return it to its original shape. It may be that the more you heal, the less you will be able to shape-shift.

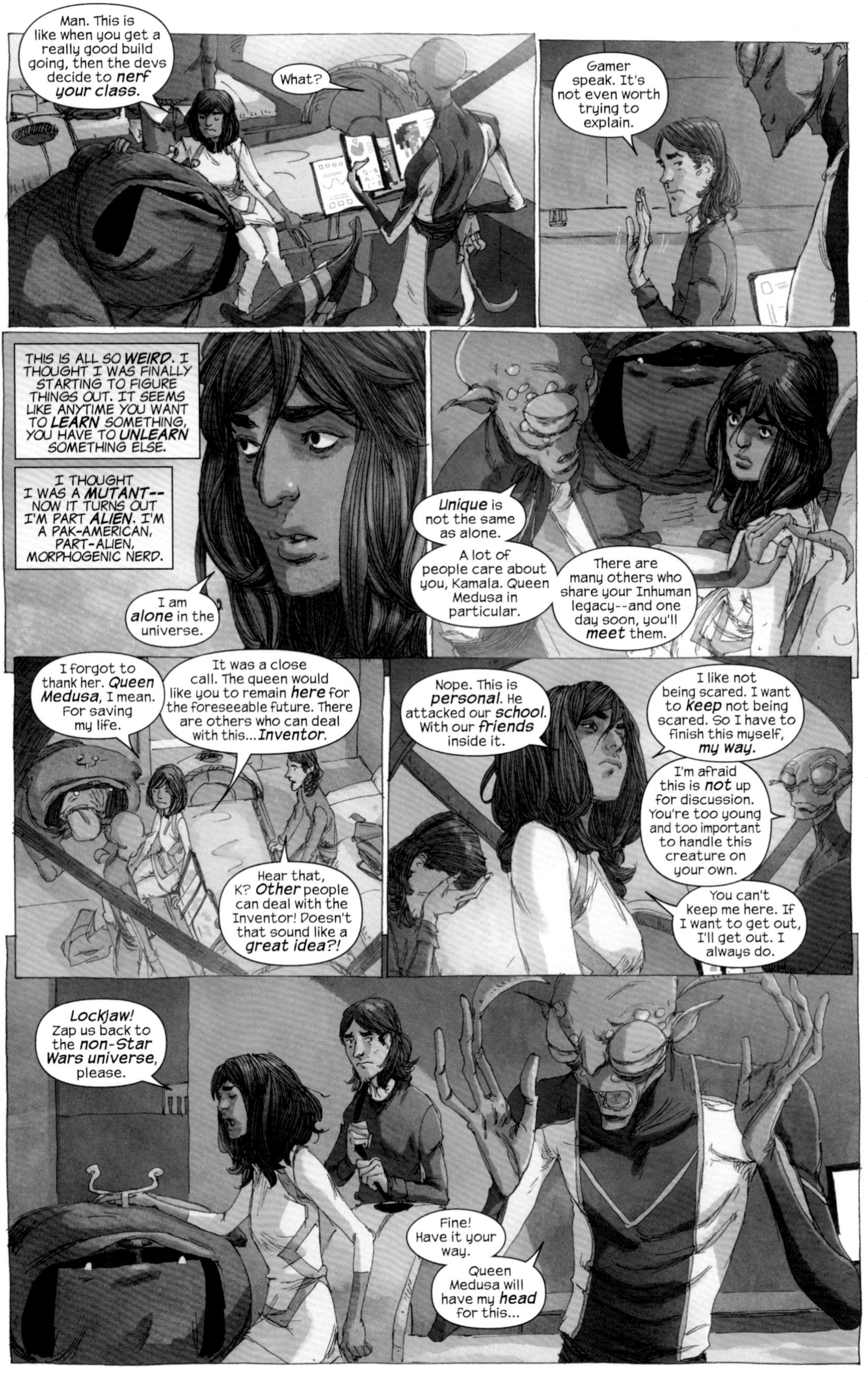

Man. This is like when you get a really good build going, then the devs decide to *nerf your class.*
What?
Gamer speak. It's not even worth trying to explain.
THIS IS ALL SO *WEIRD*. I THOUGHT I WAS FINALLY STARTING TO FIGURE THINGS OUT. IT SEEMS LIKE ANYTIME YOU WANT TO *LEARN* SOMETHING, YOU HAVE TO *UNLEARN* SOMETHING ELSE.
I THOUGHT I WAS A *MUTANT*-- NOW IT TURNS OUT I'M PART *ALIEN*. I'M A PAK-AMERICAN, PART-ALIEN, MORPHOGENIC NERD.
I am *alone* in the universe.
Unique is not the same as alone.
A lot of people care about you, Kamala. Queen Medusa in particular.
There are many others who share your Inhuman legacy--and one day soon, you'll *meet* them.
I forgot to thank her. *Queen Medusa*, I mean. For saving my life.
It was a close call. The queen would like you to remain *here* for the foreseeable future. There are others who can deal with this... *Inventor*.
Hear that, K? *Other* people can deal with the Inventor! Doesn't that sound like a *great idea?!*
Nope. This is *personal*. He attacked our *school*. With our *friends* inside it.
I like not being scared. I want to *keep* not being scared. So I have to finish this myself, *my way*.
I'm afraid this is *not* up for discussion. You're too young and too important to handle this creature on your own.
You can't keep me here. If I want to get out, I'll get out. I always do.
Lockjaw! Zap us back to the *non-Star Wars universe*, please.
Fine! Have it your way.
Queen Medusa will have my *head* for this...

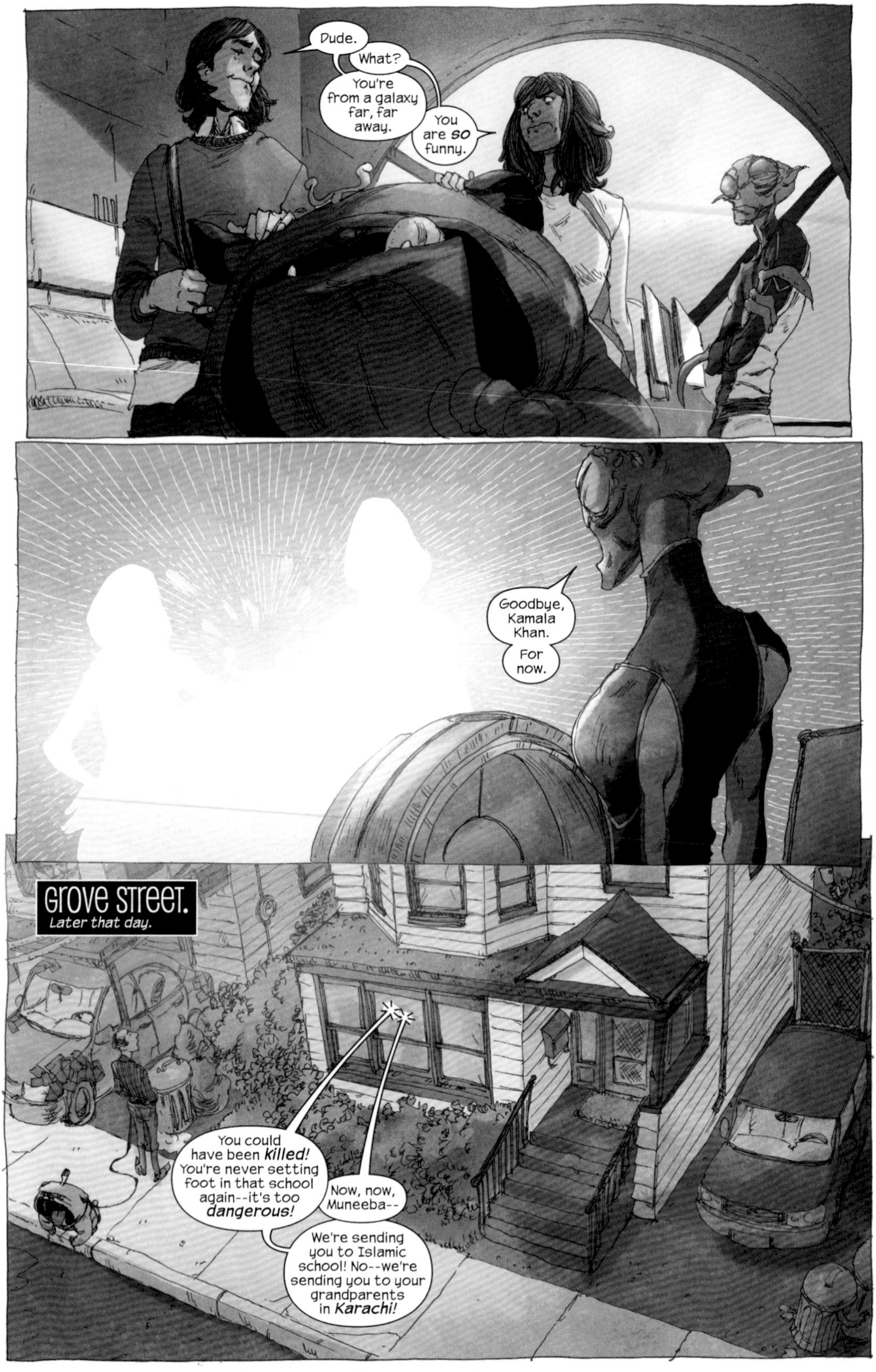
Dude.
What?
You're from a galaxy far, far away.
You are *SO* funny.
Goodbye, Kamala Khan.
For now.
GROVE STREET.
Later that day.
You could have been *killed!* You're never setting foot in that school again--it's too *dangerous!*
Now, now, Muneeba--
We're sending you to Islamic school! No--we're sending you to your grandparents in *Karachi!*

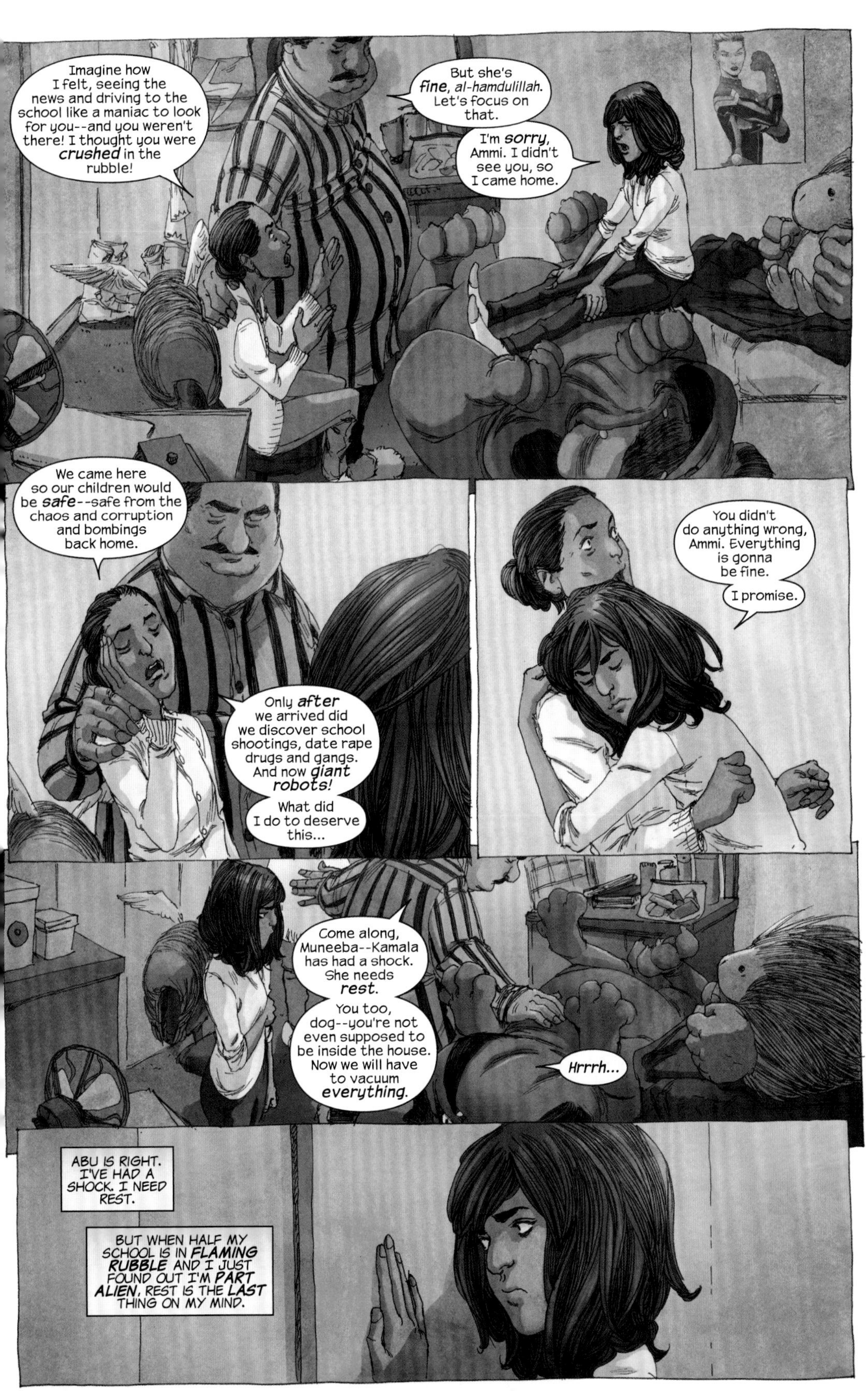

Imagine how I felt, seeing the news and driving to the school like a maniac to look for you--and you weren't there! I thought you were *crushed* in the rubble!
But she's *fine*, *al-hamdulillah*. Let's focus on that.
I'm *sorry*, Ammi. I didn't see you, so I came home.
We came here so our children would be *safe*--safe from the chaos and corruption and bombings back home.
Only *after* we arrived did we discover school shootings, date rape drugs and gangs. And now *giant robots*!
What did I do to deserve this...
You didn't do anything wrong, Ammi. Everything is gonna be fine.
I promise.
Come along, Muneeba--Kamala has had a shock. She needs *rest*.
You too, dog--you're not even supposed to be inside the house. Now we will have to vacuum *everything*.
Hrrrh...
ABU IS RIGHT. I'VE HAD A SHOCK. I NEED REST.
BUT WHEN HALF MY SCHOOL IS IN *FLAMING RUBBLE* AND I JUST FOUND OUT I'M *PART ALIEN*, REST IS THE *LAST* THING ON MY MIND.

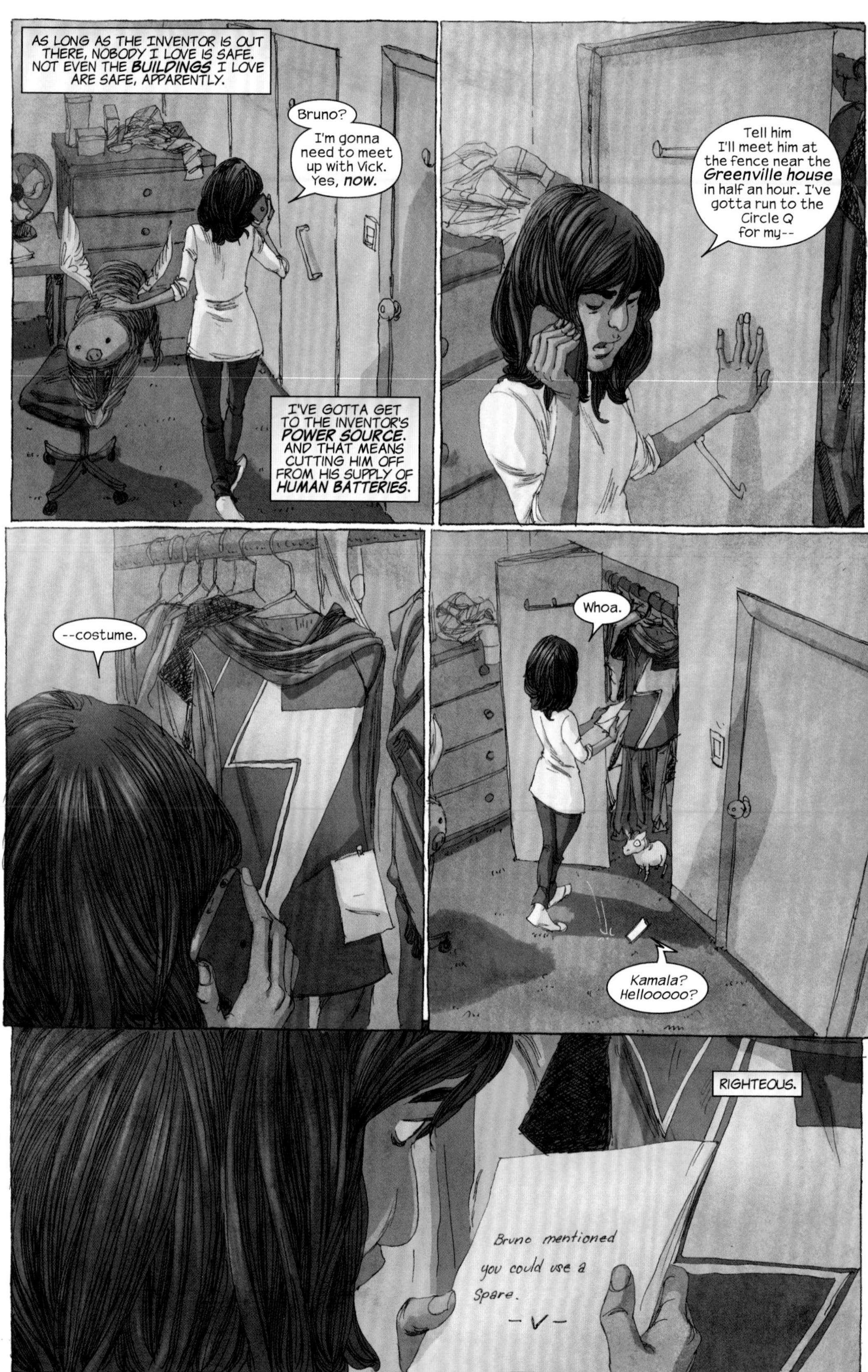
AS LONG AS THE INVENTOR IS OUT THERE, NOBODY I LOVE IS SAFE. NOT EVEN THE BUILDINGS I LOVE ARE SAFE, APPARENTLY.
Bruno?
I'm gonna need to meet up with Vick. Yes, now.
I'VE GOTTA GET TO THE INVENTOR'S POWER SOURCE. AND THAT MEANS CUTTING HIM OFF FROM HIS SUPPLY OF HUMAN BATTERIES.
Tell him I'll meet him at the fence near the Greenville house in half an hour. I've gotta run to the Circle Q for my--
--costume.
Whoa.
Kamala? Hellooooo?
RIGHTEOUS.
Bruno mentioned you could use a spare.
-V-

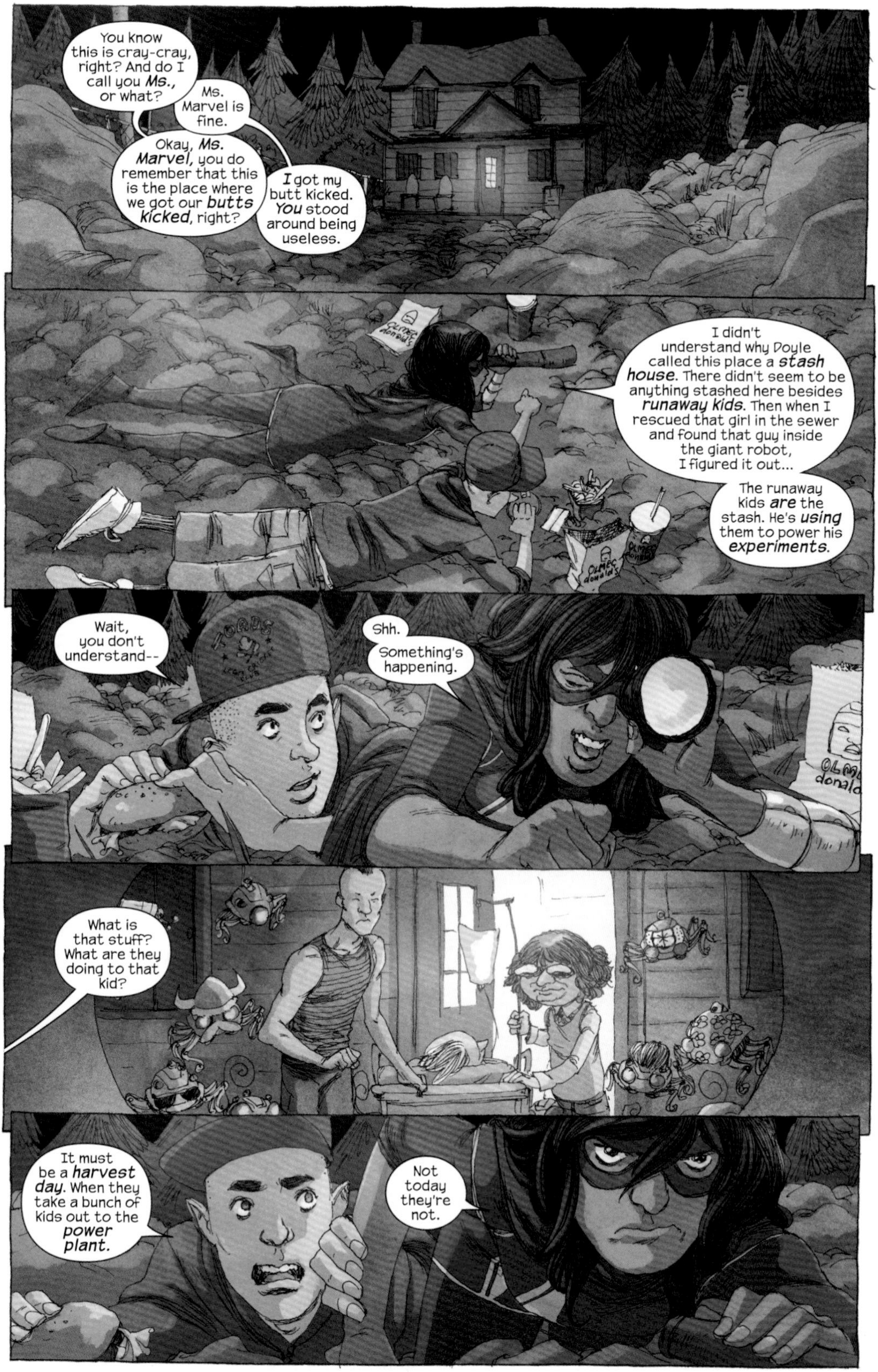
You know this is cray-cray, right? And do I call you Ms., or what?
Ms. Marvel is fine.
Okay, Ms. Marvel, you do remember that this is the place where we got our butts kicked, right?
I got my butt kicked. You stood around being useless.
I didn't understand why Doyle called this place a stash house. There didn't seem to be anything stashed here besides runaway kids. Then when I rescued that girl in the sewer and found that guy inside the giant robot, I figured it out...
The runaway kids are the stash. He's using them to power his experiments.
Wait, you don't understand--
Shh.
Something's happening.
What is that stuff? What are they doing to that kid?
It must be a harvest day. When they take a bunch of kids out to the power plant.
Not today they're not.

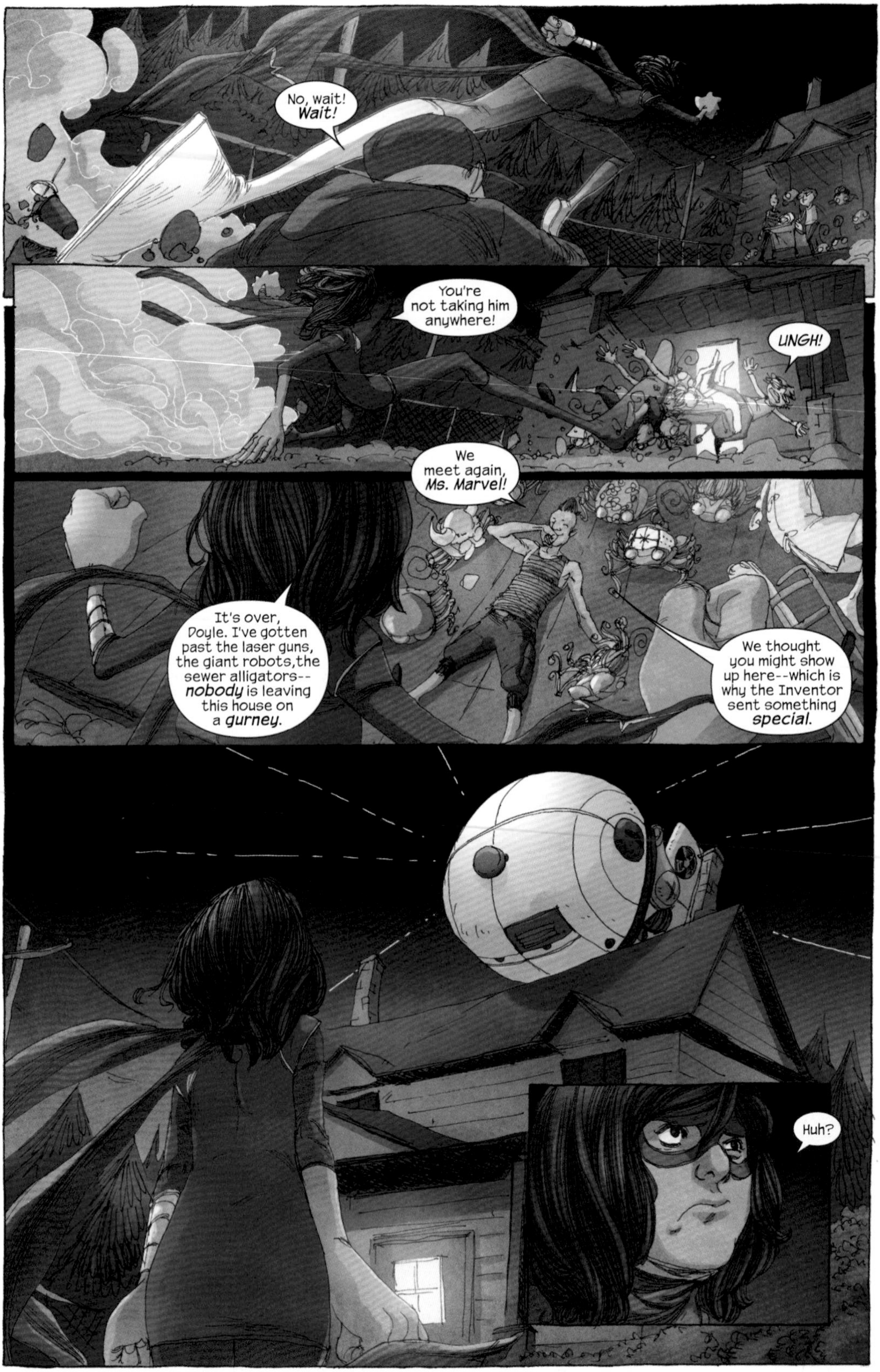
No, wait! Wait!
You're not taking him anywhere!
UNGH!
We meet again, Ms. Marvel!
It's over, Doyle. I've gotten past the laser guns, the giant robots, the sewer alligators-- nobody is leaving this house on a gurney.
We thought you might show up here--which is why the Inventor sent something special.
Huh?

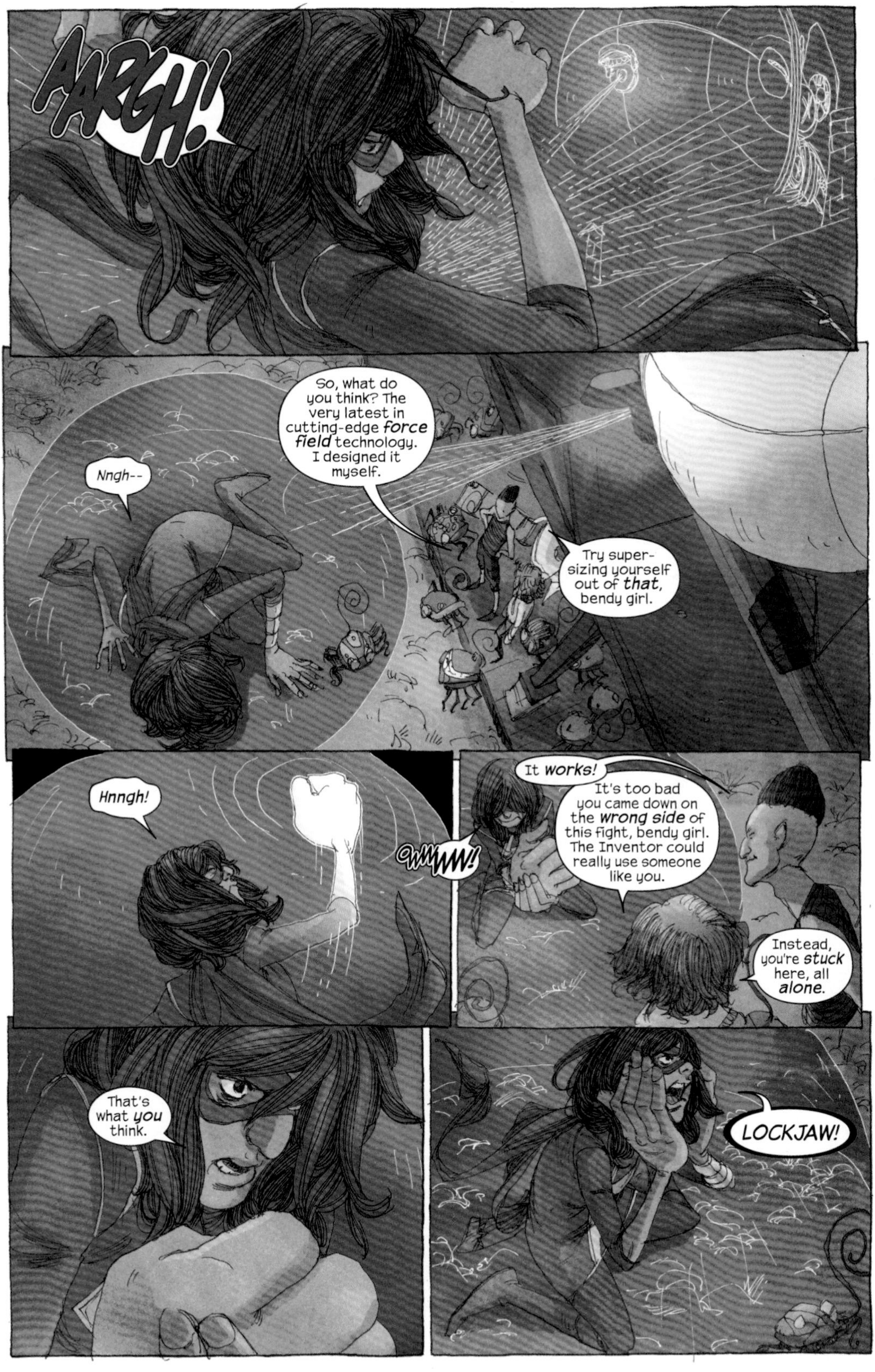

AARGH!
So, what do you think? The very latest in cutting-edge force field technology. I designed it myself.
Nngh--
Try super-sizing yourself out of that, bendy girl.
Hnngh!
WMMWW!
It works!
It's too bad you came down on the wrong side of this fight, bendy girl. The Inventor could really use someone like you.
Instead, you're stuck here, all alone.
That's what you think.
LOCKJAW!

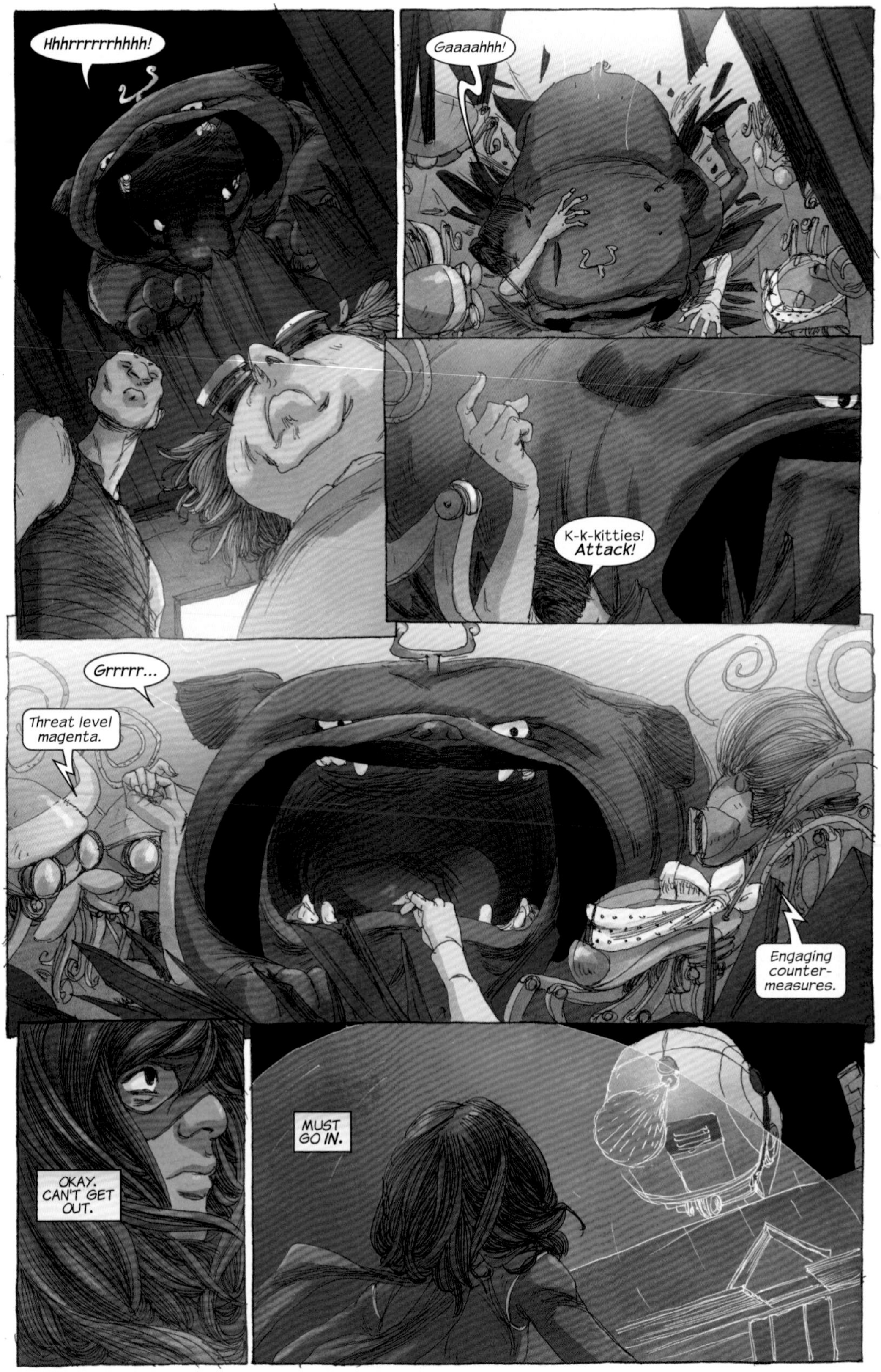
Hhhrrrrrrhhhh!
Gaaaahhh!
K-k-kitties! Attack!
Grrrrr...
Threat level magenta.
Engaging counter-measures.
OKAY. CAN'T GET OUT.
MUST GO IN.

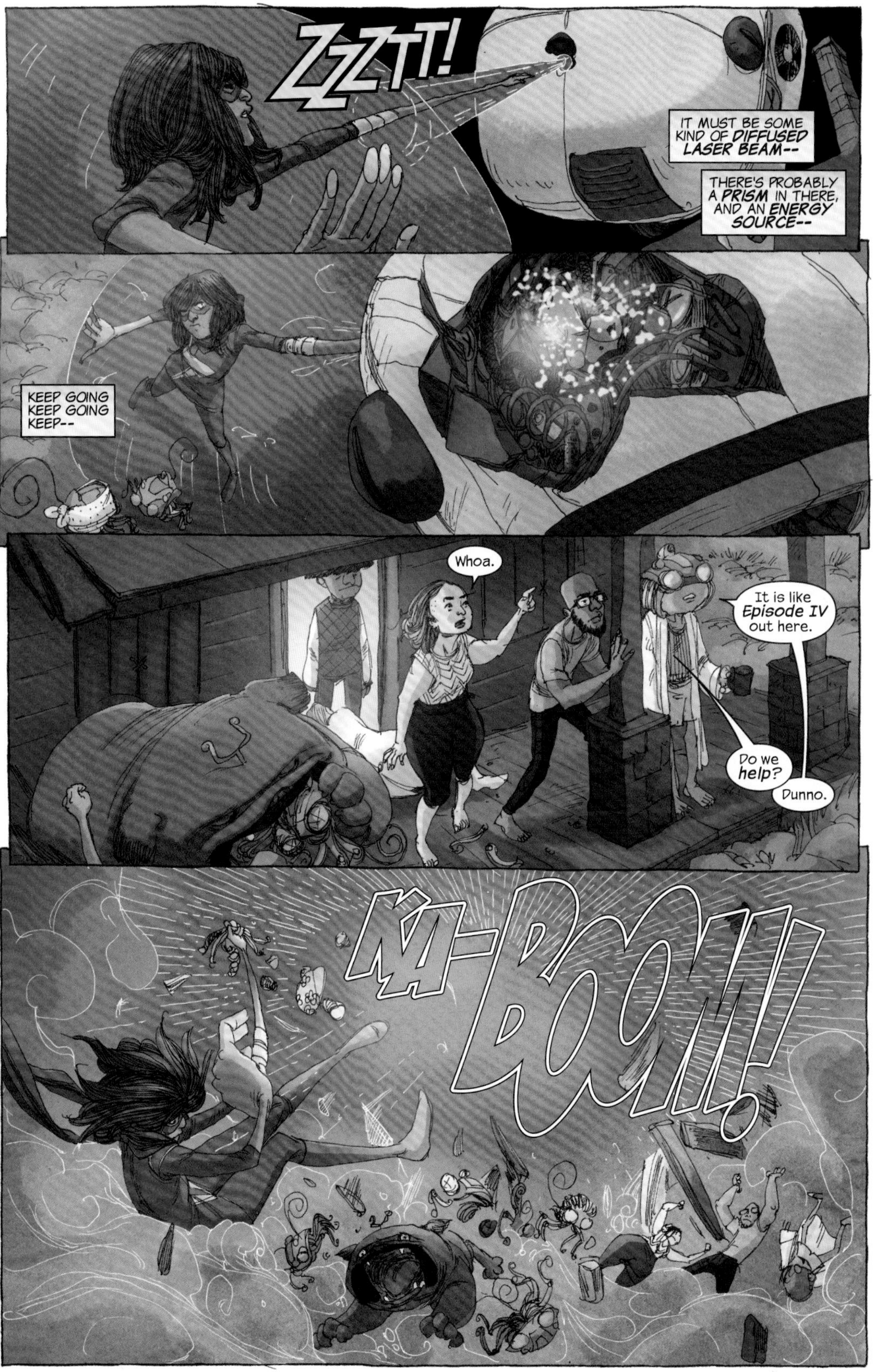
ZZZTT!
IT MUST BE SOME KIND OF DIFFUSED LASER BEAM--
THERE'S PROBABLY A PRISM IN THERE, AND AN ENERGY SOURCE--
KEEP GOING KEEP GOING KEEP--
Whoa.
It is like Episode IV out here.
Do we help?
Dunno.
KA-BOOM!

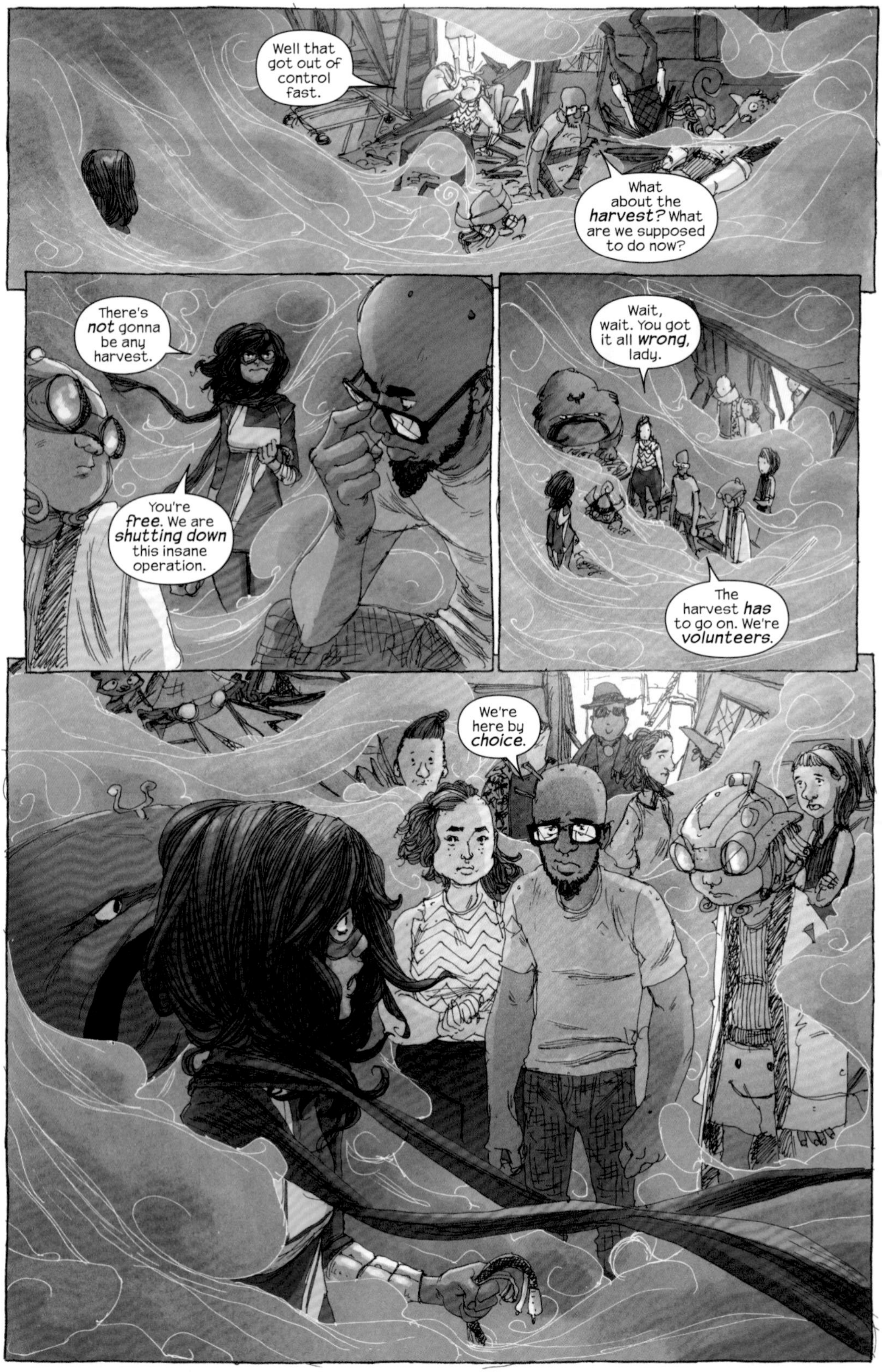
Well that got out of control fast.
What about the harvest? What are we supposed to do now?
There's not gonna be any harvest.
You're free. We are shutting down this insane operation.
Wait, wait. You got it all wrong, lady.
The harvest has to go on. We're volunteers.
We're here by choice.

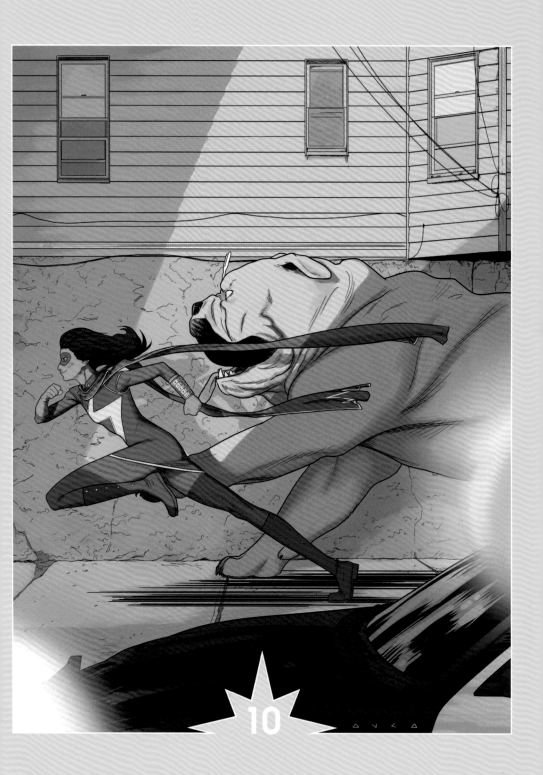

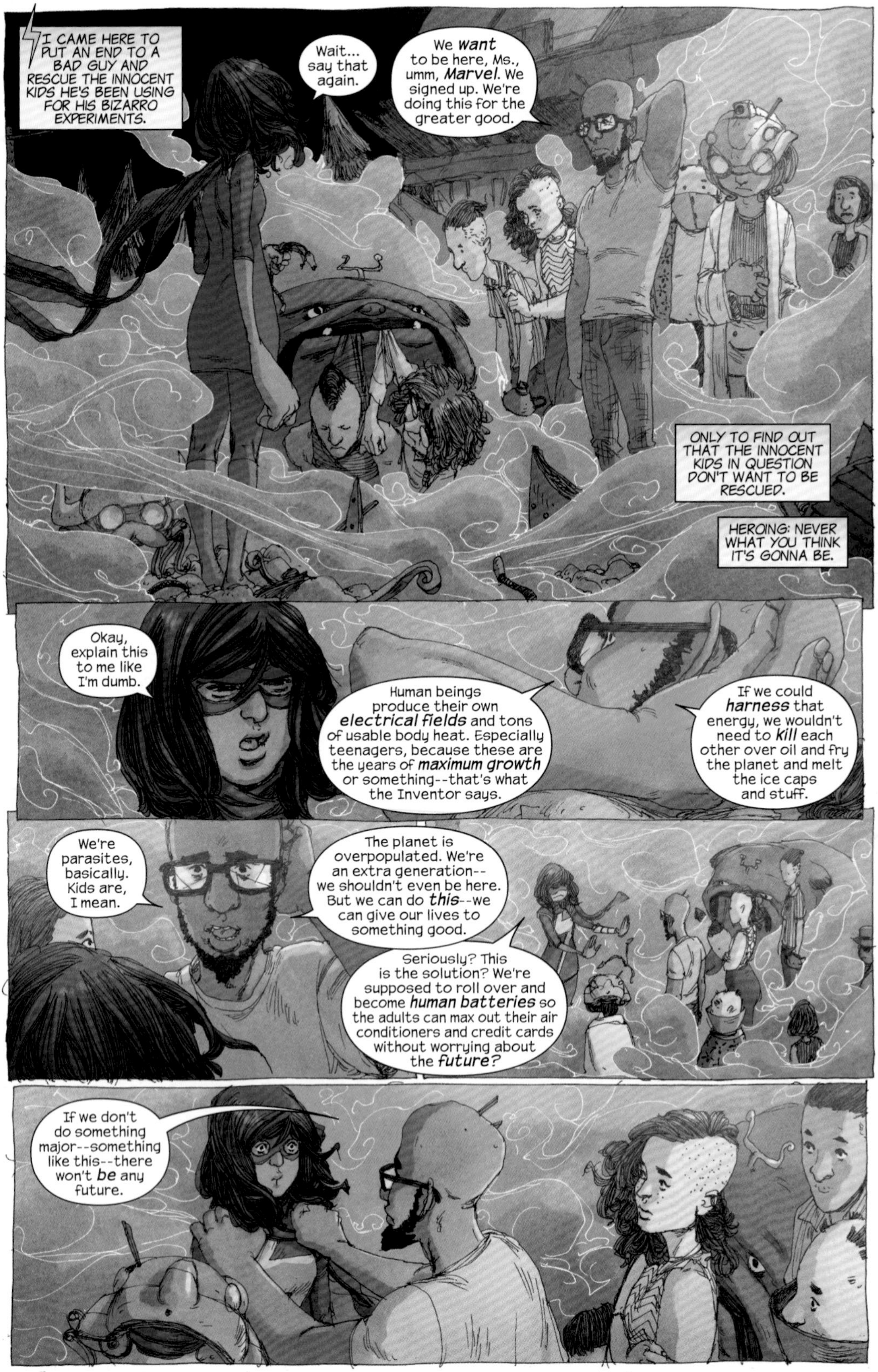
I CAME HERE TO PUT AN END TO A BAD GUY AND RESCUE THE INNOCENT KIDS HE'S BEEN USING FOR HIS BIZARRO EXPERIMENTS.
Wait... say that again.
We want to be here, Ms., umm, Marvel. We signed up. We're doing this for the greater good.
ONLY TO FIND OUT THAT THE INNOCENT KIDS IN QUESTION DON'T WANT TO BE RESCUED.
HEROING: NEVER WHAT YOU THINK IT'S GONNA BE.
Okay, explain this to me like I'm dumb.
Human beings produce their own electrical fields and tons of usable body heat. Especially teenagers, because these are the years of maximum growth or something--that's what the Inventor says.
If we could harness that energy, we wouldn't need to kill each other over oil and fry the planet and melt the ice caps and stuff.
We're parasites, basically. Kids are, I mean.
The planet is overpopulated. We're an extra generation--we shouldn't even be here. But we can do this--we can give our lives to something good.
Seriously? This is the solution? We're supposed to roll over and become human batteries so the adults can max out their air conditioners and credit cards without worrying about the future?
If we don't do something major--something like this--there won't be any future.

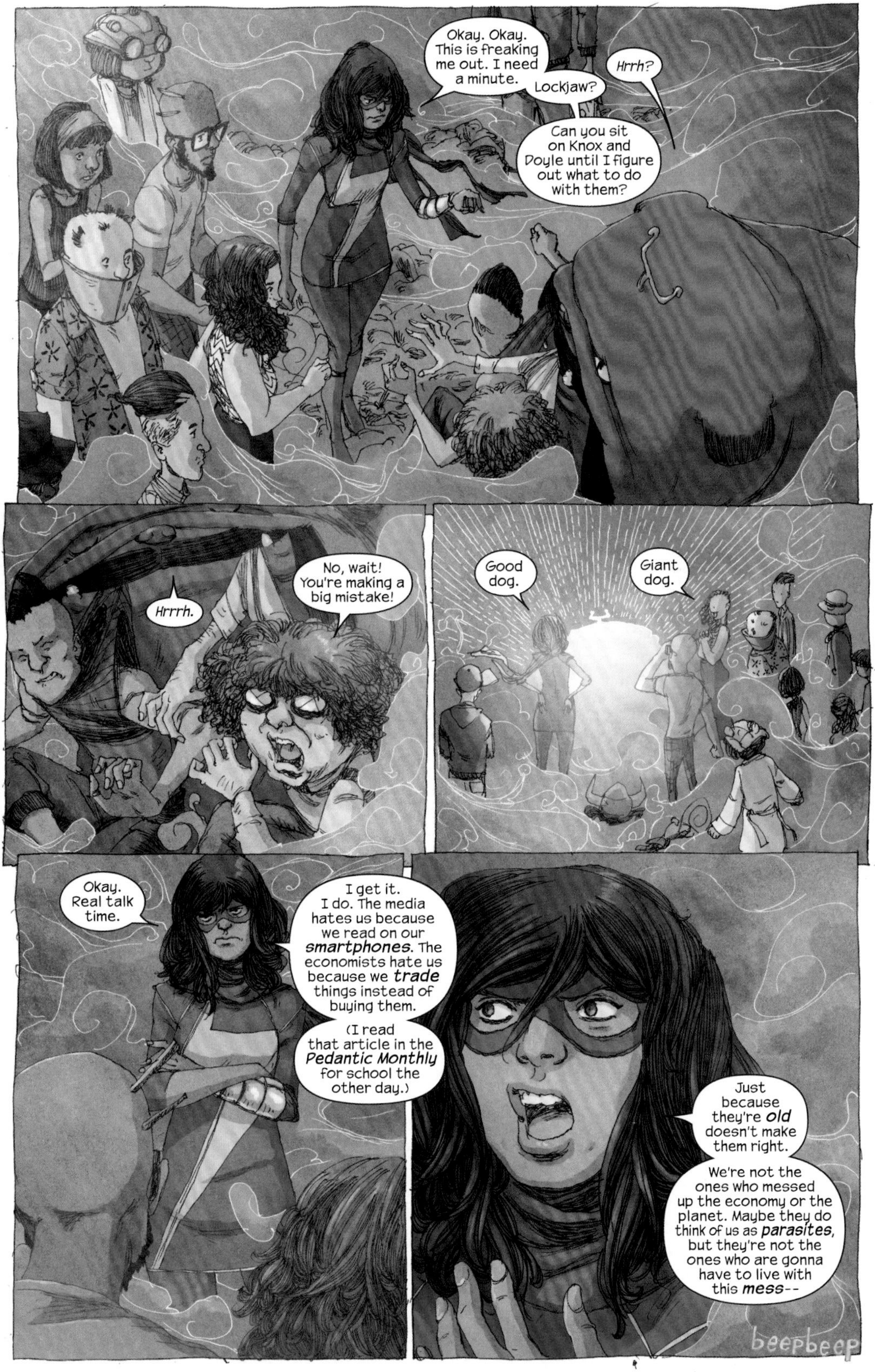
Okay. Okay. This is freaking me out. I need a minute.
Lockjaw?
Hrrh?
Can you sit on Knox and Doyle until I figure out what to do with them?
Hrrrh.
No, wait! You're making a big mistake!
Good dog.
Giant dog.
Okay. Real talk time.
I get it. I do. The media hates us because we read on our smartphones. The economists hate us because we trade things instead of buying them.
(I read that article in the Pedantic Monthly for school the other day.)
Just because they're old doesn't make them right.
We're not the ones who messed up the economy or the planet. Maybe they do think of us as parasites, but they're not the ones who are gonna have to live with this mess--
beepbeep

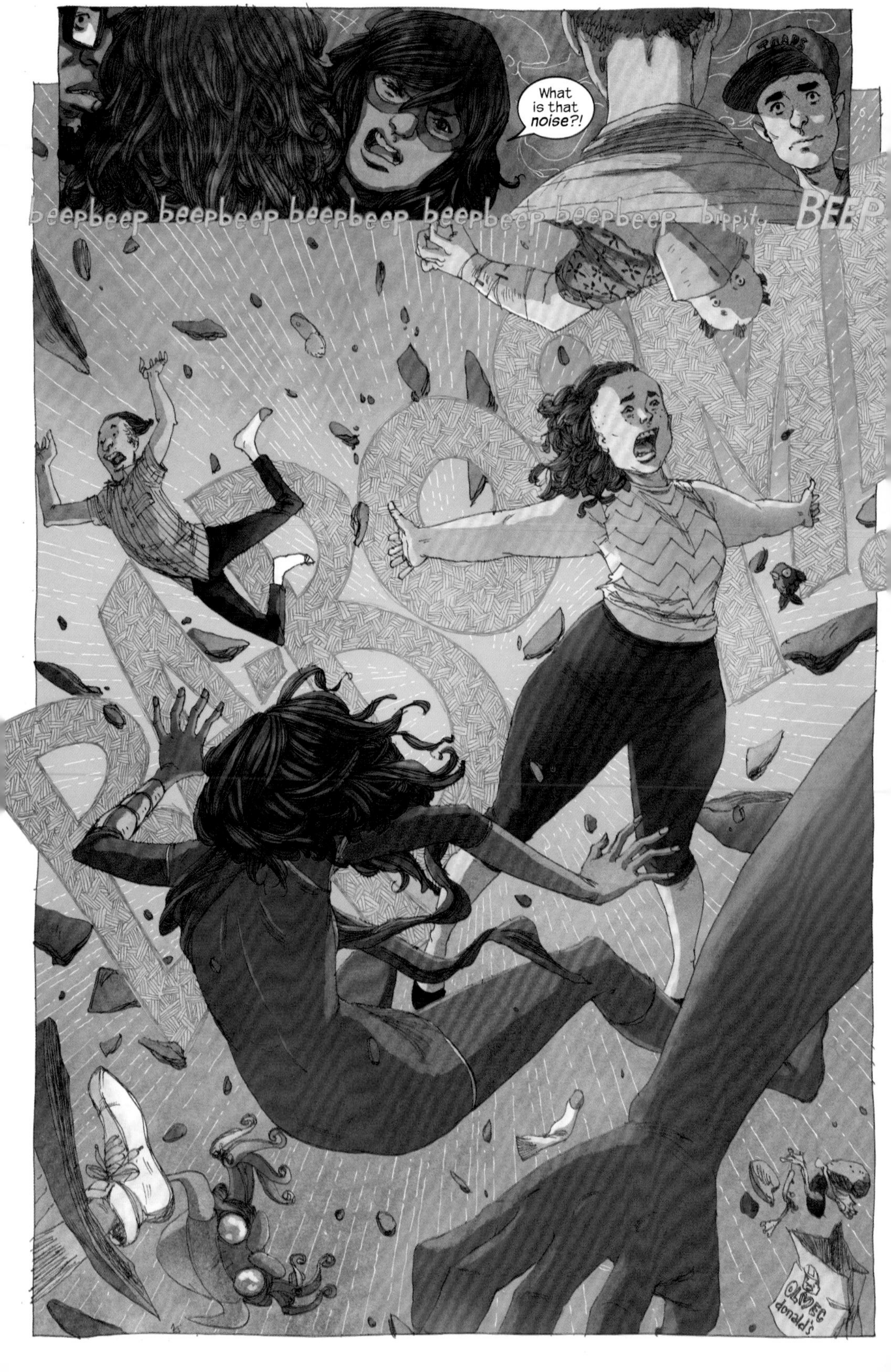
What is that *noise*?!
beepbeep beepbeep beepbeep beepbeep beepbeep bippity BEEP

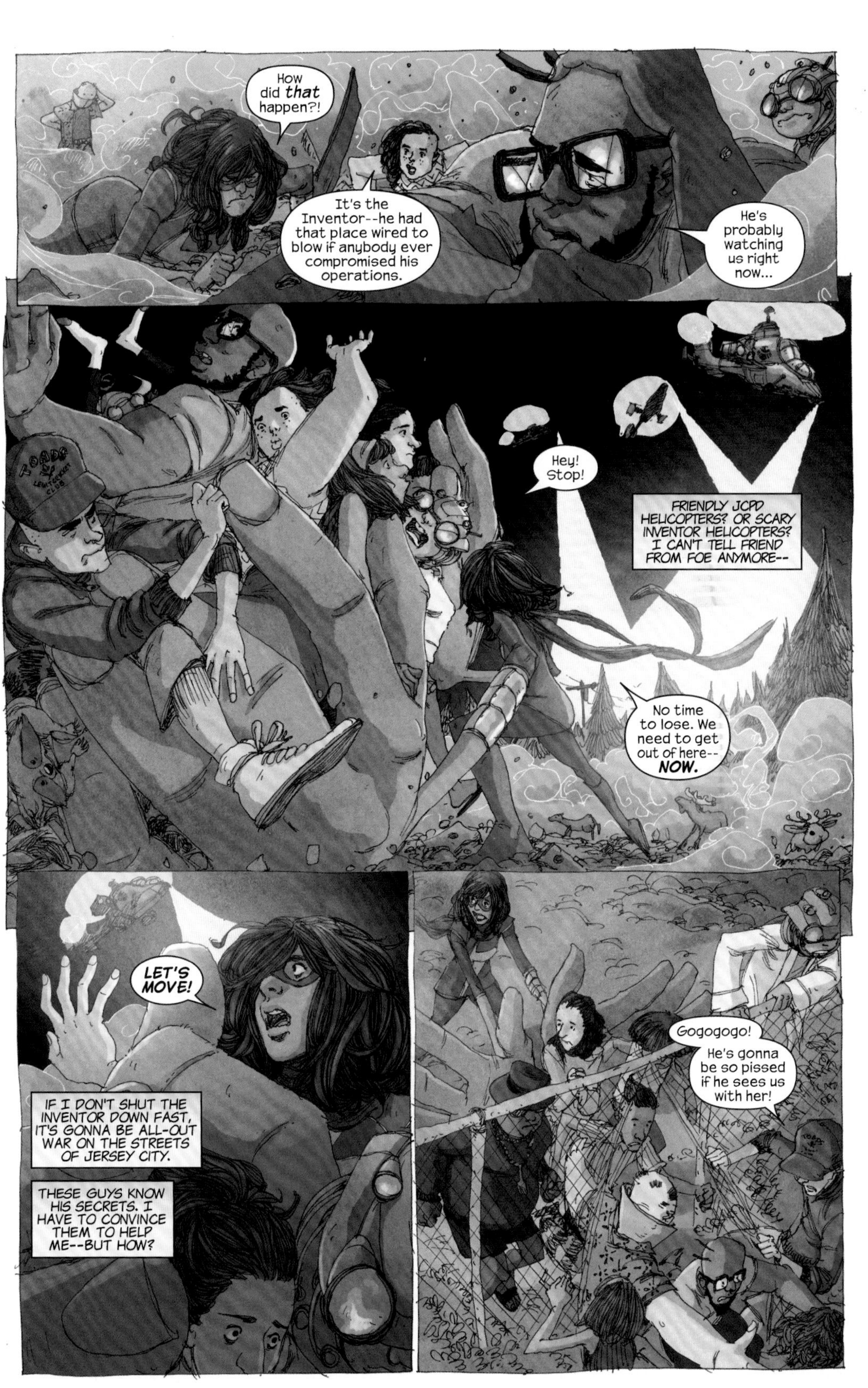
How did *that* happen?!
It's the Inventor--he had that place wired to blow if anybody ever compromised his operations.
He's probably watching us right now...
Hey! Stop!
FRIENDLY JCPD HELICOPTERS? OR SCARY INVENTOR HELICOPTERS? I CAN'T TELL FRIEND FROM FOE ANYMORE--
No time to lose. We need to get out of here-- **NOW.**
LET'S MOVE!
IF I DON'T SHUT THE INVENTOR DOWN FAST, IT'S GONNA BE ALL-OUT WAR ON THE STREETS OF JERSEY CITY.
THESE GUYS KNOW HIS SECRETS. I HAVE TO CONVINCE THEM TO HELP ME--BUT HOW?
Gogogogo!
He's gonna be so pissed if he sees us with her!

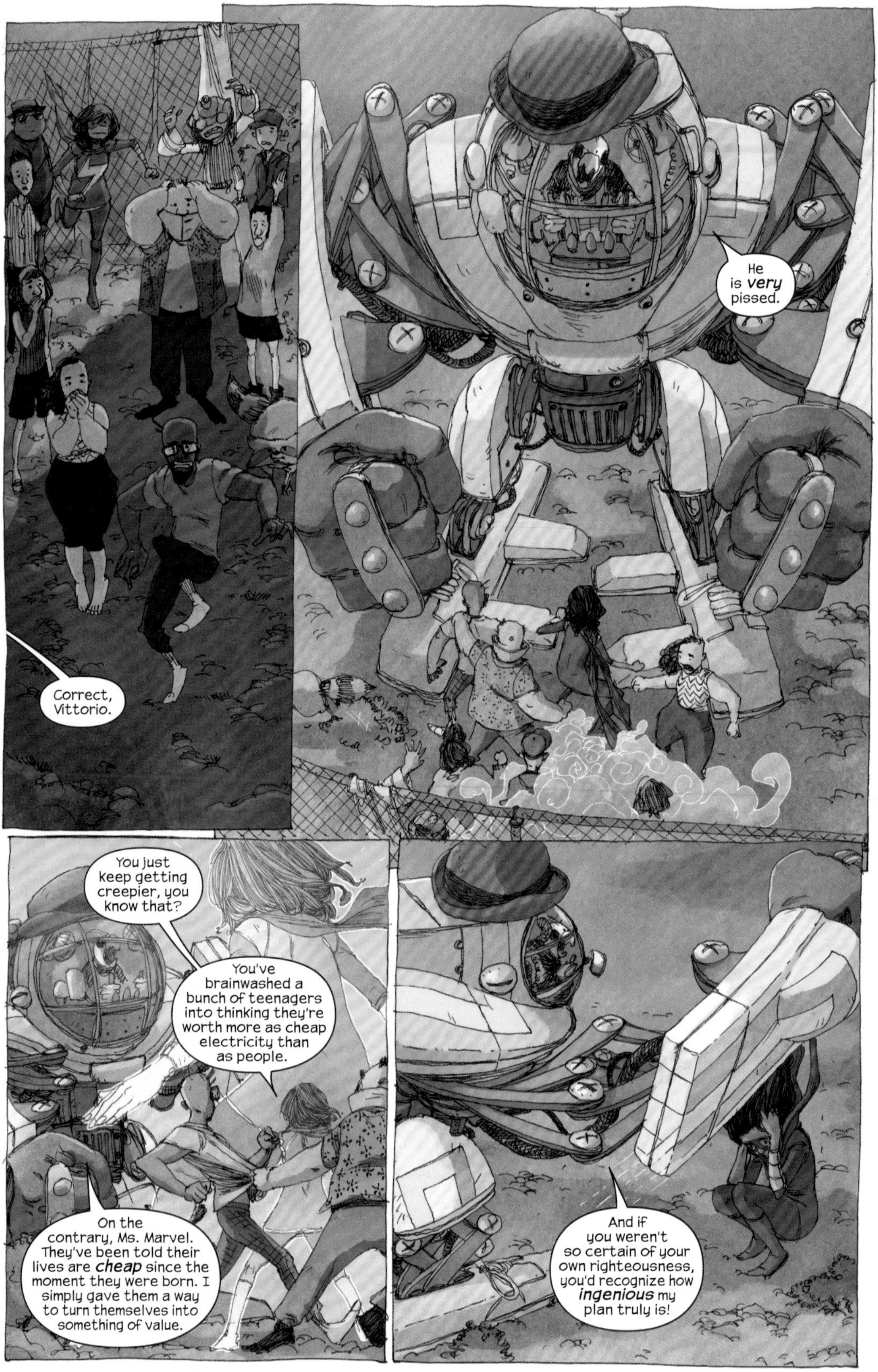
He is *very* pissed.
Correct, Vittorio.
You just keep getting creepier, you know that?
You've brainwashed a bunch of teenagers into thinking they're worth more as cheap electricity than as people.
On the contrary, Ms. Marvel. They've been told their lives are *cheap* since the moment they were born. I simply gave them a way to turn themselves into something of value.
And if you weren't so certain of your own righteousness, you'd recognize how *ingenious* my plan truly is!

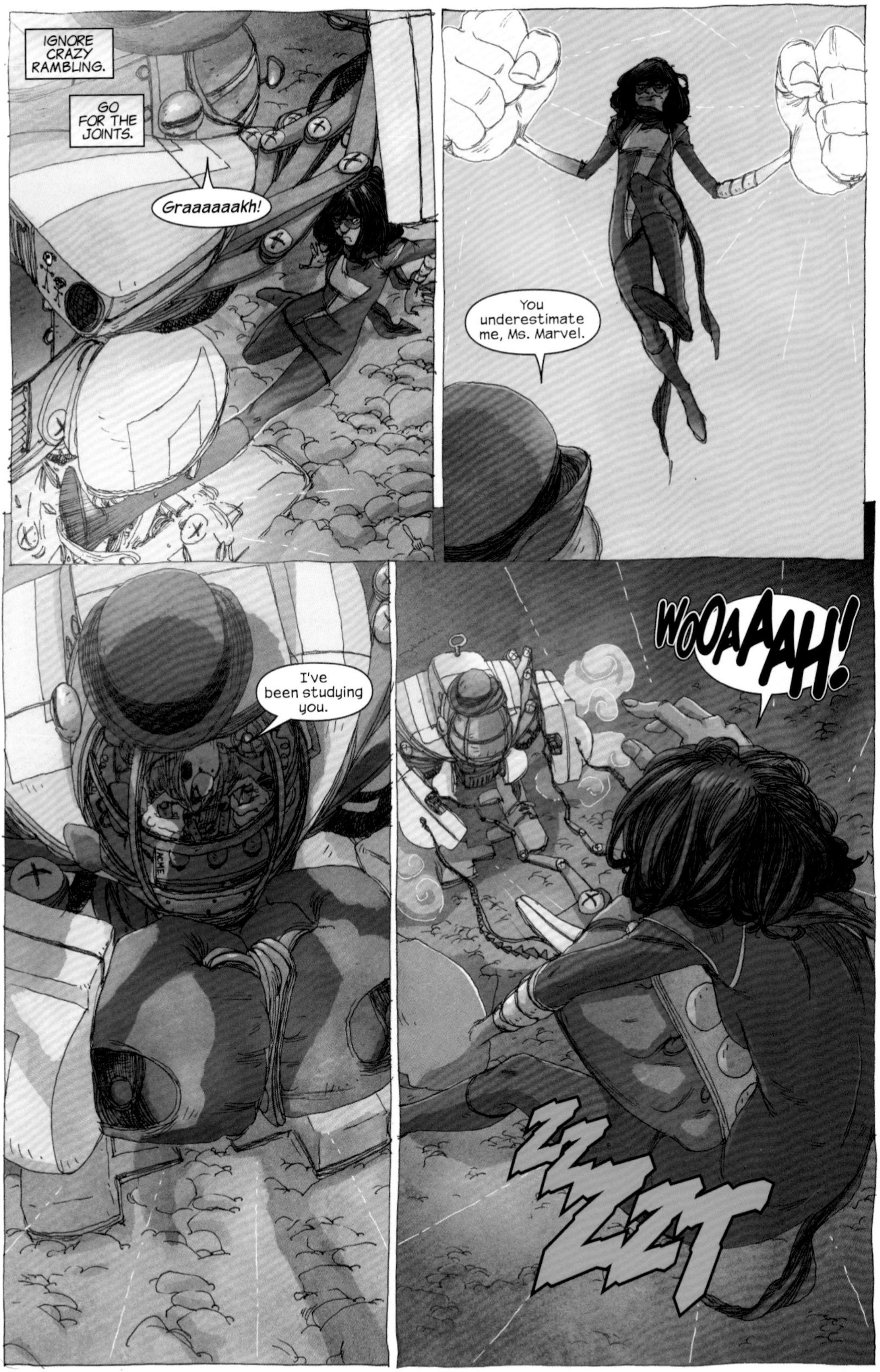
IGNORE CRAZY RAMBLING.
GO FOR THE JOINTS.
Graaaaaaakh!
You underestimate me, Ms. Marvel.
I've been studying you.
WOOAAAH!
ZZZZT

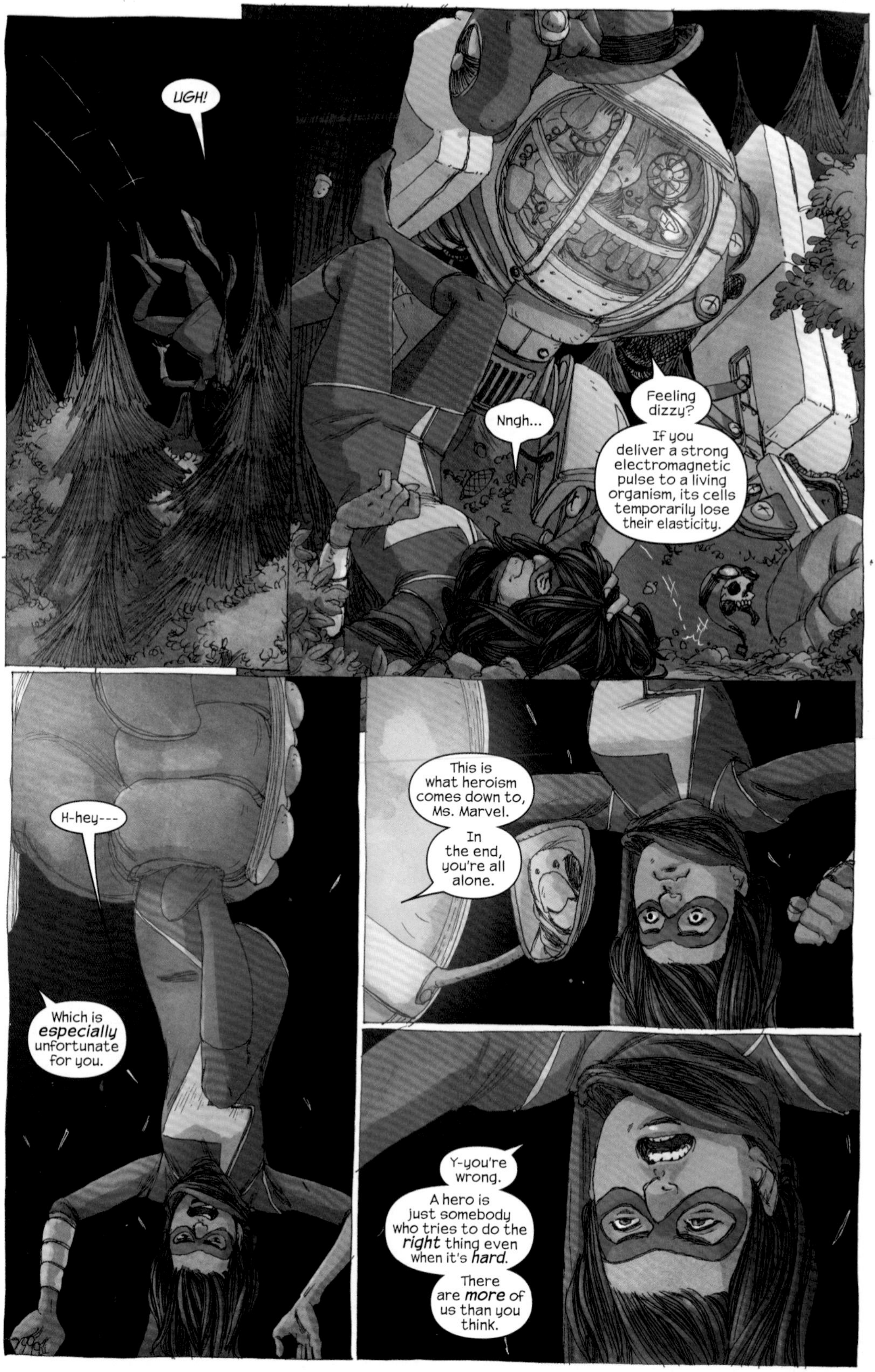

UGH!
Nngh...
Feeling dizzy?
If you deliver a strong electromagnetic pulse to a living organism, its cells temporarily lose their elasticity.
H-hey---
Which is *especially* unfortunate for you.
This is what heroism comes down to, Ms. Marvel.
In the end, you're all alone.
Y-you're wrong.
A hero is just somebody who tries to do the *right* thing even when it's *hard*.
There are *more* of us than you think.

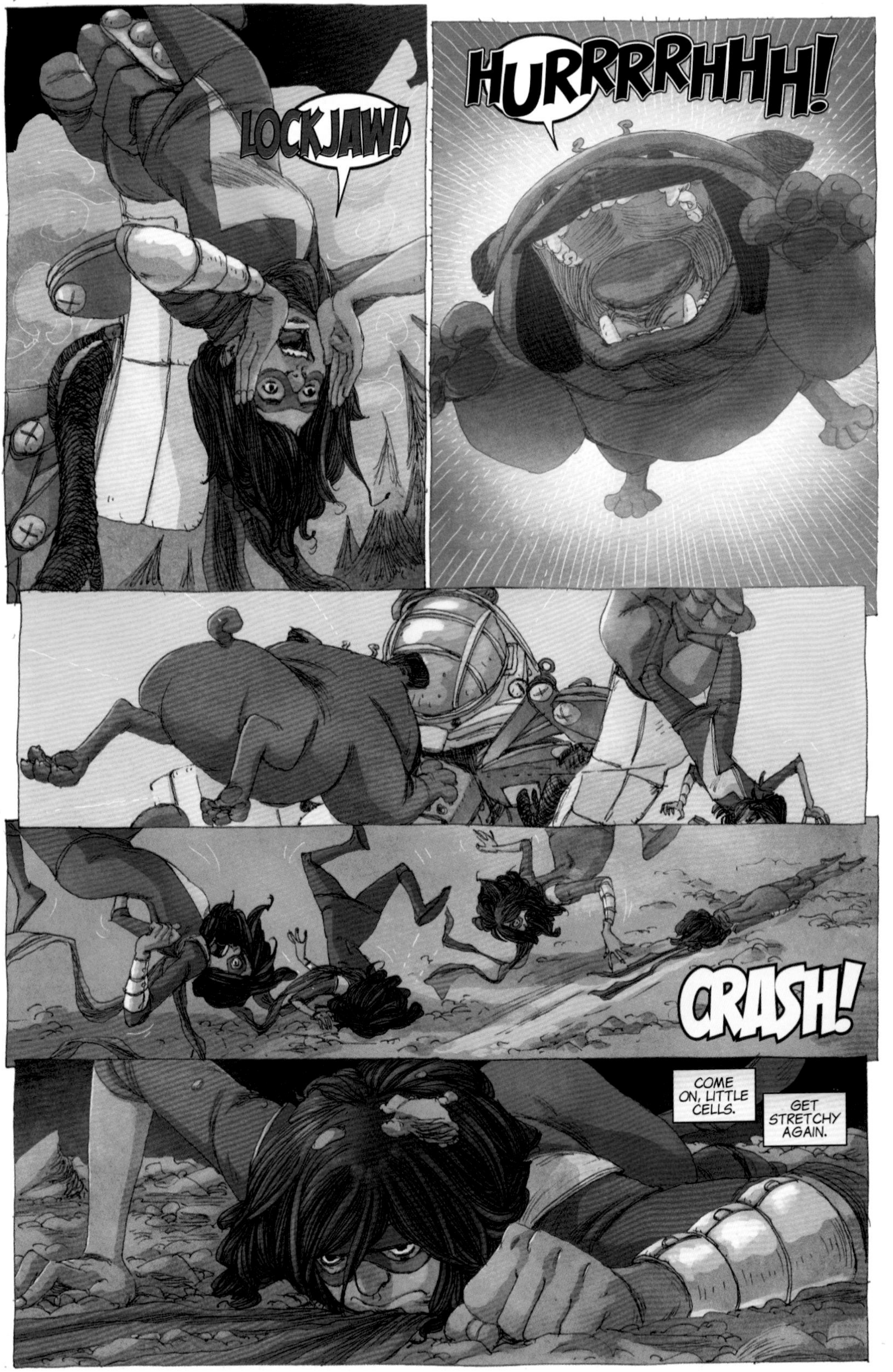
LOCKJAW!
HURRRRRHHH!
CRASH!
COME ON, LITTLE CELLS.
GET STRETCHY AGAIN.

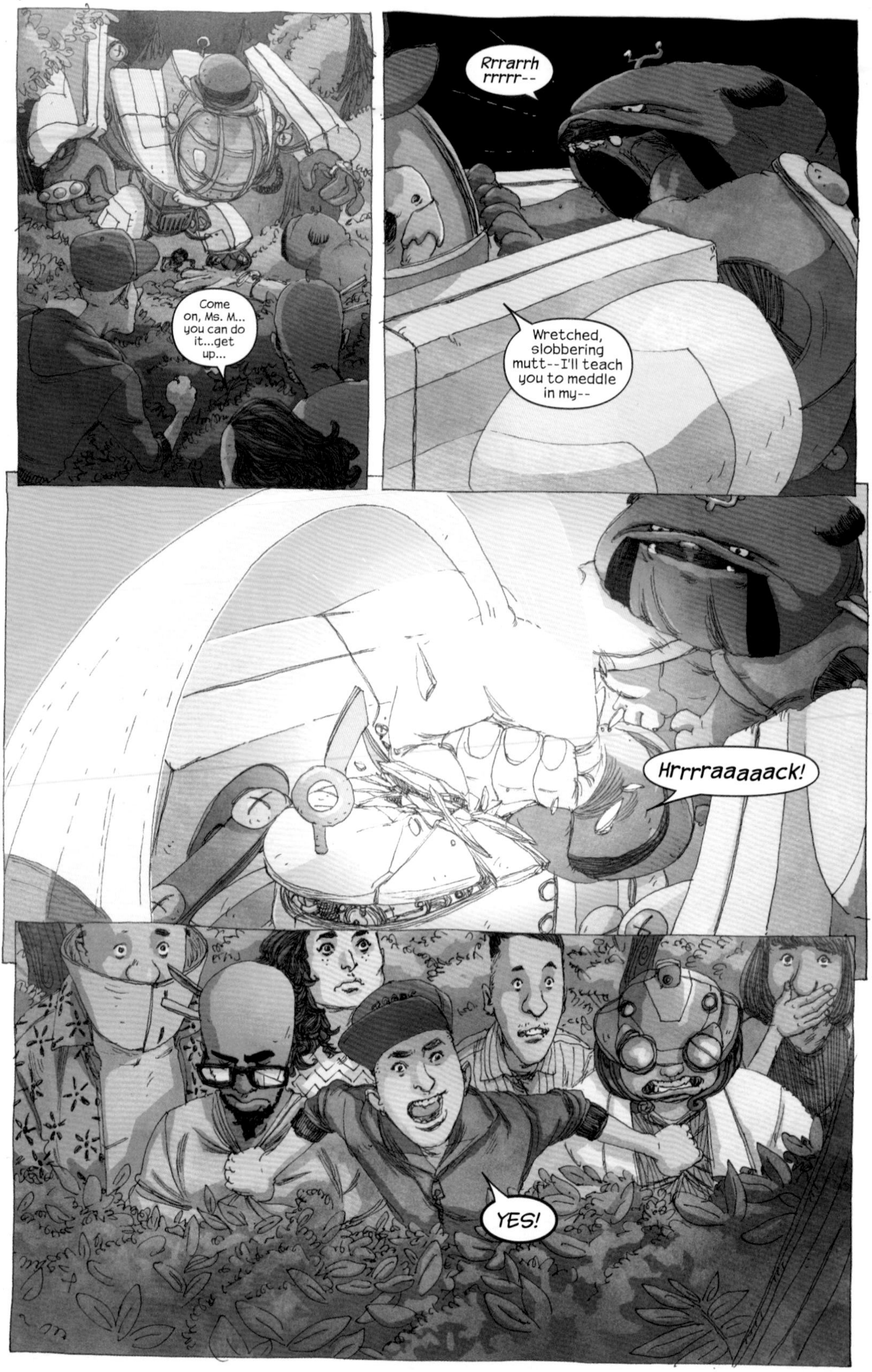
Come on, Ms. M... you can do it...get up...
Rrrarrh rrrrr--
Wretched, slobbering mutt--I'll teach you to meddle in my--
Hrrrraaaaack!
YES!

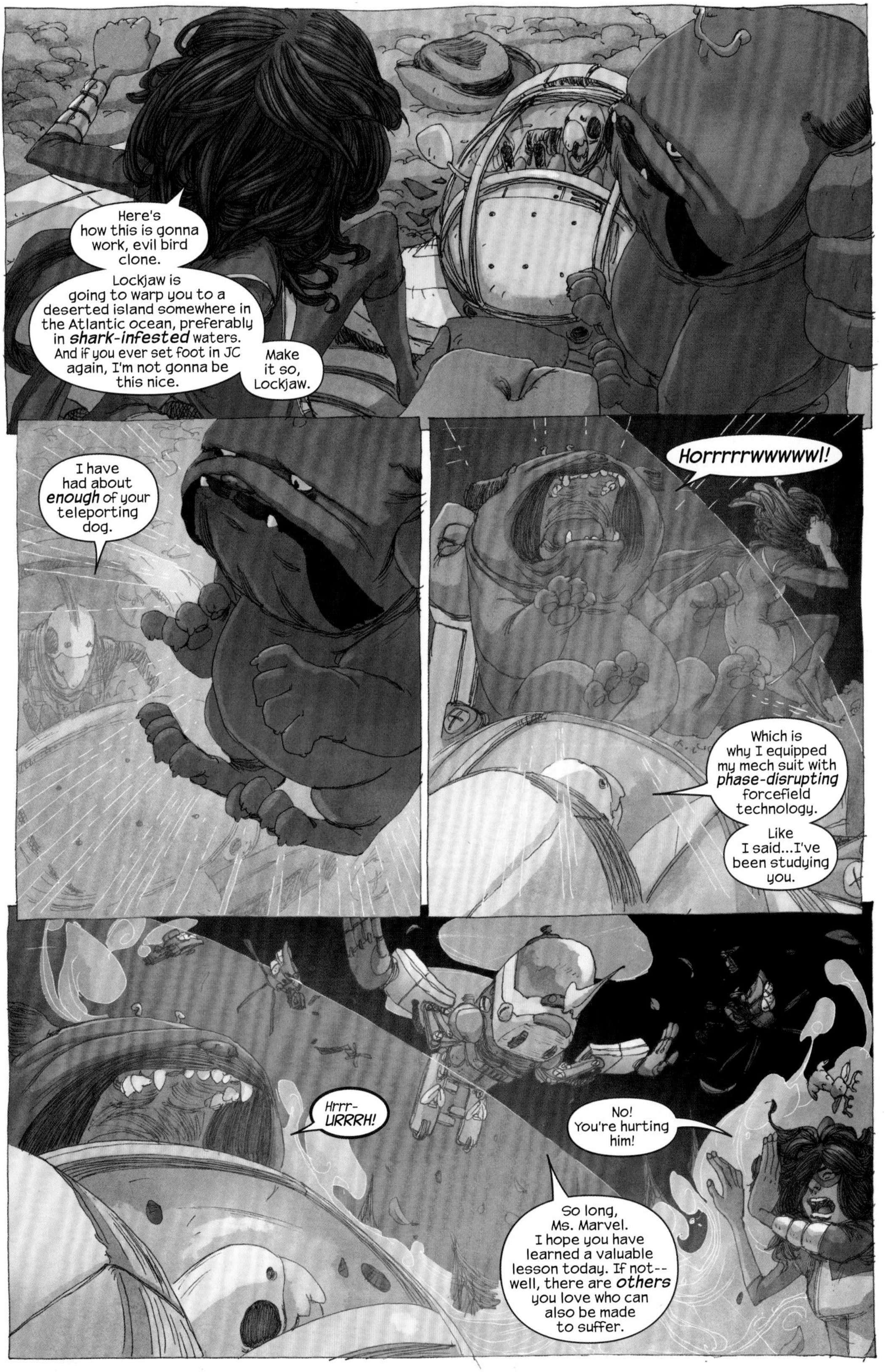

Here's how this is gonna work, evil bird clone.
Lockjaw is going to warp you to a deserted island somewhere in the Atlantic ocean, preferably in shark-infested waters. And if you ever set foot in JC again, I'm not gonna be this nice.
Make it so, Lockjaw.
I have had about enough of your teleporting dog.
Horrrrrwwwwwl!
Which is why I equipped my mech suit with phase-disrupting forcefield technology.
Like I said...I've been studying you.
Hrrr-URRRH!
No! You're hurting him!
So long, Ms. Marvel. I hope you have learned a valuable lesson today. If not--well, there are others you love who can also be made to suffer.

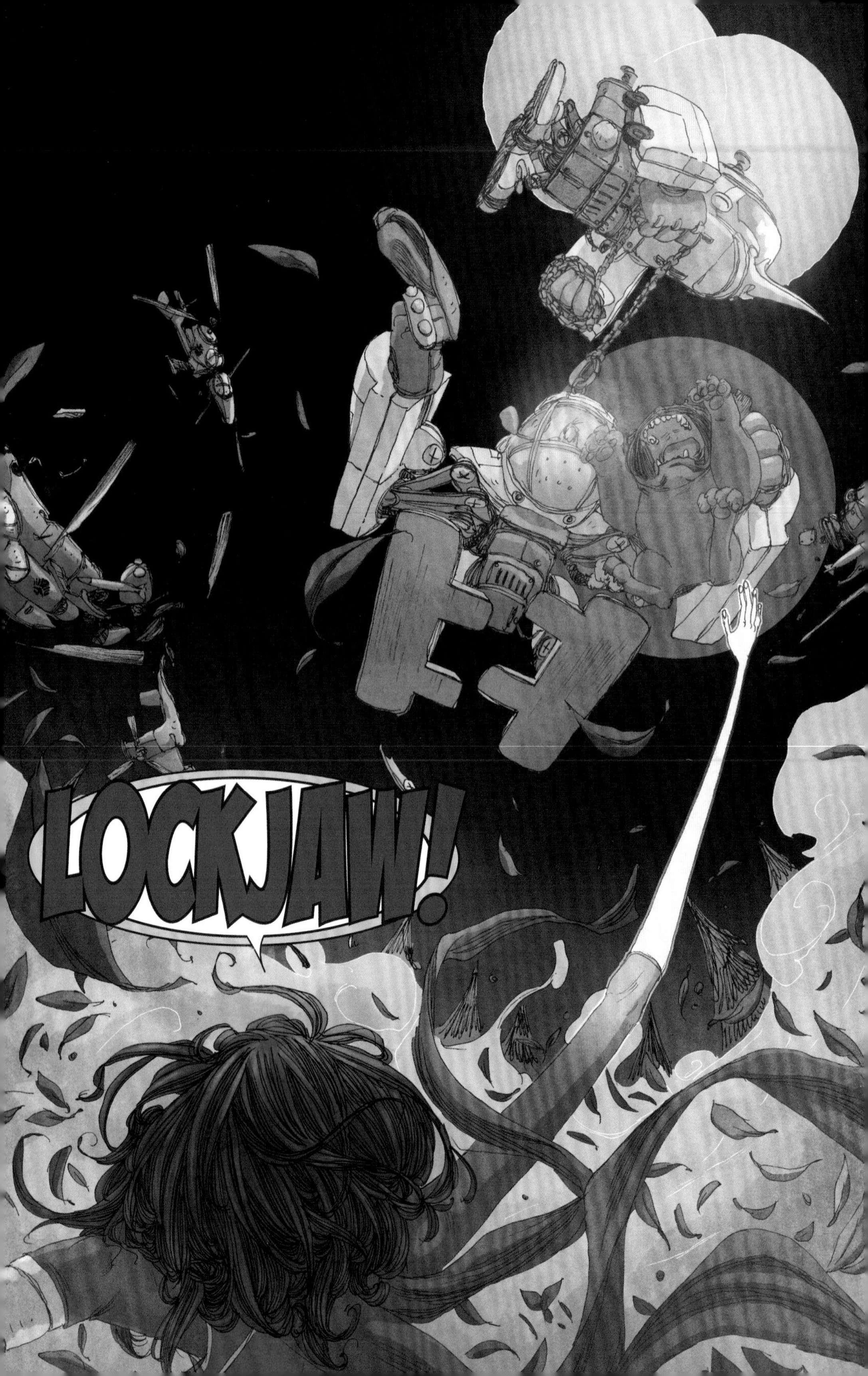
LOCKJAW!

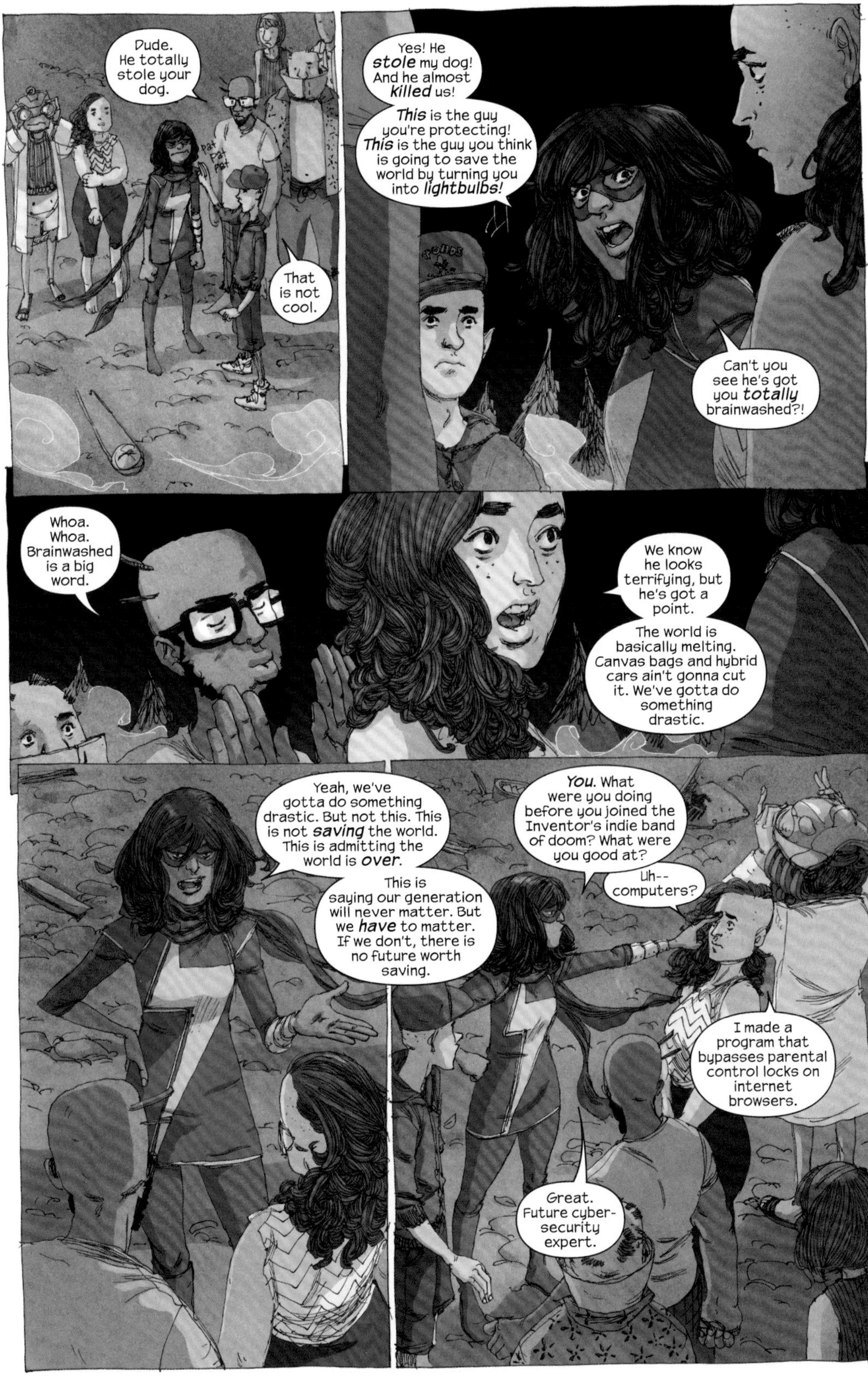

Dude. He totally stole your dog.
Pat Pat Pat
That is not cool.
Yes! He stole my dog! And he almost killed us!
This is the guy you're protecting! This is the guy you think is going to save the world by turning you into lightbulbs!
Can't you see he's got you totally brainwashed?!
Whoa. Whoa. Brainwashed is a big word.
We know he looks terrifying, but he's got a point.
The world is basically melting. Canvas bags and hybrid cars ain't gonna cut it. We've gotta do something drastic.
Yeah, we've gotta do something drastic. But not this. This is not saving the world. This is admitting the world is over.
This is saying our generation will never matter. But we have to matter. If we don't, there is no future worth saving.
You. What were you doing before you joined the Inventor's indie band of doom? What were you good at?
Uh-- computers?
I made a program that bypasses parental control locks on internet browsers.
Great. Future cyber-security expert.

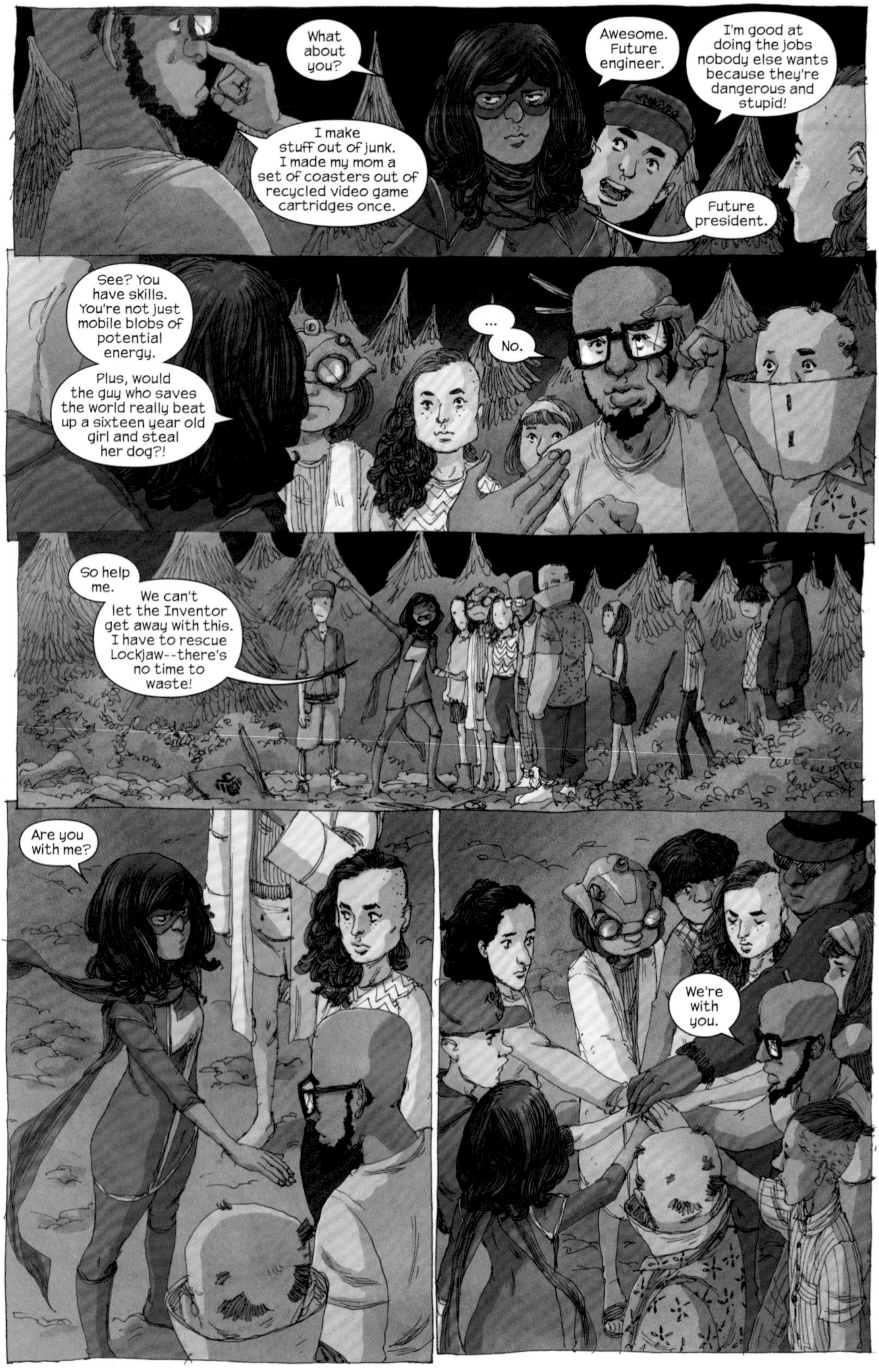
What about you?
I make stuff out of junk. I made my mom a set of coasters out of recycled video game cartridges once.
Awesome. Future engineer.
I'm good at doing the jobs nobody else wants because they're dangerous and stupid!
Future president.
See? You have skills. You're not just mobile blobs of potential energy.
Plus, would the guy who saves the world really beat up a sixteen year old girl and steal her dog?!
...
No.
So help me.
We can't let the Inventor get away with this. I have to rescue Lockjaw--there's no time to waste!
Are you with me?
We're with you.

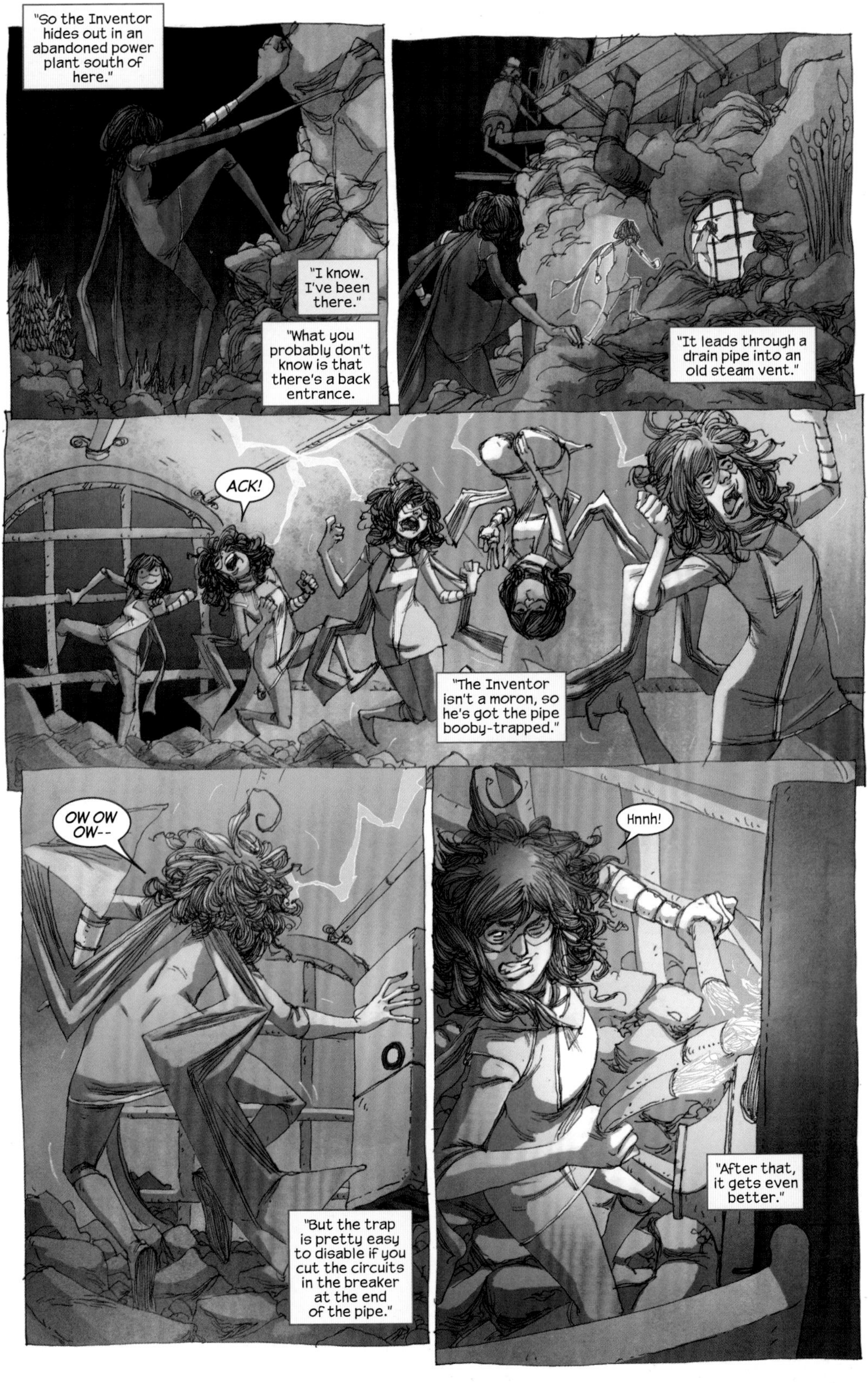
"So the Inventor hides out in an abandoned power plant south of here."
"I know. I've been there."
"What you probably don't know is that there's a back entrance.
"It leads through a drain pipe into an old steam vent."
ACK!
"The Inventor isn't a moron, so he's got the pipe booby-trapped."
OW OW OW--
"But the trap is pretty easy to disable if you cut the circuits in the breaker at the end of the pipe."
Hnnh!
"After that, it gets even better."

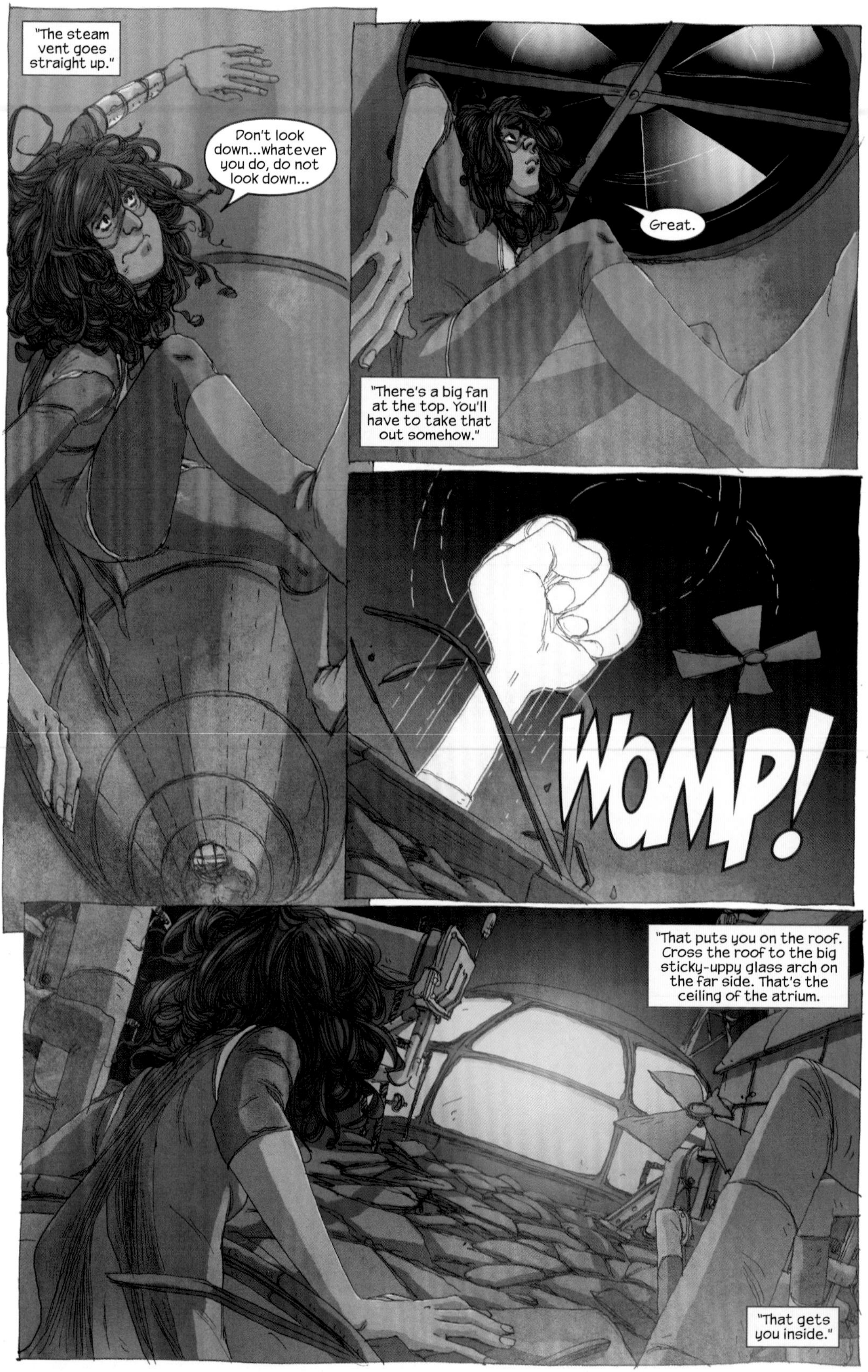
"The steam vent goes straight up."
Don't look down...whatever you do, do not look down...
Great.
"There's a big fan at the top. You'll have to take that out somehow."
WOMP!
"That puts you on the roof. Cross the roof to the big sticky-uppy glass arch on the far side. That's the ceiling of the atrium.
"That gets you inside."

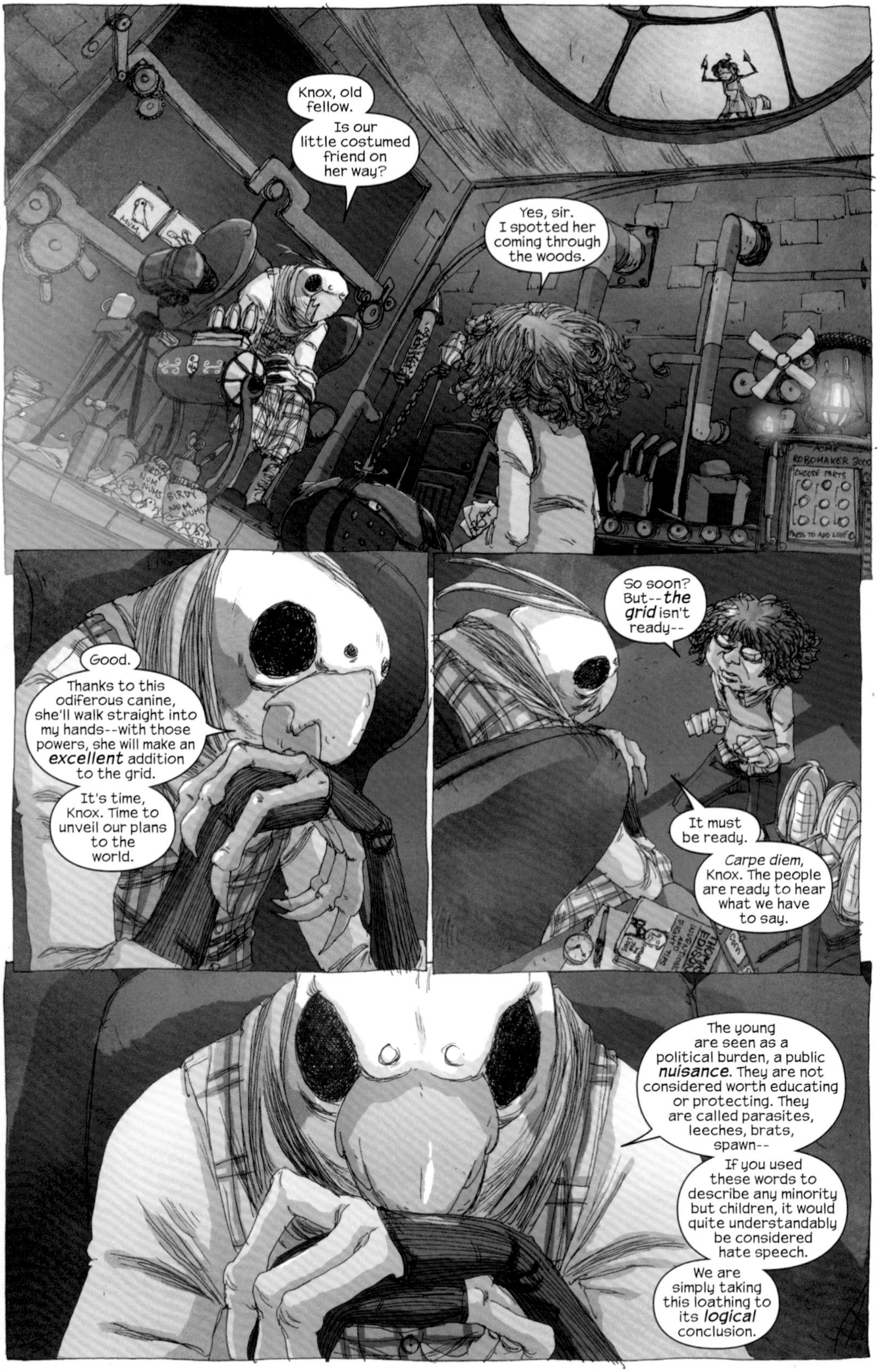

Knox, old fellow.
Is our little costumed friend on her way?
Yes, sir. I spotted her coming through the woods.
MUM
BIRDY NUM NUMS
BIRDY NUM NUMS
ROBOMAKER 3000
CHOOSE PARTS
PRESS TO ADD LOVE
Good.
Thanks to this odiferous canine, she'll walk straight into my hands--with those powers, she will make an *excellent* addition to the grid.
It's time, Knox. Time to unveil our plans to the world.
So soon? But--*the grid* isn't ready--
It must be ready.
Carpe diem, Knox. The people are ready to hear what we have to say.
The young are seen as a political burden, a public *nuisance*. They are not considered worth educating or protecting. They are called parasites, leeches, brats, spawn--
If you used these words to describe any minority but children, it would quite understandably be considered hate speech.
We are simply taking this loathing to its *logical* conclusion.

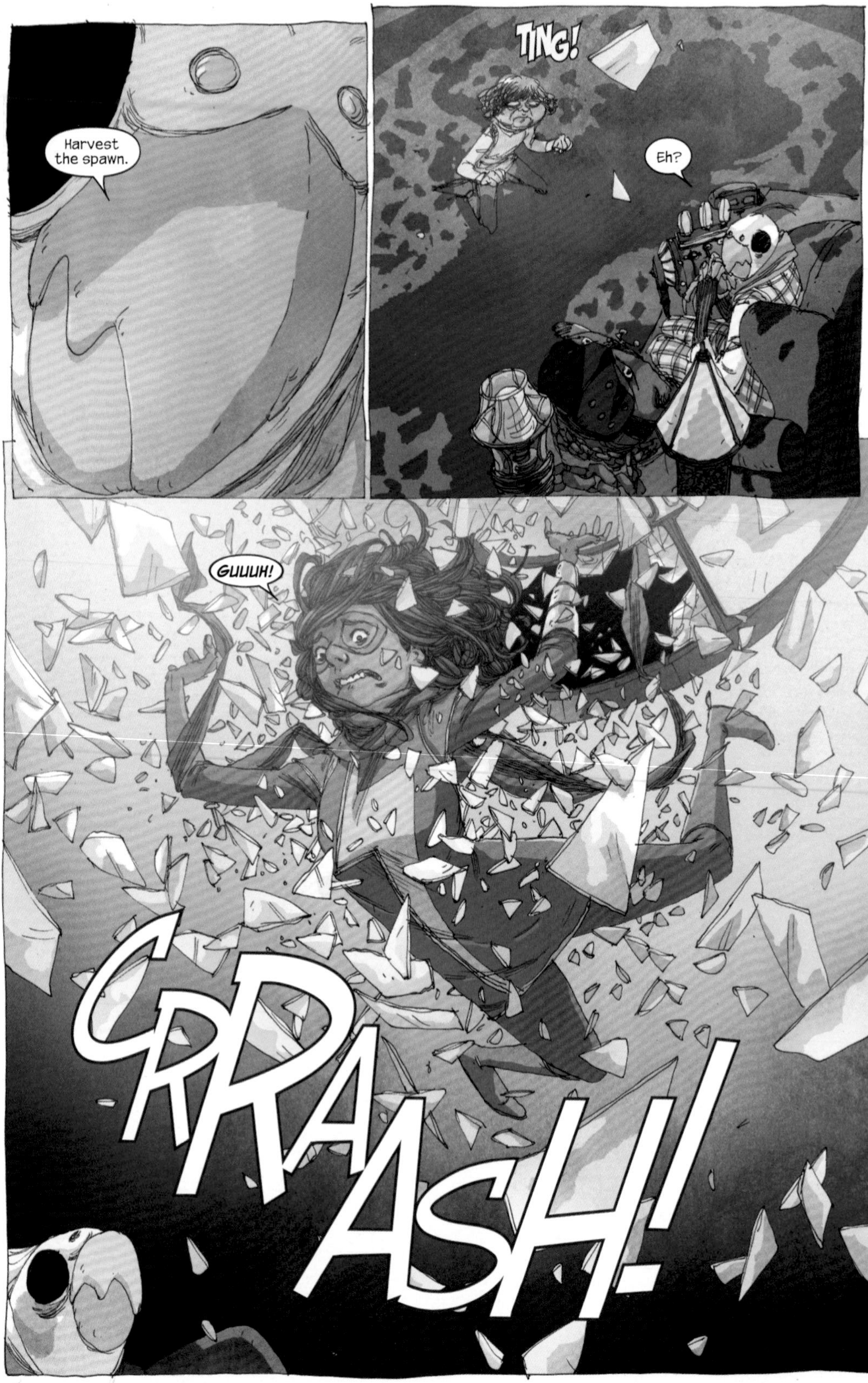

Harvest the spawn.
TING!
Eh?
GUUUH!
CRRAASH!

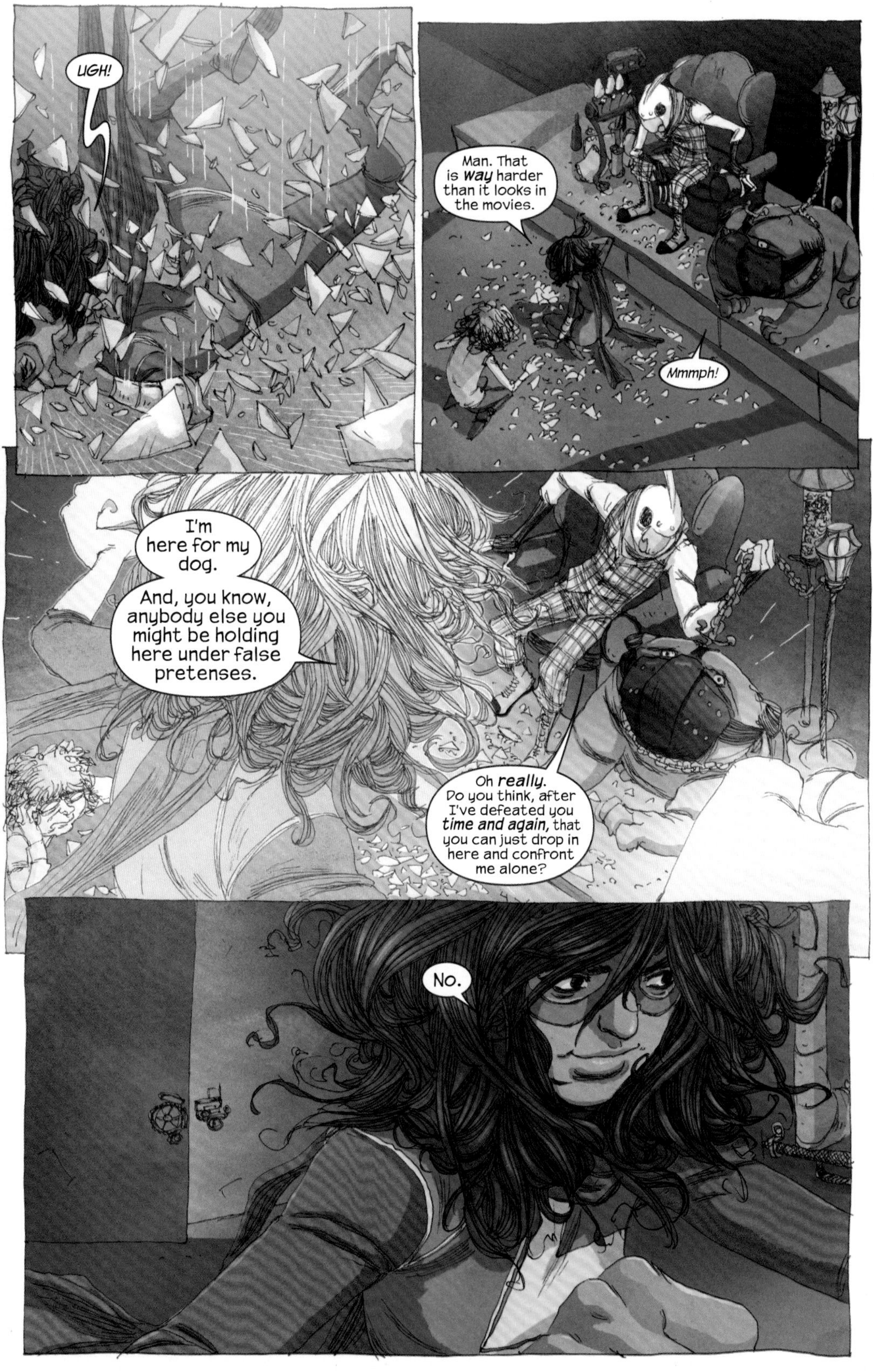
UGH!
Man. That is *way* harder than it looks in the movies.
Mmmph!
I'm here for my dog.
And, you know, anybody else you might be holding here under false pretenses.
Oh *really*. Do you think, after I've defeated you *time and again*, that you can just drop in here and confront me alone?
No.

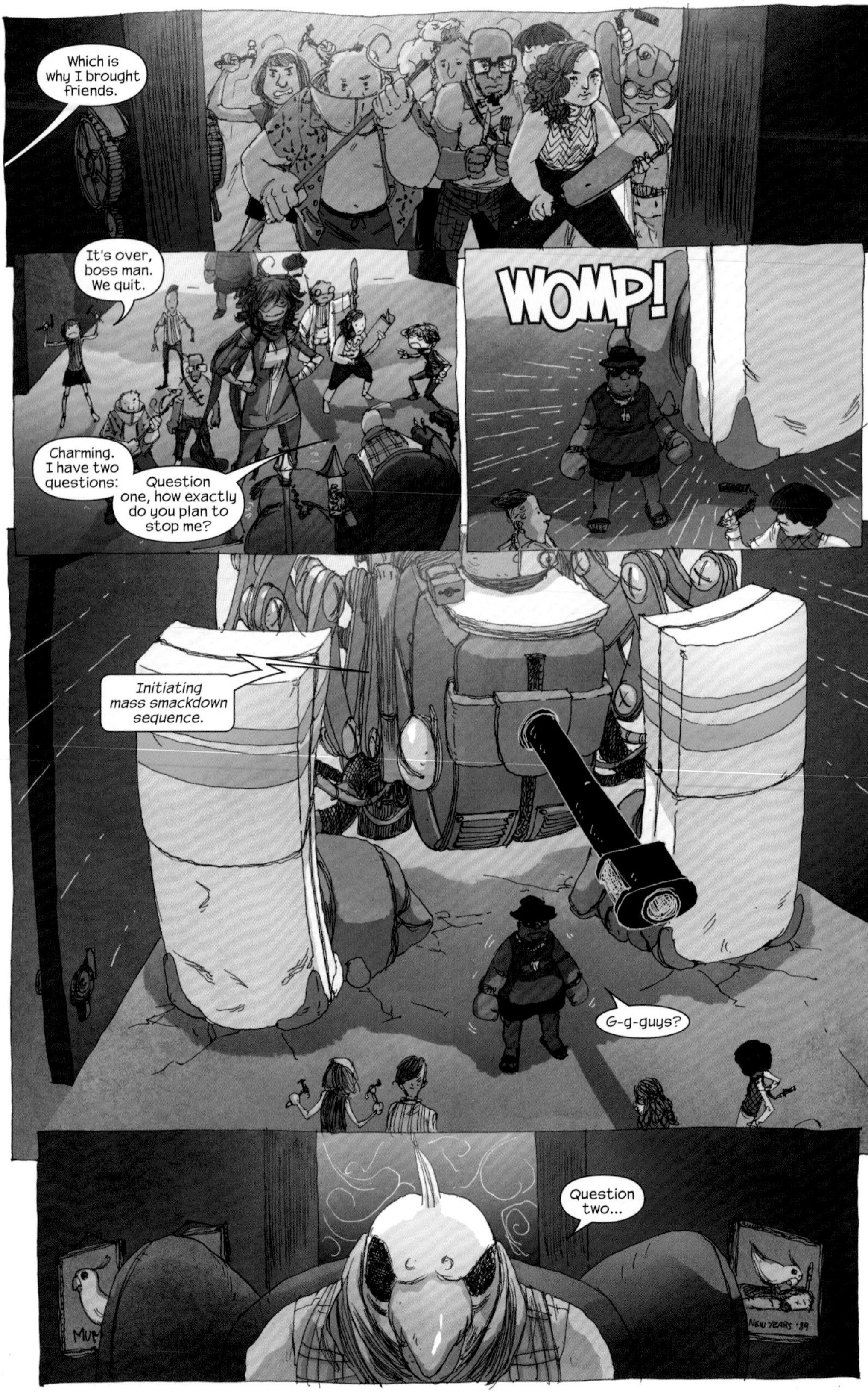

Which is why I brought friends.
It's over, boss man. We quit.
Charming. I have two questions:
Question one, how exactly do you plan to stop me?
WOMP!
Initiating mass smackdown sequence.
G-g-guys?
Question two...
MUM
NEW YEARS '89

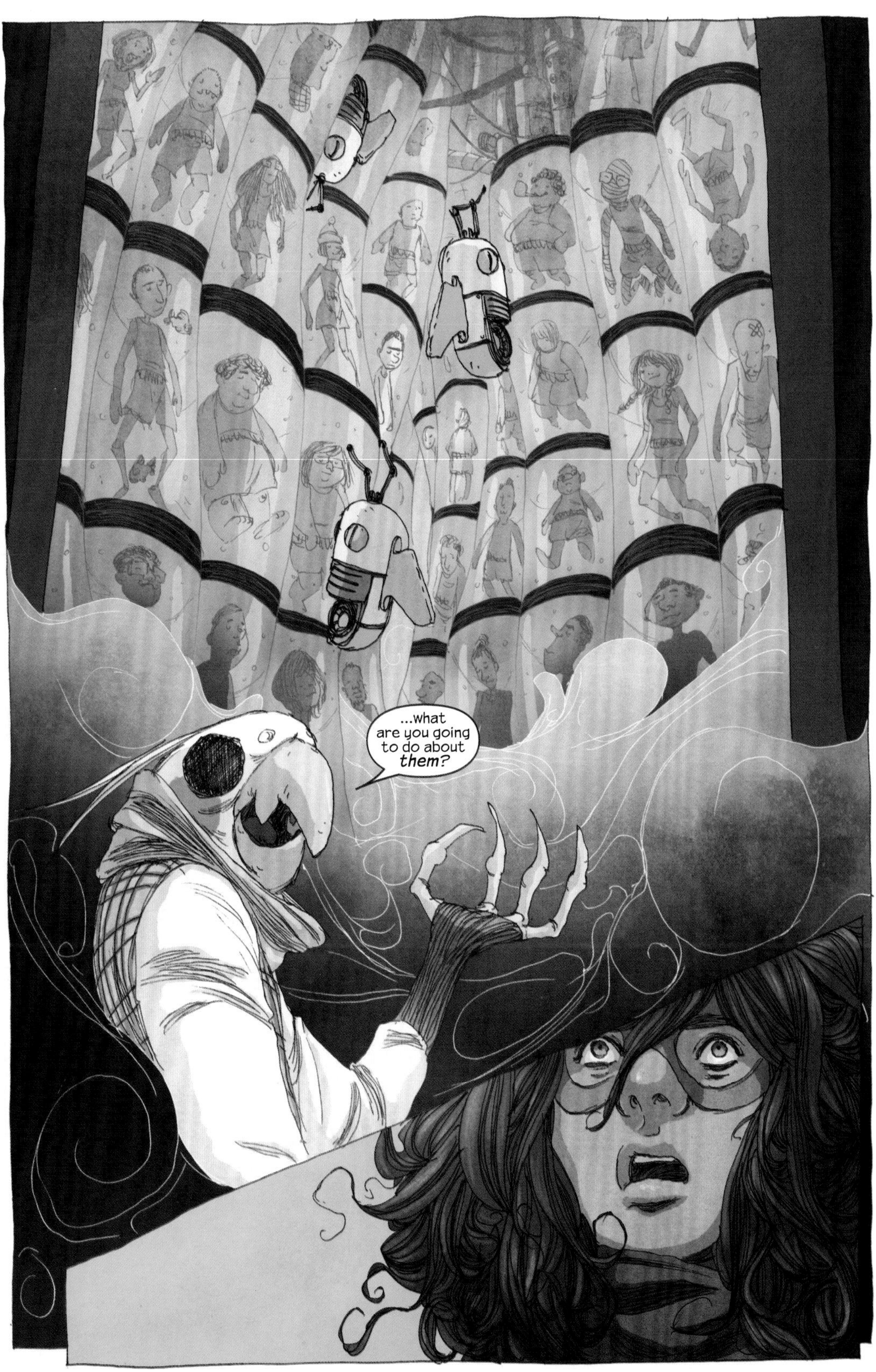
...what are you going to do about *them*?

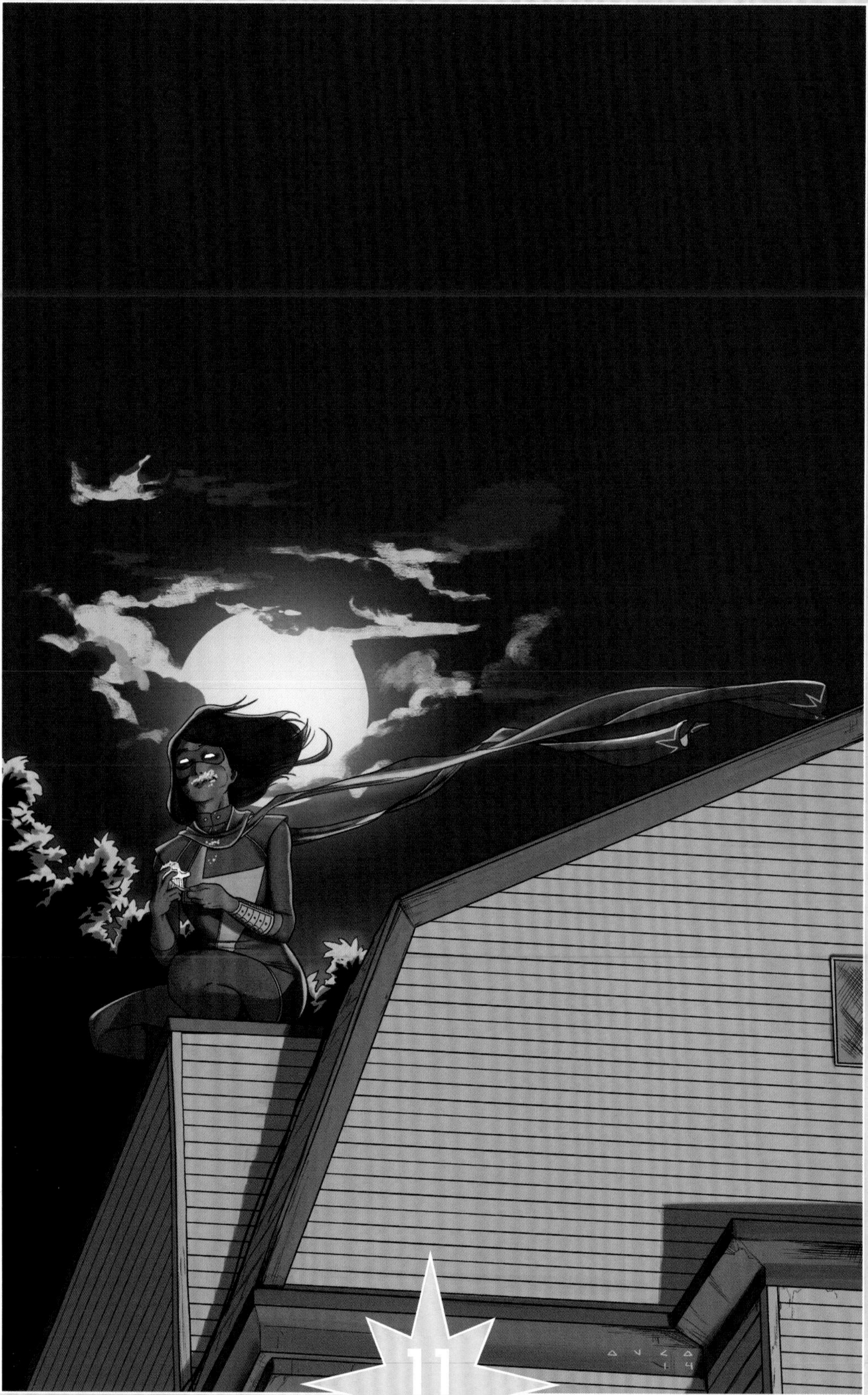
11

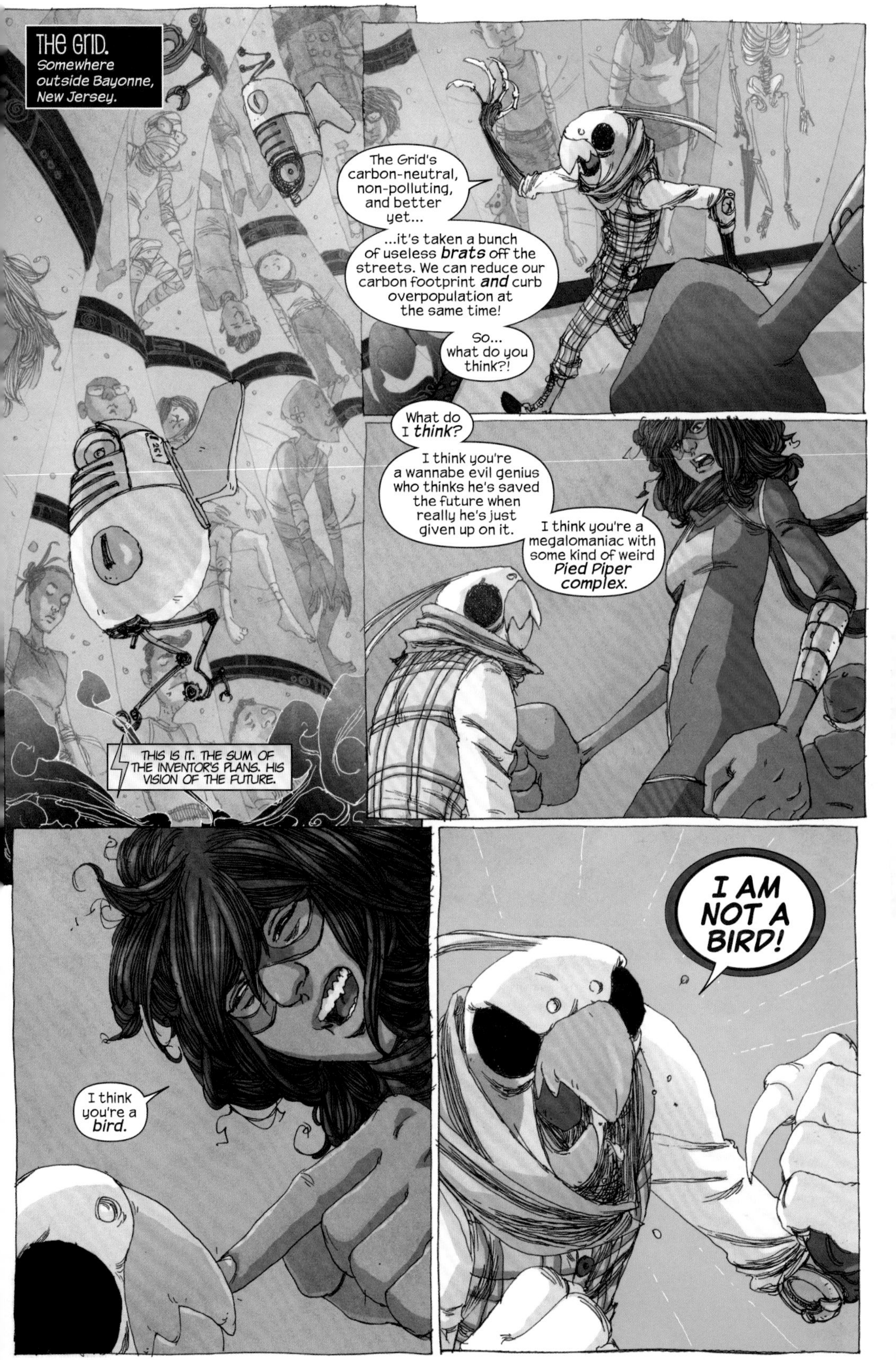

The Grid.
Somewhere outside Bayonne, New Jersey.
The Grid's carbon-neutral, non-polluting, and better yet...
...it's taken a bunch of useless *brats* off the streets. We can reduce our carbon footprint *and* curb overpopulation at the same time!
So... what do you think?!
What do I *think*?
I think you're a wannabe evil genius who thinks he's saved the future when really he's just given up on it.
I think you're a megalomaniac with some kind of weird *Pied Piper complex*.
THIS IS IT. THE SUM OF THE INVENTOR'S PLANS. HIS VISION OF THE FUTURE.
I think you're a *bird*.
I AM NOT A BIRD!

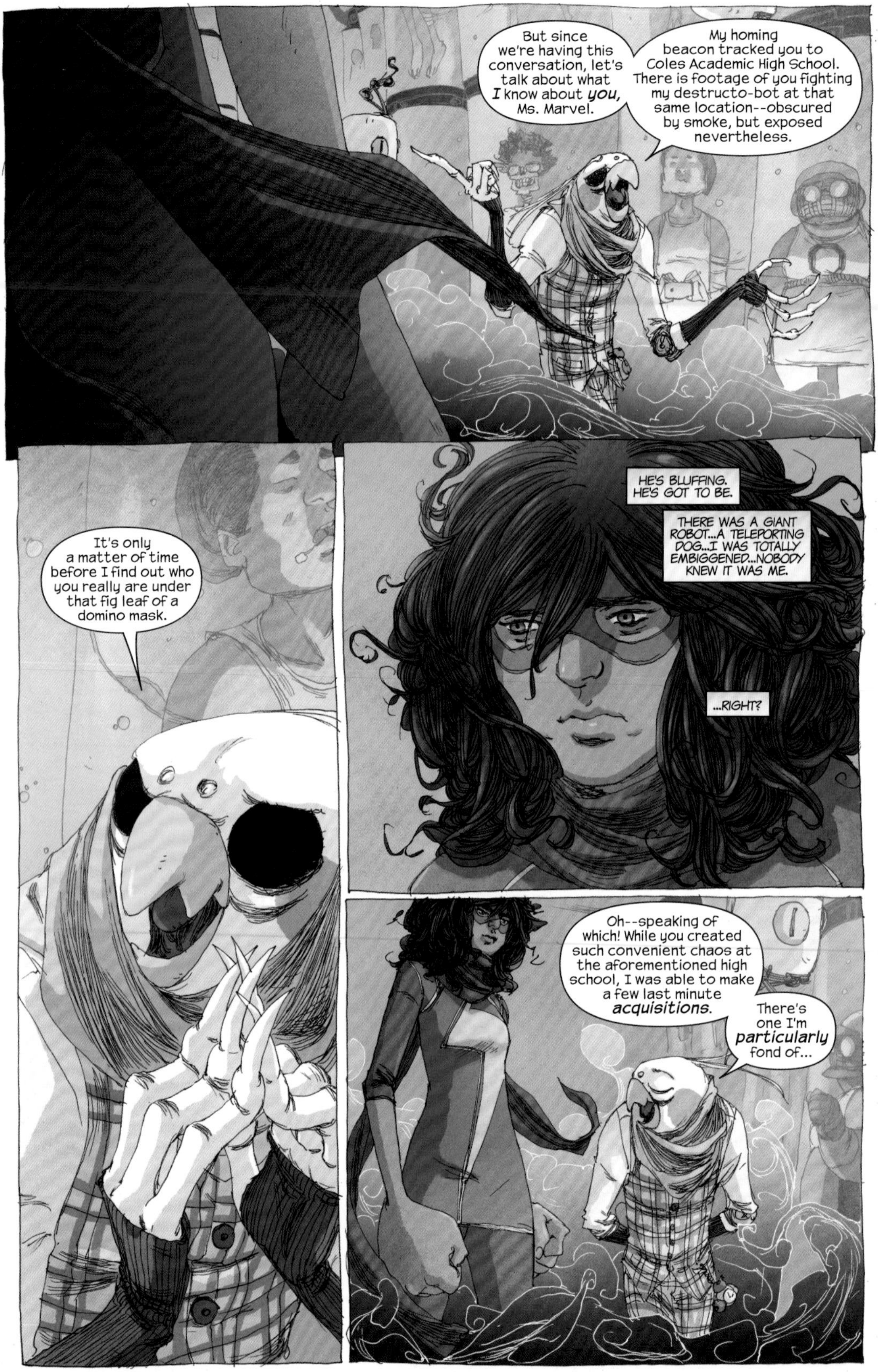

But since we're having this conversation, let's talk about what *I* know about ***you,*** Ms. Marvel.
My homing beacon tracked you to Coles Academic High School. There is footage of you fighting my destructo-bot at that same location--obscured by smoke, but exposed nevertheless.
It's only a matter of time before I find out who you really are under that fig leaf of a domino mask.
HE'S BLUFFING. HE'S GOT TO BE.
THERE WAS A GIANT ROBOT...A TELEPORTING DOG...I WAS TOTALLY EMBIGGENED...NOBODY KNEW IT WAS ME.
...RIGHT?
Oh--speaking of which! While you created such convenient chaos at the aforementioned high school, I was able to make a few last minute ***acquisitions***.
There's one I'm ***particularly*** fond of...

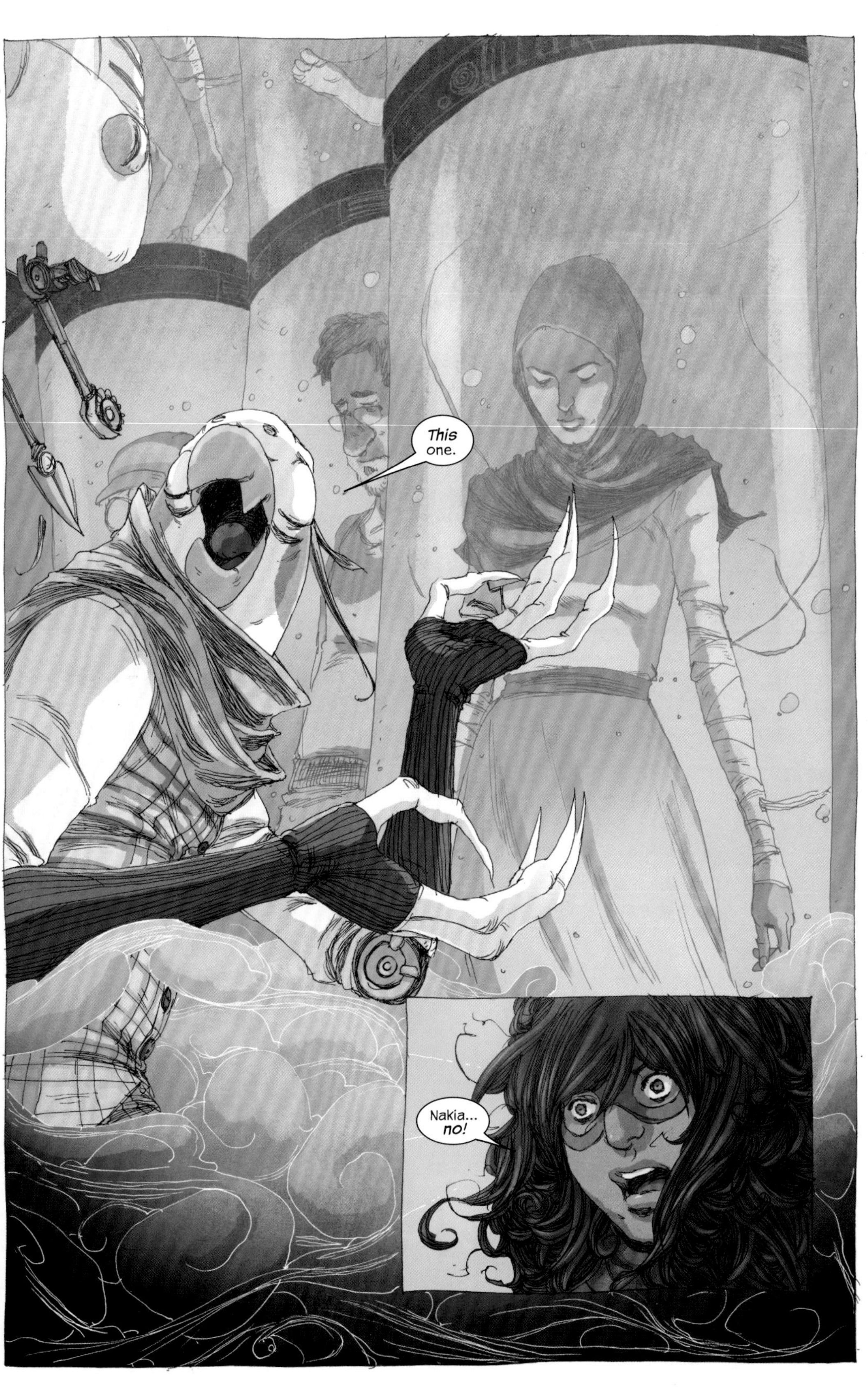
This one.
Nakia... no!

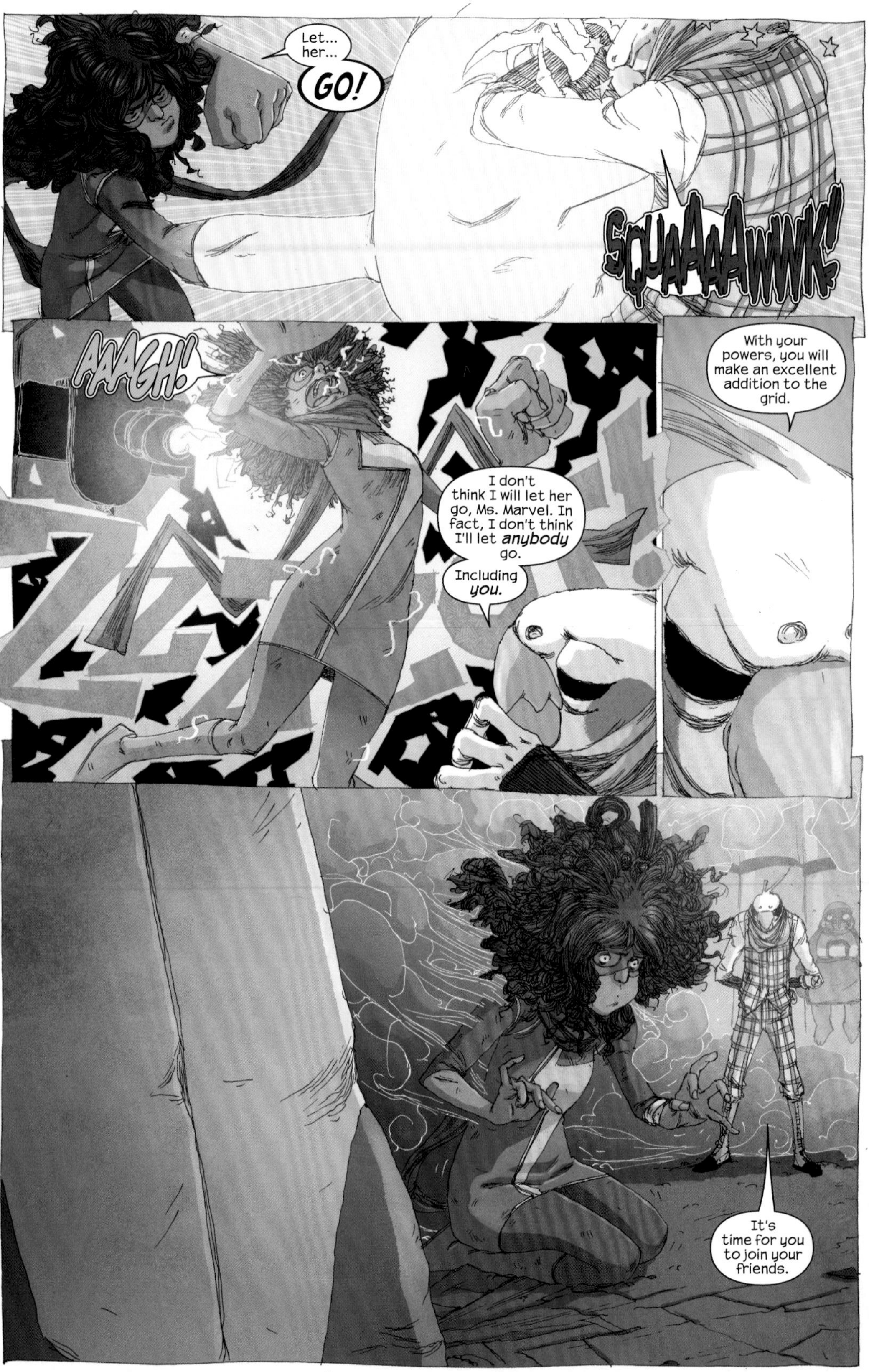
Let... her... GO!
SQUAAAAWWK!
AAAGH!
ZZZAK
I don't think I will let her go, Ms. Marvel. In fact, I don't think I'll let *anybody* go.
Including *you.*
With your powers, you will make an excellent addition to the grid.
It's time for you to join your friends.

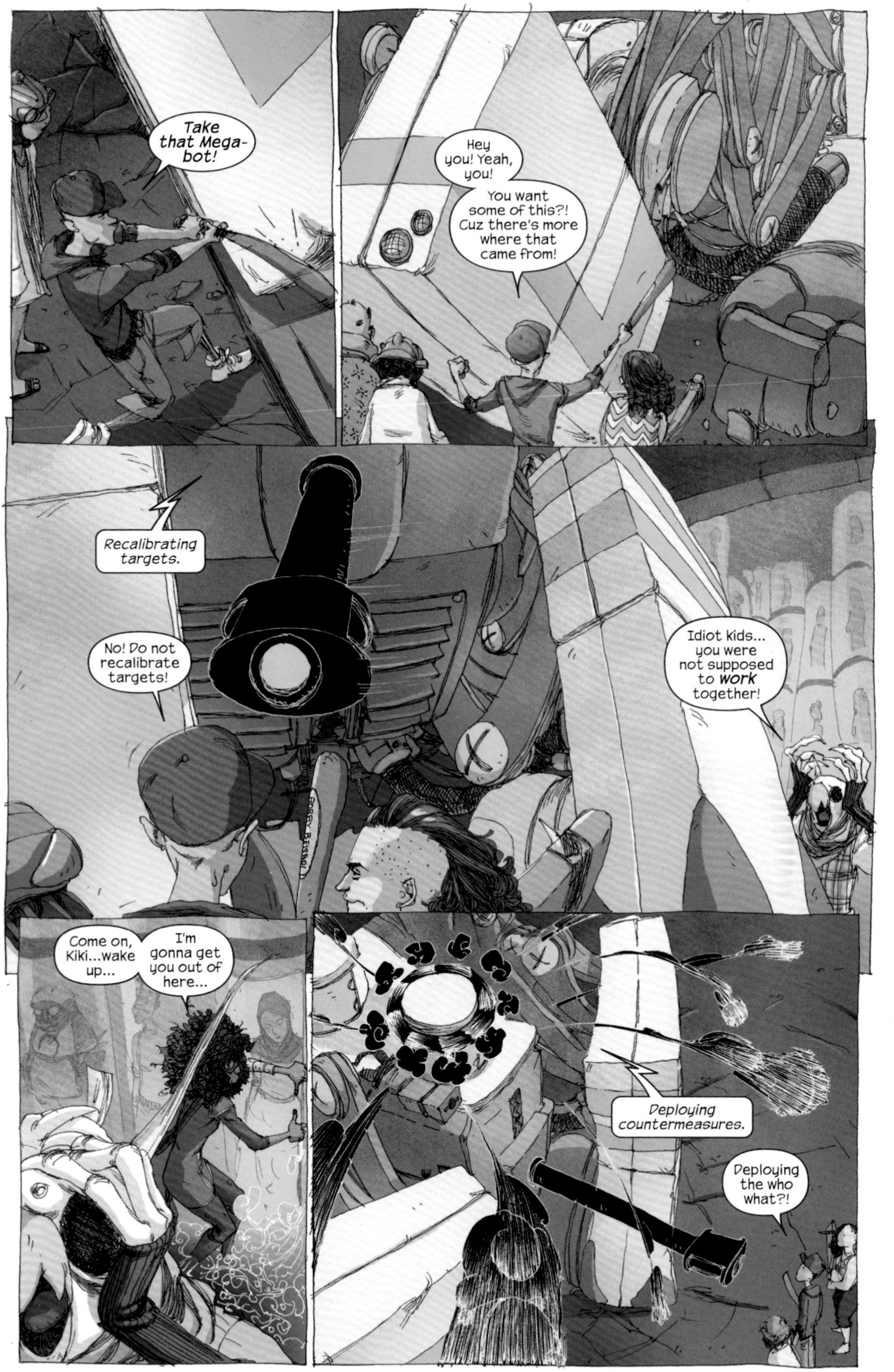
Take that Mega-bot!
Hey you! Yeah, you!
You want some of this?! Cuz there's more where that came from!
Recalibrating targets.
No! Do not recalibrate targets!
Idiot kids... you were not supposed to work together!
Come on, Kiki...wake up...
I'm gonna get you out of here...
Deploying countermeasures.
Deploying the who what?!

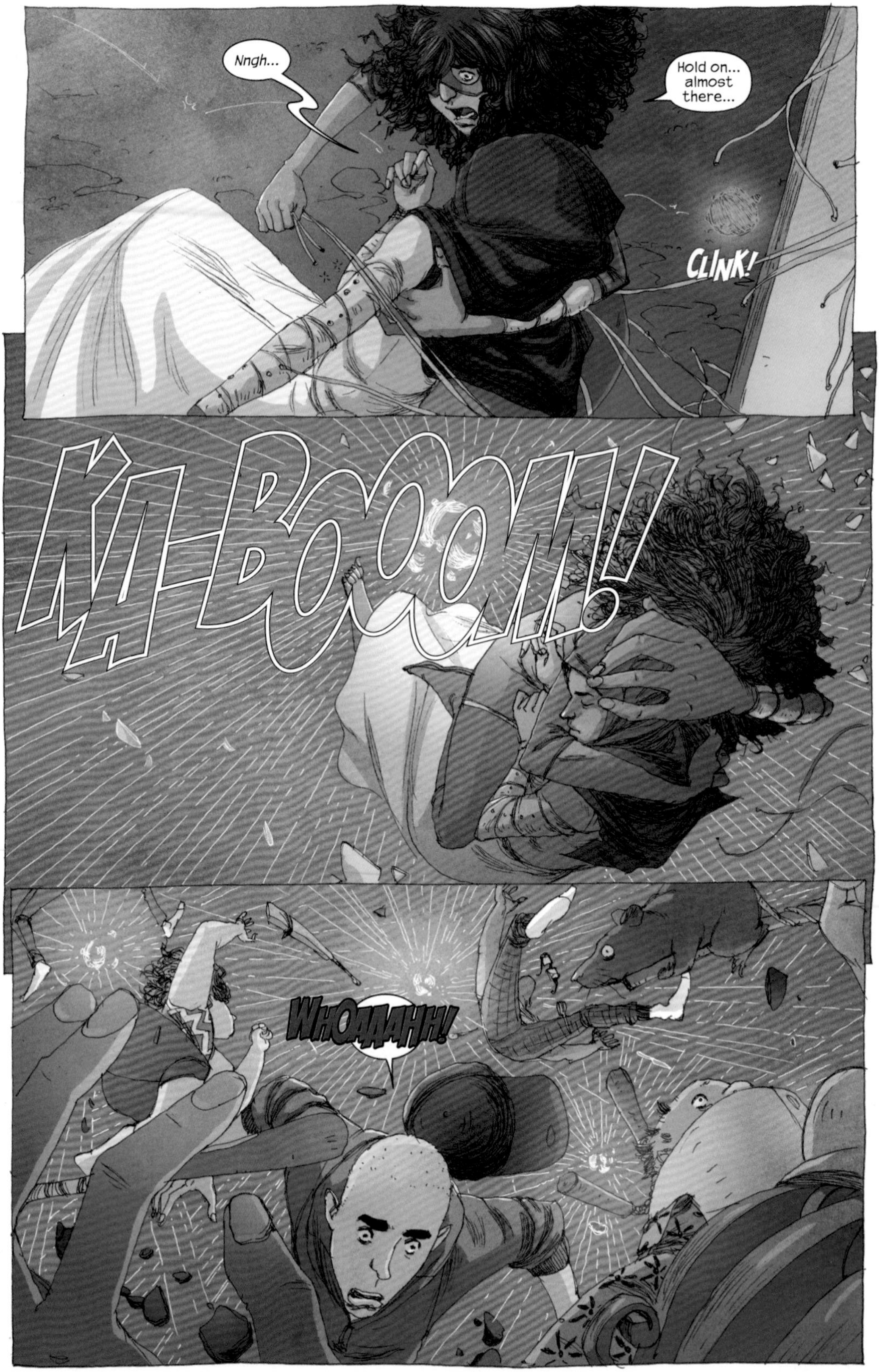

Nngh...
Hold on... almost there...
CLINK!
KA-BOOOM!
WHOAAAHH!

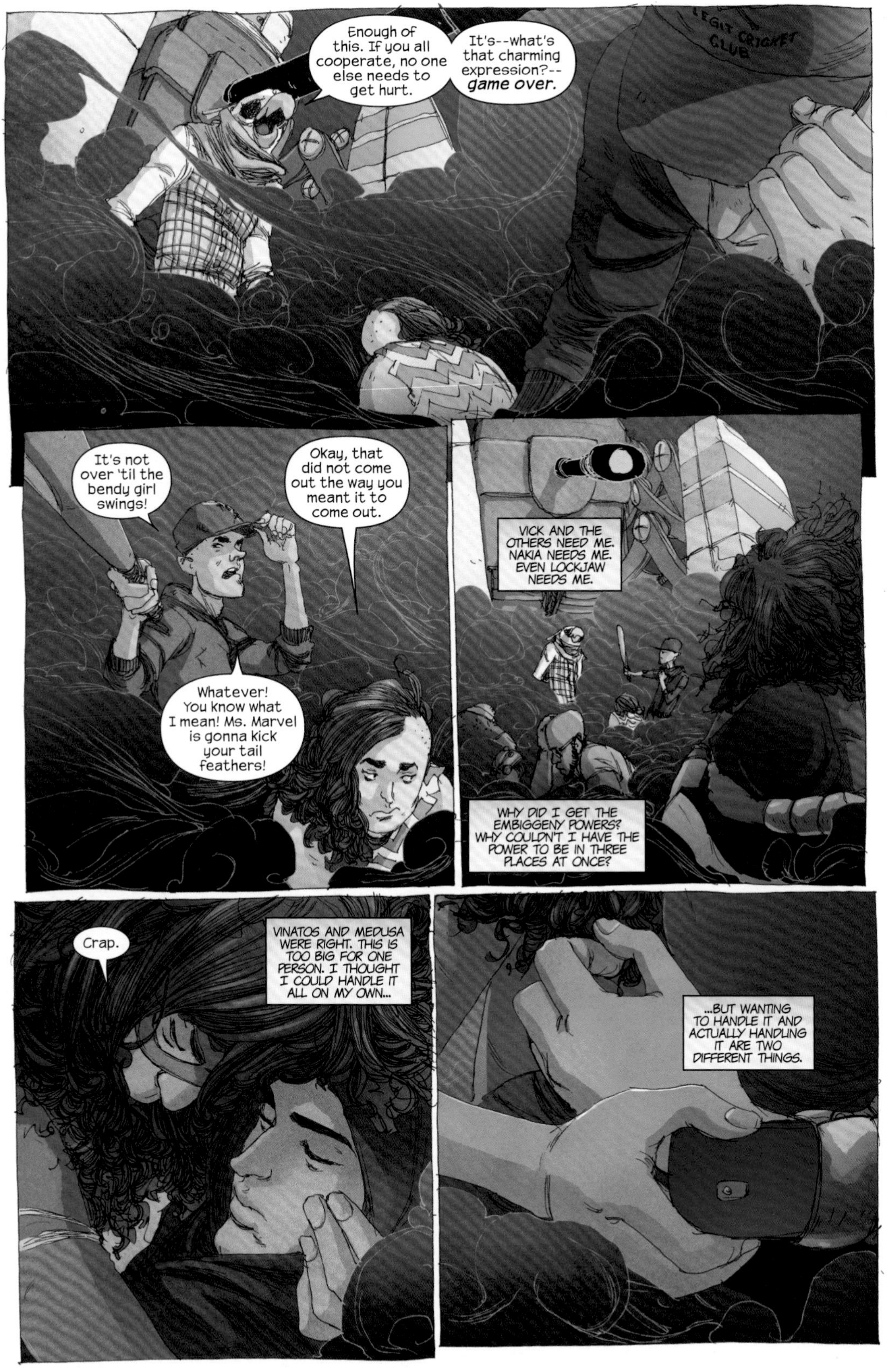

LEGIT CRICKET CLUB
Enough of this. If you all cooperate, no one else needs to get hurt.
It's--what's that charming expression?-- *game over.*
It's not over 'til the bendy girl swings!
Okay, that did not come out the way you meant it to come out.
Whatever! You know what I mean! Ms. Marvel is gonna kick your tail feathers!
VICK AND THE OTHERS NEED ME. NAKIA NEEDS ME. EVEN LOCKJAW NEEDS ME.
WHY DID I GET THE EMBIGGENY POWERS? WHY COULDN'T I HAVE THE POWER TO BE IN THREE PLACES AT ONCE?
Crap.
VINATOS AND MEDUSA WERE RIGHT. THIS IS TOO BIG FOR ONE PERSON. I THOUGHT I COULD HANDLE IT ALL ON MY OWN...
...BUT WANTING TO HANDLE IT AND ACTUALLY HANDLING IT ARE TWO DIFFERENT THINGS.

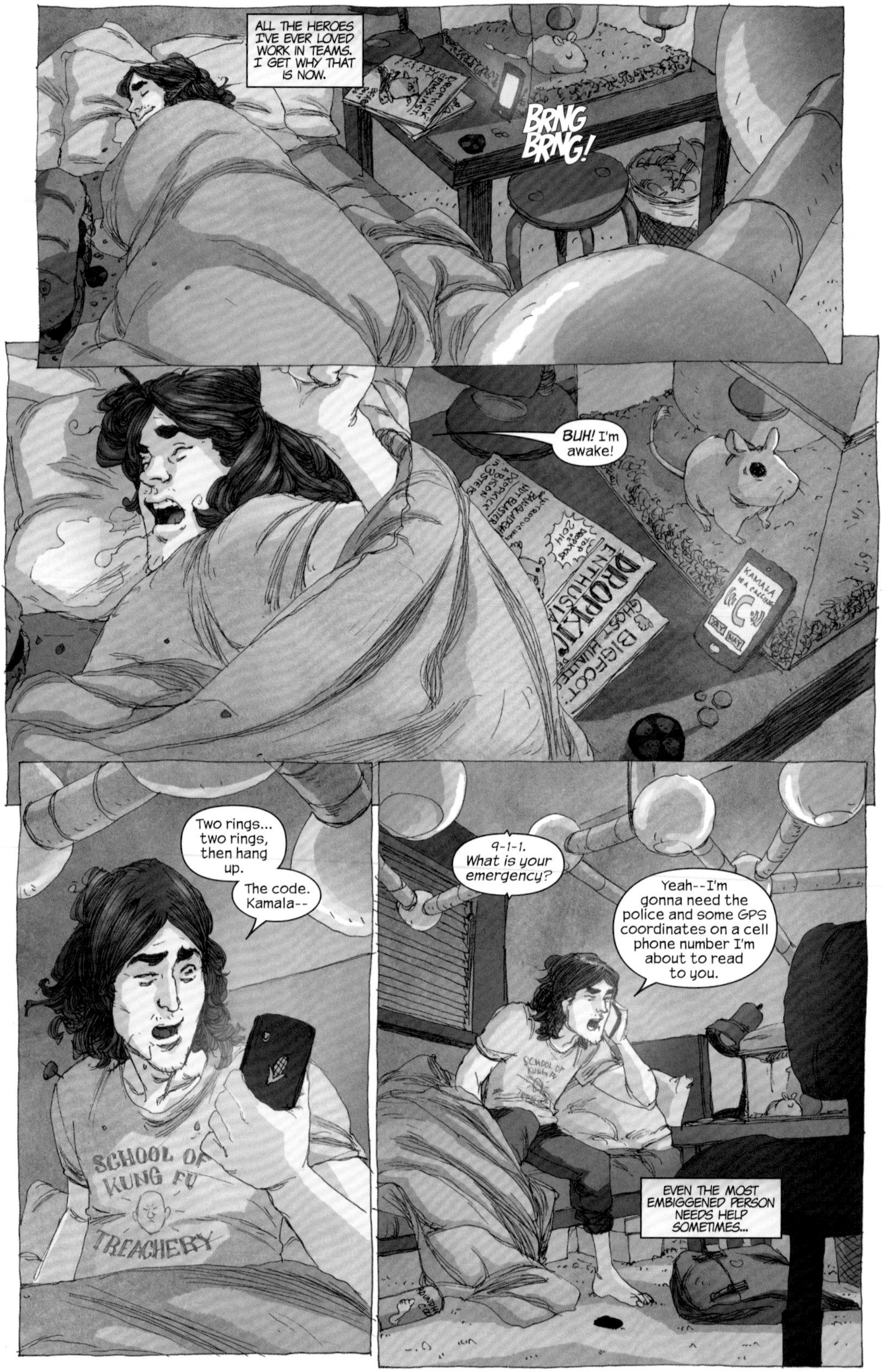
ALL THE HEROES I'VE EVER LOVED WORK IN TEAMS. I GET WHY THAT IS NOW.
BRNG BRNG!
BUH! I'm awake!
Two rings... two rings, then hang up.
The code. Kamala--
9-1-1. What is your emergency?
Yeah--I'm gonna need the police and some GPS coordinates on a cell phone number I'm about to read to you.
EVEN THE MOST EMBIGGENED PERSON NEEDS HELP SOMETIMES...

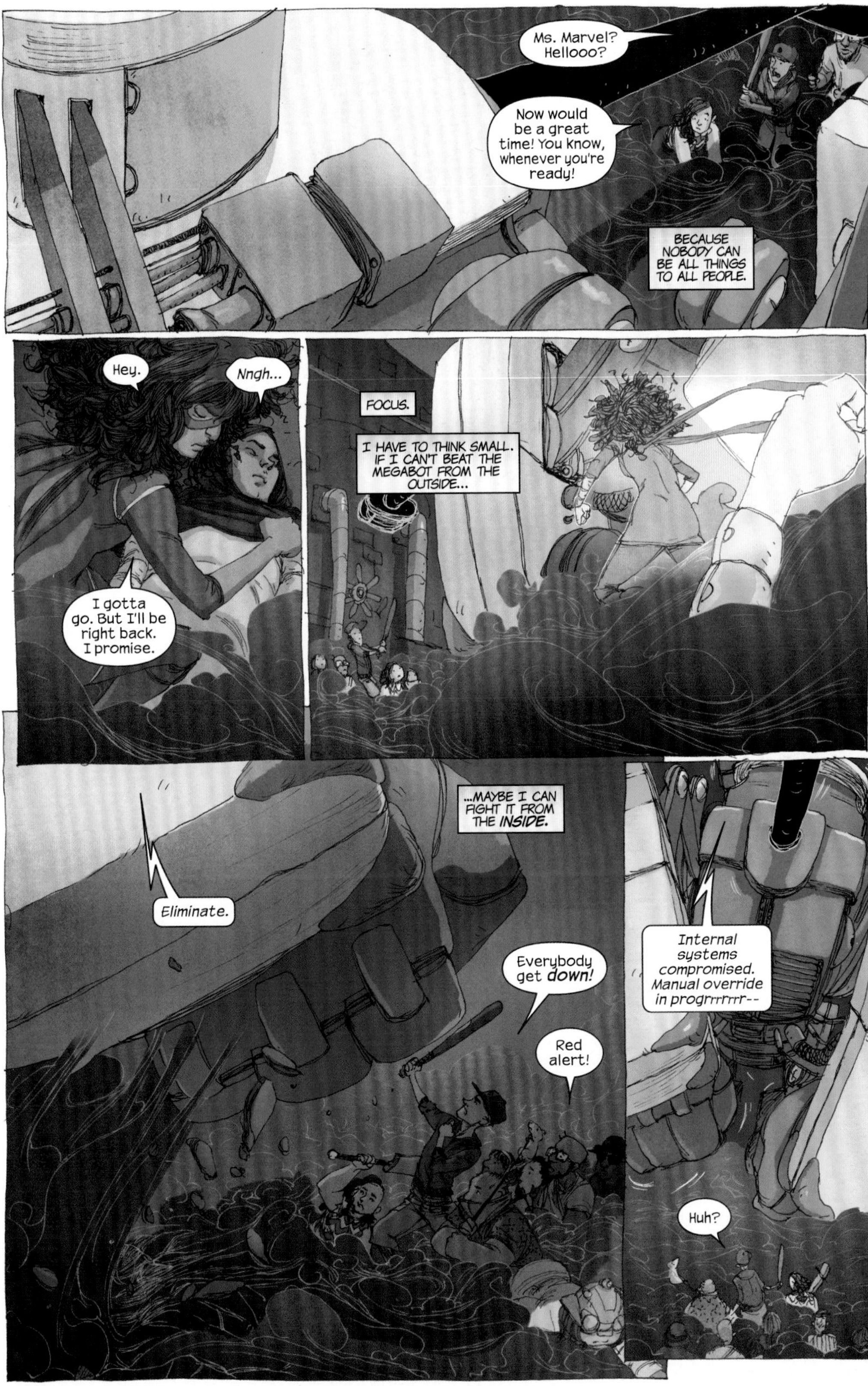

Ms. Marvel? Hellooo?
Now would be a great time! You know, whenever you're ready!
BECAUSE NOBODY CAN BE ALL THINGS TO ALL PEOPLE.
Hey.
Nngh...
I gotta go. But I'll be right back. I promise.
FOCUS.
I HAVE TO THINK SMALL. IF I CAN'T BEAT THE MEGABOT FROM THE OUTSIDE...
...MAYBE I CAN FIGHT IT FROM THE INSIDE.
Eliminate.
Everybody get down!
Red alert!
Internal systems compromised. Manual override in progrrrrrrr--
Huh?

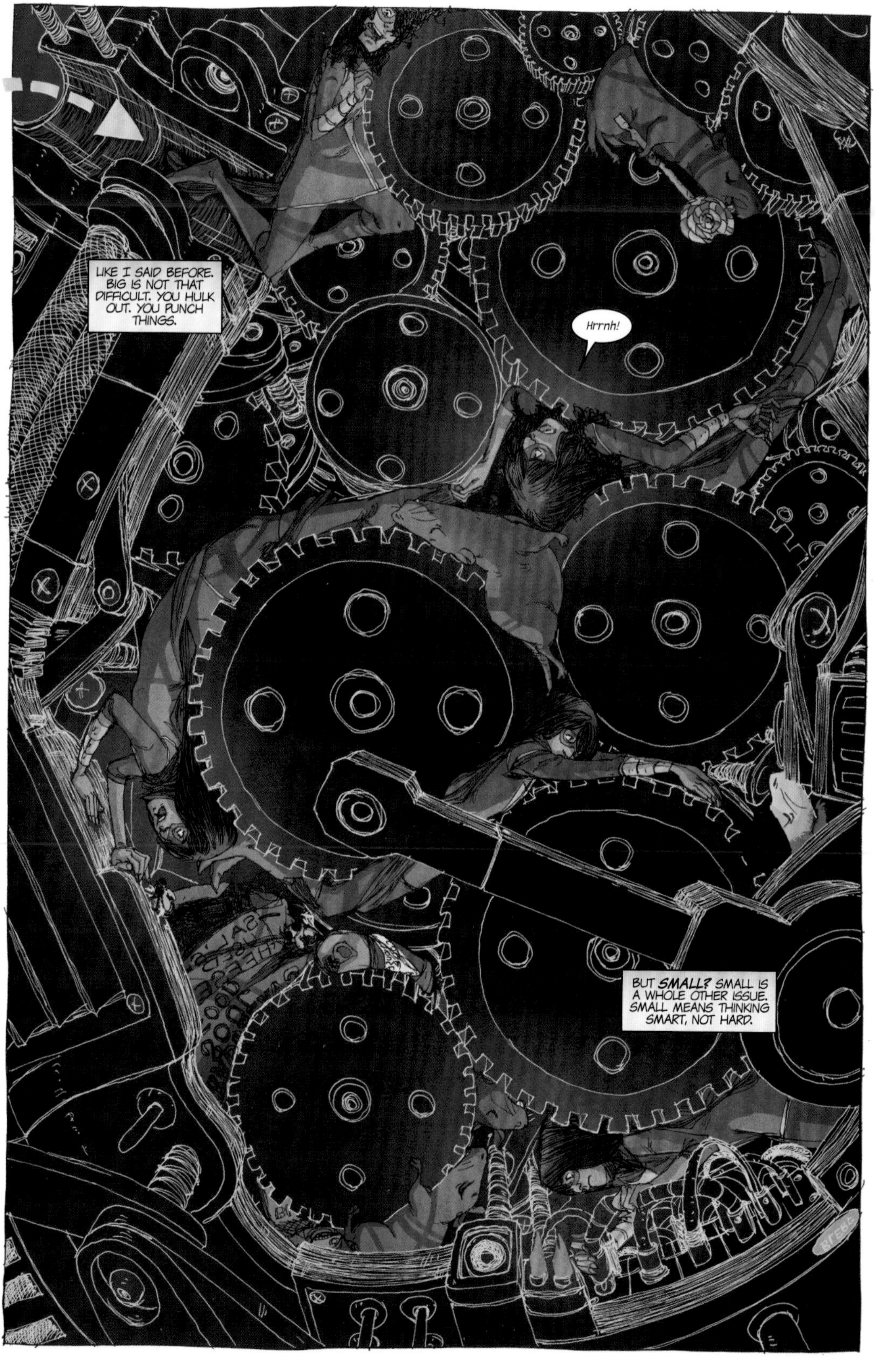
LIKE I SAID BEFORE. BIG IS NOT THAT DIFFICULT. YOU HULK OUT. YOU PUNCH THINGS.
Hrrnh!
BUT SMALL? SMALL IS A WHOLE OTHER ISSUE. SMALL MEANS THINKING SMART, NOT HARD.

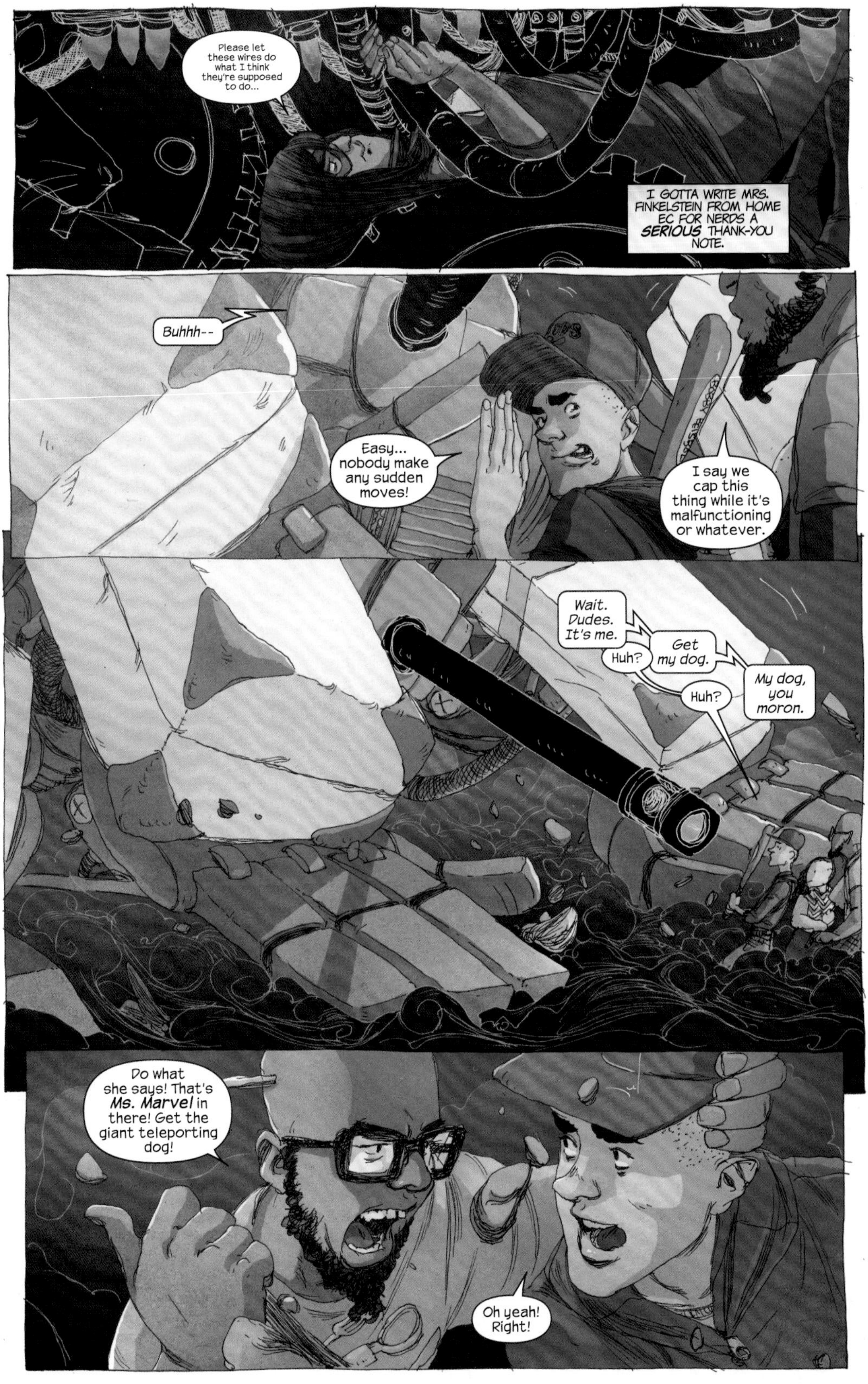
Please let these wires do what I think they're supposed to do...
I GOTTA WRITE MRS. FINKELSTEIN FROM HOME EC FOR NERDS A SERIOUS THANK-YOU NOTE.
Buhhh--
Easy... nobody make any sudden moves!
I say we cap this thing while it's malfunctioning or whatever.
Wait. Dudes. It's me.
Huh?
Get my dog.
Huh?
My dog, you moron.
Do what she says! That's Ms. Marvel in there! Get the giant teleporting dog!
Oh yeah! Right!

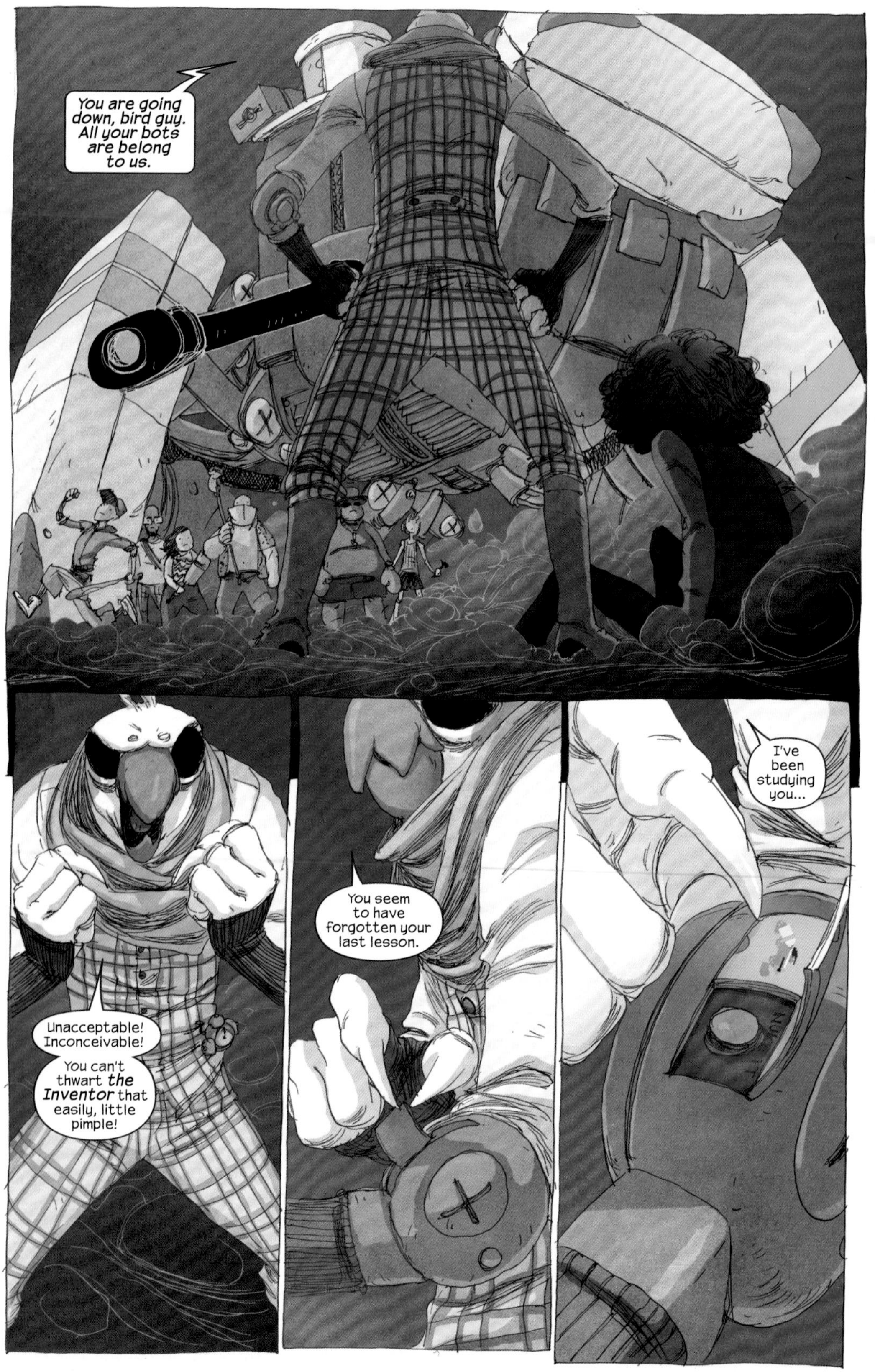
You are going down, bird guy. All your bots are belong to us.
Unacceptable! Inconceivable!
You can't thwart **the Inventor** that easily, little pimple!
You seem to have forgotten your last lesson.
I've been studying you...

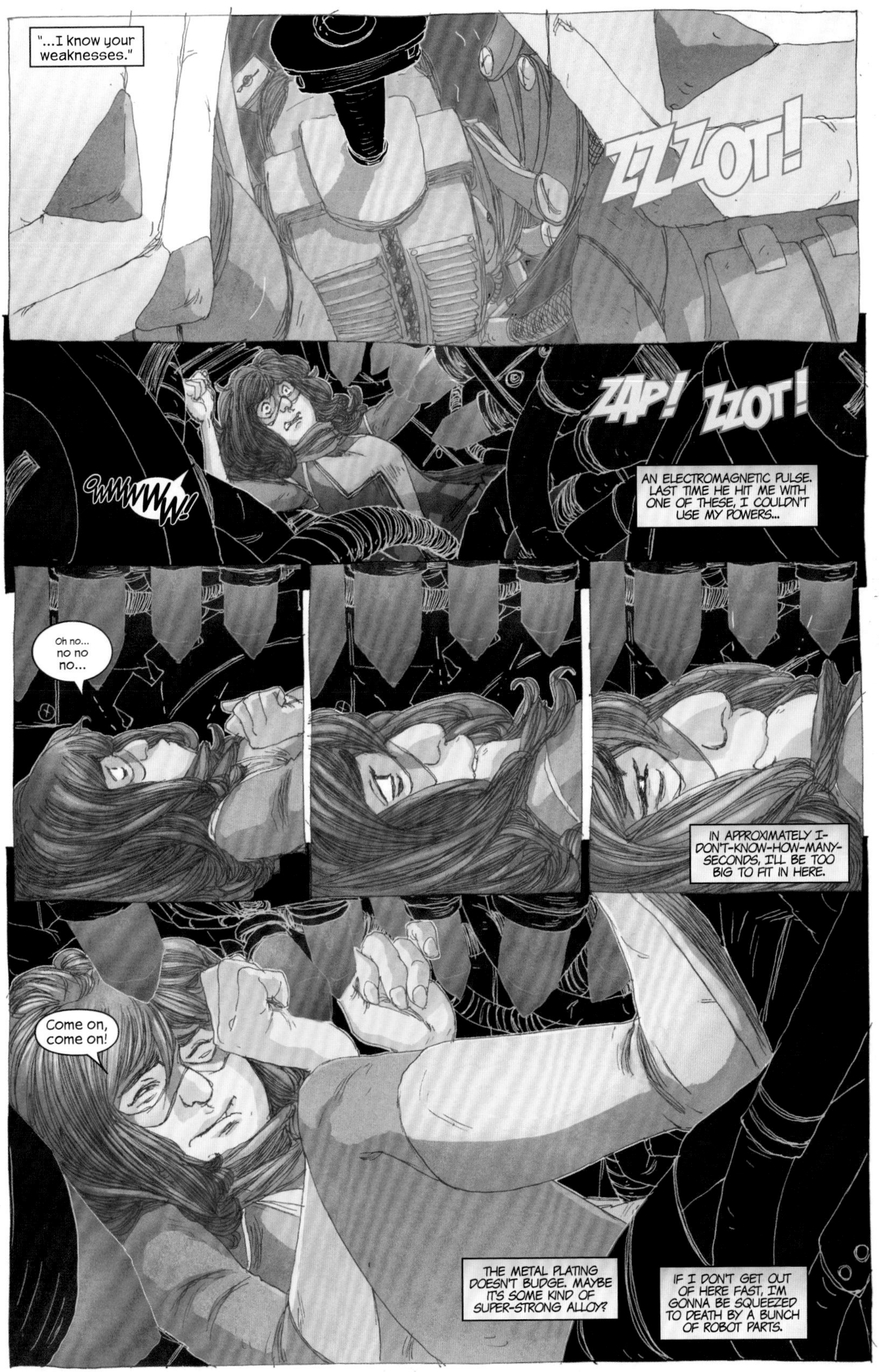
"...I know your weaknesses."
ZZZOT!
ZAP! ZZOT!
WHMWWW!
AN ELECTROMAGNETIC PULSE. LAST TIME HE HIT ME WITH ONE OF THESE, I COULDN'T USE MY POWERS...
Oh no... no no no...
IN APPROXIMATELY I-DON'T-KNOW-HOW-MANY-SECONDS, I'LL BE TOO BIG TO FIT IN HERE.
Come on, come on!
THE METAL PLATING DOESN'T BUDGE. MAYBE IT'S SOME KIND OF SUPER-STRONG ALLOY?
IF I DON'T GET OUT OF HERE FAST, I'M GONNA BE SQUEEZED TO DEATH BY A BUNCH OF ROBOT PARTS.

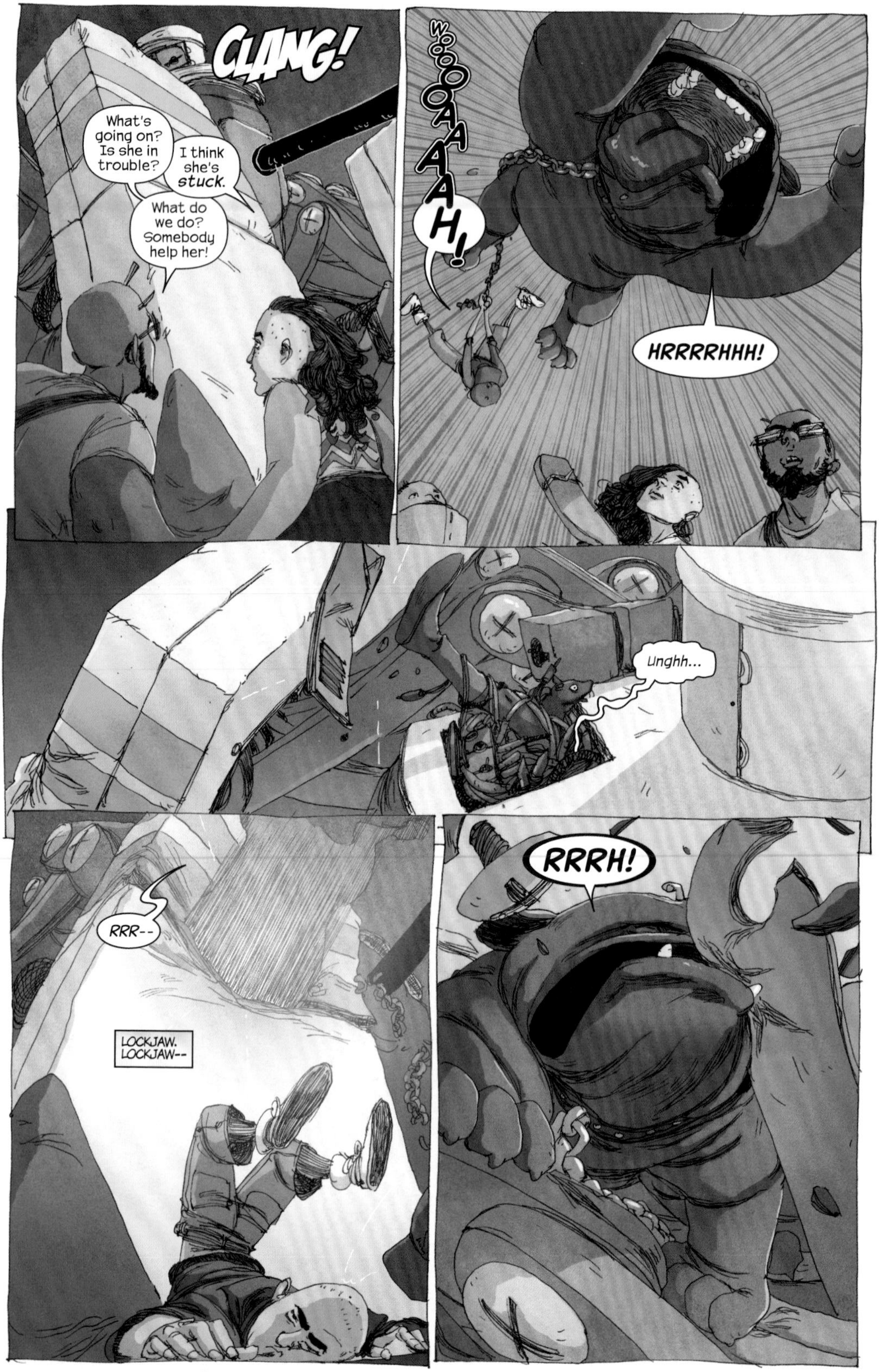
CLANG!
What's going on? Is she in trouble?
I think she's stuck.
What do we do? Somebody help her!
WOOOOAAAAAH!
HRRRRHHH!
Unghh...
RRR--
LOCKJAW. LOCKJAW--
RRRH!

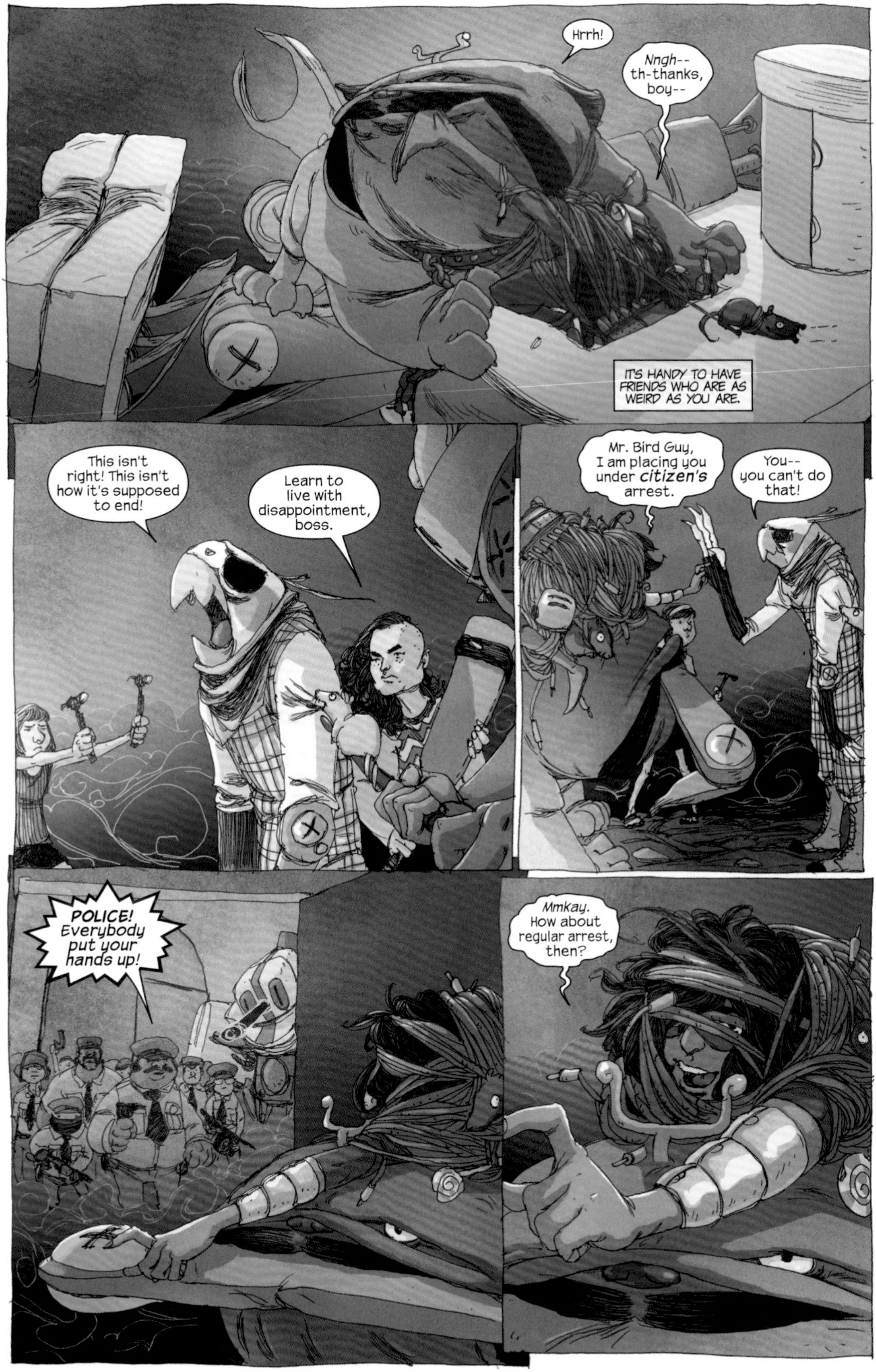
Hrrh!
Nngh-- th-thanks, boy--
IT'S HANDY TO HAVE FRIENDS WHO ARE AS WEIRD AS YOU ARE.
This isn't right! This isn't how it's supposed to end!
Learn to live with disappointment, boss.
Mr. Bird Guy, I am placing you under citizen's arrest.
You-- you can't do that!
POLICE! Everybody put your hands up!
Mmkay. How about regular arrest, then?

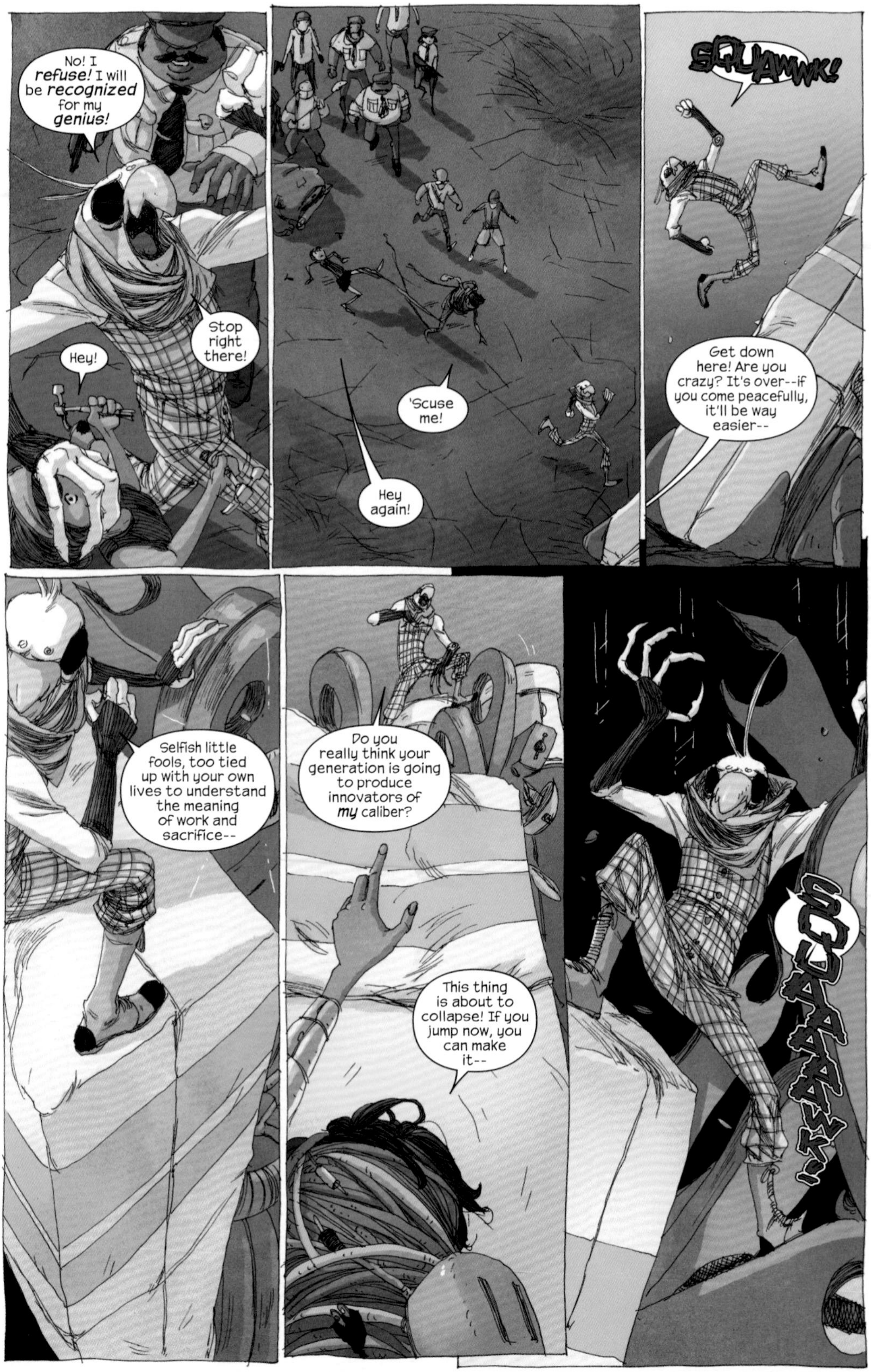
No! I refuse! I will be recognized for my genius!
Hey!
Stop right there!
'Scuse me!
Hey again!
SQUAWWK!
Get down here! Are you crazy? It's over--if you come peacefully, it'll be way easier--
Selfish little fools, too tied up with your own lives to understand the meaning of work and sacrifice--
Do you really think your generation is going to produce innovators of my caliber?
This thing is about to collapse! If you jump now, you can make it--
SQUAAAAWK!

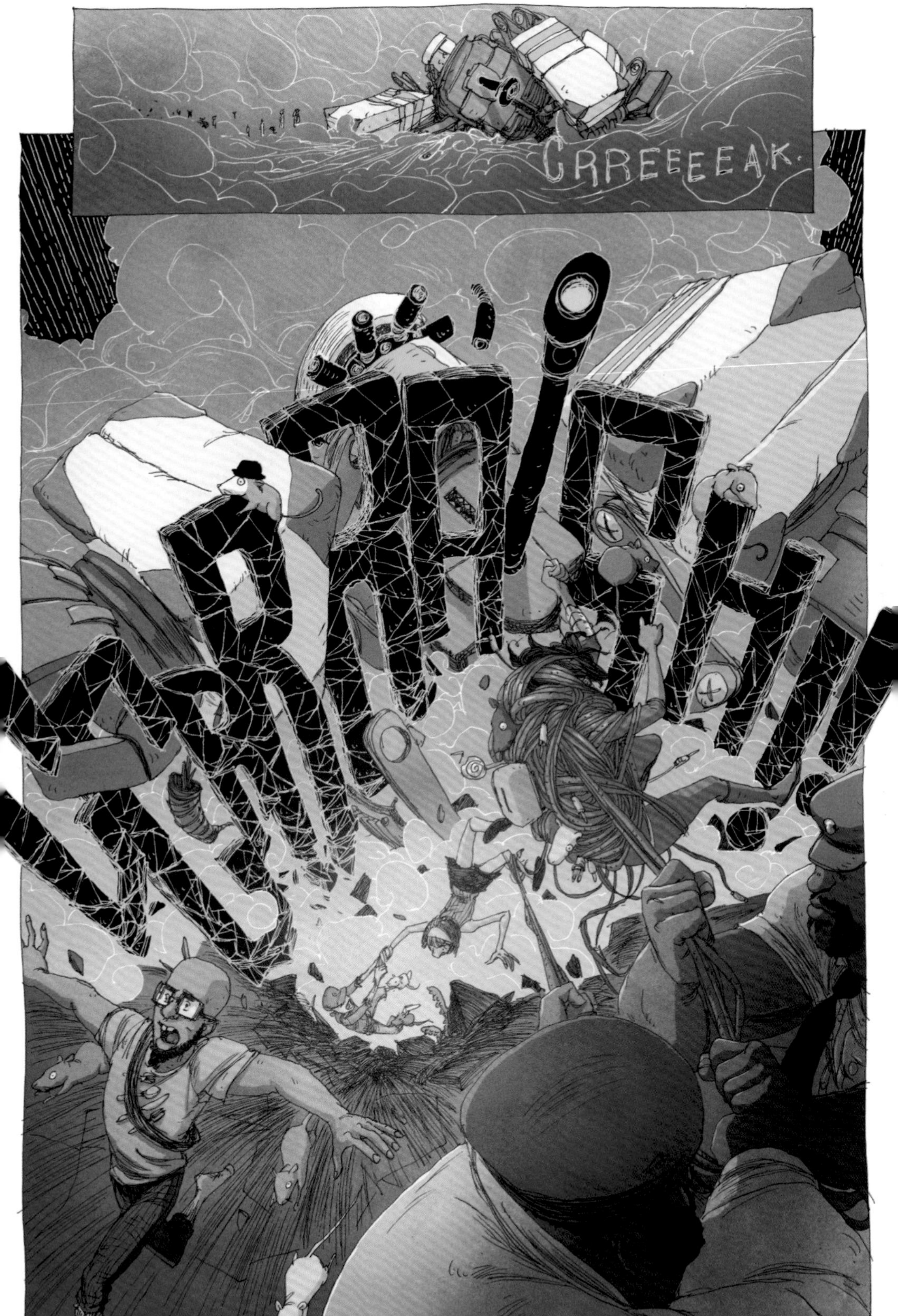
CRREEEEAK.

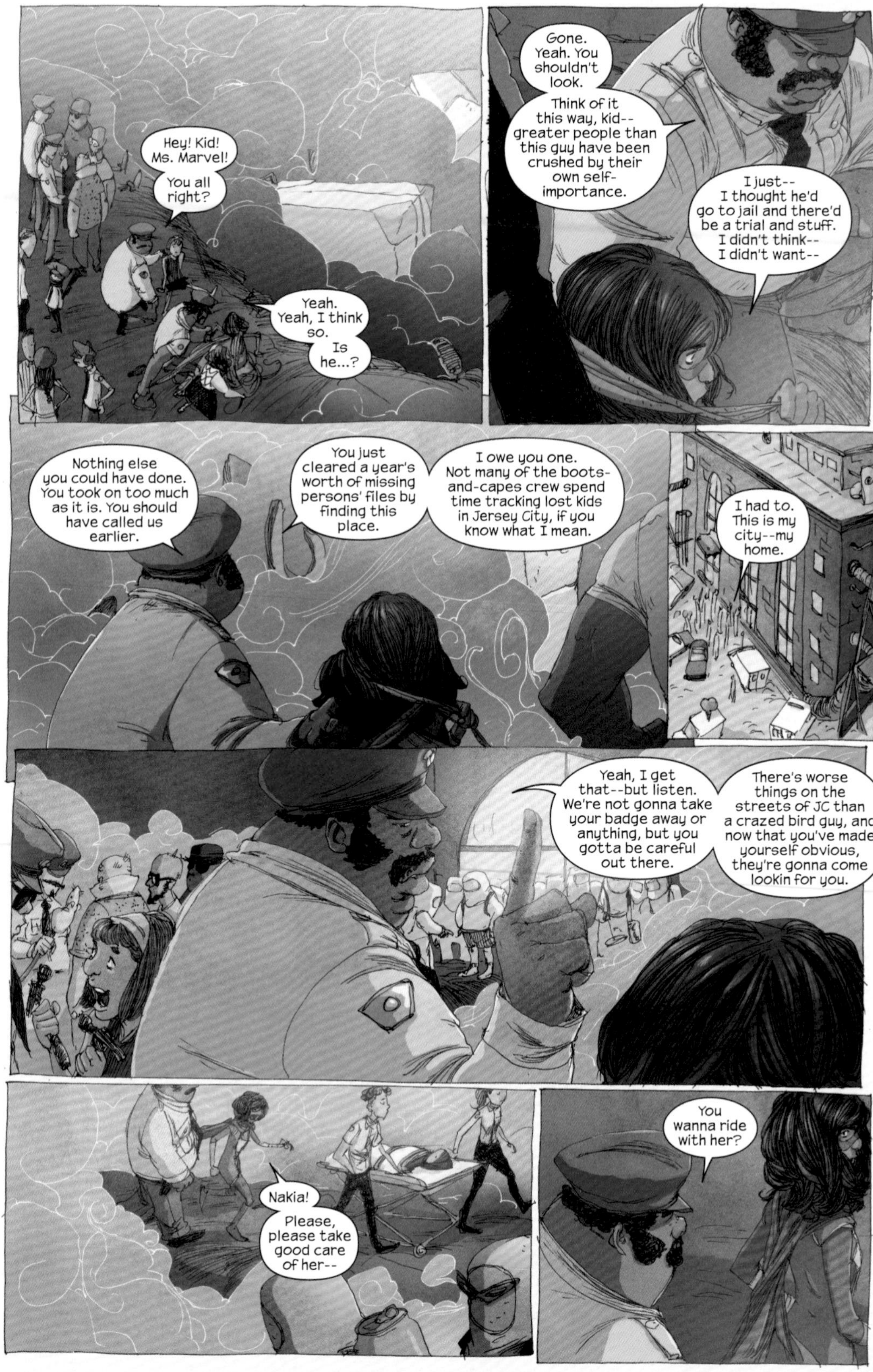
Hey! Kid! Ms. Marvel!
You all right?
Yeah. Yeah, I think so.
Is he...?
Gone. Yeah. You shouldn't look.
Think of it this way, kid--greater people than this guy have been crushed by their own self-importance.
I just--I thought he'd go to jail and there'd be a trial and stuff. I didn't think--I didn't want--
Nothing else you could have done. You took on too much as it is. You should have called us earlier.
You just cleared a year's worth of missing persons' files by finding this place.
I owe you one. Not many of the boots-and-capes crew spend time tracking lost kids in Jersey City, if you know what I mean.
I had to. This is my city--my home.
Yeah, I get that--but listen. We're not gonna take your badge away or anything, but you gotta be careful out there.
There's worse things on the streets of JC than a crazed bird guy, and now that you've made yourself obvious, they're gonna come lookin for you.
Nakia!
Please, take good care of her--
You wanna ride with her?

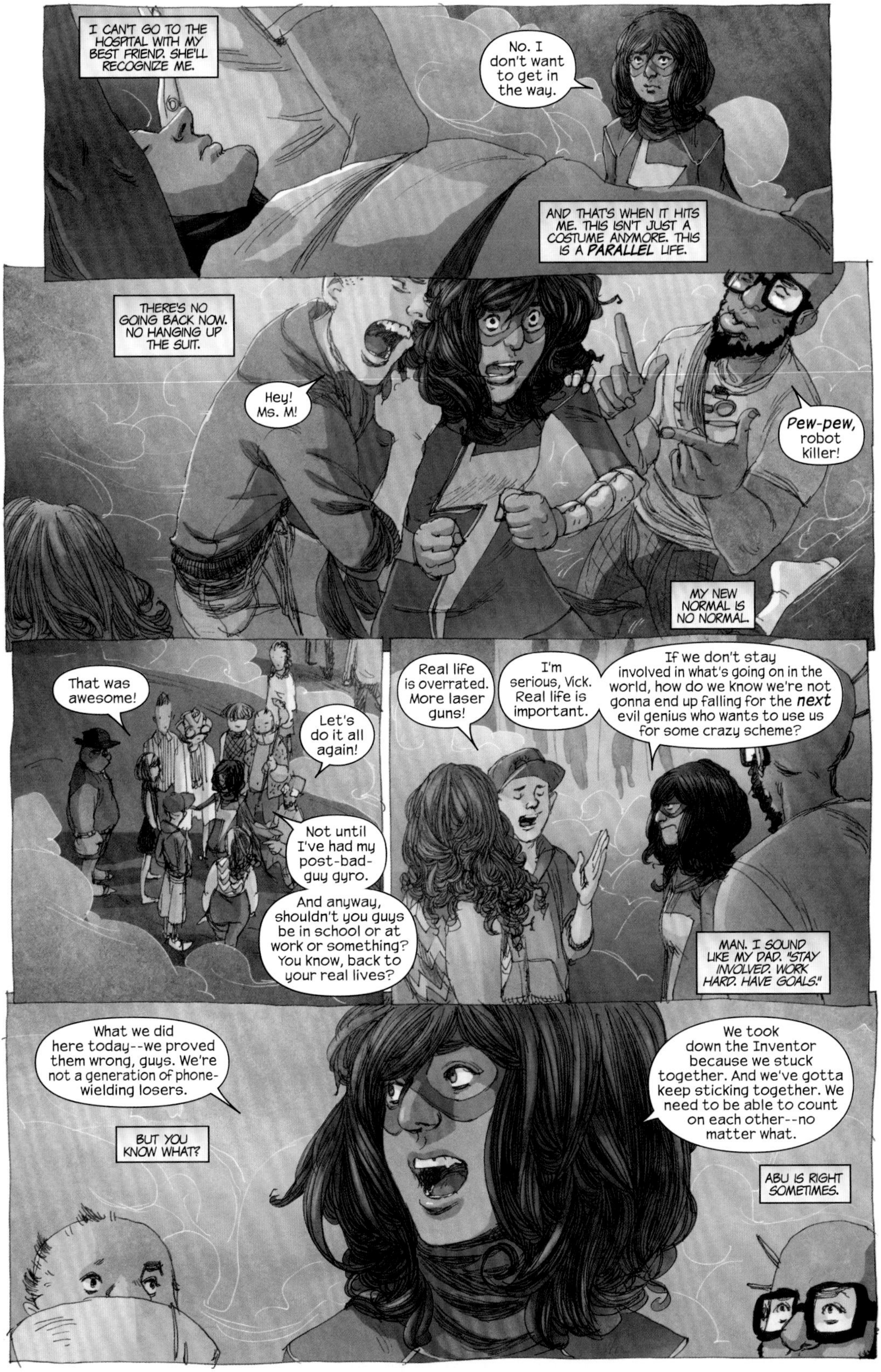

I CAN'T GO TO THE HOSPITAL WITH MY BEST FRIEND. SHE'LL RECOGNIZE ME.
No. I don't want to get in the way.
AND THAT'S WHEN IT HITS ME. THIS ISN'T JUST A COSTUME ANYMORE. THIS IS A PARALLEL LIFE.
THERE'S NO GOING BACK NOW. NO HANGING UP THE SUIT.
Hey! Ms. M!
Pew-pew, robot killer!
MY NEW NORMAL IS NO NORMAL.
That was awesome!
Let's do it all again!
Not until I've had my post-bad-guy gyro.
And anyway, shouldn't you guys be in school or at work or something? You know, back to your real lives?
Real life is overrated. More laser guns!
I'm serious, Vick. Real life is important.
If we don't stay involved in what's going on in the world, how do we know we're not gonna end up falling for the next evil genius who wants to use us for some crazy scheme?
MAN. I SOUND LIKE MY DAD. "STAY INVOLVED. WORK HARD. HAVE GOALS."
What we did here today--we proved them wrong, guys. We're not a generation of phone-wielding losers.
BUT YOU KNOW WHAT?
We took down the Inventor because we stuck together. And we've gotta keep sticking together. We need to be able to count on each other--no matter what.
ABU IS RIGHT SOMETIMES.

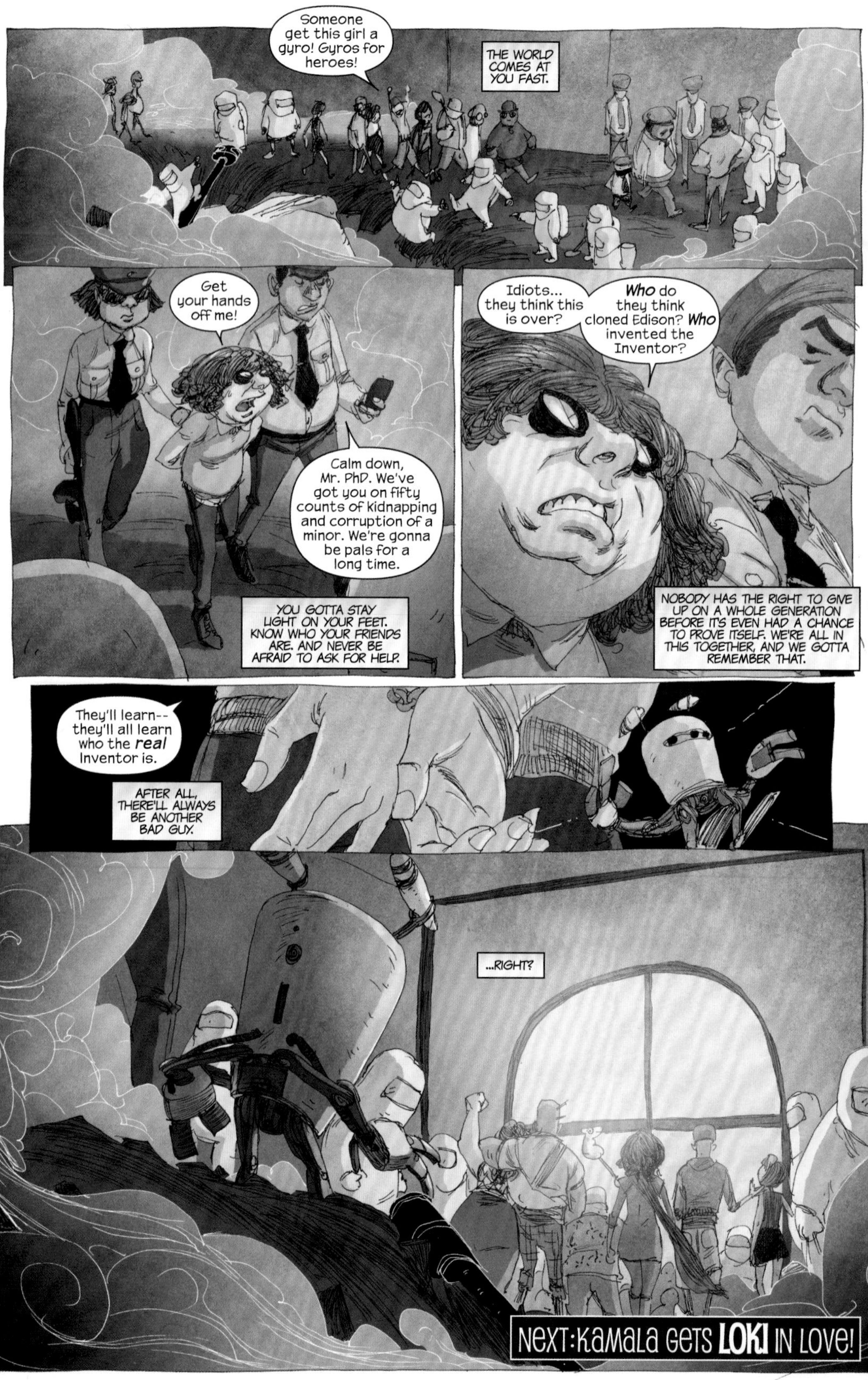
Someone get this girl a gyro! Gyros for heroes!
THE WORLD COMES AT YOU FAST.
Get your hands off me!
Calm down, Mr. PhD. We've got you on fifty counts of kidnapping and corruption of a minor. We're gonna be pals for a long time.
YOU GOTTA STAY LIGHT ON YOUR FEET. KNOW WHO YOUR FRIENDS ARE. AND NEVER BE AFRAID TO ASK FOR HELP.
Idiots... they think this is over?
Who do they think cloned Edison? Who invented the Inventor?
NOBODY HAS THE RIGHT TO GIVE UP ON A WHOLE GENERATION BEFORE IT'S EVEN HAD A CHANCE TO PROVE ITSELF. WE'RE ALL IN THIS TOGETHER, AND WE GOTTA REMEMBER THAT.
They'll learn-- they'll all learn who the real Inventor is.
AFTER ALL, THERE'LL ALWAYS BE ANOTHER BAD GUY.
...RIGHT?
NEXT: KAMALA GETS LOKI IN LOVE!

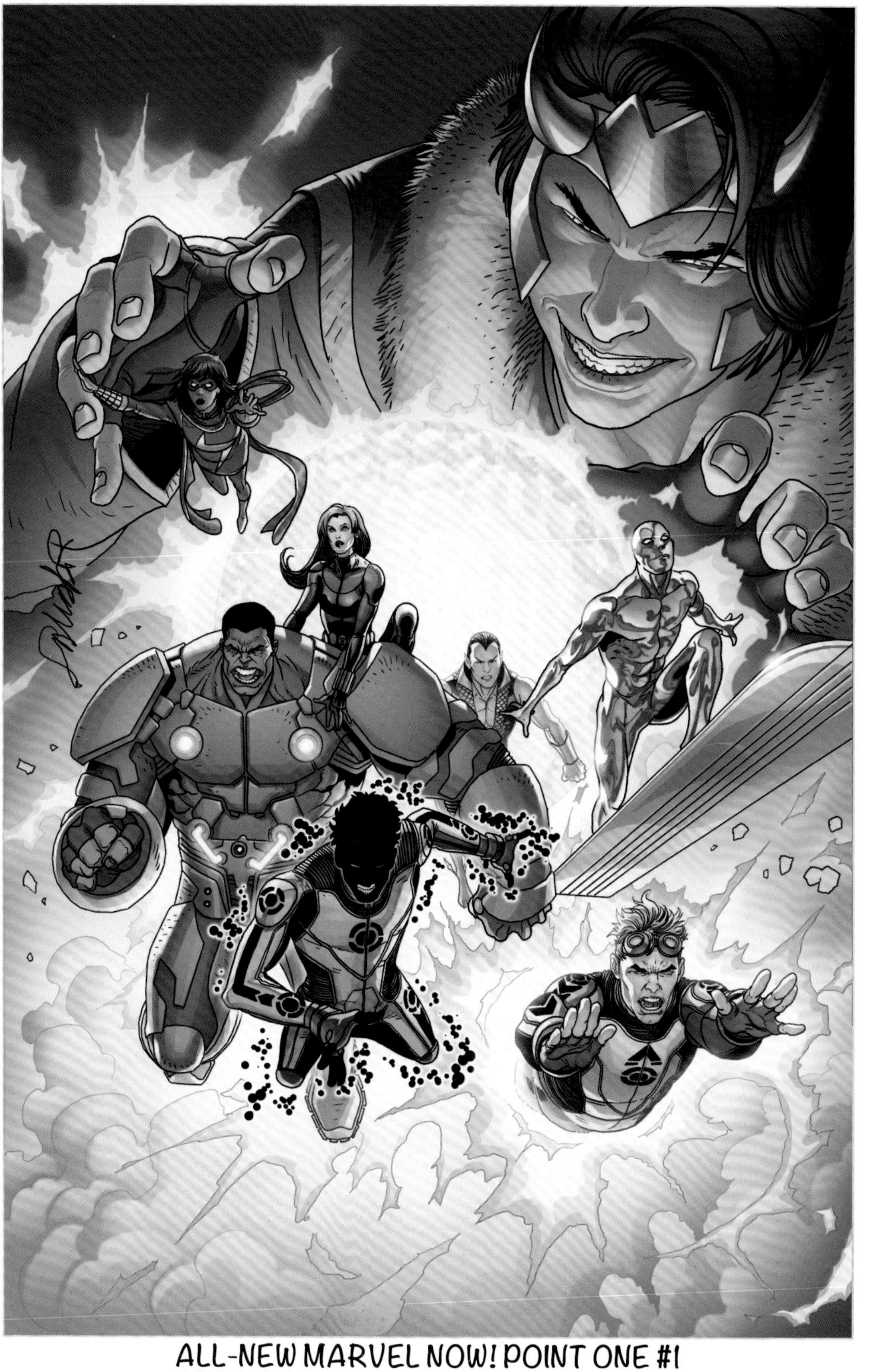

ALL-NEW MARVEL NOW! POINT ONE #1
COVER BY SALVADOR LARROCA & LAURA MARTIN

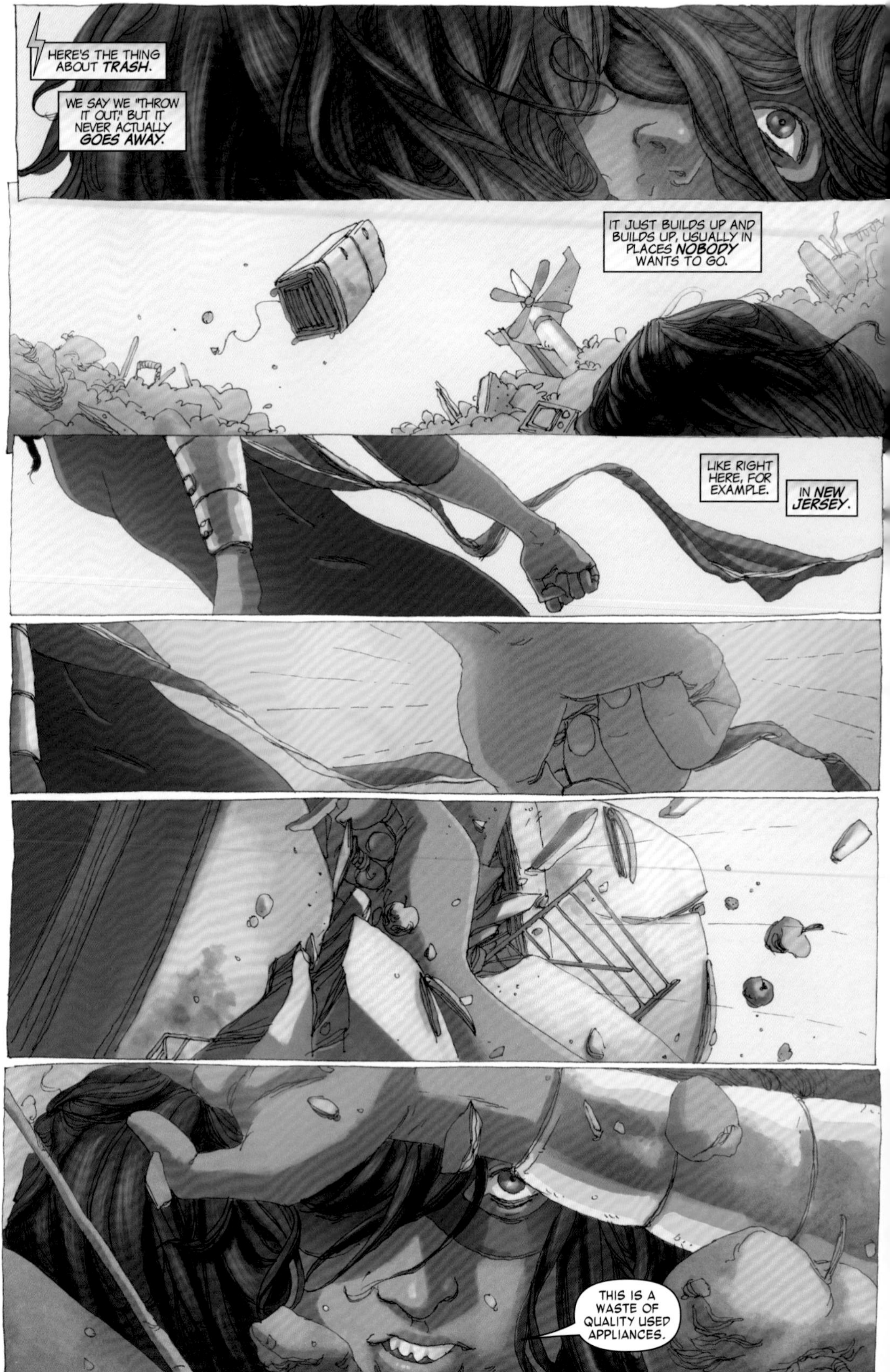
HERE'S THE THING ABOUT TRASH.
WE SAY WE "THROW IT OUT," BUT IT NEVER ACTUALLY GOES AWAY.
IT JUST BUILDS UP AND BUILDS UP, USUALLY IN PLACES NOBODY WANTS TO GO.
LIKE RIGHT HERE, FOR EXAMPLE.
IN NEW JERSEY.
THIS IS A WASTE OF QUALITY USED APPLIANCES.

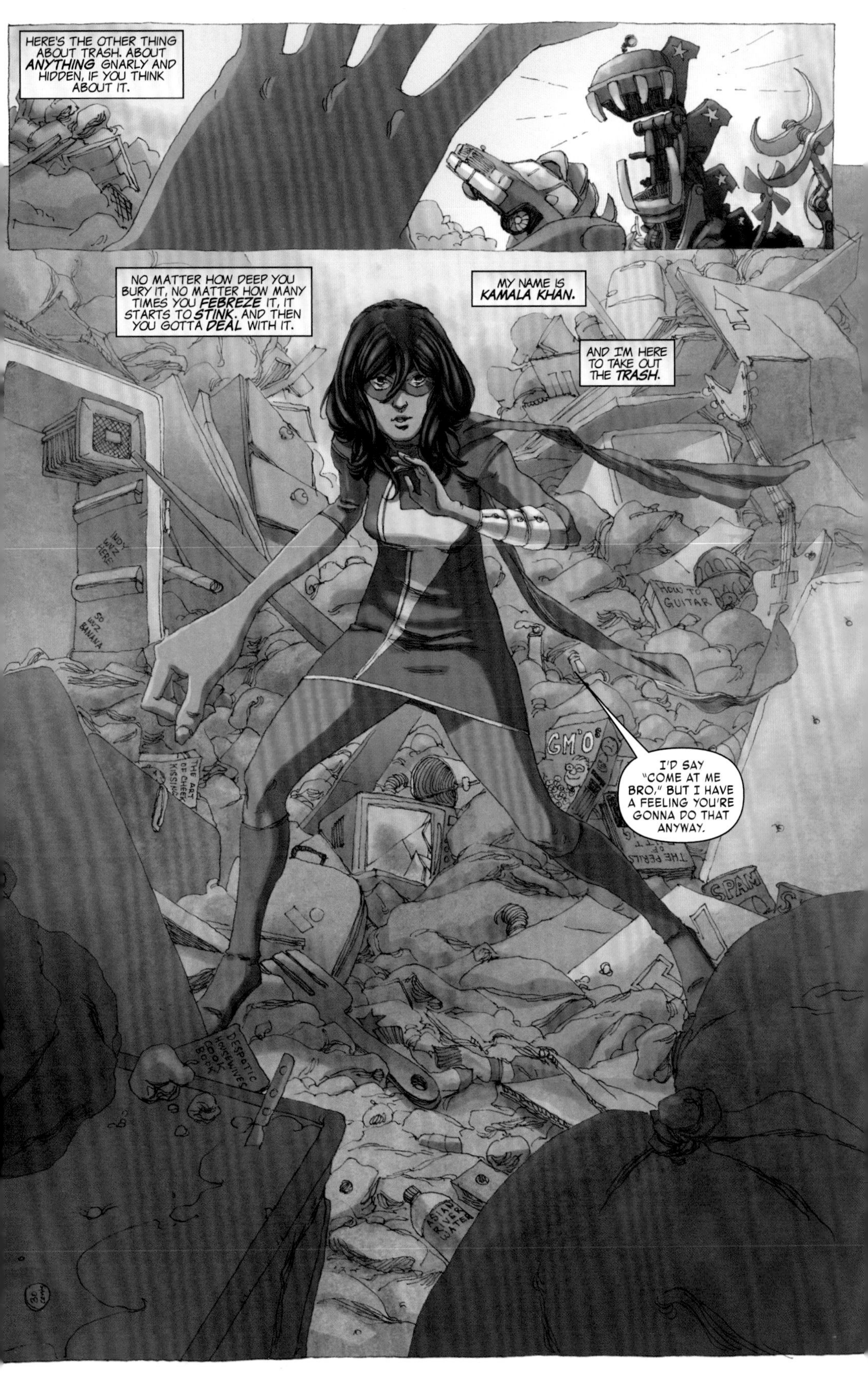
HERE'S THE OTHER THING ABOUT TRASH. ABOUT ANYTHING GNARLY AND HIDDEN, IF YOU THINK ABOUT IT.
NO MATTER HOW DEEP YOU BURY IT, NO MATTER HOW MANY TIMES YOU FEBREZE IT, IT STARTS TO STINK. AND THEN YOU GOTTA DEAL WITH IT.
MY NAME IS KAMALA KHAN.
AND I'M HERE TO TAKE OUT THE TRASH.
I'D SAY "COME AT ME BRO," BUT I HAVE A FEELING YOU'RE GONNA DO THAT ANYWAY.
HOW TO GUITAR
THE ART OF CHEEK KISSING
GM'O
THE PERILS OF
SPAM
DESPOTIC HOUSEWIVES COOK BOOK
ASIAN RIVER WATER

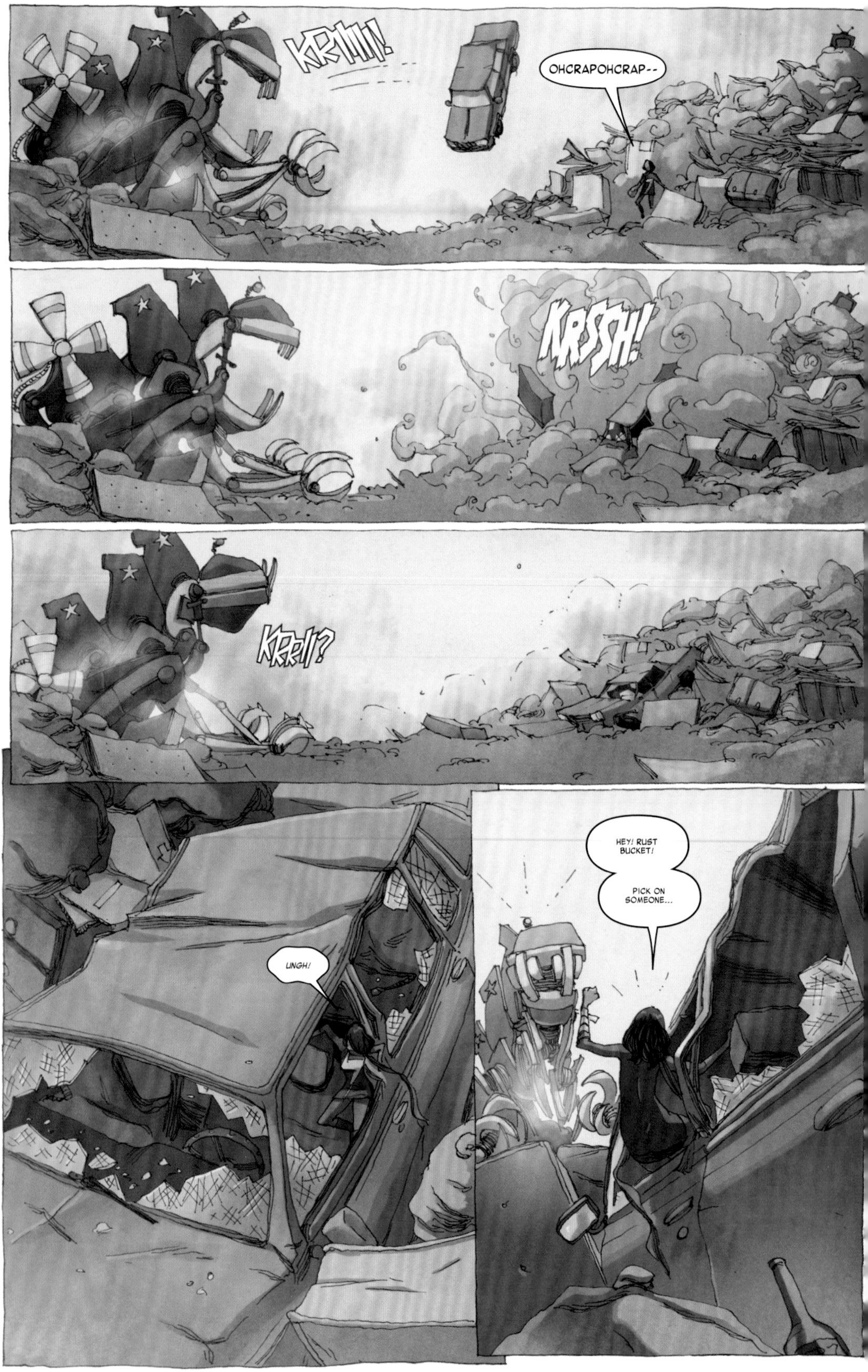
KRMMM!
OHCRAPOHCRAP--
KRSSH!
KRRRLL?
UNGH!
HEY! RUST BUCKET!
PICK ON SOMEONE...

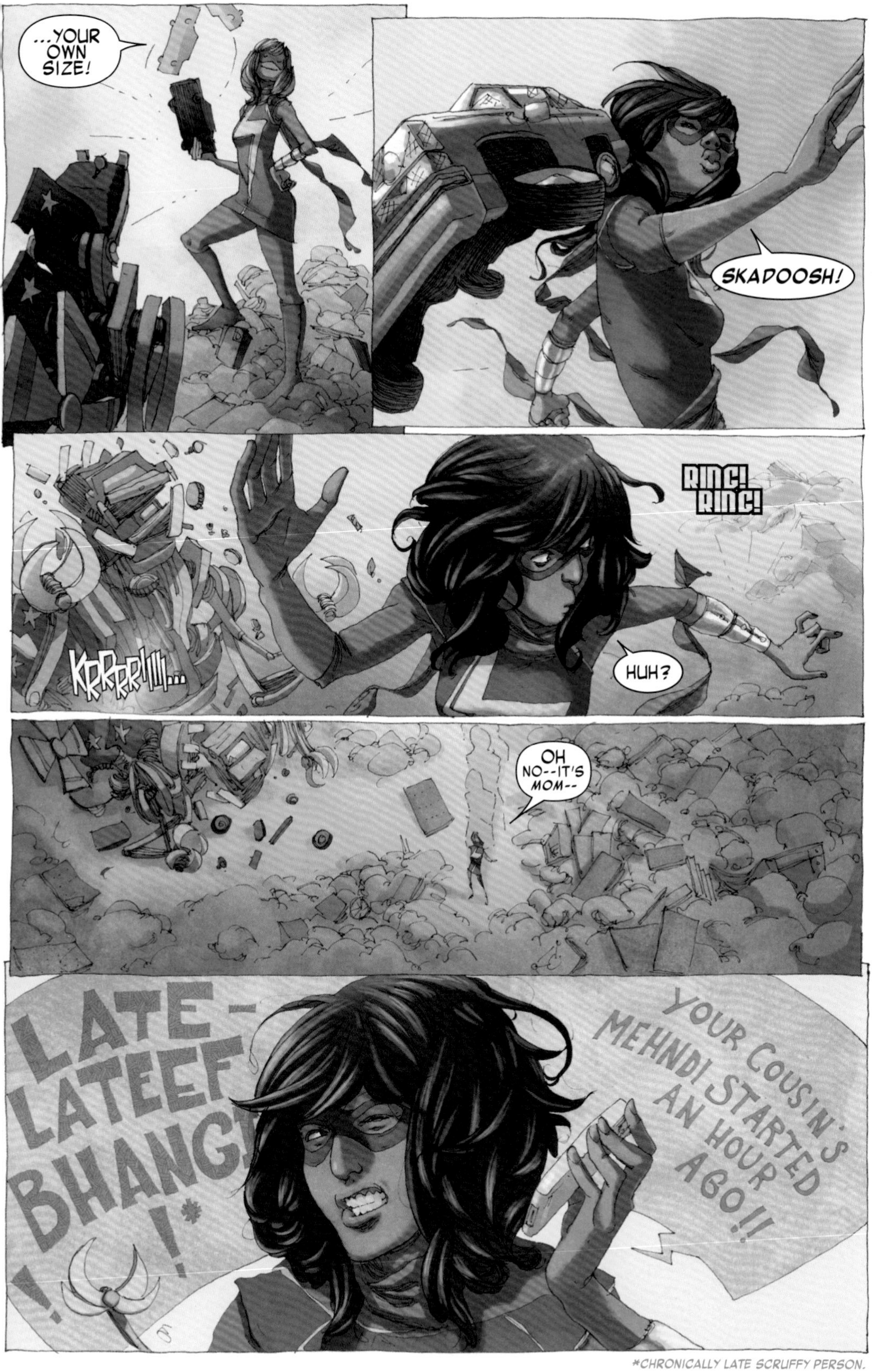
...YOUR OWN SIZE!
SKADOOSH!
RING! RING!
KRRRRRIIIII...
HUH?
OH NO--IT'S MOM--
LATE-LATEEF BHANGI!*
YOUR COUSIN'S MEHNDI STARTED AN HOUR AGO!!

*CHRONICALLY LATE SCRUFFY PERSON.

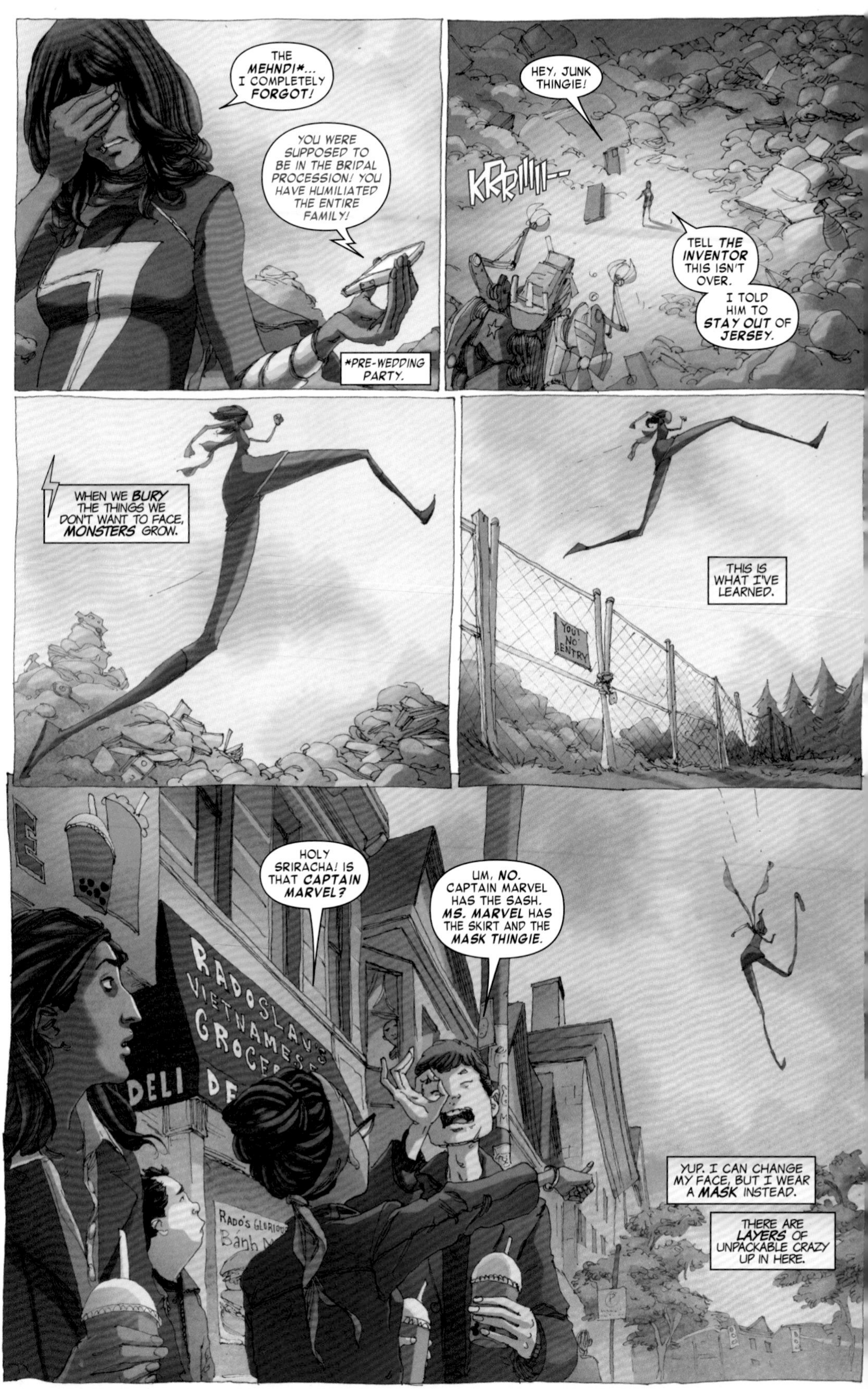

THE MEHNDI*... I COMPLETELY FORGOT!
YOU WERE SUPPOSED TO BE IN THE BRIDAL PROCESSION! YOU HAVE HUMILIATED THE ENTIRE FAMILY!
*PRE-WEDDING PARTY.
HEY, JUNK THINGIE!
KRRIIIII--
TELL THE INVENTOR THIS ISN'T OVER.
I TOLD HIM TO STAY OUT OF JERSEY.
WHEN WE BURY THE THINGS WE DON'T WANT TO FACE, MONSTERS GROW.
THIS IS WHAT I'VE LEARNED.
YOU! NO ENTRY
HOLY SRIRACHA! IS THAT CAPTAIN MARVEL?
UM, NO. CAPTAIN MARVEL HAS THE SASH. MS. MARVEL HAS THE SKIRT AND THE MASK THINGIE.
RADOSLAV'S VIETNAMESE GROCERIES
DELI
RADO'S GLORIOUS
Bánh
YUP. I CAN CHANGE MY FACE, BUT I WEAR A MASK INSTEAD.
THERE ARE LAYERS OF UNPACKABLE CRAZY UP IN HERE.

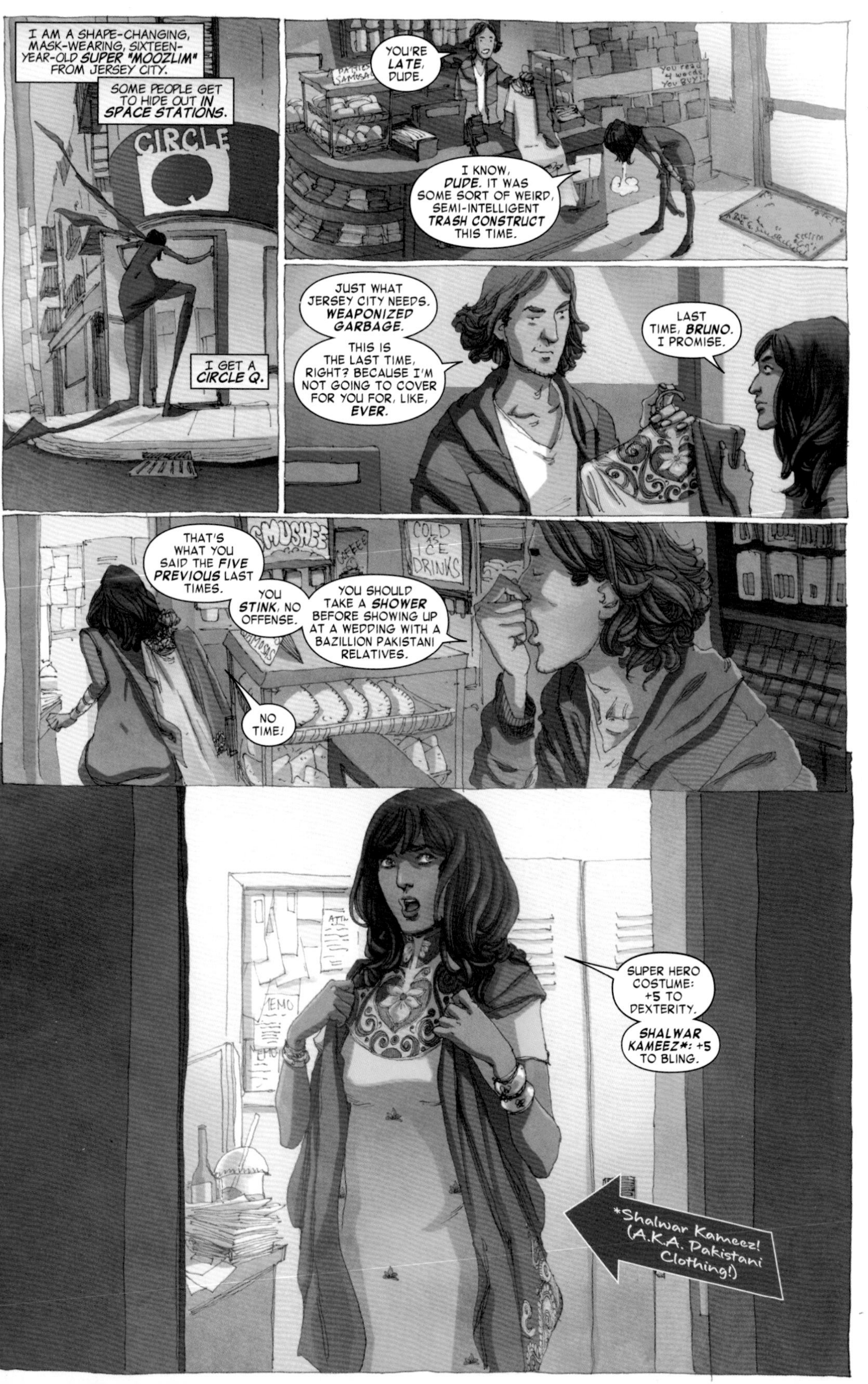
I AM A SHAPE-CHANGING, MASK-WEARING, SIXTEEN-YEAR-OLD SUPER "MOOZLIM" FROM JERSEY CITY.
SOME PEOPLE GET TO HIDE OUT IN SPACE STATIONS.
CIRCLE
I GET A CIRCLE Q.
YOU'RE LATE, DUDE.
I KNOW, DUDE. IT WAS SOME SORT OF WEIRD, SEMI-INTELLIGENT TRASH CONSTRUCT THIS TIME.
JUST WHAT JERSEY CITY NEEDS. WEAPONIZED GARBAGE.
THIS IS THE LAST TIME, RIGHT? BECAUSE I'M NOT GOING TO COVER FOR YOU FOR, LIKE, EVER.
LAST TIME, BRUNO. I PROMISE.
THAT'S WHAT YOU SAID THE FIVE PREVIOUS LAST TIMES.
YOU STINK, NO OFFENSE.
YOU SHOULD TAKE A SHOWER BEFORE SHOWING UP AT A WEDDING WITH A BAZILLION PAKISTANI RELATIVES.
NO TIME!
COLD ICE DRINKS
SUPER HERO COSTUME: +5 TO DEXTERITY.
SHALWAR KAMEEZ*: +5 TO BLING.
*Shalwar Kameez! (A.K.A. Pakistani Clothing!)

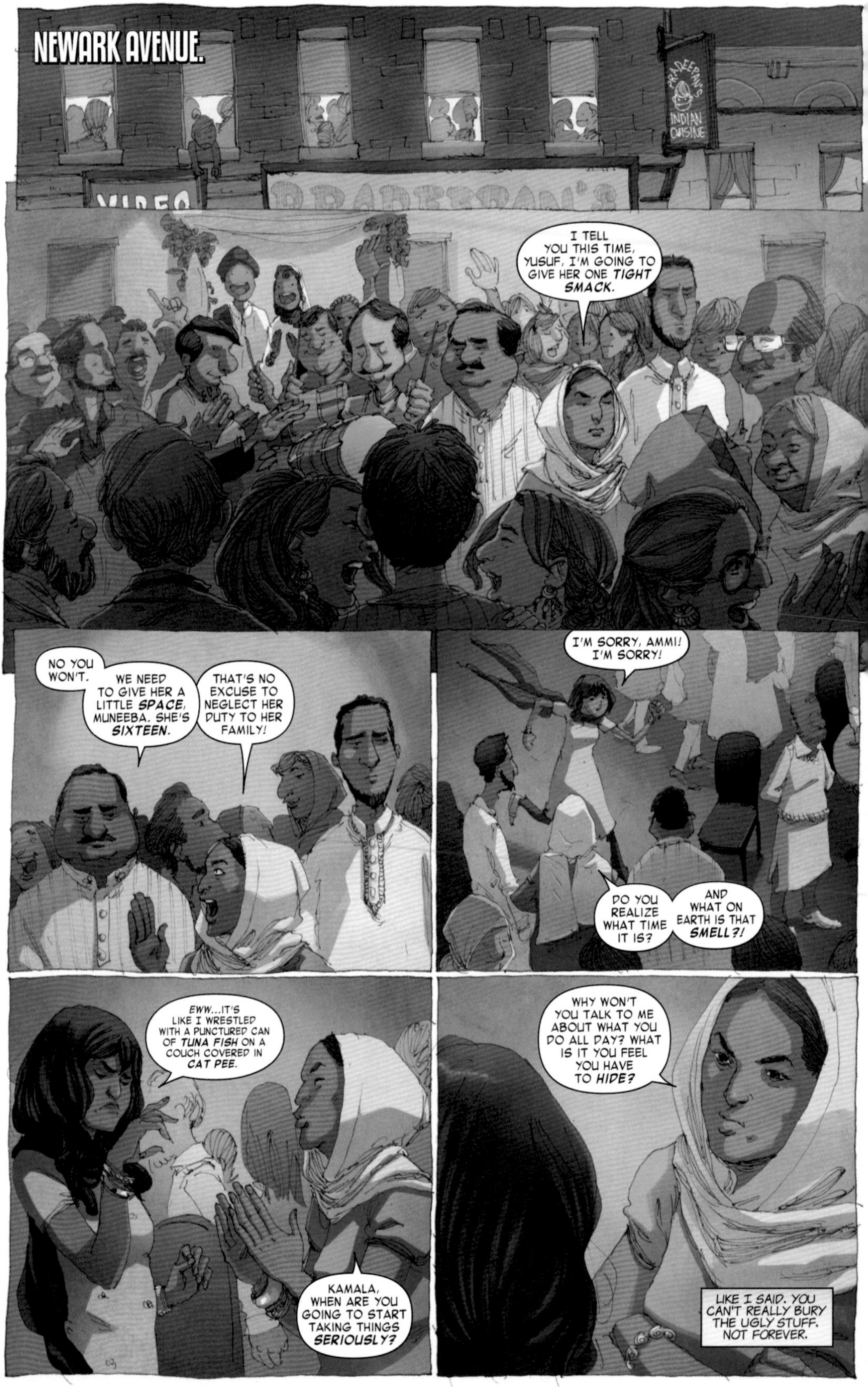
NEWARK AVENUE.
PRADEEPAN'S INDIAN CUISINE
I TELL YOU THIS TIME, YUSUF, I'M GOING TO GIVE HER ONE TIGHT SMACK.
NO YOU WON'T.
WE NEED TO GIVE HER A LITTLE SPACE, MUNEEBA. SHE'S SIXTEEN.
THAT'S NO EXCUSE TO NEGLECT HER DUTY TO HER FAMILY!
I'M SORRY, AMMI! I'M SORRY!
DO YOU REALIZE WHAT TIME IT IS?
AND WHAT ON EARTH IS THAT SMELL?!
EWW...IT'S LIKE I WRESTLED WITH A PUNCTURED CAN OF TUNA FISH ON A COUCH COVERED IN CAT PEE.
KAMALA, WHEN ARE YOU GOING TO START TAKING THINGS SERIOUSLY?
WHY WON'T YOU TALK TO ME ABOUT WHAT YOU DO ALL DAY? WHAT IS IT YOU FEEL YOU HAVE TO HIDE?
LIKE I SAID. YOU CAN'T REALLY BURY THE UGLY STUFF. NOT FOREVER.

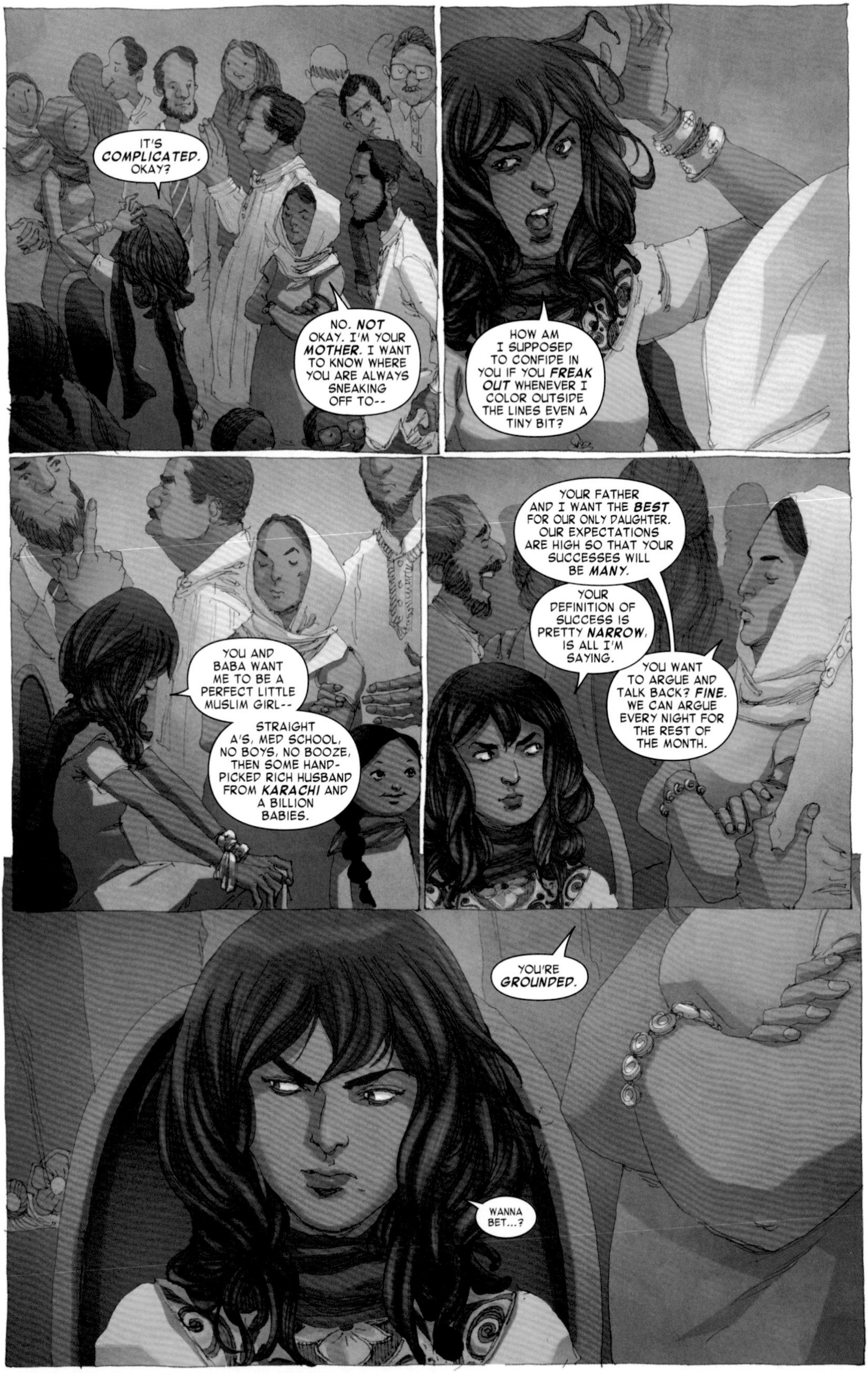

IT'S COMPLICATED. OKAY?
NO. NOT OKAY. I'M YOUR MOTHER. I WANT TO KNOW WHERE YOU ARE ALWAYS SNEAKING OFF TO--
HOW AM I SUPPOSED TO CONFIDE IN YOU IF YOU FREAK OUT WHENEVER I COLOR OUTSIDE THE LINES EVEN A TINY BIT?
YOU AND BABA WANT ME TO BE A PERFECT LITTLE MUSLIM GIRL--
STRAIGHT A'S, MED SCHOOL, NO BOYS, NO BOOZE, THEN SOME HAND-PICKED RICH HUSBAND FROM KARACHI AND A BILLION BABIES.
YOUR FATHER AND I WANT THE BEST FOR OUR ONLY DAUGHTER. OUR EXPECTATIONS ARE HIGH SO THAT YOUR SUCCESSES WILL BE MANY.
YOUR DEFINITION OF SUCCESS IS PRETTY NARROW, IS ALL I'M SAYING.
YOU WANT TO ARGUE AND TALK BACK? FINE. WE CAN ARGUE EVERY NIGHT FOR THE REST OF THE MONTH.
YOU'RE GROUNDED.
WANNA BET...?

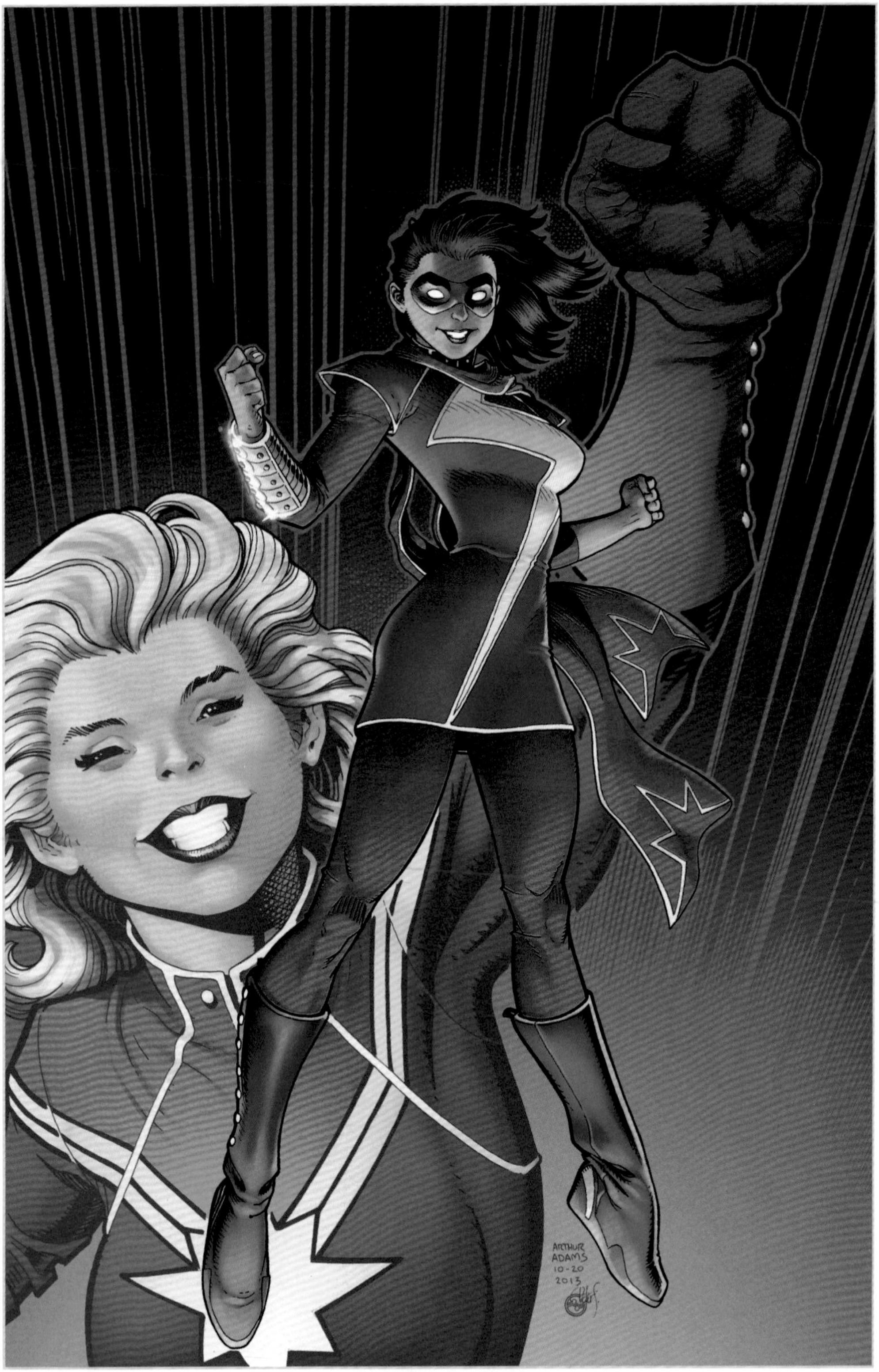
ARTHUR
ADAMS
10-20
2013

MS. MARVEL #1 VARIANT

BY ARTHUR ADAMS & PETER STEIGERWALD

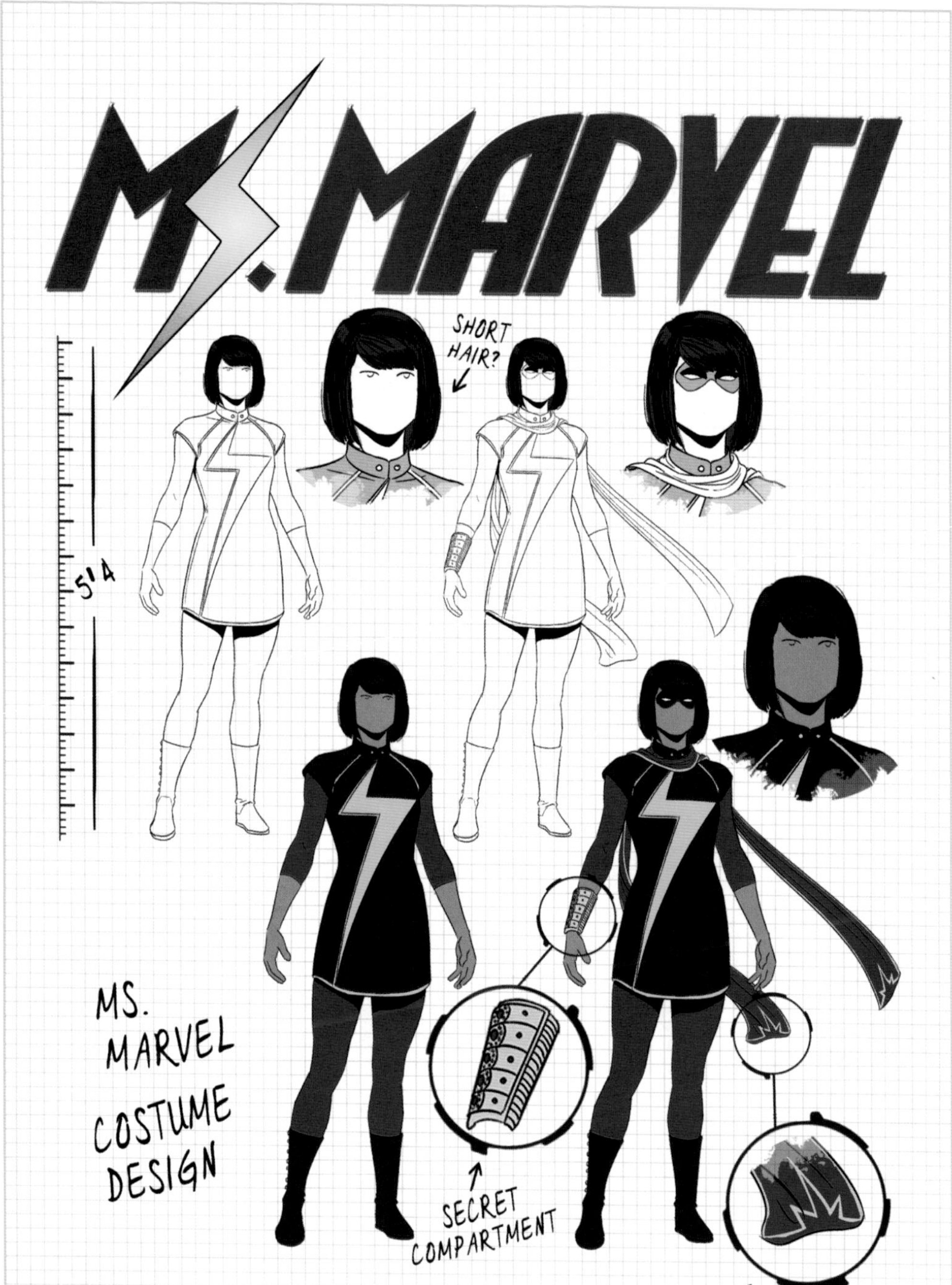
MS. MARVEL
SHORT HAIR?
5'4
MS. MARVEL COSTUME DESIGN
SECRET COMPARTMENT
HINT OF ORIGINAL COSTUME WITH CM DESIGN

MS. MARVEL #1 DESIGN VARIANT
BY JAMIE McKELVIE

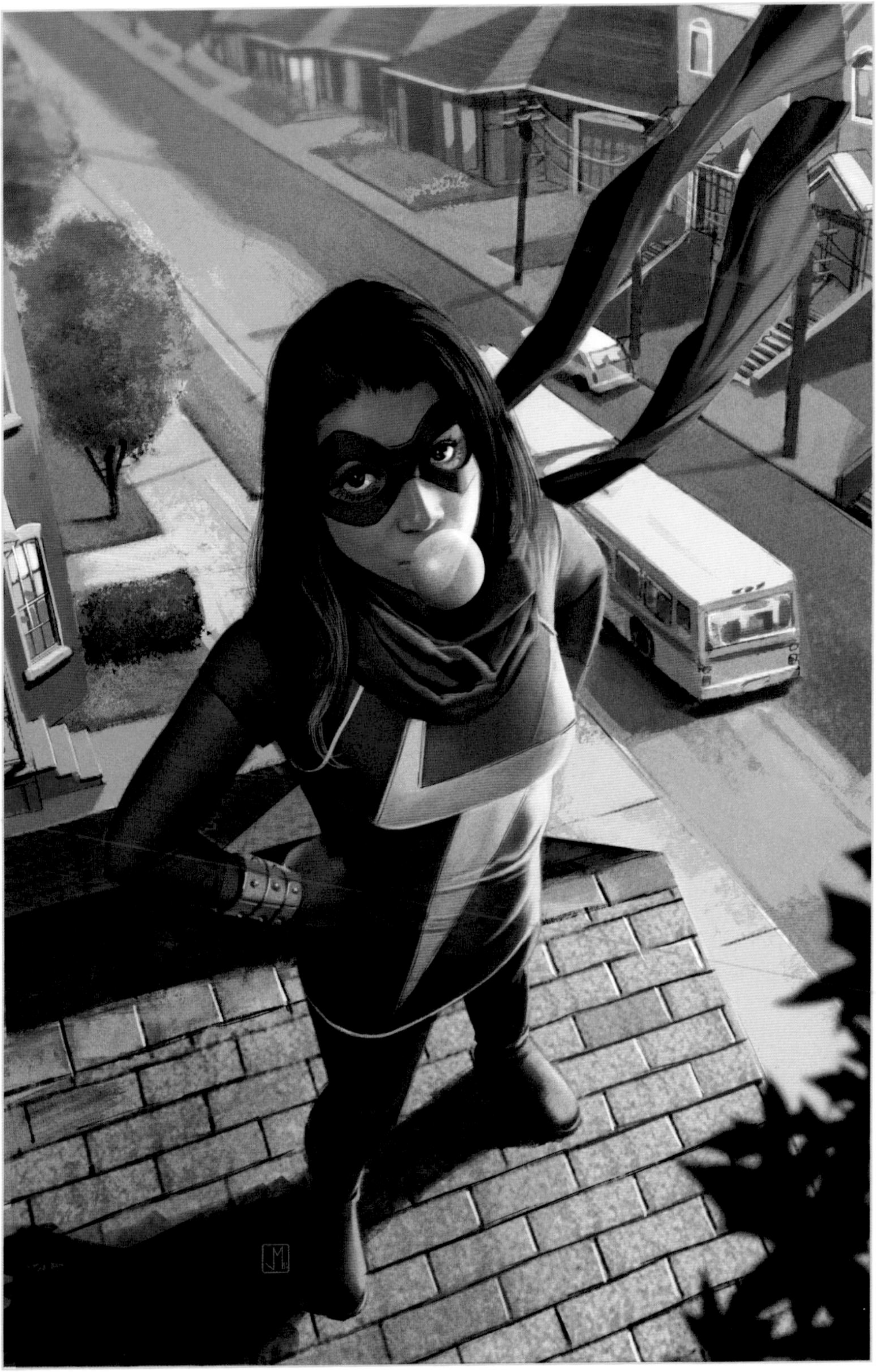

MS. MARVEL #2 VARIANT
BY JORGE MOLINA

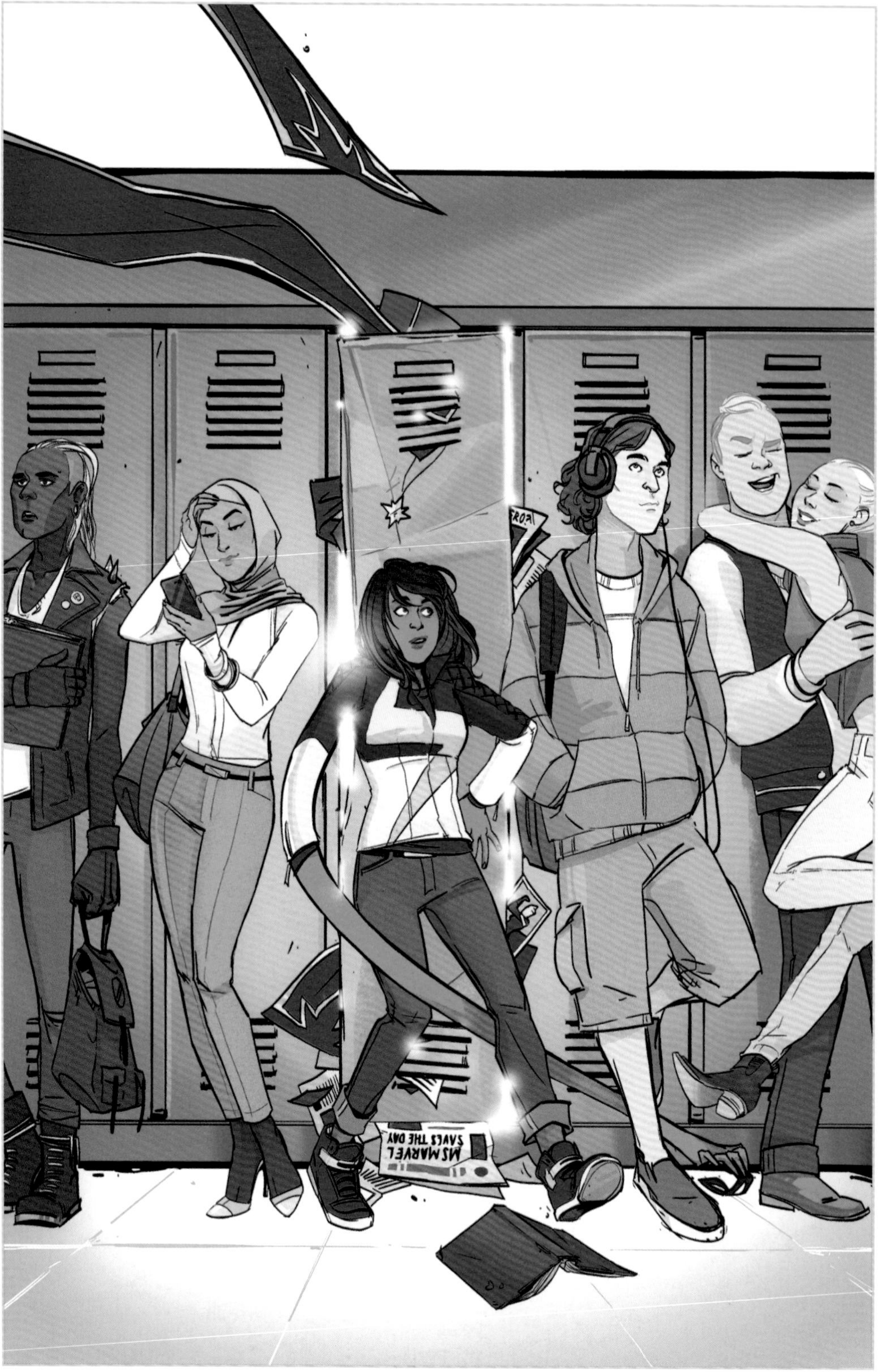
MS MARVEL SAVES THE DAY

MS. MARVEL #3 VARIANT

BY ANNIE WU

inks to color process

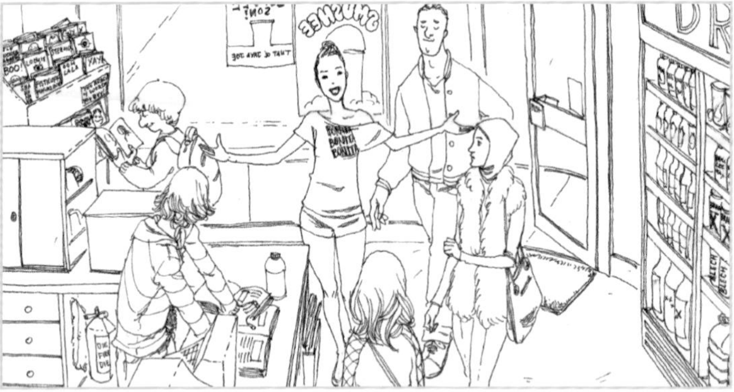
BOO!
YAY

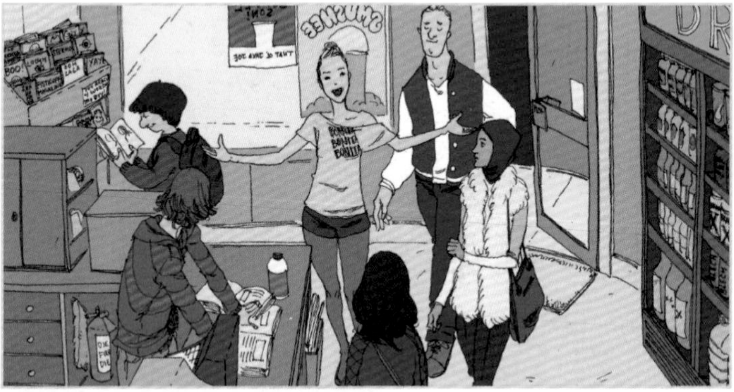
BOO!
YAY

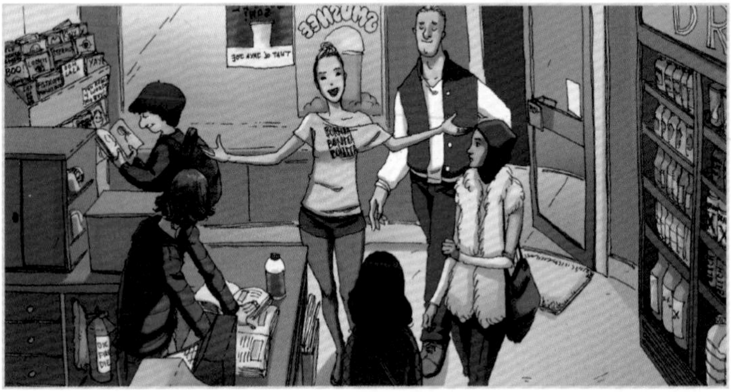
BOO!
YAY

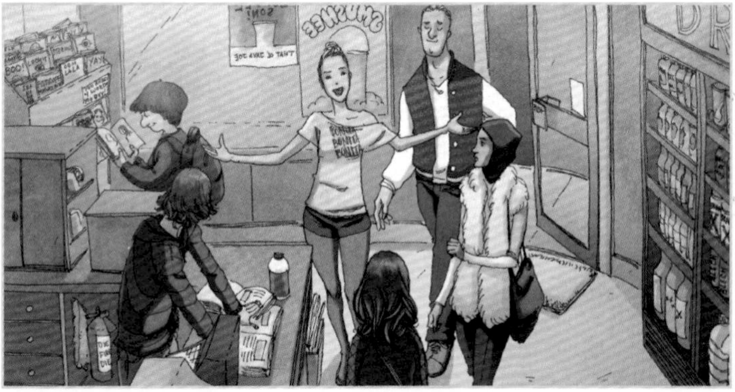
BOO!
YAY

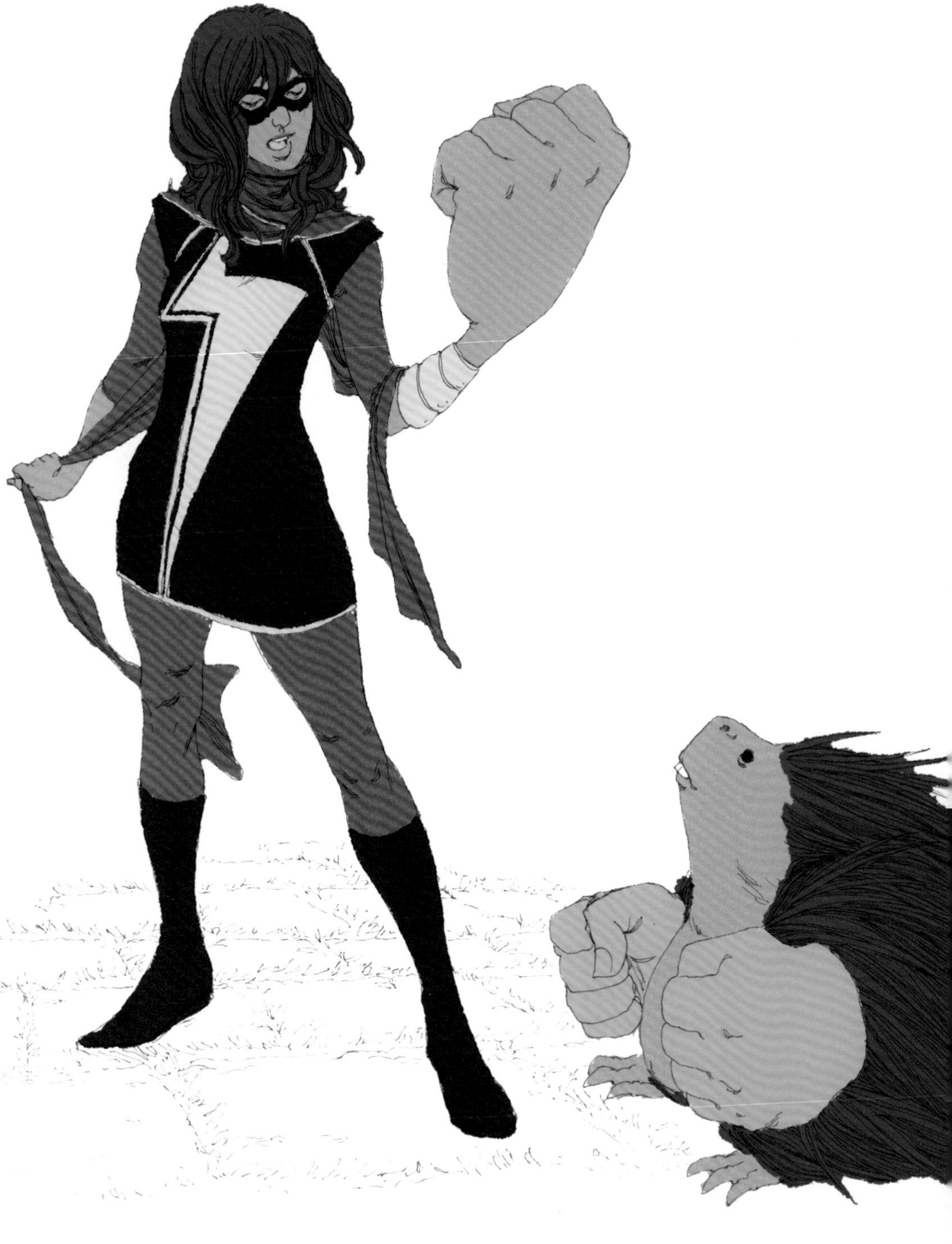

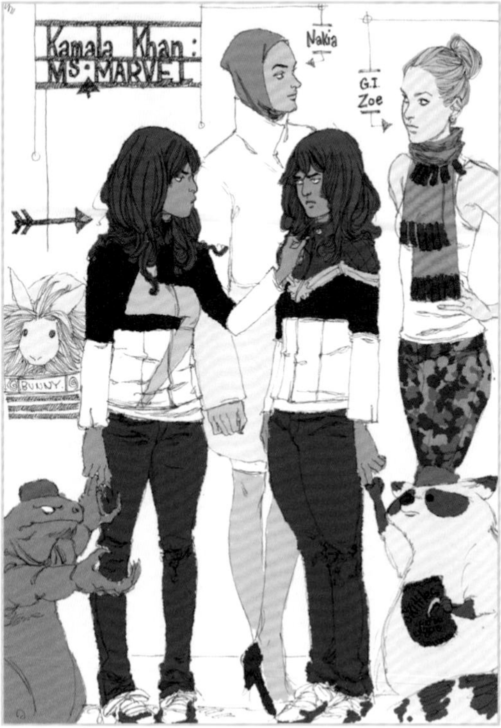

Kamala Khan :
MS. MARVEL
Nakia
G.I. Zoe
BUNNY.

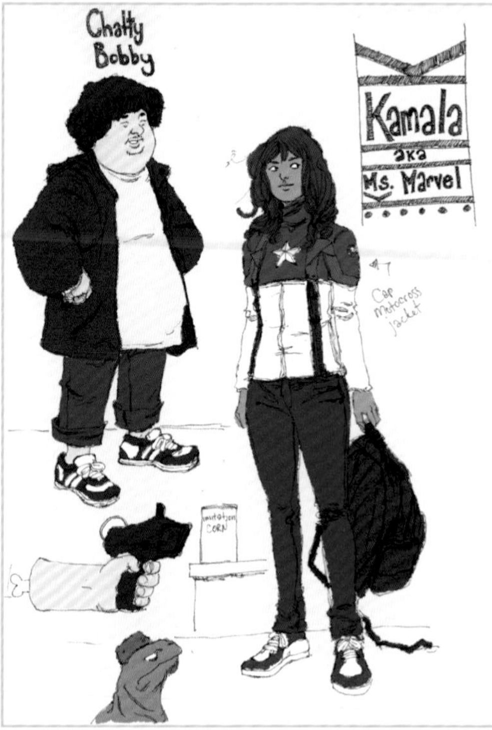

Chatty Bobby
Kamala
aka
Ms. Marvel
Cap Motocross jacket
imitation CORN

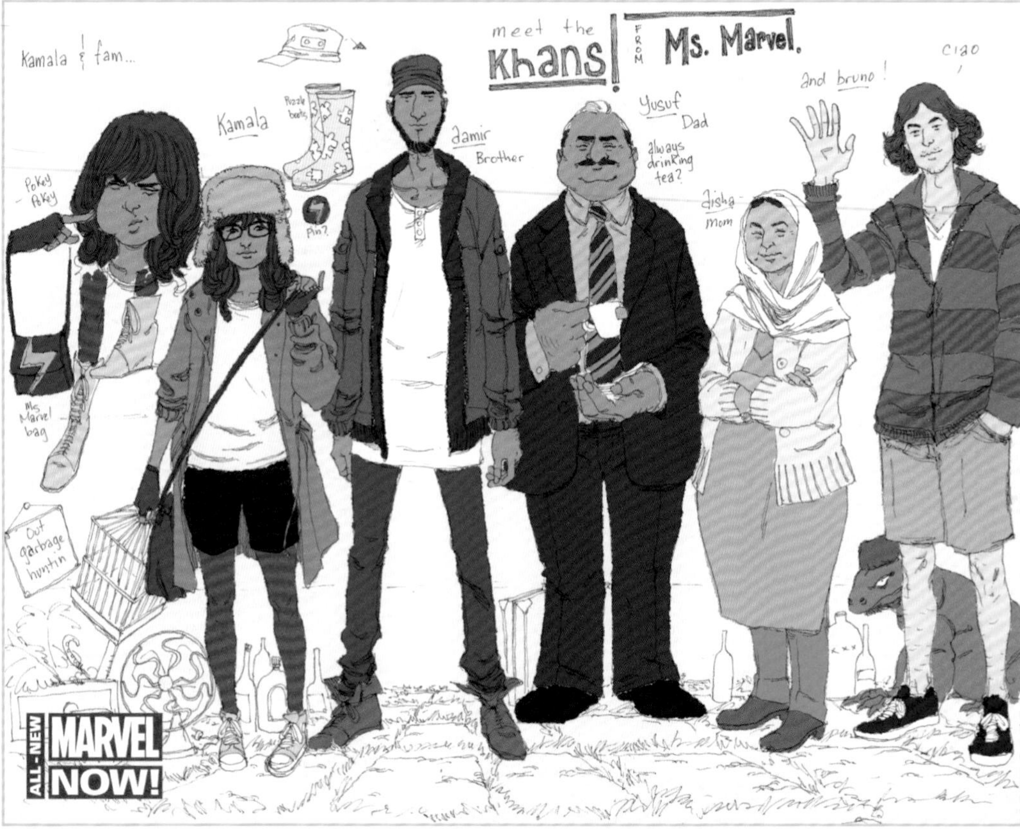

Kamala & fam...
meet the Khans! FROM Ms. Marvel.
ciao
and bruno!
Kamala
Puzzle boots
Aamir
Brother
Yusuf
Dad
always drinking tea?
Aisha
mom
Pokey Pokey
Pin?
Ms Marvel bag
Out garbage huntin
ALL-NEW MARVEL NOW!

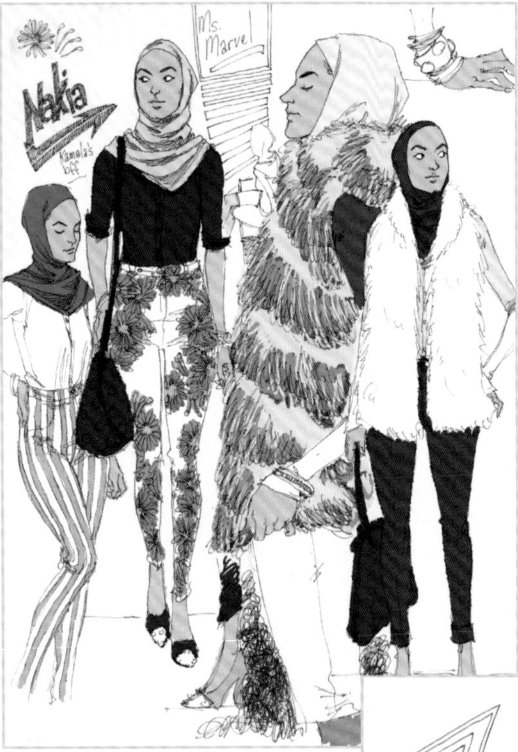
Nakia
Kamala's bff
Ms. Marvel

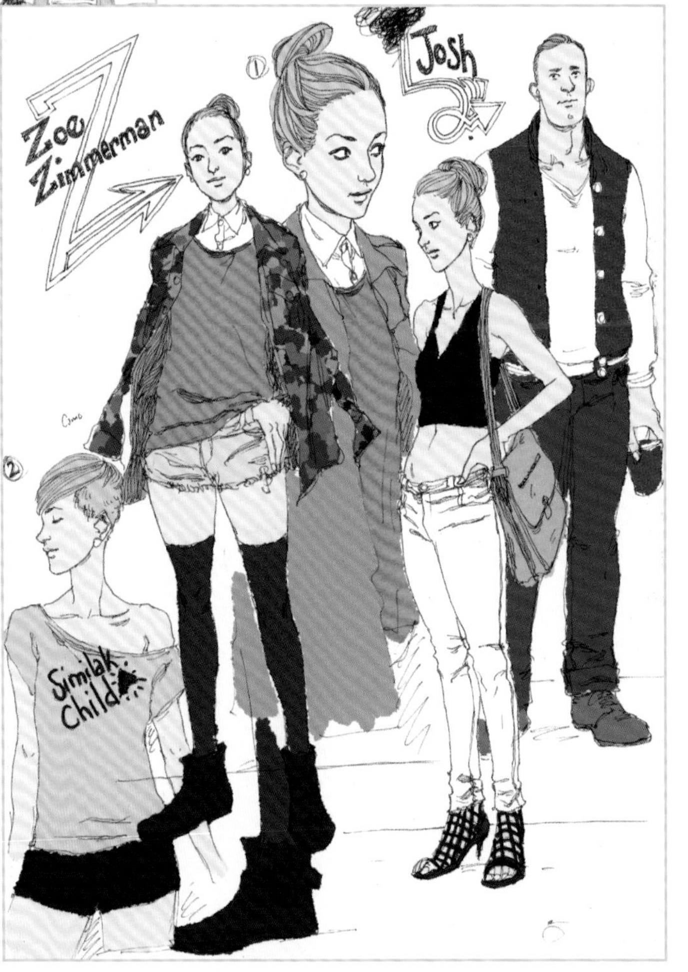
Zoe Zimmerman
Josh
Similak Child

#8, page 2 by adrian alphona

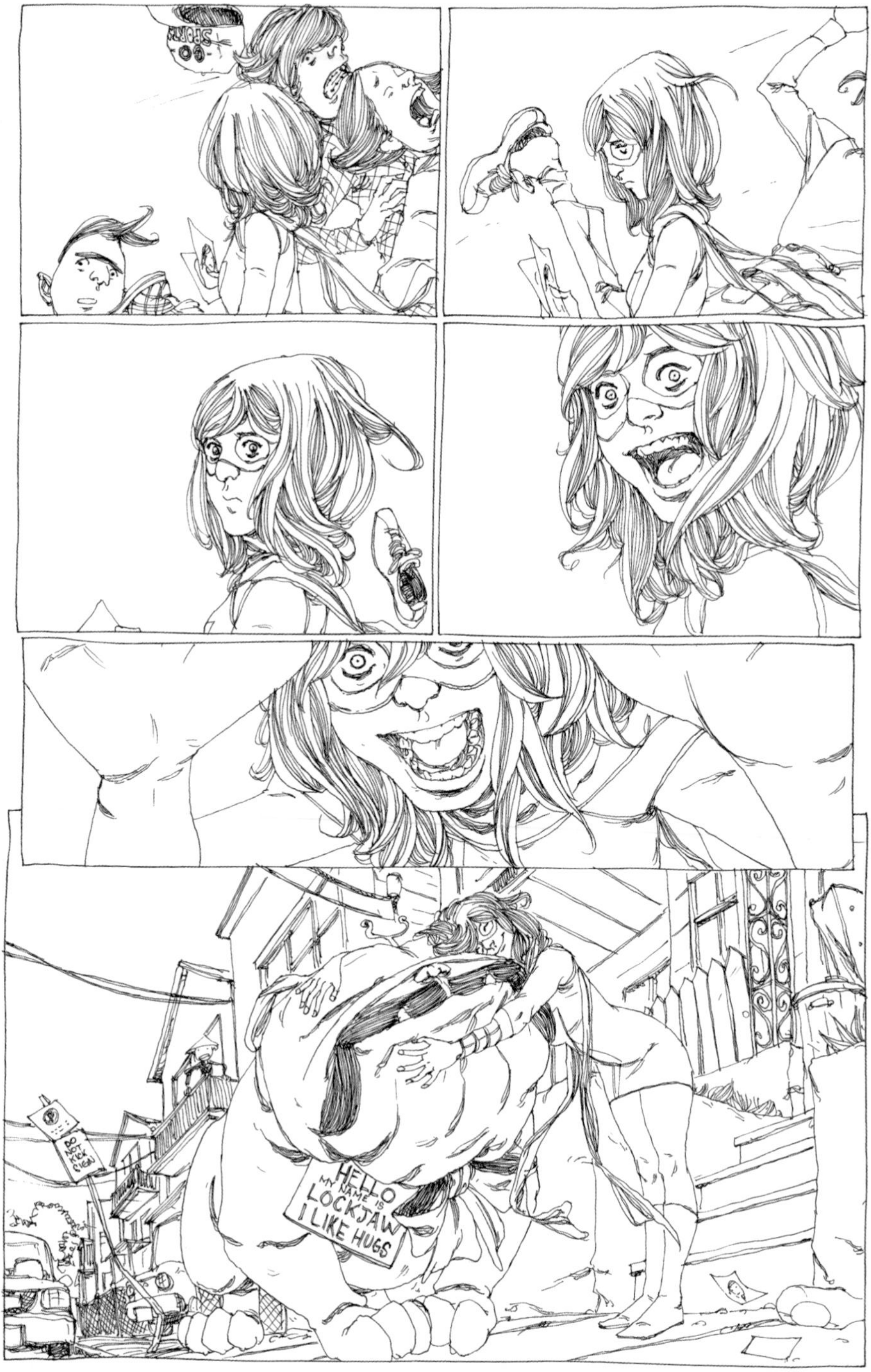
SPORT
DO NOT KICK SIGN
HELLO MY NAME IS LOCKJAW I LIKE HUGS

#8, page 15 by adrian alphona

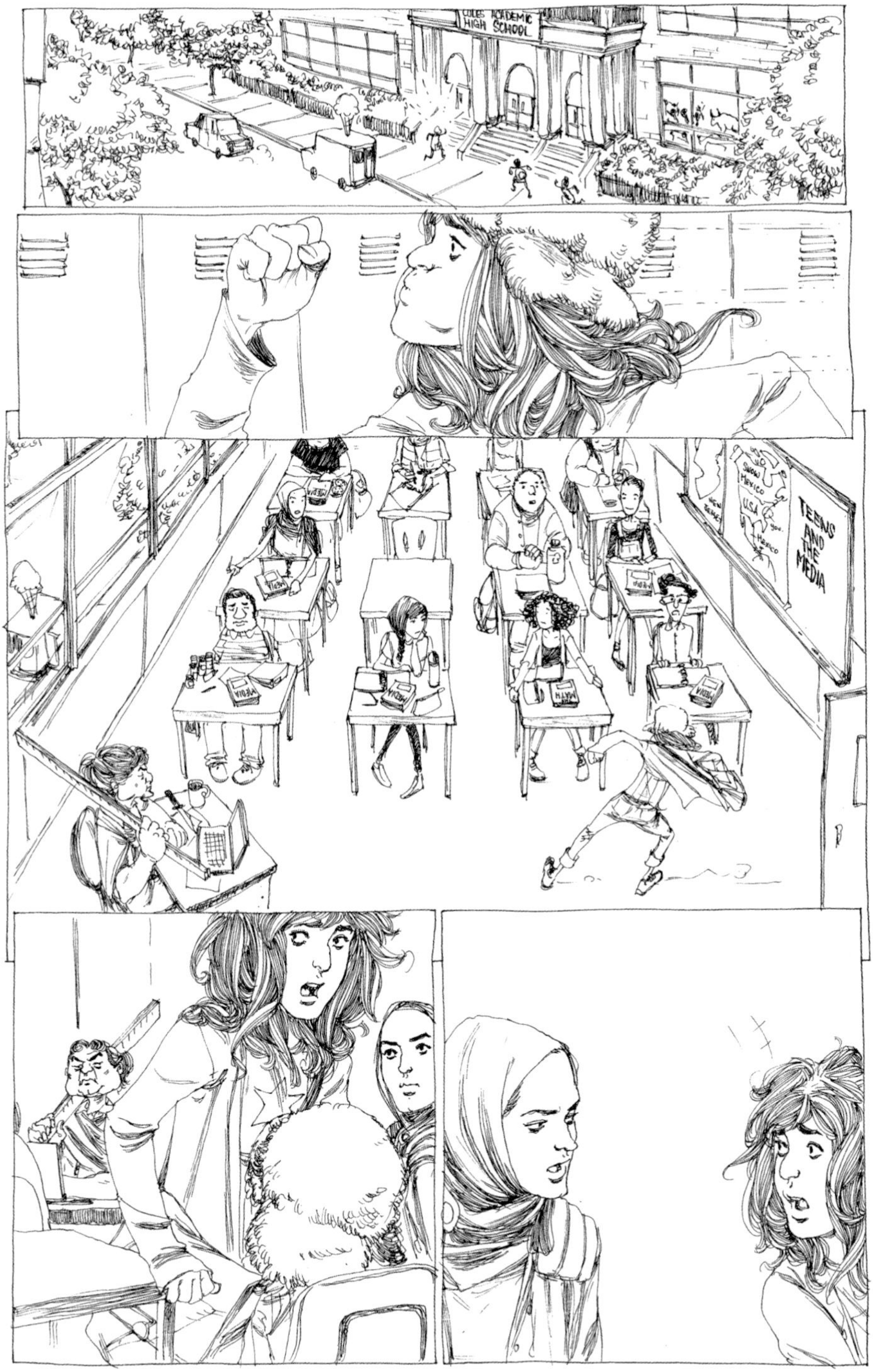
COLES ACADEMIC HIGH SCHOOL
TEENS AND THE MEDIA

#9, page 7 by adrian alphona

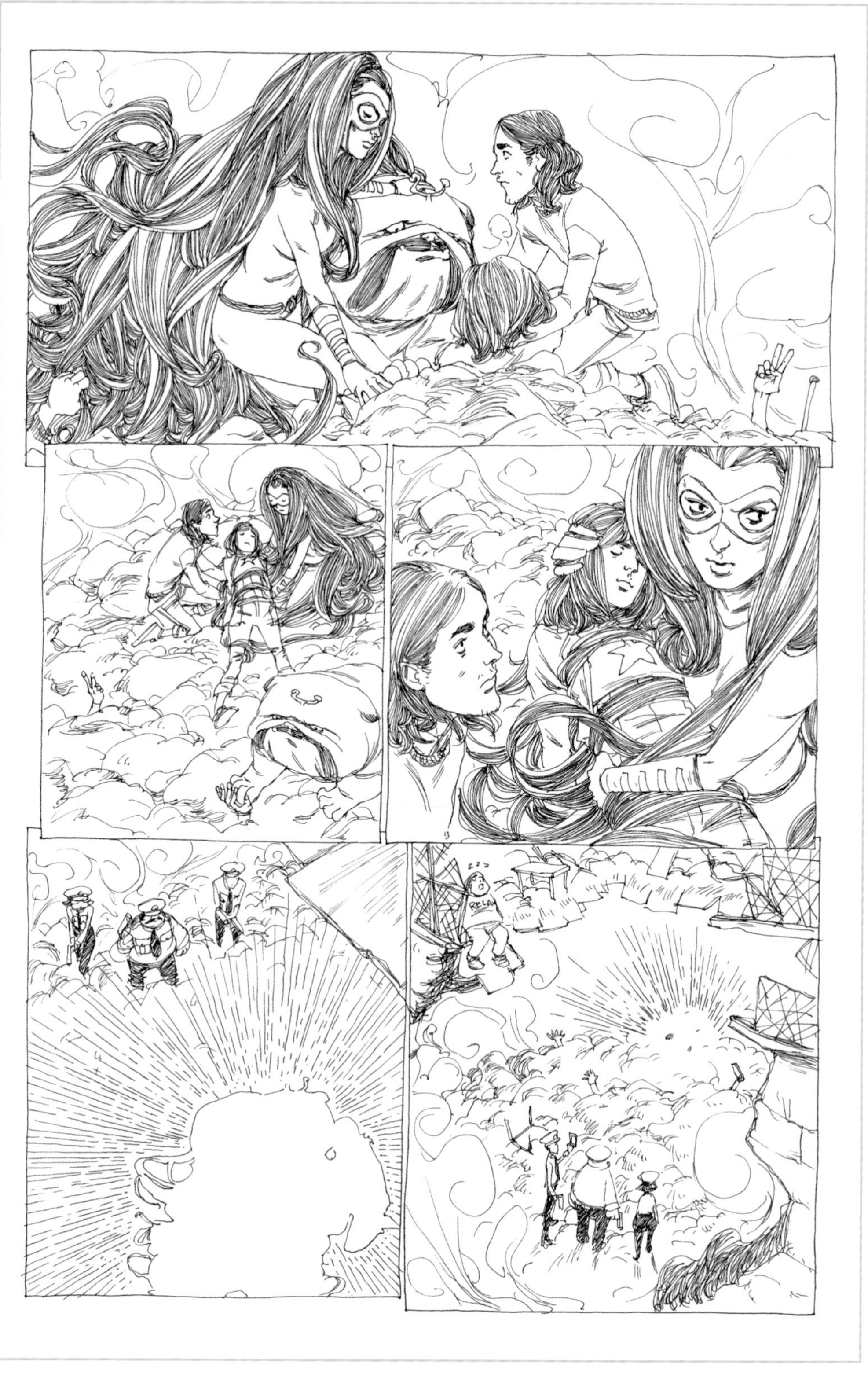

#10, page 3 by adrian alphona

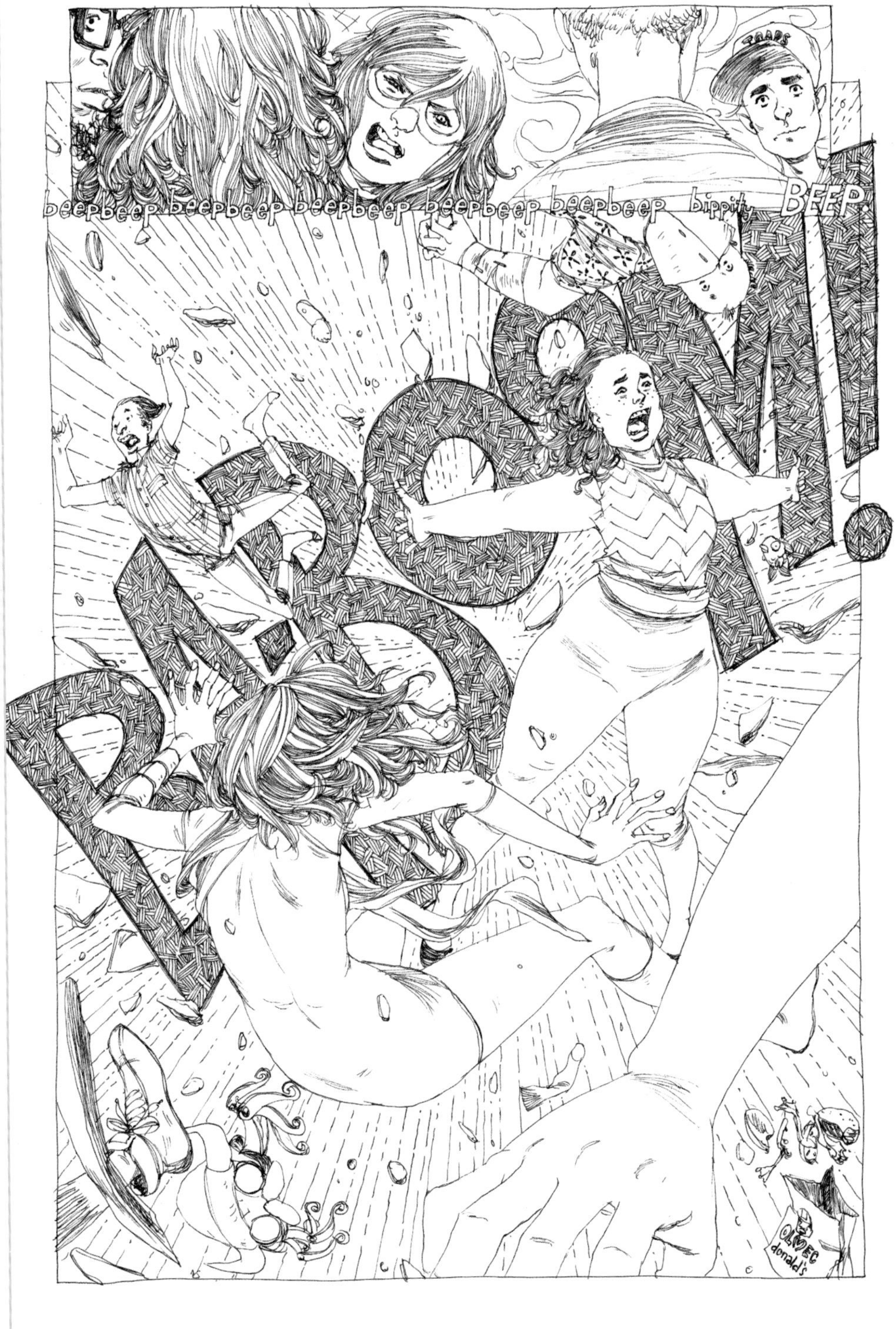
beepbeep beepbeep beepbeep beepbeep beepbeep bippity BEEP
BOOM!
OLMEC
donald's

#10, page 8 by adrian alphona

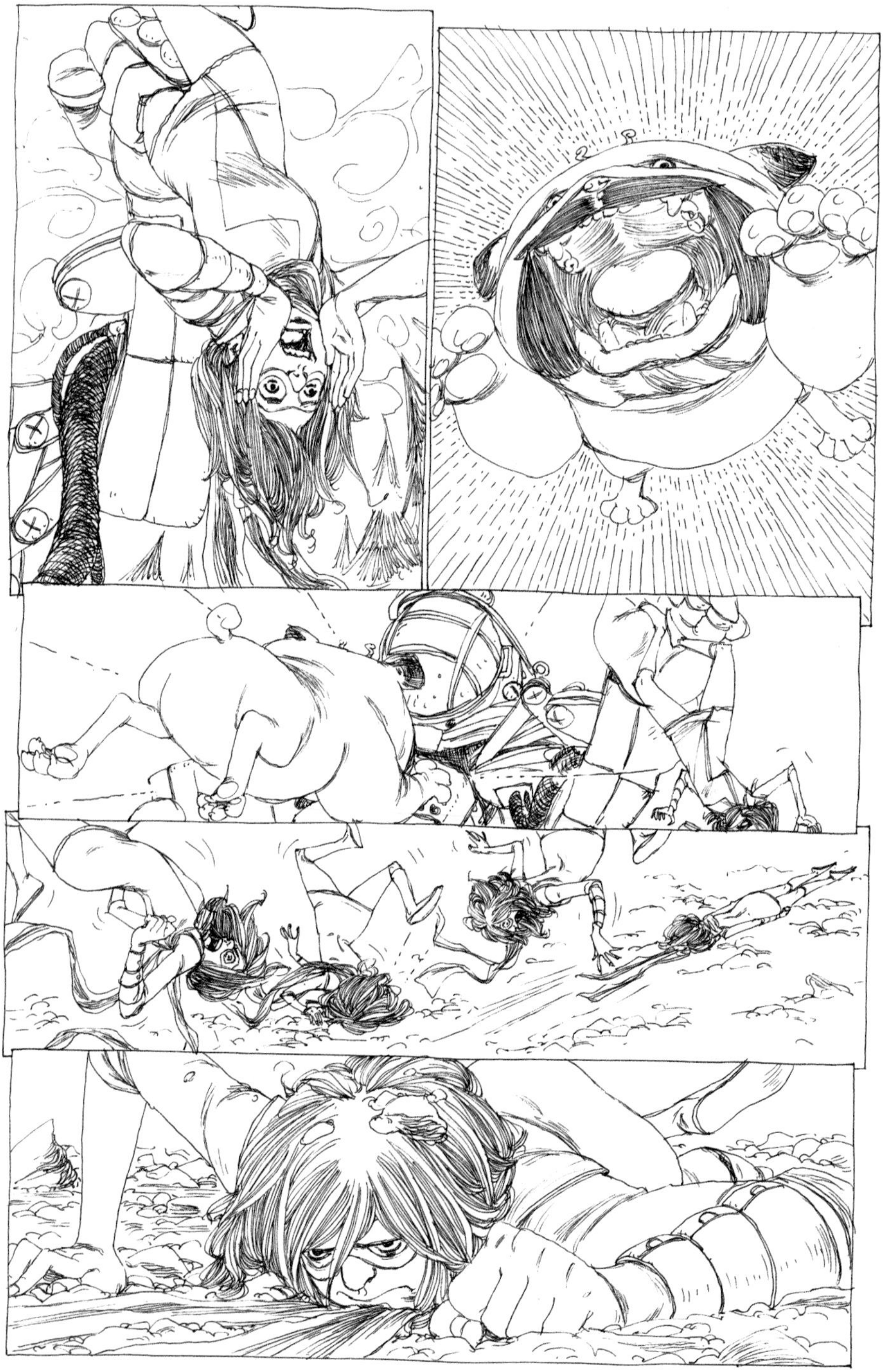

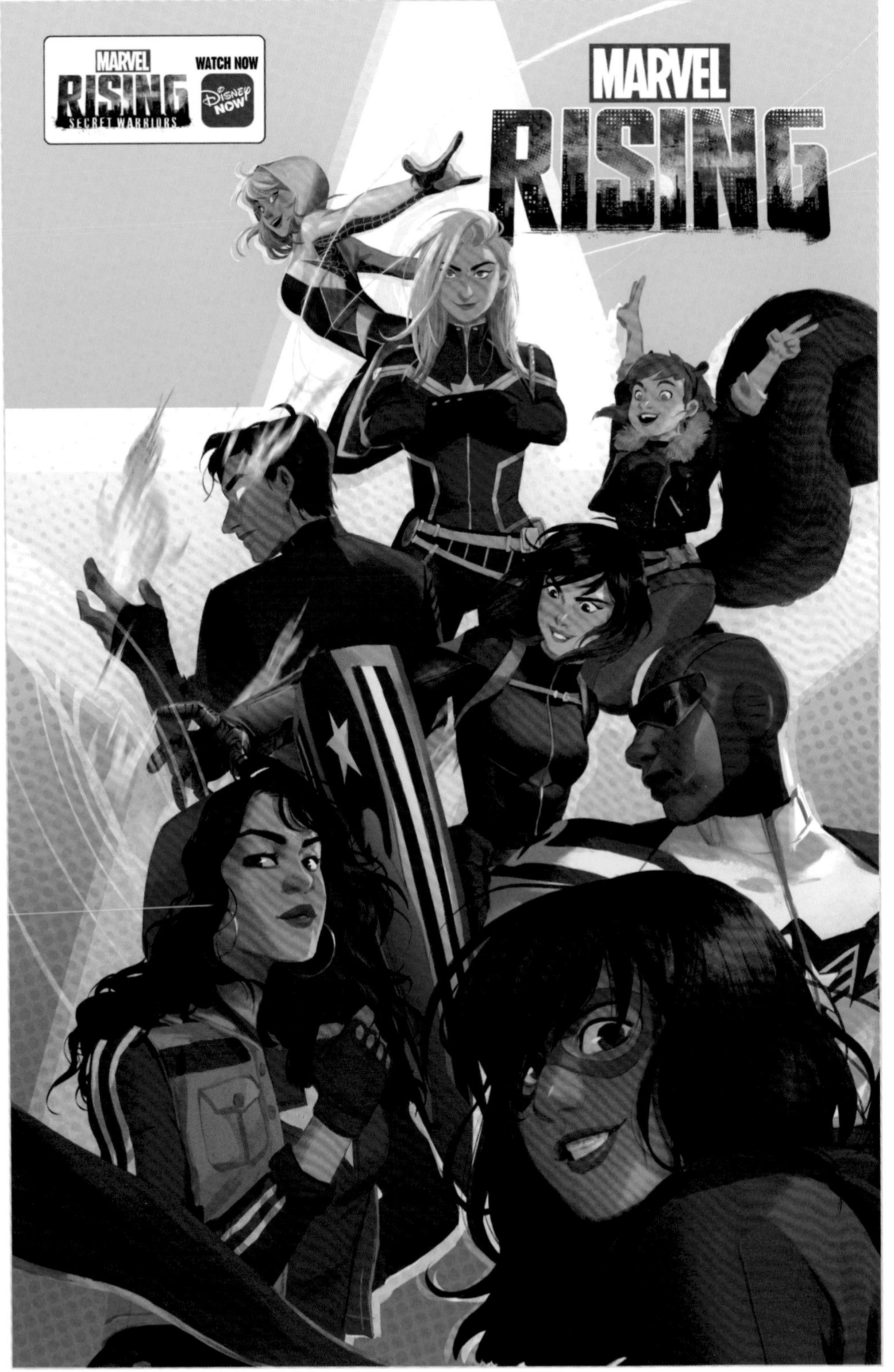

MARVEL
RISING
SECRET WARRIORS
WATCH NOW
DISNEY NOW
MARVEL
RISING

INTRODUCING MARVEL RISING!

MARVEL RISING

THE MARVEL UNIVERSE IS A RICH TREASURE CHEST OF CHARACTERS BORN ACROSS MARVEL'S INCREDIBLE 80-YEAR HISTORY. FROM CAPTAIN AMERICA TO CAPTAIN MARVEL, IRON MAN TO IRONHEART, THIS IS AN EVER-EXPANDING UNIVERSE FULL OF POWERFUL HEROES THAT ALSO REFLECTS THE WORLD WE LIVE IN.

YET DESPITE THAT EXPANSION, OUR STORIES REMAIN TIMELESS. THEY'VE BEEN SHARED ACROSS THE GLOBE AND ACROSS GENERATIONS, LINKING FANS WITH THE ENDURING IDEA THAT ORDINARY PEOPLE CAN DO EXTRAORDINARY THINGS. IT'S THAT SHARED EXPERIENCE OF THE MARVEL STORY THAT HAS ALLOWED US TO EXIST FOR THIS LONG. WHETHER YOUR FIRST MARVEL EXPERIENCE WAS THROUGH A COMIC BOOK, A BEDTIME STORY, A MOVIE OR A CARTOON, WE BELIEVE OUR STORIES STAY WITH AUDIENCES THROUGHOUT THEIR LIVES.

MARVEL RISING IS A CELEBRATION OF THIS TIMELESSNESS. AS OUR STORIES PASS FROM ONE GENERATION TO THE NEXT, SO DOES THE LOVE FOR OUR HEROES. FROM THE CLASSIC TO THE NEWLY IMAGINED, THE PASSION FOR ALL OF THEM IS THE SAME. IF YOU'VE BEEN READING COMICS OVER THE LAST FEW YEARS, YOU'LL KNOW CHARACTERS LIKE MS. MARVEL, SQUIRREL GIRL, AMERICA CHAVEZ, SPIDER-GWEN AND MORE HAVE ASSEMBLED A BEVY OF NEW FANS WHILE CAPTIVATING OUR PERENNIAL FANS. EACH OF THESE HEROES IS UNIQUE AND DISTINCT--JUST LIKE THE READERS THEY'VE BROUGHT IN--AND THEY REMIND US THAT NO MATTER WHAT YOU LOOK LIKE, YOU HAVE THE CAPABILITY TO BE POWERFUL, TOO. WE ARE TAKING THE HEROES FROM MARVEL RISING TO NEW HEIGHTS IN AN ANIMATED FEATURE LATER IN 2018, AS WELL AS A FULL PROGRAM OF CONTENT SWEEPING ACROSS THE COMPANY. BUT FIRST WE'RE GOING BACK TO OUR ROOTS AND TELLING A MARVEL RISING STORY IN COMICS: THE FIRST PLACE YOU MET THESE LOVABLE HEROES.

SO IN THE TRADITION OF EXPANDING THE MARVEL UNIVERSE, WE'RE EXCITED TO INTRODUCE MARVEL RISING--THE NEXT GENERATION OF MARVEL HEROES FOR THE NEXT GENERATION OF MARVEL FANS!

SANA AMANAT
VP, CONTENT & CHARACTER DEVELOPMENT

▶ **DOREEN GREEN** IS A SECOND-YEAR COMPUTER SCIENCE STUDENT — AND THE CRIMINAL-REDEEMING HERO THE UNBEATABLE SQUIRREL GIRL! THE NAME SAYS IT ALL: AN UNBEATABLE GIRL WITH THE POWERS OF AN UNBEATABLE SQUIRREL, TAIL INCLUDED. AND ON TOP OF HER STUDYING, NUT-EATING AND BUTT-KICKING ACTIVITIES, SHE'S JUST TAKEN ON THE JOB OF VOLUNTEER TEACHER FOR AN EXTRA-CURRICULAR HIGH-SCHOOL CODING CAMP! AND WHO SHOULD END UP IN HER CLASS BUT...

▶ **KAMALA KHAN,** A.K.A. JERSEY CITY HERO AND INHUMAN POLYMORPH MS. MARVEL! BUT BETWEEN SAVING THE WORLD WITH THE CHAMPIONS AND PROTECTING JERSEY CITY ON HER OWN, KAMALA'S GOT A LOT ON HER PLATE ALREADY. AND FIELD TRIP DAY MAY NOT BE THE BREAK SHE'S ANTICIPATING...

MARVEL RISING
PART 0

DEVIN GRAYSON
WRITER

MARCO FAILLA
ARTIST

RACHELLE ROSENBERG
COLOR ARTIST

VC's CLAYTON COWLES
LETTERER

HELEN CHEN
COVER

JAY BOWEN
DESIGN

HEATHER ANTOS AND **SARAH BRUNSTAD**
EDITORS

SANA AMANAT
CONSULTING EDITOR

C.B. CEBULSKI
EDITOR IN CHIEF

JOE QUESADA
CHIEF CREATIVE OFFICER

DAN BUCKLEY
PRESIDENT

ALAN FINE
EXECUTIVE PRODUCER

SPECIAL THANKS TO RYAN NORTH AND G. WILLOW WILSON

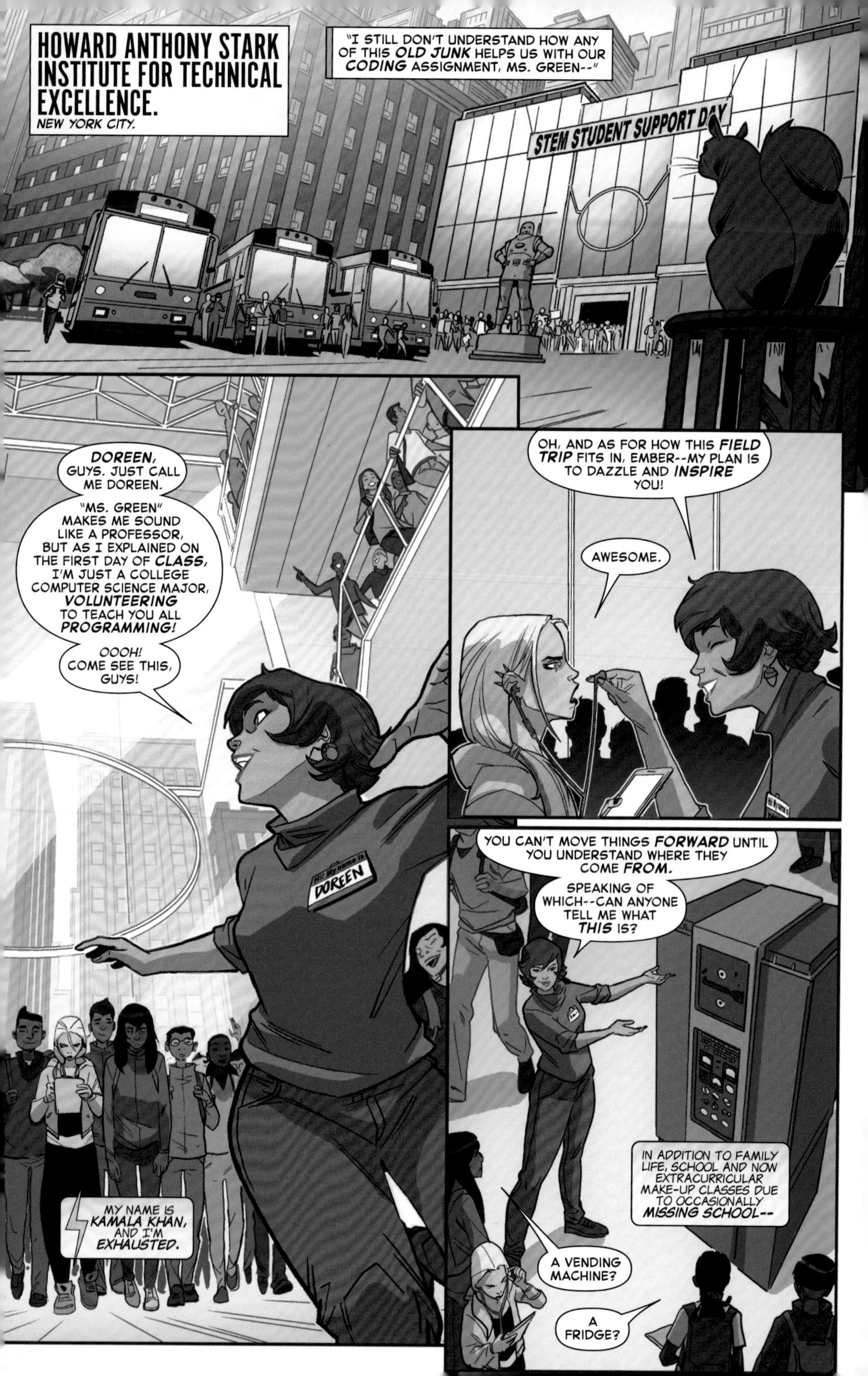
HOWARD ANTHONY STARK INSTITUTE FOR TECHNICAL EXCELLENCE.
NEW YORK CITY.
"I STILL DON'T UNDERSTAND HOW ANY OF THIS OLD JUNK HELPS US WITH OUR CODING ASSIGNMENT, MS. GREEN--"
STEM STUDENT SUPPORT DAY
DOREEN, GUYS. JUST CALL ME DOREEN.
"MS. GREEN" MAKES ME SOUND LIKE A PROFESSOR, BUT AS I EXPLAINED ON THE FIRST DAY OF CLASS, I'M JUST A COLLEGE COMPUTER SCIENCE MAJOR, VOLUNTEERING TO TEACH YOU ALL PROGRAMMING!
OOOH! COME SEE THIS, GUYS!
HI! My name is DOREEN
MY NAME IS KAMALA KHAN, AND I'M EXHAUSTED.
OH, AND AS FOR HOW THIS FIELD TRIP FITS IN, EMBER--MY PLAN IS TO DAZZLE AND INSPIRE YOU!
AWESOME.
YOU CAN'T MOVE THINGS FORWARD UNTIL YOU UNDERSTAND WHERE THEY COME FROM.
SPEAKING OF WHICH--CAN ANYONE TELL ME WHAT THIS IS?
IN ADDITION TO FAMILY LIFE, SCHOOL AND NOW EXTRACURRICULAR MAKE-UP CLASSES DUE TO OCCASIONALLY MISSING SCHOOL--
A VENDING MACHINE?
A FRIDGE?

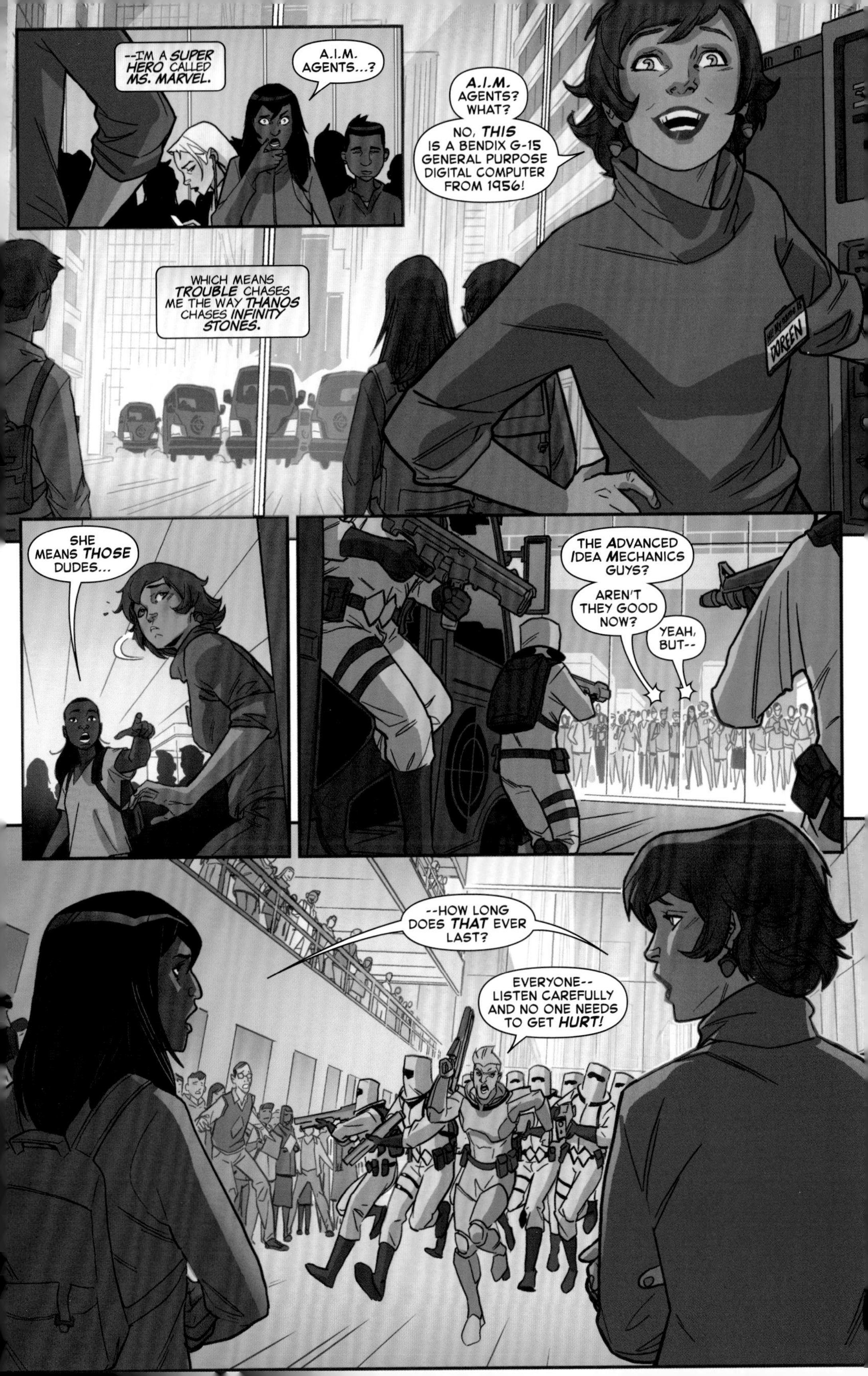
--IM A SUPER HERO CALLED MS. MARVEL.
A.I.M. AGENTS...?
A.I.M. AGENTS? WHAT?
NO, THIS IS A BENDIX G-15 GENERAL PURPOSE DIGITAL COMPUTER FROM 1956!
WHICH MEANS TROUBLE CHASES ME THE WAY THANOS CHASES INFINITY STONES.
SHE MEANS THOSE DUDES...
THE ADVANCED IDEA MECHANICS GUYS?
AREN'T THEY GOOD NOW?
YEAH, BUT--
--HOW LONG DOES THAT EVER LAST?
EVERYONE-- LISTEN CAREFULLY AND NO ONE NEEDS TO GET HURT!

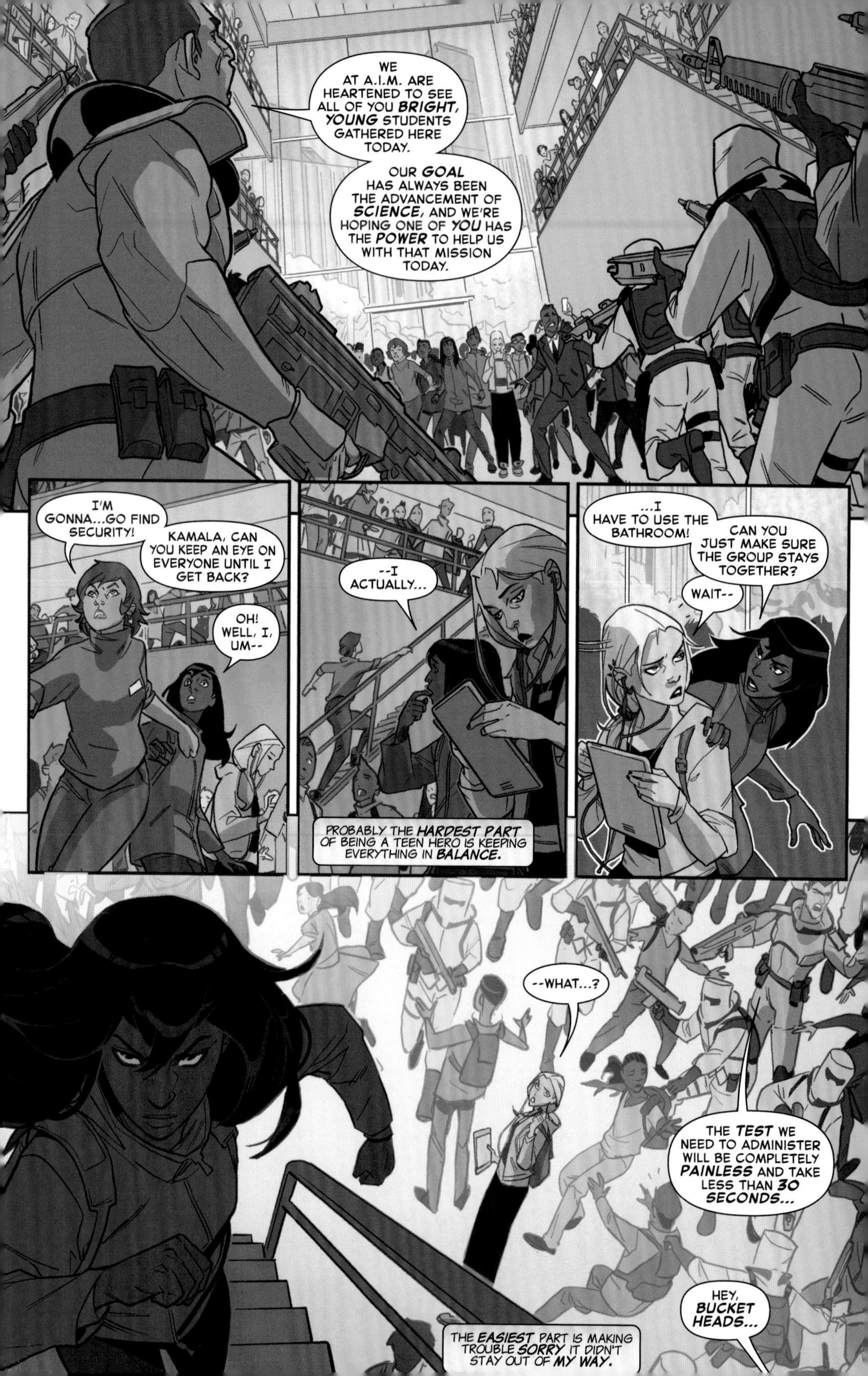

WE AT A.I.M. ARE HEARTENED TO SEE ALL OF YOU BRIGHT, YOUNG STUDENTS GATHERED HERE TODAY.
OUR GOAL HAS ALWAYS BEEN THE ADVANCEMENT OF SCIENCE, AND WE'RE HOPING ONE OF YOU HAS THE POWER TO HELP US WITH THAT MISSION TODAY.
I'M GONNA...GO FIND SECURITY!
KAMALA, CAN YOU KEEP AN EYE ON EVERYONE UNTIL I GET BACK?
OH! WELL, I, UM--
--I ACTUALLY...
PROBABLY THE HARDEST PART OF BEING A TEEN HERO IS KEEPING EVERYTHING IN BALANCE.
...I HAVE TO USE THE BATHROOM!
CAN YOU JUST MAKE SURE THE GROUP STAYS TOGETHER?
WAIT--
--WHAT...?
THE TEST WE NEED TO ADMINISTER WILL BE COMPLETELY PAINLESS AND TAKE LESS THAN 30 SECONDS...
HEY, BUCKET HEADS...
THE EASIEST PART IS MAKING TROUBLE SORRY IT DIDN'T STAY OUT OF MY WAY.

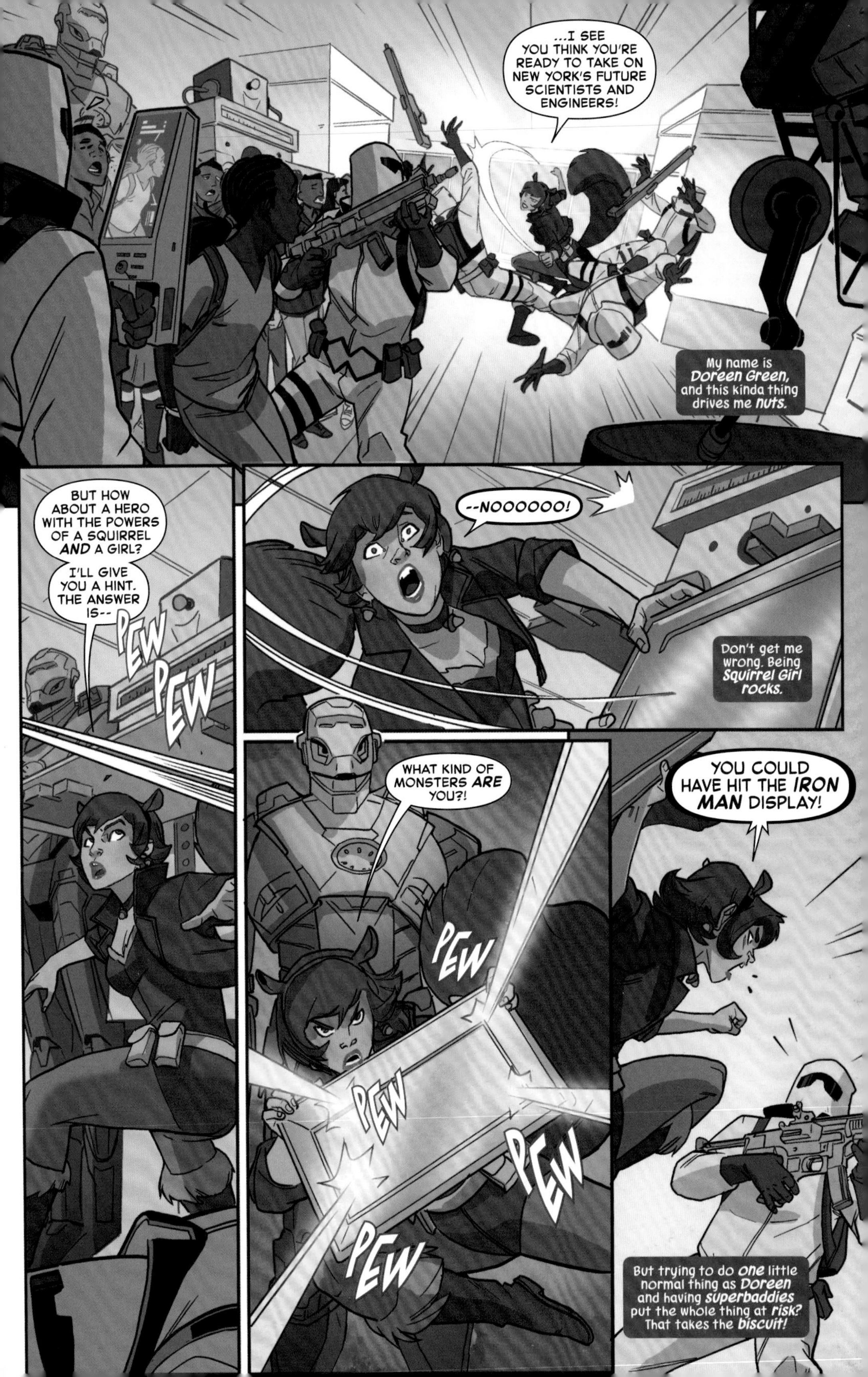
...I SEE YOU THINK YOU'RE READY TO TAKE ON NEW YORK'S FUTURE SCIENTISTS AND ENGINEERS!
My name is Doreen Green, and this kinda thing drives me nuts.
BUT HOW ABOUT A HERO WITH THE POWERS OF A SQUIRREL AND A GIRL?
I'LL GIVE YOU A HINT. THE ANSWER IS--
PEW PEW
--NOOOOOO!
Don't get me wrong. Being Squirrel Girl rocks.
WHAT KIND OF MONSTERS ARE YOU?!
PEW
PEW
PEW
PEW
YOU COULD HAVE HIT THE IRON MAN DISPLAY!
But trying to do one little normal thing as Doreen and having superbaddies put the whole thing at risk? That takes the biscuit!

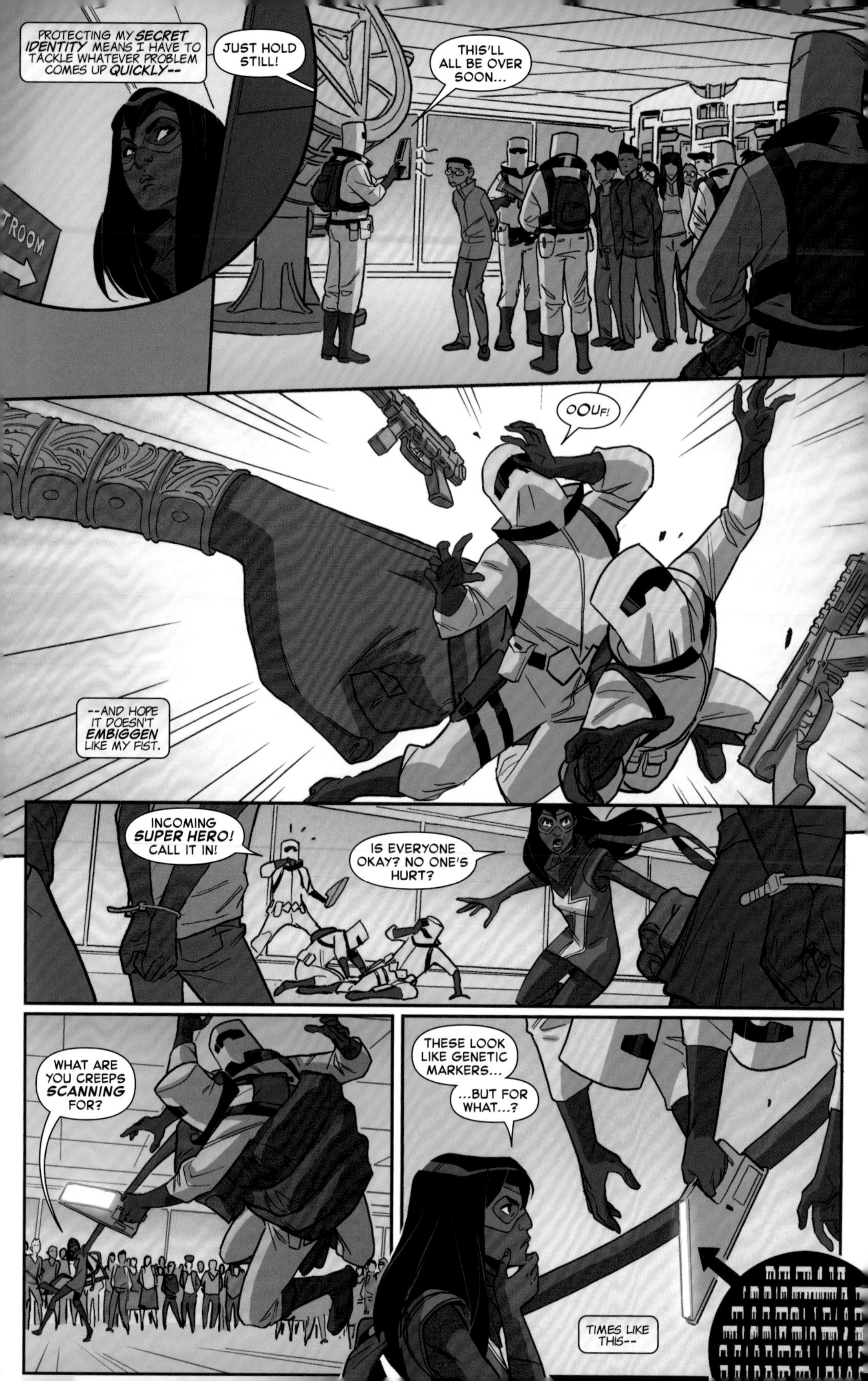
PROTECTING MY SECRET IDENTITY MEANS I HAVE TO TACKLE WHATEVER PROBLEM COMES UP QUICKLY--
JUST HOLD STILL!
THIS'LL ALL BE OVER SOON...
TROOM
OOUF!
--AND HOPE IT DOESN'T EMBIGGEN LIKE MY FIST.
INCOMING SUPER HERO! CALL IT IN!
IS EVERYONE OKAY? NO ONE'S HURT?
WHAT ARE YOU CREEPS SCANNING FOR?
THESE LOOK LIKE GENETIC MARKERS...
...BUT FOR WHAT...?
TIMES LIKE THIS--

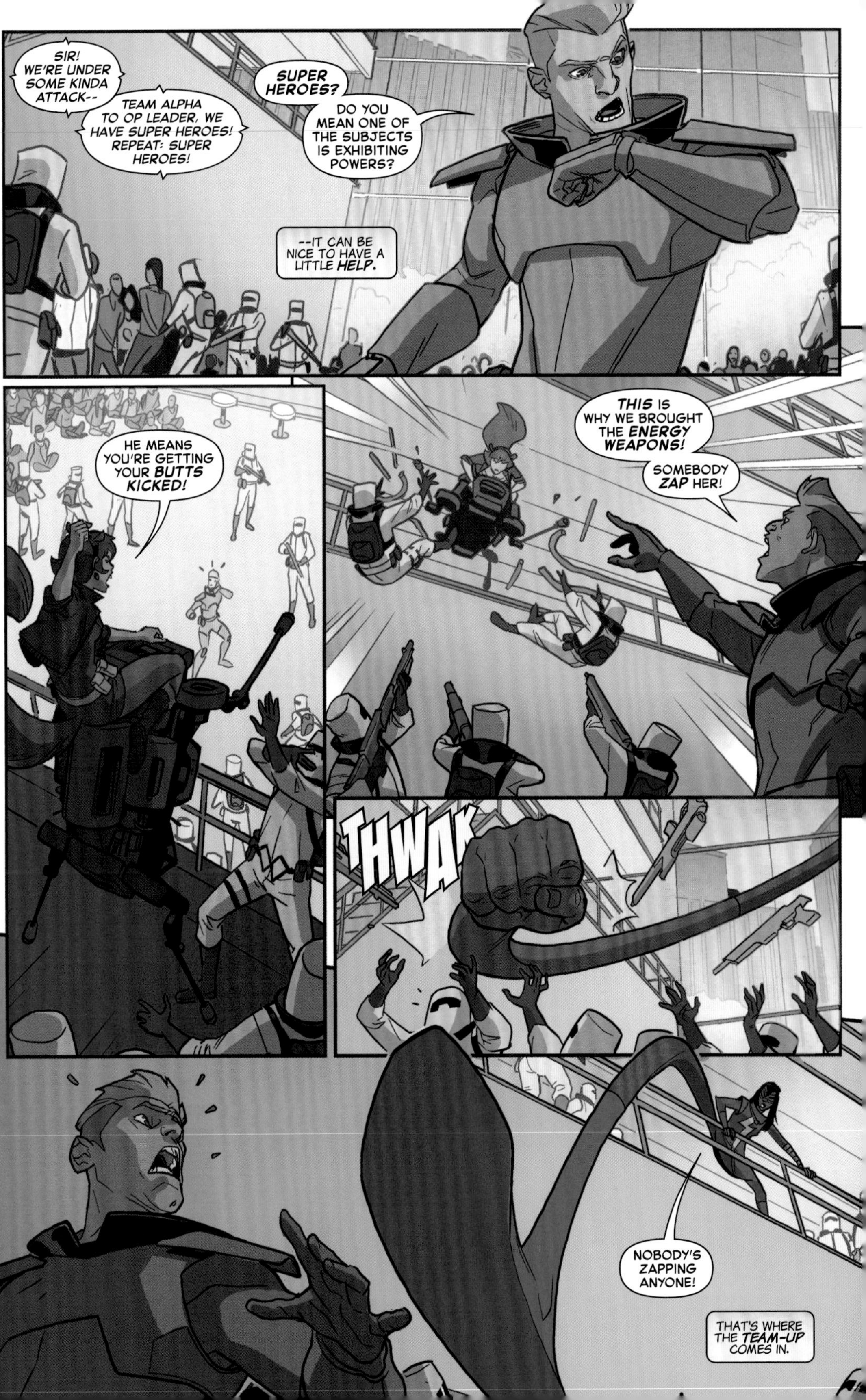
SIR! WE'RE UNDER SOME KINDA ATTACK--
TEAM ALPHA TO OP LEADER, WE HAVE SUPER HEROES! REPEAT: SUPER HEROES!
SUPER HEROES?
DO YOU MEAN ONE OF THE SUBJECTS IS EXHIBITING POWERS?
--IT CAN BE NICE TO HAVE A LITTLE HELP.
HE MEANS YOU'RE GETTING YOUR BUTTS KICKED!
THIS IS WHY WE BROUGHT THE ENERGY WEAPONS!
SOMEBODY ZAP HER!
THWAK
NOBODY'S ZAPPING ANYONE!
THAT'S WHERE THE TEAM-UP COMES IN.

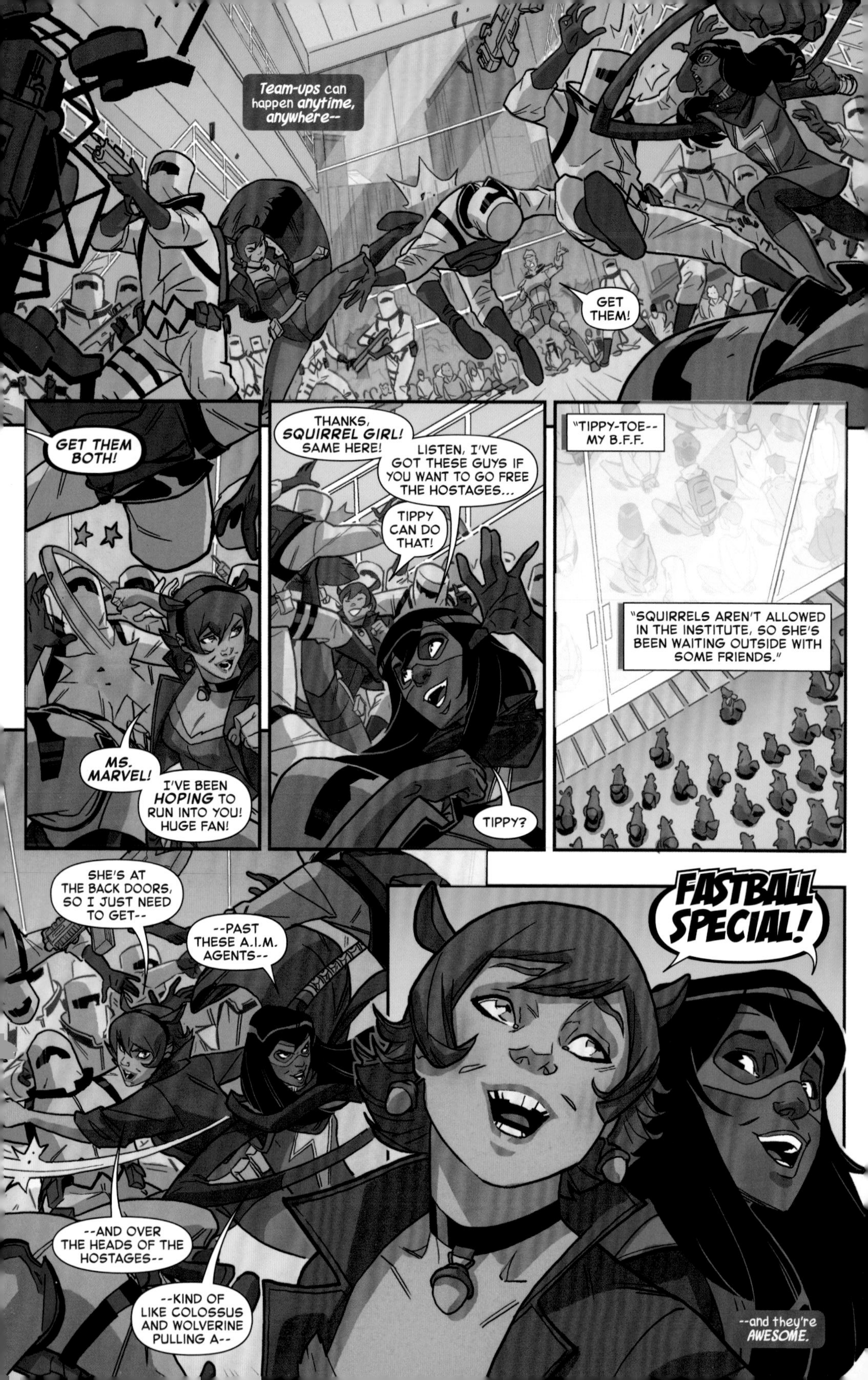
Team-ups can happen anytime, anywhere--
GET THEM!
GET THEM BOTH!
MS. MARVEL!
I'VE BEEN HOPING TO RUN INTO YOU! HUGE FAN!
THANKS, SQUIRREL GIRL! SAME HERE!
LISTEN, I'VE GOT THESE GUYS IF YOU WANT TO GO FREE THE HOSTAGES...
TIPPY CAN DO THAT!
TIPPY?
"TIPPY-TOE-- MY B.F.F.
"SQUIRRELS AREN'T ALLOWED IN THE INSTITUTE, SO SHE'S BEEN WAITING OUTSIDE WITH SOME FRIENDS."
SHE'S AT THE BACK DOORS, SO I JUST NEED TO GET--
--PAST THESE A.I.M. AGENTS--
--AND OVER THE HEADS OF THE HOSTAGES--
--KIND OF LIKE COLOSSUS AND WOLVERINE PULLING A--
FASTBALL SPECIAL!
--and they're AWESOME.

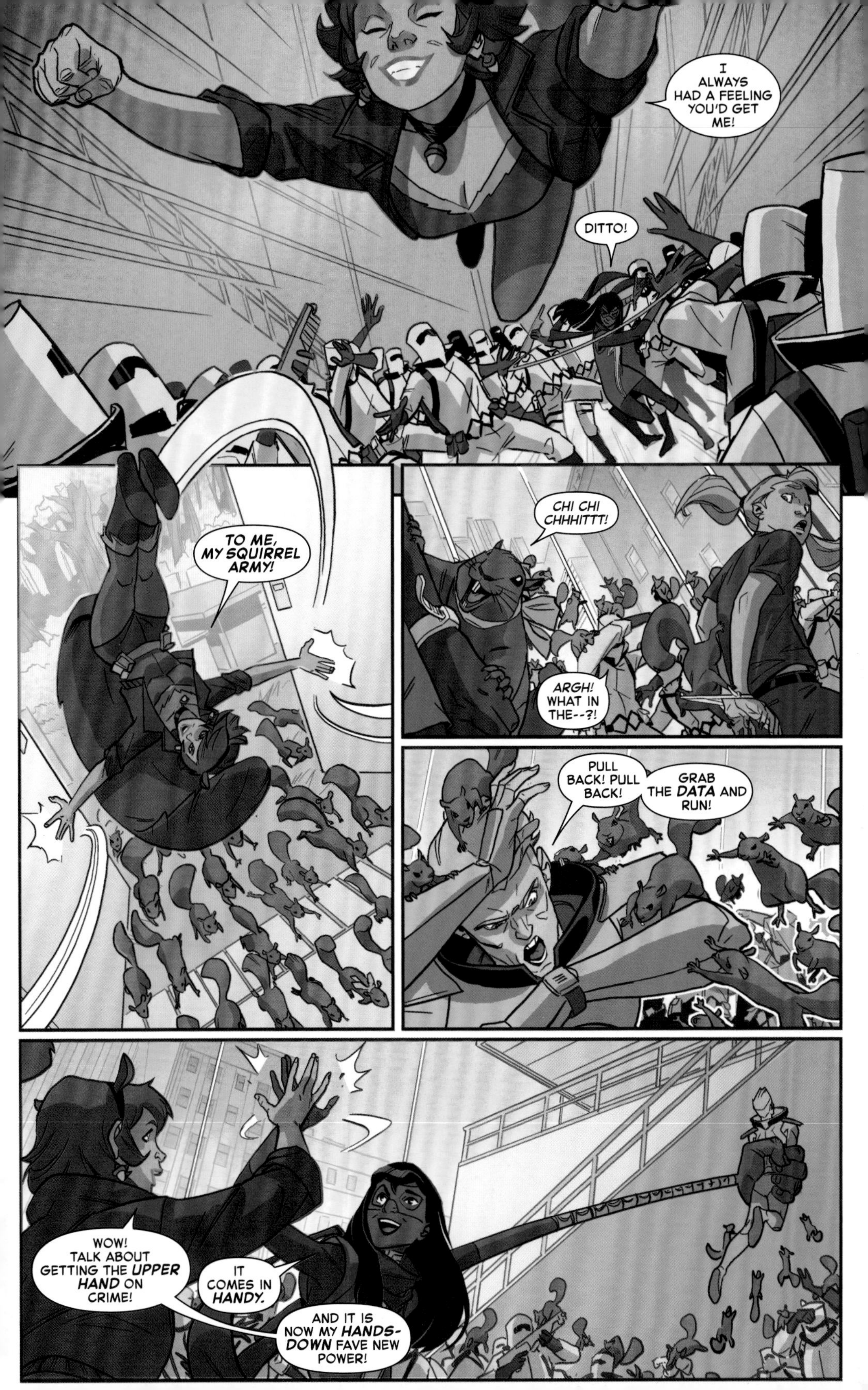
I ALWAYS HAD A FEELING YOU'D GET ME!
DITTO!
TO ME, MY *SQUIRREL ARMY!*
CHI CHI CHHHITTT!
ARGH! WHAT IN THE--?!
PULL BACK! PULL BACK!
GRAB THE *DATA* AND RUN!
WOW! TALK ABOUT GETTING THE *UPPER HAND* ON CRIME!
IT COMES IN *HANDY.*
AND IT IS NOW MY *HANDS-DOWN* FAVE NEW POWER!

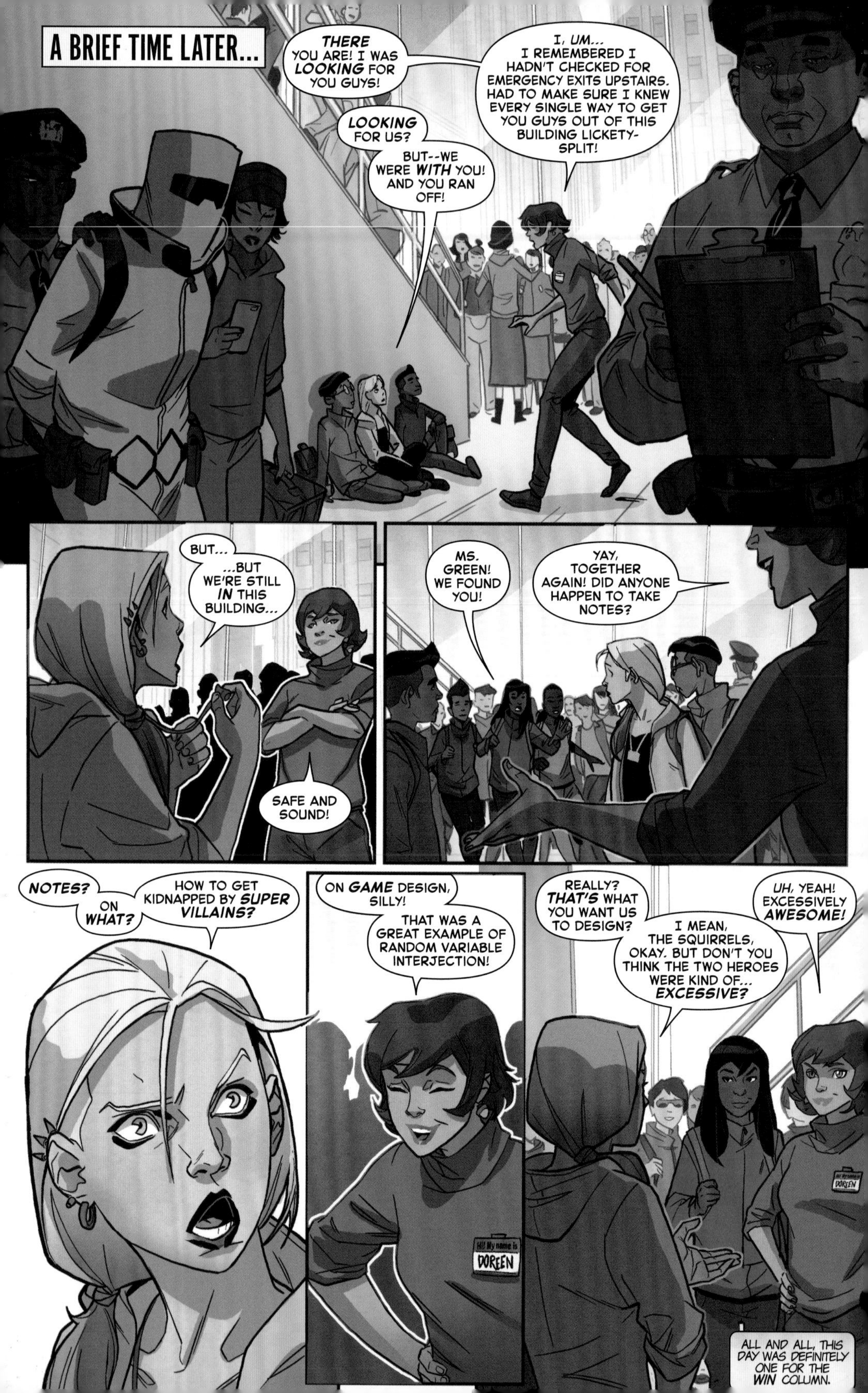
A BRIEF TIME LATER...
THERE YOU ARE! I WAS LOOKING FOR YOU GUYS!
LOOKING FOR US?
BUT--WE WERE WITH YOU! AND YOU RAN OFF!
I, UM... I REMEMBERED I HADN'T CHECKED FOR EMERGENCY EXITS UPSTAIRS. HAD TO MAKE SURE I KNEW EVERY SINGLE WAY TO GET YOU GUYS OUT OF THIS BUILDING LICKETY-SPLIT!
BUT... ...BUT WE'RE STILL IN THIS BUILDING...
SAFE AND SOUND!
MS. GREEN! WE FOUND YOU!
YAY, TOGETHER AGAIN! DID ANYONE HAPPEN TO TAKE NOTES?
NOTES? ON WHAT?
HOW TO GET KIDNAPPED BY SUPER VILLAINS?
ON GAME DESIGN, SILLY!
THAT WAS A GREAT EXAMPLE OF RANDOM VARIABLE INTERJECTION!
HI! My name is DOREEN
REALLY? THAT'S WHAT YOU WANT US TO DESIGN?
I MEAN, THE SQUIRRELS, OKAY. BUT DON'T YOU THINK THE TWO HEROES WERE KIND OF... EXCESSIVE?
UH, YEAH! EXCESSIVELY AWESOME!
ALL AND ALL, THIS DAY WAS DEFINITELY ONE FOR THE WIN COLUMN.

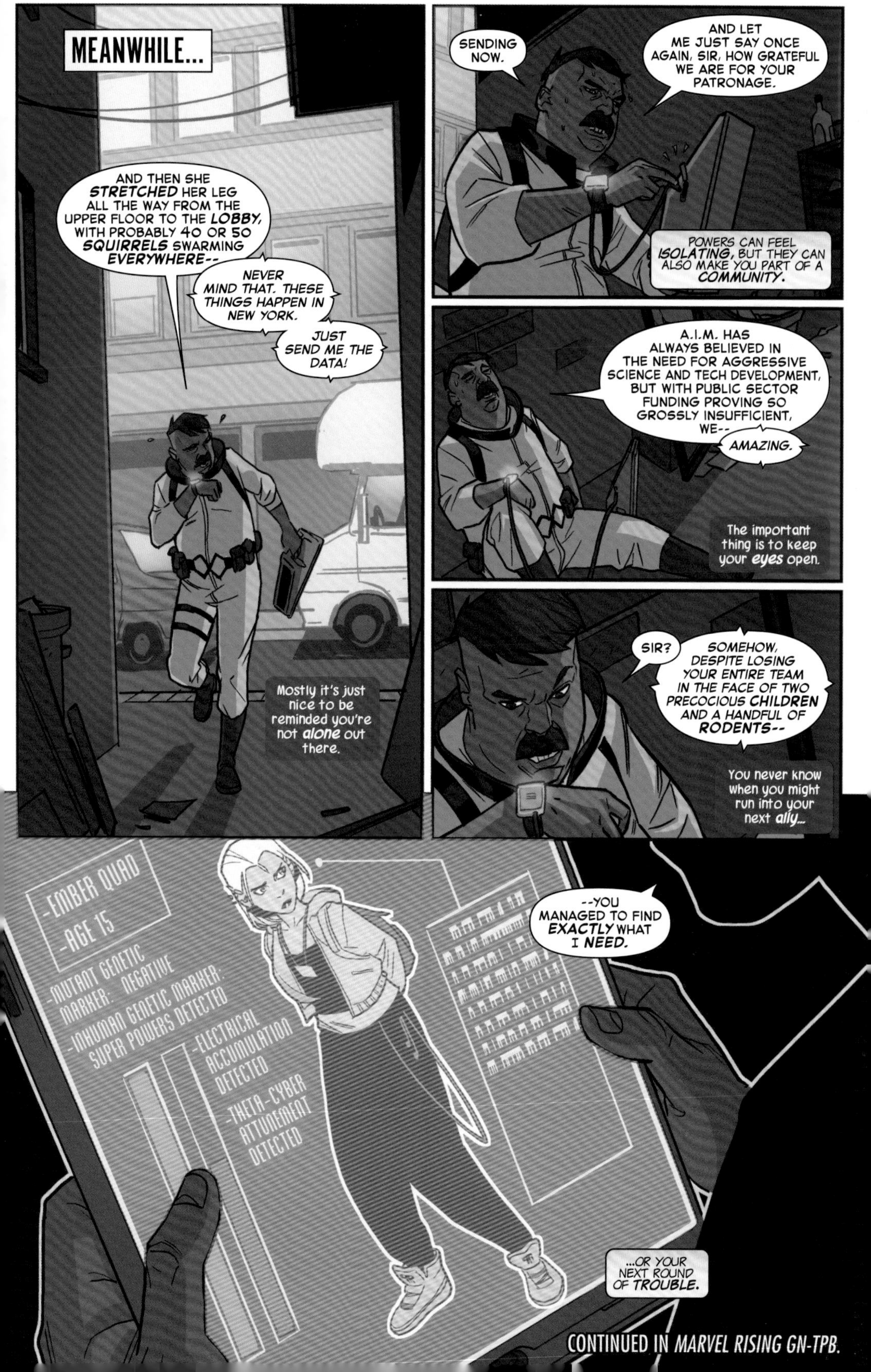
MEANWHILE...
AND THEN SHE STRETCHED HER LEG ALL THE WAY FROM THE UPPER FLOOR TO THE LOBBY, WITH PROBABLY 40 OR 50 SQUIRRELS SWARMING EVERYWHERE--
NEVER MIND THAT. THESE THINGS HAPPEN IN NEW YORK.
JUST SEND ME THE DATA!
Mostly it's just nice to be reminded you're not alone out there.
SENDING NOW.
AND LET ME JUST SAY ONCE AGAIN, SIR, HOW GRATEFUL WE ARE FOR YOUR PATRONAGE.
POWERS CAN FEEL ISOLATING, BUT THEY CAN ALSO MAKE YOU PART OF A COMMUNITY.
A.I.M. HAS ALWAYS BELIEVED IN THE NEED FOR AGGRESSIVE SCIENCE AND TECH DEVELOPMENT, BUT WITH PUBLIC SECTOR FUNDING PROVING SO GROSSLY INSUFFICIENT, WE--
AMAZING.
The important thing is to keep your eyes open.
SIR?
SOMEHOW, DESPITE LOSING YOUR ENTIRE TEAM IN THE FACE OF TWO PRECOCIOUS CHILDREN AND A HANDFUL OF RODENTS--
You never know when you might run into your next ally...
-EMBER QUAD
-AGE 15
-MUTANT GENETIC MARKER: NEGATIVE
-INHUMAN GENETIC MARKER: SUPER POWERS DETECTED
-ELECTRICAL ACCUMULATION DETECTED
-THETA-CYBER ATTUNEMENT DETECTED
--YOU MANAGED TO FIND EXACTLY WHAT I NEED.
...OR YOUR NEXT ROUND OF TROUBLE.
CONTINUED IN MARVEL RISING GN-TPB.

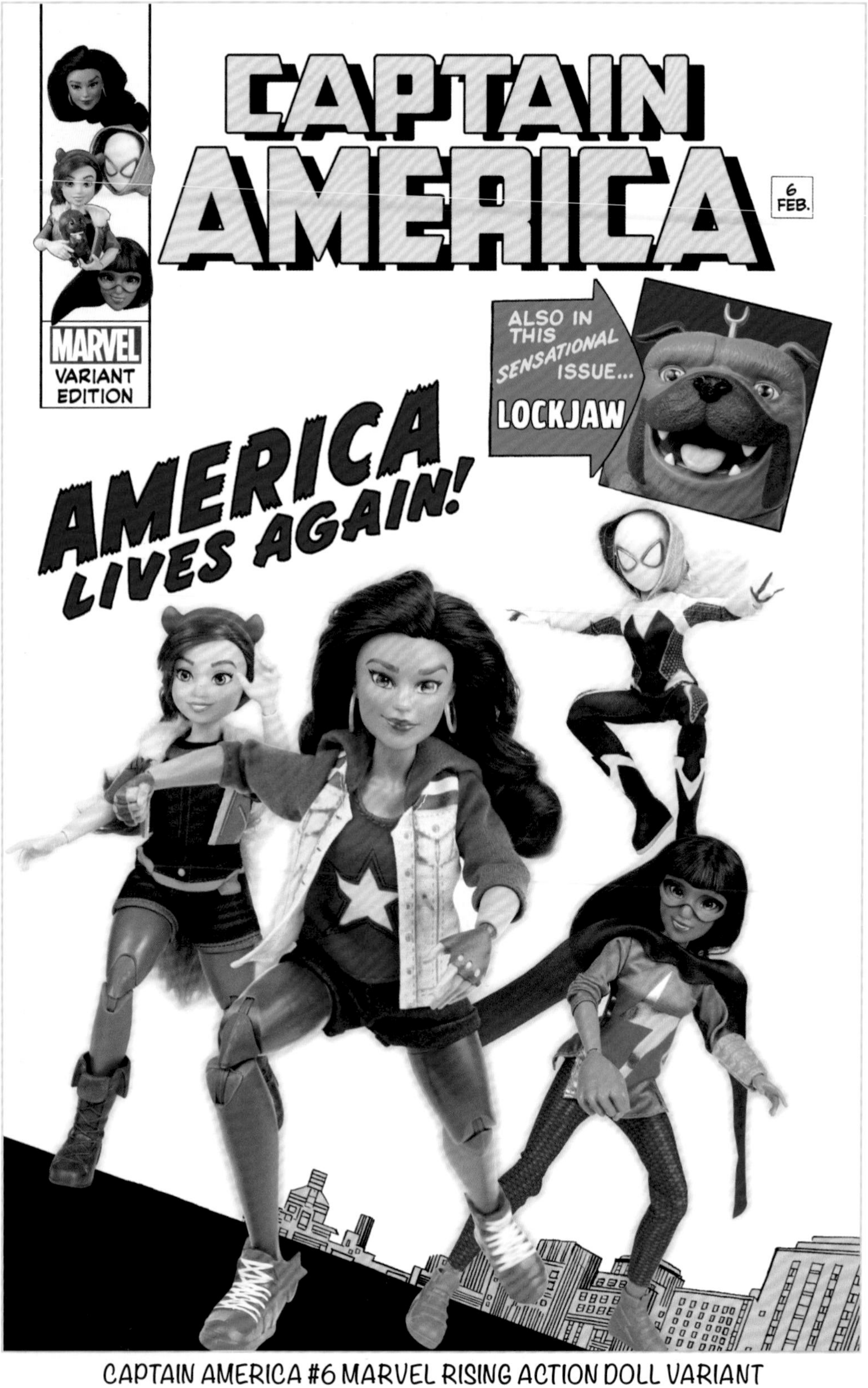
CAPTAIN AMERICA
6 FEB.
MARVEL
VARIANT EDITION
ALSO IN THIS SENSATIONAL ISSUE...
LOCKJAW
AMERICA LIVES AGAIN!

CAPTAIN AMERICA #6 MARVEL RISING ACTION DOLL VARIANT

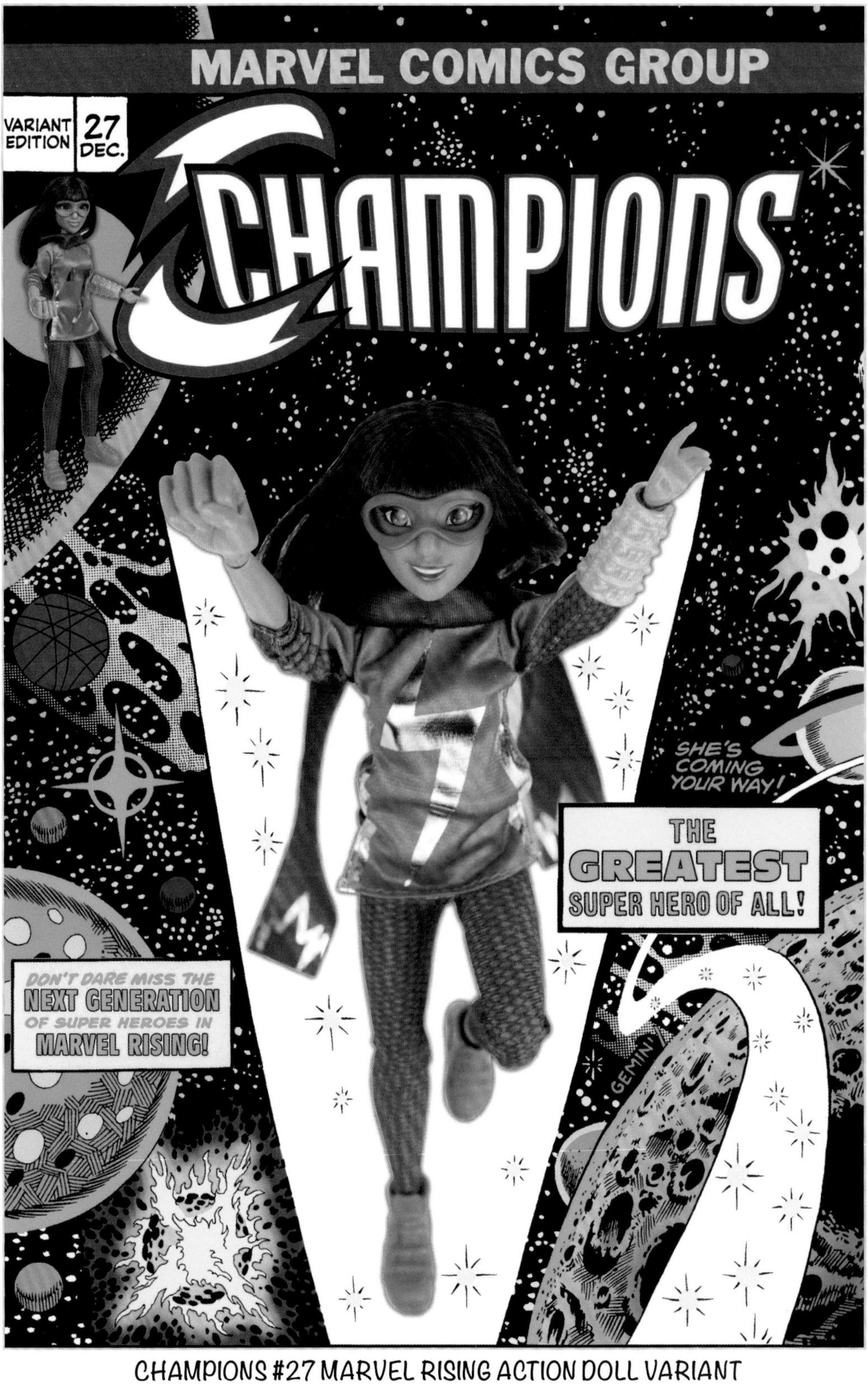
MARVEL COMICS GROUP
VARIANT EDITION
27 DEC.
CHAMPIONS
SHE'S COMING YOUR WAY!
THE GREATEST SUPER HERO OF ALL!
DON'T DARE MISS THE NEXT GENERATION OF SUPER HEROES IN MARVEL RISING!

CHAMPIONS #27 MARVEL RISING ACTION DOLL VARIANT

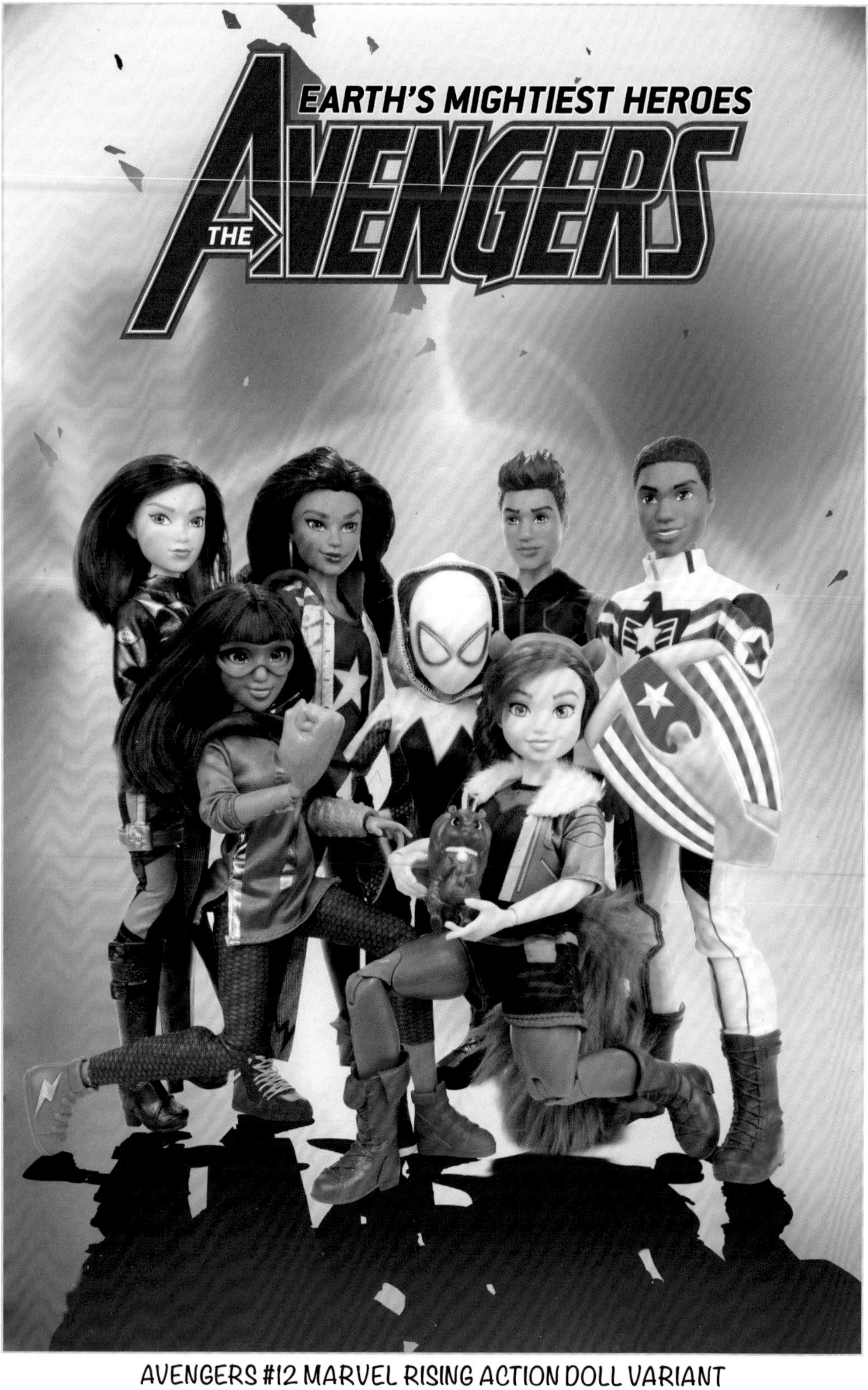
EARTH'S MIGHTIEST HEROES
THE AVENGERS

AVENGERS #12 MARVEL RISING ACTION DOLL VARIANT